THE WORLD'S CLASSICS

MR. FACEY ROMFORD'S HOUNDS

ROBERT SMITH SURTEES was born at The Riding, Northumberland, in 1805. His father was the Squire of Hamsterley, County Durham. Though articled to solicitors in Newcastle and London he soon abandoned the law as a profession. In 1830 he became Hunting Correspondent of the *Sporting Magazine* and a year later founded the *New Sporting Magazine*. He succeeded to Hamsterley Hall in 1838 and subsequently became Deputy Lieutenant, and in 1856 High Sheriff, of County Durham. He died in Mutton's Hotel, Brighton, in 1864.

His books include *Jorrocks's Jaunts and Jollities* (1838), *Handley Cross* (1843), *Hillingdon Hall* (1845), and *Mr. Sponge's Sporting Tour* (1852).

JEREMY LEWIS read history at Trinity College, Dublin. He has worked in publishing since 1967, and is a director of Chatto & Windus. A monthly columnist for the *New Statesman*, he has been a regular book reviewer for *The Times* and the *Sunday Telegraph*, and has contributed occasionally to the *Spectator*.

THE WORLD'S CLASSICS

R. S. SURTEES

Mr. Facey Romford's Hounds

With an introduction by
JEREMY LEWIS

Oxford   New York
OXFORD UNIVERSITY PRESS
1984

Oxford University Press, Walton Street, Oxford OX2 6DP

London Glasgow New York Toronto
Delhi Bombay Calcutta Madras Karachi
Kuala Lumpur Singapore Hong Kong Tokyo
Nairobi Dar es Salaam Cape Town
Melbourne Auckland

and associated companies in
Beirut Berlin Ibadan Mexico City Nicosia

Oxford is a trade mark of Oxford University Press

First published as a World's Classics paperback 1984
Introduction and Chronology © Jeremy Lewis 1984

British Library Cataloguing in Publication Data
Surtees, R. S.
Mr. Facey Romford's hounds.—(The World's classics)
I. Title II. Lewis, Jeremy
823'.8[F] PR5499.54
ISBN 0-19-281657-8

Library of Congress Cataloging in Publication Data
Surtees, Robert Smith, 1805-1864.
Mr. Facey Romford's hounds.
(The World's classics)
I. Title. II. Title: Mister Facey Romford's hounds.
PR5499.S4M48 1984 823'.8 83-23737
ISBN 0-19-281657-8 (pbk.)

Printed in Great Britain by
Hazell Watson & Viney Limited
Aylesbury, Bucks

CONTENTS

INTRODUCTION

ONE of Rudyard Kipling's stories, 'My Son's Wife', features a rather tiresome young man called Midmore, a high-minded aesthete and member of the 'Immoderate Left' who idles his days away discussing how the world can be brought 'a step nearer the Truth, the Dawn and the New Order'. Midmore inherits a country estate from a widowed aunt named Mrs. Werf, and reluctantly decides to pay it a patronizing visit. Bored and ill at ease away from London, and reduced to thumbing through the books in the library, he suddenly realizes 'with horror what the late Colonel Werf's mind must have been in its prime': for the colonel—like Kipling—was an enthusiastic reader of Surtees, the nineteenth-century hunting novelist; and the unsuspecting Midmore finds himself made uncomfortably but compellingly aware of an attitude to life—sceptical, brisk, tough-minded, utterly unsentimental—completely different from his own. 'It was', Kipling tells us in a lurid encapsulation of Surteesian society, 'a foul world into which he peeped for the first time—a heavy-eating, hard-drinking hell of horse-copers, swindlers, match-making mothers, economically dependent virgins selling themselves blushingly for cash and lands, Jews, tradesmen and an ill-considered spawn of Dickens and horsedung characters (I give Midmore's own criticism), but he read on, fascinated.' Midmore eventually reels off to bed clutching a copy of *Handley Cross*, one of Surtees's milder and more benevolent creations; 'and a lonelier Columbus into a stranger world the wet-ringed moon never looked upon'.

Although he has retained a devoted following among the dwindling denizens of country houses (latter-day equivalents of Colonel Werf), members of the crustier London clubs, and assorted backwoodsmen, many of whom read little else, Robert Smith Surtees has never been greatly esteemed by the literary or academic worlds: and considering the nature of his subject-matter and his agreeably coarse-grained prose style this is not altogether surprising, despite some sporadic advocacy from Siegfried Sassoon, George Orwell, Joyce Cary (in his masterly introduction to the World's Classics edition of *Mr. Sponge's Sporting Tour*), V. S. Pritchett, and—surprisingly and somewhat circuitously—Virginia Woolf. From among Surtees's fellow Victorians, Tennyson and William Morris were alleged admirers; while Thackeray not only recommended to Surtees his fellow Carthusian, John Leech, whose magnificently gloomy engravings of rain-swept fields and bottle-nosed huntsmen perfectly complemented the novels, but is said to have remarked that he would have given all he had to have written *Mr. Facey Romford's Hounds*, an early draft of which he read shortly before his death.

Twentieth-century Surtees-lovers tend to facetious but heartfelt claims that *Mr. Sponge's Sporting Tour* and its successor, *Facey Romford*, are, if not the profoundest novels ever written, at least among the funniest and the most boisterously entertaining—their sporadic anxiety to spread the word being tempered with a defensive dread of a private passion becoming part of the accepted wisdom, and the subject of stupefying doctoral theses. The 1920–2 volume of Sassoon's Diaries finds him making doomed efforts to convert his fellow guests at Garsington (Midmores to a man, no doubt): but he tells us elsewhere of how 'when I mentioned him to Arnold Bennett he merely enquired "Can he . . . really be perused?" Whereupon I went straight to a book-seller's near the Reform Club and ordered Sponge and Romford to be sent to him. A few days later I received a postcard. "Many thanks for putting me right on Surtees. Romford is the real thing."'

Written in the winter of 1863–4, when its author was fifty-eight, *Mr. Facey Romford's Hounds* is the last of Surtees's nine completed novels, and—along with *Mr. Sponge's Sporting Tour*—is thought by many to be his best; like all his novels, it was published anonymously, and initially in serial form. Both novels perfectly display Surtees's brusque North Country qualities of pace, vivid dialogue and characterization, ruthless (and often hilarious) humour, and an unillusioned, unmoralizing toughness more reminiscent of Smollett than of Fielding; and unlike his earlier Jorrocks novels, or so much of Dickens, neither of them carries an ounce of spare flesh.

Surtees had succeeded his father as the squire of Hamsterley Hall in County Durham in 1838, after spending much of the previous thirteen years in London, briefly as a lawyer (which he loathed) and then as a rather quarrelsome, even vindictive, sporting journalist and the editor-founder of the *New Sporting Magazine*; a taciturn, reserved figure, he seems to have been the kind of old-fashioned Tory who combined a cynical view of human nature in general with private kindliness, fiercely opposing the extension of the franchise yet proving himself an honourable and conscientious landlord and Justice of the Peace, and—in his own words—'a decided Friend to Improvement in every Shape—and Way'. Surtees was no egalitarian, but he disliked the dandified exclusivity of the fashionable hunts as much as he derided the pretensions of those on the make: alternating as it does between the hunting field and the drawing-rooms of remote and draughty country houses, *Mr. Facey Romford's Hounds* is the ultimate embodiment of his brisk and bracing world of hard-riding, hard-boiled country squires, humbugs, predatory mothers, slovenly, cheating servants, crooked horse-dealers (the used-car salesmen of the day), and London tradesmen who have made their packets and set themselves up as country gents, complete with bogus family portraits and impressive pedigrees.

The plot of *Facey Romford* is simplicity itself: Facey Romford, like Soapey Sponge before him, is a confidence trickster who takes advantage of country society's greed and gullibility, and gets away with it. Readers of *Mr. Sponge's Sporting Tour*—which first appeared some fifteen years earlier, in 1849—may remember that Facey Romford was the only man to get the better of its hero as Soapey travelled round the country with his reconditioned nags, sponging off country-house owners and exciting matrimonial expectations among hostesses foolish enough to be taken in by rumours of 'a house in Eaton-square, a yacht in Cowes, and a first-rate moor in Scotland, and some said a peerage in expectancy'. Facey invites Sponge to join him in some shooting at his 'Oncle Gilroy's place', Queercove Hill; unable to stay any longer with the breathless Jogglebury Crowdey, who has resorted to bawling instructions about Sponge's imminent departure outside his guest's bedroom window (and makes a welcome reappearance in *Romford*), Sponge eagerly accepts, only to find himself sharing seedy, bug-ridden digs above a saddler's shop with Romford, who proceeds to feed him on pork, strong cheese, and gin, rob him at cards, and deafen him with atrocious playing on the flute. Sponge manages to make his escape without settling up the 'sivin pund ten' he owes his host—a debt Romford carries forward to the next book—and the novel ends with Soapey marrying the dashing Lucy Glitters, late of Astley's Royal Amphitheatre and a fellow guest of the drunken, hiccuping Sir Harry Scattercash, and setting up shop in The Sponge Cigar and Betting Rooms of Jermyn Street.

Sponge himself makes only fleeting, furtive appearances in *Mr. Facey Romford's Hounds*, dodging out of the back door when Romford comes to collect his debt, and then bolting to Australia 'with all the spoons and the loose cash', leaving Lucy to fend for herself. Romford, in the mean time, has suffered a mighty blow to his expectations: unaware that his recently deceased 'Oncle Gilroy' has left behind him 'a left-handed wife and promising family in the sylvan retirement of St. John's Wood', he finds himself cheated out of what he regards as his rightful inheritance by a 'great masculine knock-me-down-looking woman' with a 'strongish shading of moustache on her upper lip', and realizes that he will have to live off his wits to make ends meet. Facey may be a villain, but he is also—like Sponge—a resourceful and enthusiastic sportsman, and he decides to advertise his services as a Master of Foxhounds in the expectation that 'his hunting would get him shooting, and his shooting would get him fishing, and all three would get him into society, and there was no saying but that he might get an heiress after all'. As private packs of hounds were replaced by subscription packs in the first half of the nineteenth century, local farmers and gentry were often dilatory and unforthcoming when it came to digging into their own pockets, and small provincial packs, unable to raise a full-time Master of Foxhounds from among their own numbers, were reduced to importing outsiders: so making room for unscrupulous adventurers like Facey, prepared to drive the hardest of bargains and indulge in some dubious horse-dealing on the side.

Already adept at pretending to be other than he is, Facey is lucky enough to share the same names as an entirely respectable huntsman, Mr. Frank Romford, J.P., of Abbeyfield Hall: he passes himself off as the 'real' Mr. Romford with the worthies of the Heavyside and Larkspur Hunts, while the absentee Lord Lovetin lets him Beldon Hall on the assumption that he must be the Romford he knew at

Eton. (Needless to say, his lordship receives not a penny-worth of rent, and eventually has to pay Romford and his hangers-on to leave the premises.) Facey takes with him the deserted Lucy Sponge—posing as his half-sister and 'the widow of an India officer'—and Lucy's mother, Mrs. Sidney Benson, a retired theatrical dresser; Mrs. Benson's unaristocratic origins are hard to conceal, and she is kept discreetly in the background. Lucy herself uses her skills as a former circus equestrienne to show off a particularly vicious horse they have brought with them to sell to some unsuspecting local: however, the old-fashioned gentlemen of the Heavyside Hunt are stuffily unamused when Lucy acts as whipper-in after Swig and Chowey, Facey's alcoholic huntsmen, have disgraced themselves at The Bald-Headed Stag, and they have to pay Facey handsome compensation for taking his services elsewhere. Once installed in Beldon Hall, all accounts are charged up to Lord Lovetin or the innocent Mr. Romford and, more often than not, sent down on the London train (for 'London is the real place for unhesitating compliance with specious orders'): and so equipped, Facey sets out to enjoy as much hunting as he can, and to indulge in the life of a country gentleman, albeit of an odd and antisocial kind.

Anxious as he is to land himself an heiress, Facey is far too gauche and unconventional a social climber, and far too devoted to the unadorned practicalities of sporting life, to want to waste his time on the niceties of the social round and the elaborate rituals of country-house visiting: and it is his rather charmless bluntness and absence of social humbug (elementary manners, some would say), together with his unflamboyant devotion to hunting, that make him, one feels, infinitely preferable in Surtees's eyes to the social climbers, nincompoops, and incompetent 'Leadenhallers' by whom he was surrounded. 'He was', we learn, 'just turned of thirty-one, tall and muscular, with a broad, expansive chest, heavy round shoulders, and rather knock knees. His large backward-growing-all-round-the-chin-gingery-whiskered face was lit up with a pair of little roving red-lidded pig eyes, that were constantly on the watch—sideways, lengthways, cornerways, all ways save frontways'; on top of which he had an engaging habit of 'twitching out a liberal sample of his cane-coloured beard as he spoke', which he used to examine closely under the light after extraction. Facey has little time for life's pleasantries: he reports a nightmare in which 'he had dreamt that he had tumbled on a poodle in the drawing room, and squirted a bottle of porter right into a lady's face'; his idea of a dinner party—very different from Lucy's elaborate dainties, sent down on the London train by Fizzer, Confectioner to the Queen—consists of 'rabbit poie and cheese' washed down with gin. Returning to Beldon Hall after an elegant evening out, he broods on 'how much snugger it was to roll about in Tweeds and be waited on by a Dirty [the Dirties being a particularly grubby family employed at Beldon Hall] than to undergo the penance and persecution of a party—the persecution of wine, the persecution of fish, the persecution of food in general, the persecution of footmen, the persecution of finery'; for 'What good did it do him dinin' off plate? He could eat off pewter quite as well, if not better. As to a fine bed, it was all lost upon him: he was none the better for snoozin' in one—could sleep in a barn for that matter—under a haystack, if it didn't rain.' Surtees loves to dwell on the angry, resentful panic occasioned in a household when the guests' carriage is heard crunching up the drive, with the flustered host flinging himself into a comfortable chair with a copy of *The Times* or a volume of sermons just as the visitors are announced, and affecting a languid surprise and pleasure as a servant ushers them in; and much of the humour of *Mr. Facey Romford's Hounds* derives from Facey's brutish refusal to be impressed by the convolutions of social life, or to make polite, double-edged conversation about the weather or the latest news from London.

Facey may be—in Joyce Cary's disapproving words—'an oaf as well as a crook', but only the most censorious could fail to relish the ways in which he and Lucy take their equally scheming but more conventional neighbours for a ride: Lucy asking her friend Betsey Shannon to scour London's theatrical costumiers for 'a couple of rich lace-bedizened job liveries for two substantially-built footmen'; Goodheart Green, the cheerfully crooked London ''oss dealer', uncomfortably aware that 'he knocked his Hs about', struggling to enunciate correctly while posing as 'Sir Roger Ferguson, Bart.', and being set upon by swarms of mercenary but misguided mothers; Betsey Shannon passing herself off as the aristocratic 'Miss Howard' and promptly hooking her man (none too bright, but with compensatory assets); Facey's unromantic impatience with the blandishments of Miss Watkins and Miss Hazey, the two rivals for his hand and his putative fortune. Both Facey and his creator seem to have had a fairly glum view of women in general while retaining an agreeably soft spot for dashing, cigar-puffing members of the *demi-monde* like Lucy or Betsey Shannon. Even so, we find Facey indulging in some familiar grumbles about Lucy's behaviour on the hunting field ('Dash you and your tea! You women are always wanting tea—should go about with a kettle tacked to your saddles' or 'Rot the women . . . they are never happy unless they are pokin' their noses into each others' houses').

As we have seen, Surtees disapproved of the fast-riding, snobbish swells who hunted the fashionable shires of Leicestershire and Northamptonshire—exciting the awed admiration of 'Nimrod', the most celebrated sporting journalist of his day, and the subject of Surtees's unkind contempt—as much as he scorned the sporting incompetence and social pretensions of former tradesmen like Mr. Large, the retired teapot-handle maker, or Mr. Bonus, the ex-Chairman of the Half-Guinea Hat Company, remarkable for his 'skew-bald fan beard, formed of alternate tufts of yellow and white hair, just like the tufts of a kettle-holder'. Jaundiced as he undoubtedly was, Surtees was not entirely despondent about human nature, however. Ralph Lambton, a celebrated North Country M.F.H., remained Surtees's ideal of an English gentleman, and his spirit perhaps makes a fleeting appearance in the form of Facey's reserved and unusually decent neighbour, Stanley Swerling, who shares Facey's belief that 'Good foxes are becomin' very scarce—too many Leadenhallers about', and is one of the two male characters in the book who is neither fool, villain, nor humbug: the other being the Northumbrian coachman, Independent Jimmy, who regards the comings and goings of the locals with a pleasingly disrespectful eye. (Facey asks him what the preening, *nouveau riche* Mr. Watkins does with himself all day. 'Nout. Brush his hair mainly ar should say', replies the voice of Surteesian cynicism.) Jimmy, incidentally, spends much of his time meeting people off the train, from London and elsewhere: Surtees always wrote particularly well about railway travel, and the effect trains were having on Victorian country society, 'opening out the great matrimonial market' and leading to 'a consequent improvement in Society—improvement in wit, improvement in wine, improvement in "wittles", improvement in everything'.

It would be a great mistake to assume that Surtees's novels can only be enjoyed by hunting buffs. As Sassoon has pointed out, 'many of his admirers have been people without personal experience of the sport': those of us whose knowledge of hunting is drawn from the place-mats of country hotels, or who instinctively feel that the only approachable horse is one whose jaw has been safely strapped shut and whose legs have been mounted on castors, can skip or skim the hunting scenes or—much more sensibly—enjoy them as, in Jorrocks's words, 'the image of war without its guilt, and only five and twenty per cent of its danger', relishing them for the excitement of the chase and the vivid evocations of crisp wintry mornings, ploughed fields, leafless copses, and angry, stentorian voices bellowing 'Hold hard, gen'lemen' as some impetuous buffoon over-rides the hounds.

Sad to say, neither Surtees nor the excellent John Leech lived to see *Mr. Facey Romford's Hounds* in print. Leech completed only fourteen of the twenty-four colour plates, leaving the rest to be finished by Hablot K. Browne ('Phiz'); two months before Bradbury & Evans began serialization, in March 1864, Surtees himself died suddenly while staying with his wife at Mutton's Hotel in Brighton. Brighton was, perhaps, an appropriate place in which to die: Surtees had spent much time hunting on the downs when living in London; he wrote well about the predatory social life of seaside towns; and, as Joyce Cary has pointed out, the raffish world of Regency England lingers on in his novels, as it does in those of his admirer, Thackeray. *Romford* ends with Facey and Soapey Sponge setting up as bankers in Melbourne. 'Good luck attend their exertions, say we!' Surtees writes in the concluding words of the book. 'We expect to hear of their setting up a pack of hounds together next.' Would that we had.

JEREMY LEWIS

A CHRONOLOGY OF
R. S. SURTEES

1805   May. Robert Smith Surtees (R.S.S.) is born at The Riding, Northumberland. His father, Anthony, was the Squire of Hamsterley, Co. Durham, and—according to Nimrod—'a true sample of the old English squire, and as good a judge of a horse, a hound, a bottle of port-wine and an oak tree as any man in England'.

n.d.   Educated at Ovingham School. The headmaster, the Revd James Birkett, 'had the most ludicrous propensity for making and hoarding up walking sticks that ever was heard of. He could not see or hear of a promising sapling but he would be at it, and having converted it into a walking stick, would add it to his redundant collection.' (cf. Jogglebury Crowdey in *Mr. Sponge's Sporting Tour*.)

1818–19   Attends Durham Grammar School.

1822   Articled to a solicitor in Newcastle.

1825   'Further articled' to a Mr. William Bell, of Bow Churchyard in London.

1825–8   Hunts with the Old Surrey, the headquarters of which was Croydon. The hunt was much favoured by City tradesmen like Mr. Jorrocks, the Cockney grocer.

1828   Admitted in Chancery, but shortly thereafter abandons the law as a profession.

1829   Pays the first of many visits to Brighton.

       Visits Paris. In Boulogne he is presented with—and hunts—a pack of hounds after its English owner has been imprisoned for debt; and is granted permission to hunt the royal forest at Samer, where 'a very harmonious evening closed with so grand a debauch of *Eau de Vie* that towards midnight Monsieur Saurange was carried home on a shutter'.

Begins to indulge his 'taste for scribbling': shows his first attempt at a novel to two friends who 'so laughed it to scorn that I put it on the fire and half resolved to abandon the pursuit of letters for the future'.

1830 Feb. Replaces the celebrated Nimrod as Hunting Correspondent of the *Sporting Magazine*, signing his contributions 'Nim South' or 'A Durham Sportsman'.

1831 His brother Anthony dies of smallpox: R.S.S. becomes heir to Hamsterley Hall.

Publishes *The Horseman's Manual*, the only one of his books he allows to be published under his name. Dedicates the book to his Durham neighbour, Ralph Lambton, a celebrated huntsman and 'a perfect specimen of a highly polished English gentleman'.

Feb. R.S.S. breaks with the *Sporting Magazine*.

May. Founds the *New Sporting Magazine* (*NSM*) in partnership with Rudolf Ackermann: Ackermann is the printer and publisher, R.S.S. the editor and Hunting Correspondent. Persuades Nimrod to contribute.

July. 'John Jorrocks of Great Coram Street, Grocer and Tea Dealer of St. Botolph's Lane in the City of London' makes his first appearance in the third issue of the *NSM*, and appears there regularly until Sept 1834.

1836 Dec. R.S.S. gives up the editorship of the *NSM*: he may have had some differences of opinion with Ackermann, and needs to spend more time at Hamsterley. But he retains his interest in the magazine, and continues to contribute to it.

1837 March. Is persuaded to stand as Tory candidate for Gateshead ('I am a decided Friend to Improvement in every Shape—and way'), but withdraws before polling day.

R.S.S.'s mother dies.

1838 R.S.S.'s father dies, and he succeeds to Hamsterley Hall: in addition to hunting—he acquires a pack of hounds, but disbands it in 1840—he appears to have been a fair and conscientious landlord and a firm advocate of agricultural improvement.

Jorrocks's Jaunts and Jollities published in book form

by Walter Spiers, with 12 uncoloured illustrations by 'Phiz'. 2nd edn. 1839.

March. *Handley Cross*—the second part of the Jorrocks trilogy—begins its serialization in the *NSM*.

1841   May. Marries Elizabeth Jane Fenwick.

1842   Appointed JP, and Deputy Lieutenant for Co. Durham.

Jorrocks's Jaunts and Jollities reissued by Ackermann, with 15 coloured plates by Henry Alken.

1843   *Handley Cross* published in book form by Colburn; no illustrations.

Feb.–June 1844; *Hillingdon Hall*—the concluding volume of the trilogy—is serialized in the *NSM*: illustrations by Wildrake and Henry Heath.

Death of Nimrod, only months after R.S.S. had derided him as 'Pomponius Ego' in *Handley Cross*.

1844   Joins a committee established in Durham to combat agitation to repeal the Corn Laws.

1845   *Hillingdon Hall* published in book form by Colburn; no illustrations.

1845–6 Contributes a series of articles on hunting to *Bell's Life in London*: published in 1846 as *Analysis of the Hunting Field*.

1846   Oct. *Hawbuck Grange* serialized in *Bell's Life in London* under the title 'Sporting Sketches'; concluded June 1847. No illustrations.

1847   Son, Anthony, born.

Hawbuck Grange published in volume form by Longmans; illustrations by 'Phiz'.

1849   Jan. *Mr. Sponge's Sporting Tour*—R.S.S.'s first popular success—begins its serialization in Harrison Ainsworth's *New Monthly Magazine*; concludes April 1851.

1851   Ackermann reissues Nimrod's *Life of John Mytton*, together with R.S.S.'s 'Memoir of Nimrod'.

Young Tom Hall begins its serialization in the *New Monthly Magazine*: R.S.S. never completes this novel after breaking with Harrison Ainsworth, who had

xviii A CHRONOLOGY OF R. S. SURTEES

made use of his name in an advertisement, and so broken his rule of anonymity (Jan. 1852).

1852   *Mr. Sponge's Sporting Tour* is reissued in 13 parts by Bradbury and Evans; and, for the first time, one of R.S.S.'s novels is illustrated by John Leech. R.S.S. originally asked Thackeray if he would provide the illustrations: Thackeray replied that 'I have not the slightest idea how to draw a horse, a dog, or a sporting scene of any sort', but went on to say that 'My friend Leech, I should think, would be your man—he is of a sporting turn, and to my mind draws a horse excellently.'

1853   March. *Handley Cross* is reissued in 17 monthly parts, with illustrations by Leech.

1856   R.S.S. is appointed High Sheriff for Co. Durham.

1857–8   *Ask Mama* is issued in 13 monthly parts by Bradbury and Evans, with illustrations by Leech; published in one volume 1858.

1858–60 *Plain or Ringlets* is similarly published in 13 parts by Bradbury and Evans, with Leech's illustrations; published in one volume 1860.

1863–4   R.S.S. works on his 'Social and Sporting Recollections'—fragments of autobiography which were eventually published in E. D. Cumings's *Robert Smith Surtees (Creator of Jorrocks) 1805–64* (Edinburgh, 1923).

R.S.S. writes *Facey Romford's Hounds*, in which several characters from *Sponge*—Romford himself, Soapey Sponge, Lucy Glitters, Robert Foozle—make a welcome reappearance. Unfortunately, both R.S.S. and Leech died before Bradbury and Evans began publication in 1864: Leech completed 14 of the 24 plates, and—appropriately enough—'Phiz' completed the series. *Facey Romford's Hounds* was issued in one volume in 1865.

1864   March. R.S.S., who had taken to wintering in Brighton with his wife, dies on the night of 16 March, in Mutton's Hotel.

MR. FACEY ROMFORD'S
HOUNDS

CONTENTS

CONTENTS

MR. FACEY ROMFORD'S
HOUNDS

CHAPTER I

OUR HERO—THE WOMAN IN BLACK

IT was lucky for our friend Mr. Romford—or Facey
Romford as he is sometimes familiarly called—that
there was another Mr. Romford in the world of much
the same tastes and pursuits as himself, for our Mr.
Romford profited very considerably by the other Mr.
Romford's name and reputation. In the first place they
were both called Frank,[1] and in the second place they
both kept hounds; on different principles, to be sure,
but still they both kept hounds, and the mere fact of
their doing so was very confusing. Added to this, our
friend Facey being of the pushing, acquisitive order,
accepted the change without doubt or hesitation.

We don't mean to insinuate that he went about saying
"I am the rich Mr. Romford, owner of Abbeyfield Park,
patron of three livings, J.P., D.L.," and all that sort of
thing; but if he found he was taken for that Mr. Romford,
he never cared to contradict the impression. Indeed, if
pressed, he would mount the high horse and talk patronis-
ingly of the other Mr. Romford—say he was a deuced
good fellow, if not much of a sportsman, and altogether
pooh-pooh him considerably. To hear Facey talk, one
would think that he had not only persuaded himself
that he was the right Romford, but had made the right
Romford believe so too.

Of the Facey pedigree we would gladly furnish the
readers of this work with some little information, but

[1] Our friend was called Charley at school, but his real name
was Francis—hence, perhaps, "Facey."

unfortunately it does not lie in our power so to do, and for the self-same reason that prevented Nimrod from detailing that of Mr. Jorrocks', namely, that we do not happen to know anything. When in his cups (which, however, is but seldom), Facey has been heard to observe that he was "nobbut well bred on one side of his head." "My moother," he used to say, "was a lady, but my fatther was a gardener." The illiberal, indeed, have asserted that the parentage was pretty equal on both sides of the head, for that the moother was a lady's-maid, and the fatther a gardener, a union that certainly does not seem so inconsistent as the other.

Be that however as it may, Facey in early life had constituted himself heir to a maternal uncle, one Mr. Francis Gilroy, a farmer in the country, and a great cattle jobber in London. Gilroy was his godfather, and Facey was called Francis Gilroy Romford out of compliment to him. Now a cattle jobber is to the bovine world what the dealer is to the horsey world, and it requires an uncommonly cute, sagacious sort of chap to make a successful jobber. All this "Oncle Gilroy" was. He had a pair of little penetrating beady black eyes, set in a great red-faced chuckle-head, that could almost look into an animal, see what sort of an interior it had, what sort of a thriver it was going to be, and tell what weight it was likely to get up to. He was a capital judge of stock, and had a fine discriminating genius that taught him the propriety of charging a gentleman customer a good deal more than a farmer. "Nothin' like changin' your stock often," he used to say to the former, which, considering that Gilroy had a commission at both ends, to say nothing of very comfortable pickings in the way of luck pence, and market charges, etc., in the middle, was a very judicious recommendation. He was supposed to have choked more gentlemen off the cattle department of farming than any other salesman going. Indeed, so pleased were the graziers in one county with his perform-ances in that line, that they presented him with a testimonial—a silver tankard. It did not make the noise these absurdities usually do, either from a lack of eloquence on the part of the chairman, or because

"This eternal blazon must not be."

but came off very quietly.

"Francis Gilroy," said the Chairman, producing a silver cup from his pocket after the market dinner, and stripping it of its pink tissue and whity-brown paper. "Francis Gilroy, there's the mug," handing it to him.

"Gentlemen," said Gilroy, taking it, "I thank you for the jug;" and so ended the ceremony. But they all knew what it meant. The inscription, "Gilroy, the Farmers' Friend," told that.

Now Gilroy, who lived very economically in the country, was supposed to have accumulated a vast deal of money, and Facey Romford, who had been apprenticed or articled, or whatever they call it, to a civil engineer, thought there was no use in his toiling and slaving too ; so he gave up the theodolite, intending to wait for his uncle's shoes, which Facey reckoned Gilroy would not be long in being done with. And having a decided turn for sporting in all its branches, he laid himself out for it by fair means and foul, doing a little poaching when he couldn't get it otherwise. And being a bit of a vet, he generally had an old horse to cobble up, on which he used to scramble after the hounds, and sell when he would pass for sound. So he went on from year to year, living, as Gilroy said, "verra contagious to his farm," now fluting to and flattering the old fellow that he would live for ever, now most devotedly wishing that he would, what he called, "hop the twig." And the neighbouring farmers and people, seeing the terms they were on together, put up with a good deal more trespass and nonsense from Facey than they would otherwise have done. Thus Gilroy increased in years and corpulence, and Facey matured to a man, each trusting the other just as far as he thought right. Gilroy never said in as many words to Facey, "Francis, my dear fellow, all you see here and a great deal more will be yours," but he always directed his letters F. Gilroy Romford, Esq., as if proud of the connection, encouraged him to look after his farm in his absence, to protect his Talavera wheat from Squire Gollarton's pheasants, and see that he got a fair day's work out of his women people at harvest and turnip time. And as there is perhaps no man so happy as an heir-apparent, Facey lived on in little village lodgings, beguiling his days with his rod and his gun, and his evenings with a tune on the flute, varied with mental calculations as to how much Gilroy was worth.

"There must be lots of money somewhere," Facey used to say, as he sat smoking his cavendish in his diminutive sitting-room ; "there must be lots of money somewhere—bills, bonds, post obits, I O U's ;" for Facey reckoned rightly, his uncle was too good a judge to put his money out to ordinary interest. "Shouldn't wonder if there was twenty thousand pund," he used to say confidentially to himself. "Fancy me with twenty thousand pund, boy jingo !"

Nay, he has been known, under the influence of his third glass of gin, to get it up as high as thirty thousand, on which occasions his imaginings were very magnificent. He would have the best kennel of pointers and setters in the kingdom, and, like Mr. Sawyer, would go to the Shires with such a stud of hunters as never were seen. Money ! Money would be no object to him ! He'd give anything for a good horse ! Hope deferred never made the Romford heart sick ; on the contrary, he rose with the occasion, flattering himself that the cash was only accumulating.[1]

One dull winter afternoon, on which day had scarcely gained its supremacy over night, as Facey Romford was taking a stroll with his dog and gun round his absent uncle's farm—the dog down in the dell on Squire Gollarton's side, Facey all right for a shot either way—what should he see but the unwonted apparition of a dark luggage-laden vehicle crawling leisurely up the rutty lane leading to the house. Facey stood transfixed, like a pointer to its game, regardless of Juno's feathering below.

"Who have we here?" muttered he, stopping and grounding his gun on his navvy-shod foot. The dingy-looking vehicle went crawling on as before.

"No go, there," continued Facey, as the driver now stopped and descended from his box to open the last gate, which having propped back with a bit of stick that he found lying on the ground, he remounted and drove up to the door with as much dash as he could raise. Facey stood looking, and calculating how long it would be ere the white horse's head reappeared at the end of the varie-gated holly hedge, that protected the Gilroy hereditaments from the cutting east wind. Then he wondered whether

---

[1] For further particulars of Mr. Facey Romford's antecedents, consult "Mr. Sponge's Sporting Tour," p. 381.

the fellow would have the sense to shut the gate, or would just leave it open as it was.

"Dash it, I shouldn't wonder if he was to leave it as it is," said Facey, watching; "these town fellows have no idea of cattle trespass, or anything of that sort, and think gates are just put to divide people's properties, or for larking fox-hunters to leap over." So Facey looked and looked, keeping one eye on the gate and the other on the old red cow, who knew just as well as a Christian when there was the chance of a dash at the great Scotch cabbages at the back of the garden. Still no horse's head, no vehicle appeared. "Devilish odd," said Romford, staring; "must be me Oncle Gilroy with a friend. Some one p'r'aps come down to see some stock. But it's never like him to hire a fly with his own gig mare only doing half-day's works. Hope his friend pays for it. Never do to have him wasting the inheritance in that way. Must go and see," continued Facey. Whistling up Juno, and shouldering his Joe Manton, he went striding away, closely followed by Juno, looking somewhat disconcerted at being done out of her fun. Facey was a capital hand across country, whether on foot or on horseback, and soon put the intervening fields between him and the house behind him. His heart beat quicker as he advanced, for he felt there was something unusual in the sight. He had never seen a shut cab at his uncle's before. It couldn't be that the long-expected event had happened. Hardly, he thought. What was all the luggage for? However, he would soon see. On he went for the purpose. Kicking the little prop out from under the gate, so as to let it close on the swing, he hurried round the corner, and soon had the familiar house full before him. The fly was gone, gone to the stables behind. Couldn't be Oncle Gilroy, he wouldn't stand that, Facey knew. No fly-horses baited there; Red Lion was the place. Hark! sounds of mirth proceed from the parlour, children's voices screaming and shouting, Barley me this, Barley me that. "Oh, what a drum this will make!" exclaimed another, thumping away at Uncle Gilroy's hard hat.

"Who the deuce have we here?" muttered Facey, now lost in astonishment. Pushing through the partially opened sash door, he traversed the passage, and presently stood in the widely opened portals of the parlour. A great coarse-looking woman in deep mourning was arranging her crape bonnet in the diminutive mirror above the little imitation marble mantelpiece just opposite the door, while a perfect sliding scale of children, all clad in black too, were romping and rioting about in a way quite inconsistent with grief—one had the Gilroy testimonial in its hand. The lady started as she saw Romford in the glass, and wheeling round, turned a very brandified face, surmounted by a most palpable flaxen front, full upon him.

"Who are you ?" ejaculated Facey, eyeing her intently.

"And who are you ?" demanded she, putting her arms a-kimbo, and staring him full in the face.

She was a great masculine knock-me-down-looking woman, apparently about five-and-forty, red faced, grey eyed, with a strongish shading of moustache on her upper lip. Facey trembled as he looked at her. He got the creeps all over.

"Me Oncle Gilroy's not at home," at length ejaculated Facey.

"Hut, you and your Uncle Gilroy ! D'ye s'pose I don't know that ?" exclaimed she, with a horse laugh.

"Well, but who are you ?" demanded Facey, bristling up.

"Who am I ?" retorted she. "Who am I ? I'm the mistress of this 'ere 'ouse," replied she ; "and this is the young Squire," patting a boy on the head, so painfully like Gilroy as to be perfectly ridiculous—big bristly head, beady black eyes, capacious mouth, and lop ears.

The truth flashed upon Facey with terrible velocity. His uncle was dead, and had deceived him. Frightful idea ! Facey quivered all over. His knock knees smote each other. It was but too true. Gilroy, instead of re-tiring to the Royal Oak, or the King and Queen on Paddington Green, there to enjoy a quiet frugal glass before turning in to his seven-shillings-a-week lodgings, as he always represented to Facey and his friends, had a regular establishment in the sylvan retirement of Lisson Grove, St. John's Wood, where he had reared the covey of little Gilroys who now disported themselves profusely over his parlour. Gilroy was dead.

While Facey stood as it were transfixed, the lady had dived into her pocket and fished up a document that Facey saw at a glance was the will. "There !" exclaimed she, flourishing it open, so as to display the well-known

Gilroy signature, "there's the writin's. Now have you got anything for to say?" demanded she. Facey was mute.

"I've heard of you, you nasty, sneakin', mean-spirited wretch," continued she, "thinkin' to rob me and mine of their dues. I've eat your cock fizzants and your 'ares, you nasty warmint, and laughed at your folly for sendin' them;" and thereupon she set up a chuckle that shot through Facey's every nerve. A waft of the will would almost have been enough to knock him down.

Just then old Mother Maggison, the housekeeper, who had already attorned to the new régime, came hurrying in with a red-hot poker to light the fire, and Facey gladly availed himself of the opportunity to beat a last retreat. He rushed frantically through the familiar fold-yard, nearly upsetting the fly-man, who was crossing with a pail of water for his horse, then struck down the deep lane past the Lizzards, swung through Woodgate Marsh, and on to Ballishaw Barn, bottling up his grief until he got home. Arrived at his little lodgings at Dame Trotter's, he rushed upstairs, disregarding the liver and bacon he heard hissing for dinner, and entering his little partitioned-off room, threw himself on the stump bed, and groaned loud and audibly.

"Oh dear me! Oh dear me! Oh dear, what shall I do!" Just as if he had got the stomach-ache. Then clasping his right knee with both hands, as he lay on his back, he held his leg up towards the ceiling, and apostrophised himself as follows:—" Oh, Francis Gilroy Romford, moy beloved friend, you are reglarly floored—done brown! That wretched old oncle has sold you! Oh, Francis Gilroy Romford, discard the detested name of Gilroy, and be for ever after Romford only. Oh, Francis Romford, Francis Romford, what are you now to do—what are you now to do? Here for years have you been feasting and serving that vicious old man, sending him fish, sending him game, looking after his farm, nearly breaking your wind by playing the flute to him, and now—oh heavens, that it should ever have come to this!" and thereupon relinquishing the leg, he buried his face in his hands. Just then Dame Trotter, who had heard his groans and his moans, came hurrying in with her never-failing specific, a glass of hot gin and bitters, which Facey bid her set down on the drawers and retire. Then finding he was overheard, he moderated the expressions of his grief, well knowing that very little clamour would raise a trouble-some body of creditors about him. Taking the gin and bitters, therefore, into his sitting-room, he halloaed down-stairs to Mrs. Trotter to give his dogs their dinners, add-ing that he didn't want any himself; and drawing his wooden-bottomed semicircular chair to the fire, with a foot on each hob, and a pipe of tobacco, he quietly con-templated his condition. It was very bad; there was no denying that. Gilroy had been too many for him. He now understood why he so often had cattle left from one market-day to another, and which he must needs stay in town to look after. The woman in black explained all that.

Wicked old man, where could he expect to go? Would surely get quilted below. It was not only the money Facey had lost—the thousands and tens of thousands—but all the fine chances of preferment he had thrown away on the strength of being Gilroy's heir. He might have married Susan Burtree, who was reputed to have five thousand pounds—three certainly—with great expec-tations from an aunt. Miss Cropsey, now Mrs. Jimmy Dobson, would have been delighted to have had him; and the rich widow Sago had set her cap at him, only she, as Facey said, was past mark of mouth. In the heyday of heirship he was rather particular and difficult to please. Moreover, he was a prudent Facey, and would never make up to a girl until he knew exactly what she had, because —as he used to explain to the mammas—his Oncle Gilroy would be sure to disinherit him if he made an improvi-dent match. So he never laid himself open to an action, or the charge of having used a girl infamously. He now felt he had built too much on Oncle Gilroy and too little on himself. If he was not altogether handsome, he was of goodly stature—six feet high—and there was something about him, he said, that the girls couldn't resist. But perhaps the reader would rather have his portrait drawn by a more impartial hand than his own. Well, then, at the time the aforesaid calamity befell him, he was just turned of thirty-one, tall and muscular, with a broad ex-pansive chest, heavy round shoulders, and rather knock knees. His large backward-growing-all-round-the-chin-gingery-whiskered face was lit up with a pair of little roving red-lidded pig eyes, that were constantly on the watch—sideways, lengthways, cornerways, all ways save frontways. He looked as if he was always premeditating a parable, but somehow never produced it. Not that he was a fool—far from it, as those who had had anything to do with him in the betting or horse-dealing lines could testify ; but he looked like a satirist who could cut a man in two with a sarcasm, only, like a generous giant, he refrained from doing so. In short, a sort of you'd-better-leave-me-alone-looking man.

Well, then, this stout, strong, able-bodied man, without a grey hair in his head, was suddenly thrown on his beam-ends without the slightest notice, or provocation on his part. A long, weary apprenticeship to his Uncle Gilroy's fortune regularly thrown away ! The position was critical, for the woman in black would be sure to proclaim it, after which Facey felt there would be no quietus for him. And deeply he pondered on his alarming condition, and voluminous were the clouds of smoke he raised in his aid. Dame Trotter's cuckoo clock chimed three before he turned into bed, and the bird announced four, and the bird announced five, ere he dropped off into an unquiet sleep, greatly dreading the terrors of the coming dawn.

CHAPTER II

A FRIEND IN NEED

SOMEHOW Facey Romford awoke better than he expected. The reality of his position was mercifully continued to him, instead of having to be gathered in disjointed fragments and put together again. His quick apprehension, too, suggested a resource.

On the south side of the village of Hezelton, where Facey lived, about equidistant from his Uncle Gilroy's, was Puddingpote Bower, the seat of Mr. Jogglebury Crowdey, or Jogglebury Crowdey, Esq.,[1] as we suppose he ought to be called ; a fat, estimable gentleman, who devoted himself to the administration of the poor law, the propagation of his species, and the manufacture of fancy-headed walking-sticks. Of children, he had twelve, with the prospect

[1] *Vide* " Mr. Sponge's Sporting Tour," p. 303.

of more, to each of whom he flattered himself if he could leave a sufficient number of walking-sticks he would make them very independent. So he cut and hacked and hewed and fashioned ashes, hollies, blackthorns, etc., into the heads of great people—poets, authors, statesmen, and so on.

To this and his other pursuits Mr. Jogglebury Crowdey had at one time united those of shooter and occasional fox-hunter, more perhaps to promote the grand object of stick-hunting than from any decided inclination for either sport; but his waistband increasing in size he had long relinquished the saddle, and had latterly entered into an arrangement with Mr. Facey Romford, whereby the latter was to have the free range of his manor (which indeed Facey had long taken without leave), in consideration of a certain equivalent in the way of game. So Crowdey, who was a good shooter, but a bad hitter, got a small supply of birds—as many as Facey thought were good for him—while he saved not only the cost of his certificate, but also of his powder and shot, to say nothing of the exertions of himself and his plethoric dog, Ponto, who like his master had become fat and lazy. This gunning arrangement, of course, brought Mr. Romford occasionally to Puddingpote Bower, and Mrs. Crowdey, ever anxious for the welfare of her numerous progeny, and perhaps rayther mistrusting Jog's sticks, had conceived the notable idea of securing the Gilroy fortune, after Facey was done with it, for one of her youngsters. So she made up to Facey a good deal, always had him to dine when there was a goose (not her husband, but the bird), and put Master Marcus Aurelius forward as the most promising boy in the parish.

And Facey feeling all this, and thinking that perhaps the Puddingpote intimacy might now end, resolved to conclude it with a loan, which present circumstances favoured the prospect of getting. So, arraying himself immediately after his porridge breakfast in a glossy suit of black that he had long kept in lavender to be ready for his oncle, he craped his Sunday hat deeply, and drawing on a pair of new black kid gloves, took the way across the fields, avoiding Bickerton and Branshaugh, to the Bower. Arrived there he found Jog feeding his Cochins, who started at the sight, and nearly broke the brown earthenware bowl in which he had the barley-meal.

"Oncle dead," whispered Facey, with a knowing look and a solemn shake of the head.

"Poor (*puff*)!" ejaculated Jog; "when did it (*puff, wheeze*) happen?"

"Only heard of it last night," replied Facey lowly.

"(*Puff*) in, and (*gasp*) Mrs. Jogglebury," said Jog, taking Facey's muscular arm and leading the way through the back kitchen to the dining-room, where Mrs. Jog was just sweeping the chips Jog had made in cutting a Lord Palmerstonian-headed stick under the grate.

"My (*puff*) dear, here's (*gasp*) Mr. Romford," said Jog, opening the door and putting his friend forward to bear the brunt of the action in case it should be wrong. Mrs. Jog started, too, for she had never seen Facey in anything but his somewhat miscellaneous coloured clothes, and the contrast was rather appalling. She soon jumped to a conclusion.

"Poor man!" exclaimed she, clasping her hands, "when did it happen?"

"Only heard of it last night," replied Facey sorrowfully, as the woman in black flashed across his mind.

"Indeed! Then was he from home?"

"Been away for a week," replied Facey; "was to have come home on Tuesday."

"Only think!" ejaculated Mrs. Jogglebury, turning her eyes up to the ceiling, as if with a fine moral reflection, but in reality calculating Aurelius's chances. "What, died in London, did he?"

"Died in London," assented Facey.

"Then you'll be going up to see about things, won't you?" asked Mrs. Jogglebury, anxious for Marcus Aurelius's interest.

"That's just it," said Facey, looking out of the corners of his little ferretty eyes at Jogglebury, "that's just it. You see the bankers won't let me have any money till the will is proved, and I've just come down to see if you can let me have a——"

"Oh (*gasp, puff, wheeze*) yes, they will," ejaculated Jog. "When my (*wheeze*) uncle (*gasp*) Crowdey died, Blunt and Buggins let me have as much as I (*gasped*)."

"Ah, that was in the country," observed Mrs. Jog, thinking to clench the Aurelius interest with a loan.

"That was in the country," said Facey, adopting the

idea. "London is a very different place; they'll hardly change you a fi' pun note without a reference."

"Well, but your (*gasp*) uncle would have an account in the (*wheeze*) country as well," observed Jog.

"Not he," replied Facey; "me oncle wasn't the man to tell his right hand what his left hand did. However," continued he, raising the craped hat from the floor, "I must just see what the Londoners will do, for time is precious, and things must be looked after." So saying, Facey rose as if to depart, whereupon Mrs. Jog essayed another *coup* at her husband.

"Well, but Jog, my dear, I daresay you could let Mr. Romford have what he wants."

"My (*puff*, *gasp*) dear, I have only (*gasp*) pound in the house," replied the excited Jog, stamping, and turning perfectly scarlet.

Now (*gasp*) pounds being an indefinite sum, and having the missus on his side, Facey did not like to say it would do, so, pretending indifference, he said he was only providing against possible contingencies, and did not know he might want it at all. That comforted Jog considerably, for he did not like lending money to anybody; but Mrs. Jog speedily dispelled the delusion by observing that perhaps he could give Mr. Romford a cheque for what he required.

"Ah, that might do," said Facey, brightening up, "and then I could cash it or not, as I wanted it;" and Jog, seeing that a storm was imminent, after a long leisurely hunt for his keys, at length found them, and proceeded to unlock a great brass-bound mahogany writing-desk, out of a secret drawer of which he produced the important little money sheaf of a cheque-book. Then he had to look for a pen that would write, next for some ink that would mark, after that for his almanack, and finally for his spectacles. Still Romford, though in such a desperate hurry, did not back out. So Jog, having consumed all the time that he could, at length filled in the date, and then came to the next blank after the word pay. Messrs. Blunt and Buggins, pay—"Pay who?" asked Jog, looking up.

"Oh, pay me," replied our friend. "Pay me—Mr. Romford—pay Mr. Romford or order—say, fifty pund—not that I dare say I shall want it, but it will make even money, and I can send you down a fifty-pun note—cut in two, you know ; " adding, " dessay I shall find plenty of specie when I get there—only one likes to be provided."

This last observation had a consolatory effect upon Jog, who, after a hunt for his blotting-paper, at length found it, and stamping it severely on the cheque as if he would knock its wind out, took a last farewell, and tearing it abruptly from the book handed it over to Facey, with a feeling as though he were parting with his heart's blood.

" All right," said Romford, glancing at it, and then folding it up, he placed it in his betting-book and pocketed it.

" You'll let us hear from you in London, I suppose," observed Mrs. Jogglebury Crowdey, as Facey prepared to depart.

" Certainly," replied Facey, " certainly—write to you as soon as I get there—most likely send you your cheque back." So saying, he shook each heartily by the hand and hurried away through the kitchen.

Without waiting for the bang of the back door, Jog's pent-up wrath exploded with a " I wonder you are such a (*gasp*) as to (*puff*) away money in that way."

" Oh, nonsense, Jog, you *are* so suspicious. You have no spirit or enterprise about you. I declare the poor children might be all paupers for anything you do."

" Paupers (*puff*) ! enterprise (*wheeze*) ! I think you are much more likely to make them (*puff*) paupers than (*wheeze*) me."

" Nonsense, Jog ; I tell you you don't know the men as well as I do. Leave me to manage these matters. Just as Marcus Aurelius's chance is at the best, you try to throw all my endeavours away."

" Ah, (*puff*) that's just what you used to say with regard to Gustavus (*wheeze*) and Mr. Sponge. Nothin' was too (*puff*) for Mr. Sponge—he was sure to (*wheeze*) Gustavus James everything he had, and must have the best of everything,—all the delicacies of the season,—and then he goes and marries a (*gasp*) actress. Wish I had the (*puff*) expenses of that (*wheeze*) visit in my (*gasp*) pocket. Would come to a pretty round sum, I know."

This agreeable dialogue was at length interrupted by a double knock at the half-open door, indicating the presence of a listener. It was the cook, come to say that Betty the fishwoman was in the scullery with soles,

haddocks, and skate. Mrs. Jog gladly beat a retreat to
hold a conference with her, for Betty dealt in gossip as
well as fish, and always had the latest intelligence. So,
after a slight survey of the fish, she asked her if there was
anything going on. "Well, no, I think not, mum," replied Betty, who was more tenacious about the freshness
of her news than that of her fish, and always opened as if
the news was old. "Well, no, mum, I think not. You'll
have heard of the doin's at Mr. Gilroy's doubtless?"

"Doings!" exclaimed Mrs. Jog, "why, he's dead."

"Dead, yes, and left a widdy and large family," replied Betty.

Shriek! screech! scream! went Mrs. Jog, rushing to a
vacant chair by the cistern.

"Oh, mum, what's happened?" exclaimed Betty,
standing aghast.

"What's the (*puff*)?" demanded Jog, rushing in with
the Palmerstonian stick in his hand.

"Oh, tell him—tell him, take him away and tell him,"
shrieked Mrs. Jog, covering her face with one hand and
motioning them away with the other.

When Jog heard the sad news he was quite beside himself. Summoning his man-boy the two got the phaeton
ready, and drove off at such a rate, to stop the cheque at
the bank, that they threw down the old family mare,
breaking one of the shafts and both her knees. But
Facey was too many for them. He never went near the
bank, but just walked round to Mr. Holmside, the
treasurer to the Poor Law Union, saying, as that worthy
appeared at his door, " I say, here's one of your old broken-
winded Chairman's cheques—just give me money for it,
that's a good fellow." And Jog being a very great man
in the eyes of Mr. Holmside (Chairman of the Stir-it-Stiff
Union, comprising no less than ten townships), immediately produced his money-bags, and asking Mr. Romford
how he would have it, handed him five five-pound notes and
five-and-twenty sovereigns. Facey then telling Holmside
that there were a brace of partridges and a hen pheasant
(one of Squire Gollarton's) at Mother Trotter's that he
might have for sending for, bade him adieu, and was
quickly out of sight. Arrived at home, Facey trundled
his clothes into his box, and consigning his dogs to the
care of his landlady, drove off in the postman's gig to
catch the mail train at the Hyndleyburn Station. And

the almost broken-hearted Jog vowed that he would
never have anything more to do with Faceys or Soapeys
or men of that sort, for the interests of his children would
be much better promoted by sticking to the sticks. So he
hacked and hewed and carved away with redoubled
vigour, and is hacking and carving away to this hour for
aught we know to the contrary. Last scene of all that
closes this portion of our sad eventful history was the
coming of the county court bailiff, who swept away all
that friend Facey had left at his lodgings—his wide-awake
hat, his "flay craw" clothes, his shabby mackintosh, his
mud boots; above all, his valuable library — his
"Boxiana," his "Fistiana," his "Bell's Life," and "White's
Farriery."

CHAPTER III

THE SPONGE CIGAR AND BETTING-ROOMS

ARRIVED in the great metropolis, Facey's earliest
visit was to the well-known Soapey Sponge, in
Jermyn Street, St. James's. Soapey in bygone days had
been a guest of Facey's, and had lost a certain sum of
"sivin pun ten" to him at Blind Hookey, which no
amount of coaxing or bullying had ever been able to
extract from him. Indeed, latterly the letters had been
returned to Facey through the dead-letter office. This
was not to be borne, and Facey was now more than ever
determined to have his dues, or to know the "reason
why." We may mention that Soapey, on his marriage
with the fascinating actress, Miss Lucy Glitters, had set
up a cigar and betting shop, a happy combination, that
promised extremely well at the outset, but an unfeeling
legislature, regardless of vested interests, had presently
interposed, and put a stop to the betting department. So
Soapey had to extinguish his lists, and Lucy and he were
reduced to the profits of the cigar shop alone—" WHOLE-
SALE AND RETAIL, AND FOR EXPORTATION," as the
circular brass front and window blind announced.

Now, though Lucy's attractions were great, and though
she never sold even one of her hay-and-brown-paper

cigars under sixpence, or ever gave change for a shilling; still Soapey and she could not make both ends meet; and when poverty comes in at the door, love will fly out of even a glittering cigar shop window. So it was with the Sponges. Deprived of his betting recreation, Soapey took to idle and expensive habits; so true is the saying that

> "Satan finds some mischief still
> For idle hands to do."

He frequented casinoes and billiard-rooms, danced at Cremorne, and often did not come home till daylight did appear. All this went sadly against the till; and the rent and the rates and taxes, to say nothing of the tradesmen's bills, were more difficult to collect on each succeeding quarter. With this falling fortune friend Facey arrived in town to further complicate disasters. He took twopennyworth of Citizen 'bus from Lisson Grove as far as the Piccadilly Circus, and then, either not knowing the country, or with a view of drawing up wind, threw himself into cover at the St. James's Street end of Jermyn Street, instead of at the Haymarket end, where one would have thought his natural genius would have suggested the Sponges would have been found. To be sure he had not been much about town; Oncle Gilroy, for obvious reasons, having kept him as much as he could in the country. As we said before, it being the winter season, when day is much the same as night in London, Facey lounged leisurely along the gaslit street, one roguish eye reading the names and callings of the shops on his left, the other raking the opposite side of the way; but though he drew along slowly and carefully, examining as well the doors as the windows, no Sponge sign, no cigar warehouse, greeted his optics. Fish, books, boxes, bacon, boots, shoes, everything but Sponges.

So he came upon the 'bus-crowded Regent Street, not having had a whiff of a cigar save from the passers-by. There then he stood at the corner of the street biting his nails, lost in astonishment at the result. "Reg'lar do," muttered he; "beggar's bolted," looking back on the long vista of lamps he had passed. "Well, that's a nice go," said he; "always thought that fellow was a sharper." Just then an unhandsome hansom came splashing and tearing along the way he had come, and dashing across Regent Street pursued the continuous route beyond.

"May as well cast across here," said Facey to himself, picking his way over the muddy street, taking care of his buttoned boots as he went. His sagacity was rewarded by reading "Jermyn Street" on the opposite wall. "For-rard! for-rard!" he cheered himself, thinking the cigar shop scent improved as he went. Indeed he quickly came upon a baccy shop, green door, red blinds, all indicative of a find, for no sooner does one tradesman get well-established than another comes as near as he can get to pick away part of his custom.

Just then Facey's keen eye caught sight of two little overdressed snobs stopping suddenly at a radiant shop window a few paces farther on, and advancing stealthily along, as if going up with his gun to a point, the words "Devilish 'andsome" fell upon his ear. Looking over their shoulders there appeared the familiar figure of Mrs. Sponge behind the counter. Mrs. Sponge, slightly advanced in *embonpoint* since he saw her, but still in the full bloom of womanly beauty. She was dressed in a semi-evening costume, low-necked lavender-coloured silk dress, with an imitation black Spanish mantilla thrown gracefully over her swan-like neck and drooping well-rounded shoulders. The glare of the gaslight illumined her clear Italian-like complexion, and imparted a lustre to a light bandeau of brilliants that encircled her jet black hair. Altogether she looked very bewitching. There was a great hairy fellow in the shop, as big as Facey, and better made, who kept laughing and talking, and " Lucy "-ing Mrs. Sponge in the familiar way fools talk to women in bars and cigar rooms. The little snobs were rather kept at bay by the sight ; not so friend Facey, who brushed past them and boldly entered the once famous "Sponge Cigar and Betting-Rooms." Lucy started with a half-suppressed shriek at the sight, for Romford at any time would have been formidable, but a black Romford was more than her nerves could bear. Added to this she knew who had returned the dunning letters, and feared the visit boded no good.

"Well, and how goes it?" said Facey, advancing, and tendering his great ungloved hand.

"Pretty well, thank you, Mr. Romford," replied Lucy, shaking hands with him.

"And how's the old boy?" asked Facey, meaning Soapey.

"He's pretty well too, thank you," replied Mrs. Sponge.
"At home?" asked Facey, with an air of indifference.

"Well—no," hesitated Lucy, "he's just gone out to his drill. He is one of the West Middlesex." (He was upstairs dressing to go to the billiard-room.)

The hairy monster, seeing he was superseded, presently took his departure, and the little snobs having passed on, the two were left together ; so Facey taking a chair planted himself just opposite the door, as well to stare at her as to stem the tide of further custom. It was lucky he did, for Sponge coming downstairs peeped through the dun-hole of the little retiring-room, and recognising his great shoulders and backward-growing whiskers, beat a retreat and stole out the back way.

"And may I ask who you are in mourning for?" inquired Lucy, as soon as the first rush of politeness was over.

"Oh, me oncle, me Oncle Gilroy," replied Facey.

"Gone at last, is he," said Lucy, who recollected to have heard about him.

"Gone at last," assented Facey, with a downward nod.

"Well, and I hope he's left you something 'andsome," observed Lucy.

"Leave ! Oh, bless you, I never expected nothin' from him. He had a wife and ever so many bairns."

"You don't say so !" exclaimed Lucy, clasping her beautiful hands ; "I always understood he was a bachelor. Well, Mr. S. *will* be astonished when he hears that," added she, turning her lustrous darkly fringed eyes up to the ceiling.

"Fact, however," said Facey significantly.

"You surprise me," said Lucy, fearing the little debt would not be wiped off. "Well," continued she, "it's lucky for those that can do without."

"Ah, that's another matter," muttered Facey, who saw how it bore on the sivin pun ten. "Money's always acceptable," continued he, looking round the shining shop and wondering if he would ever get paid. There seemed plenty of stock, provided the barrels and canisters were not all dummies. How would it do to take it out in kind ? Better get money if he could, thought he. Facey then applied himself to sounding Lucy as to where Sponge was likely to be found. Oh, he would be sure to find him at any time ; could scarcely come wrong. He hadn't been gone five minutes when Mr. Romford came. Would be so vexed when he returned to find he'd missed him. Facey rather doubted this latter assertion, and was half inclined to ask why Soapey had not answered his letters, but Lucy being too pretty to have any words with, and appearing to believe what she said, he pretended that he did too, and shortly afterwards left to get a beefsteak dinner at the Blue Posts in Cork Street. As he turned out of the shop he encountered a blear-eyed, brandy-faced man, with a numbered badge on his breast, and an old red cotton kerchief twisted carelessly round his battered hat, whose seedy greasy clothes seemed greatly in want of a washing. The wearer started at the sight of our friend. It was none other than Soapey Sponge's late job stud-groom, Mr. Leather, crawling from the cab-stand for his weekly stipend of eighteenpence of hush-money for a certain horse robbery he had been engaged in with Mr. Sponge before he married Lucy, and the aged head within the battered hat was the one that butted the Romford stomach, and knocked its owner neck and crop backward downstairs. (*Vide* "Mr. Sponge's Sporting Tour.") Romford, however, did not recognise it, and Leather, wisely thinking the reminiscence would not be productive of a tip, let him pass ; so, after strolling into the Haymarket, Leather returned leisurely to Lucy, and told her that he real*lie* did believe he'd seen that Mr. Romford Facey wot wanted to steal his old master's clothes. And Lucy said he had. The fact was that Romford Facey, as Mr. Leather called him, had wanted to detain the clothes for this identical sivin pun ten he now came in quest of, and Leather showing fight had ultimately been the victor, butting Facey backward downstairs and putting his shoulder out. Leather had long tried for sixpence a week extra for this service, but had not succeeded in getting it.

CHAPTER IV

THE BRIGHT IDEA

LONDON was very empty. There were as many waiters as guests at the Carlton, and White's was equally deserted. A man might walk a long time before he would be hailed—a very long time before anybody would ask him to dine.

Mr. Facey Romford vacillated between the Blue Posts in Cork Street, John o' Groat's in Rupert Street, and Soapey Sponge's in Jermyn Street. Still he never could find Soapey at home. Call early, call late, call when he would, he was never to be seen. Lucy was charged with excuses, and she did her spiriting so kindly and gently that Facey almost began to be reconciled to not seeing him. Still, sivin pun ten was a deal of money, a deal at any time, a great deal to a man who had just been defrauded of an ample fortune, and had to begin the world afresh. Ah, indeed! groaned Facey, as he lay in his attic bed above the ham and beef shop at his new lodging in Beak Street, thinking it over. What should it be? If that old scoundrel hadn't deceived him he might have made a great fortune as a civil engineer; been a second Stephenson or Brunel; for our friend had a good opinion of his abilities—few men better. Facey was quite puzzled what to do. He couldn't return to his theodolite, to levels and surveys—

"And drag at each remove a lengthening chain."

He wouldn't mind being an auctioneer, or stationmaster, if there was a good salary and he could steal away for a little shooting now and then. He wouldn't mind being a chief constable, or even a super, if they would let him hunt his horse occasionally—could trap a thief with any one. His decided *forte*, however, was for dogs and horses. He wouldn't mind a farm, provided he had the game also; but then, under this confounded new system of improvement, it required capital; so did a horse-dealer, so did everything. That was what floored him. In vain he thought of something horsey, out-of-doorish, and exhilarating, that could be worked without any money; nothing of the sort ever occurred to him.

A man's bright ideas generally come when he least expects them; they occur to some in shaving, some in smoking, some in drinking, some in batting, some in boating. Romford caught inspiration by staring into a saddler's shop window in Oxford Street. There he saw sundry busy men in their shirt sleeves, sewing and stitching and hammering away at saddles and horsey things. These being interesting to horsey men, he stuck his thumbs into his armlets and stood straddling and eyeing the operation, looking at saddles in every stage of advancement, from the trees up to the final finish. "Dash it, why shouldn't I be a saddler?" thought he; "could fit one on as well as any man." And then the confounded money question arose again.

Well, but he might be master of the horse to some great man who had not as much leisure and experience as himself. *That would do!* Mr. Romford master of the horse to an earl or a duke say. That would sound well! Would buy the horses and the forage, pocket the percentage, and ride for nothing. And he was half inclined to step into Wilkinson and Kidd's and ask if they knew of anything of the sort—ask as if it were for a friend—a young man in whom he took an interest. While he was thus cogitating, his keen eye caught sight of a man fitting a hunting-horn to a saddle, which carried him away on the moment. From the horse to the hound is an easy and natural transition, which, coupled with the mastership of the horse, then uppermost in Facey's mind, struck the train of thought right into the kennel line, and caused him to hit off the idea of being a master of hounds. A master of hounds! That was the thing—the very thing for his money—or rather, his no money—and he gave his great thigh a slap that sounded like the report of a pistol. "Well done, ingenuity!" cried he, swinging his right arm about, sending an old apple-woman into the gutter, as he rolled away from the window, feeling a new, renovated, regenerated man. A pack of hounds was the very thing to his mind, the very thing of all others that he would have liked best if he had got that wicked old man's money, though he now thought it had been so ill made that it would never have prospered with him. And Facey wondered that the idea had never struck him before: it seemed so natural and obvious, that he could not think how it had happened. Money! It required no money! The people who wanted the sport would find the money. He would find discretion and judgment. He knew all the ins and outs of management,—how a twenty pund horse was made into a fifty,—where to buy meal, where to buy oats, where to buy hay, where to buy everything. Then he would hunt the hounds himself—do for pleasure what others did for pay—and could soon fashion a light, active, 'cute lad with brains in his head into a whip. He knew how to get helpers at the exact market price,—he would be his own stud-groom,—master of horse to himself. His hunting would get him shooting, and shooting would get him fishing, and the three would get him into society, and there was no saying but he might get an heiress after all. And Facey congratulated himself uncommonly on his sagacity, and retraced his steps to the Blue Posts, and then back to Soapey's, with a light elasticity that he had never known since the death of Oncle Gilroy. Still there was no Soapey to be seen in Jermyn Street. Lucy was there, neat and pretty as usual, with the accustomed levee of nincompoops, all looking out for a smile. A mortgagee to the extent of sivin pun ten might well exercise acts of ownership, and Facey rolled in with such an air of importance that several of the small fry slunk away in alarm, thinking Facey was Soapey, and might perhaps spin them into the street. And as Soapey knew better than appear when Facey was there, the latter had the shop pretty much to himself; a presence, however, that did not at all contribute to the increase of custom. But as Facey had no share in the profits, and found the shop a very convenient lounge, he just dropped in whenever it suited him, getting his pipe and his porter from the Black Horse over the way. Lucy was always neat and nicely dressed, and partly from having an excellent figure of her own, and partly because the space behind the counter was rather contracted, she did not counteract Nature's gifts by making herself into a haystack with hoops, but just put on as much something as made her clothes stand out below. She was always busy with her needle—always either making her own clothes or mending Soapey's, which latter were sometimes rather dilapidated.

Facey on his part kept the mastership project firmly and steadily in view. The letters M.F.H. met him in the morning, they accompanied him throughout the day, and closed his eyes at night. He apostrophised the Bow bells' address to Whittington—

> "Turn again Whittington,
> Thrice Lord Mayor of London."

into,

> "Turn again, Romford,
> Thrice Master of Fox-Hounds."

He felt fully persuaded he would be a master, just as Mr. Disraeli felt fully persuaded he would be an orator, and Louis Napoleon that he would be an emperor—it was fated so. He visited all the likely haunts of horsey and hunting men, from Tattersall's down to some of the enterprising gentlemen who offer invaluable horses for half nothing, with every opportunity of investigation and trial. Though most of these thought Facey looked like a clown, yet there was something about his roguish physiognomy that prevented their trying it on with him. One thought he was a coper in disguise, and asked him, with a knowing wink, if he wasn't in their line himself. And though Facey had gone into the yard with a considerable swagger, he did not resent the imputation, but said, in a low confidential sort of tone, " Well, no, but p'r'aps I could give you a lift." And the man being ever anxious to do some one, after feeling his way a little further, fraternised with Facey, and but him up to a thing or two. So Facey went about from place to place, always with an eye to the main chance—that of getting a country, and talking as if he had lately abandoned one.

Still, running about and making inquiries instead of advertising for what one wants is very much like sending one's letters by a special messenger instead of availing oneself of the post. One good advertisement in the right quarter, the right medium of communication, will do more towards suiting people than whole reams of letter paper, and months of personal effort and inquiry.

Of course Romford, wanting a country, did not advertise in the " Record," or the " Saturday Review," but went to the appropriate office of " Bell's Life in London," where with the aid of a clerk he combed out a very taking advertisement. It stated that a gentleman, to whom subscription was a secondary consideration, was ready to treat for a country where he could get a little shooting and fishing as well. " All letters and communications to be addressed to Francis Romford, Esq., at the Sponge Cigar Warehouse, Jermyn Street, St. James's, S.W., Facey thinking that Jermyn Street, St. James's, sounded better than Jermyn Street, Haymarket, which perhaps it does. And having thus laid the foundation of future fame, he went about with a copy of the paper in his pocket, pricing saddles and bridles, and things, showing the fortunate victim by the advertisement where to send them to ; and sportsmen being always in high repute with tradesmen. he very soon got a goodly collection together. He looked in at Bartley and Hammond's, intending to have his boots and breeches from them ; but somehow, though these great professors took his measure, and complimented him on his proportions, they did not care to execute his orders. Bartley told him he would back him to lick Sayers, but still he would not make him a pair of boots to fight in. However, as Facey said, there was no harm done, and he inwardly wished himself better luck another time.

CHAPTER V

THE H.H., OR, HEAVYSIDE HUNT

BEING about the middle of the hunting season it was not to be expected that friend Romford would have many applications for his immediate services ; but these being the days for getting one's sport out of other people's pockets, he had plenty of feelers as to what he would do against the next one. Some of the writers evidently thought they were communicating with the other Mr. Romford, who if they could but get to adopt their country, it would save them all further trouble about subscribing— sport being evidently the object of the advertiser, not subscription—indeed, Mr. Romford was known to be very rich. Facey entered into correspondence with some of these, and one gentleman came all the way from Uttoxeter to see him, to the serious detriment of a five-pound note ; when finding they were both of the same kidney, he was weak enough to try to get Facey to pay half his expenses—a light for a cigar was all he got out of Romford. Still, our friend continued his advertisement, and at length it brought forth,—if not golden,—at all events some fruit. The members of the old-established Heavyside Hunt had quarrelled among themselves, and it had been resolved to re-cast the establishment altogether, and have a dictator instead of many masters.

The hunt, as many of our readers are perhaps aware, is one of very great antiquity, being called after its founder, Mr. Simon Heavyside, of Heavyside Hall. From one of his capacious clasped red pockets in which he used to dot down the doings of the day, the horses he bought, the corn he sold, the lambs he reared, we learn that, so far back as 1751, he had hired a youth called Mark Buck to go with Harry the huntsman and hounds, the same being, as Mr. Heavyside noted, "cappital when settled to their fox, but rather mettlesome before," most likely very riotous, and Buck was to be whipper-in under the inferior title of couple-boy. The hunt, therefore, must have been in existence some time before this, though how long we are unable to say. Mr. Heavyside kept the establishment, such as it was, and having the whole county to operate upon he used to make royal sporting progresses wherever he heard there was good wine to drink and foxes to hunt. Very cheery and jolly the old cocks were, hunting, and drinking, and talking enthusiastically of the sport. Very circumspect they were about their port—four years in wood and twenty in bottle was the youngest they could drink, and solemn and sententious were the judgments they delivered ere a pipe was considered perfect. Then they went ahead till it was finished. They never hunted two days together —three days a week was considered very handsome ; but they used to assemble at the kennel on the intervening ones, and chat over the pedigrees and merits of those hounds that had particularly distinguished themselves on the preceding days,—how Firebrand led up to the Gibbet on Harrowden Heath, and how Trimbush and Trueman took it up and maintained the lead all the way to Billington Hill. It was all the hounds they talked about, not themselves or their horses. No telling of how Brown beat Smith, or how Tomkins set the field. Indeed, the horses were not adapted to that description of work, being merely what would be called machiners at the present day ; but they could trot and clamber along, and a hunt not being a hunt unless it lasted three hours, there was great harmony between them and the hounds. They would paw and whinny with delight as some sage veteran of the chase made long-drawn proclamation of the scent, to be ratified and confirmed by each particular hound for himself. They used not to take much upon credit. Each hound had to be satisfied, and enthusiastic would he be when he was so—not a yard would they go without a scent.

We have been favoured with a sight of a picture of old Mr. Simon Heavyside painted about the fortieth year of

his reign, in which the old bottle-nosed hero is depicted
on an old crop-eared grizzled horse with a whitening-brush
tail, a flat flapped saddle, and a snaffle bridle in his mouth.
The squire, a good eighteen stoner, is attired in a velvet
cap, with a squarish peak, from whose black sides a profusion of snow-white locks protrude, gathered and tied
into a comprehensive pig-tail behind. His abundant,
almost superabundant, single-breasted scarlet coat-laps
reach a long way below the mahogany-coloured boot-tops,
which are kept over the calf of the leg by a pair of broad
tanned straps across the knee, thus showing a sufficiency
of the bright blue woollen interregnum, a buff vest high
in the throat and long in the waist, with ample flap-
pockets, a straight spur, a spare stirrup leather across the
shoulder, and a most formidable-looking hammer-headed
whip, the thong dangling at the side of the leg, complete
the costume of this ancient worthy. Around him are
several couple of hounds, great long-eared, lumbering
animals, and in the distance sundry stacks of chimneys are
seen in full smoke rising among the trees, indicative of the
extent of hospitality at the Hall. It was said that no one
ever left it either sad or sober—it was a sort of free public
house for the country at large, and as the squire brewed
his own ale, killed his own meat, and made his own cheese,
there was a great deal of wear and tear for the teeth at no
very serious sacrifice. At length the old trump being
unable any longer to partake of the pleasures of the chase
himself, bethought him of providing for the amusement of
posterity by securing the continuance of his hounds in the
country to which he was so much attached. To this end
he made his will, of which the following is an extract :—

"I Simon Heavyside, of Heavyside Hall, Esquyer, being
of hole and perfect mind and memorie, thoughe verie
craysed and sore wounded in body, do make this my last
will and testament in manor and forme folowienge ; that
is to say : To my well beloved friends and brother sports-
mene Oliver Rookeburn, of Ringland Hill, and Thomas
Dawson, of Chaldon Hall, Esquiers, and their Heirs, all my
most truly valuable hounde dogges, with the cooples them
thereunto belonging, together with £62 by yere, or as
much more as my landes in Lamsheles and Allenton will
let for by the yeare, for the keep and maintenance of the
saide hounde dogges, and their desendents for ever."

And he gave to his friend Tom Tidswell of Hayford for a token, his racking grey nage, alsoe to Joe Smith, of Westfield, his donne horse, and to Ned Armstrong, of Windrush, a browne horse that he bought of Nicholas Rattler.

And he ordered that his huntsman, George Grimwell, should have meat and drink in his house during his life, with 40s. by the yere for tobacco and snuff.

And Simon being greatly respected, as most men with bottle noses are, the hunt resolved itself into a Heavyside club at his death, the members of which all took the surname of Heavyside, and addressed each other by the title of brother, sinking their own surnames and using the prefix to their Christian ones only, thus, Brother Nicholas Heavyside, Brother Solomon Heavyside, Brother Timothy Heavyside, the parties' real names being Fairbank, Woodney, and Heaton. Then at the hunt dinners, the memory of their great founder was drunk standing with solemn silence, and those who had hunted with him and those who had wined with him shook their grey heads, and said they should never see his like again. But Time, the soother and reconciler, gradually lessened the veneration, as younger men with smaller waists and greater activity began to supply the places of the original members. Then they wanted a younger huntsman, quicker hounds, shorter runs, and smarter cords.

At first the mere mention of any innovation was looked upon as rank heresy, and the irritated elders peered over their formidable broad-rimmed spectacles (for specs were specs in those days) to see who was guilty of such treason ; but as the specs gradually gave way to eyes that could see, there was a growing inclination in favour of pace.

But Lawyer Lappy, who was an original Heavysider, and, moreover, had attained the distinguished weight of nineteen stone, insisted that according to the terms of the will the hounds must be the lineal descendants of the old stock, or they would forfeit the endowment, so they could do little in the way of improvement as long as the lawyer lived. At length Brother Lappy paid the debt of nature, whereupon the new generation abolished the term brother and substituted a smart hunt button—dead gold with a bright border, and the letters H.H. entwined so affectionately and hieroglyphically together as to make it extremely difficult to say what they were. Then old Grimwell was turned adrift on his baccy and beer, the throaty old patriarchs of the pack were put in repose, and swallow tails superseded the flowing bed-gown like coats. Crop-eared horses disappeared, and whitening-brush tails were succeeded by long switches.

Still there were always two parties in the hunt, those who admired the old system, and those who advocated the new, and Lawyer Lappy's oracular decision operated very prejudicially upon pace. They would not like to lose the rents, which had increased amazingly since Mr. Heavyside's time. So they jangled and wrangled on season after season, each side declaring the others were the most stupid and impracticable people imaginable. At length they got to the point of dissension that resulted in the application to Mr. Romford. They could bear each other no longer, and wrote to know if Mr. Romford would undertake to hunt their country three days a week for £800 a year, each side being determined to screw the other up to the utmost.

Now though £800 a year seems a very small sum when compared with the book estimates, and considering the great opportunities a pack of hounds afford for spending money, yet £800 a year well administered will go a good way towards sport, especially with a man like Mr. Rom-ford, who knew the value of money, and meant to work the thing himself. Then too the H.H. had a fat hunts-man, one Jonathan Lotherington, who absorbed the best part of £100 a year, and yet wouldn't ride over a water furrow, an aggravating circumstance to gentlemen who liked to see a man come gallantly over a hedge, and calculate what they themselves would do or try to do it for. This £100 Facey would save by hunting the hounds himself, and there were many other little items that he knew how to lop off or reduce. Of course he didn't tell the H.H. gentlemen this; on the contrary, he pooh-poohed the subscription, declaring it would do nothing for him, but that was only to excite them to further endeavours, and enforce the propriety of early and punctual payment. He determined from the first not to miss it, unless of course he saw his way to something better.

Indeed he talked, or rather wrote, so magnificently that some of them wished he mightn't be too great a man for their money. Lucy, who wrote a good hand and

managed the literary department for him, was much
struck with the grandeur of his views, and wondered that
a gentleman who could do so much should make such a
noise about a trumpery sivin pun ten. Meanwhile the
H.H. gentlemen were staunch and anxious, only too eager
to close with such a desirable gentleman, and the anxiety
was not diminished by a reference to Burke, which showed
that the owner of Abbeyfield Park was a bachelor, heir
presumptive, his brother Augustus Umfreville.

Some of the young ladies thought they would like to
save Augustus Umfreville the trouble of thinking of it.
At length they got a bargain struck : So much money
down, so much more in the middle, so much at the end of
the season, and Facey strutted up Regent Street as if both
sides of the way were his, and the middle too. It was Mr.
Romford, M.F.H., Mr. Romford, master of the Heavyside hounds. And he drank his own health in a copious
bowl of Blue Posts baked punch, and then bought Lucy
a splendid tiara of brilliants in Burlington Arcade. Price
two pound ten. *Hoo-ray!* for Mr. Romford !

CHAPTER VI

GONE AWAY !

AS ill-luck would have it, the very day that saw Mr.
Romford elevated into a master of hounds, placed
him in an awkward position with Mrs. Sponge. Soapey, as
we said before, had not been a good husband. So long as the
betting lists lasted, and he could pigeon the greenhorns, he
was all very well, and attended to the shop, but when
they were abolished, and Sir Richard Mayne's cab-fares
superseded those of his favourite author Mr. Mogg, Soapey
grew more and more out-of-door-ish, horsey, and Hornsey
Wood-ish, until at last upon Lucy devolved the entire responsibility of making the pot boil. Still, they might
have done pretty well with the cigar shop alone ; for the
abolition of the betting lists operated favourably in the
baccy line by drawing a goodly number of young swells
into the shop, who had theretofore been kept at bay by

the appearance of Sponge; but unfortunately he spent more than the swells brought in, so the concern was rapidly retrograding. At this juncture came Facey Romford, as before mentioned, whose great athletic frame and keen watchful eye cleared the course like a constable. The lawful owner even, too, durstn't show, for there was that sivin pun ten scored against him, and as the take in the till grew daily less, the less Sponge cared to come to count it. And now, on this auspicious day, when Facey came to crown her with the tiara on the glorious termination of the hound treaty, he was met by Lucy with the serious announcement that Mr. S. (for she did not care to mention the name) had bolted—bolted with the spoons and all the loose cash.

She had just received a letter with the Euston Square postmark upon it, saying, he was off to Liverpool, to catch one of the Black Ball line of clipper packets for Australia, and would write to her again when he got there.

"Bolted!" exclaimed Facey, his lively imagination realising the position as quickly as did that of the old gentleman who had the child pawned off upon him in the City omnibus.[1] "Bolted!" repeated he, twitching out a liberal sample of his cane-coloured beard as he spoke, and examining it by the fan gaslight of the counter.

Facey did not like it; Lucy neither. Though Soapey had not been a good Sponge to her of late, still she now realised her old aphorism, that a bad husband was a deal better than none. Facey feared to have a woman thrown upon him just at this critical moment of his preferment, when he thought he saw heiresses rising in shoals to contend for his hand. He now wished he had forfeited the sivin pun ten.

"Whatever am I to do?" exclaimed poor Lucy, clasping her hands, with tearful upturned eyes. "Nathan

---

[1] "Would you have the goodness to hold the baby while I get out?" asked a young woman of a respectable-looking gentleman sitting next her, at the same time placing it on his knee. The next thing he saw, was the young woman disappearing in the thick of the crowd by the Mansion House. The omnibus went on, the gentleman sitting with his little charge, saying nothing. When, however, it stopped again, at the end of Cheapside, he repeated the operation on his next neighbour, saying, "Would you have the goodness to hold the child while I get out?" When, having done so, he instantly disappeared up St. Martin's-le-Grand.

Levy has fixed to be here at twelve o'clock to-morrow for
his rent, and there isn't a halfpenny to meet it with."

"Humph!" growled Facey, taking another pull at his
beard.

"He'll seize whatever he finds," ejaculated Lucy.

"Then the less you leave him to find the better," replied
Facey. "Whose are these things?" asked he, knocking
the mahogany counter with his knuckles, and nodding
promiscuously at the gas and general fittings around.

"Some are his, and some are ours," replied Lucy.

"Well, then, I'll tell you what, you just go and convert
them," said Facey, "and bolt too."

"But where am I to go? What am I to do?"

"Plenty of places to go to!—plenty to do," rejoined
Romford, with the confidence of a man well established
himself.

Lucy hesitated assent.

"Set up a register-office, start a school, teach dancing,
give lessons in riding, return to the stage—a hundred
ways of making money in this great, rich metropolis."

Facey determined that, come what might, he would not
be encumbered with her himself. He was a very moral
man, especially when it was his interest to be so, and was
not going to prejudice his chance of getting an heiress by
—even the semblance of an illicit connection.

"But why not go to your mother?" asked Facey, who
he knew was a theatrical dresser, living at Hart Street,
Covent Garden.

"Oh, my mother has as much as she can manage to keep
herself," sighed Lucy.

"Well, but you can stop there, at all events, for the
present," observed Facey, "till summut turns up."

The result of a long conference was, that the little slipshod girl of the house was sent to Wardour Street for a
furniture broker, to whom Lucy sold everything for ready
money, with a stipulation that it was all to be cleared
away that night, and, having packed up her clothes,
together with the remaining stock of cheroots and manillas,
she drove off in a four-wheeled cab to her mother in Hart
Street, there to ruminate on the past and contemplate the
future.

Next morning, "THE SPONGE CIGAR WAREHOUSE,
WHOLESALE, RETAIL, AND FOR EXPORTATION," was closed!

And when Nathan Levy heard the said news, he wrung

his hands in anguish, vowing that he was utterly and inextricably ruined. Never ! no *never*, should he get over it.

And selfish Facey, having established Mrs. Sponge, presently took his departure to look after his hounds, very glad that things had terminated as they had done, for at one time he thought they looked very ominous.

The reader will therefore now have the goodness to accompany Mr. M. F. H. Romford into the country.

CHAPTER VII

MINSHULL VERNON

RAILWAYS have destroyed the romance of travelling. Bulwer himself could not make anything out of a collision, and trains, trucks, trams, and tinkling bells are equally intractable. No robbing, no fighting, no benighting, no run-away-ing. One journey is very much like another, save that the diagonal shoots across country are distinguished by a greater number of changes. But with the exception of certain level crossings, certain mountings up, certain divings down like a man changing his floor at a lodging, there is really nothing to celebrate. It's, "Away you go !" or, "Here you are !"

The H.H. country had scarcely been screeched and whistled awake by the noise of railways. It had few requirements that way.

There were no factories, no tall chimneys, no coal pits, no potteries, no nothing. The grass grew in the streets of what were called the principal towns, where the rattle of a chaise would draw all heads to the windows. The people seemed happy and contented, more inclined to enjoy what they had than disposed to risk its possession in the pursuit of more. In fact, they might be called a three per cent. sort of people in contradistinction to the raving rapacity of modern cupidity.

It was long after dark ere the little dribbling single line branch railway, that Mr. Romford had adopted by means of a sort of triumphal arch on quitting the main

one at Langford Green, deposited him at the quiet little
town of Minshull Vernon, the nearest point to the H.H.
kennel. He had been in and out of so many trains,
paced the platforms of so many stations, and read the an-
nouncements of so many waiting-rooms, that he felt as if he
had traversed half the kingdom, and was thankful to get
his luggage out for the last time in a quiet, unhurrying
way. The train was twenty minutes behind time as it
was, and the guard did not seem to care if he made it
thirty before he got to the end of his short but slow
journey. Minshull Vernon was a very small station, too
insignificant for any advertiser save a temperance hotel-
keeper and a soda-water maker to patronise. Even their
placards looked worn and dejected. There wasn't a bus
or a cab or a fly or a vehicle of any sort in attendance,
only a little boy, who, however, was willing to carry any
quantity of luggage. Such a contrast to the leaving in
London.

Finding there were but two inns in the place, the
White Swan, and the West-end Swell, our friend, true to
his colours, patronised the latter, and was presently
undergoing the usual inquiry "what would he like for
supper," from a comely hostess, Mrs. Lockwood, the
widow of a London groom, who in all probability had
christened the house after his master. Romford wasn't
a dainty man, and having narrowed the larder to the
usual point of beefsteaks and mutton-chops, he said he'd
have both, which he afterwards supplemented by a large
cut of leathery cheese. Two pipes and two glasses of
brandy-and-water, one to his own health, the other to
that of the hounds, closed the performance, after which
he rolled off to bed in a pair of West-end Swell slippers.
He was soon undressed, in bed, and asleep.

Facey couldn't tell where he was in the morning. The
excitement of the journey, the rapidity of events, all
tended to confuse him.

He wasn't at Mother Maggison's, for he had no curtains
to his bed there; besides, that game was all up. It
wasn't Beak Street, for those were brown and these were
green; then it came across him where he was, and with
a victorious swing of his great muscular arm, he bounded
out of bed with a thump that nearly sent him through
the old dry rotting floor. Mrs. Lockwood thought it was
the chimney-stack coming down.

Never having heard of Minshull Vernon before, of course Facey had not formed any expectations as to appearance; but when he came to look out of his window he found quite a different sort of place to what it looked over night. In lieu of a dull, formal street he found himself on the reach of a beautiful river with its clear translucent streams sparkling in the morning sun. "Dash it, but here's fishing," said Facey, as he eyed the still trout holes —adding, "I'll be in to you, by fair means or foul." Having made a general survey of the scene, he then halloaed downstairs for hot water just as he used to do at old Mother Maggison's, and forthwith proceeded to shave and array himself.

Having ordered his breakfast—coffee and sausages, for which latter Minshull Vernon is famous—Facey put on his buttoned boots and turned out for a stroll in the street. It was a seedy-looking place, all the shops doing double duty, with no apparent pre-eminence among them. Jugs and basins commingled with ladies' hoops, flour and fruit stood side by side, marbles and mustard were in the same bowl. Besom-makers and beer shops seemed to predominate. At length Facey found a saddler's, or rather half a saddler's, for he dealt in cheese as well, far different to the saddler's in whose window he drew in inspiration in Oxford Street. This was Toby Trotter, a first-rate gossip and liberal tipper of servants who brought work to his shop. To hear the tippees talk, one would think there wasn't such another shop in the kingdom. Such leather, such sewing, such workmanship generally. Toby was what they call a jobbing saddler, a man who worked out by the day, either so much money and his meals, or so much money without his meals; but as people found that Toby managed to get his meals either way, they mostly adopted the system of paying and feeding him. This gave him a fine opportunity for picking up news, and many a story and many an arrangement that people thought quite snug all among themselves was pro-mulgated at Toby's shop. All the queer rumours and scandals in the county could be traced up to him. He had heard, when taking his usual nightcap, that there was an arrival at the West-end Swell, and was on the lookout for a view. He now saw Facey coming, and began busying himself with the arrangement of a bunch of brass-nailed cart-whips hanging at the shop door.

Toby was a little bald, turnip-headed, roundabout, white-aproned man, who looked as if you could trundle him down street like a beer barrel. At first he thought Facey was a bagman—we beg pardon, representative of a commercial establishment—a conjecture that was speedily dissipated by his stopping short and asking for a set of spur straps. Toby had none by him, but would make him a set in a minute, which was just what Facey wanted, the imparlance, not the leathers, being the object of his visit. A saddler's is always the place to pick up sporting news, just as a confectioner's is the one to pick up matrimonial intelligence. So our friend entered and took a seat on a stool while Toby busied himself for what he wanted. Nay more, Facey made a mental inventory of the shop, and estimated its contents, cheese and all, at some eighteen pound odd. This, too, while he was talking on indifferent subjects with Toby. Our friend's honours were too novel and recent to admit of his keeping them to himself ; and Toby, who was a bungler, had scarcely begun to cut ere Facey let out that he was the new master of the Heavyside Hunt. Great was Toby's awe and astonishment, and his hand shook and his cutter jibbed in a way that made very slovenly workmanship. Nevertheless his tongue went glibly enough, and he presently inducted Facey into his country, told him who kept a good house, who kept a middling one, who kept a shabby one, whose keeper shot the foxes, whose sold the pheasants, whose trapped the hares, whose wanted palming. Altogether, gave him a very satisfactory insight into what he might expect. And Toby declined taking payment for the spur leathers, handing Facey a card, and hoping he would allow him the honour of opening an account with him, a request that Facey was obliging enough to grant.

CHAPTER VIII

THE H.H. HOUNDS

THERE are few things so faithful as a dish of sausages, not the indigestible leadeny things cooks make in the country, but the light savoury productions of the

practised hand ; and friend Facey having eaten about a
pound and a half of Minshull Vernon ones felt equal to
any emergency ; he didn't think he would ever be hungry
again, so he didn't pocket his customary crust. Finding
that the kennel was only seven miles off by the fields, he
determined to attempt the expedition by the usual mysti-
fying directions of the local bumpkins : " Ye mun gan
to the Old Wood toll-gate and then torn to the left and
then to the reet, and then keep straight endways till ye
come to the pound, and then take the Hay Bridge Hill
road till ye come to a four lane ends, after which ye cross
the common and come oot by Newbiggin toon end," all
very plain sailing to a practised person, but quite be-
wildering to a stranger. However, Facey was used to
country people's directions, and by dint of keeping the
kennel question steadily in view, he succeeded in reaching it in about double the distance he expected. Still, he
did not care much for the *détour*, consoling himself with
the reflection that he was seeing the country, and would
be able to rectify his mistakes in returning. He now
pulled up on a rising ground, a short way off, to contemplate the unmistakable brick and slate structure standing
on the slope of a corresponding hill opposite.

> "Its courts
> On either hand wide opening to receive
> The sun's all-cheering beams, when mild he shines
> And gilds the mountain tops."

"Va-ry good," muttered Romford, eyeing it, "va-ry
good, the stables I see are behind, clock in the middle,
corn lofts above—have seen many a worse-looking place
than that." Facey feeling his own consequence involved
in the appearance.

He then sunk the hill, and crossing along a little rustic
footbridge over a gurgling stream, presently deserted the
footpath for the more generous amplitude of the kennel-
surrounding carriage way.

Our friend was now at one of the hunt-endowed farms,
Allerton by name, greatly altered and improved since Mr.
Heavyside's time. Indeed, its value had been more than
quadrupled.

A bright green door, with a highly polished brass
knocker placed between diamond-patterned paned
windows, now announced the huntsman's house, and

making for it, a very slight rat-a-tat brought a little hooped servant girl to answer it.

" Mister What's-his-name at home ? " asked Facey, who had either never heard, or had forgotten, the huntsman's patronymic.

" Mr. Lotherington's in the kennel, sir," replied the girl, dropping a curtsy.

"Then tell him Mr. Romford's here," said Facey, thinking to have the whole establishment all out in a rush.

" Please, sir, Mr. Bamford's here," said the girl.

"Bamford, Bamford, know no such name ; tell him to coom in," said the Yorkshireman, who was busy in a kennel conference.

Jonathan Lotherington was a self-sufficient man, who firmly believed in the perfection of everything around him, consequently he never went from home, for change or advice. People might imitate him, he said, but he copied nobody. His was the glass to dress by. Jonathan had been many years with the Heavyside hounds, and though he came out beef-ier and beef-ier every season, he never recognised any change in himself. He thought, indeed, he rather improved than otherwise. He now rode eighteen stone, a grand weight, he said, for making horses steady and careful at their leaps.

Still, he had his admirers among the H.H., few more sincere than Colonel Chatterbox, with whom he was then conversing. The Colonel had been one of the old " Brothers Heavyside," and always regretted the change that had taken place in the name. When Jonathan and he joined their sapience together they were very convincing. They could unravel a run and kill foxes over again. They were in the middle of a long towl about a twenty years' old run from Lovedale Gorse to Brierly Banks, when the little girl interrupted the narrative. Though they were both very "'cute," according to their own accounts, and were in daily expectation of the new master, yet they neither of them thought Bamford might be Romford, and so returned to the point where the confounded coursers headed the fox on Frankton open fields and drove him off the finest line of country that ever was seen.

When Romford rolled in, the fat huntsman was standing before the fat Colonel, each poking away at the other's ribs, as they made their successful hits and recollections of the run. They were quite enthusiastic on the subject.

Romford had no difficulty in recognising the huntsman, for he was attired in the last year's robes of office, viz. a purply lapped coat, warm breeches and boots—a hat instead of a cap, and the absence of spurs, was all that denoted the non-hunting day. The Colonel was green-coated, buff-vested, white-corded, and leather-gaitered. Carmelite had taken the liberty of wiping his feet on his cords, leaving him the only consolation that they were the second day on. Jonathan and he were now both prepared against further assaults in the shape of kennel-whips held under their arms.

Though they both saw Romford coming, they neither of them thought a man in such a shabby hat, and seedy paletot, with his Sydenham trousers turned up at the bottom, worth their attention, so they just went on poking and talking as before.

"Well, old boy," said Romford, laying his heavy hand on Jonathan Lotherington's shoulder, "I've come to see these 'ere canine dogs."

"Presently, sir, presently," snapped Lotherington, as much as to say, who are you, pray, that thus interrupts?

"Presently!" retorted Romford; adding, "I'm Mr. Romford, the new master."

Lotherington started at the announcement. Off went the hat with a sweep, commensurate with a five-pound tip, looking as if it would never be restored. The Colonel, too, raised his a little, and salutations being over, Facey renewed his application to see the hounds.

"Certainly, sir, certainly," replied Lotherington, pre-senting Facey with a dress-protecting switch, holloaing at the same time, "Michael! here, lad! coom!" to his whip.

The lad, who was about sixty, came shambling along in the peculiar manner of dismounted horsemen, and passing out of the flagged court in which the Colonel and Lotherington had been having their kennel lecture, they entered the first lodging-house yard beyond. The door being opened, the hounds were turned off their warm benches by the lad, and came yawning and stretching themselves, giving an occasional bay, as much as to say, what are you bothering us about now? Mr. Romford, like a general at a review, then took up a favourable position from which he could criticise their looks. There were several throaty, splay-footed, crooked-legged animals among them, and Mr. Romford thought there was scarcely one

that he could not find a fault in. However, that he kept
to himself, pretending to imbibe all Lotherington and the
Colonel said in their praise. At length, the Yorkshireman
having rather over-egged the pudding with his praise, Mr.
Romford observed that he thought some of them must be
kept for their goodness rather than their beauty. This
only made the parties more vehement, and as Facey had
not the means of confuting them, he made what he thought
the *amende honorable* by saying they might be better than
they looked. They then proceeded to the other yard. It
was ditto repeated. More blear eyes, more flat sides, more
weak loins. But Lotherington assured him he could carry
their pedigrees right back into the last century.

"So much the worse," muttered Romford. Then he
continued his silent criticism. "Well," at length said he,
"the proof of the puddin's in the eatin', and I'll see them
in the field before I say anything. Let me see," continued
he, diving into his paletot and fishing up his "Life,"
"Wednesday, that's to-morrow, Shivering Hill ; Saturday,
Oakenshaw Wood. What sort of a place is Oakenshaw
Wood ?" asked Romford.

"Very good, sir," said Lotherington.

"Very good," assented the Colonel.

"Then I shall most likely be there," said Romford,
returning Lotherington his switch, adding, "and now I
must be off, for the days are short, the roads dirty, and I
don't know my way." So saying, with a sort of half bow,
half nod, to the Colonel, he rolled out of the kennel.

But that Abbeyfield Park kept it down, the Colonel
would have said "he's a rum 'un." Lotherington, less
awed, thus expressed his opinion to his friend Grimstone,
the head groom, who, as usual, came, crab-like, down from
the stables to hear what was up.

"Ar think nout o' this Romford, mister," said he.
"Why, he cam to kennel i' buttoned boots ! cam to kennel
i' buttoned boots !" as if it was impossible for a man to be
a sportsman who wore such things. And Grimstone shook
his head as much as to say he "wouldn't do."

CHAPTER IX

THE DÉBUT

NO man with money in his pocket need ever be long in
want of a horse ; this Mr. Facey Romford well knew,
having bought four-legged ones, three-legged ones, and
two-legged ones—all sorts of horses, in fact.   He had
bought horses with money and without—more perhaps
without than with.   He would take them on trial, buy
them if he saw he could sell them for more than was
asked, or pay or promise so much for their use if returned.
And being a bold, resolute rider, people had no objection
to seeing him shove their horses along, feeling perhaps
that they came in for part of the credit of the performance.
Many of them thought what they would give to be able
to spin them along as Facey did.

Having regained Minshull Vernon, with the omission
of several of the angles he had made in going to the
kennel, he refreshed his inner man, and then bethought
him of further cultivating the acquaintance of his morning friend, Toby Trotter.   Toby was in the West-end
Swell, being a member of the Jolly Owls' Club, which
met there every other night, and gladly availed himself
of the invitation to drink at Mr. Romford's expense
instead of his own.   Besides, the honour of the thing was
very considerable.   A Master of Foxhounds !—He had
drank with many eminent men—commercial gentlemen
—representatives, as they called themselves,—but never
with anything approaching such eminence.   So he pulled
up his pointed gills, readjusted his cameo brooch, and
proceeded to answer the summons.   At first the Owl was
inclined to stand, but Romford insisted upon his sitting,
and each having got his favourite beverage, rum to the
Owl, gin to the Master, together with pipes, they drew to
the fire and had a very discursive discussion with regard
to the country and its sporting capabilities generally.
From him Facey learned that there were several young
farmers with goodish-like horses who might be equitably
dealt with—men who wouldn't ask three hundred when
they meant to take thirty—and Facey having got the

names and addresses of some of these, borrowed Bullock the butcher's pony the next morning and set off in quest of the needful. He wanted a mount for the Saturday, and almost the first place he came to, viz. young Mr. Dibble of Cumberledge, supplied the deficiency : Dibble was going to be married to the pretty Miss Snowball and wouldn't want his horse during the honeymoon, and finding who he had for a customer, he unhesitatingly placed him at Mr. Romford's disposal, declining all mention of money. If Mr. Romford liked him, well and good—they then could talk about it after ; if not, he could return him, and would be welcome to the loan. Dibble was not one of the swell order of farmers, who ride in scarlet and spurt the mud in their landlord's faces, but a quiet-going respectable young man, who got his day or two a week out of a great raking, snaffle-bridled, cock-thropped, chestnut horse, with white stockings ; like Facey, himself rather deficient on one side of his head, his "fatther" being the gentleman, and his "moother" a cart mare. However, he could "gollop," as Lotherington said, and leap almost anything when he was not blown. Independently of the usual trimming, these sort of animals always want about the heels, a farmer's condition is seldom first rate, and the Dragon of Wantley, as the horse was called, would have been better for a little trimming all over ; but this was precisely where Facey was deficient— he had no idea of neatness, let alone style, and put hunt-ing upon much the same rough footing as shooting. "What's the use of dressing up fine when one's going to dirty oneself directly ?" he used to say ; so the Dragon of Wantley and his rider were much upon a par. Facey not having thought it worth his while to get the dribbling cow-boy ostler of the West-end Swell to take the long hairs off the horse any more than to try to put any lustre upon his own rusty Napoleons ; and being quite a man for the morning, our friend, having made a most sub-stantial sausage breakfast, mounted betimes to ride the Dragon of Wantley quietly on to the meet, calling as he went down street at Toby Trotter's for one of his pig-jobber-like whips in lieu of the Malacca-cane-sticked one he had left at Mother Maggison's for the inexorable County Court Bailiffs. And now, being fully accoutred, Facey got the Dragon by the head, and giving him a touch of his persuasive spurs, tried his pace along the Westfield road. He was a strong, light-going horse for his size, above sixteen hands, and seemed rather pleased than otherwise at carrying a pink, making Facey hope for his better acquaintance before night. So they proceeded gaily along through highways and byeways according as the pioneering grooms directed the course, from whom, however, Facey did not receive many complimentary caps. He arrived at the meet just as the hounds came up.

It having transpired that Mr. Romford would be out at Oakenshaw Wood, there was a great gathering of the H.H. to greet the new master, and many were the times Lotherington was asked by ambling up horsemen if "Mr Romford had come," the inquirers taking the shabby old scarlet sitting slouching among the hounds to contain young Tom Snowball, the bride's brother, going to take his change out of the Dragon of Wantley, during the aforesaid honeymoon. And of course there was a good deal of awkwardness and many pantomimic gestures necessary to prevent further explosion, and stop people from saying what perhaps they ought not to say. It is very disagreeable to be talked of as if one was absent.

And, as ill luck would have it, neither of the gentlemen with whom Facey had corresponded were out, and Colonel Chatterbox, the only member of the hunt who had seen him before, had got a bad attack of rheumatism from his day on the flags, where they met. So that there was really nobody to receive and introduce the owner of Abbeyfield Park to the field. However, Facey didn't care much about that sort of thing, and having stared at the hounds as much as the field stared at him, he asked Lotherington if they hadn't better be moving.

"Generally give a quarter of an hour's law," replied Lotherington, with a semi-touch of the cap.

"Do you?" retorted Facey; "devilish bad plan—I'd advertise an hour, and keep to it."

"Well, sir, what you please, sir," rejoined Lotherington, in a more subdued tone, for there was a determination about Facey that as good as said he meant to be master.

"Be off, then," said Facey, getting the Dragon of Wantley short by the head, giving him at the same time a refresher on the shoulder with the pig-jobber whip, and a touch of the spur in the flank. This then gave the field, who had only hitherto enjoyed a side and a back view of our friend, the benefit of a front one also, thus exhibiting his watchful pig eyes, a peculiar expression of countenance, his battered hat and shabby shirt. No one knows how ungentlemanly he can look, until he has seen himself in a shocking bad hat. The field drew into line as he passed with the hounds to have a good stare, which Facey returned with a scrutinising sidelong glance at them all, embracing both riders and horses, with a running commentary in his own mind, as to which were the fifties, which the twenties, and which the ten pound subscribers to the hounds. But there was no salute or recognition on either side, and as the Dragon of Wantley was well known, there was great curiosity excited on the subject. "Where the deuce did he get the Dragon of Wantley?" asked one. "Did you ever see such a coat?" asked another. "Bought it off the pegs, I should think," observed a third. "Boots and breeches are a dead match," observed a fourth. "How much for the lot?" exclaimed a fifth. "Hard-bitten-looking beggar," observed a sixth. "Let's be on and see what he does," added another, spurring in front and thus leading the field.

CHAPTER X

OAKENSHAW WOOD

IF Jonathan Lotherington thought little of Mr. Romford in his buttoned boots, he thought less of him now that he saw him in his hunting costume mounted on the familiar Dragon of Wantley. He hadn't seen such a coat, such a hat, such breeches and boots, he didn't know when. They looked fitter for an earth-stopper, or a cad down Tattersall's entry, than for a master of hounds. Jonathan on his part was spicey and gay, having on his first-class coat, first-class cap, first-class everything, in addition to which he was mounted on his best horse, North Star, and sat as corkily in his stirrups as a man of his years and weight could do. In fact there was a little affected activity in his movements, as if he wished to make Mr. Romford believe he was young. But for Facey's impudence at the kennel, Jonathan would rather have pitied him riding solitarily along with nobody noticing him; as it was, he thought to patronise him through the medium of his horse.

"Got Mr. Dibble's old hoss, I see," observed he, looking the Dragon of Wantley over.

"Ay, what sort of a nag is he?" asked Romford, giving the horse a familiar slap on the ribs with his hand.

"Good hoss—gallops well," replied Jonathan. "Loups too."

This was satisfactory to Romford, who hoped to put both qualities to the test before evening. So they trotted on familiarly as before, each party examining the other critically, Jonathan thinking there wouldn't be much credit in serving buttoned boots, buttoned boots thinking Jonathan was not at all like a man for his money.

"P'r'aps you'd like to see me find my fox," now said Jonathan consequentially, as they neared the little bridle gate leading into the east end of Oakenshaw Wood.

"Go along," replied Facey, and at a wave of the hand away went the hounds, distributing themselves equably over the ground, sniffing and snuffing and questing as they went. Then Jonathan, who had a musical voice and could find a fox if he couldn't hunt one, began yoicking and cheering and cracking his whip, little doubting that buttoned boots would be very much struck with his skill—if he wasn't, Jonathan thought he wouldn't give much for his judgment. And as hounds know where the fox lies nearly as well as their masters, Pillager and Pilgrim were quickly feathering on the line, but not yet venturing to speak. At length Pillager gives a whimper, Pilgrim gives a challenge which Driver and Duster endorse with their usual vehemence, and Jonathan caps the whole with one of his XX stentorian cheers. Then the chorus fills, hounds come tearing pell-mell to the place, horses jump and plunge with delight, while their riders funk or rejoice according to the stuff of which they are made. The wood rings with the melody, driving every denizen out save the fox, who takes a liberal swing of its ample dimensions to see which side affords the most convenient point of egress. He is a long-toothed, full-brushed, gray-backed old fellow, who has had many a game of romps with Jonathan and his followers, and does not despair of beating them again (though he has had rather a heavy supper) as he has beaten them before, only he wants a fair start and not to be bullied on leaving, chased by a cur or a lurcher, or turned over by a great daft greyhound whose followers take him for a tiger. Twenty couple of hounds are enough for any animal to contend with, even when light and full of running. So he plods diligently along, eyes well forward, ears well back, listening to where he hears his noisy friends and their vociferous huntsman. Coston Corner is blocked by a great leather-legged man with a gun. Three or four unfortunates who never come to the meet arrive at the high gate just as the fox comes up, or he would have tried his luck for the third time over Amberley Common and away for the main earths at Frankton Wood. However, the fall of the ground here gives him a view of the adjacent country, and the green fields of 'Longville look very inviting, so running the wood well as long as it served, he drops quietly down into the deep Dillington Road, and presently swerving to the left, by keeping the low ground, is never seen until he is half over Warrenlaw Hill. And the hounds having been brought to a check at the wall, Jonathan, never suspecting such an unhandsome cat-like performance, is holding them back into the wood, thinking the fox may have lain down in a drain, when the first distant note of surprise ripens into a nearer holloa, and the man with the gun next gives a most unmistakable TALLY-HO! as he views him stealing quietly over the crown of the hill. Oakenshaw Wood is again electrified, horses are got shorter by the head, seats adjusted, and riders prepared to follow their respective leaders. Some men are quite lost in a wood.

And now friend Romford, who has kept well down wind hearing every note and cheer that was given, gets the Dragon of Wantley hard by the head, and lets in his Latchfords, determined to see what he is made of. He presently gets into a deep clanging ride, whose distance was closed by a group of flying red coats, and setting the Dragon's head straight that way, he scuttled up its length, and emerged with the last of the tail into the Billington road.

"Which way?" "which way?" was the cry as the sportsmen looked right and left for the double line of hedgerows denoting a road.

The first thing Mr. Facey saw on coming up was the hounds considerably in advance of the huntsman, the

next thing was said huntsman dancing and prancing at
his fence. At length he went over, and a great show of
activity then took place as he spurted up a wet furrow.
Then there came another fence and another furrow, so
that if the hounds had been a quick mettlesome pack they
would infallibly have run clean away from him.

As it was they were laboriously respectable, like the
merchants of old, who made their fortunes more by
saving than by rapid dashing adventure. Give the
hounds time and they would generally wind up their fox,
but they must do it carefully and systematically, taking
nothing on trust, retaining, in fact, a good deal of the old
Heavyside style of suspicious proceeding.

Their noses were always in the right place, they had
plenty of music, were very truthful, and could get on
with a bad scent better than many; but they were a
lobbing set of goers, that a light-drawn fox would leave
immeasurably in the lurch. They were quite a peep-of-
day pack, notwithstanding their pretension to later hours.
Lawyer Lappy and the Brothers Heavyside had effectually
kept them back.

Romford seeing at a glance how things were going,
readily .accepted the *pas* the hesitating field seemed
disposed to yield him, and ramming the Dragon at a
high mortar-coped wall, sent his coat laps and his character
flying up together.

"Well done, seedy boots!" exclaimed dandy Captain
Hollybrook, who, however, did not offer to follow him.

"Dash my buttons, but he can ride!" exclaimed ugly
Tom Slam, with a jerk of his head, as he pulled his dun
horse sharp round preparatory to clattering along the
Billington road. Then a greater length of tail followed
suit. In truth the H.H. were not rash men across
country. They retained much of the prudence and
caution of the original Brethren, and always liked to see
which way the fox inclined before they began to bump.
On this occasion there were Peel's three courses open to
him, Frankton Woods, Gatheridge Craigs, and Bewley
Hills. The fox was evidently undecided at first which
line to take, and until he settled the point, the field
hesitated to commit themselves to the perils of the chase.
The roads were very convenient. Jonathan was more
venturesome than usual, but that was because he thought
to astonish Mr. Romford, whose going powers he greatly

doubted. It was therefore with no very pleasurable sensations that on looking back he saw our Herculean master sailing along on the Dragon of Wantley, shoving him at his fences regardless of the gaps, in a very determined sort of way.

Worst of all he began "for-ward, for-ward, forwarding!" to the hounds as he came up, as though he were huntsman as well as master.

"Gently, *hurrying*!" exclaimed Lotherington, holding up his hand as if afraid Romford would drive them beyond the scent.

"Hurrying!" exclaimed Romford, cracking his cart-whip, "why, man, you don't call this going!" adding, "a fox will last them a week at this pace."

And Jonathan's broad back heaved with anger at the speech. "Was there ever such a man?" thought he.

The run then continued without further incident over Soberton Meadows, past Holden Mill to Marwell, the pace somewhat better, with easy fencing, and most accommodating gates. Here a short check occurred which the hounds hit off by themselves, and then a swerve to the left is answered by a turn of the upward road to the right, and they cross the Little Paxton Lane just as the ecstatic field come clattering along full of enthusiastic delight.

"Hold hard!" is the order of the day, horses are pulled up, and all eyes are strained to see the Invincibles carry the scent over the road. Beautiful! beautiful! were there ever such hounds? Truest pack in the world! as each particular Solomon issued his proclamation, that the fox was on.

Up then comes Mr. Jonathan Lotherington on North Star, Jonathan sadly out of his bearings, for he has been tempted into a field excursion, instead of leaving the throaty old line-holders to carry the scent to Rickwood Thicket, where they are evidently going, while he trotted gallantly round by the road. Worst of all, they have crossed at a most unfavourable place, there being no way out of the field, on the lane side, save over a very un-inviting ragged blackthorn fence with a wide ditch on the far side. Jonathan had often contemplated it from the road, but never with any eye to leaping it; now he began dancing and prancing and wishing himself well over.

"Clear the course, old man!" now exclaims Mr. Romford,

coming up at a canter, holding the Dragon of Wantley
well by the head, with his cart-whip brandishing on high,
to give him a refresher.

"Old man !" snapped Lotherington, looking round
irately.

"Then old woman !" retorted Romford, giving the cock-
tail a cut that sent him over with a bound—horse and
rider landed well in the road before the assembled field.
Without waiting to pick up the compliments, Facey then
rammed the Dragon at the opposite fence, a stiff stake
and wattle, with a rail beyond, and was again in the same
field as the hounds—Lotherington then led over.

And Romford, being now in possession of the pack,
shot alongside the head hounds, capping and cheering
the tail ones on the line. The pace improved with the
encouragement, and they went brisker and keener over
Otterton Moor, past Thatcham Hill, skirting Lockham
Green, and down into the depths of Fursdon Wood, than
they had done any period of the run.

Meanwhile Mr. Jonathan Lotherington, having accomplished his lead over, being highly enraged at buttoned
boots' interference with the pack, and knowing the run
of the fox, hustles North Star along, and comes up the
low ride just as the pack are swinging a cast at the
brook at the bottom of the wood ; some thinking the
fox was back, others that he was forward, Facey that he
had caught sight of a shooter, and turned short to the
left.

And Lotherington being determined to have the
hounds from Facey, even if he rode them astray, out with
his horn and blew a discordant blast as he cantered past,
pretending he was going to a holloa. But certain of the
sages being of Romford's opinion that the line was to the
left, persevered on that way, in spite alike of Jonathan's
horn and Michael's holloa. And scarcely had they got
clear of the cold rutty cart road than Affable struck a
scent on some very indifferent seeds, which Dashwood
immediately endorsed with clamorous energy, and away
they went, followed by about hàlf the pack who had
hesitated which side to obey. And Facey off with his
shocking bad hat, and cheered them to the echo. The
field, too, thinking better of him than they did at the
meet, adopted his line ; so the now greatly disconcerted
Lotherington had to return at his leisure. "Oh dear !

oh dear!" exclaimed he, knocking his horn-mouth against his cords, as he eyed Facey tearing away. "Too mony huntsmen mak bad work,—too mony cooks spoil the broth,—too mony huntsmen mak bad work." So he trotted sulkily along with the field, while Mr. Romford stuck to the hounds along Bleaberry Banks, past Duck End and Lawford Grange, cheering and encouraging them to run as he went.

The chase has now lasted about an hour, which, according to Mr. Romford's ideas, ought to be about enough; but had the fox been light with the start he got, and never having been pressed, he was well qualified to go on for a week. The country, too, was favourable, the fields being large, the hedges easy, and the population small. But the hounds didn't get on as they ought under the circumstances, and the fox has more than once stopped to listen if they were coming at all. Facey sees their defects and pities their infirmities. "Dash it, but ye want heading and tailing," says he, "and then I don't know that I'd give much for the middle." Some of them, he thought, would run if the others would only let them; but they were a devilish tiresome set. "G-a-r away, ye loiterin', lumberin' beggars!" exclaimed he, cracking his cart-whip to set them forward. And away they went at a somewhat amended pace.

Now if Mr. Romford missed his fox it is quite clear he would have been set down as a humbug, at all events as an officious intruder. Mr. Lotherington would have declared he could have killed him if master would only have let him alone, just as a cow-leach always says he could have cured a horse if the groom had sent for him instead of the vet. And now with this evident issue before him, the Dragon of Wantley shut up at the time he was most wanted in a very summary and unexpected manner.

Facey had been so anxious pressing and forcing the hounds, that he did not feel the occasionally turnip-fed Dragon gradually sinking beneath him, until on putting him at a very low fence, he stood stock still, tail erect, nostrils distended, eye staring and fixed. "Rot it!" exclaimed Romford, jumping off, "that's a bad job!" looking at the horse's heaving sides and wooden frame. It was clear he was beat.

"Here!" exclaimed he to a countryman, who now

came running down the hill in a pair of very impeding clogs. "Take this horse up to yon house," pointing to a whitewashed one on the left, "and see him taken care of till I come."

As luck would have it, this was a led farm of Mr. Dibble's, and the countryman having scratched his head and given a good stare, exclaimed, "Whoy, deare me, it surelie be our master's huss."

"Ah, Mr. Dibble's," replied Romford.

"Yeas!" said the man.

"Well then, take and use him kindly," rejoined Mr. Romford; adding, "There's sixpence for you, and I'll give you another when I come for him if I find him all right;" so saying, he resigned the horse to the man and was preparing to follow the hounds on foot.

"Fox be doon the Quarry Banks," observed the man, pointing to the right.

"How d'ye know?" demanded Mr. Romford.

"Mar dog torned him," replied he, thinking Jowler had done a very clever thing.

"Tell me where?" rejoined Mr. Romford.

"Just by yon bit bush beyond the stone heap."

Facey then off with his hat and holloaed the now baffled hounds back on the indicated line. It was as the man said. Craftsman hit off the scent with vehement energy, bringing all his comrades to the cry, and away they went round the end of Preston Hill and up the rough gorse-grown quarry banks. The pace and the music here slackened. The rougher the banks became the less vehemence there was. Romford soon saw they would require all the encouragement he could give them. The Heavyside hounds were not fond of gorse, it pricked their sides too much. They had plenty of natural covers, and preferred drawing them. Besides, going in now after the fatigue of a long and to them very sharp run was rather unreasonable. If anybody would kick the fox out for them they would pursue him in the open, but routing him out for themselves was both hard and sharp. Facey saw this, and though he had very indifferent cords on and no drawers, and much of the gorse was of vigorous growth, in he went as though it were a field of oats.

"*Eloo in there! Eloo in!*" cheered he, trying to get the reluctant hounds to give cry. Just as he was in the midst of his endeavours up came General Lotherington with the combined forces, and distributed themselves along the brow of the hill, Lotherington laying himself ten shillings to one that the fox beat the new master. Facey then continued his exertions down below with the eyes of England upon him—Argus himself, in fact. The cover was long and straggling, lying against the rather steep slope of the hill, thick here and open there, through which a quick, mettlesome pack would soon force a fox' but where a judicious dodger was pretty safe from the Heavysides.

In vain Romford hooped and holloaed and dashed forward on the line, trying to bring the nearest forces to bear on the scent. When the ground was open they put in a bustling appearance, but soon withdrew when the prickles were troublesome. And the fox knowing his ground and watching his opportunity, at length slipped back upon the foiled ground, thus making the difficulties doubly great. Still Romford continued his exertions, and if the gentlemen on the hill were cold, he was warm. He also coaxed in several of the now assembled foot people, assuring them the pricks were nothing, and they'd catch the fox amongst them directly. He didn't say anything about paying them. Mr. Jonathan Lotherington sat sulkily on the hill contemplating the commotion below.

"If Mister What's-his name kills this fox I'll eat him, pads and all," said the huntsman, making the bet twelve to one instead of ten. Then some of the field began to slink off. "All U P," said one; "Starvation work," said another; "Home, sweet home," sang a third.

And certainly appearances were now greatly against Mr. Romford, for the fox had got into strong quarters, while the number of ejectors became fewer and fewer. There were not above two couple of hounds in earnest. Still Romford persevered on, now scrambling, now diving, now swimming as it were through the sea of almost impervious gorse to where the light whimper told him the fugitive was ensconced. He spared neither his arms nor his legs nor his lungs. At length even the light whimper failed, and Facey was left alone in his labours. "*Con*-found the beggar!" muttered he, as he stood scratching his head in the high gorse.

"*Told you so!*" said Mr. Lotherington triumphantly; adding with a smile and a knowing shake of his head, "Taks a huntsman to kill a fox, taks a huntsman to kill a fox." And Jonathan began fumbling at his horn as if to blow the hounds out of cover.

Yap, yeau scranch! the gorse shakes violently about ten yards from Romford, and taking a header he disappears in the thick of it.

Up he comes with a great ruddy dog-fox in his hand, whooping and holloaing as hard as he could shout.

" Hoo-ray ! " cheered the horsemen on the hill.

" Hoo-ray ! " cheered the foot people below.

" Hoo-ray ! " responded Romford, holding him up.

Away Facey went, dragging his prize along amid the baying of the lazy hounds, who now seemed inclined to eat him without onions. Making up to Lotherington he says, " There, old man ! there's your fox," giving it to him, and while the last obsequies of the chase are performed, our friend receives the compliments and congratulations of the field. " Never saw anything better ! Wonderful performance ! Deserves to be immortalised ! "

So ended Mr. Romford's first day with the Heavysides.

CHAPTER XI

THE TENDER PARTING

THE reader will observe that we have not "Brown, Jones, and Robinson" in the field, Mr. Brown, Mr. Romford ; Mr. Jones, Mr. Romford ; Mr. Robinson, Mr. Romford ; and for this reason, that, with the exception of an earnest and not uncommon desire to take care of their necks, there was nothing very particular about the H.H. gentlemen ; and the fact was Mr. Facey did not stay very long with them. Of course, after the run described in the last chapter, he rose rapidly in public estimation, and his fame kept increasing every time he went out—increasing with every one save Mr. Lotherington, who liked Facey less every time he saw him. At length, having ridden another borrowed horse to a stand-still, Facey most unhandsomely dismounted Lotherington, under pretence of assisting at a mutual "lead over," when, getting on to Lotherington's horse, Facey galloped away, leaving the huntsman in the lurch. This

indignity Lotherington could not brook; and having
feathered his nest pretty well, the expenditure of the
hunt having been a good deal under his control, he
anticipated Romford's dismissal by giving him up, which
he did rather cavalierly—so much so, indeed, that Facey,
who was by no means fastidious, told him he was uncommon welcome to go, adding that he need not apply to him
for a character. Whereupon Lotherington, embodying
all the slights and contumely he had received at Facey's
hands—the old man'd, old woman'd, slandered as no fox-
killer, robbed of his horse—embodying all these, we say,
in one bitter pill, Lotherington replied—.

"I'm sure, sir, if you never mention I've lived with
you, I never shall, for I'm most *heartily 'shamed of it.*"

Facey, however, cared little for that sort of thing;
indeed, it was rather in his favour, for it put him in
possession of Lotherington's horses, which belonged to the
hunt, thereby saving him the trouble of begging and
borrowing others. And Minshull Vernon being rather
wide of the kennel, he presently removed to more convenient quarters at the snug little hostelry known by the
sign of the Dog and Partridge Inn, by the side of the
Marlingford and Rockland road.

It was a quiet little solitary, stone-slated, six-roomed
house, and standing in a clump of venerable elms; and
Facey got a comfortable carpeted parlour, with the usual
complement of stuffed birds, samplers, and sand-boxes,
with a bedroom above, for ten shillings a week, fire and
cooking included. And here he did very well, getting
his hunting and shooting for nothing, without the persecution of visitors; for though the H.H.'s were a most
respectable twenty shillings in the pound set of men, they
did little or nothing in the way of extraneous gaiety. No
balls, no breakfasts, no dinners, no nothing, and it is
much to be questioned if they had not the endowment
whether they would have had any hunt either. This,
then, seemed just the very thing to suit a rough-and-
ready customer like friend Facey, and why it did not
must be reserved until we have introduced one or two
more of our dramatis personæ to the reader. We may
however, state that Facey did uncommonly well in the
country. He was most assiduous in showing sport, no
day being too long or distance too great for him; and he
rode in a way that astonished the natives, saving his

horse where saving was right, but never saving him to the detriment of sport. They had never seen such a pounder before. He never turned away from anything, and if he couldn't leap he would lead over, his only anxiety being to get to his hounds. Even these he improved considerably, getting them to come quicker to holloas, and not lie on the scent, as old Lotherington had let them. So Facey really seemed to have benefited by the loss of his "oncle's" fortune. If he had got it, in all probability he would have been nothing but a mere farmer, whereas now he was a master of hounds, courted and consulted, with people touching their hats to him, and paying him for enjoying himself in hunting the country. Nothing could be better. He only wished the woman in black could see him, and those terrible little imps of hers that he still saw dancing in his mind. And Jog, poor old Jog! What an ass the old stick-cutter was. He wondered what Jog would think of him, and what he would take for his chance of getting his (Jog's) fifty pounds back again. Soapey Sponge had hit Jog hard —he (Facey) had eclipsed Sponge altogether.

The H.H. being an early country, and the season whose doings we are recording an unusually dry one, Facey did not care to prolong it to the prejudice of the vixens, especially as there were no itinerant sportsmen who must either hunt or sleep, all the H.H.'s having something to do either in the way of farming, or draining, or driving, or doctoring, or what not.

So Facey having killed his ten brace of foxes, making, with Lotherington's five foxes, twelve brace and a half, shut up by giving two grand entertainments to the keepers and earth-stoppers, at the Dog and Partridge Inn, at which he himself presided, thereby making the acquaintance of a very important class of men, with a good deal of summer amusement in their power; and though Facey was a big hen-speckled fellow, none of them could ever see him doing what he ought not to do, either in the way of fishing, shooting netting, or what not. So he seemed landed in clover, and being a wise man, set about improving his position.

And Facey having a good idea of what a pack of hounds should be—say, three-and-twenty inches high, with bone and substance, pressers, but not hurryers, with plenty of music—bethought him of improving the H.H.'s by head-

ing and tailing the pack, and introducing a liberal in-
fusion of fresh blood among them. To this end he wrote
to the huntsmen of several of the best packs in the
kingdom, the Belvoir, the Beaufort, the Bramham, and
others, engaging their draughts, young and old, particularly mentioning in each letter that they were not to be
sent to Abbeyfield Park, but to some quiet, out-of-the-
way railway station therein specified, where they would
be met by people who knew nothing about Facey, and
again transferred to others who did; and the letters
being written on good paper—best cream-laid—and
sealed with the right Romford crest—a Turbot sitting
upon its tail on a cap of Dignity—the huntsmen had no
hesitation in complying with the orders, feeling, perhaps,
rather flattered than otherwise at their draught going into
such good hands. The seal, we may mention, was a bread
one, made by Facey from an impression on a letter, or
rather on an envelope from the other Mr. Romford,
enclosing a dunning shoemaker's bill to friend Facey,
that somehow or other, after boxing the compass, had
found its way to Abbeyfield Park, in the extraordinary way
the lost hounds and letters do cast up. And a most useful
adjunct this bread seal was; for, independently of other
advantages, Facey got a most valuable lot of hounds
together by it, and, though perhaps rather anticipating
our story, we may add that he never paid for them, our
independent master either treating the letters with silent
contempt, or writing such abusive answers to the applications for the money, denouncing the hounds as a skirting,
babbling, overrunning, sheep-worrying lot, not worth
hanging, as perfectly astonished the worthy huntsmen,
who, thinking they must be deceived in their judgment,
or that the hounds had been changed on the journey, felt
rather sorry than otherwise at having disappointed so
good a sportsman as the Turbot on its tail, Mr. Romford.

And Facey, being a thorough dog man, liked his bargains—or rather presents—amazingly, and very different
were the reflections that passed in his mind as he stood
weeding his cane-coloured beard on the flags whilst inspecting his pack, and the denunciations he had hurled at
the huntsmen when they ventured to ask for their money.

And having invested our hero with the material of a
good pack of hounds, let us now turn to the requirements
of the necessary adjuncts of horses.

CHAPTER XII

MR. GOODHEARTED GREEN

AMONG other equestrian acquaintances made by our
friend Mr. Romford while in London, was that
of the extensive philanthropist Mr. Francis Green, or
Goodhearted Green, as he is commonly called, Brown
Street, Bagnigge Well's Road. Goodheart is a sort of
horse-dealing bat, veering between the plaited straw,
yellow sand magnificence of Piccadilly and Oxford Street,
and the queerly smelling back slum quarters of the check-
stealing fly-by-night chaunters and copers. Though
Goodheart spurned the latter, he was on friendly terms
with many of the former, easing them of many objectionable horses that mistaken judgment or ill-placed confidence had put them in possession of, rearers, restives,
runaways, wicked, vicious, unmanageable animals
generally.

We don't mean to say that Goodheart dealt in nothing
but incurables, for he had a happy knack of blending the
useless with the dangerous, and was always ready to
exchange a low-priced slave for a high-priced savage, or
vice versa. And there was such a fine, frank, open-hearted
taking manner about him—coupled with his snow-white
hair, his roseate hue, sporting attire, Bedford-cords, and
top-boots, with a green cut-away, that, unlike the generality
of dealers in cheap and damaged articles, he has been
known to do the same flat a second time. Then he was
so feeling and affectionate—quite the philanthropist in
everything. "Really, sir, really," he would exclaim,
after listening to a victim's list of enormities perpetrated
by a notorious offender. "You don't say so—you *don't*
say so. Well, I *ham* distressed. I did think, if there
was an 'oss I could 'scientiously 'commend a comely
looking gentleman of some fifty years of age, residing and
carrying on business at No. 13 Brown Street, it was that
'ere bay Sultan 'oss. But you are quite right, sir—quite
right," Goodheart would continue. "Don't keep him an
hour longer than you like him, sir—send him back by all

means—or shall I send for him?" stepping out as if about to appeal to the ostlers' bell outside the little office-door, but in reality inveigling the customer into a stable of soft ones, out of which he was welcome to choose himself what Goodheart called a "cheery one." And if the too fastidious customer did not like that, Goodheart would let him have another of the same sort, always, of course, subject to the usual penalty of a few five-pound notes. But a man's hobby never costs him anything, and Goodheart gained as much credit by the one transaction as he lost by the other.

London being now accessible to everybody—accessible either by the flying express, the moderate twopence-a-mile, or the still more reasonable Parliamentary trains, according as time or money is most valuable to the traveller, people get sucked up to the capital almost incontinently, and talk of going to town just as their fore-fathers talked of going to sessions or assizes. And there being little fatigue consequent on the journey, there is no occasion for the prolonged stay for recruiting that used to be considered necessary ere the intrepid voyageur again committed his precious person to the care of all the jibbers, and kickers, and vicious horses in the country. People talk of the dangers of railways, but all horse owners know that there was no little danger attendant on the coaches. If a man had a vicious animal he always sold it to a coach proprietor.

And Romford, ever anxious to be doing, and being now a great man—a master of foxhounds—sought the capital, like his equals, and renewed his acquaintance with the large swelling bosom of Goodhearted Green. Goodheart was well in stock with troublesome animals, having what Mr. Rarey would call some very incorrigible offenders, constantly passing and repassing through his hands. Never a week elapsed without his either receiving a most fuming letter from some provincial dupe, or some resident cockney walking Lincoln and Bennett in hand up his yard, to show the destruction done to his head-gear.

Then Goodheart, inflating his canary-coloured vest with grief, would sigh and exclaim, "Oh dear, dear, dear, was there ever sich doings! Here, Michael! Robert! William!" hallooing to his men, "did any of you ever see any symptoms of vice or depravity about that 'ere

cockolorum 'oss ?" Then they all exclaimed, as with one
voice, " Oh, never, sir, never ! quietest 'oss that ever was
seen," and then retired to their respective dens to watch
the further proceedings.

When Mr. Romford came, which was towards the close
of the London season, Goodheart had some seven or eight
horses that a timid rider could make nothing whatever of,
horses that, if the purchaser wanted to go to Barking,
would perhaps insist upon carrying him to Brompton, or
may be to Hoddesdon instead of Hyde Park. There were
others with less objectionable properties, but still troubled
with qualities that made them unmarketable to general
purchasers.

Now Goodheart, who could read a man pretty quickly,
recognised in Romford the materials of a determined rider,
and opened his expanding breast accordingly, telling him
the peculiarities of each, and recommending such as he
knew were full of courage and endurance.

First on the list was that noble weight-carrying hunter,
bought as "The Cur," but re-christened by Goodheart
"Honest Robin." The Cur — we beg pardon — Honest
Robin was a bright, sixteen-hands chestnut, with light,
lively action, a capital fencer, and fast, but unfortunately
having been ridden to a stand-still in his youth, and not
relishing the performance, now shut up whenever he
thought he'd had enough. In the middle of a run, when
the rider thought he was going gallantly, expecting to cut
everybody down, the Cur would suddenly collapse, and
refuse to proceed a step farther, leaving the laughing
field to pass him like a milestone. No, neither bullying
nor coaxing had any effect on the Cur. He would kick,
and strike, and plunge, and wheel round and round, but
as to going any farther, that he resolutely declined—it
was quite out of the question. "A fair day's work for a
fair day's food," was the horse's motto ; and of course the
animal himself was the best judge of what was fair. And
this sort of performance not being at all relished in the
hunting-field, he passed quickly from country to country,
becoming more hardened in his profligate habits at each
change—until he introduced the practice of the hunting-
field into his ordinary road performances. He wouldn't
go any farther than he liked on a journey, and if his rider
insisted on pushing him forward, he would either run
away or kick him over his head, and return home without

him. And a horse that will neither ride nor drive not
being of much use to anybody, he at length came into
Goodhearted Green's hands, who, knowing how the world
is governed by appearances, thought to turn him to
account.

The Cur not being at all an endearing or marketable
name, Goodheart quickly changed it to its opposite,
Honest Robin, a confidence-inspiring one, which, coupled
with his appearance (barring a certain sulk of the eye),
was well calculated to produce a favourable impression.
Then, to see Goodheart appraising him to a purchaser,
shaking his head, and drawing in his breath, as though
he were taking a prolonged suck at a stick of barley-sugar,
was a fine piece of acting.

Green had sold him for three hundred guineas, and
thirty back ; for two hundred, and twenty back ; for one
hundred, with nothing back ; and now put him into
Romford at thirty pounds, or half of whatever he made
beyond that. Of course Facey didn't put anything down,
" honour among thieves " being the motto.

The next of Goodhearted Green's horses that it will be
necessary to introduce to the reader, was a black horse
called Brilliant, some sixteen hands and a half high,
and nearly a perfect model of a weight-carrying hunter.
At first sight, he appeared to be two inches lower than he
really was, his great frame having been well developed by
good meat when he was young. He stood slightly over
before, rather an advantage to Goodheart than otherwise,
for suspicious purchasers invariably took exception to his
legs, and required to be specially guaranteed against their
going ; a request that Goodheart readily complied with,
for he knew that the horse had been foaled so, and subscribed to the doctrine that the legs of horses so foaled
never failed.

Still Brilliant—and be it observed, he had never passed
under any other name—had his peculiarities, being, as
Goodheart amiably observed, a " playful rogue," that is to
say, a most inveterate savage in the stable. He would kick,
and bite, and fly at even the man with his food, in a way
that was perfectly alarming, and Goodheart had always to
pay a helper two or three shillings a week more for looking after Brilliant than the regular tariff of the yard.
Still, when at the door and in the hunting-field, Brilliant
was quite quiet and tractable ; but then the difficulty was

to get him to the door, it being obvious to everybody that a horse is of no use to any one unless he can be got there. And many a time Green's too sensitive bosom had been wrung with recitals of the horse's malpractices ere Mr. Romford's manly form relieved him of him. Brilliant had nearly eat so many men, that Goodheart feared a "crowner's 'quest" from him, and didn't know but he himself might be involved in the consequences. So he put him in very low, twenty pounds, or half of whatever Romford might get beyond that for him.

The third was Leotard, the wondrous Leotard! a beautiful cream-coloured lady's pad, with an Arab-like head, and silver mane and tail—a picture to look at, but a profligate in practice. Leotard had no notion of doing anything he didn't like, and as remonstrance was vain, and pretty sure to end in a backward over rear, it was Goodheart's humour to show him in a plain snaffle bridle, as if he could be turned with a thread. And there were times when Leotard would do exactly what he was wanted; at other times he seemed to be possessed of a devil, and would do nothing but either run away or rear. Still, he had the redeeming quality of generally showing off to advantage before strangers, especially to purchasers, and had brought Goodheart in considerable gains. But his peculiar colour was against him—as was his character. He came back too often, and people began to quiz Goodheart about the cream-colour's notorious performances, so that altogether he wasn't sorry when Romford decided upon making Leotard the third in his horse-box. And having said that he wasn't "altogether to be depended upon," he left Facey to find out what were his deficiencies. Leotard was put in low, ten pounds, or half profit as before. So the new friends parted, mutually pleased with each other, Goodheart thinking he had done Romford, and Romford thinking he had done Goodheart.

And now, humbly following in the footsteps of the immortal author of the "House that Jack built," and having got some hounds to follow the fox that stole the goose that Facey meant for his dinner, and also some horses to live with the hounds that followed the fox that stole the goose that Facey meant for his dinner, let us see about getting some men to ride the horses and live with the hounds that followed the fox that stole the goose that Facey meant for his dinner.

CHAPTER XIII

SWIG AND CHOWEY

WHAT dilapidated specimens of horsey humanity one sees down Tattersall's yard on a full Monday in the height of the London season. Men in every stage of sporting decay, from the covered button roseate groom of yesterday's dismissal, down to the threadbare, calfless scarecrow of irreconcilable garments, who does not look as if he had had a meal for a month. Were there ever such queerly cut clothes, so oddly put on; such shaggy heads, such baggy shorts, such faded, careless ties, such uncouth vests, such extraordinary coats, so rich in little oddly placed pockets, made for holding the mythical never-coming coin! What sticks, what legs, what sticks of legs! Two to one but every other man wants a back button to his coat. And yet these incongruous garments often cover those who have been clad, if not in purple and fine linen, at all events in pink—men who have been hailed by my Lord and noticed by Sir Harry, as they jogged on to cover with their hounds; or may be they contain men who, in the soberer costume of stud grooms, and the full arrogance of office, have even refused their masters admission to their own stables, now perhaps only too happy to lead a newly purchased horse at the hammer all the way to Hackney or Hoxton for a shilling.

If the talented author of Dick Christian's lectures could inveigle a few of these men down into the Turf tap, and opening their hearts with a little of Mr. Maish's best brandy, he might gain matter for instruction on servitude that would be extremely useful both to master and man—to the masters in teaching them not to give way to the men, to the men as teaching them not to presume with their masters. We incline, however, to think the demon drink would be·found to have been at the bottom of most of their misfortunes. Not that the men themselves would admit the fact, but would say they had been most handsomely used, or made the victims of base conspiracy or unfounded suspicions. Drink! oh no, they never mention drink.

It was at Messrs. Tattersall's repository of bad legs and brandy noses that Mr. Romford sought to supply the vacancies caused by Mr. Lotherington's retirement, and the subsequent succession of his coadjutor Mr. Michael. Romford wanted two whippers-in to aid in breaking and entering the hounds so surreptitiously obtained, and our master giving his own personal superintendence to every department of the kennel, he did not care more about character than a groom generally does when he engages a helper. Knowledge of their business, with lightness of weight, were Facey's principal requirements; and as most men out of place are light, and summer is the season for choice, he soon had plenty of applicants—some with whole bones, some with broken; some with teeth, some without, some with a few scattered here and there. They were all most willing to work; no asking who did this or that, or inquiring how many suits of clothes Mr. Romford allowed in a year. Fancy old Facey giving his servants what he didn't allow himself! He had so many remnants of humanity to choose from, that he scarcely knew which to select. Now he thought Joe Harford, late of the Blazers, whose face was his character, would do; then Harry, late of the Beckingham Bruisers, superseded Joe, and was in turn eclipsed by the hard-riding—too hard-riding—Rat from the Cheshire. Just as he was closing with the Rat, who, as Facey said, seemed as light as a bladder, up came the residuum of that hard-bitten, hard-drinking creature Daniel Swig. Daniel, clad in three waistcoats and no coat, the outer waistcoat worn open, like a spencer, a pair of very critical-looking cords, and dirty leather leggings, with sadly patched shoes. Daniel had lived with the great Lord Scamperdale, who had put up with his nonsense so long that he thought his Lordship would stand him for ever, and now, finding his mistake, he could never sufficiently atone for his faults by airing his Lordship's name on all drunken occasions. He seemed to think it a perfect talisman against mischief, and would go hallooing out, "Mind! I'm Daniel! I'm the Right Honourable the Hurl of Scamperdale's Daniel!" as if it would be perfect high treason to meddle with such a man as Daniel. Facey knew Daniel, and also that he knew his business, so he threw the Rat over (who had but one eye), and installed Daniel instead. He soon picked up a match for him in the forlorn figure of little Tom Chowey.

Who doesn't know little Tom Chowey?—Chowey, the man with the india-rubber-ball-like mouth?—Chowey, the mildest-mannered, civilest-spoken, most drunken little dog in the kingdom? Chowey had been with half the hunts going, thus forming a large acquaintance, and so enabling him to earn a precarious livelihood when out of place, by touching his hat, and reintroducing himself to itinerant sportsmen, or gentlemen down Tattersall's yard. "Remembers your Lordship when I lived with the Crammers," with a saw of the air with his arm. "Caught your 'oss, Sir Harry, when you got that juice of a fall with the Varickshire" ("juice" being the nearest approach to an oath that Chowey ever indulges in). "Was out, Mr. Crasher, when you swam the Lune on Lehander," and so on. A horsey scamp will generally get a shilling out of a sportsman, while a combey or a staylacey one would plead in vain. The most remarkable part of Chowey, however, was his mouth. This, as we said before, was like an india-rubber ball, and once seen could never be forgotten. In repose it was like the neck of the ball tied ; when, however, the owner was excited—say, by the sight of a fox—it gaped again, just like one of the Dutch toys into whose mouth children try to chuck balls. When he screwed it up, it looked like the incipient trunk of an elephant. The whole of the lower part of his face seemed to converge to that feature. It was a most remarkable one.

Swig, with his three waistcoats on, was a few pounds heavier than Chowey, the two together weighing less than friend Facey. They were as lean as laths, just like so many feet of galvanised gristle. Both had piercing grey eyes that roved in all directions, like Daniel Forester's on dividend days. Their ages might be anything—anything between thirty and sixty. Swig's wardrobe went into a little valise that swung in the air as light as a pen-case, while Chowey carried his in the crown of an extinguishing bell-shaped hat. These two geniuses, Romford, after due deliberation and much cautioning, at length engaged, and having paid their third-class fares by the Parliamentary train, and giving them each a penny roll and sixpence apiece, sent them off to Minshull Vernon, thinking they could not do much harm till he came. And like a majestic master as he now began to be, he followed next day with his newly acquired horses.

CHAPTER XIV

CUB HUNTING

HAVING already intimated that Mr. Romford did not stay very long with the Heavyside Hunt, and not having Brown, Jones, and Robinson in the field, the reader will not expect us to dilate much on the peculiarities of the country, or to tell who gave Mr. Romford

> "white bread,
> Who gave him brown;
> Who gave him plum cake
> And sent him out of town;"

but would doubtless rather that we trotted on with our story to the more permanent scene of his great sporting career.

To this end, therefore, we shall be very brief, merely observing that he got through his summer very comfortably, fishing where he liked, shooting where he liked, and, generally speaking, doing pretty much what he liked. The harvest was early, the corn was cut and carried in good order, and he satisfied himself that the litters of foxes were both numerous and strong. He had heard nothing of Jog or his cheque; nothing of Mr. Holmside, the treasurer of the Stir-it-Stiff Poor Law Union; nothing of Mr. Nathan Levy and his rent; and nothing of Mr. Soapey Sponge, either about his shop or his wife. Altogether, Mr. Romford felt like a new man—like the Turbot on its tail himself If he ever thought of Oncle Gilroy, it was only to bless the day on which he stared into Wilkinson and Kidd's shop window, and was instigated to become a master of foxhounds. Thanks to the generosity of his brother masters, or the gullibility of their huntsmen, he had now a most promising entry of hounds. If they were only as good as they looked, thought he, they would indeed be hard to beat. And he would stand by the hour in the kennel, criticising their shape and their make, incontinently culling samples of his beard, until he was actually sore with the operation. And as the glad day approached for trying the pack, he was more and more in the kennel, until he seemed absolutely to begrudge himself his rest and relaxation. At length came the time for trying their prowess, as also that of his horses and men.

Most masters would have felt rather nervous in taking the field with two such coadjutors as Chowey and Swig, but Mr. Romford knew no fear, for he looked carefully after them himself, and there being no public-house within three miles of the kennel, save the Dog and Partridge Inn, where he himself lived, and whose every nook and cranny he could command from his sitting-room, they dare not come there, while he hardly gave them time to get elsewhere. Moreover, they had no money, and were not likely looking customers for people to trust. So they had to "behave themselves" whether they were inclined to do so or not.

What with the H.H. and his own, Facey had nearly a hundred couple of hounds in kennel, and meal being costly, it was his interest to reduce their numbers as quickly as possible. So he would be at it by daybreak, making the welkin ring with their melody, long before Hodge and his ploughmen awoke from their slumbers. Often, as our sportsmen have been returning home, all dust and perspiration, after handling a cub or two, they have been asked when they were "gannin to cast off?" And Swig and Chowey, seeing they had a master mind in our friend, readily seconded his efforts, and played into his hands with skill and enthusiasm. The presentation hounds wore indeed capital, and Facey, having satisfied himself that he couldn't do wrong whichever he kept, again had recourse to the good bread-seal, offering most superior drafts to outlying distant masters, at what he called the very moderate price of five guineas a couple ; and some of them knowing the Turbot on its tail personally, others by character, they readily accepted the offer, and Facey got a great number of five-pound notes in a very easy, agreeable manner. "Nothin' like bein' a master of hounds," said he, as they came rolling in post after post. And he revolved in his mind what other packs he could draw further supplies from. It was clear that either his own credit or that of the other Mr. Romford was extremely good, and he saw no reason why he should not profit by it. It was lucky that he had dropped the name of Gilroy, thought he.

At length, the Romford orchestra being properly tuned, and all things ready for an opening, Swig and Chowey clad in good second-hand clothes, bought off the pegs, the fox-hunting curtain arose early in November, to the old familiar H.H. audience.

Facey had matched his hounds admirably ; they could both hunt and run, and the foxes having been well disturbed, flew as they had never done before. The new horses, too, were admired ; and, altogether, the Romford star seemed in the ascendant. Still, there was nothing flash or showy in the establishment—indeed, our master had not even treated himself to a new coat, the Romford theory being that a hunting-coat, like a shooting-jacket, should be worn as long as it would hang together. But the plum-coloured coats brought many a fox to hand, one a day being the rule, instead of one a week, as it was in old Lotherington's time.

We now come to what broke up all this apparent prosperity ; and, as there is a lady, or rather two ladies, involved in the case, we will begin a fresh chapter.

CHAPTER XV

MRS. ROWLEY ROUNDING

WE do not know that we have ever mentioned it before, but if we have, we venture the observation again, —that among other great advantages afforded by railways, has been that of opening out the great matrimonial market, whereby people can pick and choose wives all the world over, instead of having to pursue the old Pelion on Ossa or Pig upon Bacon system of always marrying a neighbour's child. So we now have an amalgamation of countries and counties, and a consequent improvement in society—improvement in wit, improvement in wine, improvement in "wittles," improvement in everything. Among the members of the Heavyside Hunt who profited by this state of things during the summer of Mr. Romford's noviciate, was the rich Mr. Rowley Rounding, of Grandacres Hall, a good turnip-headed, turnip-growing squire, whose faculties generally served him about twenty or five-and-twenty minutes after they were wanted. Being on a gaping excursion all along the Southern coast, he was perfectly galvanised with the beauty of the fair-haired, blue-eyed, brisk young widow, Madame de Normanville (*née* Brown), of Boulogne-sur-Mer, who came upon him at Ramsgate, in such a succession of bonnets, as almost to deprive him of reason, and at first prevented his laying that and that together, and deciding that if he couldn't be Monsieur de Normanville, she, at all events, might be Mrs. Rowley Rounding.

For first of all, being a Madame, he had to ascertain and digest the fact that she might be and indeed was single; then it opportunely occurred to him that he was single too, after which he came to the conclusion that there was no reason why—though he wasn't in search of a wife—he shouldn't try to catch the widow and carry her down into the H.H. country. To be sure, Bob Ricketts, Billy Meadows, and Charley Westrope might laugh and deride him, but they had not his means, and, moreover, had never been tempted by—such extraordinary beauty and bonnets as hers. If she wasn't an angel, she was as near hand one as could be—but he thought she was one entire. He only wished he could make up to her. But what the "juice," as Chowey would say, is a country gentleman with no acquaintance but the landlord of his hotel to introduce, to do under such circumstances?

The lady, however, soon solved that mystery. Madame de Normanville seeing she had Basilisk'd the booby, presently afforded him an opportunity of making her acquaintance by dropping her finely laced and ciphered kerchief as she floated before him on the pier, when she gave him such a pearly-teeth-showing smile of gratitude on restoring it as immediately finished the business.

Next day she had him as handy as a French poodle, and looking about as sensible as one. And widows being generally pretty good men of business, short, sharp, and decisive, she brought him up to the "what have you got, and what will you do?" gate, without giving him a chance of leading her over it. Indeed, her beauty ought to have exempted her from any such operation as that, for though inclining to *embonpoint*, she had a beautiful figure and complexion, set off by the best of modistes and milliners, as Rowley found when the rather long-standing bills came pouring in—some dating even as far back as the time when she was Miss Brown—or Brown Stout, as the impertinent young fellows of that day called her.

To make a long story short, however, which was more than Rowley could do by the bills, he married her off hand, and then, of course, according to the old needles and pins song—

"his sorrows began."

Of course he took her down into the country, and here we may observe that we cannot imagine a greater change than from the light elastic gaiety of southern watering-places to the sober realities of dull out-of-the-way country quarters, where the ladies were all prolific, and their talk was of children or nurses, and cooks, and how many candles each used in the kitchen.

Mr. Rowley Rounding, though a very good man, and a capital judge of a cow, had very little in common with his sprightly wife, who having no family, required the excitement that children supply. And as it is not often given to the same man to be a good judge of a horse as well as of a cow, our squire cared little about the former, and could not enter into the spirit of the equestrian performances of his wife, who was known for her capering qualities to all the small riding-masters along the Southern coast. Indeed, at Brighton they used to charge her rather more than other people in consequence of her weight and galloping propensities.

Having exhausted her country circle, got all their histories and grievances by heart, domestic economy included, she now took it into her head she would like to resume her riding, alleging that it was no use wasting a good habit; and although Mr. Rowley Rounding pointed out that a habit ate nothing, and did not cost anything keeping, she stood to her point firmly, and insisted that she ought to ride, that she would be much better if she rode, that horse exercise would do her a great deal of good, that Doctor Senna had strongly recommended her to ride, the doctor having said, in reply to her inquiry if he didn't think she would be better if she rode, that "perhaps she might."

And she talked and teased so much about a horse, declaring she couldn't do without a horse—that she must have a horse—that she would be perfectly happy if she

had a horse, that Mr. Rowley Rounding, greatly appreciat-
ing peace and quietness, agreed to buy her a horse, and
forthwith she besieged all her friends and acquaintance
with inquiries if they knew of a horse, a lady's horse, a
horse with a flowing mane and tail—a whole coloured
horse with racing-like points—that she wouldn't be
ashamed to ride in Hyde Park, for she had some notion
of getting up to town in the spring if she could. And a
person wanting to buy a horse being a novelty in the
H.H. country, where they almost all bred their own, and
wore them from end to end, it was talked of a good deal,
and it seemed to be the general opinion that the wonderful Leotard was the likeliest horse to suit our fair friend.
Not that Romford had said anything about selling him,
but people thought he didn't seem to be of much use to
him, and he might perhaps be tempted to part with him.
So our old friend Colonel Chatterbox, who dearly loved a
commission of that sort, and also, with some ten or a
dozen others, fancied himself a great favourite of the
lady's, deputed himself to sound our master on the subject,
and pretending the horse was for himself, Mr. Romford
accommodated Chatterbox with him for a hundred—a
cool hundred—Facey observing that it was absolutely
giving him away. And though Colonel Chatterbox
thought it was plenty of money, yet as he seemed the very
thing Mrs. Rowley Rounding wanted, and he knew she
wouldn't like to ride a cheap horse, he closed with the offer
by giving Mr. Romford a draft on Checksby and Shorter's
bank at Ridwell, which of course Facey immediately
cashed, and felt very comfortable in consequence. So the
wondrous Leotard again changed hands, and of course
furnished abundant food for comment and criticism in
his new quarters, no two connoisseurs agreeing in their
opinion of him.

At first Leotard, having been kept on low diet by Romford, and exercised with the hounds, of which he was
very fond, behaved pretty well ; but common grooms being
so fond of stuffing themselves, that they think they can
never sufficiently stuff horses, so crammed him with corn
that he soon began to relapse into his former bad ways.
After one or two minor ebullitions of temper, Mrs. Rounding and Leotard came to a decided difference of opinion at
the cross-roads between Crowfield and Linghurst Hill,
Mrs. Rowley Rounding wanting to go to the right, Leotard

evincing a decided preference for the left, though there
was no earthly reason why he should care for either.   And
Mrs. Rowley Rounding being little accustomed to be
thwarted, and never considering that a pampered, over-
fed, under-worked pad differed from the obedient rocking-
horse animals she had been accustomed to do what she
liked with at the watering-places, struck him rather
smartly on the shoulder with a gold-mounted, amethyst-
topped riding-whip, which Leotard instantly resented by
rearing almost perpendicularly, and sliding her down
over his tail into a soft newly scraped mud-heap on the
roadside.   Then, having deposited her as in a pudding,
he struck off home, where he arrived to the terror and
consternation of the household, and rushing into his stable,
proceeded to eat the remains of a feed of corn that he
found in another horse's manger.   And Mrs. Rowley
Rounding, with her dirty habit, presently arrived in the
postman's gig, none the worse, but very angry at what had
happened.   Then there was a council of war held as to
what should be done with the horse, one recommending
that he should be ridden back to the place and made to go
the way he was then wanted to go ; another, that he should
be taken into the adjoining fallow and well lathered for
his pains ; a third, that he should be well licked in the
stable ; a fourth, that he should be beat at the door.   And
as they were all very angry, and imparted a portion of
their ire to the horse by scolding and slapping him whilst
he was eating, they did not at all improve the prospects
of his obedience, and when the tea-tray-groom postilion
came to mount him to give him a good round in the
paddock, the active Leotard very soon sent him, pink jean
jacket and all, flying over his head.   Then there was a
fresh commotion, fresh anathemas at the horse, fresh
recommendations as to what should be done with
him.

And as there is always some great, heavy-fisted horse-
breaker in every neighbourhood who will undertake to
ride anything, Tom Heslop, of the Bee-hive beershop,
the hero of that district, was sent for, who undertook to
Rarey-fy the rebellious spirit forthwith.

Leotard let the dirty Heslop mount very quietly, and
obeyed his dictation pretty readily, until an unlucky
brewer's dray happened to come along the road, when,
catching suddenly at the bit, he sidled up to it and pro-

ceeded to rasp Tom's leg against the wheel, rubbing it backwards and forwards till he made him bellow like a bull. Then the drayman got to the fractious horse's head, and after a desperate conflict succeeded in rescuing the unfortunate man from his intolerable oppression. Heslop then jumped off, and led the refractory horse home.

Another council of war was presently held, at which the butler, the gardener, and Matilda Mary the lady's-maid severally contributed their quota of wisdom, when they all agreed that Leotard was vicious, and a most improper 'oss for missus to ride. So Heslop and another man were dispatched to Colonel Chatterbox's with Leotard, and a request that he would be good enough to return the horse to Mr. Romford, and get back the money.

Now returning the horse was one thing, and getting back the money was another, for Mr. Romford particularly refused to refund one single farthing; alleging first, that it was an out-and-out sale, without any warranty or condition whatever; secondly, that the horse was sold to Colonel Chatterbox, and was quite quiet with anybody who could ride,—a double reflection, seeing that it involved an imputation both on the Colonel and Mrs. Rowley Rounding's horsemanship. But Facey politely added, that the horse might stand in his stable at the usual remuneration of four-and-twenty shillings and six-pence a week, all of which was repeated and commented upon by the gentlemen of the H.H. hunt, to the disparagement of Facey, who was thought to have been rather too sharp in the matter. But the Colonel having stretched a point as well as Facey, they could not make much of the transaction, and Mr. Rounding was at length glad to take twenty pounds for his bargain, in payment of which our master assigned him Mr. Tom Slowcome's subscription to the hounds, which there was always great difficulty in getting,—Facey alleging, as he gave the order on Slowcome for the money, that he never gave cheques for such "trifles as twenty pounds." So the wondrous Leotard returned to Mr. Romford's stable, there on diminished fare to undergo fresh discipline.

Still, Mrs. Rounding being pretty and popular, and her husband giving good dinners, the spleen of the country was not satisfied, though it had not to wait long for an opportunity to break out in another quarter. Though Mr. Romford rode Leotard to cover himself, to show he was quite tractable, they insisted that Mrs. Rounding had been cheated.

It was quite a different thing, they said, being quiet with a great Herculean monster like our master, and with a timid, delicate woman like Mrs. Rounding.

"It was a monstrous shame to sell a lady a horse that was vicious," said one in Facey's hearing.

"And at such a price too!" exclaimed another, a hundred guineas not being an everyday price in the country.

Lotherington went so far as to say, that a man ought to be hung who sold a lady such a horse.

All these sayings in due time came to our master's ears, with, of course, a due allowance of exaggeration; and though our friend was not particularly thin-skinned, he yet feared that the Leotard transaction might operate prejudicially, as well on future sales of horses, as on his present position and popularity as a master of hounds. He hadn't got on far amiss as it was, his undoubted keenness and great money-reputation helping him along.

Facey, of course, didn't mean to contend, even to himself, that Leotard was a perfect lady's pad; but he well knew that, by judicious management, he could be made sufficiently tractable to last long enough to throw on the new owner the blame of spoiling him by bad riding. And in the course of his cogitations, Lucy's beautiful horsemanship, as seen with the late Sir Henry Scattercash's hounds, occurred to recollection, and he said to himself, "Ah! that is the woman that could do it, if she liked." Twist him any way, and do whatever she liked with him. Never saw such a hand on a horse as she had. "She *was* a rider," said Romford to himself, twitching his beard as he said it. "Dash it, but he would like to see her on him," added he, throwing the sample away.

At length, galled by the reproaches and rebuffs which increased rather than diminished, he thought seriously of having her down to contradict their ungenerous assertions, by showing that Leotard was perfectly tractable with a lady. It was only the dread of expense, and the fear of exciting scandal, that prevented him; but the expense he, at length, thought might be previously settled, and the consequences averted by judicious arrangement. He really thought it feasible. He had still eighty of the hundred

guineas to the good, and wouldn't mind standing a trifle
to vindicate his character.

He should like to see her cutting down some of the
spurters who thought they could ride, and leading the
lumberers over the heavy into grief and humility. "Cutting them down and hanging them up to dry," as they say
in the Shires.

At length he took courage, and wrote to Lucy, directing
to the care of her mother in Hart Street, saying
that, if she had a mind for a mount with his hounds, he
would "stand Sam" for the Parliamentary train, directing
her, if she came, to stop at the sign of the West-end
Swell, at Minshull Vernon, whither the horse should be
sent on the morning of the meet; but by no manner of
means to think of coming on to the Dog and Partridge
Inn.

Lucy jumped at the offer, for she was well-nigh suffocated
with fog and bad air, and felt that a run into the country
would do her an infinity of good. Moreover, she had been
keeping her hands in by taking part in the monster
steeplechase at the Royal Agricultural Hall at Islington,
under the title of Madame Valentine de Mornington, to
the great admiration of crowded audiences. So her hat
and her habit were in very good order. She was presently
packed and away.

And the arrangement was most opportune, for Swig and
Chowey, we are sorry to say, had rather relapsed into
their former habits, and the Dog and Partridge Inn being
closed against them by reason of Mr. Romford's residence,
they had been compelled to go farther a-field for their
liquid fire; and a hunt servant, a man who rides where
he likes in a red coat and cap, being always an object of
admiration in the country, they had no difficulty in
borrowing Farmer Roughstubble's dog-cart to drive to the
sign of the Bald-faced Stag, on the Ashcombe Road,
where the Old Tom rum was capital, the gin pure, and the
drink generally both strong and heady. Here, being
Saturday night, they fell in with several gentlemen of
their acquaintance—Jack Arrowsmith the farrier, Peter
Marston the mole-catcher, Jack Miller, Squire Thompson's
keeper, with Jacob the coachman, Geordy Banks the
standing sot of the house, and others, all of whom were
most desirous of trying the alcoholic test of friendship
upon them, which they did so effectually that our sports-

men required a good deal of helping, and hoisting, and
holding in their vehicle ere they ventured to drive off,
being then fully impressed with the conviction that they
were the two finest fellows under the sun.

It being a moonlight night, the road straight, and the
horse steady, they had little difficulty in driving. Swig,
who acted as charioteer, giving the horse his head, who
kept well on the middle of the road, turning all ap-
proachers aside, until within a few miles of home, when
they had the misfortune to meet Billy Barber the flying
higgler's spring-cart, and Billy, being as drunk as themselves, charged right into them, shooting Swig one way,
and Chowey another, then driving on with a damaged
steed, despite of Swig's vociferations that he was "Daniel,
the Right Honourable the Hurl of Scamperdale's Daniel!"
while little Chowey lay on his back, his india-rubber-ball-
like mouth contracting and dilating as he muttered, in his
usual bland way, "By all means, shir, by all means,"
thinking he was helping a gentleman through a hedge
with his horse, and wondering whether he would get half
a crown or a shilling for his trouble. Both were put,
what Chowey elegantly called "*horse des combat*," by the
collision. So Mrs. Sponge now took their place.

CHAPTER XVI

LUCY ON LEOTARD—THE LADY WHIPPER-IN

A HABIT in the hunting-field was quite an unknown
article in the Heavyside country, where nearly
all the ladies had ample domestic duties to occupy them,
and the gentlemen found it was about as much as they
could manage to mount themselves, and, moreover, had
no particular fancy for being outdone by their wives;
so the first flaunting of Lucy's elegant fan-tailed, blue
and black braided habit, as she rode along with Facey
and the hounds, created quite a sensation, which was
little allayed by seeing it was borne by the refractory
Leotard. Not only was it borne by Leotard, but the
fair equestrian was absolutely going to act the part of

whipper-in to the hounds: Swig and Chowey having got such "juices" of shakes, as Chowey said, by their upset, as made them more like mummies than men. But for this untoward accident Facey might have passed Lucy off for a chance lady who had come down to look at the horse.

The meet was on Calderlaw Common—not a common by courtesy, as many now are, but a real unenclosed common of wildness and waste—rather a favourite fixture, for the roads were most accommodating, the country open, and, without being hilly, was undulating, very favourable for seeing, in fact; moreover, being mostly drained land, there were no agonising ditches to add to the terror of too formidable fences. So there was generally less "which way, Tomkins?"—"which way, Jenkins?" when the hounds met there, than when they were lower down in the vale.

The early birds of the hunt, those who rode their own horses on, Friar, Friskin, Coglin, and others, were now surprised by the unwonted appearance of a habit.

"What's up now?" exclaimed Friar.

"Woman, as I live!" rejoined Friskin.

"Why, it's Mrs. Rowley Rounding," muttered Coglin, staring intently.

"Not a bit of it," replied the first speaker, who knew her figure better.

"It's her horse, however," observed Friskin, eyeing the cream-colour as he ambled along.

"Was," rejoined Coglin, who knew all about the sale and return.

And now, as the widely spreading pack came straggling along the green lane leading on to the common, there was a general move that way to see who it was.

"I'll tell you what, I shouldn't be s'prised," said Coglin, seizing Friar by the left arm, and whispering in his ear as they rode along together—"I'll tell you what, confidentially, I shouldn't be s'prised if it's that Mrs. What's-her-name from the West-end Swell."

"Not Mrs. Spicer?"

"Oh no, that's the landlady. This is the mysterious lady who has just come down. My groom heard of her yesterday."

"Indeed!" exclaimed Friar, now staring intently, wondering what Mrs. Friar would say when she heard of it.

Facey, who gave his hounds plenty of liberty on the road, now rather contracted their freedom by a gentle rate to Favourite, who had got somewhat too far in advance, and the head receding, while the tail advanced, the pack came up in a perfect cluster of symmetrical beauty. There's a lot of charmers, thought Facey, as he looked them over, and then proceeded to nod to, and "how are ye?" the field. Our master's greetings were responded to, but the parties evidently seemed as if they expected something more—viz. to be introduced to the lady. This, however, Facey had no notion of doing, keeping, as he said, the coat's and the petticoat's account distinct, so he proceeded up the common to the usual halting-place—viz. the guide-post, where the Low Thornton and Hemmington roads intersected the waste.

Here was a fresh gathering—the cream of the hunt— the gentlemen who came late, in fact, Newton and Snobson, and Hastler, and Spooner, the two Bibbings, with Spencer Jones, and Burgess and Scarratt, with the usual concomitant grooms. Great were the nudgings, and starings, and what-next-ings as the cavalcade approached. The like had never been seen in the Heavyside Hunt.

"Well done, Romford!" exclaimed one.

"Who'd ha' thought it?" muttered another.

"A lady whipper-in," observed a third.

"A deuced pretty one, too," observed young Spooner, drawing his horse round to have a good stare at her.

And very pretty she was. Nicely hatted, nicely habited, nicely horsed, nicely arranged altogether.

So thought they all as she passed along, looking down demurely, as if she thought of nobody, and thought nobody thought of her. That of course was a little acting.

"Mornin'," said Facey, "mornin', mornin'," continued he, giving two or three random shots of nods at the different groups of sportsmen as he passed, several of whom took off their hats to the lady. He then made for a piece of rising ground a little to the left of the guide-post, in order to give his hounds a roll on the greensward prior to throwing off. And as he showed no symptoms of a desire to introduce his fair friend to this the first-class portion of his field either, they renewed their criticisms as soon as the cavalcade was past.

"Why, that's Mrs. Rounding's horse," observed Jones.

"So it is," said Mr. Newton. "Thought there couldn't be two of that colour."

"They say he's vicious," observed Hastler.

"Nothing of the sort," replied Newton. "Mrs. Rounding has no hand. See! that lady can do what she likes with him," added he, watching Lucy's light hand, as she twisted and turned the horse about at her will.

"Who is she?" asked Mr. George Bibbing, pressing up.

"Don't know," answered Hastler, with a shake of the head.

"I do," observed Jones, with a knowing wink.

"Well, who?" asked several.

"The lady at the West-end Swell, to be sure," replied he, after a pause.

"Oh, nonsense," rejoined Bibbing, "not a bit like her."

"As like as ladies generally are in hats and habits to what they are in dresses."

"Well, they do make a great difference to be sure," observed Snobson, who had mistaken Mrs. for Miss Noakes once.

"But what is she doing here?" demanded Spooner.

"Better ask the master that," replied Bibbing.

Facey, however, didn't look at all like a man to take liberties with, as he sat in the midst of his hounds, his little watchful ferrety eyes peeping and peering about in all directions, to "see how," as he said, "the cat jumped."

Lucy, on her part, took things very quietly, apparently paying more attention to the hounds than watching who was looking at her, though of course she still kept an eye out for admiration. Leotard also behaved most amiably, answering the touch of her light hand on the plain snaffle-bit, now turning Pillager, now following Rummager, as though he were personally interested in the order and decorum of the pack. At length, time being up—a quarter to eleven — Facey gave Lucy a nod, and after a wide-spreading run through the common, a slight twang of the horn brought the hounds to his horse's heels, and away they all jogged for Falcondale Wood.

"You take the high side," said Facey to Lucy, as they now approached the cover—a long straggling wood, placed on a steepish hillside. "You take the high side, and blow this whistle if he breaks," continued he, giving her a shrill dog-whistle as he spoke; whereupon Lucy scuttled away up the rough side at the east end of the wood, closely followed by sundry swells, who preferred watching her to keeping along the low fields as usual.

"Cover, hoick!" cried Facey to his hounds, with a slight wave of his arm, and in an instant they were tumbling and scrambling head over heels through the blind fence into the wood. Facey, mounted on Brilliant, then rode quietly along on the line, keeping a watchful eye as well on the now wide-spreading pack in the cover as on the Lucy-pressing youths up above. He had only sixteen couple of hounds out, having brought nothing but what he could depend upon. They had not been in cover many minutes, ere old black-and-tan Vanquisher, who had hurried along a path with a palpable but still unproclaimable scent, struck up a little fern-covered ravine, and as nearly as possible had old Reynard by the neck. But the fox bounced with a desperate energy that aroused the whole pack ; a crash sounded through the wood as they hurried together, while the shrill sound of the whistle presently proclaimed he was gone. Facey got his horse by the head, and cramming into the ragged fence, cleared the wide water-channel beyond, and forced his way up the wooded bank, regardless alike of stubs, briars, and thorns. Another effort over a broad rail-topped mound, with a yawner on the far side, landed him handsomely on Farmer Bushell's fallow, just as the hounds, closely followed by Lucy, were straining over the large grass-field beyond. There was a rare scent. Every hound threw his tongue, making the welkin ring with the melody. So they raced up Amerton Hill, past Nutwell grove and Kellerton Law, through Oakley Wood beyond. The pace presently slackened ; hunting became more the order of the day, to the satisfaction of the majority of the field, who preferred seeing the intricacies of the chase unravelled, to being borne furiously along at a pace that did not allow them to look after anything but themselves. Thus they hunted steadily past Brackenhill Green, skirting Orton Moor, leaving the Scar on the left, down the banks by the Winwick road, into the Vale of Heatherfield below. Lucy and Facey, or rather Facey and Lucy, kept their places gallantly, Leotard going with the greatest temper and moderation, as though he were the best-behaved horse in the world.

Whatever Facey took, Lucy took ; and whatever Lucy took, the young H.H.'s felt constrained to take, for the

honour and credit of the hunt. So there was more
dashing riding and heavy fencing on this occasion than
usual. Romford, to do him justice, was always with his
hounds, though Daniel Swig and Chowey both knew how
to shirk. The steady hounds still kept pressing on,
carrying the scent over the sandy soil of Heatherfield
Vale with laudable pertinacity. This enabled the "heavy
fathers" of the stage—the paterfamilias of the hunt—to
come up, and presently the Westham and Studland road
resounded with the ringing hoofs of the horses, and the
laughing hilarity of the riders, each overjoyed at getting
such a near view. And the slower the pace, the more
they enjoyed it. "Splendid hounds! Finest run that
ever was seen! By Jove! they're away again!" And
scarcely had the fatties given their horses the wind,
and the youngsters looked down for lost shoes, ere Harmony and Desperate, having got upon a warm headland,
gave such a proclamation of satisfaction as brought all
their fellows to the enjoyment, making young and old
again drop on their reins. The hunt was up! Facey's
round shoulders were again careering in the distance, and
Lucy's plump figure was equally conspicuous. So they
raced away, the hounds passing handsomely through the
deer in Beechborough Park, round Sorrel Hill, past the
limekilns at Dewlish, and into Langley Lordship beyond.
And here the first check occurred. The fox had been
chased by a shepherd's dog, and the mischief was increased
by a complication of sheep. The stupid muttons were
just wheeling into line as Facey slipped through the farm-
yard on the hill.

"Hold hard!" cried he, raising his hand high in the
air to enforce quiet from those behind, while his hounds
made their own cast ere he interfered with them. They
spread and cast well to the front, to the right, to the
left—but no scent. The fox has been forced back on his
line, and the field are all over the ground. The steam
of the horses, the chatter of the followers, and the clatter
of the roadsters, increase the disaster. Facey sits transfixed, one keen eye watching the hounds, the other raking
the country round. At length he sees the black author of
the mischief skulking along a hedgerow to his smock-
frocked master, who appears at a railing at the far corner of
the field.

"Case for a cast," says Facey to himself; and getting

his horse by the head, he halloas "Turn them," to Lucy,
who forthwith gets round them in a quiet but most
masterly manner, and a single twang of Facey's horn,
with a crack of her whip, sent them all flying the way
Facey wanted them. He then gave them plenty of swing,
letting them use their own sagacity as much as possible,
and was rewarded at the end of a semicircular cast by
hitting off the scent at a meuse.

"Well done!" "Devilish well done!" "Capitally
done!" cried the field, more to Lucy than Facey, as the
hounds dashed over the fence into the turnip-field beyond,
and took up the running inside the hedgerow. Being on
turf, with a pleasant vista of white gates before them, the
field kept on that tack, and Facey went scuttling along,
throwing wide the portals as he passed. The best of
friends, however, must part, and the line of gates at length
came to an abrupt termination in a very rough, tangled
boundary fence between Mr. Pilkington's and Emmerson
Gunliffe's farms, at Shepherdswell Hill. It seemed as if
it was made up of all the rubbish and refuse of the country,
and zigzagged like a lady's vandyked petticoat, wasting
and spoiling a great width of land.

For the first time in the run, Facey changed his mind
as he approached the fence, turning from a tangled black
thorn lapped with mountain ash, to a still more impervious
looking ivy-blind place.

"Dash it! but this is a rum customer," said Facey to
Lucy, as he stood erect in his stirrups, looking what was
on the far side.

"Oh, throw your heart over it," said Lucy, "and then
follow it as quickly as you can."

"Heart!" muttered Facey. "I shall never find it again
if I do. It would be like lookin' for a needle in a bundle
of hay."

"Let *me* try, then," said Lucy, backing Leotard to give
him a good run at it. She then put his head straight,
gave him a slight touch of the whip and a feel of the spur,
and was presently floundering in the thick of the fence.

"I thought how it would be," said Facey, jumping off
his horse and running to her assistance. But before he
got up, another vigorous effort of the horse extricated her
from her difficulties, and landed her in the next field,
with a considerable quantity of burrs and briars in her
habit.

"Well done the lady!" cried the panting Mr. Goldthrop, now coming up, not only pleased, but grateful for the performance.

If Facey would but charge it too, the field might all be able to get through. What a place it was!

And Facey, having clambered back into his saddle, turned his horse quick round, and thrusting his hat down on his brow, claimed his right of saltation. They were all ready to yield him the *pas*, services of danger being generally at a discount, and Romford was presently planted in the midst of the thicket, which Leotard had done little to enlarge. Scramble they went, the horse fighting and struggling as if in the sea, Facey sitting with his feet out of the stirrups, ready to throw himself off clear if required. It, however, was not necessary, for Brilliant, after many flounders, with a tremendous heave, extricated himself from a woodbine-laced binder that held him, and landed on his nose on the opposite side. He was up like lightning, and Facey, who held on by the mane and his spurs, being chucked back into his seat, gathered himself together, and ere he sat, gave a cheering exclamation of "There's nothing on the far side!" But if there was nothing on the far side, there was a great deal on theirs, as many of them seem to be aware. However, it was no time for measuring, and Leotard's friend, Tom Heslop, coming up on a three parts broken cart colt, dashed manfully in, and fought a road safely through in the miraculous way peculiar to drunken men. What before was all doubt and obscurity suddenly became clear and transparent. It was then who should get at it first. No "I'll hold your horse if you'll catch mine," or friendly negotiation of that sort. Meanwhile, the hounds had shot sadly away, leaving not a trace of their melody behind; and but for the clubbing of sheep and the staring of cattle, the H.H. gentlemen would hardly have known which way to ride. To be sure, an occasional countryman, after a prolonged stare, in reply to the inquiry if he had seen the hounds, would drawl out, "Ye-a-s, ar see'd them," but none of them could muster intelligence enough to answer "where," ere the questioner was out of earshot. However, they rode on, hopefully and manfully : the young ones, as usual, abusing the fox for taking such a line, the old ones wishing they might come up with them again before they killed.

Fortune, however, always favours the brave, and after

clattering through the little straggling straw-thatched village of Reepham, bringing all the women and children to the doors in bewildered astonishment, Mr. Friar's quick eye caught sight of a red-coat topping the edge on the opposite hill, up whose sandy side ran the road they were then pursuing.

"Yonder they go!" cried he, pointing it out with his whip, though he did not know how far the hounds might be ahead of the coat. But riding to anything was better than riding to nothing, galloping about the country, exclaiming, "Have you seen the hounds?"

They then clattered down Cockenhatch Hill, across the bridge over the rushing stream, and laying hold of their horses' manes, proceeded to stand in their stirrups, and hug them up the opposite bank. That gained, some of the young ones, disdaining the road, dashed over a quickset fence into a heavy fallow, and sought the line Mr. Romford was leading, or rather following, for Lucy was leading. The old ones pounded away on the road, reaching the crown of Eccleston Hill long before the seceders, when their admiring optics were greeted with a sight of the hounds swinging down the green slope of Rippendale Hill, closely followed by Lucy and Facey. Then there was a burst of enthusiasm at the magnificent way the hounds were doing their work, slightly clouded, perhaps, by the sight of the silvery Ribble, meandering its tortuous course through the rich green fields of the vale. What if he should cross it, thought they. However, it was no time for reflection. Meanwhile, Facey and Lucy had got together, and Facey's keen eye descried the fox taking the water, and floating down the stream so as to land a good way below the taking-off place.

"Cunnin' beggar," said Facey, pointing him out to Lucy; "but I'll have you in hand for all that," muttered he.

The fox then crawled out on the opposite side, and after shaking himself leisurely among some dwarf willows, and listening to the music of the hounds, he again set off on his travels, as if in no way particularly concerned in the concert. He was an old dog-fox that had beat Lotherington and his lumberers twice or thrice before, and did not go in great fear of them. He was not aware that there had been any change in the programme, or he might have put on a little more steam. However, he kept on at a good steady pace, and being now so far from home, thought he might as well go on to Addington Woods, where there were not only plenty of rabbits, but very comfortable quarters and respectable keepers. And Facey, who saw the woods in the distance, and knew their attractions, thought to terminate the performance before they got there, not knowing when he might get out again if he once got in, with only his fair friend for a whip. So, riding inside the hounds, he cut off a wide angle, and met them at the place where the fox had crossed. Up they presently came, lashing and bristling for blood.

"Yoick, over he goes!" cried Mr. Romford, taking off his hat, as Constance and Cruiser spoke to the scent on the exact track of the fox.

Forthwith the whole pack took the water like a flock of sheep, and went fighting, and splashing, and striving to be first out. Then, after a scramble out, and a hearty preliminary shake, they again put their inquiring noses to the ground to solve the problem, "Which way has he gone?" Trumpeter struck the scent with an exulting flourish; the rest scorned to cry, and away they went, pressing and pushing as before.

"*For*-rard, away!" cried Facey, turning Brilliant about to have a run at the brook. "Well, how is it to be?" said he to Lucy, ere he dropped in his spurs to send his horse at it. "You first or I first?"

"Oh, both together," replied Lucy, turning Leotard round also to take it in line.

"Bear to the left, then," said Facey, nodding to a narrower place at an abrupt bend of the brook. "You take off by the bush there, and I'll go a little higher up, so that we mayn't break the bank with our weight."

It was a prudent resolve; for the bank, which was a great resort for water-rats, immediately gave way with the weight of one horse; and when the first of the H.H.'s came up, hoping to cross over it as our master and his lady had apparently done, they found a very frowning, yawning, formidable-looking place, that did not at all improve upon acquaintance.

However, there was no help for it: a brook is a brook, and must be either taken or let alone. Neither sober nor drunken men can do anything for us, and some of the knowing elderlies boldly wheeled round for Lowington Ford, while the younger ones charged here, there, and everywhere, two getting in for one that got over. Great

was the splashing and snorting, and snatching at hats, and
scrambling after whips, and loud the exclamations of
"Catch my horse!" "Turn my horse!" "Help me out
with my horse!" But for the inconvenience of being
beaten by a lady, very few of them would have risked a
ducking.

The country now became wilder and opener, the scent
worse, and the seeing better. You looked into the landscape with minute distinctness. The Addington Woods
were darkly visible. He would like to lay hold of him
before he got there. A fresh fox would be very inconvenient at that hour.

"*For-rard! for-rard! for-rard!*" cheered Facey, to get
his hounds on; but the land was poor and exposed, and
the line took a deal of finding.

"To guide a scent well over a country for a length of
time, and through all sorts of difficulties, requires the
best and most experienced abilities," said Mr. Romford to
Lucy, as they now trotted on, watching the proceedings.

"Dash it! yonder he goes!" exclaimed Facey, pointing
the fox out to Lucy, stealing at a very steady, serviceable
pace along the low side of a rough gorse-grown pasture,
some fields ahead.

"So it is," replied she, recognising her friend.

"Put them on to me, and I'll give them a lift," said Facey,
pulling out his horn, and clapping spurs to his horse.

Tweet, tweet, tweet! went the horn; crack, crack, crack!
went Lucy's light whip, and away the willing pack flew
after their master.

As long as Facey viewed the fox, he galloped and blew
his horn, and then stopped just at the place where he had
seen him last. The hounds then dropped their noses, and
quickly hit off the scent on much more favourable ground.
They ran in good earnest. Galloper no longer keeps his
place—Brusher takes it. See how he flings for the scent,
and how impetuously he runs! Now another takes it,
and so it is lost and caught, and caught and lost, by the
compact phalanx of competing mouths. Mr. Romford
cheers them on, for he is anxious to kill the fox, as well
for the credit of his pack as the éclat of our fair whipper-
in. So he rides, all eyes, ears, and fears, looking anxiously
out for any indication of the line. A man on a hay-rick
now holds up his hat, and our master presently views the
fox again, still pursuing the even tenor of his way towards

the large sheltering woods. He has a good steady stare, and calculates the respective paces of each, thinking the balance of speed rather in favour of the fox. He is half inclined to lift them again. If it weren't that they were hunting so well, he would do it. Just then fortune favours him. A party of practising riflemen, whom Pug mistakes for poachers, having been most unhandsomely peppered by one of the tribe, begin bang, bang, banging at the butt, causing him to make a long detour by Shirrington, and through Brandsby stone pits to Sherley. That seals his doom. He gets into a more populous neighbourhood, is headed and bothered, and driven from point to point, until baffled and flurried, he is almost driven into the mouths of the pack. Giving his horse to Lucy, Mr. Romford dives among the worrying hounds, and picks him up a lamentable victim of mistaken identity. He had had a very different pursuer to Mr. Lotherington. If he had known it was Romford, he would have made more sail.

"Who-hoop!" holloos Mr. Romford, holding him on high. "Who-hoop!" repeats he, with redoubled emphasis. "Who-hoop!" shrieked he for the third time. "Dash my buttons if I was ever so pleased at killing a fox in my life!" continued our master, throwing him on to the ground, and proceeding to examine his mouth. "A reg'lar hen-stealin', goose-gobbin', turkey-worryin' old sinner," announced he, rising, and diving into his long, baggy black-and-white tartan vest for his knife. Off went the brush, head, and pads. "There," said Mr. Romford, pocketing them, "you'll do no more mischief." Then he again raised the now mutilated carcase high in air with both hands, and with a profusion of "Who-hoops," threw it to the clamorous pack, with an equal profusion of "Worry, worry, worried."

"Clear the course there!" now exclaimed he, as the pull-devil pull-baker pack, having broken the ring, were scrambling among the crowding horses' legs. "Clear the course there!" repeated he, driving the field back with his whip like a circus-master. Then there arose inquiries for the brush and the pads, and how long it had been.

"Brush is bespoke," muttered Facey, advancing to Lucy, and decorating Leotard's head with it. "Better than the baccy-shop, this," said he, in an undertone, with a knowing wink, as he adjusted it. And Lucy thought of the time when another sportsman (Mr. Sponge) placed a well-won brush in her hat, and sighed.

He then distributed the pads, while the satisfied field expatiated on the merits of the run, the time, the distance, and the severity of the pace. Nothing could be better, they all agreed. Time, an hour and twenty minutes; distance, anything they like to call it. And they were all extremely obliged to the lady, they said. So they at length separated in various detachments, according to their respective destinations, many of them "Which-way-ing?" the country people, as though they had just dropped from the clouds. And Lucy and Facey rode home extremely well satisfied with themselves, and the hounds, and the horses, and with all they had done. Facey had no idea that Lucy was such a fine horsewoman, not knowing she had been in a circus before she took to the stage.

CHAPTER XVII

THE FRACAS—THE LARKSPUR HUNT IN DOUBLEIMUPSHIRE

WE are sorry to say that the unanimity which pre vailed in the hunting-field, respecting Lucy and her equestrian performances, was not shared in by the domestic circles of the H.H. hunt. Her appearance, instead of propitiating matters as was expected, only fanned the smouldering flame of discontent that had been lit up by the sale of Leotard to Mrs. Rowley Rounding into a downright blaze of anger and revenge.

"What! they were to have pretty horse-breakers down in the country, were they?" the ladies exclaimed. "They didn't care about Mr. Romford's wealth or his pack, or his sporting prowess, or anything about him. They would have no impropriety!"

The "H.H." had always been a most respectable, well-conducted hunt; and respectable it should be to the end of the chapter, or their husbands should have nothing to do with it. And they talked, and fumed, and stimulated each other into a grand phalanx of resistance. "No pretty horse-breaker!" was the cry. Swig and Chowey being still *hors de combat*, Lucy continued to officiate in their places to greatly diminishing fields, until one morning, at the meet at Mr. Trollinger's, Emerald Hall, instead of the usual offer of hospitality, they found the door shut, the window-blinds down, and the earths open; so when Facey thought the hounds were settling well to their fox, and about to drive him from the round hill on the left into the open, he popped into the honeycombed breeding earth behind the home farm. Pretty nearly the same thing was repeated at Starcross Court, much to Mr. Romford's chagrin; for though he cared nothing about the breakfast inside, or the sherry and biscuits at the door, he was always very anxious for what he called a "gollop."

And as the party most concerned is oftentimes the last to know the real facts, so our friend was the talk of the country, without his having the slightest idea that he had done anything wrong. At length, one gentleman more venturesome than the rest volunteered to enlighten him, and also to express the almost unanimous wish of the country that he would be good enough to resign it. Mr. Romford was petrified. He had no idea that ladies were prohibited from hunting with the H.H.; Lucy intruded upon no one, and why should they interfere with her? He didn't understand such work—dashed if he did.

All this was looked upon as the arrogance of riches, and made the malcontents more than ever determined to sever the connection. Facey at first was inclined to be pacific, not wishing to forfeit the great eminence he had attained, and he was half inclined to concede that Lucy should not come out any more; but the ladies would not let their husbands negotiate, and none of the fair dames being particularly fond of fox-hunting, which they considered a very inferior sport to shooting, they thought it would be a good thing to stop the adventurous amusement for a time, and also punish a purse-proud, arrogant man for his impertinence in thus thinking to ride rough-shod over them. So "go" was the word.

Then Mr. Romford finding himself in a fix, dislodging the Turbot for a time, mounted his own cap of dignity, and resolved, if he was to lose the country, to sell himself as dearly as he could. So he said, of course he should not think of remaining a moment if he did not give perfect satisfaction, but they must all be aware of the enormous sacrifice he had made in coming to them, and the great outlay he had incurred in hunting the country, which would entitle him to the subscription for the season the same as if he remained,—not that he cared a farthing about money, and would most likely give it to a charity, but he did not choose to be snubbed or dictated to in that sort of way. And he talked as if he was well bred on both sides of his head, instead of only on one, and as if his pockets were full to repletion—talked till he almost made himself believe he was a gentleman. So the H.H.'s, not liking to contend with a man of Mr. Romford's means, were at length obliged to succumb. And they closed just in time to enable him to restore them some sixteen couple of the old H.H. hounds, which he had out at walk in various parts of the country, whose fate veered between the members of that famous scratch pack the Gatherley hounds and the rope—the Gatherley's wanting the hounds for less than Mr. Romford chose to take. He had long since put down the most incorrigible of the old offenders, and, having now got his own pack well made, could afford to dispense with the rest. So he drafted all those with H.H. on their sides, and told his late followers that he wished them joy of their treasures.

Facey was now better in funds than he had ever been in the whole course of his life; better, indeed, he almost thought, than if he had got Oncle Gilroy's fortin'; for if he hadn't got a fortin', he at all events had learned how to acquire one, and that was by hunting a country, keeping hounds, and getting his sport at other people's expense. Far better than railway-making, turnip-snig-gling, thief-catching, or any of the promiscuous pursuits he had once thought of. Hunting a country was the thing, and though the H.H.'s might take exception to his *ménage*, as Lucy called it, they could take none whatever to his prowess as a sportsman. If they didn't know his worth, others would. It must be a very "slee fox" that could beat him. And, though Mr. Romford said it himself, there was a great deal of truth in the assertion, for he had a wonderful knack at circumventing a fox, and if there was not much style in his proceedings, there was a great deal of execution. This the H.H. gentlemen felt, and recalled how often they had seen him handling his fox when old Lotherington had been nonplussed, casting about without rhyme or reason—asking everybody's opinion and advice—" Which way do you think he's gone, Mr. Brown?" "Which way do you, Mr. Green?" That "which way" is a very posing question. However, there was no help for it, and a penn'orth of comfort being worth three-halfpence to most of them, Romford, and Lucy, and Leotard, and all had to go, and were presently back at the old quarters at the West-end Swell, Facey telling people that the H.H.'s were such a set of confounded cock-tails he had given up the country in disgust. He then took stock, and found himself master of fifty couple of most efficient hounds, with the recipe for getting more, and a comfortable sum of money in his pocket. Very well off, in fact. What he called "a very able man."

"There are as good fish in the sea as ever came out of it," said Facey, determining to take another try in the advertising line; and forthwith he concocted a very specious announcement, offering the services of a gentleman with an excellent pack of hounds, to whom subscription was a secondary consideration to sport, to hunt a country, either for a term of years or for the remainder of the season. And having dispatched the same to "Bell's Life" and the "Field," he quietly waited the result—amusing himself as best he could at the aforesaid Dog and Partridge Inn.

As luck would have it, the very first announcement brought an application from a gentleman, signing himself "Simon Greenfield, of Greenfield House, Honorary Secretary to the Larkspur Hunt," asking him what he could do that season—immediately, indeed. The Larkspur Hunt, like the Heavyside one, had long been a free-gratis establishment—so long that the natives had ceased to look upon not subscribing as any accommodation; and when old Mr. Bloomfield at length died, they had no doubt that plenty of people would be found ready to take the country on the same terms as he had had it. But experience shows, that with the great increase of wealth has not come a corresponding desire to support hounds, subscriptions being more difficult to collect now than they were fifty years ago. Formerly hunting, with shooting, satisfied a man: hunting from home, and shooting from home, both in reason and moderation. But now everybody must do everything: hunt in Leicestershire, shoot in Scotland, fish in Norway, race at Newmarket, and yacht everywhere, to say nothing of the necessity of enjoying the expenses of a London season, whether he likes town or not. As to a resident taking the hounds, that is a thing not to be thought of ; hence, we have a breed of migratory masters—men like Mr. Romford—who alight upon a country, and live out of the establishment. There were plenty of what Mr. Romford would call "able men" in Doubleimupshire (the scene of the Larkspur Hunt operations), but they were all either gentlemen enjoying life's wholesale recreations, or gentlemen most earnestly bent on making more money. The former gave their subscriptions more from coercion than anything else ; while the latter found it more to their interest to subscribe liberally than to waste time which to them was money, in interfering with what they didn't understand, and with which they would most likely burn their fingers if they meddled. So they gave their money and stuck to their trades, some hunting for fashion, some medicinally, some for air and exercise, some they didn't know why. But as they were all £ s. d. men, men deeply imbued with the spirit of gain, who had never been accustomed to the growing exorbitance of a pack of hounds, they always felt themselves imposed upon—never thought they got half enough for their money—never believed the hounds cost what they said, were always sure whoever had them was making money out of them, and so they went on until none but the worst of the migratory masters would touch, and at last even they began to fight shy. At length the country became vacant altogether, and had got so far into the season without hounds, when Mr. Romford's opportune advertisement appeared. It was looked upon as a very apropos announcement—one that ought to be cultivated, and forthwith each man began screwing his neighbour to see if he could not induce him to subscribe a little more. The usual stock-victims—the Lord Lieutenant, the County Members, and the Borough Members—of course, were applied to, it being part of their duty to find funds for all. There was plenty of money in the county, plenty of plate and powdered footmen, but somehow the parties preferred producing the latter to the former. But plate and powdered footmen alone won't draw, and the ladies soon began to feel the want of the red-coats, and the enlivening meets of the hounds. In this respect they differed from the Heavyside ladies, who thought sherry and biscuits were all that was required ; whereas the Larkspur ladies looked upon a hunt as a grand nucleus of society—the promoter of balls, breakfasts, dinners, races, conviviality of all sorts. And as the winter had opened gloomily, and threatened to be very dull, they were more than usually urgent and pressing, when they heard of the advertisement, lest some other country might catch the advertiser up ; for we all fancy other people want what we do. So Mr. Simon Greenfield, who gave his services to the hunt instead of subscribing, was instructed to reply to the advertisement on behalf of the members of the Larkspur Hunt, whose country, Doubleimupshire, was then vacant—asking who the liberal-minded gentleman was that was ready to take one. And on receipt of the note, Mr. Romford replied, sealing the letter with the invaluable Turbot-sitting-on-its-tail seal, which spoke more forcibly than whole realms of satin note-paper could have done. Mr. Romford ! Mr. Romford ! I know the name perfectly, exclaimed several. And forthwith there was a rush to the Burkes, and an anxious turn to the R.s— Rippon, Robson, Robertson, Roddam, oh yes—all right— here he is, "Romford, Francis, Esq., J.P., D.L., seat, Abbeyfield Park, patron of five livings, crest, a Turbot sitting upon its tail on a cap of dignity." Just so !—here it is (holding up the letter), "a Turbot sitting upon its tail on a cap of dignity." Well done, Romford, Francis, Esq. He would be the very man for their money.

The announcement caused great satisfaction in Doubleimupshire, for Mr. Romford's name was good, and, as he could only be changing for the sake of improvement, the superiority of their county would doubtless compensate for any little deficiency in the matter of funds. And some of the small subscribers began to wish they had put themselves down for double the amount, seeing it was not likely to be called for. So Mr. Simon Greenfield was requested to rejoin forthwith, and thereupon a reciprocity of paper-politeness took place between Mr. Romford and him, in which the latter expressed his readiness to meet Mr. Romford to confer on the matter at any place he might choose to appoint. And Facey, not caring to have him too near, replied, after a good consultation and calculation of Bradshaw, that fair play was a jewel, and he would meet him half-way, naming the Trench Crossing station of the Union Railway, at Hopton Heath, which appeared to divide the distance as nearly as possible, and being quite private, would prevent any chance of interruption; in other words, prevent any one seeing him, and letting out that he was the wrong Romford. And so a meeting was appointed to take place accordingly.

CHAPTER XVIII

THE HONORARY SECRETARY TO THE LARKSPUR HUNT —TURNING OVER A NEW LEAF

THE Trench Crossing Station of the Union Railway at Hopton Heath was an isolated shed upon a bleak, barren plain, inhabited only by a solitary snipe of a station-master, who but for the appointment would have made a capital hermit. The express trains shot past it with disdain, the first and second classes only stopped on demand, while the pick-ups and parlies alone pulled up voluntarily, and having once stopped seemed as if they would never go on again. Facey had been down that way once before on a crusade against Sir Charles Goodacre's pheasants, and knew how to change his third-class ticket for a first one at Fiddler's Ferry station so as to come up all right first class at the heath. His appearance on this occasion was very different to what it was then, his ten-penny wide-awake being exchanged for a good black hat, and his rough pouched-like garb for a very becoming sporting attire. In truth, Lucy Glitters—we beg pardon, Mrs. Sponge—had civilised him amazingly, trimming his mane, and reducing the ruggedness of his uncouth all-round-the-face whiskers. Upon this occasion he sported a neat scarlet-and-white striped tie, secured with a splendid diamond (Brighton diamond) ring, that would have been worth many hundreds had it been real, whereas he had only given eighteenpence for it. Still it looked very hand-some, and, though Mr. Facey was ugly enough, he had the size and the action that carry a thing off. Then, when he discarded his smart gray or rather lavender coloured paletot, he disclosed a neat, single-breasted, dark grey morning coat, striped buff vest, with Bedford-cord trousers, and buttoned boots. In his dog-skin gloved hand he clutched a green silk parasol-like umbrella, the property of Lucy, which looked altogether out of proportion to the monster who carried it.

A railway journey, unlike a road one, can either be made long or short, or middling, according to the taste and inclination of the traveller, and there is no limit to what steam will accomplish. Hence, it follows that time affords no criterion of the distance that a man may travel in a day. It all depends upon the train, whether he has flown by express, or taken it quietly by an ordinary train. Mr. Romford did a little of all sorts, changing from one line to another, from one class to another, as did his travelling coadjutor from the contrary direction, until, like the weird sisters in Macbeth, they at length met upon the "blasted heath." Facey came up in a slow train. Puff-whew-hew-ew-whiou, whew! and the sluggish monster at last got its cumbrous length laid alongside the little station. Out came the Snipe for a stare, never imagining that two passengers could want to alight there in one day. Two baskets he had had, and three boxes, in one day, but he never remembered two passengers. So he didn't proclaim the name of the station. Mr. Romford, however, looked out and saw it, and prepared to alight. On the little platform stood a mildly drawn looking pink and white young gentleman, of some five-and-twenty or thirty years of age. Just the sort of man that Facey would like to have to negotiate with. A glance of his keen ferreting eyes told him that he could, what he called, "talk him off his legs in no time." He was glad to see he was alone, for then he needn't mind what he said. Lowering the third of the remaining carriage window in which he was seated, he called to the Snipe to open the door, and then alighted with the stately deliberation of a man doing the consequential instead of the hurrying out of a second or third class carriage. Advancing towards where the stranger stood, he gave his new hat a groomy sort of a rap with his forefinger, accompanied by a duck of the head, and a mutter of "Mr. Greenfield, I believe."

"Mr. Greenfield it is," replied the placid stranger, with a smile, adding, "Mr. Romford, I s'pose," with a bow, whereupon Facey tendered him his substantial fist, and pump-handled him severely.

"Ticket, sir, please," said the solitary Snipe, now

coming up ; which being delivered up, and Facey having arranged his paletot becomingly across his arm, and felt that the Brighton diamond was safe, turned again to the "Honorary Secretary," saying, "Now let's go in and have a talk." Thereupon Facey led the way into the diminutive waiting-room, furnished with four black horse-hair-bottomed mahogany chairs, a round table, and a gaudy-coloured oil-cloth on the floor. In the little watch-pocket-like grate of a fireplace a few very inferior coals were gradually smouldering into white ashes.

"Bring some fuel!" roared Facey, digging his capped toe into the midst of the remnant ; and the want being supplied, he invited his friend to be seated on one of the chairs, and, taking another himself, stuck himself well before the fire, and thus opened upon him—

"Now tell me first," said he, fixing his little ferreting eyes full upon him—"now tell me, do your people eat, or do they drink, or do they hunt ? I mean," said Facey, seeing the Honorary Secretary did not understand him, "do they talk about their cooks or about their wine, or about the sport they have had with the hounds ?"

"Well, I don't know exactly," replied Mr. Greenfield, "they do a little of all three occasionally. There is a good deal of dinner company goes on, and where there is eating there will be drinking and talking too, you know."

"Ah, I don't care about dinners," replied Facey, with a shrug of his great round shoulders ; "a little shooting would be more in my way. Tell me now, are your people good-natured about their shooting, or do they kick up a dust if anybody gets on to their ground by accident or mistake ?"

"Oh, some of them are very good-natured indeed, others are only so-so—men vary, you know."

"So they do," said Romford—"so they do ; one man is no more a criterion for another man than one horse is a criterion for another, or one hound a criterion for another. Every herring must hang by its own head." He then began biting his nails and weeding his chin, as was his wont on critical occasions.

"Now tell me about the hounds," at length resumed he, coming to the real purport of the interview. "Tell me about the hounds. How many days a week do you want the country hunted ?"

"Four," replied Mr. Greenfield promptly.

"And the subscription?" rejoined Facey.

"Well, from sixteen to eighteen hundred a year," stammered Greenfield, who had been told to begin low.

"Sixteen to eighteen 'undred," muttered Facey, pulling a sample out of his beard, and examining it attentively at the fire. "Sixteen to eighteen 'undred a year," repeated he. "How comes the uncertainty? There's a difference, you know, between sixteen and eighteen, you know—difference of two, I should say, though I don't know nothin' 'bout mathematics—'rithmetic, I should say."

"There are always some people who put their names down and don't pay," replied the Honorary Secretary.

"So there are," said Facey, "and be hanged to them—so there are, as I know to my cost. Well, but I suppose we might put the subscription down at eighteen 'undred a year," continued he, pulling out his betting-book, and doing a little "'rithmetic"—"eighteen 'undred from three thousand, and twelve 'undred remains. That would leave twelve 'undred a year for me," said he, with a "can't-be-done-ish" sort of shake of the head.

"So much as that?" stared Mr. Greenfield.

"The way I should do it," replied Mr. Facey—"the way I should do it. Of course there are some of these new-fangled Marsh [1]-like masters who will do it for less, and live out of the subscription too, but that sort of work wouldn't suit me. I must do the thing properly or not at all."

Facey then arose, and diving his hands up to the hilts in his Bedford-cord trouser pockets, took a meditative fling round the little apartment, apparently lost in calculation, but in reality resolved not to miss such a chance.

"It's too much for the master to pay," at length said he pulling up short, and sticking himself John Bull-ically (a coat tail over each arm) before the fire. "It's too much for the master—but still I think it might be manished,—I think it might be manished. S'pose now," said he, sitting down again, and placing a foot on each hob, "s'pose we were to say—subscription two thousand—subscription two thousand—that would leave a cool thousand

---

[1] An ex-groom, having changed his name from Marsh, and decorated his face with mustachios, took a country, and passed muster, until he hunted a bag fox on a Sunday!

for me—quite little enough for a man who has all the
trouble and bother of the thing."

"I am afraid we could hardly raise the money," replied
Mr. Greenfield meekly.

"Oh, easy enough," replied Mr. Romford—"easy
enough. Put on the screw! there are always plenty of
fellows with more wool on their backs than's good for
them, who'll stand a little fleecing."

Mr. Greenfield sat mute, for his instructions were to
fleece Facey.

"It's a disagreeable thing to talk about money," observed Mr. Romford, with a pish and a pshaw, "but
landed property is so different to money property, where
you get every farthing paid to the day, that one's 'bliged
to be a little prudent and circumspect. Won't do to live
up to one's income, you know," added Facey, with a shake
of the head.

"True," assented Mr. Greenfield, who had some house
property of his own, which was always either standing
empty, tumbling down, or wanting a year's rent laid out
in repairs.

"Oh, I don't think there could be any difficulty about
it," resumed Mr. Romford cheerfully, after a pause;
"I don't think there would be any difficulty about it.
It's only like putting a percentage on to the present
subscriptions, you know. Just as easy to draw a cheque
for sixty as for fifty. People don't care half so much for
parting with money by cheque, as they do in notes or
sovs."

Mr. Greenfield sat mute.

"A man can't leave home without loss," observed Mr.
Romford. "When the cat's away, the mice will play,"
continued he, taking another sample out of his beard and
examining it attentively as before. The two then sat
silent for a time, Facey twisting the hair about and
viewing it in various lights.

"You'll have the country hunted as it never was before,"
at length observed Romford, throwing the hair into the
fire. "I don't like boasting, but if anybody can show
sport I can. I have a first-rate pack of hounds," added
he; "spared no expense in getting them."

Mr. Greenfield did not attempt to gainsay any part of
this, his friends of the Larkspur Hunt being quite content
to take Mr. Romford, provided they could get him at

their own price, but being a rich man they thought they should have him cheaper than if he was a poor one. And our friend, like the drunken actor who fancied himself the King, in the Coronation, and exclaimed as he crossed the stage, "God bless you, my people !"—our friend, we say, having talked so long in thousands, began almost to think that he dealt in them too, and that he was really a rich man instead of a rank impostor.

Having given the fire another poke with his toe, for they did not allow fire-irons at the Hopton Heath Station, Mr. Facey Romford got up again and gave himself another fling round the room, as if for inspiration.

"You see now," said he, resuming his erect position before the fire, "you see now, what I want is sport—sport is the first consideration with me ; but sport can't be had without money, and we ought to put our shoulders fairly to the wheel together to get it."

The Secretary nodded assent.

"Well, then, you see," said Facey, "besides what I shall lose by leaving home, I shall have to increase my establishment ; and I needn't tell you, who see me, that a man of moy weight can't mount himself for nothin'. Three 'underd is generally the figure I have to give for horses. As soon as ever the rascals hear they are for Mr. Romford, they immediately stick on the price. Then I should certainly like to know about a little shooting and fishing—not that I can say I should avail myself of either much, only it's pleasant to have an object for a walk, and to feel that one can go out if one likes. Altogether, I think we understand each other," said Facey, thinking it would be very odd if the Honorary Secretary did. "Two thousand a year guaranteed subscription, half in November and half in January, or the whole in November, if you like, for four days a week, with an occasional 'bye,' cover rents and stopping paid, and I'll undertake to show you such sport as never was seen. But 'of their own merits modest men are dumb'—only, if I can't show sport, I don't know who can ; so that's a bargain," said he, extending his right hand for a shake.

"Oh ! but I shall have to consult the gentlemen of the hunt first," exclaimed Mr. Greenfield, drawing back in alarm. "I shall have to consult the gentlemen of the hunt first."

"Or'd rot it, I thought you'd been a reg'larly 'pointed

Plenipotentiary," replied Facey, pretending disappointment at the answer. "Or'd rot it, but I thought you'd
been a reg'larly 'pointed Plenipotentiary," repeated he.
"However," said he, "you know what I want, and must
fig your fellows up to giving it. Tell them it's only the
superiority of their country that tempts me, *nothin'* else."

"I'll represent all you have said," replied Mr. Greenfield guardedly.

"And in talking about it, mind don't forget to broach·
the shooting. Say I should like a little shooting."

"I'll not forget that either," assented Mr. Greenfield.

"Nor the fishing," rejoined Facey; adding, "It would
do your heart good to see me throw a fly. I really think
the fish feel a pride and a pleasure in being hooked by
me," continued he, flourishing his right arm as if he were
in the act of handling a fishing-rod.

He had had a good deal of fishing where he was, and
what with his rod and his gun had kept the butcher's bill
down.

Our master then took a general suck of the Secretary's
brains, learning as much about the country and characters
in it as he could. They seemed to be a lively sort—
quite different to the old Heavysides. Dinners, balls,
parties of all sorts.

The shrill shriek and screech of the whistle at length
announced the coming of the down-train, and Facey, who
had arranged the visit with a greater regard to his own
convenience than that of the Honorary Secretary, now
asked him to give him a help on with his paletot, which
being adjusted, Facey gave him another pump-handling
shake of the hand, and emerging from the little
waiting-room, was presently seated conspicuously in a
first-class carriage on his way back to Minshull Vernon,
exchanging the first-class for a third one, as before. And
the big talk, coupled with the Brighton diamond and gay
get-up generally, had impressed the Honorary Secretary
so favourably, that the Larkspur gentlemen resolved to
secure Mr. Romford, and, after trying eighteen hundred
a year unsuccessfully, Mr. Greenfield was at length com-
missioned to close for the two thousand a year, the name
of Romford tickling the subscribers' fancies just as Mr.
Facey said he tickled trouts when a boy.

And Facey chuckled at his own 'cuteness when he got

the dispatch announcing their acceptance of his offer, and said the Romford star was clearly on the ascendant.

When it became known that such a swell as the Turbot-on-its-tail had taken the Larkspur country, he was beset by people with large places offering him their houses, at more or less remunerative prices.   " Nothing for nothing," is the motto nowadays.   One gentleman was going to Naples; another to Rome; a third wanted to make a tour in the East; a fourth in the West; and they would have no objection to letting their houses and gardens to a careful party without any children, and one who would not interfere with the game.   The game was to be held sacred. But for this, Facey would have had no difficulty in taking a place, and paying the rent out of his gun.

The course of his inquiries, however, made him acquainted with the fact that Beldon Hall, the beautiful seat of Lord Viscount Lovetin, on the south-east of his country, was vacant, and had been so for some time— a circumstance that generally has a mitigating influence on the expected rent.   In this case it had a considerable influence ; for his lordship had had so many cruel dis-appointments and vexations about letting it, that he was almost heart-broken in consequence.   Not that the Viscount was poor—far from it—but this was the thorn in his side—the one thing that made him miserable. Indeed, he had much changed with the unexpected acquisition of his title from his cousin, having been, when Jack Moneygull, of the Tom and Jerry Hussars, one of the jolliest fellows under the sun, ready to back a bill, bonnet a Bobby, do anything light and frolicsome; but now, as the Lord Viscount Lovetin, he had become the meanest, most morose, penurious creature possible, always dreading expense and imposition, sitting calculating interest by the clock.   He had shut up Beldon Hall and retired to the Continent, where he lived *au troisième, au quatrième, au cinquième*—anywhere rather than at home—never spending a halfpenny he could help, and talking as if he didn't know where the next day's dinner was to come from.   Then he wanted to let Beldon Hall, and he didn't want to let it.   When it came to the point, he put so many restrictions and embargoes upon the parties, that nobody would take it.   His lordship wanted the money, in fact, but did not want to give the tenants anything for it.   Mr. Challoner might have it, provided he wouldn't use the drawing-room. Mr. Coverdale might have it, provided he wouldn't use the dining-room. Mrs. Emmerson and his lordship quarrelled about the cut pile carpet in the music-room. He would have it put away, while she insisted upon keeping it down. So they separated, after consuming an immensity of paper, for they were both most voluminous letter-writers. And half a dozen other negotiations had gone off on similar quibbles, until the place was regularly blown. Nobody would look at it. People said it wasn't to let.

Mr. Romford, finding this, wrote to his lordship, saying that he had taken the Larkspur country, and, hearing that Beldon Hall was empty, he would be glad to know if his lordship would have any objection to letting it to him, adding that he would take great care of the furniture and everything belonging to it, and of course he sealed the letter with the proper Turbot-on-its-tail seal. Now it so happened that Lord Lovetin had been one of the "gilded youth of England" along with the right or other Mr. Romford at Eton, and though they had never been particularly intimate, yet his lordship perfectly remembered Frank Romford, and, moreover, had had his memory constantly refreshed by reading the meets of his hounds in the papers; and, hope deferred having long made his lordship's heart sick, he jumped at the offer, and named a much less rent than he had ever asked before. And Facey quickly concluded a bargain, which was only mentioned to Mr. Lonnergan, the agent, when it came to be ratified by directions from his lordship for giving Mr. Romford possession.

Now Mr. Lonnergan was an imperious man—one who had no notion of divided dignity, or of an owner presuming to exercise any control whatever over the property confided to his charge. There could be no two Kings of Brentford with him; and Mr. Lonnergan being at best one of your "receive-the-rents, drink-the-landlord's-health, and let-the-tenants-do-as-they-like" order, he was doubly easy and indifferent with regard to the letting of Beldon Hall, just executing his lordship's orders, and nothing more—telling Mrs. Mustard, the dirty house-keeper, that the place was let, but saying, with a significant snort and a chuck of his great double-chin, he "didn't know who to, or anything at all about it, so she needn't bother him, his lordship having thought proper to manage

the matter himself." And Lonnergan inwardly hoped
that his noble master might burn his fingers by the
transaction. Indeed, he half thought of turning his
lordship off for the offence.

So, one bright winter's afternoon, a sort of social
resurrection seemed to take place at the long-deserted
mansion of Beldon Hall, in the shape of smoke rising
from the various stacks of chimneys, to the surprise of the
passers-by along the Horton and Kingswood road, and
the astonishment of the country round about. "What's
up now?" was the general inquiry. "Is his lordship
coomin' home?" demanded the men. "Has he gotten
a wife?" asked the women. Proudlock, the gigantic
keeper, strutted consequentially with the all-important
secret—almost too large for his capacious chest to contain.

The great Mr. Romford was coming!

What a man Proudlock made him out to be! Wore
silver boots on week days, and gold on a Sunday.

CHAPTER XIX

LUCY BAMBOOZLES THE MASTER—INDEPENDENT JIMMY

SWIG and Chowey being at length restored to con-
valescence, if not to their pristine beauty—sundry
strips of adhesive plaster still remaining on their weather-
beaten faces—Mr. Romford thought that Lucy might as
well return to her scenes in the circle at Islington as
waste her time any longer at the West-end Swell. To
this end, therefore, he magnificently presented her with
a five-pound note and her fare, saying he would be glad
to see her again some other day. But Lucy, having again
tasted the sweets of country life, was not to be so easily
disposed of as friend Facey supposed, and kept loitering
on at the West-end Swell;—where, however, we are
bound to say she conducted herself in a most exemplary
manner. Soapey himself could not have taken exception
to her conduct. The fact was she had got fond of the
hounds and the horses, and would like if she could to
blend her fortune with theirs. But Facey didn't favour

the design; he felt that he was on his preferment, and that such an appendage to his hounds might injure his prospects. In vain she expatiated on the delights of the chase, on the pleasures of leading the field, of cutting down Newton and Bibbing. In vain she hinted that Swig and Chowey would be better for a little more looking after, that having a whipper-in in reserve (meaning herself) would have a beneficial effect in keeping them in order. Facey was proof against all her allurements, though he could not but admit that the last argument had a good deal of weight in it. It was a convenience, he admitted, to have some one in reserve. That opinion, however, he kept to himself. At length Lucy touched a chord that vibrated more forcibly still— it was a direct appeal to his pocket—Didn't he think it would assist his sales to have a lady to show off his horses? A woman could hardly object to a horse that another had rode, and a man would be laughed to scorn who did.

Facey was struck with the argument. That £80 had excited his cupidity and made him wish for more. He thought it might be very easily got. A very little riding of the horse by Lucy would do to establish his name for perfect temper and docility— perfect manners, as the advertisers say.

The severity of the conflict now passing in his mind was evinced by the number of samples he culled from his chin and rejected without examination. He ran the matter quickly through his mind—the profit, the loss, the risk, and so on.

"No, it won't do," at length said he; "the world is censorious, and we should only get into a scrape." Facey felt the importance of now making hay while the sun shone, viz. getting an heiress, if he could. He must start fair at all events.

But Lucy was a good coaxer, and combated his objections with great adroitness. She ridiculed the idea of her presence being the cause of the Heavyside rupture. It was all because they were jealous of her riding. She might have added "looks," but she left that for another to say—who, however, did not say it.

They then had a great discussion upon the feasibility of the thing—the possibility of Lucy again living alone as she had done at the West-end Swell without exciting curiosity; and it was decided by Mr. Romford that she could not. Still her resources didn't fail her. Why shouldn't her mother come down and live with her and make herself useful—she could graft stockings there with her quite as well as in Hart Street.

"*Humph!*" growled Facey, appealing again to his beard. "Don't see what good that would do," at length observed he, after a long pause, fearing, amongst other things, that he might have to pay for the quarters. "If your mother was to coom, she'd better coom to the Hall, where there's plenty of room," observed he.

"And why not!" exclaimed Lucy. "I'm sure she'd be most happy."

"Then folke would say, 'Who the deuce are these people he's got with him?'" replied Facey.

"Say I'm your sister," rejoined Lucy.

"Hoot! we're not a bit alike," growled he.

"Half-sister, or sister-in-law, then," said Lucy, anxious to accommodate matters.

Still Facey was afraid.

She then suggested some complicated state of relationship arising out of an imaginary double marriage of her mother that would cure all defects of looks and family connection, and argued it so scientifically, that she completely bamboozled our master. He could neither comprehend nor confute her. And the lady, as usual, got her way. After a great deal of doubt and controversy, it was at length arranged that Lucy should accompany Mr. Romford to Beldon Hall, and that her "moother," Mrs. Glitters, who will hereafter be known by the name of Sidney Benson—Mrs. Sidney Benson—should come down to keep her company, on the express understanding that Mrs. Benson was to make herself generally useful in the house, and Lucy out of doors :—Facey strongly impressing upon Lucy that it was only an experiment which might or might not answer, but that, under no circumstances, could he have anything like riotous housekeeping — "sheep - chops" and batter - puddings being Facey's idea of luxurious living. It was also further arranged that Lucy might pass as his half-sister—sister by courtesy—assuming the name of Somerville, and passing as the widow of an Indian officer.

The present is undoubtedly the age for furthering Romfordian speculations, for dress has become so queer and eccentric, and all people are put so much upon a par by the levelling influence of the rail, that a versatile man may pass for almost anybody he likes—a duke, a count, a viscount. Mr. Romford, however, was so satisfied with the distinguished name of Romford, that he had no desire to be taken for any one else; indeed, he thought Romford was just about as good a name as a man could have. If people chose to confound him with his namesake, the other Mr. Romford, it was no business of his. So, discarding the detested name of Gilroy on leaving the West-end Swell at Minshull Vernon, he directed his packages, "Francis Romford, Esquire," only; but then he added, "At the Lord Viscount Lovetin's, Beldon Hall, Doubleimupshire," which made them very commanding, and procured him great attention. They were not numerous, neither were Lucy's, but things are so procurable all the world over, that there is no occasion to travel about with any great stock. Moreover, Lucy—we beg pardon, Mrs. Somerville—on whom of course devolved the burthen of display, meant to work the Turbot-on-its-tail seal upon the London milliners as soon as she got established at Beldon Hall.

Being now aware of the importance of first impressions, Facey sent his own and his men's measures up to the celebrated Mr. Tick, the tailor in Civil Row (whose aptitude for dressing sportsmen is so universally appreciated), in order that they might not appear in the disreputable-looking garments they had been accustomed to wear with the now discarded Heavyside hounds. And he also communicated fully with Mr. Goodhearted Green, urging him to send down a supply of horses—good, bad, or indifferent—as quick as he could, adding, that if Goodheart came with them himself, he would put him up and find wear and tear for his teeth.

And all things being prepared for a start, and Facey having taken a parting glass with Toby Trotter overnight, rose with the sun the next morning, and left Minshull Vernon, with hounds, horses, servants, Lucy, and all, much to the regret of Mrs. Lockwood, the genial landlady of the West-end Swell.

The unwonted freight commanded great attention on the line. The various station-masters presented themselves respectfully at the carriage-door; the curious of each place peered in at the window; and the bustling

guard, as he hurried along the platforms, kept replying
"Mr. Romford—Mr. Romford," to the numerous inquiries
"Who it was?" So our travellers passed from line to
line till they got to the Cross Street Station at Howland
Hill, where they ought to have changed carriages, but
here a director happening to be on the platform, and
hearing who it was, came forward, bowing and scraping,
and begging that Mr. Romford and the lady would not
think of disturbing themselves, for the carriage they were
in should go on to their utmost destination. Thus they
proceeded, with great dignity and ease, laughing at the
fools who thus worshipped them.

At length, after a long pace-slackening glide, the train
stopped before a sort of Swiss cottage, and a large black
and white board in the centre announced "FIRFIELD
STATION." The porters then began running along the
line of carriages, exclaiming, "Field!—Field!—Fifield
Station! Change here for Shenstone, Comb, and Danby! Change here for Shenstone, Comb, and Danby!"

Mr. Romford having let the train fairly subside, then
lowered his window, and called authoritatively to the
head-porter to open the door. The mandate being
quickly obeyed, our master descended, with becoming
caution and dignity, and then proceeded to hand out
Lucy, the eyes and necks of the remaining passengers
being strained to get a sight of the lady. "Very pretty,"
the men said she was. "Middling," said the ladies.
With a clank of the coupling chains, off went the last
joints of the tail containing Mr. Romford's cargo; the
hounds raised a melodious cry, and the now lightened
engine presently snorted, and then shot away with the
rest of the train.

"Tickets!—Tickets, if you please," was then the order
of the day; and tickets Mr. Romford delivered up—
tickets for himself and Mrs. Somerville—tickets for Swig
and Chowey—also for Bob Short, who had replied to
Facey's advertisement for a "strong, persevering man to
clean horses"—and voluminous documents for the hounds
and stud. The "strong, persevering man" being a
teetotaller, Facey now put Swig and Chowey under his
charge, while he escorted his sister—Mrs. Somerville—to
her destination.

It must be a poor, spiritless place that does not sport
a "bus"; and though none of the three old grey-roofed

villages—or "toons," as the natives called them—viz.
Necton, Lingford, or Heatherey Clough, were important
enough to keep one themselves, yet, by clubbing together,
they not only had a bus, but also a nondescript vehicle
and pair that might be engaged by those who objected to
making the triangular tour of the "toons" by the bus.
Both vehicles belonged to the same man, one Peter Cross,
of all three places, Peter being a publican at one, a
provision-merchant at another, and paper-hanger at a
third. Peter and his man, Jimmy Jones, or Independent
Jimmy as he was generally called, drove the bus and the
"chay" by turns; and on the day of the great Mr.
Romford's arrival, Peter had the bus, and Jimmy the
"chay." Peter, who did the politeness—an article that
Jimmy was rather deficient in—seeing who they had got
to convey, strongly recommended the "chay" to our
friends, observing that they would get to Beldon Hall in
half the time that they would by the bus; and Peter
even yielded the *pas* to the "chay," keeping all the bus
passengers waiting while he helped Jimmy to load and
shove Lucy into the queer little cock-boat of a carriage,
all curtains, slides, and glides, that no one can ever work
in a shower until he is wet through.

Having, however, little to do with our "Mathews-at
Home" of a master, we will proceed to introduce the
man, who is a more important personage in our story.
Independent Jimmy was well called Independent Jimmy,
for he had a most independent way of his own : he did
not seem to care a copper for any one. If a passenger
tipped him, he took it; if he didn't tip him, he was
equally civil without : he did not seem to care which
way it was. Sometimes he sported a coat, and sometimes
he didn't; and the more likely the weather was for
wearing one, the more unlikely Jimmy was to have it on.
He never said Sir, or Ma'am, or Miss, or used any of the
circumlocutory forms of address, but just blurted out,
"Noo then!" "Get oop!" "Get doon!" "Get in!"
"Get oot!" and shoved his passengers about like so
many sheep. He was a big, burly, strongly built, blunt
Northumbrian, with the strength of a Sayers, and the
digestion of an ostrich. A man might as well pound at a
sack of beans as at Jimmy. His healthy cheek almost
outvied the bloom of his blue-glass-buttoned scarlet
plush vest. He would take a trunk away from a totter-

ing footman, and chuck it into its place like a quoit. He had been all his life among horses, either as an ostler, a helper, a post-boy, a bus-man, or a cab-driver, vacillating about the country, changing from the Rose and Crown at Heckworth to the Leopard at Bucknell, and from the Bunch of Grapes at Haywood to the Hat and Feathers at Heatherey Clough. Thus he had a very general acquaintance, and could have written or dictated a capital guide-book, giving as well an account of all the inns and places of public entertainment, as of all the private houses, with their respective staffs of servants, and the strength of each of their taps. Jimmy was free of them all—of all at least that gave anything away. There was a sort of an independence in his very gait, for his right leg gave a free-and-easy shake, as if it did not care a copper for the other. But we will let him parade himself as he goes.

We are now at the back of the Firfield Station, with the luggage on, and Lucy in, what the wags called the melon-frame. The day being fine, and Facey, not at all the man to submit to the impurities of a shut cab, as he called a close carriage, now intimated, by a jerk of his head and a turn of his wrist, that Jimmy might shut the carriage-door, which being done, Facey and he mounted the box on alternate sides, and Jimmy having tendered Facey half his old drab frieze overcoat to sit upon, clutched the hard weather-bleached reins, and with a jog and jerk and a click of his tongue, moved the old leg-weary screws slowly away out of the whinstone-covered ring at the back of the Firfield Swiss cottage station. The grinding noise subsiding as they got upon the well-kept turnpike road beyond, the two old nags—a bay and a chestnut—having first laid their heads together as if in consultation, seemed to agree that a voluntary trot might save them a rib-roasting, so, with wonderful unanimity, they both began to potter along, while Facey sat contemplating their dreary, leg-weary action, and Jimmy sat wondering what Facey thought of them.

" Not a bad shaped nag, that old white-legged chestnut ! " at length observed Romford.

" Good 'un,—varry," said Jimmy, giving the horse an approving rub in the ribs with the crop of his pig-driver-like whip.

" Where did you get him, now ? " asked Romford.

"Wor maister bought him—bought him of Hazey—
—second-hand Neddy, as ar call him," said Jimmy.

"What Hazey—the man who keeps the Hard and
Sharp hounds?" asked our hero.

"Keeps the hunds!" ejaculated Jimmy; "the hunds
more like keep him, ar should say."

"Well, but we mean the same man," rejoined Facey.

"Same man," assented Jimmy; "same man. Arn't
two such men i' the world."

"Mean man, is he?" asked Romford.

"Mean man," assented Jimmy; "man that would do
out; quite a wonderful sort of man for meanness."

"But he's rich, isn't he?" asked Romford.

"Rich, ay; rich enough. But what signifies his riches;
does things that a beggar would be sham'd on. A but
hear him buy a hus and sell a hus is quite a theatre
performance: a man wadint know that he was talkin'
'boot the same animal. Ar arways says that nobody
knows what doonright cliver lein (lying) really is who
hasn't heard Hazey. A, he's a reglar imposition," said
Jimmy, with a shake of his head and a chuck of the
coupling reins, as if to make his horses get away from
the thoughts of him.

"You wouldn't give much for him, I s'pose," observed
Romford, holding Jimmy on to the line of scent notwithstanding.

"Moch, no!" replied Jimmy. "Why, he's abun twenty
years ald, and been doon iver se mony times—doon
with the butler, doon with the coachman, doon with
the gardener, doon with ivirybody a'morst."

"A fi'-pun-note, p'r'aps," suggested Facey.

"Fi'-pun-note!" retorted Jimmy ironically, adding,
"No sink; we get twe sich as him for that money."

"The deuce you do!" observed Mr. Romford, laughing.

"We just gav three-and-thorty shillin' for him,"
continued Jimmy, unburthening his mind without further
circumlocution. "Ald Hazey wanted twe pund, but
wor ald maister's just as keen and as hard bitten as he
is, and began by bidding him thorty shillin', and efter
'boot six weeks' hard barginin', he got him for three-
and-thorty."

"Cheap enough," said Mr. Romford, eyeing his honest
pulling.

"Why, he's not iv'rybody's money, you see," replied

Jimmy. "He's o'er leet for the bus, or o'er wake for the
ploo, and if he couldn't carry the lad wi' the letters,
what could Hazey de wi' 'im? Sink ar think he did
varry weal to get three-and-thorty shillin' for him,"
continued Jimmy, rubbing the old horse again on the
ribs with the crop of his whip to coax him along.

The fall of the road favouring a trot, Jimmy then
bowled along for some half-mile in silence. Mr. Romford
at length broke it.

"Who have we here?" now asked he, as a spacious
stone mansion with a couple of crest-decorated gates
and lodges suddenly loomed upon them.

"Oh, this be Lees—Dalbury Lees. Willy Watkins—
Squire Watkins lives there," replied Independent Jimmy,
with a twirl of his whip and a chuck of his chin, as
if he did not think much of him.

"Does he hunt?" asked Romford.

"Hont! no—shut noither," replied Jimmy.

"What does he do, then?" asked Facey.

"Nout. Brush his hair mainly, ar should say," replied
Jimmy. "He whiles put on a red coat, but it's only
for show, ar should say.

"Sink," said he, half to himself and half to Romford,
"but I de think they are the biggest feuls in arl the
country. Leuk, noo," said he, "at them there lodges
with the red and gould lion crests and grand·fancy gates,
just as if they belanged to a duke. Arm dashed but
that chap was a painter and glazier, or somethin' of
that sort only t'other day," continued he, flanking the bay,
as if to get past the obnoxious gates as fast as he could.

"Painter and glazier," repeated Mr. Romford, "he
must have had a good trade."

"No, he hadn't," replied Jimmy, "a varry bad 'un—
at least he couldn't make nout on't, so he went to
Horsetria, ye see, where they dig out the gould."

"Australia, p'r'aps," submitted Mr. Romford, whose
friend, Soapey Sponge, was now there.

"Ay, Horsetrilia—that's the varry name of the place,"
replied Jimmy—"Horsetrilia. Well, there he dug a
mint o' money, and came home with a grand set-up
wife and sich a conceited darter, ar don't think ar ever
seed sich a sarcy pair, and took this place of old Squire
Dobbindale, puttin' oop these grand crests at the gates
and gatherin' all the lazy scamps o' servants i' the coountry.

They'll take anything that they say has lived with a lord. As to the darter," continued Jimmy, reverting to her, "she's just the impittantest, sarciest gal i' the world, arlways tossin' aboot and givin' gob. Noo, there's the Ladies Rosebud, Lord Flowerdew's darters, when ar gans to the Castle, for anybody there, they speak quite civil and plizant; 'Good morning, Jimmy.' 'How do ye do, Jimmy? hoo are all the little Jimmys?' (for ar ha' thorteen on 'em," added Jimmy parenthetically) "and so on, while this sarcy thing taks had of her stickin'-out claes, and cries, 'Now, man! get out of the way, man; see, man! look, man! mind, man!' just as if I were a twoad. Sink, I'd skelp her ivry other day gin she were mine;" and thereupon Jimmy gave Hazey's horse some scientific cuts, just as if he were dealing them out to Miss Watkins.

"Sink, but ar often wonders," continued Jimmy, now looking down at his lack-lustre shoes, now up at the firmament; "sink, but ar often wonders who those sort o' fondies think they impose upon. It can't be the likes o' me," continued he, "for we know all about them; it can't be the gentlefolks, for they'll ha' nout to say te them. It mun just be their arn silly sels," at length added he, solving the problem as he proceeded.

They then passed on within sight of several other country houses, of more or less pretensions, of all of whose inmates Jimmy discoursed in terms of easy familiarity, d——g one, praising another, scouting a third. It is always well for county gentlemen to keep in with the drivers of public vehicles past their places. Being abused—say twice a day—every day of the year comes to a good deal of abuse in the course of a twelve-month. To-day, for instance, Mr. Romford made the acquaintance of the most distinguished characters in our story, all through a chance journey with Independent Jimmy.

And Jimmy had his favourites as well as his foes.

"Noo this be a genleman comin'," said he, as a sporting-like man in leather leggings and a shooting-jacket came tit-tup-ing along on his pony; "though he has neither powdered footmen nor piebald gates, Storlin (Sterling)—Stanley Storlin of Rosemount."

"How are you, Jimmy?" nodded the Squire, as he now came up.

"How are you?" nodded Jimmy, as he passed along.

"Sink, now, if that had been Hazey, or Willey, or any o' them like chaps, they'd ha taken ne mair notice on me than if ard been a coo," observed Jimmy, giving Hazey's old horse another refresher, adding, "Arm dashed, but ard like to hev the lickin' o' some o' them chaps," flourishing his whip as if he would give them it well.

CHAPTER XX

BELDON HALL—MRS. MUSTARD'S MISCELLANY

A SUDDEN turn of the road to the right now brought our travellers in full sight of a noble-looking mansion, standing open, but not exposed, in a rich, well-wooded park, sloping gently down to a broad, shining river, whose sparkling reaches ran parallel with the road along which they were passing. It was, indeed, a beautiful scene: beautiful even in the sterility of winter, lovely in the rich leafy honours of a glowing luxuriant summer.

"That be your shop, now," said Independent Jimmy, nodding his head, and pointing towards the commanding edifice with his clumsy whip, adding, as he stared at it, "Sink, but it's lang sin' ar seed them chimlies smokin' i' that way."

Facey sat in mute astonishment, contemplating its vast proportions, which still kept increasing as they proceeded, —now the stables and the gardens, now the dairy, now the dovecot, appearing panorama-like, as they proceeded. He had, indeed, got a large house—a very large house; but there was no occasion to occupy it all.

They now arrived at the massive Gothic lodges, slightly disfigured by the appearance of sundry clay pipes, gingerbread horses, and glasses of lollypops in the windows, all of which would have been removed, as they always were for Mr. Lonnergan's periodical visits, had Mr. Romford come a little later. As it was, our friends took the natives rather by surprise, the young lady who at length

came to open the gates making her appearance with one
red stocking on and the other off, besides being otherwise
en déshabille.

"*Jip!*" cried Jimmy, as she at length got the iron
gates open : and, passing through, he took the old horses
by the heads, and began to bustle and prepare them for
the circuitous ascent of the hill to the house. "Sink, ar
I mind when there wasn't sic a thing as a weed to be
seen on this road," observed Jimmy, now contemplating
its grass-grown dimensions. "That was in the ould lord's
time," added he ; "not much weedin' done here now."

Lucy, meanwhile, having been aroused by the stoppage
at the gates, opened a melon-frame window, and proceeded to reconnoitre the place as successive winds of
the road presented the grand house in a variety of views,
south, east, and west. She was very much pleased with
all she saw, and felt quite equal to the occasion. Not
so friend Romford, who dreaded the expense of a large
place. "A house is a consuming animal," he always said.
He liked the simplicity of the Dog and Partridge Inn,
and the easy independence of the West-end Swell.
However, he was in for it, and must brazen it out. He
wasn't easily cowed.

The ascent being at length gained, a good piece of
trotting ground presently brought the travellers up with
a swing under the wood-paved portico of the front door.
They were now at battlemented Beldon Hall, with its
deep bay windows divided by stone mullions and
transoms, and other baronial evidences of strength.
Independent Jimmy, having chucked the reins on the
horses' backs, in apparently well-founded confidence that
they wouldn't run away, then "got doon," and proceeded
to arouse the long-dormant house with a pull at the
conspicuous brass-handled bell knob. It pealed as if it
would never cease, and echo seemingly took pleasure to
repeat the sound. It was long since echo had had any
such recreation.

Before the noise ceased, one side of the folding-doors
opened, disclosing the tawdry person of the before-
mentioned Mrs. Mustard, now struggling hard to open
the other side, so as to let the great man enter in proper
form. Mrs. Mustard was rather surprised to see a lady
in the vehicle, instead of only a gentleman, as she
expected.

"All right!" said Romford, seeing her looks. "All right! It's only my sister."

So saying, Facey handed Lucy out of the carriage, and bid her go into the house and fend for herself.

"I'm sorry I didn't know the lady was coming," observed Mrs. Mustard, dropping a curtsy as she smoothed down her faded brown silk gown; "or I would have had the drawing-room ready."

"Oh, hang the drawing-room," replied Facey. "Do very well without it—do very well without it."

"But his lordship would have wished you to find everything comfortable and proper," replied Mrs. Mustard.

"Oh, proper enough," replied Facey, taking out the cloaks. "Proper enough. I'll tell you what to do. You get her a bedroom as near yours as you can; for she hasn't brought her maid, and, moreover, is afraid of bogies and such-like things," adding, "her moother's coomin' to-morrow."

"Certainly," replied Mrs. Mustard. "Certainly—she can have the pink room, next door to mine, if you like."

"That'll do," said Romford. "That'll do. Now about the luggage. Chuck down the traps," continued he, addressing himself to Jimmy.

These were soon on the ground—gun-case, fishing-rod, landing-net, and all. Jimmy, again clutching the reins, reascended the throne, and drove off without any dallying, or loitering, or inquiring—railway-porter-like—if Facey had got this or that, in order to draw out the reluctant shilling. As Jimmy returned he met Squire Sterling again, who hailed him to stop.

"Who had you in your melon-frame just now?" asked he.

"Oh, it was Mr. What's-his-name, the new maister," replied Jimmy.

"The deuce it was!" exclaimed Mr. Sterling, wishing he had taken a better look. "Well, what sort of a chap is he?"

"Seems well enough," replied Jimmy. "Not a man of much blandishment ar should say," added he, driving on.

Mr. Romford, having seen Jimmy off, then walked into the house as if it was his own. The spacious entrance-hall showed it was a capital place, replete with comfort and every modern luxury. Pictures, vases, statues, busts, all betokening wealth and taste. Some people would have felt rather abashed at getting into such a place under the influence of a spurious broad seal, but friend Facey didn't look at it in that light. A master of hounds was a great man, and his lordship evidently wished to treat him as such. So he took possession with an air of confident ownership.

Lucy had not been long in the place ere she had explored every hole and corner—from the skylights to the scullery, wash-house, knife-house, laundry, larder, and all; and had informed Mrs. Mustard as much of her history as she wished to have promulgated—viz. that she was the widow of an Indian officer, and had come to stay with her brother, the new master of the hounds, until he was comfortably settled at Beldon Hall. And though Mrs. Mustard thought they were very little alike, yet her own daughters, whom we shall presently introduce, were very little alike either; and she felt it was no business of hers to make any observations. So Mrs. Somerville and she proceeded from apartment to apartment, the grandeur increasing as they progressed, until the whole culminated in the noble put-away drawing-room, with its gilded ceiling and brown holland balloons containing the richly cut-glass chandeliers.

Lucy was fired with a noble ambition, and thought what a glorious sight it would be to see herself seated on an ottoman—feathered, flounced, with a broad-laced kerchief in her gloved hand, arrayed for the reception of company.

"Satin damask," now observed Mrs. Mustard, lifting up the corner of a cotton print chair-cover, and showing the shining substratum of pink, adding, "I'd have had the room ready if I'd known you'd been coming, mum."

And a thought struck Lucy, that as she had come she might as well have it; so, after casting a longing eye at the lofty muslin'd mirrors, resting on their pure white marble slabs, she said—

"I s'pose it could be got ready, if wanted?"

"Certainly, mum, certainly," replied Mrs. Mustard, dropping a curtsy, wondering where all the fine-figure footmen were to come from if it was used.

And Lucy's ambition rose as she saw the opportunity of gratifying it. What a change from the cigar shop in

Jermyn Street, Haymarket! and the West-end Swell at Minshull Vernon!

Mrs. Mustard was one of the pauperised order of housekeepers, who veer between temporary places and turnpike gates. No one kept Mrs. Mustard long. She was only a job; job nurse, job cook, job anything. The regular turnpike people were shy of employing her, she required so much watching; while road trustees would as soon have thrown the gates open altogether, as appointed Mrs. Mustard to collect the money for them. Her great recommendation to Lord Lovetin's place was that she was to be had very cheap; and his poor lordship having been so dreadfully depressed by the repeated failures to let Beldon Hall, found it absolutely necessary to reduce the expenditure upon the place to the lowest sum possible. So the housekeeper's wages had gradually come down, and down, and down, under successive administrations, until they at length fell to Mrs. Mustard's mark—six shillings a week, which, however, was a shilling a week more than she got for keeping the Grableyside bar on the Shaverdale road. To be sure, she was allowed "garden stuff," which, by a liberal construction of the term, was held to include milk, fruit, and fresh-water fish. The ponds at Beldon Hall were well stocked. It was also said that she kept a pig on the sly in the pigeon-house. The great advantage of the place to her, however, was that it enabled her to harbour her three dashing daughters, Bridget, Agatha, and Ruth, when any of them came dribbling home from place, which one or other of them did every month, or oftener, their services being as little appreciated as those of their worthy mother. Mrs. Mustard, now about fifty-five years of age, had been a beauty in her day, and her daughters, though exceedingly unlike each other, were handsome, showy, dressy girls, though, like their mother, so slovenly and slatternly when not *en grande costume*, as to have earned for themselves the sobriquet of the Dirties, Mrs. Mustard herself being called Dirty No. 1; Miss Bridget Mustard, Dirty No. 2; Miss Agatha, Dirty No. 3; while Ruth, the youngest and prettiest of the whole, and who has more to do with our story than her sisters, was designated Dirtiest of the Dirty.

Ruth was very pretty, and just turned of twenty; tall, slim, and elegant, with light brown hair, large languishing blue eyes, fringed with the longest of lashes, pearly teeth, beautiful hands and feet, and a soft musical voice, with gentle and subdued manners—a being capable of being wrought into a very beautiful creature. Unfortunately, however, she had a drawback besides her untidiness, and that rather a serious one—she was an incorrigible thief. She could not be restrained from stealing. Gentlemen's places, farmers' places, publicans' places, were all alike to Ruth; she would have souvenirs from each of them. Nor was she at all abashed at being caught. Her mistress might turn the stolen goods out of her box before her face without eliciting a blush from Miss Ruth. Indeed, the chances were she would say her mistress had put them there. On one occasion, having got a month at Frownham Petty Sessions for stealing a silver spoon from Farmer Cropton's, of Byfield, she declared, when she came back from the House of Correction, that she had been at the seaside for the benefit of her health.

Now it so happened that all the Dirties were at home when the Romfords—that is to say, Mr. Romford and Mrs. Somerville—arrived at Beldon Hall, for Miss Bridget, a tall, stout, startling brunette, with the blackest of hair and the brightest of eyes, had recently been discharged from Farmer Roughfolds' of Loggan Hill, for leaving her cows unmilked one morning while she went over to Casterton to get herself photographed, and Miss Agatha had long been vacillating between the duties of an occasional dressmaker and a barmaid, in the expectation of the coming of a tall grenadier, who a gipsy had predicted would marry her. Agatha was a beauty too, though of quite a different order of beauty to that of her sisters, being of the medium height, and plump, with a noble forehead, arched in matchless symmetry by its own beautiful drapery of chestnut hair. Her complexion, we need scarcely say, was of the delicate pink of the wild-rose leaf, and her eyes of the brightest, most searching hazel. The tall grenadier could hardly have known what a beauty awaited him, or he would surely have come.

Then Mrs. Almond, the grocer's wife, at Henfield, had just paid forfeit on Ruth, Dirtiest of the Dirty, rather than have so troublesome a young lady in her establishment. All the three daughters were thus at home, forming a complete party, but still a heavy tax on the six shillings a week, for the girls spent all their earnings in dress and decoration, gaudy bonnets, glass beads, and brass-eyed boots. It was, therefore, an important point with Mrs. Mustard, Dirty No. 1, to get some of them fastened on the Romfords if she could, and Mr. Lonnergan's imperious conduct favoured the design.

Having, therefore, chaperoned Mrs. Somerville all round about the house, and now brought her to a standstill in the magnificent drawing-room, she began sounding her on the important topic of servants, asking where Mrs. Somerville would like her maid to sleep, and how many beds Mrs. Mustard should get ready for the rest of the domestics. Now this question was rather a poser, for Lucy had never had a maid, let alone an establishment of servants, having always lived in lodgings, where the people of the house did everything for her. But, being a woman of ready wit, she parried the question by saying she really couldn't tell, so much depended upon her brother, Mr. Romford, but she supposed they could get an occasional servant or two in the neighbourhood until they decided about bringing their own. Whereupon Mrs. Mustard exultingly replied, "Oh dear, there could be no difficulty about that; there was herself and her three daughters, all of whom would be most happy to do anything in their power; she" (Mrs. Mustard) "was not a professed cook, but she had lived in some great families, *noble* families, indeed she might say—Mr. Boyston, of Boyston, amongst the number, and her daughters were equal to all sorts of duties—indeed they were all quite finished servants, and could undertake any sort of work, but p'r'aps Mrs. Somerville would like to see them—if she would please to step into the breakfast-room, where there was a fire, she would bring them up to her," Mrs. Mustard leading the way to the indicated apartment. This was a comfortable-sized room, some eighteen feet by twenty, with a southern aspect, affording, with the aid of a fire, a much better climate than Mrs. Somerville had been enjoying while making the grand tour of the house. Moreover, it was not "put away," as the rest of the house was, having been got ready for the great Mr. Romford. And Mrs. Mustard having got Mrs. Somerville there, then closed the mahogany door and went away on her errand.

Having surveyed herself in a stately mirror over the richly carved Carrara marble mantelpiece, and compared notes by a second look in a panelled one between the windows, she came to the conclusion that, though she wanted a new bonnet, she was not looking far amiss, and would make some little sensation in Doubleimupshire. With this comfortable reflection she took a seat at the round table before the fire, and helping herself to an illustrated copy of " Rogers's Poems," began reading—

"Oh could my mind, unfolded in my page,
Enlighten climes, and mould a future age,"

while her thoughts were wandering amongst all the bonnet-shops in London.

Meanwhile Mrs. Mustard having made a rapid descent into the lower regions, for the kitchens were underground, found all her elegant daughters clustered and anxious to hear the news, so much so, indeed, that they would hardly listen to her exhortations to get themselves ready to go upstairs to see the lady.

Indeed, the command caused an evident disappointment, for they thought Mr. Romford was a bachelor, and hoped accordingly. Mrs. Mustard seeing this, rectified her error by announcing, "No! no; he's not married! She's only his sister! but come quick, one of you; come upstairs, and see the lady."

Now it so happened that, upon this occasion, Dirtiest of the Dirty was the cleanest of the three, having on an only three days' worn blue-and-white striped print, with magenta-coloured stockings, and being decidedly the least marketable of the three, Mrs. Mustard was glad to show her first, so giving her uncapped head a rub over with the old joint-stock hair-brush, she told her to pull her shoes up at the heel, and follow her, and to mind curtsy and speak civil. As they ascended the staircase together, she charged her to assent to all she (Mrs. Mustard) said, and by no means to let out anything about the low places she had been in, particularly to keep the seaside visit quiet. With these and similar injunctions they reached the door of the room that held the great lady, and, a respectful knock being answered by a "Come in!" the two entered, and curtsied to our fair friend.

"My daughter Ruth," said Mrs. Mustard, whereupon Dirtiest of the Dirty curtsied again, and Mrs. Somerville began questioning her just as the managers of theatres used to question her herself when she sought an engagement. Dirty acquitted herself so well, that Lucy, albeit no great admirer of her own sex—indeed she used to say that the only thing that reconciled her to being a woman was that she could not by any possibility have to marry one—was very much taken with her. Dirty, from her own account, could do anything—wash, sew, darn, mend, get up fine linen, and all. Of course, when asked if she could dress hair, she replied, " No, but she could learn."

Lucy then adroitly took hold of the hairdressing deficiency to disparage her other acquirements, observing, she was afraid she must have her own maid down, when Mrs. Mustard, fearing she was going to lose her market, asked Mrs. Somerville if she wouldn't be pleased to take her daughter on trial, mother Mustard well knowing that Dirtiest of the Dirty would soon make up for a little deficiency of service if there was any money or jewellery left lying about. And the trial system suiting Lucy best, after due deliberation and many inquiries into Dirty's middling morals, Lucy said, that as her stay at Beldon Hall was very uncertain, and her maid was visiting a sick mother in Somersetshire, she would just see what her daughter could do, but that she would have to keep herself to herself, and be extremely neat and tidy in her person, not wearing flash or tawdry dresses, or going gossiping about the country, or letting people come to the Hall—adding, that if Ruth conducted herself properly, it might be the means of getting her into a high situation.

And Mrs. Mustard, shark-like, having thus succeeded with one daughter, then broached the subject of another, observing that she had a daughter quite equal to the housemaid-work; but Mrs. Somerville, who had been conning the matter over while she was airing her eyes with—

"Oh could my mind, unfolded in my page,"

put a peremptory veto upon that, observing that her mother was coming next day, and that Mrs. Mustard and Ruth would be quite equal to all that was required for the present. She then told Ruth to go and heat a poker, and light a fire in her bedroom, whither, accompanied by old Dirty, she then proceeded, walking through the stately hall and corridors with great satisfaction.

CHAPTER XXI

MR. PROUDLOCK, THE KEEPER — LORD LONNERGAN AND
HIS SON, COMMONLY CALLED THE HONOURABLE
LOVETIN LONNERGAN

WHILE Mr. Romford's adopted sister, Mrs. Somerville, was thus making the tour of the fine house, friend Facey, on his part, was at work reconnoitring the out-of-door accommodation of the place. His fine natural instinct soon led him to the stables, partially concealed though they were from the north front of the Hall by a line of magnificent ground-sweeping cedars. These premises were quite in keeping with the mansion, having been built by the same noble lord who surmounted the old Hall with the dish-cover. Indeed some said it was the apparent inequality of the increased house and the old stables that made his lordship think it necessary to re-build the latter entirely, though the old stables were in reality a great deal larger and better than anything he himself wanted. There is often a laudable desire among noblemen and gentlemen to make their places as complete as they can for their successors, regardless of the selfish aphorism, that "posterity has done nothing for them." Be that, however, as it may, friend Facey presently stood in the centre of a very magnificent pile of building. He needed no cicerone to induct him into the arrangements. There stood the stables forming three sides of a square, open in front, with a lofty archway in the centre leading to the places of deposit behind. On the right he read, as it were, the words "stables, straw-house, hay-house," in the centre again the words "saddle-room, harness-room, stables, and straw-house," while large folding-doors on the left proclaimed an infinity of standing-room for carriages. Above the whole line were granaries and apartments for servants.

"V-a-ry good, v-a-ry good," ejaculated our friend, as with a stick-propped chin he stood straddling, contemplating the edifice. "V-a-ry good indeed," added he, as his little pig eyes had taken in the whole arrangement.

If it had but stood at Allington Banks or Greenhope, he thought, it would have been the most convenient residence a master of hounds could possibly have had ; might have reached every cover in the country without lying out, that lying out being a terrible bug-bear to Mr. Facey, on account both of the expense and the irregular habits of Chowey and Swig. However, Mr. Romford consoled himself by thinking that his lordship would be very sly if he got any rent out of him. He then proceeded to inspect the interior of the premises, beginning, of course, on the right, so as to end at the less interesting portion of the building containing the coach-houses. While thus engaged, a footfall sounded behind, and looking round, Mr. Romford confronted the before-mentioned Mr. Proud-lock, the keeper, a big black-eyed, black-haired, bushy-whiskered man of some five-and-thirty years of age or so. There was no mistaking his calling : his billycock hat, his baggy black velveteen coat, his lusty leggings, above all, his half-insolent air, proclaimed what he was. Proudlock was a man whose supposed strength and stature had pro-cured him admission into good places, but whose bad conduct had immediately lost him them again, sometimes almost as soon as obtained. He stood six feet three, stretchable into nearly four with his navvy-nailed boots and upright bearing. He was large chested, full limbed, and broad generally, and, having been drilled as a militia-man, had a very erect, imposing appearance, just the sort of man to salute a coming party of shooters, or to take the lead at a battue.

He was, however, such a mischievous, lying bully—always backbiting and getting his employers into hot water—that he came tumbling down the ladder of servi-tude till he finally landed among the grand body of poachers.

His size, however, which was a recommendation as a keeper, was a disadvantage to him here, for he could be easily identified, and that at a great distance, and, more-over, the exertion was more than he liked ; so, after two or three unsatisfactory appearances at petty sessions, he relinquished the trigger for a time, and took to showing himself as a giant, in conjunction with the celebrated Pig-faced Lady ; but the confinement of the caravan was too great for him, and, the engagement having terminated, he again sought the freedom of the fields.

He was then to be had very cheap—twelve shillings a week, a house and coals, with two couple of rabbits, being all he asked; and that being within the scope of Lord Lovetin's means, especially as just at the time he had every expectation of Mr. Emmerson taking Beldon Hall, whereby he would have got rid of an immense indoor expense, after very mature consideration he allowed Mr. Lonnergan to engage him at that remuneration; his lordship, however, stipulating that though Proudlock might have his coals led by the antediluvian horse that drew them to the gardens, yet Proudlock must pay for the fuel himself, that being, as his lordship truly said, the best means of checking an undue consumption; and Lonnergan and his lordship carried on a correspondence that would have filled a number of "Bailey's Sporting Magazine" on the subject.

At the time of our story, Proudlock had been a year and a half at Beldon Hall, during which time he had ascertained the exact length of Mr. Lonnergan's foot, as well as the ways and means of all the surrounding country. Lonnergan was fond of woodcocks, and Proudlock was too happy to supply them. Mrs. Lonnergan liked hare soup, and Proudlock knew how to snare them on some one else's property. Though often caught, he was always ready with an excuse, how he had followed that scoundrel, Jack Mason, off their manor on to the preserve he was found upon, or was lying *perdu* to see who came to take up the trapped pheasant on the other side of the hedge. Altogether, though he was much disliked and strongly suspected, yet no one cared to tackle with a nobleman's servant, especially one notoriously supported by the deputy nobleman, "Lord" Lonnergan, as the agent was called. So Proudlock strutted, and swaggered, and vapoured, and bullied, always presuming on his great size and proportions, and, though often threatening, never coming into actual collision with anyone. Independent Jimmy, indeed, was the only man in the country who had ever stood fairly up to him; but the generous giant said he refrained from touching him on the score of inequality of size, and that people would accuse him of having crushed a worm. Jimmy, however, who was very handy with his fists, hearing of this, then addressed him through the usual medium of communication — viz. the pugilistic column in "Bell's Life in

London"—stating that Independent Jimmy was ready to fight the Big Bully of Beldon Hall for three pounds a side, in a roped ring at the back of the Firfield Station, any day between the coming of the 9.30 a.m. train and the going of the south mail; but Proudlock did not take any notice of this either, merely observing in general company that a nobleman's servant could not demean himself by fighting with a bus-man.

Such, then, was the genius who encountered Mr. Romford on his visit of inspection of the Beldon Hall stables; and, as next to a bit of pink, a bit of velveteen came nearest home to the heart of our hero, he returned the keeper's semi-military salute with a " How are you ? " and a wave of his right hand, as though he had known him before.

Thus emboldened, Proudlock made him a bow, observing that he was glad to see Mr. Romford amongst them, and hoped he would have good sport.

"Thank'ee," said Romford — "thank'ee ; " adding, " That depends a good deal upon gentlemen of your cloth, however. I know you are a good feller, and will do all in your power to promote it."

" *Certainly*," replied Proudlock, with an emphasis— "certainly," repeated he, as though he had never shot a fox in his life, or turned down a bag-man either.

"Not at all great fox-preservers down here, I believe," observed Mr. Romford, pretending to know a good deal more than he really did.

"Well (hum), there are (hum) scaly people in all countries," observed Mr. Proudlock; " but, upon the whole, I should (hum) say they are (haw) as good here as elsewhere."

Proudlock's preservation depended altogether upon the payment of his fees, for which he sent in his bill at the end of the season, as regular as a boot or shoe maker,—so much for a litter, so much for a find, so much for stopping, or " stoping," as he spelt it.

But, though Mr. Romford asked about foxes, he was quite as anxious to know about pheasants—who was tenacious, who was extra fierce, who took it easy, and who might be poached upon with impunity. So, in the course of a running dissertation on racks and mangers, boxes and stalls, Mr. Romford managed to blend a very useful inquiry into the particulars of the country generally, keeping foxes apparently to the fore, but at the same time casting about for general information.

Having criticised the stables, with their appurtenances, and pronounced them extremely good, our friend and his cicerone now found themselves before the spacious coach-houses on the left-hand side of the building, a few paces in front of which Mr. Romford stationed himself, as if to stare them out of countenance : the idea floating uppermost in his mind at the moment being, that they would make very capital kennels ; and a further investigation and division of the whole into four satisfied him on that point. And, having got on so well with Proudlock, he saw no reason why he should not take his opinion on that point.

"I say," observed he, looking him steadily in the face —"I say, don't you think these coach-houses might very easily be converted into kennels ?".

Proudlock drew breath and bit his thick lip, for he well knew that if there was one thing his noble master, Lord Lovetin, was more particular about than another, it was having the Hall and offices kept in perfect apple-pie order ; not that his lordship cared about seeing them, but he liked to know that they were so, and that he could occupy them at a moment's notice whenever he chose to return to England. It was that feeling that prevented his letting Mrs. Emmerson have the cut-pile carpet. He was afraid she would wear it down below the orthodox standard of other things, and so derange the grand order of uniformity. It *had* been down some time.

"Well, what do you think?" asked Facey, seeing Proudlock rather craned at the question.

"Oh, it could be altered easy enough," replied the man of powder and shot. "The only question in my mind was, whether his lordship—that is to say, Mr. Lonnergan —might like it or not."

"And who's Mr. Lonnergan ?" demanded Facey, it being the first mention he had heard of the name.

"Oh, Mr. Lonnergan," replied the keeper, in the deferential tone due to a man in authority — "oh, Mr. Lonnergan, you know, is my lord's representative here—he and his son, Mr. Lovetin Lonnergan, at least ; and we never do anything without consulting one or other of them."

The fact was, Lonnergan had been the last lord's agent,

and had hardly been able to realise the fact that he (Lonnergan) was not the real owner of the property, and the present Lord Viscount an intruder.

"And where do they live ?" asked Mr. Romford.

"At Flush House, near Bury St. Bees, about nine miles from here," replied the retired giant, pointing in the direction in which it lay.

"Well, then, I'll tell you what ; you go over there, with my compliments, in the morning, and say that, as I've taken the place, I s'pose there'll be no objection to my makin' a few little temporary alterations, which I'll restore before I leave."

"Yes-'ir," said Proudlock; adding, "Shall I say what they are, sir ?"

"Well, no," replied Romford. "No ; you see I can't 'zactly know myself ; but just say, generally, triflin' alterations—triflin' alterations."

"Just so," replied Mr. Proudlock, who now saw the give-an-inch-take-an-ell principle upon which the inquiry had to proceed. And, after a few more inquiries and inspirations, the friends separated, each with a high opinion of the other.

It was a wise step on the part of friend Romford sending Proudlock over to Flush House, for it concili- ated Mr. Lonnergan, and procured an answer from that promising youth, commonly called the Honourable Lovetin Lonnergan, whose father was away, that very materially assisted Mr. Romford's further proceedings, namely, that Mr. Lonnergan had no instructions from Lord Lovetin on the subject, but that as a friend of the family, "one of them," as he familiarly said, Lovetin Lonnergan had no doubt Mr. Romford might do as he liked. And, of course, the first thing he liked was to convert the aforesaid coach-houses into kennels, which he did in the most liberal way, by not only employing Lord Lovetin's joiners, but making the estate supply him with the necessary material, Facey observing that it would be none the worse for his work after it was done. So, having made himself two capital lodging-rooms with airing-yards in front, he set up his boiler behind, and converted the harness-room into a feeding-house.

And here for a word on the Lonnergans.

Lord Lonnergan was one of a now nearly bygone generation, whose antiquity is proclaimed by their dress.

He wore a large puffy shirt-frill and a puddingey white
tie with flowing ends, a step collared buff vest, and a blue
coat with bright buttons. He had long adhered to tights
and Hessians, and it was only when he found himself left
alone in his glory that he put his fat legs into trousers.
He was a porcupine-headed little man, who tied his cravat
so tight as to look as if he were going to throttle himself.
He was a short, sallow, plethoric, wheezing, scanty-
whiskered man, with eyes set very high up in his head,
like garret windows; a long unmeaning-looking face,
surmounted with a nose like a pear. His mouth was
significant of nothing except an aptitude for eating. As
we said before, he had a voluminous double-chin.

He drew his great warming-pan-like watch up from his
fob with a massive kitchen-jack-like gold chain, to which
was attached a bunch of seals, the largest and most striking
whereof had been purchased with the surplus cash from a
tea-service testimonial presented to Mrs. Lonnergan by
the tenants on Lord Lumbago's Lubberey estate in
Easyshire, and contained around a plough the significant
motto, "RENTS SHOULD NEVER RISE." And rents certainly
never did rise with Lonnergan, for he would always
rather excite the landlords to compassion than urge the
tenants to activity; still he had some capital forms of
agreement to the fulfilment of which he never attended.
Of course he did not use the "rent-should-never-rise"
seal when he wrote to any of his employers, but another
butterpat-like production with his initials "J. L.," John
Lonnergan, cut in the open-hearted, undisguised capitals
of the old engravers. No writhing hieroglyphics for
him.

He had lived in good times, when gentlemen were
gentlemen, and trusted their land agents implicitly,
never troubling themselves with farming or interfering
with their tenants' occupations in any shape or way,
taking everything for granted, including both facts and
figures. Still Lonnergan was a noted old screw in his
own affairs, never missing a chance anywhere, and always
on the watch for discount. He was too good a judge
to receive tenant-farmer testimonials himself, but Mrs.
Lonnergan was open to the reception of any number—
vases, inkstands, butter-coolers, fruit-stands, etc. A guest
leaving his house one dark night mistook his lordship for
the servant in the passage, and gave him a shilling, saying,

"There, there's a shilling for you, and mind your master doesn't get hold of it."

Lord Lonnergan did not encourage his son, Lovetin Lonnergan (so called, of course, after the last lord, who was his godfather), in anything like show or extravagance, but endeavoured to hold him on steadily in his own line, and make his father's large accumulations still more. "Stick to the shop, and the shop will stick to you." "Take care of the pence, and the pounds will take care of themselves." "When has a man got enough money, Lovetin?" "When he has got a little more than he has," were aphorisms of almost daily inculcation by old Lonnergan; but, somehow, Lovetin Lonnergan did not like the doctrine, and longed for a little more freedom and independence.

Not that Lovetin was extravagant; on the contrary, he neither shot, nor coursed, nor hunted, but he would like to ride about in a chaise. Riding about in a chaise was, he thought, the summit of all earthly happiness. He always looked upon Independent Jimmy's friend, lolling along in his carriage, as the happiest of human beings, and longed to emulate him.

Lovetin Lonnergan, "the Honourable," as he was called, was the exact counterpart of his father, making allowance, of course, for the difference of dress and the disparity of years. The same long, lugubrious, scanty-whiskered, sallow face, with the garret-window eyes, the same incipient pear nose, and the same absence of expression about the mouth.

In lieu of the warming-pan with the jack-chain and the butterpat-like appurtenances, he had a smart Albert chain attached to a small Geneva watch; and instead of excommunicating his chin with his tie as his excellent father did, he gave its looming proportions ample latitude over the turn-down collar and diminutive neck-string of the day.

Lovetin Lonnergan was now just turned of five-and-twenty, and had plenty of young ladies after him, plenty of mammas sounding his praises; but Lord Lonnergan was difficult to please, always asserting that it was utterly impossible for his son Lovetin to marry other than "a lady of fortin." Lovetin was proud of his father's wealth, and fond of expatiating upon its amount, not unfrequently winding up his discourses with a shake of the head and the filial ejaculation of "Ah, now, *if father would but die!*"

This youth, becoming a semi-hero in our story, we have introduced him more at large than we should otherwise have done. Let us now go into Beldon Hall, and see about something to eat.

CHAPTER XXII

THE INTERNAL ECONOMY OF BELDON HALL—GOODHEARTED GREEN AGAIN

PART of Lucy's—we beg pardon again—Mrs. Somerville's luggage consisted of the remains of her larder at the West-end Swell—viz. half a loaf of brown bread, three-quarters of a loaf of white, a pound and a half of pork-chops, a slice of leathery cheese, a nip of tea, and some fivepenny sugar, Lucy observing that it was of no use leaving anything behind her. And, indeed, it was lucky she brought something, for an inspection of the Beldon Hall larder would lead to the supposition that the Dirties lived entirely upon air. There was not even the wretched bare shoulder-blade that generally seems to act the part of scarecrow in the most destitute of houses. Two eggs and a bunch of thyme was all the provender the larders of the proud Hall produced.

Still there never was a place yet where drink was not to be had, and Facey having now returned to the Hall, and found Lucy making herself quite at home in the breakfast-room, produced a half-crown piece, and told her to send somebody out for a quart of ale, and the rest of the money in gin, so that they might have their dinners as soon as possible, for Facey always dined when he was hungry without waiting for any specific hour of the day. And while Dirty No. 1 was busy cooking the pork-chops, and Dirtiest of the Dirty was laying the cloth, Lucy lionised our master over the magnificent mansion, taking much the same line as old Dirty had done. Friend Facey was greatly impressed with the magnitude of his venture, and almost doubted whether he was equal to the occasion. He wished that he mightn't have put his foot in it. A house, he said, was a consuming animal, and people

would think he was deuced rich, living in such a large
one. He must be prudent and circumspect.

"X was expensive, and soon became poor ;
Y was the wise man who kept want from the door"—

he inwardly chanted. And having dined, he whiffed his
pipe and sipped his gin, and at length retired to bed, full
of caution and prudential considerations.

Morning, however, and the return of Proudlock from
Flush House, with the satisfactory reply from Lovetin
Lonnergan, that Mr. Romford was to do as he liked,
brought him confidence, and taking the Honourable at his
word, he forthwith began to exercise his privilege in the
most summary manner, for finding there was an excellent
cellar of wine, he sent for Tom Hooper, the blacksmith,
and bid him pick the lock, telling Dirty No. 1, in
Hooper's hearing, to be 'ticklarly careful in preserving
the bottles in order that he might restore an equal
quantity of wine when he left. As there was a large
stock of champagne, which Facey said would not improve
by keeping, Lucy and he indulged in it most freely,
Facey acquiring, as he said, very gentlemanly ideas with
the beverage. So much so, indeed, that after a pint, or
perhaps three-quarters of a bottle, he did not feel so much
out of his element at Beldon Hall as he did on his first
coming. Lucy on her part took to grandeur quite
naturally, and Dirty No. 1, having supplied her as well
with the "Beldon Hall" seal as a good stock of coroneted
paper (kept ready against Lord Lovetin's contemplated
return, which he always said might take place any day),
she diffused her orders freely through the land. London,
however, is the real place for unhesitating compliance
with specious orders, and thither Mrs. Somerville directed
her chief attentions, patronising all the shops and establishments that she used to envy and covet, and look upon
as utterly impossible, while living with Mr. Sponge in
Jermyn Street, Haymarket.

She reviewed her wardrobe, estimating its capabilities
by her improved condition—sister of a master of foxhounds—mistress of a nobleman's mansion—and, finding
it rather deficient, she wrote off to Madame D * * *, of
B * * * Street, for sundry semi-mourning dresses, Para-
matta twill, glacé silk, with flowers, black velvet with black

satin, jet ornaments, and other articles, all of which came
down with the usual alacrity of high-sounding orders.
One obsequious milliner indeed directed her bonnet-box
to "The Honourable Mrs. Somerville," an addition that
caused Independent Jimmy to observe, as he handed it
down from the bus to Dirtiest of the Dirty, "Sink, ar
didn't ken yeer mistress had a handle tir her name."

Handle, however, or no handle, things came down with
the utmost dispatch—wonderful alacrity—not only the
outward and visible articles of dress, but the more delicate
items of Edith nightdresses and under attire.

When the gentlemanly ideas were in, Facey did not so
much grudge the orders, but with the evaporation of the
champagne came prudent thoughts and fears for the
future. Still, as Mrs. Somerville ordered them all in
her own name, he consoled himself with the reflection
that he could not be made liable, and didn't know but
it was just as well to have a handsome, well-dressed
woman about the house as a dowdy. He only hoped
that none of the Heavyside Hunt, or any of his promiscuous acquaintance, would come and expose her—
of that, however, he must take his chance, as he had
chanced many a difficulty before.

And, in truth, she required a refit, or rather, perhaps,
an outfit, for, without going at all into the minutiæ of
her wardrobe, it must be evident to every one that what
did extremely well at the West-end Swell would be very
insufficient for Beldon Hall. Nor, considering the precarious nature of her tenure, can she be much blamed for
taking advantage of her opportunity.

> "Who can observe the careful ant,
> And not provide for future want?"

thought Lucy, as she again applied the key to the drawer
in the library table containing the coroneted note-paper
with the talismanic words "Beldon Hall" in gilt
characters on the top, in order that she might again test
the liberality of the Londoners for shoes, scents, gloves,
French cambrics, embroideries, cosmetics, and miscellaneous articles generally.

Mrs. Glitters—now Mrs. Sidney Benson, we should
observe—arrived in due time, being as anxious for a run
into the country as her daughter had been. When
Independent Jimmy met her at the Firfield Station, in

her large hoop and small stock of linen, he thought she was Mrs. Somerville's lady's-maid, and told her "her missis was arl safe at the Harl."

Facey was rather disappointed when he saw what he had imported, for Mrs. Benson, being only accustomed to dress those who strutted upon the stage, not doing any "My name is Norval"-ing herself, had none of the easy self-possession that distinguished her elegant daughter. However, Facey consoled himself with the reflection that she would not be much seen, while her homely air and attire might enable him to get more work out of her than he might otherwise have done had she been fine. If she looked after the Dirties, and Lucy after the stables when he was away, the arrangement might answer and not be very onerous; but he dreaded the inflammation of his weekly bills, and, as he said, "was more afraid of the old lady's appetite than he was of her drinkite." This latter requirement Lord Lovetin's cellar would supply, but the imperative butcher's bills would be his.

There being no plant or stock-in-trade belonging to the Larkspur Hunt for Mr. Romford to take to, he had to make up an establishment as well and as quickly as he could. So soon, therefore, as he got a bargain struck with the Doubleimupshireites, he wrote to Goodhearted Green, detailing his present position and equine wants, urging Goodheart to supply the latter as quickly as he could, adding, if he had not the exact ticket, to send as near as possible; and Romford concluded by saying that he would be glad to see Goodheart down at his new residence, Beldon Hall, in Doubleimupshire, where he would mount him and find wear and tear for his teeth for a week or ten days, whenever he liked. Goodheart's great bosom swelled with honest emotion, for he had recently sent away some most remarkable malefactors— horses that kicked, horses that struck, horses that flew at people like tigers, horses that nobody could shoe, horses that nobody could saddle when they were shod, horses that nobody could ride when they were shod and saddled some very notorious savages, in fact, as Mr. Rarey would say.

"Oh dear! oh dear!" exclaimed he, stamping his foot and smiting his forehead, as the concluding paragraph of Romford's letter touched him in the quick. "Oh dear!

oh dear! If I had but got this last week, I could have
fit him with such a stud as would have astonished the
natives. There's Bounding Ben, to be sure," continued
Goodheart, thinking over what he had left. "There's
Bounding Ben—he's hup to sixteen stun; but he's
uncertain in his bounding, or he wouldn't be called
Bounding Ben. Ah! if I 'ad but kept Pull-Devil-Pull-
Baker!—he'd ha' shone conspikiously brilliant. Neck-
or-Nothing, too, would ha' bin a grand 'oss for Mr. Romford. But it's no use cryin' over spilt milk," continued
Mr. Green, tinkling his little yard bell to summon his
head man, Aaron Peacock, to his presence.

That worthy now emerged from his hiding-place, and
came shuffling up the yard with the usual groom-like,
crab-like action. He was a little, weasely, ginnified-
looking man, with scarcely a hair on his head, or an
ounce of flesh on his bones, but keen, twinkling, little
grey eyes, that penetrated a horse in an instant. He
looked right into them, as it were. He seemed to dress
up to the character of Peacock, being gay and gaudy in
his costume, and very various: scarlet tie, Lincoln green
vest, lilac shirt, baggy breeches that had once been white
and tight, yellow leather leggings, with mother-of-pearl
buttons.

Though he was not an original liar—could not lead
the gallop himself—yet he was a capital coadjutor, and
would swear to anything that Goodheart said; so, what
between Goodheart's generous volubility and Aaron's
shakes of the head and solemn sententious sayings, a
youngster was pretty sure to be handsomely cheated
between them. Let us now see them together.

"Ah, here's that big Mr. Romford written for 'osses,"
said Goodheart to Aaron, flourishing the letter, as the
little man got up to his master.

"So-o," replied Aaron, drawing his breath, adding,
"'ow many may he please to want?"

"Oh, ten or a dozen," replied Green, as if it was quite
an impossible number.

"Harn't that in the 'ole stables," observed Aaron—
"leastways, not fit to go."

"Not with such a robustious giant as Mr. Romford,"
assented Goodheart, preparing to take a stroll of the
premises, more with a view of arranging his thoughts
than in the expectation of finding horses.

The yard was spacious—larger than it looked—for there were supplementary stables at the low end belonging to houses in Sylvia Street, which Goodheart let off in dull times to one Roughhead, a cab-master, and altogether he had standing for forty or fifty horses. Still, the exigencies of an unusually open season had depleted them, and he had not above twelve or fourteen horses in hand at the time of Mr. Romford's sudden demand, and these were mostly of the weak, washy order—good flat-catchers, but good for nothing for work—all the real "playful rogues," as Goodheart called them, being away, practising their vagaries in the provinces, much to the horror of huntsmen and masters of hounds therein. There is nothing so formidable as a rash young man on an intemperate horse, for he thinks he must ride as well to distinguish himself as to get his change out of his quadruped. Hence, he is always in the midst of the hounds—always rasping on, pulling and hauling, and taking a ten-acre field to turn his brute about in. These are the boys that baffle the sport.

The horses, as we said before, were almost all good flat-catchers, well calculated to please the eye, which Green knew was half the battle with the youngsters, and, moreover, like the aforesaid Bounding Ben, were generally christened with high-sounding names diametrically opposite to their respective qualities. Thus, "Everlasting," a handsome sixteen hands horse, with black points, and all the shape and strength necessary for a weight-carrying hunter, slackened his pace as soon as ever he got upon rising ground, and gradually subsided into a walk as he ascended a hill. He couldn't go up one, so it was no use trying to force him.

"Hearty Harry," again, wanted no end of codlin and linseed-teaing; "Twice-a-Week" would hardly come out once a fortnight; while the "Glutton" looked as if he had lived altogether upon toothpicks and water.

"That Boundin' Ben 'oss is most like big Mr. R.'s work," observed Peacock.

"Yes, he is," assented Goodheart—"yes, he is. Put him in as one."

"'Op Along,' then," suggested Aaron.

"Why, yes, he's a neat 'oss—a takin''oss—with a very high bred determined hair about him," replied Goodheart; "but he's lame of three legs, and not very sound on the fourth."

"Only to lame the fourth, and make him all right,"
observed Aaron.

"Well, that might do," assented Goodheart ; "but we
mustn't call him 'Op Along,' you know ; call him 'True
Blue,' or 'Bell Metal,' or something of that sort."

"Ah, 'Bell Metal's' the better name—a very taking
name. Bean him, and call him 'Bell Metal.' He'll be
No. 2. Now for another. Well, there's 'The Brick,'"
suggested Aaron.

"'The Brick?'" repeated Goodheart, for he had had so
many of that name that he could not hit off the horse at
the moment.

"The brown 'oss with the star, and the dead side to his
mouth—not the nutmeg grey that we bought of the
soldier hofficer," explained Peacock.

"Ah, that soldier officer's 'orse was a do," sighed Goodheart ; "does nothin' but kick in the stable, and won't
pass a wheeled vehicle of any sort or kind without
scrubbin' his rider's leg up against it, to see which is
'ardest. To be sure he might do for a servant's 'oss," continued he ; "servants arn't so 'tickler 'bout their legs as
their masters ; besides, there are no vehicles in the hunting-
field for him to get to and scrub against. Oh, I would say
christen him 'Perfection,' and send him," said Goodheart.

"And 'The Brick'?" asked Aaron.

"And 'The Brick' too," assented Goodheart. "His
only fault is that he won't face water, but a whip can
always go round by a bridge, or cross in a boat, or keep
out of the way of water altogether. Then how about
'Oliver Twist'?" continued Goodheart, pleased at the
progress he was making.

"Oliver's not a bad 'oss," replied Aaron, "barrin' that
his forequarters are rather at wariance with his hind, but
it don't make much matter which end of an 'oss gets
through an 'edge fust, so long as they both land on the
right side together at last."

"True," assented Goodheart—"true ; put him in for
another. How many's that?" continued he, telling them
off on his fingers. "Ben, one ; Op—that's to say, Bell Metal,
two ; The Brick, three ; Perfection, four ; Oliver, five ; and,
say—Everlasting or Twice-a-Week, six."

"Oh, Twice-a-Week will do nothin' for nobody,"
observed Aaron, with a shake of his head. "Better send
the Glutton than him."

"But he's such a hungry-looking scarecrow," replied Goodheart.

"Then say Heverlastin'," rejoined Aaron. "He's 'andsome enough with his great harms, magnific shoulders, and lean 'andsome 'ead."

"'Andsome enough," assented Goodheart, "but he's more fit for some bathing or watering-place buck, who wants to do the show-off of the meet and the streets, than such a ramming, cramming customer as this Mr. R."

And while yet they stood debating whether to send the Glutton or Everlasting, a blue and red telegram-boy came dribbling down the yard, fumbling for something in his leather-case as he came.

"Ah, now, here's mischief!" exclaimed Goodheart, advancing and taking the note from the boy, muttering as he opened it, "Somebody's got his skull split or been carried triumphantly over the moon. No, all right!" continued he, swinging joyfully round on his heel— "all right!—all right! only Placid Joe (late Pull-Devil) been too many for Mr. Martin Muffington only Placid Joe been too many for Mr. Martin Muffington. What could he expect, a little Titmouse of a man like him getting on to an 'orse fit to carry an 'ouse! Told him he wouldn't suit him, but he would 'ave 'im. Thought he knew better than me. Many of these young gents do." Goodheart then read the telegram again. Thus it ran :—

"MR. MARTIN MUFFINGTON, AT THE WHITE SWAN INN, SHOWOFFBOROUGH, TO MR. GREEN, BROWN STREET, BAGNIGGE WELLS ROAD, LONDON.

"That brute, Placid Joe, has no more mouth than a bull. He's carried me right into the midst of the hounds, and nearly annihilated the huntsman. I will send him back by the 9.30 a.m. train to-morrow, and won't pay you a halfpenny for his hire."

"Ah, well, all right," said Goodheart, "will have to pay his expenses both ways, at all events."

And here we may observe that Goodhearted Green behaved well in the matter, for he didn't want Martin to have him ; but Martin, seeing the horse's name,

"PLACID JOE," put conspicuously up in black and white letters on a board in front of his stall, became enamoured of him, and attributed Green's objections to letting him, have him to another cause, namely, his wanting to keep Joe for somebody else. So Martin would have him. though we dare say if Green had made similar objections to Muffington having Placid Joe under the name of "Pull-Devil-Pull-Baker," he would have been equally anxious, Muffington having the vanity to think that he could ride anything.

The fact was, the Baker was only placid when he was either ground down with work or "rarefied," but as soon as ever the rarefaction wore off he was just like an uniced glass of champagne—not good to be taken till he was iced again.

Still he was just the horse for Mr. Romford, a sixteen-hands bay, blood-like, and handsome, with great substance, and plenty of liberty. Everlasting and he were as handsome as horses could well be, with the most opposite qualities, the Baker being as hard as the other was soft. Everlasting, however, was such a gay deceiver, and Mr. Romford had so many opportunities of placing him advantageously, that Mr. Green determined to send him instead of Bell Metal. Having thus made up his mind, he retired into his little den of an office and poured forth all his hopes and fears upon paper to Facey, beginning at the top of a large sheet, and going right through to the end of the fourth page, with one continuous paragraph, full of the flow of the milk of human kindness, regrets, promises, hopes, and expectations. How, if he had known only three days before, he could have suited Mr. Romford to a T, but how that the season was then at its height, and everything with the slightest pretension to hunting was caught up in an instant, but how that many of his stud wouldn't suit everybody, and, as sure as ever anything came back worth its keep, it should be sent off direct without a moment's delay to Beldon Hall in Doubleimupshire, while others should follow as fast as they could be procured; and the ominous letter, equal to two pages of this work, concluded by a grateful acknowledgment of the compliment Mr. Romford had paid Green by asking him to Beldon Hall, where he assured him he would visit him before the end of the season, for he felt a real and sincere interest in his distinguished customer's comfort and convenience. Never, indeed, had he known any one in whom he took so great an interest.

And Placid Joe returning as advised, the next day's post conveyed the following invoice :—

"FRANCIS ROMFORD, Esq.,
    "BELDON HALL, DOUBLEIMUPSHIRE.

"Please receive at the Firfield Station by the 2.20 p.m., train the following horses :—

"1. Bounding Ben ; a whole coloured dark-brown horse, up to sixteen stone.
"2. Pull-Devil-Pull-Baker ; a high-couraged bay, up to almost any weight and work.
"3. The Brick ; a brown horse, up to twelve stone.
"4. Everlasting ; a bay ; a splendid weight-carrier, and very handsome.
"5. Perfection ; a nutmeg grey ; a good servant's horse, and smart.
"6. Oliver Twist ; a black horse ; quiet in harness, and has carried a lady."

These, with what Facey had before, viz. Honest Robin, Brilliant, and Leotard, made him up a tolerable starting stud, reinforced as it was to be with further consignments from the same orthodox quarter.

All things now conduced to that period of excitement when the orchestra having at length tuned their instruments to their satisfaction the leader flourishes his baton, and forthwith the music strikes up. The Swig and Chowey garments had come, also Mr. Romford's upper things, and though Bartley and Hammond declined clothing the extremities, there were plenty of others proud of the honour of working for the great Turbot on its tail.

The coming of a new family into a county, especially to occupy such an important place as Beldon Hall, was sure to make a considerable sensation, but when with the strange family was coupled a new bachelor master of hounds, the excitement was intense. Things, too, had been managed so quickly and quietly that though there were two parties in the hunt, there was no time for the reaction of inquiry and pulling to pieces. All parties, hunting and non-hunting parties, agreed that it was a most fortunate thing for the country to get such a man as Mr. Romford to take it, and the acquisition of Beldon Hall stamped the transaction so conclusively, that if any one had had the impudence to get up and say this Mr. Romford is a penniless impostor, and "I'll prove it," he would have been looked upon as mad. There was, therefore, no doubt or hesitation about calling at Beldon Hall — no, not even any looking into the "Landed Gentry," to see if it was all right about this widowed sister. All was taken for granted as readily and agreeably as either Mr. Romford or Mrs. Somerville could have wished. The only contest seemed to be who should be first to call upon the newcomers, a feat that was accomplished by our, or rather Independent Jimmy's friend, Mr. Watkins.

And this distinguished family now forming a prominent feature in our story, we will take the liberty of introducing the members of it before we throw off with the hounds.

CHAPTER XXIII

MR. AND MRS. WILLY WATKINS AND MISS WATKINS

HAVING now introduced the reader as well to the outdoor offices as the indoor magnificence of Beldon Hall, let us proceed to dilate a little upon its immediate neighbourhood, and on Doubleimupshire generally. And taking parties pretty much in the order in which they figure in our story, we will first revert to Independent Jimmy's dandified hair-brushing friend, Mr. Watkins of Dalberry Lees, commonly called Willy Watkins, who has already had the advantage of that free-spoken gentleman's opinions passed upon him, as Jimmy charioteered Mr. Romford along in the melon frame. Jimmy, it will be remembered, made a sort of rough guess at Willy's antecedents, which we will now supplement with more reliable information.

Well, then, we may commence our introduction of these important personages in our story, by saying, that when Willy Watkins went to the "diggins," he had exhausted

friends, credit, and estate. Everybody was sick of
Willy Watkins. It was—"Oh, 'D' Willy Watkins!"
and "'B' Willy Watkins! I never want to hear more of
Willy Watkins!" Now, however, he was quite another
Willy Watkins.

But before displaying him as he now is, let us glance at
what he once was. Willy's misfortune was, being a good-
looking fellow without any brains. That misfortune was
aggravated by his looking wise, for it was not until a man
had worked and tried Willy in all ways, that he saw
what an empty-headed creature he really was. He was
tall, nearly six feet high, well set up and well propor-
tioned, with a clear dark complexion, intelligent eyes, and
good features generally.

He began life with a splendid pair of whiskers, and a
head of dark glossy hair, which he petted and tended with
the utmost care and solicitude. He was always feeling,
and smoothing, and coaxing his side-locks. Even at the
period of our story, when old Father Time had tithed
them severely, he still kept fingering and feeling and
putting them right, when he had nothing to do, which was
pretty often.

Well, Willy's looks had been the ruin of him, for first
one silly woman, and then another, had smiled and
flattered him into folly, until he fully believed he could
marry a countess, or any one he liked. With Willy, as
with Facey himself, we are not prepared to give any
pedigree, which we must leave to the reader to infer from
his calling.

Willy had tried his hand at various trades before he
finally settled on emigration. First of all, it was thought
his good looks would ensure him success behind the
counter, and he was duly installed with a yard-wand, at
Messrs. Flimsey and Figments, hosiers and haberdashers,
High Street, Brittlesworth. Here, however, he was such a
lazy dog, that he could never get the shutters down in
proper time, and the shop used to remain closed till half-
past eight or nine o'clock in the morning, much to the
amusement of Messrs. Scamp and Scurryworth's genteel
young people opposite, and the inhabitants of the High
Street generally. Flimsey and Figments couldn't stand
this, and after two or three ineffectual scoldings they
gave Willy up, who presently obtained a clerkship in a
brewery, at Brackenworth, but here the dull monotony of

counting cash and measuring malt contrasted so forcibly with the gay *insouciance* of selling silks and satins to the ladies, that Willy emancipated himself at the end of a month, and, after nibbling at an auctioneer's, turned gentleman at large for a time. This, however, is but a poor trade—desperately poor when a man has to sponge on his friends for his meals, who give him his food with the sort of churlishness that one gives a strange dog a bone.

Willy soon became a seedy swell, a deplorable object at any time, and one that gets daily worse. His hat became glazy, his coat got threadbare and scrimpy, and his boots were patched like the driver's of an omnibus—for we believe nobody ever yet saw a driver of an omnibus with a whole pair.

In this dilemma, his friends subscribed and set him up a photographic studio, but Willy Watkins soon proved that he was no hand at high art. He made such frights of his friends that he scattered his business before it had well taken root—drove them away with walking advertisements of his incompetence in their hands. He then found it was easier to cozen the ladies with their linen than with their likenesses.

So the sun of his success soon set.

He first got rid of his barker, then of his boy, then of the apparatus itself, and finally, at the early age of twenty, went off to the diggings, in Australia, with the proceeds of the sale. And people were heartily glad when they heard he was gone, and didn't care if he never came back. Those who had lent him money wrote off the amount in their books, and those who had been photographed by him put themselves quietly away in whitey-brown paper, to see if, like port wine, they would improve by keeping.

Time wore on, and years elapsed, ere anything was heard of Willy Watkins. Gradually, however, it became bruited in Brittlesworth, and elsewhere, that a man of the name of Watkins had lit on his legs, and was doing uncommonly well—found no end of Ballarat nuggets, in fact. Further accounts confirmed the statement, and the Watkins family began to consider quietly among themselves who was his heir. There was, however, no occasion to give themselves any trouble on that score, for Willy had anticipated their views by marrying a very aspiring lady, the daughter of a gentleman who had formerly "left his country for his country's good," and who, by land speculations, wool speculations, and a little usury, had amassed a very considerable fortune. He had been transported for forgery under the name of Peter Corcoran, but on completing his term of servitude (fourteen years) he assumed that of Fitzgerald, Granby Fitzgerald, and married the daughter of a gentleman who had been transported for burglary, who had also discarded his own name, that of Thomas Duffy, for Conrad Cunningham. With Duffy, however, we have nothing to do.

The Fitzgeralds, on the contrary, furnish an important personage in our story. Well, they soon set up for great people. The Old Bailey reminiscences were merged in the Australian prosperity. They made out that they were the younger branch of an old English family, who had emigrated for elbow room, and always talked of returning to the old country next year, just as Boulogne gentlemen talk of going to London next week; but somehow they never go.

Old Fitzgerald kept his own counsel, and chuckled at the 'cuteness of his children, of which he had several; to wit, three sons and four daughters. Hearing that Willy Watkins was in for a good thing, he invited him to his house, Britannia Park, near Port Philip, where the eldest and most presuming of his daughters, Miss Letitia, was allowed two clear days' start of her sisters, to enable her to capture Willy, which she did with the greatest ease, and presented herself to her sisters as a fiancée on their return from visiting the elegant family of a third ex-convict. Those were days when they did transport culprits, instead of giving them tickets of leave to hug honest people at home. Well, Willy and Miss Letitia were presently married, and one, and only one, child blessed the aristocratic union—viz. Independent Jimmy's fair friend, christened by the high-sounding names of Cassandra Cleopatra. And Willy's wealth increasing, though his family did not, as that solitary piece of perfection verged towards womanhood, he, with his aspiring spouse, resolved to revisit England, there to seek for Cassandra's equal in marriage—if, indeed, such a *parti* was to be found.

Willy, too, longed to display his wealth in his native country, to drive up and down the High Street of Brittlesworth, and show off before the counter-skippers of Flimsey

and Figments. Some people would have shirked that
sort of scene, and broken fresh ground, but Willy did
not appreciate the position, and his wife did not know
of it. So, having appointed his excellent father-in-law
manager of his property, the trio proceeded to England,
and, after one or two changes, established themselves at
Dalberry Lees a year or two before Mr. Romford's accession
to the country. Willy was then about five-and-forty, with
just as much solicitude about his side-locks as he had
when the now nearly bald crown was covered with a
glorious crop of curly dark hair. He was always tending,
and feeling, and plastering, and looking in the glass to
see whether the side-locks were diminishing or any
hairs absent without leave.

Mrs. Watkins was just then in the prime of life and the
full development of her matronly beauty. She was fair
and stout, with a commanding presence, and a very
determined look about her,—a pushing, self-asserting,
doubtful sort of woman, who would push her way if she
could. It was very difficult to keep Mrs. Watkins out of
a house that she determined to be into.

Her daughter was very like her in both mind and
person, though on a smaller scale, of course, fair—indeed,
rather white—with either a natural or an affected lisp,
which she seemed rather to cultivate than correct.
Seeing that her father had carriages, and horses, and
everything that her mamma said constituted gentility,
Miss concluded they were great people, and conducted
herself accordingly. Independent Jimmy's description of
her wasn't far from the truth—she was very saucy.

Character is often shown in trifles, and perhaps a copy
of a letter from Mrs. Watkins to Mrs. Scarsdale about a
cook will elucidate that of Mrs. Watkins better than anything we can write. Mrs. Scarsdale, we may observe, was
a quiet, unassuming lady, who with her husband were
people of very old family. They, however, unfortunately,
were not so rich as they had been. Thus the letter ran :—

"To Mrs. Scarsdale,
     "Manor House.
                              "Dalberry Lees, *Tuesday.*

"Madam,—Mrs. Lubbins, your late cook and housekeeper, has referred me to you for a character in those

capacities, though indeed I only require her in the former one, as my establishment requires the constant supervision of an experienced housekeeper.

"I shall therefore feel obliged if you will inform me if you can recommend Lubbins as honest, trustworthy, sober, steady person, also a *thoroughly* good cook, sending up dinners in good style for eighteen or twenty, and in her *everyday* dinners attentive to send up nicely ; understands *soups well*, made dishes, sweets, and confectionery. The head gardener makes the ices. I am particular in inquiring about *soups*, as we require them daily and good. Indeed, we want everything good, as we keep a great deal of company, and that good. May I ask if Lubbins does her own work fairly and well, not trusting too much to the kitchen-maids, of which we keep two, besides a dairy-maid, who helps on emergencies. I should like to have Lubbins's last character, if you have it.

"I am, Madam, yours truly,
"LETITIA WATKINS.

"An early answer is requested."

It will be observed that in this document Mrs. Watkins speaks of "my establishment," ignoring friend Willy until she comes to the eating part of the inquiry, and that was pretty much the way she treated him on all occasions, hitching him in as a sort of contingent, and because she thought it looked better to have a man with her than to go bowling about the country with her daughter alone. Willy, however, always had to sit with his back to the horses. Besides eating, dressing, and, as Independent Jimmy said, "brushin' his hair," Willy had no sort of occupation. He neither farmed, nor gardened, nor hunted (except he couldn't help it), nor coursed, nor shot, nor walked, nor rode. He read as little as possible. He said it was bad for the eyes. Willy, poor, empty-headed Willy ! was thrown on dress and equipage as his only resource. He got himself up elaborately every day—not in what is called the "ditto" style, coat, waistcoat, and trousers all of a piece, but in the colour-matching, colour-choosing, cut-varying, velvet-facing, silk-lining order of former times. This changing with the season, coupled with an extensive wardrobe, enabled him to appear differently every day. Now in a fine tightly fitting surtout, with white vest and bloodstone buttons ; next in a red and

yellow ribboned deer-stalker hat, with a tie to match,
silk velvet shooting-jacket, white flannel-looking trousers,
turned up at the ankles to show his red stockings and
Balmoral boots. His dressing-room was like a museum.
Every species of coat, costume, and raiment that could be
devised, varied with skull-caps, slippers, and dressing-
gowns without end. He dressed four times a day. Morning *déshabille*, Turkish trousers and dressing-gown;
luncheon, a sort of etching of what he was to come out
after; then, grand costume for the carriage drive; after
which, full or moderate evening attire, according as they
had company or not. And as they paced the weary turn-
pike-roads, the pompous grey horses propounding their
magnanimous legs with the true airing action, the whole
party thought they were the envy and admiration of the
world. They little knew what the Independent Jimmies
said of them.

Such swells coming into the country, sporting two crests
and a portentous coat-of-arms on their carriage, the man
swell giving his £100 a year to the hounds, were sure to
get into a certain society; but the neighbours, having
mastered the Watkins' establishment, gradually withdrew
from the plate, linen, and china contest, and the longer
the Watkinses lived at Dalberry Lees the less they were
visited. Lubbins had very little to do—very few "up-
roars," as she elegantly called parties, to provide. Each
fresh dinner was only a repetition of the last, and people
got tired of the same thing over and over again. That is
the case in most countries. Railways have gone far to
annihilate that sort of society. London now has the
monopoly.

At this juncture came the Romfords. Mr. Romford, a
single man—master of hounds—living at Lord Lovetin's—
enough to stamp him with respectability; Beldon Hall,
just a nice drive from Dalberry Lees. And there was
Miss Watkins, a charming young lady, longing to be
settled, with a most enterprising mamma to guide her in
the right course. Mrs. Watkins saw her opportunity, and
determined to improve it. She knew that by dashing at
the newcomer she might gain an ascendency that it would
be difficult to dispossess her of; and, moreover, appearing
to be intimate, might ward off invidious detraction, which
it is always desirable to do. So they brought out their
cards to call at Beldon Hall at the earliest possible

moment—rather, indeed, as it happened, before Mr. Romford was ready to receive them; though, if they had waited for that event, they would never have got there at all. Facey did not hoist the flag of reception, though there was one attached to the dome of the house.

CHAPTER XXIV

THE MORNING CALL

IT was a fine bright winter's day, slightly inclining to frost, that our friends at Dalberry Lees, having taken an early lunch and got themselves up with extra care, stepped into their well-appointed London barouche, to shed their cards at Beldon Hall. The greys had on new rosettes. Spanker, the swell coachman, sported a well-curled wig, and John Thomas showed his quivering calves in pink silk gauze. Mrs. and Miss were radiant; Mrs. all ermine and feathers, Miss exhibiting a grand floricultural trophy on her head, the produce of her great London milliner, Madame Mirabel Marvellouslongbille, of Upper Grosvenor Street.

Country calling requires a good deal more tact and consideration than it does in London, where ten minutes will make up the difference anywhere, and people get nothing but a grin or a shake of the hands when they come. First, there is the distance to be considered; then the state of the roads; next, perhaps, the state of the horses. Then comes the grand question,—to lunch or not to lunch; for if you don't mean to lunch, the call should be postponed till such a time as to prevent any mistake as to your intentions, else you may have the lady ringing the bell, and without giving an order letting you in for a second lunch, whether you will or not; a penance only to be equalled by that of a second breakfast at a lawn meet. Well, then, if you don't lunch, there is the second calculation as to whether the time of year will allow of your getting there and back before dark, with the state of the roads, the state of the horses—the old subject over again. But ladies' horses can do anything, so here let the Watkinses go. Let us suppose them in and away.

Spanker, the coachman, tired of the six miles an hour monotony of airing, seemed glad of an excuse for springing his horses, and put them over the intervening miles in double-quick time. Gasper, the roadman, who worked by the day and spent half his time in gossiping with the passers-by, wondered what had happened. He had never seen the Lees folk, as he called them, having some doubt of their quality, in such a hurry before.

Arrived at the still pipe-decorated lodges, the opposing gates flew open with the rapidity due to such an exalted equipage, and the greys were coaxed into a canter against the now rising ground.

Mr. Willy Watkins looked at his watch to see that they were not anticipating the revised dress of the Romford footman, and Mrs. and Miss began feeling their hair, adjusting their gloves, and arranging their company faces. They were presently under the portico of the front door. John Thomas, who, like all the Watkins' men, was a London servant (working-up a lost character in the country), having alighted from his seat, rang an amazing peal at the bell, and was instantly alongside the carriage for orders, in anticipation of an immediate outburst of servants—butler, groom of the chamber, footman, etc.

"Mrs. Somerville," said Mrs. Watkins calmly, slightly removing the rich sable coverlid from her side of the carriage, as if to get out. But John Thomas stood listening at the hall-door, like a terrier at a rat-hole, without receiving any internal response to his summons. The fact was, these were the first callers the Romfords had had, and nobody seemed to know what to do. If the master and mistress were not at home, however, it was clear the servants were, for a bunch of uncropped, Frieze-land hen-like heads were seen clustering in a second-floor window of the opposite wing, after the manner of well-conducted establishments. These, we need scarcely say, were the Dirties—Dirty No. 1, Dirty No. 2, and Dirtiest of the Dirty—who all seemed more bent on admiring the unwonted equipage than desirous of affording the inmates of it any information. Thus they talked—

Dirty No. 2.—"Can it be for us?"

Dirtiest of the Dirty.—"Wonder who it is."

Dirty No. 1.—"Oh! those Watkins folks."

Dirty No. 2.—" No doubt come to look after the Squire ; " meaning Mr. Romford.

"Better ring again," at length muttered the coachman, who saw what was passing in front ; and forthwith John Thomas gave another astonishing peal, that almost pulled the bell-handle out of the socket.

This scattered the Dirties ; and Lucy—Mrs. Somerville—who had whipped a pair of stockings, on which she was engaged, into an ottoman at the first alarm, now met the flying group in the back passage, and rallying them while censuring their flight, she desired that one of them would go and open the door directly.

And as on this occasion Dirtiest of the Dirty being again the cleanest of the three, she went circling along in her palpable hoops, showing her well-shaped legs as she went. She opened the door, and exhibited herself in its portals.

But that she was pretty, John Thomas would have felt rather demeaned at being thus confronted with a female. As it was, he looked benignly at her, and said, with a simpering smile—

"Missis at 'ome, Miss ?"

And Dirtiest of the Dirty, having no orders to the contrary, and not exactly understanding the meaning of the term, dropped a curtsy, and incontinently answered "Yes" ; whereupon John Thomas reapproached the carriage to liberate the party, instead of taking the cards, which they had been sorting in full expectation of a different answer. Out got Willy, followed by the ladies, piloting their petticoats, to the admiration of the remaining Dirties, who had again congregated at the opposite window.

Oh, what fine ladies the Dirties thought them, and how they envied their smart clothes.

Our visitors looked rather disconcerted at the escort, but attributing the deficiency to the confusion of shifting, they followed Dirtiest of the Dirty across the lofty black and white marble-floored hall, through the vestibule, to the breakfast-room, where Lucy, nothing loath to see what was up, had subsided at an elegant work-table, with a strip of book-muslin in her hand.

"The ladies," now said Dirtiest of the Dirty, opening the door ; and forthwith Lucy arose, and with a profound stage curtsy to each, welcomed mother and daughter, and then, with a somewhat slighter curtsy and a graceful wave of her right hand, indicated a couple of advanced chairs, on which she begged they would be seated.

"MISTER WATKINS," now announced Mrs. Watkins, slowly and distinctly, bringing her flash man forward, so that there might be no mistake as to who they were. And Lucy gave a still more modified curtsy to him, and begged that he too would take a chair. All four having thus at length got themselves seated, Mrs. Watkins adjusted her fine lace-fringed kerchief, and arranged her company-smile for a task.

It is a great advantage to have trod the stage—to have played at kings and queens. It gives people wonderful composure under company circumstances. But for Lucy's experience that way, she might have felt rather awkward in the presence of two such highly dressed ladies, she only in a plain semi-mourning costume, waited upon by a woman—"Mamma," we may say, was busy baking, and did not show. Still Lucy's quiet, graceful manner, coupled with her aristocratic residence, completely deceived Mrs. Watkins, and deprived the latter of her usual condescending patronage, making her think that Lucy was a person to look up to. So, instead of bringing out her Court card of the greatest personage she knew, as people in the country generally do, or talking about the splendour of Dalberry Lees, she began toadying, and apologising for this early intrusion on the score of their anxiety to be the first to pay their respects to Mrs. Somerville; all of which Lucy received with great propriety, and many bows and thanks for their neighbourly consideration. They then indulged in a slight dissertation on the weather —in the course of which Lucy considered whether to offer them any luncheon, but thinking they looked like people who could eat at any time, and recollecting the dilapidated state of the establishment—nothing but Dirties—she wisely refrained, and entered with great glee on that safe, sure-footed subject of the climate, hoping the fine weather might continue, frost and snow were so very disagreeable —particularly snow, which put an end to everything, and made the country like a great prison. The snow question soon brought them to the subject of hunting, and Mrs. Watkins continuing her toadyism at high pressure, by expressing their great delight with having got Mr. Romford to take the hounds—the country was so dull without them—for though, she said, Mr. Watkins only hunted for conformity, still it was a great advantage to everybody having hounds, not only in showing sport to the gentlemen who liked to have their faces scratched, but in promoting sociality, balls and parties, and making everything pleasant.

To this Lucy, who knew Facey's forte was not capering in a ball-room, made no reply ; but Mrs. Watkins followed up the charge briskly by saying, she supposed Mr. Romford had an excellent set of dogs.

Lucy said he had, and spared no expense in procuring them. And Mrs. Watkins heard he was an excellent sportsman too. Lucy replied that he was.

And now, Mrs. Watkins having laid a foundation of flattery, proceeded to raise a superstructure of inquisitiveness upon it. She hoped Mrs. Somerville was going to stay among them. Indeed, she didn't see how Mr. Romford could do without her, though Mrs. Watkins inwardly thought he would do much better with her beautiful daughter Cassandra Cleopatra. Lucy parried this home-thrust, by saying that she would most likely stay till she saw her brother comfortably settled an answer that might involve any period of time, seeing that the comfort is so much a matter of opinion. Some people might think the West-end Swell comfortable; others, again, might require the elegancies of the Clarendon or of the Lord Warden at Dover, before they returned a verdict to that effect.

"Well, but as the winter was so far advanced," observed Mrs. Watkins, returning again to the charge, "Mrs. Somerville would most likely stay it out."

Lucy couldn't say. It would depend a good deal upon the weather.

"Was she afraid of cold?"

"Not particularly," replied Lucy, "only the country is always colder than the town."

"But this seems a warm, comfortable house," observed Mrs. Watkins, looking round the well-furnished room. "Had they taken it for any length of time?"

Lucy couldn't tell; didn't know whether it was a lease, a loan, or what it was; Mr. Romford and Lord Lovetin had managed the matter between them.

"His lordship's a peculiar man, I th'osse," now lisped Miss, who, at one time, thought she might perchance be Lady Lovetin.

"Is he?" said Lucy, who did not feel at all inclined to lead the charge against their noble landlord.

"Oh, very," assented Mamma; "quite a recluse. Does he lock up all the things, and just let you have the bare walls?"

"Oh no," replied Lucy; "we have whatever we want."

"Ah, then Mr. Romford will be a friend," suggested Mrs. Watkins—"Mr. Romford will be a friend. I know a party who wanted to take the place, and his lordship would hardly let them have anything for their money— wanted to be paid extra for everything."

"Indeed," said Lucy; "he's quite different with us— I mean with my brother. He has all he wants, and more."

"It's a good houth, I th'osse?" lisped Cassandra Cleopatra.

"Very," assented Lucy; adding, "Would you like to see it?"

Miss would, and so would mamma—the latter particularly, for, independently of the natural taste all ladies have for seeing over houses, she wanted to see what servants they had. So Lucy, handing Mr. Watkins last week's "Bell's Life" (Facey's sole instructor) to amuse himself with during their absence, opened the door, and away they floated on the grand tour of the house— upstairs and downstairs and in my lady's chamber. Whatever Mrs. Watkins saw that was fine, she determined to have at Dalberry Lees.

Meanwhile friend Romford, who was busily engaged cleaning his gun in his shirt-sleeves in the butler's pantry down below, was sorely put out by the repeated rings at the door bell, and severely objurgated all the Dirties for letting the callers in, telling them, as he met them on the wing after the mischief, always to say that they were "*not at home*" when anybody came. And he then returned to his former occupation, now wishing the Watkinses were gone, now wondering why they came, next dreading lest they might eat his dinner for luncheon, then thinking how he came to miss his last woodcock that morning. "It was that confounded mountain-ash in the way," said he.

In the midst of his speculations the rustle of robes and the sound of female voices came softened down below, and, listening attentively, friend Facey distinctly heard

Lucy's voice pioneering the marauders. "This is the servants' hall," said she, "and beyond it is the butler's pantry," the voice advancing that way.

"And, rot it, they're comin'," said he, depositing his gun and ramrod on the table, and making his escape by the opposite door. He got into the still-room—no still room, however, for him, for the voices presently approached that door, driving him into the housekeeper's room, from whence there was no escape save through the scullery and up by the coal-cellar grate. Determined not to be caught—especially in his shirt-sleeves—he dashed valiantly at the iron bars, and, mistaking the side of the cellars, crawled out right in front of the Watkins' horses' heads, to the astonishment of Mr. Spanker and the magnificent footman, who at first thought it was the long-expected ale-jug coming. Not being, however, easily disconcerted, friend Facey just asked them, in a careless, indifferent sort of way, if they had seen a rat come up, and, being answered in the negative, he turned in again at a side door as if nothing particular had happened, the Watkins' men wondering if it was the gardener, or who it could be.

The ladies, having at length completed their tour, dairy, pantry, larder and all, began to arrange their features for farewell ; Mrs. Watkins considering whether she should offer Mrs. Somerville her hand, or wait for Mrs. Somerville to tender hers ; Mrs. Somerville thinking how to get them out of the house without an irruption of Dirties to show them the way. The Watkinses then recollected that they hadn't got Willy, so, returning to the breakfast-room, they found that worthy in the act of examining his side hair minutely in the mantelpiece mirror. "Come, Willy, come !" cried the imperious dame, and forthwith Willy relinquished the arrangement of his locks, and proceeded to recover his hat. That gained, Mrs. Watkins assumed his arm, and, thus fortified, then came the terrible conflict about the adieu. Whether 'twere nobler to make a curtsy and move on, or go in boldly for a shake of the hand. Momentous question !

That little ceremony has caused many a coolness—a coolness with some if you don't offer it, a coolness with others if you do. Mrs. Watkins would like to shake hands, but then came the terrible bugbear of the cold shoulder. She would like to get a footing at Beldon

Hall, if it were only for the sake of Cassandra, but then, which was the likeliest way to obtain one?

In the midst of this dilemma, and just when the case seemed hopeless—the theatrical lady knowing the right time better than Mrs. Watkins did—having got them to the room door, released the easy fold of her arms and tendered her hand to Madame, who grasped it with fervour. There is a great deal of significance in the shake of a hand. Miss quickly followed suit, and then Willy closed the affair by offering his and bowing himself out of the room. Mrs. Somerville gave a random ring at the bell, more for the sake of the sound than in hopes that any of the Dirties would show themselves to open the hall-door. And Facey, having planted himself at the window of observation lately occupied by the Mustards, saw the visitors depart, observing to himself as Miss settled into her seat in the carriage, "Not a bad looking lass that." He then ran into the larder to see what damage they had done to the meat, and finding all right, he went to discuss the visitors with Lucy. What she said, what they said, all how and about it; in fact, Facey thought the "Somerville" dodge would do.

But he couldn't have any callers admitted—might ring as much as they liked at the bell, and leave their cards in any quantities; but coming in was quite out of the question, quite another pair of shoes. And, by way of checking the expected influx, he presently set up a garden-rake, which he kept behind the Indian screen in the entrance-hall, wherewith he used to recreate himself by raking the gravel before the front door, so that he could tell whether there had been anybody there or not.

Let us, however, now attend to the departing visitors.

Well, Spanker having piloted his party safe off the premises, and Mrs. Watkins having conned matters over in her own mind, came to the conclusion that it would be well to look knowing; accordingly, without consulting Willy, she uttered the homeward route, telling the coachman to drive by Peasmeadow Park, in order that she might show off before Mrs. Clapperclaw, a lady with a great determination of words to the mouth. She was at home; and, the usual salutations over, with a short cut at the weather, Mrs. Watkins opened fire briskly— for Mrs. Clapperclaw's clock was twenty minutes too fast —by saying, "Well, they had been to Beldon Hall, and

seen Mrs. Somerville—really a very nice sort of person—
not above thirty or five-and-thirty years of age"—(this
was an exaggeration, for Lucy was then only twenty-
nine)—"evidently used to the best (dressed) society.
Mr. Romford was not in ; but the hounds had come,
and would hunt—Monday, Ashley Law ; Tuesday, Thor-
ney Row ; Friday, Pippin Priory ; Saturday—she forgot
where."

Indeed, it would not have been much matter if she
had forgotten them all, for Monday, as we shall presently
see, was Pippin Priory, and the other two places were
transposed. All meets, however, are alike to the ladies,
save at their own houses.

With regard to the establishment and prospects of
gaiety, Mrs. Watkins could give no very satisfactory
information. No doubt Mr. Romford was a friend of
Lord Lovetin, and seemed to have complete control of the
place ; but the Mustards were all the servants the Watkinses saw, though there might be others elsewhere, or
coming. If Mr. Romford lived there as a bachelor, he
might not entertain ; but if Mrs. Somerville remained,
there was no reason why they shouldn't give calls and
take a prominent part in the festivities of the country.
Indeed, Mrs. Watkins observed, that, to her mind, entertaining and promoting conviviality was one of the principal uses of a master of hounds ; for, as to the mere
scampering over the country after a parcel of dogs—
getting their faces scratched and their clothes torn, she
didn't believe that one man in ten who went out really
cared for it—she was sure Mr. Watkins did not : indeed,
nobody knew how unhappy he always was the night before
hunting. "Nothing but a high sense of duty," Mrs.
Watkins was sure, "could induce him to go out." And
Willy, who knew that doctrine wasn't the ticket, kept
frowning at his imperious wife while she delivered the
opinion. "You know it's a fact, W.," said she, turning
upon him with the effrontery of a brow-beating counsel ;
and, as there were none but ladies present, rather than
have an argument, Willy admitted that he did not care
much about it.

Mrs. Watkins—having thus delivered her budget, and
sipped her second glass of sherry—began to feel at her
crinoline ; and Miss doing the same, mamma caught at
the first pause in the conversation to arise ; and, after

much grinning, and handling, and teeth-showing, the exploring party retired, and "Home" was the word, for Dalberry Lees.

Then Mrs. Clapperclaw—who dearly loved to be knowing—having digested all Mrs. Watkins had said, presently "three-black-crowed" the information, by telling Mrs. Marcus Sompting, the next caller, that there were going to be grand doings at Beldon Hall. That Mr. Romford was a gay young bachelor, with a dashing widow sister, who doubtless would keep the game a-going, and contribute very materially to the enlivenment of Doubleimupshire. And the news flew with great rapidity, and caused very general satisfaction, for the natives wanted stirring up sadly. Indeed, for long they had had nothing to do but abuse each other, which becomes tiresome after a time. It is marvellous how country people hate, and yet hug one another!

CHAPTER XXV

MR. ROMFORD'S DÉBUT IN DOUBLEIMUPSHIRE

THAT first impressions are everything is a truism that more people are ready to admit than to act up to; else how can we account for so many ladies disporting themselves in London in their old attire instead of waiting quietly till their new things come home from the milliners, thus stamping themselves as dowdies in the minds of their friends for the rest of the season. Who can expect that last great act of social fellowship—walking down St. James' Street, arm in arm with a swell—if he is not properly attired for the critical occasion.

Many a man has been turned adrift at the Piccadilly crossings without knowing the reason why.

Mr. Romford's début with the Larkspur Hunt, in Doubleimupshire, was very different to what it was with the Heavyside one. Instead of the old pen-wiper-looking scarlet with its strong characteristic aroma of James' horse blister, he sported a smart new "tick coat," built on the semi-frock principle of the simpering gentleman

sitting on the wooden-horse in the tailor's shop window
in Regent Street ; and though Hammond and Bartley
rejected his orders, other less eminent artistes, as we said
before, were only too happy to execute them.

"Francis Romford, Esq., at the Right Honourable
Lord Viscount Lovetin's, Beldon Hall, Doubleimupshire,"
looked well on the new deal packing-cases standing conspicuously at their shop doors. So, what with Lucy's—
that is, Mrs. Somerville's—orders to London tradesmen,
and Facey's favours in the sporting and general way, Independent Jimmy was constantly leaving something or
other at Beldon Hall lodge—new saddles, new bridles, new
dresses, new boots, new bonnets, new everything. It is
of no use people stinting themselves when they are not
going to pay for what they get.

At length all the orders, all the coats, and boots, and
breeches, all the Goodhearted Green exertions, culminated
in the throwing-off point, and the Larkspur Hunt was
about to be revived under the auspices of the renowned
Mr. Romford.

Swig and Chowey were severely admonished as to
their drinking propensities—told that if they ever trans-
gressed again they should not only have the full weight
of Mr. Romford's right arm, the biceps muscle of which
he invited them to feel, but that he would spend a whole
golden sovereign in paper and postage stamps, to write
to every master of hounds in the kingdom, cautioning
them against engaging two such offenders. And by dint
of big talk, Facey made them believe he was a very
great man, and capable of demolishing them entirely.

And Mrs. Somerville, who understood stage effect, and
the advantage of uniformity, saw that Swig and Chowey
were properly dressed, clean shaved, clean white cravats,
good gloves, and well put on well-polished boots, which,
with their new London caps and coats, made them look
as unlike themselves—as unlike the remnants of men
that they were when Mr. Romford picked them up at
Tattersall's, as could possibly be.

Facey, too, was very fine—very different to what he
was when he mounted the Dragon of Wantley, to take
his first day with the Heavyside hounds. He was not
only well dressed, but he had lost a good deal of the
shaggy Lion Wallace appearance he had about the face,
by judicious trimming and polling. Then his clothes

were quite unexceptionable, for if a man will only employ good London tradesmen, they will always take care that he doesn't make a guy of himself. All he then has to do is, to put them on properly.

And when they were all mounted, Romford on the magnificent Pull-Devil-Pull-Baker, late Placid Joe; Swig riding Everlasting; and Chowey on Perfection, the nutmeg-coloured grey with the *penchant* for carriages, the blooming, well-conditioned pack of hounds around them, they really looked remarkably well—thanks to " tick " and their other numerous friends and benefactors. Thus, with eighteen couple of picked hounds, Mr. Romford set off to undergo the scrutiny of the assembled science of the Larkspur Hunt.

Trot trot, bump bump, trot trot, they went—Facey thinking if Swig and Chowey looked so well, what must he do ; new hat, new coat, new everything—besides being such a good-looking fellow. Oh! for a good line of plate-glass windows to admire himself in. He felt as if he had lit on his legs. And in the exuberance of spirit he chucked Tony Parker, the pikeman at Bewley side-bar, a shilling, without ever asking what the toll was.

Tony picked it up, saying as he did it, " Now that's a *real* gemman, that is."

The meet was at Pippin Priory, the elegant mansion of Mr. Joseph Large, who having taken a prominent part in the resuscitation of the Larkspur Hunt, under Mr. Romford's auspices, was well entitled to have the first show-off of the new establishment, on the verdant lawn before his gaudy house.

Mr. Large was not a sportsman, nor yet a regular Doubleimupshire squire, being nothing more nor less than a teapot-handle maker—a great teapot-handle maker—carrying on business both in London and Birmingham. And, though it seems a curious trade, yet, if we consider the enormous number of people there are with teapots—each, of course, with a handle—and how few men there are in the handle-making line (we question if the reader ever met with one before), it is no wonder he made a good thing of it. Joseph was rich—very rich : we wish we could give the reader an adequate idea of his riches, but he kept all his balance-sheets to himself, not even showing them to beloved Mrs. Large. He did not go about saying,

"I am the great Mr. Large, with a redundancy of money;" but if anybody were mentioned who was not in similar circumstances, he would say, with a scornful, up-turned lip, "Poor man—very poor man. Could buy him fifty times over—a hundred, if that was all."

Singular enough, Large was a good deal of the teapot build himself, being short and squat, with a very sallow complexion, and a stiff row of black curls round his otherwise bald head, somewhat resembling a coachman's wig. It was hard to say whether his vulgar, vacant face or his great sticking-out stomach was the most offensive; for he used to bring the latter to bear upon one in the most arrogant way, as much as to say, "There! there's a stomach with good fat capon lined! Match it if you can!"

Young Large—Joseph Bolingbroke, as he was magnificently called—was the exact counterpart of his father, barring the disparity of years, and that he had a full crop of curly black hair instead of the ivory-like apex of papa. He also sported a moustache, and had whiskers extending all round the chin up to the mouth. He was quite as purse-proud, though still not so good a man as his father, for he would have nothing to do with hunting, having, indeed, been trundled off both fore and aft; so papa, who had a very exalted opinion of the advantages of the chase, was obliged to do the dangerous both for self and son. It was hard upon the old boy, who, the reader will see, was not at all adapted for the sport; but pride feels no pain, and he went at it like a man—not horse—tight boots, round legs, wash-ball seat and all. He had been an ardent supporter of Mr. Romford, fully believing he was the Turbot on its tail, and thinking that Romford might be useful in getting Bolingbroke into that high society wherein he could pick up a nobleman's daughter, a connection with the peerage being the height of the teapot-handle maker's ambition.

So now he was going to reap the first fruit of his patriotism, by entertaining the new master at a grand hunt breakfast at Pippin, or Pipkin Priory, as, of course, the wags called it, a spacious Elizabethan mansion built of yellow brick, with bands and arches of red ditto. It stood on a gently rising eminence, well sheltered at the back and sides by a judicious mixture of evergreen trees and oaks. It had been the site of an old Hall house, though, of course, not a quarter the size it is now.

There had been a great gathering of fowls, and hunting of eggs, and coaxings of cream in the immediate neighbourhood, and now the thing was to get people to come in and partake of the feast so provided. The hunt, we may say, had been divided between the merits of Mr. Romford and those of that popular sportsman, Mr. Jovey Jessop, and some of the malcontents showed their displeasure at the choice by remaining outside. Indeed, Mr. Romford would much have preferred staying with his hounds, but both Lucy and her mamma had charged him to go in and make himself agreeable to the ladies, especially to Mrs. Large, assuring him that all women liked attention.

So, when the gaudy green and gold Johnny came tripping over the lawn, taking care of his stockings, to summon him inside, Facey surrendered his horse to a servant, and left the hounds in charge of old Swig. It was a dangerous move ; for ere Facey's substantial form darkened the Priory portico, a white-aproned man was seen fluttering along the yew-tree walk, bearing a sort of hen and chickens, in the shape of a black bottle with a brood of little wineglasses clustering around on a tray. At first sight Swig's good resolution said " No." " No ! " it should be " No, no, I thank you, sir," at least, as became the ci-devant servant of an earl. But as the white-aproned man turned out of the walk by the little green gate, the jingle of the wineglasses sounded rather too musically on Swig's ear, and looking at the tray, he saw some biscuits upon it. Taking a biscuit could do him no harm, he thought ! so he suffered the tempter to approach him.

" Good mornin', Mr. Swig," said the man ; for the aphorism that " more people know Tom Fool than Tom Fool knows," holds particularly good as regards huntsmen and field servants. " Good mornin', Mr. Swig," said he, in the confident tone of a man who feels sure of a welcome.

" Mornin'," said Swig, still riding the good horse Resolution.

" Take a dram this morning ? " continued the footman, balancing the tray on one hand, while he took the silver-headed stopper out of the bottle with the other.

He was now close up against Swig's horse's shoulder, and the aroma of the gin (for it was that beautiful beverage) mounted most generously up to the Swig snub-nose. This was too much for the veteran. Daniel ! the Right

Honourable the Hurl of Scamperdale's Daniel! couldn't resist it.

"Just a thimbleful," said he, as the servant began trickling the gin out of the full bottle into the clear glass. "Nay, man, that's a glass!" exclaimed Daniel, more in pleasure than in anger. Nevertheless, he quaffed it off, saying, as he raised it to his lips, "Sir, I looks towards you;" meaning thereby that he was drinking the man's health.

Chowey then unscrewed his proboscis, and took his dram down without any emotion.

Thus fortified, the two turned to the hounds, and gave them a brisk, cheerful sweep down the Park, returning, like moths, to the gin candle up above, and they then took another thimbleful each.

But we must now follow friend Facey, who has got among the Philistines in the house.

There was a great gathering inside, for Mr. Large looked upon a grand breakfast as part of the ceremony of the hunt; and friend Facey, having been duly eased of his hat, whip, and gloves in the entrance-hall, and run his fingers through his hair, was presently at the lofty mahogany door of the dining-room.

"Mr. Romford, I think?" said the obsequious butler, turning half round as he laid hold of the ivory handle.

"Mr. Romford it is," said Facey, in a tone that as good as said, "Can there be any doubt on the point?"

The door then opened, disclosing a goodly assemblage of ladies and gentlemen, all apparently busy on masticating enjoyments, but still keeping a disengaged eye for the newcomer.

"MR. ROMFORD," now announced the butler in a clear sonorous voice to our bald-headed host, as he sat with his back to the door; whereupon up jumped the teapot-handle maker, with his mouth full of ham, and, getting Facey by the hand, proceeded to give him a most spluttering welcome, working him up the room towards his wife as he went.

"Mr. Romford, my dear," gasped he, as he got him there; whereupon the well-developed matron, all gorgeous in peach-coloured, lace-bedizened moire antique and jewellery, half arose from her chair, and smiled him into a seat on her right, that had evidently been reserved for the hero of the day. Friend Facey having got himself settled, then cast one roguish eye at her, the other glancing down the table, to see what sort of a set he had got amongst. He thought they would do.

"Will you take tea or coffee?" now asked Mrs. Joseph Large, who seemed well primed with both, having great further tea capabilities in the richly chased silver urn before her.

Oh, Facey didn't care much about either. "Well, tea," he thought, muttering something about "porridge, and one breakfast a day serving him." He then took a general survey of the table and room. Everything was very fine—plate, linen, and china; flowers, and vases, and fruit. It seemed breakfast and dinner combined. He had never seen anything half so fine before. Wouldn't have touched his own eggs and bacon if he'd known what was in store for him. He had now got his tea, also sugar and cream, and the hum of conversation that had been interrupted on his entry was gradually resumed, though those in the immediate neighbourhood kept their ears open to hear what was said. Facey having pronged a piece of breakfast cake to avoid the persecution of the servants, who were now offering him everything he didn't want, then bethought him of Lucy's injunctions, and proceeded to play what he thought the agreeable to the hostess.

"How many children have you?" asked he.

"Five," replied Mrs. Large.

"Five, have you (humph)—two couple and a half. How old are you?" Facey eyeing her intently, as if making his own calculation.

Mrs. Large was not going to answer this question, so she parried it by telling the footman to hand Mr. Romford the butter.

"What's your Christian name?" was the next question.

"Mary," replied his hostess.

"Mary (humph)—just plain Mary, is it?"

"Just Mary," assented our hostess, who did not consider herself plain by any means.

The conversation then proceeded much as follows :—

Facey.—"Is this place yours, or do you rent it?"

Mrs. Large.—"Oh, it's our own."

Facey.—"Much land about it?"

Mrs. Large.—"A good deal."

Facey.—"Two or three thousand acres, p'r'aps?"

Mrs. Large.—" Perhaps."

Facey.—" Much game ?"

Mrs. Large.—"A good deal."

Facey.—"Is what's-his-name—your husband there—
(nodding towards Mr. Large) nasty particular about it ?"

Mrs. Large.—"Well (hem), not more (cough) than other
(hem) people."

Facey.—"Wouldn't mind one walking over it occasionally with one's dog and one's gun if it came in one's
way, I s'pose ?"

The conversation or rather interrogatories were interrupted at this critical point by "What's-his-name" rising
at the other end of the table, and calling upon the company
to fill their glasses—to fill bumpers to a toast he was
about to propose, for which purpose the servants had been
planting elegant grape-wreathed Dobson and Pierce glasses
at regular intervals round the table. The champagne
corks now began to fly. Mr. Joseph Large, who dearly
loved the sound of his own voice, then opened a volley of
laudatory observations on friend Facey, talking of his
great prowess as a sportsman, and the high compliment he
had paid the Larkspur gentlemen in leaving his native
county, with his great local influence and associations, to
hunt their inferior one, though Mr. Large hoped the
welcome the Larkspur gentlemen would give him would
compensate for the sacrifice. He then glanced at the great
advantages of a pack of hounds in a county, which he was
well qualified to do, seeing that he only hunted medicinally, and because he was told it was right.

Among the many merits of champagne may be mentioned
that of its tendency to cut short long-winded speeches, for
no one likes to sit nursing a glass of the sparkling beverage
in his hand until its effervescence subsides, and premature
cries of "Your health, Mr. Romford !—your health, Mr.
Romford !" caused the speaker to conclude without the
cut at the Jovey Jessopites he meant to have indulged in,
while the clatter of the china, to get Facey up to reply,
making Mrs. Large feel for her cups, she at last asked Mr.
Romford if he had not better rise.

Then the man, "whose moother was a lady, but whose
fatther was a gardener," drew his Bedford cords slowly
and deliberately from under the table, and, having gained
his utmost altitude, essayed his maiden speech, amidst the
most profound and anxious silence.

"Gentlemen," said he, "I'm no speaker, but I'm a sportsman—(applause). If you'll let my hounds alone, and give them fair play and room to hunt, I'll be bound to say I'll show you sport, but if you override them—I—I—don't know what I'll do," said he, with a shake of the head, amidst a roar of laughter. "S'pose then," continued he, after a pause, "that we drink 'Foxhunting,' and be off to it!" So saying, he drained his glass, and, pocketing his napkin, which he thought was a present, with an outward bulge of his person towards Mrs. Large, he rolled out of the room.

"He's a rum 'un," whispered one, as Facey got out of hearing.

"He is that," muttered another.

"Good sportsman," observed a third.

"Man of large pror-perty," said Mr. Large, as he felt bound to support him.

"Presumes upon that, perhaps," rejoined a fifth.

Then the ladies canvassed him freely.

"How old should you say he is?" asked Mrs. Large of the company generally.

"Perhaps five-and-thirty," said Mrs. Cumberledge.

"Oh, far more than that, mamma!" exclaimed Miss Cumberledge, who wished to deter Miss Agnes de Flouncey from thinking of him.

"He's such an ugly man," said Miss Agnes, going on the running-down tack also.

"I shouldn't say he was ugly, Agnes," rejoined Mrs. Joseph Large—"plain man, but pleasant. He has a good deal to say for himself."

"A good deal of money, I suppose," sneered Miss Cumberledge, as if she was quite above any mercenary consideration.

"He looks like a great, rich man," observed little Miss Ellerby, who, pleading guilty to twenty-five (as she was in reality thirty-three), would have had no objection to have him.

Still, notwithstanding these expressions of opinion from the few, it would have been extremely difficult to arrive at any satisfactory conclusion from the many, as to Mr. Romford's character and qualifications—his independent manner, coupled with his reputed vast possessions, confusing, if not misleading, the judgment. Here, again, if the parties had only known that he was a mere hound-stealing, penniless adventurer, they would have had no hesitation whatever in the matter. "Great clown," or "great lout" would have been the verdict. As it was, however, they seemed rather to concur with Independent Jimmy in thinking that he was not a "man of much blandishment." But having seen him in the house, let us now follow him to the field, teapot-handle maker, company, and all.

"To horse!—to horse!" is now the cry.

CHAPTER XXVI

A FICTITIOUS FOX

MR. FACEY ROMFORD'S substantial figure under the handsome portico of Pippin Priory had a very salutary influence on Daniel Swig, who was just trotting his hounds gaily back to the bottle, unable any longer to resist its seductive influence.

He had had three glasses already, and another would in all probability have made him revert to the glorious days when he was the "Hurl of Scamperdale's Daniel!" to the disparagement of his service with our Master. Not but that he was a great deal better done by than he was with the Heavyside Hunt, but still the recollection of the Hurl, and the contrast with Facey, were sometimes too much for Daniel's sensitive, excitable temperament.

Chowey, on the other hand, was more cosmopolitan in his views. He was ready to praise any master with whom he had ever lived, provided he thought the praise would be likely to put a shilling or two in his pocket.

He, too, had done homage to the gin bottle, and between visits, had been composing his extraordinary proboscis, and casting about, looking at the field to see whose acquaintance he could claim, whom he could compliment on a desperate leap with the Hatherstone, or remind that he had seen him swim a river, like a harm of the sea, with the Berkshire. Was he as hard a rider now? Ingenious Chowey! Who could resist such soft sawder as that? But to our meet.

The plot had greatly thickened since Mr. Romford entered the Priory.

Instead of the mole-catcher, the rat-catcher, the earth-stopper, the man with the three-year-old filly in the breaking bridle, and the usual circus-like ring of pedestrians, there were groups of knowing sportsmen clustering here and there, following and intercepting the hounds when they moved.

"What's that hound, huntsman?" demanded a gentleman in scarlet, in a very hundred-pounds-a-year sort of voice.

"Wich, sir?" replied Swig, with a respectful touch of his new velvet cap, not knowing what the inquirer might be good for in the way of a tip, when tipping time came.

"There, that, the lemon-pied one, just under your horse's head!"

"Oh, that's Comforter, sir. Comforter, good dog!" continued Swig, as Comforter looked up on hearing his name.

"Ah, Comforter; by the Cottesmore Combatant, isn't he?" asked the gentleman.

"No, sir; by the Burton Bellman. Bellman was by Lord Yarborough's Boisterous, Boisterous by the Cheshire Bluster, Bluster by the Bedale Buster by Sir Tatton Syke's Barbarous, Barbarous by the Right Honourable the Hurl of Scamperdale's Brilliant."

So Swig shut the inquirer up with a perfect torrent of fabulous pedigree.

Facey, who knew what they were after as well as they did themselves, paused, and looked on with a smile at their pointings, and winkings, and nudgings, feeling satisfied they could take no exception to his hounds. His horses might have some little peculiarities about them, but they were more mental than bodily defects, and clipping and shaving did all that the most scientific, self-sufficient stud groom could accomplish in the way of condition. So he came, lowering his hat string, looking carefully into the crowd to see if there was any one who could blow him—any one who could knock the Turbot off its tail—any of the Heavysides or Gilroy set.

Dash it! that square cut wide-buttoned coat was uncommonly like Oliver Jogglebury's, thought he; so were the boots, and the legs, and the action. Dashed if Facey didn't think it was Oliver. By Jove! what a go it would be if it were a nephew of old Jog's.

Just then the alarming party turned round, and in lieu of Oliver's dark, almost copper-coloured face, disclosed a nearly white one, with stubbly ginger whiskers, and white eyelashes.

"Thank heavens, that's all right!" gasped Mr. Romford, now relieved by the sight. "Thank heavens, that's all right!"

But scarcely had he regained his composure, ere a pair of very luxuriant, inward curling, jet-black whiskers, struck him as impossible to belong to any one but Colonel Bannerman.

Couldn't be two such pairs in the world, thought Facey, and again his heart mounted to his mouth, as he remembered the trifle he owed the Colonel on the Derby, and how he had warranted a three-legged horse to him as sound. Fortunately, however, our friend was again deceived. The whiskers belonged to Mr. Bradley Smith of Rushden, a member of the Larkspur Hunt, a gentleman not in the least like the blackleg Colonel. And Facey was again comforted. Fortune favoured the brave, he thought, so vaulting gaily over the light palisade that separated the green slope on which the Priory stood from the Park, he advanced confidently towards the parti-coloured crowd—now clustered about the pack— still culling and criticising their size, colour, and condition.

The hounds now raised a half-melodious, half-rebellious sort of cry at Swig and Chowey, as our Master advanced, that as good as said, "All you are only the servants that look after us, this is the boy that shows us sport." Some of the more independent then broke away altogether, jumping and frolicking towards Mr. Facey.

"Gently, Blithsome!" cried our Master, swinging his whip round as Blithsome wiped her paws right down his fine new coat-back. "Get away, you fool," added he, with a frown and stamp of his foot, as if Blithsome ought to know he had got his new coat on, as well as he himself did.

At this juncture, up waddled his host in a pair of excruciatingly tight boots, and getting our Master familiarly by the handle, proceeded to push and steer him up to several groups of sportsmen, presenting him to them at random. Mr. Blanton — Mr. Romford, Mr. Brogdale—Mr. Romford, with such rapidity, that it was utterly impossible for Facey to follow him, so adopting the old poacher's advice to his son, of always blazing into the "brown on 'em," he gave two or three general aerial sweeps with his arm, as he kept sidling away for his horse.

A little to the left of the pack walked the magnificent "Baker," late "Placid Joe," in all the pride of superlative condition, looking as demure as a Quaker, and as if he had never done anything wrong. He had, indeed, been greatly admired ; his size, his strength, his substance : and it seemed to be generally agreed that such a horse could not be procured under a couple of hundred guineas. Some said three hundred, but those were the boys who never gave more than thirty themselves.

Then Mr. Facey having gained him, and thanked the man in charge for his trouble, which was all he was in the habit of doing, he swung himself into his saddle, and felt all the better for being there. Drawing the thin rein he felt him lightly with his leg, and proceeded to pass on to the pack. Meanwhile his host had raised fresh recruits for the honour of presentation ; and the old process, Mr. Kickton—Mr. Romford, Mr. Bullpig— Mr. Romford, was resumed.

At length Mr. Facey, thinking he had been sufficiently exhibited, got his horse short by the head, and, hallooing to his host to know what he should draw first, with Swig in advance and Chowey a little behind, he moved gaily away, with the glad pack now clustering and frolicking around him—the presentation napkin just peeping out of his pocket as he went. There was a large field—fifty or sixty horsemen, perhaps—which of course a generous public would call a hundred, Jessop-ites, Romford-ites, Any-thing-else-ites. And great was the talk and commotion the hounds raised. It seemed to be generally agreed that it was an undeniable turn-out, but some thought Facey's manners *brusque*, and that he did not make sufficient distinction between the large subscribers and the small ones. Poor Facey couldn't tell by their looks what they gave.

A lawn meet generally involves a little deception, or what Independent Jimmy would call "blandishment," and Facey had to run his hounds through several im-

probable places that had never held a fox in the memory
of man, and in all probability never will. Still, it was
part of the programme, and, of course, he conformed to
it. First he tried the laurel walk, and the rhododendron
beds, then he went to the deodara grove, and was moving
on to the summer-house hill when a green and red
gamekeeper came up and announced that he had seen
a fox sitting under the projecting ridge of Silverstream
Slate Quarry. This was Mr. Charley Slinker, a gentleman
pretty well known in gunning circles, as also in the
public-house and advertising lines, being constantly
offering his services, either as a park-keeper, gamekeeper,
head or single handed, sometimes indeed descending as
low as an under gamekeeper, or even one who would
devote himself entirely to trapping. But Charley, in
his glory, was the occupant of such a place as he now
had, living with a master who, knowing nothing about
the matter, listened to his stories and worried anybody
upon whom Slinker hounded him. There is no greater
mischief-maker than a second-class gamekeeper. They
are always hunting and frittering away character.

Well, up came Slinker to Romford, in manner aforesaid,
and though friend Romford thought he looked like a
scamp, he accepted the information, and telling him to
lead the way, bid him put the fox away quietly, and
hold up his white hat when he was gone. Facey then
made a little *détour* with the hounds while Slinker
performed his part of the ceremony. And the man's
manner and official position tending to raise hopes, all
the pedestrians and several of the equestrians followed
to see what would happen. On Slinker stalked, full
of consequence and expectation that Mr. Romford would
tip him a sovereign at least for the find. Arriving at
the top of the quarry he clapped his hands loudly, and
"*shew, shewed!*" expecting to see the fox bolt on the
instant. Nothing of the sort, however, happened, some
jackdaws flew out of the quarry, but no fox appeared.
Looking rather disconcerted, the hero of the gun then
stooped, and picking up a stone threw it at the place
where he still thought he saw the fox lying. Another
jackdaw then appeared. *Crack! crack!* now went several
whips, in the midst of which Slinker descended, and,
making for the spot, found the brown substance he had
been taking for a fox was some fox-coloured fern!

Nothing daunted, however, he returned boldly to the front, inveighing bitterly against the foot people, declaring that half of them ought to be hung—that he had seen the fox there every morning for the last month, and now they had put him away just when the hounds had come to hunt him. But he knew who had done it! He knew who had done it! It was that Geordey Mason, because he wouldn't let him come to the rook-shooting. He'd pay him off, that he would.

Mr. Romford, little chagrined, for he did not expect much from his man, then took his further directions from Mr. Joseph Large, who, wishing to get out of his tight top-boots as soon as he could, told our Master he had better go at once to Winstable Wood, and not potter about wasting time any longer. Whereupon Mr. Romford's broad shoulders assumed the jerk of activity, which, having communicated itself to the rest of the field, away the whole party went, bump bump, trot trot, trotting to the bob, bob, bobbing of the men's caps in advance. So they passed through the hamlets of Shinley and Crumpton, to the delight of the children and the astonishment of the poultry, each, particularly one old hen, thinking the whole force of the movement was directed against her.

As the teapot-handle maker, in his purgatorial tops, was borne along on a very fractious rough-actioned chestnut horse, he inwardly thought that the trouble of hunting was greater than the pleasure. He thought he would like to do it by deputy. Send the coachman out instead. Why should he be tormented in this way? —riding a nasty, capering, hot-headed brute that wanted to have the whole road to itself, and, if he gave it its head, would infallibly run clean away with him?—Why, indeed! "Rot the brute! there it goes again!" exclaimed Joseph, as the irritated chestnut threw up its head and nearly flattened his snub nose. And Joseph inwardly wished he had him in a good rough ploughed field, where he could give him the slack rein and ride him to a standstill to punish him for his impetuosity. Why couldn't he take things quietly?—and thereupon he gave him a cropper that made the horse worse. Thus Joseph proceeded on his way anything but rejoicing. Meanwhile Bolingbroke was comfortably at home feeding his pigeons.

CHAPTER XXVII

A REAL FOX

THERE were good foxes in Doubleimupshire, only they required a little finding. They lay in queer out-of-the-way places, old buildings, ivy-mantled crags, and one gentleman had his billet up a hollow box-tree.

Some men are good at finding foxes and bad at hunting them; others are bad at finding, and good at hunting them : while others again are good at neither operation. Mr. Facey Romford combined both qualities, he could find as well as hunt. He had an intuitive knowledge of the nature and habits of the animal, and seemed to say to himself as he approached a cover—his little pig eyes raking it in all directions—"Now, Francis Romford, moy beloved friend, if you were a fox, where would you lie ? Would you choose the east side by the road, with the chance of intrusion from every stray cur and stick-stealing besom-maker; or would you take the west, where it is quieter with worse lying; or would you mount half-way up the hill where there is a sunny sand-bank to bask upon, with a nice close gorse in the rear ?" and whichever part of a cover Facey fancied, there generally was to be found the fox. Sometimes he would whip them out of places that nobody ever thought of trying, straggling bushes, briery banks, angular nooks—quarters that offered the benefit of seclusion without attracting notoriety by their size. "How can you be sure he's not there," Facey would say, "if you don't try?" Not that he went with the pack, and the *posse comitatus* at his heels, but he sent Swig or Chowey or some one to whip the place in passing. He never gave a keeper a chance of saying that he drew over his foxes, or left them behind.

Whitstable Wood was a sure find—at least as sure as anything can be that is dependent upon the will of a wild animal, and, not having been disturbed for some time, expectation ran high on the point. Moreover, after two or three failures, even the funkers begin to wish for something better than the mere cheer of the huntsman or the rate of the whips. It is being hurried into hot action, without a moment's preparation, or time to get on terms with one's horse, that makes people quake and wish themselves out of it. A great staring stone wall or a bottomless brook to begin upon are sad dampers to ardour and energy. Leaping should be gradual and progressive. A little one first, then a somewhat larger, and a little bigger after that, and so on. Not a great choker at starting. It should be conducted on the principle of a French dinner, where the grand *pièce de résistance* comes last.

But we are now at the cover—a twenty-acre wood of stately oaks, with capital lying, and already Romford & Co. have dissolved partnership, Swig taking the right, Chowey the left, each keeping wide of Mr. Romford, so that, as Beckford says, a single hound may not escape them. Facey coaxes as many of the field as he can into cover, but the rides being deep and the clay holding, it is not a popular measure. Mr. Joseph Large never went into a wood, because he never could find his way out again; but, on this occasion, thinking the holding clay might be serviceable to the fractious chestnut horse, he went boldly in, determined to give him a bucketing if he could. Still Joseph's example was not seductive— very few followed him. Mr. Kickton wanted to ride against Mr. Pyefinch, who had said he was a tailor; while Mr. Blanton, Mr. Bullpig, and Farmer Tuppen wanted to be ready to slip down Lavenham Lane, in case the fox went to the west. Each man has a pet reason for not going in. And as few nowadays care to see a fox found, Facey has it pretty much to himself. On he goes, slowly and carefully, inwardly hoping that his gratuitous pack might distinguish itself. If there was any truth in breeding they would, and he knew he had spared no lies in getting them.

And the hounds had not been long in cover ere the feathering of Trumpeter and Tuneable (both from the Badminton) satisfied our distinguished master that a fox was at home, and, getting the Baker horse by the head, he dashed into the thickest of the brushwood, followed by such of the pack as had witnessed the move. "*Yooi, push 'em up!*" cheered Facey, with a slight crack of his whip, and on the instant a great ruddy-coated, white-throated, irate-looking dog fox dashed out of his grassy lair in full view of Trumpeter, who raised such an exclamation of joy and surprise as electrified the rest of the pack, and brought them pell-mell to the spot to share in the crash and the triumph. What a commotion was there! A pack of vigorous foxhounds, all getting a whiff of the scent by turns, each particular hound giving as it were a receipt in full for the whole. What a crash they make! and the old wood echoes and re-verberates the sound with most usurious interest. Then the critics, both hostile and friendly, began cocking their ears for censure or for praise, while the unprejudiced sportsmen sat revelling in the melody, half wishing the fox would break cover, and yet half that he would stay, and have a little more taken out of him ere he fled. And sly Reynard, apparently considering the matter, and leaving the dreadful clamour behind him, thought he had better get a little farther ahead before he ventured to leave his comfortable quarters, so, running a couple of liberal rings, he so foiled the ground as to bring the clamorous hounds to their noses, and give him a much better chance of escape. And as the music sensibly lessened and some were beginning to abuse the scent, and Facey was cheering on the hounds that could hold it, the twang of a horn came softened through the wood, changing the whole course of the performance.

It was Daniel! the Right Honourable the Hurl of Scamperdale's Daniel! doing with his horn what he was unable to do with his husky voice, and its notes were caught and immediately drowned by the clamour that followed them.

The fox was indeed away! Well away; for he must have been a bold one to return in the face of such a yelling.

Meanwhile Daniel was on with the leading hounds, leaving Facey and Chowey to bring the rest after him. There was a rare scent, and he chuckled to think they would never catch him up. So he sailed gallantly over Mapperton Meadows, taking Babington Brook in his stride. Then Romford, who had nothing but his quick ear to guide him—never having seen a yard of the country before—settled himself in his saddle, and went tearing and crashing away through the cover to where he thought he heard the last notes of the horn, while the well-informed field diverged to the right or the left, according as their former experience guided them; some thinking the fox was away for Heslope Hill, others that he was sure to go to Hurlestone Crags, and the leader of each detachment coursed over the country, so as to lead his followers to the point with as little risk to life or limb as possible. Each party came in view just as Romford, with a gallant effort, superseded Swig, who now fell back upon the mouth-extended, gaping Chowey. "For-rard! for-rard!" was the cry, though it was scarcely possible for hounds to go faster.

Most hunts have their crack rider, a man whom they think can beat everybody; and Captain Spurrier, of Cherrymount, had long held that honourable office with the old Larkspur Hunt. Not that it is usual to ride at the master or huntsman; but the other Mr. Romford not having the reputation of being a great horseman, the Captain thought it might be well to show him how they did things in the far-famed Doubleimupshire. But for this he would have preferred retiring into private life now on the accession of a new master, for a strong tinge of hoar-frost had shot across his once dark brown whiskers, and hardish falls had somewhat quenched the love of leaping. Still, men don't like admitting they are not so good as they have been, and persevere on, in hopes that it is only a temporary depression, from which they will speedily rally. Each time they go out they think they will just show off that day, and be done; but somehow they always think they will just have another last day, and then one more, and so on, till they get beat, and give up hunting in disgust.

Happy are they who go out to please themselves, and not to astonish others.

So thought Mr. Joseph Large, as, having taken the fiery edge off the chestnut in the deep-holding clay rides of the cover, he gained the hard road, and resolved to stick to it as long as ever he could. "Pretty thing it would be for a man of his means to break his neck after a nasty, crafty, hen-stealing fox." So saying, he knotted his curb-rein, and letting it drop, proceeded to take his change out of the chestnut, now that he had got him subdued. He even ventured to spur him, not very severely, but still sufficient to let the horse know that he had a pair on.

With the before-mentioned erroneous impression of the prowess of friend Facey, Captain Spurrier hustled his horse and hardened his heart, determined to ride as of yore; and great was his surprise when, on clearing the cover, he saw the pusillanimous Romford, as he thought, sailing away, taking the large bull-finchers just as they came in his way, without swerving either to the right or the left.

"Spurting rider!" muttered Spurrier, grinding his teeth, adding, "he'll change his tune before he gets to Collington Woods," for which the hounds seemed then to be evidently pointing. So saying, the Captain put spurs to his little thoroughbred steeplechase horse, and shot in between Facey and Daniel Swig, who was now careering along in the wake of his master.

A great and widespread avalanche of sportsmen followed, some by one route, some by another, the programme widening towards its base, just like the pyramids of Egypt, or a lady's petticoat. The ground sloped gradually to the sight, giving all those who had time to look after anything but themselves a fine panoramic view of the chase—hounds in a cluster—Romford close up—Spurrier hard upon him — Swig next Spurrier, and Chowey mixed up in a miscellaneous group of horsemen, —now a red coat leading, now a black, now a red again. The air was bright and rarefied, and echo multiplied the music of the hounds. It was both a good seeing, a good scenting, and a good hearing day—quite a bespeak for an opening day.

The farther they went, the more Captain Spurrier was lost in astonishment at Mr. Romford's masterly performance. He didn't seem to care a halfpenny for anything. All he looked to was being with his hounds. Brooks, banks, walls, woods, all seemed equally indifferent to him. "What nonsense people talked about Romford not being a rider," thought he. "Was just about the hardest rider he had ever seen. Little Spratt was nothing to him." And Spurrier inwardly congratulated himself upon not being bound to beat Mr. Romford. Such a back and such shoulders he had never seen in conjunction with such a powerful horse. Altogether, Spurrier pronounced Romford a very formidable opponent. And he wondered if Romford would introduce him to Lord Lovetin. Mrs. Spurrier would like it very much, if he would. So they sailed away over Sharperow and Strother lordships, past Tasborough, leaving Thirkeld on the right and Welbury on the left, till the ploughed lands of Portgate slackened their paces and brought the hounds to their noses.

"Hold hard !" was at length the cry, and gratefully it sounded to the ears of the forward ; grateful it was, too, to those behind, who by now putting on might yet hope to get a saving view of the scene. So they hurried forward in clamorous vigour, determined to be able to say how it was up to Heatherwicke Green, at all events ; and a great wave of sportsmen surged to the front ere Mr. Romford, having let the hounds make their own cast, now essayed to assist them in full view of a panting but still critical field.

We are all great judges of hunting. Romford, nothing flurried, had employed the brief interval in watching the spreading and trying of the hounds, and surveying the same.

"Francis Romford," said he to himself, "if you were the fox, what would you do under these circumstances? You may have been headed by that noisy long-tailed team, with the man riding on the stilts, or you may have been chased by that ill-conditioned cur, who has a very felonious look about him ; but, anyhow, I think, Francis Romford, with that range of rocky hills in front, you would get on ahead, and try to ensconce yourself amongst them." So saying, Facey determined to make a wide cast in front, and try to recover his friend. And the perspiring field sat watching the move—if successful, to call it a good one ; if not, to denounce it as the wildest cast that ever was made.

Facey didn't get his hounds together like a flock of sheep, but allowed them to spread and use their own sagacity, going at a very gentle pace, without any hurrying or blustering from the whips. Two fields ahead brought him to the rapid-running eddying Fleet, now even with its banks from the effects of recent rains. It was neither jumpable nor fordable, but it was swimmable, and as such Facey took to it.

He blobbed in and scrambled out. Swig blobbed in and scrambled out. The hounds blobbed in and scrambled out.

Chowey declined.

It suddenly occurred to him that Raschid was missing.

Captain Spurrier looked at the still agitated water, and said, "Ah! that would not have stopped me, but I've got a dose of camomile in me this morning." He then joined the ruck, and rode round by the bridge at Belting-ford Burn. A hard road here favoured them, and as the field clattered along, they commented in fragmentary ejaculations on the rashness of swimming, and the general disagreeableness of water in winter.

"He must have viewed the fox," said Mr. Tuppen, "or he would never have risked his life in that way;" adding, "Have known many a man drowned in that river."

"Or is going to a halloo!" suggested Mr. Markwell, who had just joined.

"A rare 'un to ride!" observed Mr. Joseph Large, proud of his *protégé*.

But Romford had neither viewed the fox nor heard a halloo. He was simply following his own instinct that the fox was forrard; and if he didn't find him forrard, he would have swum it again to try back.

But Fortune does favour the brave, and Facey had no occasion to give his new coat-laps or Bedford cords another wetting; for, after a hearty shaking, the bustling pack again spread to pursue their sniffing investigations on the south side of the river; and at a reverse in the second hedge-row dividing a ploughed from a pasture field, the Beaufort Brilliant gave such a note of exclamation as electrified the pack, and in an instant the rickety fence cracked and bent with their weight.

"Hoop!" cheered Facey, delighted with his prowess. He didn't care a copper for his Bedford cords, nor yet for his new coat-laps.

Meanwhile the hounds shot away with renewed melody, renovating the roadsters, and making the country ring with their energy. The face of the landscape now changed, inclining upwards towards the dark frowning hills, which divided the vale from the moorlands above. The enclosures, too, got larger and larger—twenty, thirty, and forty acres each—while the surface was more openly exposed, flat, and expansive, with very weak hedges, and few hollows for concealment or out-of-sight running. The hounds now showed to great advantage, striving and racing for the mastery. A sheet would cover them.

"Dash it! but they are a rare lot!" muttered Facey, eyeing their performances. "And didn't cost much either," chuckled he, thinking how he got them. "*Forrard! forrard!*" cheered he, fanning the flame of their ardour. So they went screeching and pressing to the front—now Prosperous leading, now Terrible, now Tuneable. Dash it! He didn't know whether the Beaufort or the Belvoir were the best. Didn't think even Bondsman himself could beat some of the former. Monstrous lucky he was to get them.

Facey next views the fox stealing steadily over what was once Coltsfoot Common, with an attendant canopy of crows hovering over him, indicating his course. *Yow! yow! yap!*" went the bustling hounds. "Caw! caw! caw!" went the birds. So the poor fox had a double set of pursuers.

On he went, however, steadily and perseveringly. He had beat the old Larkspur hounds twice, and did not see why he should not beat Mr. Romford's. But nearer and nearer came the notes of the pack, commingling with the vociferous cawing of the black gentry above. It was hard to say which seemed the most inveterate against the unfortunate fox. Still, the many-caverned rocks were close at hand, and if he could but gain them, they might work for a week before they got him out. There they girded the horizon in frowning altitude, the dark interstices looking most inviting for a refuge. Facey saw the difficulty. If the fox and hounds held on at the same pace, the fox would inevitably gain the rocks and beat the hounds. This was not to be desired, especially on a first day after a good run. So clapping spurs to Pull-Devil-Pull-Baker, now, indeed, made into Placid Joe, he capped them on from scent to view; and, after a smart race, the Belvoir Dreadnought pulled the fox down by the brush, just as he was ascending the first reef of rocks.

"WHO-HOOP!" shrieked Romford, in a voice that made the hills ring and reverberate. *Who-hoop!*" repeated he, throwing himself from his horse, and diving into the midst of the pack, to extricate the fox from their fangs. Up he held him triumphantly, with the baying pack jumping and frolicking around. "Take my horse away now," cried Facey to Swig, and the coast being then clear, Facey advanced a few steps to where a soft mossy bank seemed to invite the performance of the last obsequies of the chase.   There, on the bright green cushion, he cast the nut-brown fox.

Meanwhile, the field having availed themselves of the facilities of Beltingford Bridge, were now making the air and the hard road ring with their voices and the noise of their horses' hoofs, all in a deuce of a stew lest they should lose the hounds, or not be up at the kill.   They had not yet arrived at the elegant point of indifference that makes men turn their horses' heads homewards as soon as they hear " who-hoop ! " and most satisfactory (though of course none of them admitted it) Romford's death-note sounded on their ears.

They had all about had enough.   The gallant Captain Spurrier had lost a shoe, Mr. Blanton had lost two, while Mr. James Allnut and his son had lost five between them.

Mr. Romford took no advantage of their circumlocution, but keeping the fox on the green bank, maintained the ardour of the pack by repeated hoops and halloos.   So there was a very lively circle when the last of the field came up.   Facey and the fox in the centre, the baying hounds all around, Chowey and Swig outside, contributing their occasional quota of noise to the scene.

" Well (puff) done ! " exclaimed Mr. Bullpig, mopping himself.

" Capital (gasp) run ! " shouted Allnut, who had only seen half of it.

" Never saw better (puff) hounds in my life ! " asserted Mr. Large, who had never seen any but the Surrey.

Then all having come up, Chowey, at a signal from Facey, proceeded to divest the fox of his brush and his pads, prior to presenting the remainder to the hounds. Up then went the carcase, which was caught by a myriad of mouths as it fell.   Tear him and eat him, was then the cry.   And tear him and eat him they did.   The master of the circle, Facey Romford, then quitted the ring, now somewhat difficult to maintain in consequence of the struggling efforts of the fox-devouring hounds, and having decorated Master Allnut's pony with the brush, and given the pads to those who would have them, proceeded to the outer ring, to hear how things were going on there.

There was a great discussion about the time and distance.

Mr. Pyefinch said it was nine miles as the crow flies.

Doctor Snuff, who had joined promiscuously on a cob, thought it was hardly that, but it was good eight.

Mr. Kickton thought it was more than eight. It was seven to Stewley Hill, and the rocks were two good miles beyond it.

Then they appealed to Mr. Romford.

"How far should you say it was, Mr. Romford?" demanded Mr. Joseph Large, who thought he had come twenty at least.

"Faith, I've no notion!" replied Facey, adding, "he was a right good fox, anyhow."

"Capital!" ejaculated Mr. Large; adding, "It was almost a pity to kill him."

"Not a bit," retorted Facey; "always kill 'em when you can. The more you kill, the more you'll have to kill."

The teapot-handle maker didn't understand that doctrine, but took it for granted. He inwardly hoped there were not many such foxes in the country.

Then Facey, pretending that the run was nothing out of the way, remounted his horse, demanding where they should go next; whereupon they all cried "Content!" recommending him to go home and change, for he must be very wet, and began asking their own individual ways, for some people will live in a country all their lives, and yet never know where they are after hunting.

Then Mr. Bullpig, having identified Hazelton Hill, and Mr. Blanton the far-off Castlefield Clump, the respective cohorts filed off together to be further distributed as they proceeded. And Mr. Romford having looked over his hounds, and found them all right to a fraction, moved away in the direction of Middlethorpe Steeple, well pleased at having given the field such a stinger at starting. And he smoked his pipe, and played the flute with great glee, at Beldon Hall, that evening; telling Lucy and her mamma that he had given his new friends a "*deuce of a dustin'*."

CHAPTER XXVIII

MR. HAZEY AND HIS BOY BILL

A HUNTSMAN'S fame rises and falls with the sport he shows, and after such a run as that described in our last chapter, no wonder Mr. Romford's was in the ascendant. People said there was no mistake about him. He was the right man in the right place. And the tide of public opinion turned entirely in his favour. His unadorned eloquence, queer questions, and napkin-pocketing *gaucheries* were forgotten or merged in the brilliant nature of his exploits. He was a trump, and no mistake.

The run was talked of far and wide—magnified and exaggerated beyond all bounds. It was twelve miles, it was fifteen miles, and it was twenty miles. Facey swam the Lune (a navigable river), and rode up a precipice a hundred and ten feet high. It was talked of at my Lord's, at Sir Charles's, at the Hall, the House, and Grange, at the Barley Mow, the Coach and Horses, the Fox and Hounds, the Red Lion, the White Horse, the Black Horse, the Bay Horse, at all the houses of public entertainment within the limits of the Larkspur Hunt.

As it gradually reached the confines of the Larkspur country, a sort of reaction took place, and people began to be more sceptical; doubted whether Facey swam the Lune ; doubted whether he rode up the precipice ; doubted whether the run was as long as they said. If it was there must have been two foxes.

When the news got into Independent Jimmy's friend, Mr. Hazey's country, it became more and more doubted still, and some of the members of the Hard and Sharp Hunt seemed to take it amiss if any one mentioned it. Distance? Nonsense ! it was nothing of the sort. Mr. Jiggerton Jones, who was born at Brickley Hill, and knew every yard of the country, said it was barely eight miles —not eight as the crow flies. The Lune never came in the way. It was the Fleet Mr. Romford swam—anybody could leap it on foot when the waters were down. So they crabbed the great run.

Mr. Hazey heard the news with misgivings, for he had had some difficulty in holding his own even against the old Larkspur Hunt, and it was only by letting the large subscribers hoop and halloo, and do as they liked with his hounds, that he managed to keep them together. But for this they would have been straggling all over the world, some to the Larkspurs, some to Captain Copperthwaite's harriers, some to Mr. Stotfold's staghounds. Railways make sportsmen very ubiquitous. One day they are with the Queen's, another with the Quorn, a third with the Craven, or perhaps the Cheshire.

Still, Mr. Hazey hoped if Mr. Romford was the great man people represented him to be, he might yet manage to retrieve himself by a little curative horse-dealing with him.

Mr. Hazey was one of the new-fangled order of horse-dealing masters of hounds—and hunted the country for the sake of what he could make by it. We don't mean to say that he lived out of the hounds like friend Facey, because he went to a certain expense in their maintenance and education himself, but he never missed a chance of making that expense as little as possible by selling either horses or hounds to advantage. He was one of those provoking, persecuting creatures who are always pestering people about their belongings, praising their horses until one would suppose no money would induce them to part with them, and then all at once they chop over and announce that the paragon of perfection is for sale, all the previous palaverment merely tending to excite competition and enhance the price. A man doesn't deserve a good horse who is always wanting to sell him. The respectable dealers would have nothing to do with Mr. Hazey. They would meet him at the thresholds of their yards with a bow, and a " Sorry, sir, we have nothing at home that will suit you," well knowing that he would turn every horse in the yard out, and then haggle with them for a halfpenny at the end. The great Mr. Thoroughpin of Oxford Street used to say he would rather do business with two Jews than one Hazey. Then, to hear Hazey running down a horse that he wanted to buy, and afterwards running him up when he wanted to sell, was what Independent Jimmy called quite "a theatre performance." No one would suppose he was talking about one and the same animal. In buying of the farmers, he was far worse than the

regular dealers in his persecution for luck-pence and
returns, and would take anything that they would give
him—a sack of potatoes, a goose, or even his gig-hire, if
he could get nothing else. Then what trials he required
before he could be satisfied of their soundness, and how
little he gave when he came to buy ! His plan was to
canter a horse for three-quarters of an hour or so, then
take him back to the stable, and, after he had got him
cool, to shake down a veterinary surgeon as if by chance,
to scan and scrutinise his then appearance and condition.
In selling, he sternly repudiated the services of the
brotherhood, observing, they were a class of men he never
allowed to come into his stables—knew their tricks too
well for that—"gentlemen should place implicit confidence
in each other," Hazey said.

In this honourable career he was ably assisted by his
groom, James Silkey, a man who could lie like truth, and
who would swear to anything that Hazey said. Having
been long in Hazey's service, and, of course, in at a good
many robberies, Silkey had acquired a perfect mastery
over Hazey, much to the latter's inconvenience, who could
neither do with Silkey nor without him—Silkey could
expose him whenever he liked.

Not that Hazey cared a great deal for exposure ; but
Silkey, by enabling parties to put that and that together,
might bring him within reach of the law, which would be
very disagreeable in a pecuniary point of view. Indeed,
he had had once or twice to refund as it was, not caring
to trust Silkey to the cross-examination of that teasing
counsel, Serjeant Werrit. Silkey had long discarded
livery, set up a broad back, and strutted consequentially
in brown cut-aways and gaiters, talking of moy hounds,
moy horses, moy this, and moy that—but never about moy
master.

After this introduction, perhaps the reader would like
to know what sort of a looking gentleman Mr. Hazey was
—tall or short, thick or thin, dark or fair, old or young,
or middling, or how. Well, he was of the middle stature
and middling substance, stood five feet nine, and rode
eleven stone two—a convenient weight for mounting, and
dressed in a sort of semi-groomish, semi-country gentle-
manish style—cut-away coat, light vest, fancy tie, with
generally tightish drab trousers and Balmoral boots.
Being no rider, his hunting costume, of course, was a cap,

huntsmanish-cut coat, and everything very stout and substantial.

As to his age, we can hardly fix it, for he was one of those light-complexioned gentlemen who wear so well, had no whiskers, and no striking feature save cold grey eyes that wandered restlessly about a room. It wasn't the quick, piercing eye of Mr. Romford, but the sly, circumventing one that makes a man feel far more anxious for his pocket than the other. He had a son now old enough to want top-boots, viz. Mr. William Hazey, or, "my boy Bill," as his father fondly called him. Bill had left two schools with the reputation of being the worst boy at both. Being, however, his father's facsimile in mind as well as looks, he was his especial favourite, and everything seemed to be made subservient to my boy Bill. My boy Bill must have a gun-room ; my boy Bill must have a billiard-room ; my boy Bill must have a smoking-room ; my boy Bill must have everything he wanted.

To hear Mr. Hazey talk, one would fancy that his boy Bill was the best done-by boy Bill in the county ; but those who were behind the scenes said that, unless Bill's views coincided with those of his worthy father, Bill had very little chance of getting what he wanted. My boy Bill, to all appearances, had a couple of horses, and Hazey used to point him out ostentatiously to parties as Bill changed from one to the other at the cover side, exclaiming—

"*There!* there's my boy Bill ! Show me the man who turns his son out better than I turn out my boy Bill !"

But if anybody would buy my boy Bill's horse, Bill might go on foot till Hazey picked him up another twenty-pounder, to be again converted into a fifty, and sold as before.

And now, as Bill grew up to manhood, he became a sort of chaunter to his excellent parent—praised his hounds, praised his horses, praised his sport, praised everything belonging to him—was quite equal to supersede Silkey, if they could but get rid of him. Nay, more, Bill could not only praise, but anticipate objections, palliate weak points that he saw might arise, either to hounds, horses, or anything. If the Hazey carriage was not quite so good as it might be, Bill would say to a stranger as it came round to the door, "Ah, this is a coachmaker's carriage—ours is getting done up" ; or, if the horses were shabby, "Ah, these are our night-horses." So with his hay, his straw, his oats, his everything that was Hazey. Silkey, on the other hand, rather magnified deficiencies, thinking, perhaps, to make his master rectify them thereby.

CHAPTER XXIX

BILLY BALSAM AND BOB SHORT

BELDON HALL underwent a great change in its domestic arrangements soon after the visit of our friends the Watkinses, when Dirtiest of the Dirty had to act the part of footman, receive and announce the company, and reconduct them to their carriage. This proceeding Lucy did not approve; she felt it was derogatory to the dignity of the place, and inconsistent with her brother's elevated position of Master of the Larkspur Foxhounds. So, with her ready wit, she set about seeing how it could be rectified.

Now the Viscount Lovetin kept a gardener, one Billy Balsam, or Sweet William, as Mrs. Mustard lovingly called him, who, like herself, was of the poverty-stricken order; a man who was ready to turn his hand to anything in a slovenly makeshift sort of way—leaving it to the parties who employed him to judge whether he did his work properly or not. There are plenty of these sort of creatures in all countries. He had sixteen shillings a week from the Viscount for what Balsam called looking after the garden; that is to say, seeing that no one ran away with the trees, the tool-house, and anything of that sort; and the sixteen shillings a week coming in regularly, whether he worked for Lord Lovetin or not, Balsam had plenty of time for doing little things for other people— stacking hay, taking bees, killing pigs, getting in coals— any of the hundred-and-one odd jobs that are constantly occurring in the country. "Send for Billy Balsam!" was always the last resource of the destitute, just as housekeepers used to say, "Send for one of the Mustard girls!" in case of a domestic emergency.

Billy was a stout-built, well-legged man, of about sixty years of age, with a large, full, red face—the nose slightly

indicative of drink—the whole surmounted by a most
respectable silvery-grey head—just the sort of man that
a stranger would suppose had lived all his life in one
family, instead of having been in twenty different places
at least, before he alighted at Beldon Hall.

Bob Short, who dignified himself with the title of stud-
groom, being the man who answered Facey's advertisement for a "strong, persevering man, to clean horses," was
much of the same build, though possessing more brains
than Sweet William. Indeed his abundance of brains had
got him into trouble ; for, living coachman with a gentleman of large fortune who knew nothing whatever about
horses or stable-management, Bob (who quite understood
his business) had so imposed upon his master's credulity
as to bring himself within the scope of the criminal law—
that inconvenient Act, we believe, which enables justices
to dispose of certain thefts in petty sessions. Be that as
it may, however, Bob Short fell from his high estate, as
the reader may suppose, when we find him accepting such
a situation as Mr. Romford's—not that the place was
degrading, but the pay was so poor. Well, it occurred to
Lucy that one or other, or perhaps both, of these worthies
might be made available in raising a suitable Beldon Hall
establishment, and, both of them being extremely ready,
she enlisted them as occasional footmen—Sweet William
in ordinary, and Bob and he on a Sunday.

She then turned her attention to dressing them. It is
a good thing to have walked the stage ; for, besides the
easy-self-possession acquired by so doing, it not only
teaches people how to dress themselves or others up for
any particular part, but also where to get the right properties for the occasion—crowns for emperors, wreaths
for victors, helmets for soldiers, liveries for servants. And
turning to the column headed "Public Amusements" in
"Bell's Life," to see what places were open, she found her
old stage friend, Miss Betsey Shannon—of whom more
hereafter—figuring under her assumed name of Gertrude
Dalrymple at the Royal Amphitheatre over the water,
and who, she knew, would have great pleasure in executing
any commission for her. So to Miss Shannon she wrote,
asking her to send her down to Beldon Hall, in Doubleimupshire, as soon as ever she could, a couple of rich lace-
bedizened job liveries for two substantially built footmen,
in the baronial style ; adding, that she did not care so

much about price as having the liveries smart and capable
of bearing the garish light of day. And, by way of
stimulating Miss Shannon to extra exertion in the matter,
she told her, if all went right, as Lucy expected things
would, Mr. Romford would be glad to see Miss Shannon
down at the Lord Viscount Lovetin's, at Beldon Hall, to
spend the Christmas holidays. And Miss Shannon—who
dearly loved an outing into the country, and, moreover,
entertained a lively regard for her old friend and coadjutor
(then Lucy Glitters) in the sawdusted ring—exerted herself to the utmost, going from Nathan's to Levy's, and
from Levy's to Abraham's, and from Abraham's to
Solomon's, bartering and bargaining with the hook-
nosed *costumiers* till she finally settled on a couple of very
passable pea-green coats with gold aiguillettes, yellow
vests, and yellow plush breeches, at Moses Mordecay's
well-known establishment in the Minories. They had
their imperfections, it is true ; the coat buttons bearing
a lion rampant, those of the shorts "an eagle"; but
callers are generally in too great a flurry, and too busy
thinking of themselves and their own attire, to pay
attention to such minutiæ. In other respects the clothes
were very passable, and, being slightly worn, showed at
all events that the owner was not just then setting up his
servants. Indeed, it was arranged that Mrs. Somerville
should call the servants hers, which got rid of any difficulty about the Turbot-on-its-tail crest.

These liveries, then, with pink silk stockings and
buckled shoes, Miss Betsey Shannon engaged by the week,
with a considerable reduction in price if they were kept
any time, or the option of purchasing them if Mrs.
Somerville liked. Indeed, Miss Shannon executed her
commission so adroitly, flourishing Lord Lovetin's title
so imposingly, as to make Moses Mordecay believe that
the due execution of the order would be the forerunner
of a good deal of custom, and actually induced him to
part with the garments without any deposit. And no
sooner did they arrive at Beldon Hall than Lucy opened
them out and sent forthwith for Billy Balsam, notwithstanding she knew he was then particularly engaged in
killing Mr. Proudlock's pig. Billy, with the aid of hot
water, having presently made himself Sweet William again
after the operation, was then requested to try on both
suits, and present himself to Lucy in whichever fitted

him best. This he presently did, and came along a perfect figure of fun to himself and all the Dirties. "*He, he, he! ho, ho, ho! haw, haw, haw!*" laughed they. Dirty No. 2 could hardly contain herself. She thought she had never seen such a sight—no, never since the mountebanks came down.

Then Lucy took Billy through her hands : told him to hold up his head, turn out his toes, and walk as if he were a drum-major, and not as if he were wheeling a barrow full of greens along the garden walk. And she marched him round the room two or three times, telling him to look in the mirrors, and see how much better he looked with his head erect than doubled up as if he had got a touch of the stomach-ache, or had stolen a pat of butter and had it in his pocket. And Billy thought there was something in what she said, which, coupled with the promise of a shilling a day for his services, reconciled him to the situation. The ladies, in all probability, would give up laughing after they had seen him once or twice. And what a quantity of spirits the money would buy ! So he went fairly in for his lesson.

She then proceeded to show him how to open the drawing-room door and announce the guests.

"Now," said she, "this devonport," laying her pretty hand upon one at which she had been writing, "this devonport will be me ; I will be the guest—the caller, you know—Lady Kingsborough, say—and you must open the door and show me into the room, announcing me as Lady Kingsborough."

So saying, Sweet William and she withdrew, and Mrs. Somerville closed the door after her, in order that they might go through the whole ceremony. They were then in the vestibule, Mrs. Somerville now turning round to be piloted. Sweet William, however, hesitated.

"Please, mum," said he, scratching his white head, "is it to be Lady Devonport or Lady Kingsport ?"

"Oh, stoopid, no !" exclaimed Lucy ; "the devonport —the thing I showed you—is supposed to be me, and I'm Lady Kingsborough come to call upon Mrs. Somerville ; but, as I can't possibly know by intuition who is coming, you must inform me by announcing the name."

"But how am I to know ?" asked Billy Balsam.

"Oh, by asking ; or they'll tell you," replied she, adding, "you mustn't expect to find them labelled like one of your Dutch flower-roots. Now, then, walk on, chuck up your chin, open the door boldly, and conduct me up to the devonport."

Billy then did as he was bid, and after two or three attempts succeeded not so far amiss.

Then came the finishing stroke to the instructions; namely, answering the front-door bell. For this purpose, Lucy put on her hat of the day, and followed by Balsam proceeded along the passage, across the grand hall, and out at the front door, which she closed after her, telling Billy before she did so to open it boldly and well when the bell rang, and not to peep through an aperture, as if he expected a bailiff or dun. And Lucy presently sounded an alarming summons—a summons as if all the crowned heads in Europe had come—that startled old Balsam, and brought all the Dirties to the old window of observation to see what was up.

"Hut! it's only the missus," said Dirtiest of the Dirty, who had hoped to see a fine chay; and forthwith the sisters slunk off, leaving only old Mustard to witness the manœuvres of Sweet William—see him receive and set off on the return voyage of convoy—which he accomplished not amiss, though not so well as Bob Short, who had far more brains, would have done. But then the strong, persevering man had his stable to attend to, and could only be relied upon on Sundays, or for an hour or two on the very few days of the week that Mr. Romford did not hunt.

Moreover, Bob, who had worn gaudy liveries and waited occasionally, required less coaxing to get him to invest himself in the Moses Mordecay suit than Billy Balsam had done.

However, there was no help for Short's absence, and the dignity of the house was obliged to succumb to the convenience of the stable. Still, it was a great thing to have gained even two temporary footmen at a bound. And Mrs. Somerville wrote to thank Miss Betsey Shannon most sincerely for her trouble, adding that she supposed "old hook-nose" would be in no hurry for his money for the liveries—at least she hoped not—for she was sure she would be in no hurry to pay him.

CHAPTER XXX

MR. HAZEY'S MORNING CALL

THE Hazeys, like the Watkinses, were duly sensible of the importance of establishing an early acquaintance at Beldon Hall, as well for the purpose of cultivating an intimacy, as of warding off evil communications, which too often spoil good speculations. The Hazeys, too, had an enterprising daughter, of whom more hereafter. So Mr. Hazey thus had two strings to his bow, he thinking to do a little business on his own account with Mr. Romford in the horse-dealing way, Hazey's creed being to "do" other people, as he said they would "do" him if they had the chance. Then he had a good many backbiting informants to guard against, who might be stopped from telling if they knew he was on a friendly footing at Beldon Hall. For instance, there was old Mr. Mugglesworth, of Fatfield Hall, to whom he had sold a confirmed runaway as an invaluable cob for an elderly gentleman ; young Mr. Topsfield, of Meadow Bowers Bank, to whom he had sold a most incorrigible rearer as a horse a child might ride ; middle-aged Mr. Thurrock, of Barnsdale, to whom he had sold an inveterate jibber and kicker as the steadiest horse in harness that ever was seen, but which, as Silkey said, reduced the family phaeton to lucifer matches in a minute. Altogether, Hazey had a long list of victims whose tongues he would like to deprive of their sting.

Indeed, Hazey was never happy unless he was cheating somebody. No matter how much money he had, no matter how recent and vigorous had been the "do," he was always ready and eager for another. His cold, lustreless grey eyes sparkled with animation at the mere mention of a victim. He immediately set about thinking how he could circumvent him—what he could offer him—how he could coax and sneak to inveigle him. When Hazey heard that Mr. Romford had taken Doubleimupshire he was quite delighted, for the right Romford stood well with the sporting world, and Hazey's kennel being

of the third-class character, our Mr. Romford of course
had not complimented him with an order for hounds, so
the Romford reputation stood bright and unsullied. Indeed, it would have been matter difficult to come over Mr.
Hazey, for he always required payment on delivery—
horses and hounds being, he used to say, ready money.
So sly Silkey the groom used always to be charged with
a note when he delivered a horse, wherein Hazey, alluding
to the uncertainty of human life, used to request the
favour of a cheque by the bearer. Jawkins the huntsman,
too, used to have a similar missive with hounds, for which
he went snacks with his master, and therefore of course
looked to the interests of both.

Mr. Hazey's house, Tarring Neville, was about nine
miles from Beldon Hall by the road, but only some six
or seven by the fields and those convenient cuts that fox-
hunters establish during the season. Being upon two
distinct trusts, however, with an intervening mile of township road, the distance could be lengthened or contracted
according to the wishes and views of the speaker. Thus,
for instance, if Mr. Hazey wanted Mrs. Hazey and Miss
to call upon Mrs. Somerville and leave his card for Mr.
Romford, the distance would only have been seven miles
by the road ; but as Mr. Hazey disliked riding in carriages,
especially with women in hoops, the distance suddenly
elongated to eleven—"far too far," as he said, "for
calling on a short winter day, travelling over newly
metalled roads without any moon."

Moreover, Mr. Hazey wanted to look at a horse belonging to Farmer Lightcrop, of Hollywell Lane, and which
Jawkins the huntsman said had gone pretty well with
their hounds on the Friday, and which Hazey thought
might be picked up a bargain. And Sunday being a day
on which farmers' horses do not get much exercise, Hazey
thought to come upon the horse *au naturel*, without its
having had any of the bandagings and hand rubbings that
Silkey and he were so well up to giving. So when Mrs.
Hazey began hinting and suggesting, half to him, half to
her daughter, that they ought to be calling upon Mrs.
Somerville, Hazey lengthened the road, extinguished the
moon, and mounting the "friendliness-among-foxhunters
horse," proclaimed that Bill and he would ride over and
make all square with the master.

"But Mrs. Somerville ! There's Mrs. Somerville to be

considered—she can't be squared like a sportsman," exclaimed Mrs. Hazey.

"Oh yes, we'll make her all right, too," said Hazey; "I'll pretend that you didn't know that she had come, but that you will drive over and pay your respects at the earliest possible opportunity."

"But why not all go now?" asked madam.

"Oh no," retorted Hazey; "it will be far better for Bill and I to go over together and reconnoitre—see what sort of people they are, and then you will know how the land lies against you go over. Besides," added he, "Mrs. Somerville may be serious, and not like to be called upon on a Sunday."

And, this latter argument prevailing, the ladies had no alternative but to submit, and let Hazey and Bill, duly attired in duplicate riding jackets and Chipping Norton trousers, canter over together.

It was lucky for the interests of our story that it suited Mr. Hazey to go on a Sunday, and that, too, on the very first Sunday that our friends at the Hall were qualified to receive him with a proper display of footmen. Somehow, Mrs. Somerville thought there would be callers, and she not only got herself and her servants up with extra care, but hid her mother, who, in truth, was not very producible, and put old Billy Balsam through his facings, beginning at the front door and ending in the music-room, which she had fixed upon as her reception apartment. This was a beautiful, circular, domed, gilt-ceilinged apartment, fitted up with violet-coloured brocaded satin damask, a splendid Tournay carpet, and magnificent mirrors, interspersed with costly statues, china, and articles of *vertu*. It was second only to the drawing-room in point of size and magnificence.

Mr. Romford had been an advocate for living altogether in one room—the breakfast one—where, as he said, he could have his pipe and his newspaper and his flute and all things to hand; but Mrs. Somerville insisted that it would cost nothing more to live in large rooms than in small ones, and that living in the latter would add very much to their comfort and consequence. So friend Romford, who had no objection to be made a great man of, provided it cost nothing, consented, more readily perhaps when he found he could get coals from the garden for nothing—at least for a trifling tip to the cartman who led

them. Added to this, Lucy said it would keep the Dirties
better employed, and give them less time for flirting with
young Proudlock, the keeper's son, or the butcher's boy,
proceedings of which she greatly disapproved. Thus
they got into form on this conspicuous Sunday, when the
knowing Mr. Hazey came over on his complimentary
visit of inspection.

Lucy had scarcely got Balsam through his facings, and
instructed Bob Short how to support him during the
advance, than, almost with the regularity of stage effect,
the front-door bell rang a sonorous peal ; and Mrs. Somerville, after taking a last hasty glance at herself in the
statuary marble mantelpiece mirror, subsided—in a half-
recumbent attitude, with a volume of "Blair's Sermons"
in her hand—upon a richly carved and gilt sofa, covered
with violet Genoa velvet and silk fringe.

"Who can it be ?" exclaimed she.

"I wonder !" ejaculated Romford, taking a chair—an
elegant gilt one, stuffed and covered *en suite* with the sofa,
as the upholsterers would say.

"Soon see," rejoined Lucy, listening intently, with
upraised hand to keep silence.

"Must be women, with their confounded pettikits !"
observed Facey ; "and can't get out of the carriage."

"Hark, they come !" added Lucy, dropping her hand
as the solemn tramp, tramp, tramp of old Balsam's heavy
feet approached the door. It opened.

"MR. HAZEY !—MR. WILLIAM HAZEY !" now announced
Balsam—coming well into the room—in the clear, distinct
voice that Lucy had taught him ; whereupon Mrs.
Somerville laid aside her volume of "Blair's Sermons,"
and Facey arose from his white-and-gold chair, into which
he had just subsided.

Lucy, with folded arms, then made two of her best stage
curtsies, one to Hazey, the other to Bill, motioning them
respectively to conveniently placed chairs as she did it.
Facey seconded the motion, and all parties presently got
seated.

Mrs. Somerville, as usual, was extremely neat, and her
beautiful hair was arranged to perfection.

"Mr. Hazey !—Mr. William Hazey !" muttered Romford, conning the matter over in his mind, as he scrutinised
the two with his little, roving pig-eyes. "Mr. Hazey
and Mr. William Hazey ! Dash it ! this is the hard and

sharp man—the chap the busman told me of." And
Romford reckoned Hazey up in a minute. " Looks more
like a muffin-maker than a master of hounds," thought he.

Mr. Hazey felt rather uncomfortable, for he was now
in the presence of a highly bred gentleman, to whom a
nobleman had lent his house, thus stamping him, as it
were, with the impress of friendship ; and he thought,
perhaps, that Mrs. Hazey ought to have accompanied
him in this visit of ingratiation. Added to which, he
wasn't sure that he would be welcome on a Sunday.
However, he got over that difficulty by recollecting that
the old peacocks of footmen who let him in should have
said "Not at home," if Mr. Romford or Mrs. Somerville
did not mean to see him ; so, omitting the paragraph
he had arranged in two sections in his own mind—one
referring to his own occupations as a master of hounds
on the week days, the other alluding to the greater
certainty of finding Mr. Romford and Mrs. Somerville
together at home on a Sunday—he began to strain at
an apology for Mrs. Hazey not coming, declaring she
had got such a cold, she could hardly hold her head
up. Whereas, his boy Bill knew that Hazey would not
let her have the carriage.

And Mrs. Somerville, who didn't care much about
seeing Mrs. Hazey, accepted the apologies with the
greatest readiness, expressing her obligations for the
intention, but her hopes that Mrs. Hazey would not
think of coming until she was quite well, reflecting all
the while on the good luck that Romford and she were
in, by having got into the music-room, with the mirrors
uncovered, and all the beautiful china and statuary
displayed.

Romford's mind, meanwhile, ran upon the probability
of his guests wanting luncheon, and the unpleasantness
of seeing his dinner voraciously dispatched before his
eyes.

The weather having been duly produced and disposed
of, Mr. Romford began to sound his brother-master on
the subject of hunting—scent, hounds, horses, the system
of kennel—each thinking how he would like to have
a chance of cheating the other : Romford settling in
his own mind that the nutmeg-grey that scrubbed against
carriages would carry Hazey capitally ; Hazey, on his
part, wondering whether Lightcrop's horse would be

up to Mr. Romford's weight. He (Romford) didn't look such a monster out of his hunting things as people said he was.

"Yours is a three-days-a-week pack, I think," said Facey, with the patronising air of a man who hunts four.

"Three and a bye," replied Hazey, anxious to make the most of himself.

"Not often a bye, I should think," thought Facey, scrutinising him attentively.

"I wonder you don't hunt four reg'larly," said Facey; "if it was only for the sake of havin' the same hounds out together."

"Well—yes—no—yes!" hesitated Hazey; "only ours is a country that lames a good many hounds, and I shouldn't like to attempt more than I could accomplish satisfactorily."

"Only a question of a few more horses and hounds," replied Facey.

"Yes; but, then, horses and hounds involve £—s—d," rejoined Hazey, with a solemn shake of the head.

"Fiddle the farthins!" exclaimed Facey; "fiddle the farthins!—I mean, grudge money for huntin'! Give anything for good hounds — anything in moderation, at least," added he.

"Ah, but then we haven't all got Mr. Romford's deep purse to dive into," rejoined Hazey, with a deferential bow to our great master. Hazey always wished to impress upon his boy Bill that he was poor.

They then got into a dissertation upon hounds— Hazey expatiating learnedly upon legs and loins; Facey insisting upon nose as the *sine quâ non*.

"*Nose, nose, nose*, is my motto," said Facey, thumping Lord Lovetin's fine marqueterie centre table as he spoke. "Legs are of no use," repeated he, "if they only drive the nose beyond the scent."

Then Hazey sought to sound his brother-master on the interesting subject of subscription; whether his was guaranteed, whether it was well paid, whether he paid much for cover rent, or had the country found.

Upon this subject, however, friend Facey could really give him very little information. There was, he said, a subscription attached to the country, and he meant to maintain it, not on his own account, because in all probability he should let it accumulate, to found what he had always been most anxious to see, namely, a hospital for decayed sportsmen; but because it might not be convenient to after-comers to hunt the country without a subscription, and indeed, upon the whole, he thought it rather tended to encourage sport, inasmuch as people always thought more highly of what they paid for, than what they had for nothin'; and, altogether, Facey talked in such a magnificent way as fairly to shut up Mr. Hazey. The latter sat half lost in astonishment at Mr. Romford's liberality, yet half afraid that he might ask him to contribute to the funds for the hospital.

So they were mute for a time.

Mr. Facey saw that he had taken the wind out of his brother-master's sails, and he wondered how long he was going to sit, and whether the mention of lunch would help to send him away. He thought it might, provided it were done cleverly. He would try.

"You're *sure* you won't take any lunch," at length observed he, as if he had offered it before, muttering something about Cambridge brawn, venison pastry, rabbit pie (which latter there was); but Facey put such a decided negative upon his own proposition, that, though both Hazey and his boy Bill were extremely hungry and anxious for something to eat, yet neither of them had the courage to say that they would take any. Then, by way of keeping them up to the mark, Facey indulged in a tirade against luncheons generally, saying he never took any—he hated to fritter away a good appetite piecemeal —adding, that if a man was hungry, he had better dine at once, and not make two bites of a cherry, as some did.

The last ray of hope being thus utterly extinguished, there was nothing for it but to arise and depart; so, after a few observations about the crops and the state of the country, Hazey gave the boy Bill a wink, who forthwith used his leg like a mace, to draw his truant hat from under the table, and Hazey, having clutched his arm, arose, greatly in doubt, like the Watkinses, as to the right course to pursue, whether to offer his hand, or wait for Mr. Romford to tender his; whether to go boldly up to Mrs. Somerville, and take his chance of a shake, or to bow from where he stood, and so lose the intimation the shake, if he got one, might convey.

Romford, however, quickly cut the Gordian knot by

tendering his great heavy hand to them both, in turn ;
while Mrs. Somerville, rising from her violet-velvet
throne, first rang the bell to summon the servants, and
then, folding her arms, gave a couple of those captivating
smiles and curtsies wherewith she used to express her
gratitude to a Surrey audience after an *encore*. Nothing
could be better done, for it relieved Mr. Hazey at once,
letting him see that, though Mr. Romford was called
upon, Mrs. Somerville would not consider herself properly
visited until Mrs. Hazey had been there. Then the
smiles were so sweet as to satisfy Mr. Hazey that she considered his part of the compliment properly performed.
So he backed gaily towards the now opened door, treading
heavily on the angry corns of old Balsam, who happened
to have obtruded his great foot in the way. Then
Short, seeing what had happened, took the lead towards
the front door, leaving the now string-halting Balsam to
follow at his leisure.

"Away they go !" said Romford to Lucy, as the music-
room door closed, adding, "now let you and I go and see
them off." So saying, Facey led the way to a side door
that communicated with the back passage.

Lucy and he then ascended the back stairs, and taking
up positions on either side of the usual window of
observation, generally occupied by the Dirties, obtained
a good view of the mount.

"It will be incumbent upon us to do that beggar,"
whispered Facey to Lucy, as Hazey, with a *dégagé* air,
approached the blue-coated, leather-breeched, cockaded
groom, who now hurried his horses up to the front door,
whither the guests were conducted by Balsam and Short
in due form.

"They tell me that's the biggest rogue under the sun,"
continued Facey, as Hazey now swung himself carelessly
into his saddle, and tit-tupped away from the door,
provoking the caper that he seemed to chide.

Then, meeting old Balsam as they returned to the
music-room, Lucy complimented him upon his performance, while Facey gave him a couple of ounces of shag, and
a bottle of Lord Lovetin's Old Tom gin to drink with it.

And as Hazey trotted gaily home, he thought to
improve the occasion by pointing out to his boy Bill the
superiority of well-bred people's manners over commoner
ones, illustrating his position by a comparison of Mrs.

Somerville's with those of Mrs. Watkins', greatly to the advantage of Mrs. Somerville; and there being now the chance of an intercourse, Mr. Hazey promoted a call from his wife, cushioning that inconvenient question, "Who is Mrs. Somerville?" with a general assertion that she was an extremely lady-like woman, who would be a great acquisition in Doubleimupshire. And Hazey reported most favourably of the Beldon establishment, saying, that the butler was out, but they were received by two most respectable-looking family footmen — not little, weedy, calveless shrimps, but great substantial men, who looked as if they had lived in the family all their lives. And Mrs. Hazey thought she would like to give them a mistress as well as a master.

CHAPTER XXXI

MR. AND MRS. WATKINS AGAIN

THE usual three days' law having elapsed, our friends at Dalberry Lees began to look out for the return visit from our new master of hounds and his elegant sister Mrs. Somerville, whereupon to found the further ingratiation of an invitation to dinner. Mrs. Lubbins was anxious to be doing, not having had an uproar for some time. But from the circumstance of the tight-booted teapot-handle maker having been mainly instrumental in resuscitating the Larkspur hunt under the auspices of Mr. Romford (believing him to be the other Mr. Romford), the honour of the opening meet would most likely have been accorded to the gentleman "who hunted for conformity," viz. Mr. Watkins of Dalberry Lees, who gave his £100 a year to the hounds, and paid it punctually, which, we are sorry to say, was more than all the Doubleimupshireites did. However, the teapot-handle maker had it, and the Watkinses consoled themselves with the reflection that Mr. Romford would soon find out what upstarts the Joseph Larges were, and appreciate them (the Watkinses) accordingly. It, therefore, did seem rather strange that our captivating heiress, Miss Cassandra Cleopatra, should array herself

in her most becoming attire—one morning in cerulean
blue, another in delicate pink, a third in virgin white
with puce trimmings, and that no Mr. Romford, no Mrs.
Somerville, should draw near the scene of her attractions.
The Brogdales came, and the Bigmores came, and Mr.
and Mrs. Nackington came; but they didn't want any
of these. They wanted Mr. Romford—Romford *alone*, if
they could get him, if not, with any other person.

But when Independent Jimmy let out as he did to
Miss Florence Brown, their lady's maid, as he gave her
a lift home on the bus from Mother Floyd's, the wise
woman of the district, whom she had been to consult
when she (Florence) would be married, that second-hand
Neddy, as Jimmy called Mr. Hazey, had been at Beldon
Hall, Mrs. Watkins—all things considered—resolved that
it was time to lay aside ceremony, and go boldly in for
their dues. The Larges had not been punctilious, and
she was quite sure the Hazeys wouldn't, so she wouldn't
either. And the bloom having been taken off the in-
troductory process by the Pippin Priory breakfast, Mrs.
Watkins resolved not to wait any longer for the ceremony
of the return call, but to assume the neighbourly fashion,
and ask Mr. Romford and his sister Mrs. Somerville to
come and dine, and stay all night at Dalberry Lees, and
let the hounds meet there on the morrow.

In truth, Lubbins had rather fallen off in her cooking
for want of practice, and had it not been that the wages
were large, and the "kitchen-stuff" liberal, she would
infallibly have been turning Watkins's off; for she was
a show-off cook, and required the excitement of brandy
and constant display: she didn't undertake mere family
dinners. The kitchen-maid could do those. But as somehow people will not lend themselves out for the mere
purpose of eating and drinking and showing their clothes,
so the Watkins's invitation became more and more shirked
(causing, we fear, a considerable amount of falsehood, too
easily detected in the country), until they could hardly
raise a party at all. In vain they protracted the length
of their invitations—drew upon their acquaintances at
three weeks instead of ten days or a fortnight. It always
came to the same thing in the end—the table had to be
shortened a third, if not full half; and the least desirable
part of the company only coming under these circumstances, the reader will readily imagine how important

it was to the Watkinses, bent altogether on ostentatious display, to make the most of such an attraction as a new master of hounds—especially a master so favourably circumstanced as the great Mr. Romford of Abbeyfield Park and Beldon Hall, J.P., D.L., patron of, etc. Miss, too, as we have said before, was marriageable ; indeed had had two or three indifferent offers—a curate, a cornet, and a nibble from a count, or a person who called himself one—though some said he was only a courier. And hope deferred having made Mrs. Watkins's heart rather sick, she resolved to be doing without further delay. So, having duly consulted Lubbins as to the state of the larder, Miss Cassandra Cleopatra, who acted as amanuensis for mamma, drew forth a sheet of her highly-musked cream-laid note-paper, and with many twirls of the pen, and appeals to the ceiling for inspiration, at length produced the following document :—

"DALBERRY LEES,
" *Tuesday*.

"MY DEAR MRS. SOMERVILLE,—If Mr. Romford has not yet fixed his meets for next week, would you oblige me by having one here, and giving us the pleasure of your company the day before, when we will endeavour to get a few sporting neighbours to meet you ? We dine at seven ; but, as there is no moon, pray come early. Mr. Watkins (who promises Mr. Romford a good fox) joins in kindest regards with, my dear Mrs. Somerville. Ever yours, very sincerely,   LETITIA WATKINS."

To which, in order to prevent any mistake, Willy caused to be added the following :—

"*P.S.*—Of course you will stay all night."

The note, thus amended, was then sealed with the large butter-pat seal of the Watkins's arms—three rings, three doves, three bulls, four bears, and five stags ; and, after a division as to whether Lord Lovetin's arms should be added or not, it was decided that it would be grander to do so, and the note was ultimately addressed to—

"MRS. SOMERVILLE,
"At the Right Honourable
"Lord Viscount Lovetin's,
"Beldon Hall,"
and dispatched by a groom in the Watkins's livery.

The note produced very different sensations in the
mind of Mrs. Somerville and her pseudo-brother Mr.
Romford : Mrs. Somerville was all for going to Dalberry
Lees ; Mr. Facey was all for staying at home. He didn't
feel comfortable out, he said. The napkin business had
rather upset him, Lucy having explained to him that
they were not meant to carry away ; and she had had
the Pippin Priory one washed and returned with a note,
saying that her brother had taken it away accidentally
in his 'kerchief. Then Facey hadn't a dress-coat ; but
Lucy would undertake that Tick would have one down
in no time. Still he demurred. The women bothered
him. He didn't know what to say to them. He didn't
know how to get them in to dinner. He didn't know
how to get them out again. But Lucy combated all
the objections. She would tell him what to say ; she
would teach him what to · do. He should have one of
the Dirties in, to practise with beforehand. Very little
talk did for the mistress of the house, who was always
too busy thinking about her dinner, and praying that
the sweets might come in safe, to pay much attention
to what was said. And so poor Facey was at length
obliged to submit ; and having duly conned over his
country as far as he knew it, he determined to meet at
Dalberry Lees on the Wednesday, which would give him
the non-hunting Tuesday to get there upon. Whereupon
Lucy reciprocated the sweetness of Mrs. Watkins's note,
and sent her answer back with the turbot-seal crest.
She then wrote off to town for a dress-coat for Facey,
scarlet, with velvet collar and frosted buttons ; and then
began to consider what she herself should wear on the
important occasion.

Great was the joy at Dalberry Lees on receipt of the
Beldon Hall answer, and forthwith Miss Watkins was
reinstalled at her pembroke writing-table, issuing the
first batch of invitations for parties to come to meet
Mr. Romford and Mrs. Somerville at dinner on Tuesday
next, apologising for the shortness of the notice, and
requesting the favour of an early answer. And, as guests
will come if you can only bait the trap properly,—and
there was a good deal of excitement and curiosity in the
country about the new master and his handsome sister,—
the party was soon made up, much to the joy of the
Watkins's and the satisfaction of Mrs. Lubbins, who

had really begun to think she would never have another
uproar worth mentioning at Dalberry Lees, and who
instantly commenced a grand scouring of the country for
consumables.

CHAPTER XXXII

DALBERRY LEES

THE Watkinses were now in their glory ; dressing and
dinner-giving being about the extent of Willy's
ability, while the ladies thought simpering and expanding their persons in preposterous crinolines were -the
great end and aim of society. These are the people who
exaggerate a fashion till they make it ridiculous. They
looked forward with great pleasure to showing off their
new dresses, and felt the importance to be acquired by
entertaining the new master. Mrs. Somerville, too, was
a charming woman ; and altogether they were most
fortunate in securing them. The outside plot thickened.
So far from people shirking them, as they used to do,
they asked to be allowed to bring friends, to exchange
a son for a daughter, or vice versa. There was a great
desire to see Mr. Romford in a room. Some said he was
a bear, others that he was a beau. There was a great
difference of opinion. They wanted to judge for themselves.

The Romfords, on their part, set about maintaining
their position. Mr. Tick, of Civil Row, responded
gallantly to Lucy's order, sending Mr. Facey down a
splendid scarlet dress-coat, with crimson velvet collar,
silk linings and facings ; also a pair of speculative black
kerseymeres and two white vests ready for putting on ;
altogether rather a striking get-up, and most handsomely
packed in a new deal box, directed to " Francis Romford,
Esq., at the Lord Viscount Lovetin's, Beldon Hall. By
passenger train."

Though the address of Beldon Hall alone was tolerably
taking, still Lucy found that the addition of the "Lovetin" title precipitated orders very considerably. Indeed,

she felt as if she could have half London for sending for.
And she was no niggard in her orders, either for Facey,
her mother, or herself; writing for cloaks, Malta shawls,
mantles, muffs, and Spanish mantillas, for herself;
Stiltons, and bloaters, and nourishing stout—whatever
the Lovetin cellar was without—for Facey.

Whenever Lucy received an article of dress that she
did not like, she repacked it and sent it to Betsey
Shannon, or some of her old stage friends, as a present.
Her dashed dresses she adapted to Ruth Mustard—
Dirtiest of the Dirty, as she was originally called, but
who, under Lucy's skilful guidance, presently became
" Cleanest of the Clean."

Ruth, as we said before, was a pretty girl—pretty even
in *déshabillé*,—very pretty when cleaned and properly put
on; and she took to lying as readily as she had done to
picking and stealing.   Though Mrs. Somerville couldn't
hope to pass her off at Dalberry Lees as anything but a
Mustard, still she held out to Ruth that if her own maid,
who she said was at Tunbridge Wells for the benefit of
her health, did not get better, Ruth might, by due care
and attention, be installed in her very lucrative place;
so that Dirtiest of the Dirty was for the present entitled
to rank as a lady's maid in the table of precedence
amongst servants.

And to the now all-absorbing Dalberry Lees feast let
us now devote our attention.

It may seem strange in these gastronomic times, when
a master of hounds is supposed to be able to eat two or
three dinners a day, that Mr. Romford should have got
through so long a time with the Heavyside Hunt without
ever having assisted at any of their festivities; but so it
was, and he had now all his duties in the eating line to
learn and perform.   Of course he had often put in at
Squire This or Farmer That's for a " snack," and came out
with a wedge of cheese in one hand and a slice of bread
in the other; but those scrambles have no sort of affinity
to the stately solemnities of modern English dinner-
parties.   Lucy felt this, and greatly feared that her
brother Romford might commit himself if he had not
some little previous instruction; and, knowing the nature
of rehearsals, she got up a drawing-room scene by seating
Dirtiest of the Dirty in a chair in the breakfast-room,
while Facey hovered near till Dirty No. 2 (supposed to be

the Watkins's butler) entered the room and announced dinner; whereupon Facey, tendering his arm to Dirtiest of the Dirty, led her off to the Beldon Hall dining-room, just as he would have to lead off Mrs. Watkins or some other lady at the Dalberry Lees feast. As to talking, Lucy again assured Facey very little conversation would do; a few compliments on the ladies' dress, or remarks on the weather, or the splendour of the house, being amply sufficient. All he had to mind was, if he came after another lady, not to tread on her train. And after two or three attempts, our master of the hounds accomplished the dining-room manœuvre pretty well, though he still did not like the idea of what he had to go through after.

"All very well," muttered he, "tellin' one there's nothin' to do after; it's very much like tellin' a man there's nothin' on the other side of the fence, when perhaps there's a great yawnin' ditch big enough to hold both him and his horse."

However, friend Facey felt he was committed to the engagement, and, much as he disliked the idea, he must go through it with courage and fortitude. "Grin and bear it," as he said. So he left the rest of the arrangements to Lucy.

At length came the all-important day, and with it came Independent Jimmy, and the melon frame, to convey our party to Dalberry Lees,—Mr. Romford, Mrs. Somerville, and Dirtiest of the Dirty.

"Ye cannot all get in there," said Jimmy, looking round, as the trio appeared at the door to follow their boxes into the frame.

"No: I'm goin' outside with you," replied Facey, chucking his grey wing cape on to the box; and, leaving Lucy and her maid to cram in as they could, he bounded up, and was presently sharing the box-seat apron with Jimmy.

"*Gip!*" said Jimmy, jerking his reins as he heard the door close; and away they rumbled, Jimmy applying the brake to the wheel down the hill to the lodges, lest the vehicle should· run the old weak nags off their legs. They presently shot through them at a sort of shuffling canter.

"Dalberry Lees," now announced Facey, as they got upon the turnpike.

"Thout ye'd be gannin' there," replied Jimmy; "left some fish and pea-soup there i' the mornin'."

"Soup and fish?" said Facey. "Don't they make pea-soup at home?"

"A—why—yes," replied Jimmy, flourishing his flagellator. "It wasn't pea-soup; it was some stuff they get from Lunnon—tortle they call it; comes from the Ship and Tortle Tavern."

"The deuce!" exclaimed Facey, half afraid of the consequences; "goin' to have a reg'lar blow-out, are they?"

"Blow-out, ay! bout up half the poltry in the country."

"*Humph!*" grunted Mr. Romford, seeing his worst fears were about to be realised. He had dreamt that he had tumbled over a poodle in the drawing-room, and squirted a bottle of porter right into a lady's face. "Who's there goin' besides ourselves?" asked Romford, wishing to know the worst at once. "Better be killed than frightened to death," thought he.

"A, why, the house is full; and arre got to go for the Dobbinsons after ar set ye doon, and then for aud Mowser and the Dusts. Arm sure ar don't know when ar shall get them all there." Saying which, Jimmy gave each of his old nags a refresher with his whip, as if to say, "Let us get ye set doon as quick as ar can." So they bowled along at a somewhat amended pace.

There was indeed a great to-do at Dalberry Lees. It was so long since the Watkinses had had a great spread, that many things had "gone to pieces quite cliver" in the hands of the servants since the event. The late butler, for instance, had imposed upon ingenuous Willy by showing him a shelf full of lamp-glasses when he left, saying he "'Sposed he needn't take them all down," and when they came to be wanted taken down they were all found to be broken, the whole sides having been placed outside for show. Many other departments were in a similar state of dilapidation, so that the energies of the family were by no means confined to the acquisition of fish, soups, or poultry. Besides, a dinner-party and a house full of company are very different things. A dinner-party can combine the united services of the whole establishment; whereas a house full of company scatters the forces to the different departments, thus depriving the commander-in-chief of any extra assistance.

Then, what with men who come without valets, men who come without grooms, coachmen who won't wash their masters' carriages, to say nothing of the requirements of those most elegant and sensitive creatures, the ladies' maids—who are often much more difficult to please than their mistresses,—the house is regularly turned upside-down. The servants considering their characters for hospitality quite as much involved as those of their masters, the only wonder is that anything gets into the dining-room at all. On the last occasion, when Willy thought to have a nice dish of hashed venison for his dinner after the company were gone, he found some lingering grooms had eaten it all for their luncheons! Very different are the toils of town hospitality to those of the country.

But we are now approaching those magnificent crest-decorated lodges that aroused Independent Jimmy's wrath on the occasion of the Romfords' arrival, and the leafless trees show the glittering sun lighting up the many-windowed house as if for a complimentary illumination. A rather winding approach through a few flat iron-fenced fields discloses its further proportions; not so fine as Pippin Priory, not so large as Beldon Hall, but still very good and comfortable. Facey, however, wished himself going away from it instead of coming. A few jip-jips and jerk-jerks from Independent Jimmy lays the vehicle well alongside the blue pipe-clayed steps of the sash-windowed front-door, and Jimmy's ring immediately conjures up a tableau of livery footmen with a portly butler in the background. The melon-frame compartments then began to fold, slide, and recede, and the iron steps being clattered down, first Lucy and then Dirty, being extricated from their confinement, began to shake themselves out to their natural, or rather unnatural, proportions. Mr. Romford, too, alights, and stamps and flops himself generally—thinking that life would be very pleasant if it were not for its enjoyments.

"Ar'll tac the luggage roond," now said Independent Jimmy, regaining his box, whereupon Lucy took Mr. Romford's arm, while Dirtiest of the Dirty sheered off for the back settlements under convoy of a passing page. The procession then proceeded.

"Mr. Romford and Mrs. Somerville," announced Lucy, slowly and distinctly to Mr. Burlinson, the portly butler

who now duly received them at the hands of his subal-
terns the footmen, and forthwith proceeded to pilot them
along the passages just as he used to pilot the great guests
at his late master's, Lord Omnibus, until the exigencies
of Burlinson's betting-book compelled him to pawn his
lordship's plate. Burlinson, like Bob Short, had under-
gone captivity ; but we will draw a veil over all that.
We are now going to raise the curtain for the domestic
tableau of " reception "—or, perhaps, " deception."

Although when the Romford-Somerville alarm-bell
rang, Mrs. Watkins was half choked with anger at
Priscilla Pallister, the housemaid, for not having the
best lace-fringed toilet-cover on to Mrs. Somerville's
dressing-table, she yet managed to smother the remainder
of her rage, and had subsided into a luxurious cabriole
frame chair in burnished gold, covered in needlework,
with a copy of the " Cornhill Magazine " in her hand,
when her visitors were heralded into her splendid drawing-
room by her obsequious butler. Miss, too, who had
been busy examining the fit and folds of her new dress in
her own cheval glass, had rushed down the back stairs
and got herself settled to her harp, the exertion of
running imparting a slight glow to her naturally pale
cheek. Mrs. Watkins was so absorbed with her book that
Burlinson had opened the door and got his guests piloted
half up the room ere she awoke to a consciousness of the
presence of strangers, when, laying down the number on
the table, she hastily arose and advanced to meet them.
Standing on her own territory, surrounded with elegance
and splendour, she felt that now was her time to patronise ;
so, meeting Mrs. Somerville, she seized her eagerly with
both hands and imprinted a kiss on her right cheek.
Facey stood transfixed, for he was not sure but he ought
to reciprocate the compliment ; but Lucy, anticipating
the dilemma, just drew him a little forward, saying, with
a pressure on his arm, " My brother, Mr. Romford " ; and
the gobby girl then entering the room and joining
the group, they got through the presentations without
further confusion. Chairs were then the order of the
day.

If the half-hour before a London dinner-party is a
bore, pity, oh, pity—the sorrows of a man—a poor young
man—condemned to two mortal hours in the country
before that interesting period. Tea has somewhat come

in to the relief of the ladies, but it does nothing for men —especially those unaccustomed to take the bloom off their appetites. Indeed it was rather a stumbling-block to friend Facey; for Mrs. Watkins, having proposed some to Lucy, who declined it, said she supposed it was no use offering any to Mr. Romford, whereupon our master replied, "No; he'd come to dine, and not to tea," an observation that the gobby girl giggled at, thinking it was meant to be funny.

And here let us say a little more about our heroine— heroine No. 2, at least, for we mean to be so extravagant as to indulge in two. If Miss Cassandra Cleopatra would not have been picked out as a beauty in a crowd, she would nevertheless have passed muster as an exceedingly showy, handsomely dressed girl, being well set up and set out, with a calm, cool self-possession, betokening either perfect ease or perfect indifference. Taken, however, singly, as we have her this evening, without any competitor, surrounded by all the luxuries and elegancies of life, she was calculated to make a speedy impression, and as she lithped and talked—and lithped and talked, now about horthes, now about houthes, Facey gradually and insensibly began to be attracted by her. At first he thought her lisp was affected, and that she ought to be whipped, but he soon got used to it, and then thought it rather pretty indeed. He presently summed up his observations by a mental repetition of the opinion he delivered as he saw her getting into the carriage at Beldon Hall, namely, that she was a good-like lass.

While all this was going on, Mr. Willy Watkins, whose whole soul, as we said before, was centred in dressing and dinner-giving, was taking his last survey of the dining-room, preparatory to handing it over to Lieutenant-Colonel Burlinson. It was, indeed, a grand display. There wasn't an article of plate in the house, except perhaps Willy's silver shaving-box, but what was enlisted into the service, either on the table or sideboards.

At length, having got everything most tastefully arranged on the usual principle of appearing to have twice as much money as they had, Willy took a last lingering look, and then, passing noiselessly into the passage, crowned himself with a drab wideawake, with an eagle's feather in the parti-coloured band, and came whistling along into the drawing-room, as if unaware of any arrival.

"Ah, my dear Mrs. Somerville!" exclaimed he, with a well-feigned surprise, advancing gaily towards her with extended hand, "I didn't know you were come. Pray, 'soucse my not being in to receive you," continued he, as he squeezed the pretty widow's little hand with considerable *empressement*. Mrs W. couldn't see that, he knew.

Then, without waiting for an introduction, he turned short upon Facey, with his puddingy paw, and said—

"Most happy to see you, sir," shaking his hand as he said it. "I hope you are quite well, Mr. Romford? I hope your hounds are quite well. I hope your horses are quite well?" Just as if they formed part of the family.

Romford assured him they were all quite well, and would be ready to bucket a fox for him in the mornin'. Whereupon the dreadful word fox shot through Willy's heart like a dagger, and almost deprived him of utterance.

"Why were foxes ever made?" thought he. "Confound their nasty aroma! Confound their nasty precipitation!"

Then Facey, ever anxious to do business, began sounding him about the game at Dalberry Lees; whether there were any pheasants, whether there were many hares; if there would be any harm in his looking over the place occasionally with his dog and his gun, meaning, of course, might he shoot there. And while the photographer in vain endeavoured to read his wife's meaning by her looks, the waning day was suddenly extinguished by the entry of the servants with lights—lights—more lights.

This gave Mrs. Watkins an opportunity of saying that perhaps Mrs. Somerville might like to see her room; which offer being joyfully accepted, the drop-scene presently fell on the first act of the Dalberry Lees drama, by Mr. Watkins leading Facey off to his apartment.

It must be a great relief to a lady getting away from the forced conversation of the overture to the tranquillity of her own bedroom, there to economise and rearrange her small talk, and contemplate the coming glory— perhaps victory of dress.

On a spacious sofa, between the magnificent bed and

the sparkling wood and coal fire, lay a most voluminous coloured-ribboned and twilled and flounced and flowered *robe*, so puffy and distended that a little distance would have made it look like a lady reclining at her ease.

On a richly inlaid Indian work-table on the right lay a splendid wreath of pearls, with three important pendants.

"Oh, what loves of pearls!" ejaculated Mrs. Watkins, clasping her hands, thinking how she would cut Mrs. Somerville down with her diamonds.

Meanwhile, Mr. Watkins having got Mr. Romford into the state bedroom, looked round with an air of complacency, hoping there was every thing our master wanted, adding, that there was plenty of time to dress, the first gong not having sounded, and there would be half an hour after that. And, having withdrawn, Facey, who could jump into his clothes in ten minutes, thought, that as he might not get his pipe after dinner, he had better have it before. So drawing a lounging chair to the fire, he dived into his side-pocket for the material, and was presently blowing a cloud, with a grand illumination going on all around. He didn't care for the candles—not he. A most scientific roll of thunder then presently proceeded from the gong, reminding Lucy of the cavern scene in *Der Freischutz*, and noting the lapse of time to friend Facey. Having finished his pipe, he then inducted himself into his new clothes—so handsomely furnished on credit.

After a satisfactory contemplation of himself in the mirror, he at length left the elegant room; and, following the richly patterned crimson stair-carpet down below, he presently found himself in a confluence of comers and stayers, all making for the drawing-room door. There was Mr. Burlinson receiving the candle of one guest and the name of another, while a couple of footmen stood bowing and motioning the ladies to Mr. Watkins's study, now made into a cloak-room for them. Mr. Romford then walked into the drawing-room with the consequence of a master of hounds, combined with the air of a man having a billet for the night. The man who sleeps where he dines always has a sort of crow over the pumps and pocket-comb one, who has to turn out in the cold—snow, blow, wind, or rain, whatever may have chanced to come in the meantime. What a bore, turning

out and finding the country half a foot under snow—
getting·a shoeful of it at starting by way of convincing
one of the fact!

CHAPTER XXXIII

THE DALBERRY LEES UPROAR IN HONOUR OF
MR. ROMFORD

PEOPLE will talk to each other even up to the last
moment—while some even begin before a quick-
eared departing listener is well out of hearing. Mr.
Romford, on entering the drawing-room, now disturbed
a covey of male and female inquisitives all clustered
around Burke's bulky book of the Landed Gentry, as it
lay open on the richly covered side-table. We need
scarcely say they were down on the letter "R"—R, for
Romford—Romford, here it is!—"Romford, Francis,
Abbeyfield Park, J.P., D.L., patron of three livings"—
that's your man.

It seems that old Miss Mowser, who knew, or pretended
to know, everything, had raised a doubt as to the identity
of our hero, Miss Mowser contending that the Abbeyfield
Romford was a little man with dark hair, whereas this
Mr. Romford was said to be a big one with red or gingery
hair. Not that she had ever seen either Mr. Romford,
but—— and here her narrative was interrupted by the
entry of the big Mr. Romford himself. Hush! was then
the word. The book closed, and parties shied away from
the table as if they had not been looking at it, but at
"Ye Manners and Customs of the English" instead. Mr.
Watkins then advanced to do the duties of induction by
presenting some of the non-hunting portion of his patrons
—Mr. Romford, Mr. Lolley; Mr. Romford, Mrs. Dobbinson; Mr. Romford, Mr. Dust; and one gave him a bow,
and another a hand, and a third both bow and hand.
Then some sportsmen came wriggling up; men whom he
ought to know, but, somehow, could not identify without
their coats and their caps; and Facey addressed one man
as Silver, who he ought to have called Salver; and

another, whose grandfather had been a hatter, by his nickname of Mr. Felt, instead of that of Mr. Finch. Altogether he was very uncomfortable, and felt he was making a mull of it. Why the deuce did he come ? He had plenty to eat at home—drink too. He didn't know what to do ; whether to stand by the fire or sit on the sofa, or take up a paper and pretend to read.

Lucy, on her part, was as cool and collected as a handsome, well-dressed woman who has received the unanimous plaudits of the gods of the Victoria Theatre might be expected to be, conscious that the ladies must admire her new dress, whatever they thought of her figure and complexion. The gentlemen, she knew, would admire those and her figure not the less for being finely developed. So she twisted and turned, and smiled, and showed her fine shoulders and her fine teeth, and laid herself out for general admiration. And a good deal of admiration she got, much to Miss Watkins's mortification, who did not fancy being cut out in that way in her papa's own house. But she would try if she couldn't upset Mrs. Somerville from Beldon Hall. So she quietly bided her time.

At length Mr. Burlinson the butler's large white waistcoat was seen looming up the room, without the customary convoy of guests, and Mr. Watkins, who had previously requested friend Facey to take his wife into dinner, having finished a platitude he was enunciating about the state of the moon, now presented his great red arm to Mrs. Somerville and led her off to the radiant apartment illuminated with the joint efforts of fire, candles, and oil. It was a perfect blaze of light. Mrs. Somerville having trod the passage, entered the dining-room with measured step, like a Tragedy Queen, and subsided in her seat on Mr. Watkins's right.

Then Dirtiest of the Dirties' lessons operated favourably ; for Facey, having seen Lolley, and Dobbinson, and Dust, the man whom he called Silver (but Salver), Felt, and all duly passed off, brought up the rear with Mrs. Watkins : our master inwardly hoping, as he crossed what he called the vale of the entrance-hall, that—in schoolboy parlance—her meat might presently stop her mouth. So they sailed majestically up the spacious dining-room to the top of the table, where, by one of those masterly manœuvres that ladies understand so much better than men, Facey found Cassandra Cleopatra spreading her

napkin over her voluminous dress on his right, just as
Mrs. Watkins subsided in her great arm-chair on the left.
"Rot it," thought Romford, "but I shall be talked to
death between you." He then picked the bun out of his
napkin, and spreading as much of the latter over his legs
as his fair friend's dress allowed him to do, he took a
glance down the table to see what there was in the way of
what he called "grub."

"*Humph!* I thought it had been a dinner," observed
he, in tone of disappointment, to his hostess; "but there
seems nothin' but fruit and things, like a flower-show."

"Dinner *à la Russe*," replied Mrs. Watkins, thinking
he was joking, at the same time handing him a finely
embroidered French bill of fare.

"Ah, there's nothin' like a good cut at a round of beef
when one's hungry," observed Facey, laying it down again.

A servant, with two plates of soup, then asked him
whether he would take thick or clear turtle?

"Thick," replied Facey, thinking it would be the most
substantial of the two.

The servant then set it down before him.

"Here! give us both!" exclaimed he, seeing how little
there was in the plate he had got. He then took the other
and placed it in front of him until he was done with the
first. And he supped and slushed just like one of his own
hounds.

"What's this stuff?" now demanded Facey, as a servant
offered him a green glass of something.

"Punch, sir," replied the man.

"Set it down," replied Romford, continuing his soup.
Having finished both plates of turtle, he quaffed off the
glass, and was balancing himself on his chair, raking the
guests fore and aft, and considering whether mock-turtle
or real turtle was best, when his lisping friend on his right
interrupted his reverie by asking him if he was fond of
flowers.

"Whoy, yes," replied Facey carelessly, "they are well
enough in their way," adding, "and I'm fond of hounds,
but I don't like havin' them in the dinner-room."

Miss saw she had made a wrong cast, so did not follow
up the inquiry by pointing out the beauty of the heaths
and geraniums in the blue and silver vase before her, as
she intended doing.

Facey then got some fish, not so much as he liked, but

still he would take it on account. So, helping himself copiously to lobster-sauce—taking nearly half the boat—he proceeded to attack his turbot with great avidity.

Then came some hock and white hermitage ; next, some incomprehensible side-dishes, or rather *entrées*, for, of course, they never got on the table at all ; then some sparkling Moselle and Burgundy, followed by more anonymous viands, of all of which Facey partook greedily, not knowing but that each chance might be the last. And when he had about ate to repletion, and was balancing himself as before on his chair, a servant came and offered him some mutton, which he couldn't resist, saying, as he took it, "I wish you'd brought me that at first." Next came the "sweet and dry," to which he paid the same compliment, of wishing it had come before, observing confidentially to Mrs. Watkins, that he thought champagne was just the best white wine there was, adding, that Lucy and he managed a bottle between them almost every hunting day. Meanwhile Miss Cassandra, baffled with her flowers, but anxious to be doing, thought to ingratiate herself by asking him a pertinent question connected with the chase ; namely, whether he liked ladies hunting?

"No—hate it," replied he, with a frown and an angry shake of his broad shoulders.

Miss was glad of that, for she was something like Mrs. Rowley Rounding, better adapted for driving than riding. So she said she thought ladies had no business out hunting.

"Dangerous enough for the men," replied Facey, filling his mouth full of potato ; adding, "besides, they're always gettin' in the way."

Having finished his mutton, they now offered him some turkey. Facey eyed it intently, wishing it, too, had come before. "Well—no," said he, after a pause, "ar can't eat any more!" So saying, he dived his hands into his trousers pockets, and stretched out his legs, as if he was done. But his persecution was not over yet.

After another round of "sweet or dry," the game began to circulate—grouse, woodcocks, partridges, snipes—to all of which offers our master returned a testy negative. "No! no!" exclaimed he, upon a third tease, "ar've had enough."

Still there were the sweets to come—sweets without end—sweets in every sort of disguise—for Lubbins was

great in that line. And they baited Facey with creams
and jellies, and puffs and pastry, till he was half frantic.

"A man should have ten stomachs instead of one,"
muttered he, "to stand such work."

He thought the dinner never would be done : he had
never been so tormented before. If that was high life,
he didn't want any more of it. Give him his victuals when
he wanted them—what he wanted, and no more. Rot the
fellow ! there he was again !

Footman (with a silver dish).—"Little *fondieu*, sir ?"

Facey.—"No, ye beggar ! I don't want any more !"
growled he.

And, if it had not been for the look of the thing, Miss
would quite as soon that our hero had not been so interrupted, for it interfered greatly with the progress of her
proceedings. Whenever she thought she was what Facey
would call well settled to the scent, a servant was sure to
come and put her out. She wanted to know if he liked
music—she wanted to know if he liked dancing—she
wanted to know if he liked archery.

At length there were symptoms of a lull. The chopped
cheese having made its circuit, was duly followed by Port
wine, Beaujolais, Badminton cup, bitter and sweet ales ;
and Facey began to feel a little more comfortable. His
roving pig eyes raked either side of the table—now glancing at Lolly, now at Miss Mowser, now at Felt, now at
Salver, now at Lucy, and anon at Mrs. Watkins. Then
they reverted to his fair neighbour on his right. "Good-
looking lass," thought he, examining her minutely behind.
"Good head and neck, good shoulders ;" just as he would
look at a horse. And at that moment a thought struck
him that she might be his——

"Cream or water ice, sir ?" now asked a footman.

"Who said I wanted either ?" growled Facey, just as he
would to a shopkeeper who asked him, "What's the next
article, sir ?"

Miss, who thought that ices made her nose red, declined
any also ; and, passing her napkin across her rosy lips, she
prepared for a little probing.

"Is Beldon Hall comfortable ?" lisped she.

"Oh yes," replied Facey, "comfortable enough ; more
room than we want, a good deal."

"It's a good thing to have plenty of room," lisped the
lady.

"Not if you've to fix it," replied Facey.

"Is Abbeyfield large?" asked Miss.

"Tol-lol," replied Facey. "Make up twenty or five-and-twenty beds, p'r'aps."

"Indeed!" lisped Miss. "That's a good many."

"Master of hounds must be prepared for chance visitors," observed he. "Never know how many you'll sit down to dinner till the day comes."

Miss thought she would like that.

"Is there a good neighbourhood?"

"Much the same as elsewhere;" adding, "people all get sucked up to London nowadays."

"London's a charming place!" ejaculated Miss Watkins; "but I never can get par and mar to go there."

"I don't think so," replied our master. "Give me the country—give me huntin', and shootin', and fishin'," added he, "and oi'l give moy share of Lunnon to any one who likes it."

Just then a persecution of fruit commenced—pineapple, grapes, and Jersey pears arrived—thus making a break in the conversation, and removing the occasion of an argument on the London point. Miss wanted to coincide, if she could; and, luckily, a most fortunate subject came to her aid—she touched the right chord at last: "Was Mr. Romford musical?"

"Very!" replied Facey, brightening up; "play the flute beautiful!"—[Of all broken-winded, asthmatical *artistes*, Facey Romford was the most dreary and forlorn; still he flattered himself, if he had set up as a professor, he would have made a great fortune!] "Very," replied he. "Play the flute beautiful," was the answer he gave to Miss Watkins's inquiry.

"Indeed!" rejoined she, smiling. "I wish you would come and accompany me sometimes."

"Well," said he, "oi'l do that with pleasure."

"Can you play Blumenthal's *Prière des Matelots*?"

"No; but oi can play 'Dixie's Land,' 'Old Bob Ridley,' and a heap of other pop'lar airs. Nobody knows what flute-playing really is, who hasn't heard me."

And the science of "eating made easy" having been further developed by Burlinson helping them all round to a glass of wine and offering them another, an ominous lull suddenly took place in the conversation, and all the guests arose simultaneously—the gentlemen standing a pace or two back, while the ladies extricated their enormous crinolines from under the table. Then, the door being opened by the obsequious host, Mrs. Somerville sailed out of the room, with the same stately air with which she entered it; and, after a little of the usual mock-modesty about each not going first, Mrs. Watkins at length got the whole party collected, and drove them before her like a flock of sheep. And, having returned them back into the radiant drawing-room, she devoted herself to the development of her Beldon Hall friend; while the gentlemen closed up at the table, to see what they could make of old Facey. Lucy played and sang in the drawing-room, and Facey talked about hunting in the dining one, acquitting themselves with considerable ability.

The ladies thought Mrs. Somerville would be pretty, if it wasn't for her affected manner; and Facey delivered a lecture to the men on the character and habits of the fox, very much in the style of a gamekeeper. Though they might think his manner queer, they couldn't gainsay his facts.

At length our friend, who was no drinker, having passed the wine two or three times, asked his host if he hadn't better "stop the tap"? and, the proposition seeming to meet with general approval, there was another unanimous rise from the table, and a general consultation of whiskers and ties. They then followed Mr. Romford out of the room, who led the way, as he said, to the holloa of the distant music in the drawing-room. Very clear and sounding it was! How he wished he had brought his flute—would have tickled his trout in no time! He then opened the door, and astonished himself with a blaze of light—fourfold what it was when he left.

Then came a charge of tea and coffee trays and cakes, and everything a man doesn't want; and Facey was hunted about till he almost upset one. "Rot it, if this is pleasure," muttered he, when the Curaçoa man came with his picturesque bottle, "ar don't want any more of it." And he was heartily glad when the sound of wheels out-side the house proclaimed the coming conclusion; still more happy when the footmen began announcing the carriages, and the paterfamiliases commenced beckoning their wives and daughters, and talking about not keeping their valuable horses waiting, standing shivering and shaking in the cold.

At length, after many trots to the front-door, Mr. Watkins got the last of the leavers away; and, it not being prudent to indulge in the usual worry before strangers and remanets, after a slight discharge of seltzer and soda, the instincts of all the party seemed to point towards bed. So there was a general bobbing and cooing, and bidding of good-nights—with hopes that Mrs. Somerville and Mr. Romford found everything in their rooms that they wanted. And, as the only thing Mr. Facey particularly wanted was his pipe, and he had that with him, he unhesitatingly answered "Yes." And he went along, knocking his knees together, well pleased that the penance was over. Barring the mistake of old Felt, he didn't know that he had done so far amiss. Callin' Salver Silver was nothin'—just a slip of the tongue; but the other was awkward: however, it couldn't be helped. So, taking off and putting his new dress scarlet carefully away in the wardrobe, he resumed his morning jacket; and drawing a luxuriously cushioned easy-chair right in front of the fire, he adjusted and lit his pipe, and then soused himself down in its voluminous depths to enjoy his sublime tobacco.

"Well," mused he to himself, as he puffed and smoked; "well, old boy, you are well laid in here—that white-shouldered girl is evidently in love with you! Quite inclined to meet you half-way, old gal!"

It may seem strange that it should not have occurred to a fox-hunting fortune-hunter like Mr. Romford, that Miss Cassandra Cleopatra Watkins was the very sort of girl he was in search of; but then the reader must take into account the fact that he was a perfect stranger in the country, with no one but Independent Jimmy to give him any information, and that neither Mrs. Somerville nor her mother were at all likely to forward any matrimonial arrangement.

So friend Facey was left a good deal to his own devices, —to pick up what he could from this person and from that; and, having picked it up, to put that and that together, so as to make a reliable story of the whole.

To be sure, Miss Cassandra Cleopatra was good enough to inform him, very early in the day, that she was an only child; but there were a good many more things that Mr.

Facey would like to know, and that she could not inform him of—where the money was, for instance; whether it was settled, and so on; above all, how much there was of it.

"The mother-*familias*, too, seems to be quite agreeable! Wonder what the father would say? That confounded uncertificated bankrupt," as he called his host, "is far too young," continued he. "Wonder if there's any way, now, of playin' at leapfrog with the money—passin' it over the present holder's back, so as to prevent his spendin' it, and securing it to some one beyond? Should think there was," continued he, blowing a voluminous upward cloud, after a long-drawn respiration. "The lawyers can do almost anything—anything except make a scent! Scent's a queer thing!" continued he; "dash'd if it isn't. Wonder if we'll have one to-morrow?" And then he emitted another great cloud, thinking as he did it that there would be a scent in the room, at all events. Hoped the next comer would like tobacco!

And having thus done his best to secure him the luxury, and exhausted his pipe in a further consideration of the fertile subject of scent, our friend at length undressed and turned into bed, at twenty minutes to twelve.

CHAPTER XXXIV

THE HUNT BREAKFAST

MR. ROMFORD awoke at daybreak next morning with a parched mouth and a somewhat winey headache; not at all himself, in fact. The late dinner and multiplicity of dishes had disagreed with a gentleman accustomed to early hours and simple fare. He had never tried such a mixture before; "meat, puddin', and cheese" (all the delicacies of the season, as the sailor said), being the utmost extent of his wants.

But that he had been gradually inducted into magnificence through the instrumentality of Beldon Hall, he would now scarcely have known himself, stretched in a great canopy-topped state bed in a noble room, with brilliant chimney-glass, splendid cheval one, tapestry carpet, and every imaginable luxury. What did a man want with so many baths, who always took a header when he was heated!

Of course the capital Louis Quinze clock on the marble mantelpiece did not go, so Facey appealed to his own great silver watch under the pillow to know what o'clock it was, and finding it wanted several hours to breakfast, he did not see any reason why, because the bed was a fine one, he should lie in it longer than he liked; so he bounded out, and making for a window, proceeded to reconnoitre the landscape.

"Ay," said he to himself, after an identifying stare, "that is Wavertree in the distance, the village with the spire is Dronefield, and the white house beyond will be Mr. Bullinger's, of Prestonworth."

So he settled the matter satisfactorily in his own mind, and then moved the previous question,—namely, that he should dress. But where were his clothes? They had taken them away to brush, or perhaps mop up the beer-slops with in the servants' hall, and then fold and return, and there was nothing for him but the choice between his hunting things and dress ones. Neither of those would do, so he must try to recover the Tweeds. But they had put the bell where nobody could find it; and Facey had to cast about as he would for the scent of a fox. When he did find it, nobody would answer it; for the girl in charge of the numbers merely announced "Number one bell" in the hall, and every servant who heard her concluded that the occupant of such a magnificent apartment—the best room—would be sure to have a valet to answer it, and thought no more of the matter. And when Facey, having taken another rather fretful survey of the landscape, returned again to the charge, an exclamation of "Number one bell!" was all that the ring produced; and so on for a third.

"Rot the fellow!" exclaimed Facey, swinging round with vexation; and after taking a turn about the spacious apartment, he at length settled before his hunting clothes. "S'pose I must put them on," said he, taking up the Bedford cords, and proceeding to jump into his other clothes in the promiscuous sort of way of a man going to bathe. He then opened his door, and emerged from his room in search of adventures. The landings and staircase were only half awake ; and when he got downstairs he found everything in the uncomfortable state familiar only to early, too early, risers. One housemaid on her knees pipeclaying the passage, another raising a cloud of dust with her broom ; rugs, mats, pails, dusters, all higgledy-piggledy—everything in the height of confusion. The fine overnight footmen were hurrying about in caps and all sorts of queer clothes, bearing trays full of plate, linen, and china,—the ingredients of another great spread. Worming his way cautiously among the obstacles, Facey at length reached the front-door, and emancipating himself from the house, was presently in the fresh air. Very fresh and pleasant it was, and most grateful it felt to his fevered frame.

"Oh, Francis Romford, my beloved friend," said he, "you had too much wine last night. Oh, Francis Romford, this dinin' out doesn't suit you. Oh, Francis Romford, it's a great luxury to have just what you want to eat and drink, and no more. Oh, Francis Romford, it's bad to hunt with a sore head. Huntin' and drinkin' are two men's work."

Then he thought a pipe would do him good ; and a pipe he accordingly proceeded to take, sauntering along the fine Kensington gravelled drive as he made the necessary preparation for a smoke. This brought him within sight of the stables,—a well-built, rough-cast range, with coach-houses in the centre.

"Humph ! not bad-like quarters," said Facey, eyeing them. "Have seen good horses come out of much worse stables than those." And thereupon he determined to inspect them. Making for the range on the right, he found himself among the greys in the coachman's stable, with the great Mr. Spanker sauntering about, superin-tending the stablemen in the "you-do-your-work" sort of air of a man who does nothing himself. Pugs, cobs, and coachmen were things Mr. Romford eschewed. Pugs he looked upon as eyesores ; cobs he never knew the use of ; and coachmen, he thought, were men who would be grooms, only they were too lazy. A very slight inspection of the greys, therefore, satisfied him ; and returning Mr. Spanker's salute with an air of indifference, he turned on his heel, and sought the other side of the stable. Spanker, however, recognised him, and said to his helper "That is the varry gent as came up through the grating arter the rats when we was at Beldon 'All."

When, however, Facey got into the hunting stable, he found himself at home ; and Gullpicker, the presiding genius (a Melton man, whom nobody would have at Melton), seemed impressed with the importance of his visitor. He raised his cap most deferentially, and Facey having returned a nod, and a voluminous puff of smoke, then proceeded to criticise the horses.

There were four well-shaped, well-conditioned bays, well-clothed, well-littered, well done by in every respect except well-ridden. In this latter indulgence they were sadly deficient ; indeed the two that the man who hunted for conformity was going to ride that day, had been. out, getting the fiery edge taken off them with a gallop on the green. There were now a couple of straps at work upon either side of them, each hissing and thumping as if they would stave in the horses' ribs. Willy was all for having everything as it should be, and Gullpicker was the man to accommodate him. It took two men to strap a horse properly, Gull said, so two to a horse Gull had. It is strange how some fellows get places by merely trading on a name. If Gullpicker had come from Manchester, Musselburgh, or any other place beginning with an " M," Willy would never have thought of him ; but coming from Melton, he concluded he must be all right, and so gave him eighty pounds a year and his house. A livery-stable keeper would have given him twelve shillings a week, and would most likely have turned him off at the end of the first one.

Romford now stuck out his great legs, and proceeded to question the worthy, and very soon wormed out the secret of the stable,—which was a hard 'oss, which was a soft 'un, which was a show 'un. The show 'un was master's special favorite, the man said, whom he described as a very shy rider ; indeed, the groom thought if it wasn't for the sake of wearing the red coat, Mr. Watkins would never go out hunting at all. And Facey said, that was the case with a good many men he knew, adding, that it would be a good thing not to let any man ride in scarlet until he had ridden three years in black.

The servants' breakfast bell now rang a noisy peal, for the Watkinses considered it incumbent upon them to let all the neighbourhood know when there was any eating going on ; and Facey having mastered his subject, jerked his head at the groom, who renewed his deferential salute as our master rolled out of the stable. A master of hounds is always a hero in a groom's eyes.

When he returned to the house, it had got into more comfortable order. The scrapers and door-mats were restored to their proper places, the mops and pails had disappeared, and a partially revised footman was brushing and arranging the hats in the hall. To him Facey· communicated his lavatorial wants, and was forthwith recon-ducted upstairs and introduced to the dressing-room of his apartment, where he found such an array of baths, foot, hip, shower, as to a man who always took a header seemed quite incomprehensible. Discarding all these, he requested the footman to get him some hot water, wherewith and by the aid of a razor and soap, he proceeded to divest himself of the superfluous portion of his cane-coloured beard, and then treated his pretty face to a wash in the fine mazarine blue and white china basin, thinking all the while what old Gilroy would say if he saw him.

Very queer his old fourpenny shaving-brush, and two-penny soap-box,—to say nothing of his horn comb and shabby hairbrush, — looked on the fine lace-pattern toilet-cover, lined with blue silk, and edged with Honiton lace. Very different was the toilet glass, with its carved frame and spiral supporters, compared to the few square inches of thing in which he used to contemplate his too fascinating face at the " Dog and Partridge," or the " West-end Swell." And Facey wandered backwards and for-wards between the bed and dressing-room, surveying his irresistible person first in one mirror and then another, thinking what a killing-looking cock he was.

The noisy gong presently interrupted the inspection, and looking at his watch he found it only wanted twenty minutes to ten, and at half-past the hounds would be due before the door. Tearing himself away then from the mirror, he opened the door and proceeded downstairs, encountering his lisping friend full in the face at the junction of the flights.

" Good morning, Mither Romford," said she, extending her pretty white hand as she spoke.

"Good mornin', Miss," replied Facey, taking and squeezing it, adding, " I declare you look quite bewitchin' in this fine new thingumbob," taking hold of it as he spoke.

Miss smiled, and showed her pretty pearly teeth, fresh
from the application of the dentifrice ; and while Facey
was busy staring and turning a compliment, Mrs. Dust's
unlucky maid opened the green-baized door communicating with the back stairs, and spoilt the production.
Miss then gave a whisk of her crinoline, and the two
concluded the descent of the staircase together. On
entering the dining-room, they found the heads of the
house busily engaged superintending the final arrangements of the table,—marshalling the plate, adjusting the
flower vases, pointing out the position for the egg-stands,
and the places for the toast, the twists, the tea-cakes—the
light artillery generally.

"Good morning, my dear Mr. Romford," exclaimed
Mrs. Watkins, advancing gaily and tendering her hand to
our master, quite pleased to see him and her smiling
daughter arriving so amicably together.

"Good morning, Romford : how are you ?" exclaimed
Willy, now seizing Facey's hand in the hail-fellow-well-
met of a brother fox-hunter ; adding "here's a fine day—
hope there'll be a good scent."

"Oh yes, and a good fox, too," rejoined Mrs. Watkins.

"Hope so," said Facey, adding, "I'll give a good
account of him if there is."

"Do," exclaimed Willy ; "in 'Bell's Life,' and the
'Field.'"

"Hut ! you and 'Bell's Life,'" growled Facey in
disgust.

The large richly chased silver Queen's-patterned tea-
kettle now came hissing into the room, with its corresponding teapot, sugar-basin, and cream ewers, and
simultaneously an antique melon-pattern coffee-pot, with
similar accompaniments, alighted at the low end of the
table. Honey, jellies, jams, then took up positions at
regular intervals in support of the silver cow-mounted
butter-boats, and next long lines of cakes, muffins, buns,
rolls, toasts, filled up the interstices.

A Westphalia ham, a Melton pie, and a *pâté de foie gras*
mounted the plate-garnished sideboard, just as Mrs.
Somerville came sailing in, and the first ring was heard
at the front-door bell.

Mrs. Watkins, having greeted Mrs. Somerville warmly,
hoping she had slept well and not been disturbed by the
wind, then backed her into her overnight seat by her

husband, and, sailing up the room, installed herself in
her own chair, with Facey on her right again and
Cassandra next to him, just as Burlinson brought up
the first comers, in the persons of young Brogdale, Mr.
Tuckwell, and Mr. Horsington, who, after smirking and
smiling, subsided into seats and began eating as if they
had not tasted food for a week. Some people never miss
a show meet.

*Ring—ring—ring—ring; ring—ring—ring—ring—ring;
ring—ring—ring—ring—ring—ring* then went the bell,
each particular man seeming to think it necessary to ring
for himself, though the door was yet open for his predecessor. Then whips of all sorts clustered together, and
pyramids of hats and caps rose in the passage ; and the
cry was still "They come—they come !" Gayslap, and
Rumball, and Botherton, and Brown, and West, and
young Felt, and old Muggleswick, and we don't know
who else besides.

Great was the variety of hunting costume, great the
run on the cups and saucers to supply the behests of
the wearers. "Cream, if you please." "Have you got
any sugar?" "May I trouble you for the salt?" Then
arose a surge of mastication that was quite opposed to
the idea of the parties having breakfasted before. It was
very much a repetition of the Pippin Priory performance,
only the appointments were finer and grander. Mrs.
Watkins had no idea of being outdone : only let her
know what the Larges had, and she would soon get
something better. If they had had a boar's head, Mrs.
Watkins would have had a bull's or a buffalo's.

Facey, though not quite happy, was yet far more
comfortable than he had been overnight, or when he
run the gauntlet of inquisitive eyes as he made his way
up the breakfast-room at Pippin Priory. Here he sat
somewhat like a gentleman taking his ease in a penny
chair in Hyde Park, having the population paraded
before him, and if the servants would only have let him
alone, he would have done pretty well ; but either the
butler persecuted him with buns, or the footman teased
him with toast, or Miss lisped something that he couldn't
understand, and was obliged to ask her to say over
again, so that the act of deglutition proceeded slowly
and irregularly. He was accustomed to swallow his
breakfast like a foxhound. All he wanted was to

get it down, and then pocket a crust for future want, and be off.

Meanwhile more gentlemen came stamping and clanking in from all quarters, in red coats, and green coats, and black coats; in white boots, and brown boots, and black boots, all apparently ravenous and settling to the viands as soon as, having bobbed to the ladies, they could get seated at the table. Some stuck to the sideboard, trying the noyeau, the *crême de Vanille*, the *parfait amour*, the cherry brandy, and so on. The Watkinses didn't give champagne, they were told it wasn't fashionable. Sip, sup, slop, clatter, patter, clatter, patter, was the order of the day. More tea, more toast, more coffee, eggs, muffins, and butter. Many people will give away any amount in victuals, from whom you could not get a penny in cash if it was ever so.

At length there was a lull; some stuck out their legs, others began exploring their mouths with their tooth-picks, some again arose and began looking about the room at the various family pictures, Mrs. Watkins in a green satin dress, Miss in a yellow silk one, Willy in a hunt-coat, Willy in a dress-coat, Willy in a shooting-coat. Then there was a move to the window. The hounds had just come, attended by the usual cavalcade, and Facey rushed to see what sort of equilibrium the servants presented. All seemed right.

There was Daniel—the Right Honourable the Hurl of Scamperdale's Daniel—sitting erect on that uncomfortable-actioned horse Oliver Twist; there was Chowey—insinu-ating Chowey—relaxing and contracting his extraordinary proboscis as if he was going to kiss all creation; and there was the strong persevering man who cleaned horses, riding that noble long-tailed brown horse Bounding Ben, whose only fault was that he could not be relied upon for bounding. Altogether a most respectable-looking party, and greatly indebted to Tick. Then as Miss was lisping her admiration of the establishment to Mr. Romford, the hum of conversation was interrupted by her mamma rushing wildly up the room exclaiming—

"Oh, Mr. Romford! oh, Mr. Watkins! oh, Mr. Romford! I *am* so shocked—I *am* so distressed—I hardly know what to do. I wrote to that tiresome Mr. Castangs to send us a fox—a Quornite, if he could—and there's none come!—and there's none come! Was there ever

anything so provoking!—was there ever anything so
provoking! Oh, what *shall* we do, Mr. Watkins?—what
shall we do, Mr. Romford?" continued Mrs. Watkins,
appealing imploringly first to one and then to the other.

Willy, of course, didn't know what to do, and Facey
was too disgusted to answer the question; in addition
to which, a giggle of laughter ran through the room,
showing the position was appreciated. So, looking at
his watch, and seeing it was a few minutes past time, he
gladly tendered his adieux, hurrying out of the room,
exclaiming to Mrs. Somerville as he got to the door, "I
say, Lucy,. mind, pork chops and smashed potatoes for
dinner at five!" He then swung gaily into the hall,
got his hat, and made straight for his horse in the crowd.
The Right Honourable the Hurl of Scamperdale's Daniel
then saluted him with an aerial sweep of his cap, and
Chowey, relaxing his proboscis, followed suit.

Mr. Castangs having disappointed our friends, there
was no occasion for Mr. Romford to indulge in the usual
make-believe draw round Dalberry Lees; so, getting on
Pilot, he trotted quietly over Amberwicke Meadows, and,
running the hounds through Walton Wood, passed on
to Westdale Park.

But though the portly owner, Mr. Banknewton, was
an ardent supporter of the hunt, and always made a
show of insisting upon his keeper having foxes; yet, not
having notice, and of course relying upon Mrs. Watkins
supplying the wants of the day, his fox was not ready
any more than the other. So Mr. Romford passed on
from hall to house, and from hill to vale, until he got
entirely out of his stop; without, however, having
exactly a blank day, for Chowey whipped a very fine fox
off a hedgerow on Mr. Mitford's farm at Ripple Mill,
which immediately went to ground in a well-accustomed
breeding earth behind the house.

It is, however, but justice to Mr. Castangs to state that
he had not been indifferent to his good patron Mrs.
Watkins's interests; for, when Independent Jimmy came
with the melon frame to take Mrs. Somerville back to
Beldon Hall, the fox was seen sitting in his airy trellis-
work box beside Jimmy on the driving seat. It had been
carried past by the thoughtless guard of the 9 a.m.
railway train. Better, however, that he should carry the
fox past than the pea-soup. Mrs. Watkins, however,

determining not to profit by the occurrence, begged Mrs·
Somerville to take the fox back with her to Beldon Hall;
which our fair friend consenting to do, and all things
being at length ready, after a good deal of kissing and
hugging, the ladies got parted; and Lucy and Dirty,
being duly ensconced in their vehicle, drove away, leaving
the late lively Dalberry Lees to relapse into its accustomed
quiet. Dirty, we may add, had made rather a somewhat
profitable visit of it, having picked a pearl and ruby ring
off Mr. Watkins's dressing-table, a gold thimble out of
Miss Watkins's work-box, and extracted seven-and-six-
pence from a drawer in the housekeeper's room, which
none but herself would ever have suspected of holding
a halfpenny.

CHAPTER XXXV

THE BAG FOX

WHEN Mr. Facey Romford returned to Beldon Hall
after his visit to Dalberry Lees, he found what
ought to have converted the nearly blank day there into
a splendid triumph; namely, the unfortunate bag fox,
now located in his own entrance hall. Facey got a whiff
of what Mr. Watkins would call his "aroma," almost as
soon as he opened the front door; but never dreaming
of such a thing as a fox being in the house, he just
chucked his hat and whip at random in the dusk on
to the accustomed table near the screen behind which
he kept his rake, and was making onwards, thinking of
his pork chops and smashed potatoes, when a scratching
noise arrested his attention on the other side of the
spacious entrance. Facey stopped, and in the evening
gloom the apparition of a new trellis-work cage stood in
bold relief against the carved back of an old oak chair.

"Do believe it's a fox," muttered Romford. "Can be
nothing but a fox," added he, making up to it, and looking
in, as the unmistakable scent greeted his nose. "It *is*
a fox!" exclaimed he, wondering how it came there. He
then called for a candle. Dirtiest of the Dirty presently

came tripping along, with a thick-wicked tallow, in a
block-tin candlestick, in her hand ; and Romford, flourishing it over the cage, caught sight of the parchment label,
and read—

> "WILLIAM WATKINS, Esq.
>
> "Dalberry Lees.

"By rail, to be left at the Firfield Station. Keep this
side up."

"Oh, the deuce !" muttered he. "Why, this is the
gentleman that ought to have come in the morning."
Then a further inspection of the address revealed his
own name—

> "FRANCIS ROMFORD, Esq.
>
> "Beldon Hall.

"With Mrs. Watkins's kind regards,"

in the most elegant hand, added at the bottom.

"Humph !" muttered he, "this is a pretty present for
a master of hounds to receive. S'pose they'll be sendin'
me a colley dog or a pipin' bullfinch next. May mean
it for kindness; s'pose they do," continued he, thinking
of the white shoulders; "but in reality it's anything else.
Never hunted a bag fox in my life," said he, scratching
his head. "Should be 'shamed to hunt a bag fox. What
would life be without foxes ?" continued Facey, now
lowering the candle, and looking into the cage to examine
his present more minutely. Reynard, half timid, half
savage, made for a corner, disclosing, however, enough
of his proportions to let Facey see he was a fine one,—
rather light-coloured along the back, with a full brush
and a grizzleyish head. "Wonder what sort of a mouth
he's got ?" continued Facey, making for the table, whereon
lay his hunting whip, and returning to stir the fox up
with it. "Snap !" He seized the stick with an energy
that made Facey thankful it wasn't his thumb, disclosing,
as he snapped, a set of slightly failing but still very
serviceable-looking teeth. "Good fox, very," said Facey,
wondering where he came from. "Highlands, of course,"
added he, shrugging up his high shoulders, well knowing
he did nothing of the sort. "Well," mused he, "this

is the way to bring fox-hunting to an end. Steal each other's foxes, and then we shall have nothin' to hunt. Bad work, very," muttered he, "when it comes to this." And if it hadn't been for the fair daughter, Facey would have abused Watkins right well. ˙As it was, he let off his steam by abusing the sham-fox system generally, declaring he would rather hunt with a pack of rabbit-beagles on foot, than condescend to such work. "A rat in a barn, with a terrier, is worth two of it," said he.

And he was half inclined to open the box and liberate the fox at the door ; and nothing but the fear of his being ignominiously nipped up by some passing cur prevented his doing so. Facey, therefore, adjourned the consideration of the question what to do with him until after the discussion of the sumptuous fare he had ordered in the morning. So he now proceeded to his bedroom to divest himself of his hunting attire, and assume the easier clothes of the evening. Then, old Dirty having the repast ready at the appointed time, Dirtiest of the Dirty resumed her waiting avocation ; while, between chops and cheese, Lucy enlightened Mr. Romford as to the misfortunes of the bag fox, and Mrs. Watkins's anxiety for the notification of the disappointment. Lucy had told Mrs. Watkins that she did not think her brother would have anything to do with a bagman; but Mrs. Watkins was positive the other way, asserting that a fox was a fox ; adding, that surely it was much better to have one in a box ready for use, than to be at the trouble of searching and prowling about in a wood, without, perhaps, finding one after all.

"Oh, do take him," pressed Mrs. Watkins ; "Mr. Watkins will be so disappointed if you don't ; and I'm sure we have no use for him here," added she. So Mrs. Somerville reluctantly consented, and Independent Jimmy had the pleasure of the fox's company as he drove back to Beldon Hall.

There the reader has already seen him ; and the question now is, what to do with him ; for though the whiff of a fox is very pleasant and exhilarating in the open air—especially in the hunting season—yet we do not know that it is quite so agreeable in the house. So too, thought friend Facey ; and the point now was, how to get rid of him without offending Mrs. Watkins At last he thought he had it.

"I say, old gal, let you and oi get up early in the mornin' and give that bagman a dustin' with a few couple of hounds," said Facey to Lucy between the puffs of his after-dinner pipe.

"Well," said Lucy, "I'm quite agreeable."

"It's a non-hunting day," continued Mr. Romford, "and it will keep the horses' backs down and the men quiet by letting them see we can do without them. "You ride Leotard," said he, "and I'll have that invincible Baker, and see if a gag will prevent his pulling my arms out of their sockets, as he generally does."

Lucy was quite agreeable to that also. Mr. Romford then sunk into the roomy recesses of his well-stuffed easy-chair, and luxuriated in his pipe as he passed his fine gratis pack of hounds in review before him. He was a man of decision, and quickly made up his mind what to take and what to leave at home. Ten couple was just what he would take, and ten couple he had to the fore in no time. So, having finished his pipe, he arose from his chair, and, chucking a log of wood on to the fire to last till he came back, he got a candle and went and had another stare at the fox. Here he was presently joined by old Dirty, Mrs. Mustard herself, who, in reply to his inquiries where he could get a mouse or a few beetles, replied that she had a couple of mice in the trap just then, and, as to beetles, why, her back kitchen fairly swarmed with them ; so sending her away for the mice and a handful of beetles, as also for a saucer of clean water, Mr. Romford presently made his poor prisoner as comfortable as a fox could be made under the circumstances, and left him to enjoy himself as best he could.

He then proceeded to the stables, where he found Swig and Chowey in the saddle-room deeply engaged in a game of dominoes, Chowey having rather the best of it up to the time of Mr. Romford's coming. Here, too, was Short, the stud-groom, as he was now called, having some coatless, characterless helpers under him. Mr. Romford, having first ordered Leotard for Mrs. Somerville, and the Baker for his own riding out of the brilliant galaxy of stubbornness and vice with which his stable was supplied, and Chowey, having put the finishing stroke to the game, Mr. Swig was at liberty to talk to our master, who forthwith ran him through

a list of ten couple of hounds that he wanted in the
morning so rapidly that if Swig had not had his two
intelligent friends in the saddle-room to assist him, he
would infallibly have made some mistake.

"Eight to a minute!" then cried Mr. Romford, giving
a general order for all—"eight to a minute!" repeated
he, rolling out of the room, leaving his audience very
much surprised at his proceedings. But Lucy and he
were always dropping in upon them at unqualified
hours.

"What's up now!" ejaculated Short, who had calculated
upon having to act figure footman on the morrow.

"Must be going to have a hunt by themselves,"
suggested Swig.

"The same as they had with the Heavysides," observed
Chowey, pursing up his peculiar mouth as he recollected
Swig's and his own misfortune in the gig—or, rather,
out of the gig.

"Shouldn't wonder," assented the strong persevering
man.

"Gallant little 'oman to ride," observed Swig; adding,
"I *do* like to see her go."

"He's a rum 'un," muttered Chowey. "Of all the
rum 'uns I ever lived with, he's the rummiest."

So they proceeded to discuss the merits and peculiarities
of our worthy master, without disparagement, however,
to his sporting prowess, which indeed nobody could deny.

Meanwhile Mr. Romford, little caring what they either
thought or said, hurried off by the light of the moon
to the great Mr. Proudlock's, to whom, having presented
a bottle of Lord Lovetin's best Jamaica rum that he
had wrapped up in an old "Bell's Life" newspaper in
his baggy coat pocket, he propounded his intentions for
the morrow. Mr. Proudlock, thus properly propitiated,
would be most happy to do anything in his power to
serve Mr. Romford, and, after discussing various localities,
the Holly Meadows, Eddys Row, Limecoats Green,
Shortleet Moor, High Thorn Wood, and other places,
it was at length decided that Mr. Proudlock should
start away betimes and enlarge the fox in High Thorn
Wood, on the east or Hard and Sharp side of the country,
where they would be less likely to disturb any of the
tenacious game preservers' covers on any of the country
that Mr. Romford would be likely soon to draw himself.

And Mr. Romford, having thus made all preparations for the coming day, left Mr. Proudlock to discuss his rum, while he returned to his comfortable quarters at the Hall, thinking how much snugger it was to roll about in Tweeds and be waited upon by a Dirty than to have to undergo the penance and persecution of a party—the persecution of wine, the persecution of fish, the persecution of food in general, the persecution of footmen, the persecution of finery. Oh, those horrid hoops! What wouldn't he give to destroy them—smash them irrevocably!

CHAPTER XXXVI

THE BAG FOX ENLARGED

MR. ROMFORD awoke quite cool and comfortable the next morning. All traces of wineing squeamishness were gone, and he was the real original Dog and Partridge Romford, ready for hunting, ready for shooting ready for riding, ready for anything. "Humph! what's to-day?" exclaimed he, starting up in bed, as he awoke—"what's to-day?" fearing lest he might have overslept himself and be late to cover. "Ah," continued he, recollecting himself, "it's not a hunting day—it's a bye with the bagman. Well, needs must when a certain old gentleman drives," continued he. So saying he bounded out of bed with a thump that would have shook a modern-built house to the centre. He then proceeded to take his accustomed stare out of the window. It was a fine morning, still and quiet, with a slight white rind on the ground that the now rising sun would quickly dispel. "Pity but it was a reg'lar huntin' day," muttered he, surveying the scene; "think oi could give a good wild beggar a dustin'. He then proceeded to dress himself. As he descended the grand staircase, and cut off the corner of the hall on his way to the breakfast-room, he got a whiff of his overnight friend, though Dirtiest of the Dirty, whom he met dribbling along with the kettle, assured him that Mr. Proudlock had taken him away a full hour before. The fact was, the old Jamaica rum had been too potent for friend Proudlock, who, having gone to bed tipsy, had only just come for the fox, and, fearing he was late, told Dirtiest of the Dirty to say what she did; which of course she had no hesitation in doing, lying coming quite as naturally as stealing to that elegant young lady.

Mrs. Somerville was downstairs already, but not in her sporting costume, it being one of her rules, when alone, always to put on her smart things after breakfast, considering that they ran more risk of damage at that meal than during all the rest of the day put together. And though she was not now finding her own clothes, or at least could have what she liked from London for sending for, and Betsey Shannon would only have been too glad of a cast-off, still, an early acquired habit of neatness prevented her wasting the advantages afforded even by being on the free list. So she was prudent even in her extravagance. Lucy was only a light breakfast eater, Facey a heavy one—a little dry toast, a cup of tea, and an egg sufficing for her, while our master indulged in oatmeal porridge, pork chops, rabbit pies, cold game— the general produce of his gun, in fact.

So Lucy, having soon satisfied her appetite, withdrew with mamma, leaving our master of hounds to satisfy his appetite while she was adorning herself. At length he, too, was done, and pocketing a hunch of brown bread, he rang the bell, and told Dirtiest of the Dirty, who answered it, to send old Dirty to see about dinner.

"Now then, old gal," said he, as Mrs. Mustard appeared, smoothing her dirty apron as usual, "we shall be at home in good time, I s'pect—say two, at latest; so do us those woodcocks, and make us a good apple-pie, or an apple-puddin', if you like it better."

"How many woodcocks would you please to have, sir?" asked Mrs. Mustard.

"Oh, do them all," replied Mr. Romford, "do them all —only three—no use makin' two bites of a cherry. Here!" continued he, "mind, make a good big pie—as big as a foot-bath—not one of your little tartlet-like things that only aggravate the appetite, and do it no good. Besides, I like cold apple-apple," added he, now turning round to light his old brier-root pipe, which he had been arranging as he spoke at the fire. Ere he had resumed

his erect position and emitted the inaugural puff, Mrs.
Somerville re-entered attired for the chase. She was
beautifully dressed, for, though she knew there was no
meet, yet it was impossible to say who she might see ;
added to which it was so much pleasanter and more
comfortable being smart and fit to meet anybody, instead
of having to shirk and avoid people in consequence of
being shabby. So she had on a smart new hat, with an
exquisitely cut eight-guinea habit braided in front, and
beautifully made chamois-leather trousers with black-cloth
feet. Altogether as neat as neat could be.

Nor did she mar the general effect, as some ladies do,
by wearing soiled or shabby gloves. On the contrary, she
had on a pair of smart new primrose-coloured kids that
fitted with the utmost exactitude. She had got a beautiful gold-mounted whip down from London, with a light
blue silk tasselled cord through its ruby-eyed fox-head
handle.

Mr. Romford, however, did not reciprocate his pseudo-
sister's smartness, but turned out in a very rough poacher-
like garb, viz. a slouching brown wideawake, a dirty
ditto suit of heather-coloured Tweed, with the trod out
trousers thrust into the original old rusty-looking
lack-lustre Napoleons. But Mr. Romford could ride in
anything, and, moreover, thought if the fox wouldn't run,
he would come home with the hounds and go out with
his gun after the wild ducks or snipes on Mabbleford
Mere. He liked to be doing. So now let us assist him in
his laudable design of activity.

Punctual to a minute—for those who want to have
punctual servants must be punctual themselves — Mr.
Romford and Mrs. Somerville appeared at the front door
of Beldon Hall, and there were the hounds and horses
occupying the gravelled ring before the house. The array
was not very imposing, but a deal of execution lurked
under that quiet exterior. Mr. Romford did not subscribe
to the doctrine that a "hound was a hound," on the contrary, he knew there was as much difference among dogs
as there was among men, and he made it a rule to have
value received for his oatmeal. And though he had not
taken his best, yet he had drawn his ten couple with such
ability that, thanks to the excellence of their blood, they
were as formidable as many peoples' twenty couple.

"Now then !" cried Facey, as he opened the hall-door,

"bring up your missis's horse first," calling to Short, now in charge of the prank-playing Leotard.

"Better not call me missus," whispered Lucy, adding, "it might make them talk."

"Mrs. Somerville's horse!" then exclaimed Facey, in a louder tone, as if to obliterate the first order, and in an instant Leotard was alongside the doorstep. Lucy then placing her right hand on the crutch, presented her pretty little foot to our friend, who lifted her up with airy buoyancy into her saddle. A shake of the smart habit, and she had herself adjusted in a moment. Romford then vaulted gaily into his own on the back of the all-powerful Baker. Having got him short by the gag, he gave him a kick in the ribs with his spurless heel, that as good as said, "Now then, old boy, let's see whether you or oi will be master." "Cop, come away!—Cop, come away!"— he added, to the hounds, without noticing the Baker's semi-kick in return. Away they swept from the door and trotted along with the pride of the morning.

Proudlock, the keeper, had trotted off on Tom Hooper, the blacksmith's pony, some half-hour before, to enlarge the fox in the retired recesses of High Thorn Wood, but it so happened that there were two parallel ravines, viz. High Thorn Wood and North Spring Wood, so exactly alike that Mr. Romford mistook them, and ran his hounds up the first one he came to, where fox there was none, instead of following the Kingsfield Road, half a mile farther on, and turning up the clear pebbly brook on the left. The consequence was, that, though he gave his hounds plenty of time, he never got a touch of a fox; a fact that puzzled our friend considerably, seeing, as Beckford says, that a bag fox must needs smell extravagantly—especially a bag fox that had been up to Leadenhall Market, and down again, all round about the country.

Nevertheless, it was so, and Facey got to the rising ground at the top of the ravine without a challenge—nay, without even a whisper, save from Prosperous making a dash at a rabbit. He then reconnoitred the country.

"Wrong shop!" at last said he, as, casting his eye to the south, he saw the duplicate wood bounding the horizon—"wrong shop!" repeated he, turning his horse short round, giving a slight twang of his horn, and telling Lucy to put the hounds on after him. So friend Facey trotted briskly along the woodside he had just come up, followed by such of the hounds as saw him turn, while Lucy essayed to bring the rest on after him. He then retraced his steps as quickly as he could, and regaining the Kingsfield Road, went pounding along in search of his servant. There, on a white roadside gate, holding his pony, sat the all-important Proudlock, wondering what had happened to Mr. Romford.

"Wish you mayn't ha' given him o'er much law," now observed he, as Romford came trotting up.

"What, he's fresh, is he?" asked our master.

"Fresh as a four-year-old—went off like a shot," replied Proudlock.

"So much the better," rejoined Romford. "Don't care if he beats us;" adding to himself, "no credit in killin' a bag fox—rather a disgrace, oi should say."

Mrs. Somerville then came cantering up, with the remaining hounds frolicking about her horse, and Mr. Romford having now got his short pack reunited, Proudlock opened the gate into the wood, and in they all went together.

"Half-way up the ride I struck him," said Proudlock, "and he went briskly away as far as ever I could see."

"All right," said Romford, trotting on briskly.

And sure enough, just where a large wind-blown beech formed a comfortable resting-place for our friend after his exertions in carrying the fox, a sudden thrill of excitement shot through the pack as though they had been suddenly operated upon by a galvanic battery, and away they all went with an outburst of melody, that alarmed every denizen of the wood.

"That's him!" exclaimed Proudlock, coming up at a very galloping, dreary, done, sort of pace—refreshing the old pony with a knotty dog whip as he rode.

"No doubt," replied Romford, getting the now pulling Baker well by the head. Lucy did the same by Leotard, and away they scuttled up the green ride together, leaving friend Proudlock immeasurably in the lurch. It is a sorry performance to see a retired giant toiling after a pack of hounds on a broken-winded pony.

The fox, however, had not made his exit on arriving at the rough oak rails at the top of the ride that commanded the open; for though there was nothing to impede his progress, still he was confused and uncomfortable, and had not got the cramp out of his legs from confinement in the box, so that the Romford digression into the wrong wood was very convenient, and the fox availed himself of it to take a quiet trial of speed by himself along a grassy slope to the left. The farther he went, the fresher he got, till he felt himself regaining his pristine strength ; and after two or three rolls and stretches on the grassy mead, was beginning to cast about for a permanent resting-place, when the light note of Romford's horn, calling his hounds out of the first cover, came wafted on the breeze to where he was, now in the full enjoyment of his delectable liberty.

One twang was enough. It shot through his every nerve, and flourishing his brush with a triumphant whisk, he trotted away at a good, steady, holding pace, keeping as much out of sight by following the low grounds as he could. For he argued, very rationally, that even if the horn boded him no harm, still he was just as well in one strange place as another ; while if it was any of those troublesome hunters in search of one of his class, the greater distance he placed between them and himself the better. So he went steadily on, not running to exhaust himself, but going as if he felt quite grateful for his freedom, and determined to do his utmost to retain it. Meanwhile friend Romford, with his short but efficient pack, had opened on his line, and the first outburst of melody coming down wind, confirmed the fox's worst suspicions as at first excited by the twang of the horn.

He had now little doubt it was the hounds, if not after him, after one of his own species, for whom he did not care to stand proxy ; so he employed a very vigilant eye in scanning the country, with ears well back to catch any extraneous sound that might come. He wasn't going to be caught, if he could help it. And Romford being a fair-dealing man, and not at all inclined to take advantage of an over-matched animal, let his mettlesome hounds flash half over the fallow outside the wood without calling them back, though truthful Vanquisher refused to go an inch beyond the oak rails. Then when their misleading notes gradually died out, Vanquisher's deep-toned tongue was heard proclaiming the right line to the left, and back they all swung, dashing and hurrying as if to snatch the laurels of accuracy from his brow. And when they got to where the fox had rolled, there was such a proclamation of satiety as sounded like the outburst of forty mouths instead of twenty.   Still it was not a great scenting day ; but Mr. Romford did not care for that, and went as leisurely along as a master of harriers, instead of bustling and aggravating his great round shoulders into convulsions, as was his wont when he had a bad scent and a good fox before him.   Indeed, he kept looking about in all the unlikely places for a wild fox to be, fearing lest the unfortunate fugitive should fall into the jaws of the pack without a chance for his life. But our worthy master was too careless, or too conscientious, for while he was thus dallying, letting the hounds hunt every yard of the scent, the fox was pursuing the even tenor of his way, over Linton Lordship, and so across Makenrace Common to Arkenfield.

It was a captious, fleeting, catching scent, the hounds sometimes running almost mute, and sometimes tearing along with such a chorus of melody as looked as if they would change from scent to view, and run into him in a minute.

"Look out, Lucy !" Facey kept exclaiming, "look out ! he's somewhere here ;" but still the fox showed not, and first one hound and then another led the onward chorus, just as Romford expected to be handling him.   And now the cry of the hounds attracted the roving population of the country.   Mr. Makepiece, the Union Doctor, Header, the horse-dealer, Herdman, the cattle-jobber, and Bartlett, the capless butcher's boy, on an extremely fractious tail-foremost chestnut pony.

"Is it a fox or a har ?" asked Header, not knowing what to make of the medley.

"How far hev ye brought him ?" demanded the butcher's boy ; but Mr. Romford didn't deign to give an answer to either.

"Keep that fiery steed of yours off the hounds," was all the notice he took of the latter.

Then the hounds, having got upon a sound old pasture, set to running with such determined energy and vehe-mence, that, for the first time since they found, or rather went away, Facey kicked the Baker into a canter.   Away Lucy and he went at a pace that, with the aid of a hog-backed stile out of the pasture, a wall out of the next field, and a scientifically cut hedge beyond, soon shook off their recently joined comrades.

The hounds had now been running some five-and-twenty minutes or more, and Facey began to think better of the bagman than before ; he almost thought he might beat them ; didn't care if he did. "Poor is the triumph over the timid bagman," said he.

The country, which had been cramped and awkward at first, now gradually improved—more grass, larger fields, fewer trees. If the fox did not take the best line that he might, he took far from a bad one ; and, moreover, avoided all those points of publicity that too palpably betray the stranger. Lucy half thought he might be a wild one they had got on by mistake, but Facey saw by the want of confidence among his hounds, and the vacillating course of the animal, that it was not the real thing. Indeed, at times, if he hadn't known it was a fox, he would have thought he was hunting a hare. So he cheered and encouraged the hounds in an easy careless sort of way, still letting them do their own work. "No use keepin' a dog, and barkin' one's self," thought he, as he slouched his great self in his saddle on the now placid Joe Baker. "If they can't tell which way he's gone, sure I can't," continued he, watching their working. "Deuced good lot of hounds," added he, admiring their performances. Then they went away again with a screech.

At the cross roads by Welton Pound up came Timothy Scorer, the perennially drunken horse-breaker, in a high state of excitement, on a sweaty curly-coated bay filly, with its head all over entanglement, like the bowsprit of a ship. Tim had met the fox full in the face by the reservoir of Thistleworth Mill, and had not yet got over his astonishment at the sight.

"Biggest fox that ever was seen ! Had nearly knocked his mar off her legs," he said, his spluttering vehemence contrasting with Mr. Romford's easy indifference.

"Nearly knocked the mar off her legs !" exclaimed Timothy, trying to wheel her round out of the way of the hounds.

"You don't say so," replied Romford. "Why, it must have been a wolf or a ram !"

Wolf or fox the hounds kept steadily on, if not with so good a scent as before, still with a holding one that occasionally rose into running.

And getting now into a more populous country, the

magnetic influence of a pack of hounds again operated on the casual horsemen ; and by the time the pack skirted the little agricultural village of Pendleton, the field had swelled to the number of six—viz. Mr. Smith, the miller of the afore-mentioned Thistleworth Mill ; Lawson, the road surveyor ; Dweller, the auctioneer ; Faccy, and Lucy ; with a fustian-clad servant on a white pony, who seemed inclined to give the letter-bag a round with the hounds, instead of carrying it on to its destination.

Here, too, there were symptoms of landlord farming— greener fields, trimmer fences, better gates. And, a wretched tailless cur having chased the fox and in his vehemence nearly knocked his own stupid brains out against a rubbing post, the line now took over that im- proved country, with a still further diminished scent, in consequence of the encounter from the cur.

If well-kept fences are more pleasant to the eye, they have the disadvantage of being more difficult to get over ; and those that our friends now approached were so care- fully tended, so skilfully mended with old wire-rope, as scarcely to present any preferable place. It was pretty much of a muchness where they took them. However, neither Faccy nor Lucy were people to turn away : and, after two or three well-executed leaps, they were rewarded by getting into more open and park-like ground. Indeed, they were in a park—none other than Tarring Neville Park, the seat of our distinguished friend, Mr. Hazey, though a well-wooded hill at present shut out the mansion from their view. On, on they went ! Faccy more bent on watching the working of his hounds, than mindful of the country through which they were passing. And, as the line of scent inclined down the now grassy slope, of course Faccy followed down the grassy slope ; and as it then diverged along the side of a sparkling stream, why, along the side of the sparkling stream he went also, wondering, as he rode, whether there were any trout in it. " Shouldn't be s'prised if there were," he said.

And as the hounds were casting about, here, there, and everywhere—Romford acting "sleeping partner" as before —a puffing, turban-capped youth suddenly rushed up, and breathlessly demanded to know " what they were doing there ?"

" Hunting a fox, to be sure," replied Faccy, holding

his hounds on towards an enclosed belt of wood by the side of the stream.

Then the youth looked at Romford, and Romford looked at the youth; and it occurred to them simultaneously that they had seen each other before.

"Why, it's Mr. Romford, isn't it?" asked the youth, now appealing to Lucy, who was putting on the hounds to her brother; "and Mrs. Somerville," added he, taking off his cap respectfully to the handsome lady as he spoke.

"Oh, Mr. Hazey! how do you do?" rejoined our fair friend, leaning forward and tendering him her hand. Lucy's quicker perception enabled her to detect in the heterogeneous garments the smart young gentleman who accompanied his father to call upon them on the Sunday.

It was, indeed, Bill—Hazey's boy Bill—now sent out to discharge (for the thirteenth time) old Mr. Muggeridge, as Hazey thought, from towling about Tarring Neville with the rum-and-milk harriers. Finding his mistake, Bill was anxious to efface the abruptness of his inquiry, and now ran on alongside of Lucy to where Romford was still holding his feathering hounds on the waning scent. The more likely the fox seemed to beat Facey, the more anxious Facey felt to beat the fox. "Didn't do to be beaten by a bagman!" he muttered.

"Mr. Romford! Mr. Romford!" now exclaimed Lucy, coming up with Bill and a couple-and-a-half of straggling hounds; "here's Mr. Hazey! here's Mr. Hazey!"

"Hazey, is there?" retorted Romford; adding to Affable, "*for-rard on*, good bitch! *for-rard on!* How are you, sir?" continued he, looking hastily over his shoulder, adding, "Oh, it's you, is it?" seeing it was the son; "how are ye? How's the old 'un?" meaning his brother-master of hounds. "Yoicks, Challenger: good dog—speak to him again! How's the old 'un?" repeated he, turning again to his hounds.

"Nicely, thank you; how are you?" replied the boy Bill.

"You've not seen the fox, have you?" asked Mr. Romford, without noticing the inquiry after his own health.

"No," replied Bill.

"Deuced odd," rejoined Mr. Romford; "deuced odd. Ran him quite briskly up to within half a mile of this

place, since when the scent's been gettin' weaker and
weaker. Humph!" added he, as he sat watching the
energies of the hounds gradually subsiding. "Seems to
be gone altogether!" muttered he. "What place is
this?" now demanded Mr. Romford of his young friend.

"This!" replied Bill. "This is Tarring Neville—our
place, you know."

"Tarring Neville, is it?" muttered Facey. "Well,
mind," added he, after a pause, "I brought this fox out
of my own country," fearing lest old Hazey might make
reprisal upon him; adding, "and if I can kill him above
ground, you know, I may."

The scent, however, now failed altogether—even
yellow-pied Vanquisher gave it up.

"I'll just make one cast," observed Facey, half to Lucy
half to himself; and then, turning to Bill, he added,
"and we'll come up to the stables, and get some gruel
for the horses."

"Do," replied Bill, adding, "and some breakfast for
yourselves."

"Breakfast!" muttered Facey; "more like dinner,
I should think!" forgetting how early he had come out.

He then cast his hounds for the first time during the
run, making a very comprehensive semicircular advance,
which brought him right in front of Tarring Neville.

"Not a bad-like shop," observed Facey to Lucy, as
he kept one little roving pig-eye on his hounds, the
other on the house.

"No, it's not," replied Lucy; adding, "I vote we go
in and see what it's like inside;" adding, "they were
all over ours, you know."

"Too much bother," rejoined Facey; "the women
will be all astir."

"Oh, never mind that," said Lucy. "Let's see what
they are like."

Facey still kept holding his hounds on, more for the
sake of making a survey of the place, than in any
expectation of their hitting off the scent. At last he
came to a swing cattle-gate, across a widish brook at
the far end of the lawn; and, the country beyond not
appearing inviting, he resolved to give in, hoping that
Hazey might hunt the fox back into his country some
other day.

"No use potterin' on after the beggar any longer,"

said he, turning the reluctant Baker round, with a "Cop—come away! cop—come away!" to his hounds. "First bagman I ever hunted," said Facey, "and it shall be the last. Do one's hounds more harm than enough."

So saying, he kicked the Baker into a trot, and swung gaily over the green, as if to make the hounds believe he had done all he intended. He had got the Baker's back down, at all events; and would have him quiet for the next day he was wanted.

"I should like a cup of tea very much now," said Lucy, reverting to Bill's proposal.

"Dash you and your tea! You women are always wanting tea—should go about with a kettle tacked to your saddles," replied Romford.

"Well, I'm sure it's a very harmless beverage."

"Harmless enough," retorted Facey; "but it does you no good."

"Well, there's not much feeding in it, perhaps; but, still, it's very refreshing."

"Well, then, come and refresh yourselves," said Facey, turning his horse's head towards the house, with a view of encountering the crinolines.

So they jogged over the greensward to the stables, Facey thinking, as he looked at his old lack-lustre boots, that Lucy would have to do the decorative part of the entertainment, as he was only in very "so-so" guise. He would rather have his hot woodcocks at home, than damage his appetite by anything he might get at Hazey's. However, he would see how the land lay.

CHAPTER XXXVII

TARRING NEVILLE

MR. HAZEY'S boy Bill, in the exercise of a wise discretion, had run back to the house to give the alarm of "Company coming! company coming!" while Mr. Romford made his final cast for his fox about the place Bill informed his beloved parents in breathless haste as they still sat at their morning meal, that it wasn't old Muggeridge who was towling about the grounds with the rum-and-milk harriers, but no less a personage than the great Mr. Romford, who, with his sister, Mrs. Somerville, he believed was coming in to breakfast. He did not say that he had asked them, lest that should have been wrong, but left it to be inferred that they had invited themselves.

"Breakfast!" ejaculated Hazey, throwing down his "Times," and glancing at his garments.

"Breakfast!" exclaimed Mrs. Hazey, thinking of her cream, eggs, and honey.

"Breakfast!" repeated Miss, recollecting that she looked rather yellow as she dressed.

And away they all started on their respective reviser-ships. But the boy Bill, having been seen, stood his ground in the way of dress, and confined his endeavours to rousing the establishment.

"Look sharp! look sharp!" was the cry; "there's company coming! there's company coming!"

And the news flew with such electricity that when our master and Mrs. Somerville rode into the stable-yard, sly Silkey the groom and a couple of helpers were on the look out for their horses, while a lad held back the door of a loose-box for the reception of the hounds. Having dismounted and got the latter housed, Facey locked the door, and putting the key in his pocket, proceeded to assist his sister to descend from her horse. A light bound from the saddle landed her on the ground, when, having shaken out her habit, she arranged it becomingly, with a due regard to the interests of her pretty booted feet and neatly fitting trousers. In truth Lucy looked very lovely. Her smart habit showed her natural figure to advantage, and the fine fresh morning air had imparted a genial glow to her bright complexion. Her hair, too, was all right.

"Now," said Facey to Silkey, "you give these horses half a pail of gruel and a feed of corn apiece;" adding, "and don't take the saddles off, but throw a rug over each of them:" so saying he stamped the thick of the mud sparks off his rusty Napoleons, and then proceeded to follow Lucy, who was already tripping along the gravel walk to the house.

"Rot the women," muttered he, eyeing her; "they

are never happy unless they are pokin' their noses into each other's houses. Can't possibly be hungry so soon."

"Now, who are you goin' to ax for?" demanded he, overtaking her just as she gained the little iron wicket at the end of a well-kept gravel walk that evidently led to the front of the house.

"Oh, there's no occasion to ask for any one," replied Lucy; "just ring the bell; they asked us in, you know."

"Humph," rejoined Romford; "not so clear that they meant us to come, though."

"Well, if they didn't, it will teach them to be more truthful another time," replied Lucy, laughing; "besides," added she, "this will do instead of returning their call, you know."

"Hut, oi never meant to return it," growled Romford.

Tarring Neville now resembled a theatre at the critical moment of ringing up the curtain. Whatever bustle and confusion may have prevailed behind the scenes, all must be hushed and still at that momentous summons. So at Tarring Neville, when the ominous front-door bell sounded there was an end of hurry and preparation. Basket the butler suddenly dropped from a trot to a walk; Henry the footman ceased fumbling at his coat-cuffs; the breakfast tableau was recomposed, Mrs. Hazey, in command of the teapot as before, while Hazey subsided, "Times" in hand, into his arm-chair, as though he had been sitting quietly at his meal, instead of having been to his dressing-room to exchange a shabby old silk frayed surtout for a smartish coatee and fancy vest.

"Mr. Romford and Mrs. Somerville," now proclaimed stage-manager Tomkins, opening the breakfast-room door, when up started Hazey, laying down the "Times," as though quite surprised and overjoyed at the announcement. He *was* rather pleased, for he was half-inclined to think the Romfords wouldn't visit him, and then adieu to his chance of a deal.

"My dear Mrs. Somerville, how do you do?" exclaimed he, advancing and grasping her hand fervently; adding, "let me introduce Mrs. Hazey. Mrs. Hazey, Mrs. Somerville; Mrs. Somerville, Mrs. Hazey." Then, while the ladies were bobbing and curtseying and showing each other their teeth, he turned to Romford, who was making a comparison greatly in favour of Lucy, and, shaking hands with him, said, "This is indeed quite an unexpected pleasure. Up betimes this morning, I guess—early bird that gets the worm, eh?"

"Doesn't always get the fox, though," replied Facey, with a chuckle.

"What! you've been hunting, have you?" exclaimed Hazey, with well-feigned surprise, ignoring the boy Bill's visit, old Muggeridge, and all the outdoor proceedings. "Well," continued he, seeing the action of the ladies' backs fast subsiding, "let me introduce Mrs. Hazey. Mr. Romford, my dear," added he, "brother-master of hounds; so glad to see you, Romford, you can't think," continued he, knocking off the mister, and turning again to his guest, adding, "now pray be seated and have some breakfast, and tell us all about it. Where will you sit, Mrs. Somerville? Where will you sit, Mr. Romford? Stay, Mrs. Somerville, I'll pull the blind down, and keep the sun off your eyes," so saying he lowered the shade, and Mrs. Somerville, conscious of a healthy complexion, sat boldly down with her face to the light.

The footman and Tomkins then came in, the former bearing a tray with a reinforcement of cups and other crockery ware, in the midst of which rose the tall form of a coffee-pot, with its usual accompaniments of hot milk and sugar, together with hot toast, hot rolls, hot everything. Mr. Romford took tea, and Mrs. Somerville took coffee, and our master nearly knocked the bottom out of a muffin plate by leistering two layers of roll with his fork at a blow. Hazey congratulated himself that it wasn't his No. 1 set when he heard it. "Rough fellow, that Romford," thought he, eyeing his muscular arm; "strikes as if he was pronging a salmon."

And now the usual sound of eating being established, after a careful listen at the door, Miss Anna Maria made her appearance, as if for the first time that morning, taking the chance of her breakfast things either being removed, or of Mrs. Somerville not noticing them. The fact was, Miss, considering the importance of the occasion, had determined, as she glanced at herself in the cheval glass, to make a complete revision of her person, regardless of the time it would require; and so, beginning with the damask cheek, she removed the before-mentioned pallor by the slightest possible touch of rouge, and that giving satisfaction, she then proceeded to array herself in a charming *négligée* of black and violet *foullard*.

Miss Hazey was a pretty, sunny, blue-eyed girl of some twenty years of age, with a terrible taste for coquetting, which she gratified in the most liberal and promiscuous way. Lawyers, doctors, curates, soldiers, sailors, all were alike to her. Indeed, her sole employment seemed to be winning men's hearts, and throwing them away. Her own was said to be equal parts steel and whalebone. Such was the young lady who now re-entered the dining-room at Tarring Neville, with the full determination of trying the force of her artillery upon the great and desirable Mr. Romford. It was not every day that she had such a chance.

Miss gave a well-feigned start, as if surprised at the unexpected presence of strangers, which mamma seeing, and knowing her talent for dissimulation, seconded by exclaiming, "Oh, come in, my dear! come in! It's Mr. and Mrs. Romford—I beg pardon, Mr. Romford and Mrs. Somerville. They've been out hunting already this morning, while you, idle girl, have been dozing in bed." Then, turning to Mrs. Somerville, who was just chipping the shell of a guinea-fowl egg, she said, "This is my daughter, Anna Maria, Mrs. Somerville : Mr. Romford, my dear." Whereupon Miss Anna Maria gave two of her best Brighton boarding-school curtsies, and took up a favourable position, with her back to the light, immediately opposite our master. As she unfolded her napkin, she looked deliberately at him, and thought what a queer-looking man he was,—queer eyes, queer nose, queer hair, queer altogether. "Must be rich," thought she, "he's so ugly." And Facey, peering at her out of the corners of his little pig-eyes, thought she was just as smart a little girl as ever he had seen—uncommonly smart little girl—just his fancy of a girl, in fact. He then leistered the other layer of roll. And now Mr. Hazey, wishing to know to what cause they were indebted for the honour of this early visit—especially to know how Mr. Romford's hounds came to be in his country—essayed to direct the conversation into the hunting line.

"So you didn't kill the fox, you say?" observed he, reverting to Mr. Romford's early-bird rejoinder; "so you didn't kill the fox, you say?"

"No," replied Romford, "no. Fact was, I didn't care much about killin' him."

"Must have been a good fox, though," observed Mr. Hazey ; "brought you a long way out of your country, you know ;" wondering whether Mr. Romford had been drawing his (Mr. Hazey's) outside cover, Ravensclugh Gorse, on the sly.

"No, not a bad fox," assented Romford ; "not a bad fox. Indeed, that made me less anxious to kill him. You see, we had a blank day yesterday, and I thought if I could blood a few couple of hounds with a bad fox it would keep them steady for Saturday ; but, as usual, when one wants a bad fox, one gets a good 'un, and he brought us here to breakfast with you. I've left him somewhere about your place here," added he.

"Ah, well, I'm much obliged. I'll hunt him back to you some day," replied Mr. Hazey.

"Do," replied Mr. Romford, "and kill him, if you can, in the open ; but mind, don't dig him!" added he, glancing significantly at Hazey, who was rather addicted to digging.

"Oh no, honour bright!" replied his host. "Wouldn't do such a thing for the world!"

"Wouldn't trust you," thought our master, remembering the character Independent Jimmy gave him.

Ladies are generally better hands at talking and eating at the same time than gentlemen are. At all events, Lucy eclipsed Mr. Facey in that performance ; for she chattered away, while Facey, in schoolboy parlance, "let his meat stop his mouth." She talked about the opera, and she talked about the Prince and Princess of Wales, and she talked about the Court, and she talked of great people in such a social way, that Mrs. Hazey felt as if she was regularly inducted into high life. It was quite clear Mrs. Somerville moved in the highest circles ; and Mrs. Hazey thought what an advantage it would be to her daughter if Mrs. Somerville would take Anna Maria by the hand. So she smiled, and simpered, and assented to everything Mrs. Somerville said, mingling her applause with judicious appliances of coffee and tea. And Lucy, being pleased with her reception, and the evident respect that was paid to her, laid herself out to be extra-agreeable, and talked very magnificently of herself and her doings, and said that though Beldon Hall

was a very comfortable place, yet it wasn't so good a
house as she expected to find it.   And Miss Anna Maria,
who always let the gentlemen digest her beauty properly
before she began to exercise her arts and allurements,
now seeing Mr. Romford examining her attentively, just
went on playing with her breakfast, exhibiting first her
pretty hand, then her pretty teeth, next her pretty
dimples, by a smile ; until thinking he was ready for
the grand assault of the tongue, she fixed the artillery
of her beautiful, well-fringed blue eyes full upon him,
and asked if he was fond of archery.

"Oh, why, yes—no ;—oi mean oi don't care a great
deal about it. Pretty amusement enough. Day should
be fine, though," added he, " or it's very poor fun."

"Yes, the day should be fine," assented Miss Hazey,
who had been drenched in a thunderstorm at the last one
she was at.

They then indulged in a slight discussion upon fishing,
at which, of course, Facey was more at home ; in the
midst of which, breakfast being at length concluded,
Mrs. Hazey offered Mrs. Somerville the great feminine
treat of showing her over her house. Facey and Hazey
then, we need scarcely say, paired off to the stables.

While the foregoing scene was enacting in the house,
"my boy Bill," ever anxious for reliable information,
and always more happy in the stables than in the parlour,
had slunk away to the former, there to see what he
could make out of Mr. Romford's horses. And Leotard
having finished the very moderate feed of corn Mr.
Silkey, the groom, vouchsafed him, now began sniffing
and staring about, as horses will sniff and stare about
in a strange stable ; in this case, perhaps to see if there
was any more corn coming. Then, as "Satan still," as
it has been beautifully expressed, "finds work for idle
hands to do," so the boy Bill bethought him he would
give Leotard a round in the exercising ground at the
back of the stables, and put him over the leaping-bar,
and a few of the make-believe fences his father had
established for the purpose of training his horses. So
he told a helper to put on the bridle, and this being done,
and the horse led forth, Bill mounted in the confident
sort of way that a man mounts a lady's horse, thinking,
if a lady can ride him, anybody else can. And it was
lucky that Bill began calmly, for a side-saddle not

affording a very eligible investment for a gentleman's person, if Bill had begun either in the bucketing or the timorous strain, Leotard would in all probability have kicked him over his head, whereas, Bill just employing the same light hand that Mrs. Somerville had used, the horse went poking along as quietly as could be, fulfilling all Bill's behests, first over the bar, then over the hurdle, next over the rail, and finally over the furze-coped on-and-off mound. And Bill, patting him on the safe completion of the last feat, thought he was quite as safe and clever a lady's horse as it was possible to find. With this conviction he pulled up into a walk, and returned leisurely along to the stable, hoping he might not encounter Leotard's fair owner by the way. Luckily, however, he got safe back, and Silkey had the horse restored to its stall, and all the stables put into apple-pie order, ere his master came heralding the great Mr. Romford along to the stud. Some people have a wonderful pleasure in staring at horses—staring at them just as ladies stare at bonnets ; the gentlemen, doubtless, thinking how well they would look on them, just as the ladies think how well they would look in them. Still, staring at horses is much more stupid than staring at bonnets, for with horses you haven't the whole case before you. If the bonnets were enveloped in tissue, or cap paper, as the horses are in clothing and straw, a very slight glimpse would satisfy the ladies ; whereas one sees men—at Tattersall's, for instance—staring week after week at horses, who never buy a horse, who never bid for a horse, and who, if they had a horse, would very likely not know whether to mount at the right side or the left ; yet, there they go—most likely taking a couple of catalogues each, pushing, and elbowing, and asking all sorts of absurd questions of the grooms and helpers, and finding all sorts of mare's-nests for themselves and their friends.

But our brother-masters of hounds are now approaching the stables—sauntering along, each trying to make a mental estimate of the other. As in all show places, from Windsor Castle downwards, they begin with the smaller rooms first, and proceed to those of increased size and importance, until they culminate in the baronial or some great hall ; so Mr. Hazey always passed an expectant purchaser through the servants' horses stable before introducing him to the grand exhibition of his own. On these interesting occasions our delicate-minded master had hitherto always pretended to play second fiddle to Silkey, who had a most insinuating way of recommending a horse, never pressing him, indeed, but rather expressing his reluctance to part with him; always declaring in confidence to a customer that he thought he was "just about the very best 'oss he ever had through his hands, but master really was so 'ticlar and fanciful that there was no sich thing as pleasing him. If an 'oss pulled an ounce more than he liked, he would part with him; if he went a little gayer at his fences than he was accustomed to, he would cast him. Altogether there was no such thing as suiting him."

"Ah, sir," Silkey would conclude, with a sigh, and a shrug of his shoulders, "I wish I had all the money master has wasted in 'osses since I first came to him— make me a very comfortable independence, I assure you."

If Silkey had put it the other way, and said if he had all the money he had helped his master to cheat other people of, he would not have been far wrong in his assertion.

Now, however, since the boy Bill came home he had rather taken the initiative out of Silkey's hands, though, to do Bill justice, he was clever enough to strike out a fresh line of his own, and, instead of "but"-ing, like Silkey, he used to praise the horse they wanted to sell, or, rather, the horse they thought the other party wanted to buy, so superlatively—Bill declaring he didn't think his father would part with him for "any money"—that instead of taking a trifle off the price as the "but" used to do, it enabled Mr. Hazey to put something on; a much more agreeable process than the other. But Silkey waxed sulky under the change, considering that no gentleman ought to interfere with the just prerogatives of his groom.

"The idea of using me so!" said Silkey to his friend Jawkins, the huntsman. "The idea of his using me so! *I* who always treated him like a brother!"

And now Mr. Hazey, having got our great master Mr. Romford fairly through the servants' horses stables, gradually dropped astern as he came to his own, leaving the redoubtable Bill to pilot the way, and expatiate on their extraordinary merits as they went. This stable con-

tained the joint-stock stud, viz. Mr. Hazey's and the
boy Bill's, but Bill thinking it would be more to the
honour and glory of the establishment to announce them
all as his father's, inducted our master into the presence
with the observation, "Ah! these are the governor's
horses—five for his own riding, you see—rather more
than he wants, p'r'aps, for three days a week, but still
he likes to be over-horsed, and doesn't care much about
cost."

Then Bill went up first to Volunteer, then to Lottery,
then to Gay and Sure, then to the Clipper, and lastly, to
Topthorn, patting and praising and caressing them as
though they were the greatest favourites under the sun,
that no money could purchase, though in reality Volunteer was the only horse Hazey had had during the last
season, and he, too, had been sold and returned, charged
with having an incipient cataract—of which little defect,
of course, neither Hazey nor Silkey knew anything. He
was now waiting for a convenient turn of the complaint
to go up to the hammer to be sold as the property of a
gentleman who never warranted, with Silkey to do the
cajolers. "Sound an 'oss as ever stepped—master, full of
fancies, doesn't know a good 'oss when he has one." That
is, of course, always presuming that Silkey was properly
primed and propitiated for the occasion.

And now the boy Bill, having at length concluded his
loving laudations, his beloved parent came sauntering
in from the other end of the stable, and, seeing the performance was about over, just glanced his eye along the
stalls, and then asked Mr. Romford to take a seat on the
corn-bin and finish his pipe, an invitation that Romford
readily complied with, and the two were presently in
full puff.

Whiff, puff, whiff—"That's a good horse," said Hazey,
nodding at Gay and Sure.

Puff, whiff, puff—"Is he?" said Romford, eyeing him.

Whiff, puff, whiff—"Gave a vast of money for him,"
observed Hazey.

"Fifty, p'r'aps," puffed Facey.

"*Fifty!*" ejaculated Bill—"four fifties, I should think,
would be nearer the mark." They had given eighty,
and got two back.

And the ladies on their parts having equally interesting subjects to discuss, dawdled and sauntered; and Mrs.

Hazey, in return for a delicate compliment on her daughter's beauty, having favoured Mrs. Somerville with a recital of her many eligible offers, knights, baronets, honourables, our fair friend, thinking her hostess seemed like a good conduit pipe, wherein to convey spurious information, essayed to return the compliment, by giving her a slight sketch of herself and her own career. To this end she informed Mrs. Hazey that she had two thousand a year jointure, besides a pension as a field officer's widow, but that one thousand a year would go from her if she married again; that her nephew, Charley Somerville, of the Lady Killer Lancers, to whom the thousand a year would go, would gladly compound with her for five hundred a year, but that he was a very profligate young man, much addicted to casinos and sherry-coblers, and she would not further his extravagance by any such arrangement; all of which Mrs. Hazey imbibed with great interest, but seemed to think there was no occasion for Mrs. Somerville to sacrifice herself to her naughty nephew. And having, like her husband, a keen eye to business, she began asking about the nephew's age and position, thinking perhaps her daughter could reclaim him from casinos and coblers, all of which Mrs. Somerville answered satisfactorily; whereupon Mrs. Hazey very adroitly, as she thought, suggested, that if Mrs. Somerville felt a real interest in the young man's welfare, it might be the means of retrieving him from bad connections, to bring him down to Beldon Hall and give him some hunting. And Mrs. Somerville seemed at first to be rather taken with the idea, but on second thoughts, she felt it was of no use complicating matters, so she quashed the idea altogether, by saying he had a washball seat, and couldn't ride across country; adding that she never knew a casino frequenter who could; besides which, the Lady Killer Lancers were ordered to Dublin; so there was an end of the matter.

The mention of hunting, however, opened out the question how long Mrs. Somerville was going to stay in Doubleimupshire,—a point that she was not at all inclined to enlighten Mrs. Hazey upon; so looking at her pretty Geneva watch, set with brilliants (the unconscious gift of a west-end watchmaker), she exclaimed, "Oh dear, do you know what o'clock it is? I declare Mr. Romford will think I am lost. Oh, *do* let us go to the gentlemen;

I'd *no* idea it was half so late." So saying, she gathered up her habit very scientifically, and, piloted by Mrs. Hazey, proceeded to the stables by the short cut through the back yard, under a chain-rattling salute of *Bow-wow-wows* from a great black-and-white Newfoundland dog.

Entering the court, Mrs. Hazey made direct for her husband's stable, where, seated on the corn-bin, she found the gentlemen still continuing their smoking discussions.

"Ah, here you are at last !" exclaimed Mr. Romford, as he got a glimpse of the habit; "here you are at last !" adding, "thought you'd gone to bed. Well, now," continued he, "let us be moving. Where are the horses ? Bid them put on the bridles, and turn their heads where their tails should be."

So saying, he got off the bin, and, pocketing his pipe, proceeded to stamp in a very would-be-doing sort of way.

"Oh, there's no hurry," observed Mr. Hazey, "no hurry."

"Oh no, no hurry," assented Mr. Romford; "only the days are short, and one should make the most of what there is."

"Wouldn't you like to come and see our Dorking fowls and Dorsetshire ewes ?" now interposed Mrs. Hazey.

"After a bit," replied Romford, "after a bit, when one can have some mint sauce with them, you know," added he.

The sight of the habit had set the stable-men on the alert, and the bridles being adjusted, the horses were presently wheeling round in their stalls to be ready for mounting. And as Leotard's Arab-like head and snakey neck were followed by his elegant figure, Hazey stood by, drawing his breath, thinking how he would like to have the selling of him. There is nothing so lucrative, so money-making as a showy lady's horse. If the lady says "buy," it must be buy, whatever the price; if she takes a dislike, the horse must be got rid of, whatever the sacrifice.

"Ah, that's a neat 'un," said Mr. Hazey to Lucy, with more than his usual candour. He generally praised with a reservation, an "if" or a "but"; and this piece of praise was the exception to the general rule. "Ah, that's a neat 'un," said he, conning him over. "Beautiful head and neck ; best set-on tail I ever saw :" these being, as Hazey well knew, the cardinal points of a lady's horse.

"Yes, he is," replied Lucy, now tendering him her taper hand, having already saluted Mrs. and Miss Hazey, and also the boy Bill.

"Good-bye, my dear Mrs. Somerville!" exclaimed Mr. Hazey, grasping it fervently; adding, "I'm very much obliged to the fox for bringing you here. Hope you'll come of your own accord next time."

"Thank you, Mr. Hazey," replied Lucy, now slightly raising her habit, and tendering her little foot for Romford to mount her.

The man of the muscular arm lifted her up as buoyantly as a cork. Drawing her thin reins, she touched Leotard lightly with the whip, and put him with his head on to slightly rising ground.

Romford noted the movement, and thought to reward Hazey's confidence by giving him a slight insight into Leotard's character.

"That's one of the most perfect lady's pads I ever saw," said Romford, taking Hazey a few paces off, so that he might contemplate him like a picture. "But he's just one fault,—at least so my sister thinks; he wants a little driving at his fences, whereas she likes a free goer."

"Indeed!" said Hazey, noting the defect; and, being now down wind of Mrs. Hazey, he added (loud enough to be heard by Lucy), "Well, horse and rider are uncommonly handsome—perfect pictures both of them."

Then came out that magnificent weight-carrying hunter, "Pull-Devil-Pull-Baker," with his great arms, magnificent shoulders, and lean handsome head,—looking like a perfect Placid Joe, both in mind and manners.

"Ah, that's something like a horse!" exclaimed Mr. Hazey, his cold eyes sparkling with animation as he surveyed him. "That's something like a horse. Three 'undred guineas' worth, I guess."

"*Four*," replied Facey confidentially; "leastways, two two's. Oi've a patent way," continued he, "of concealing my extravagancies, by giving two cheques for one horse: one on my London banker, and the other on my country one, so that neither of them know the extent of my gullibility."

"Well, but if you want to sell," suggested Mr. Hazey.

"Oh, then the horse speaks for himself," replied Mr. Romford. "It doesn't follow because oi give too much

that another man must do the same. One always expects
to lose by a horse."

So saying, Mr. Romford then approached and mounted
the Baker, sitting in the ostentatious sort of way of a man
who is conscious that he is cocked on the top of a "good
'un."

"What do you call him?" asked Miss Anna Maria,
who had now joined the group.

"Placid Joe," replied Romford, patting him on the
neck, well knowing it wouldn't do to call him by his
right one.

"Ah, he looks very good-tempered," observed the lady.

All things being at length ready for a start, the loose-
box door was opened, out came the hounds with a cry,
when, with mutual adieux, away the cavalcade proceeded
to find their way across country to Beldon Hall.

And Mr. Hazey having watched Leotard's action over
the cobble-stones, to which he could take no exception
whatever, and having seen the last loitering hound
disappear, after a few moments lost in deep meditation,
turned round to his wife saying, "Well, now, that's as
rum a go as ever I saw in my life."

"How, my dear?" asked Mrs. Hazey, now duly impressed with the two-thousand-a-year story.

"Well, the get-up, the turn-out, the whole thing,"
replied Mr. Hazey.

"Well, but it's only a chance visit, my dear," observed
Mrs. Hazey.

"True," said Hazey, "true; but still he's a rum 'un
anyhow."

"There's a good deal of character about him, certainly,"
assented his wife.

"I like his horses better than I do himself," observed
Mr. Hazey, after a pause. "But I do wonder that a man
who can have such fine horses should not have a pair
of better boots."

"Not particular about appearances, perhaps?" suggested
Mrs. Hazey.

"That's a nice nag, that cream-colour," observed Bill,
now joining his beloved parents.

"Ah, we must keep an eye on him," said his father.
"Shouldn't wonder if there might be a penny turned by
that horse. What was it Romford said about him—that
he didn't go freely at his fences, or something?"

"I think it was something of that sort," replied his wife, who did not take much interest in equestrian matters.

"Oh, I should say he was rather a nice fencer," observed Bill.

"How do you know?" asked his father.

"I tried him—tried him when you were all in at breakfast."

"Clever lad!" exclaimed Hazey, patting him on the back. "Clever lad! Never miss a chance, that's a good fellow—always keep your weather eye open, my boy;" so saying, the trio proceeded leisurely back to the house.

And as talks-over are always mutual, Mr. Romford and Lucy had the Hazeys on the *tapis* as soon as the breadth of the Herdlaw road enabled the hounds to get away from among their horses' feet.

"Well, and what did you make of Mother What's-her-name?" asked Mr. Romford, with a backward jerk of his head to indicate who he meant.

"Oh, well, she was very affable," replied Lucy.

"Well, but did you gammon her well?" asked Romford, meaning about himself.

"Oh, beautifully! Told her I had two thousand a year jointure, and I don't know what else."

"Oh, the deuce!" exclaimed Romford, "but you shouldn't have done that."

"Why not?" asked Lucy.

"Why not?" repeated Romford; "why, because you'll have every unmarried man in the country after you."

"Well, but I told her I lost a thousand a year if I married again."

"Oh, that won't stop them," retorted Facey—"that won't stop them. Bless your heart, a thousand a year will draw men from all the corners of the earth. You should have said you lost it all, and then they would have abused Somerville, and it would have saved our door-bell. They'll eat us out of house and home," added he, thinking of the dreadful consequences of the invasion, —the disappearance of his cold meat, his cold game, his cold pie; nay, he wouldn't answer for his Saturday's resurrection puddings, consisting of all the odds and ends of the week, being safe from the intrusion of the suitors.

Mr. Romford didn't like it. No good could come of it, for she couldn't marry with old Soapey alive, and to have his house besieged by all the idle fortune-hunters of the country was more than he could endure. And he jogged on silently in a very mystified contemplative mood, with an occasional pull of his beard, thinking he would have to rake and watch the gravel ring very attentively. But in his inmost thoughts came the conviction that Miss Hazey was much prettier than Miss Watkins, and, though it was very imprudent even thinking of her, his thoughts would run that way.

CHAPTER XXXVIII

MR. AND MRS. HAZEY'S INVITATION

GREAT as was Mr. Romford's general success in Doubleimupshire, both as a sportsman and a protégé of Lord Lovetin, in no part, perhaps, was it more signal than at Tarring Neville, where they looked upon him as a most desirable acquaintance, showing, at all events, that two of a trade do not always disagree. To be sure, Mr. Hazey thought that a man who was simple enough to keep foxhounds for a benevolent object—namely, founding an hospital for decayed sportsmen—might very likely be easily victimised in the matter of a horse; while Mrs. Hazey thought the owner of Abbeyfield Park, J.P., D.L., patron of three livings, would be an extremely eligible *parti* for her daughter. Not that she was mercenary; only she liked to see affluence. Love in a cottage found no favour with her. Love in a castle was a far better thing.

With feelings such as these, it was easily settled that the unexpected morning visit caused by the bag fox should stand in the place of a regular call; a return, in fact, of the pilgrimage that Hazey and the boy Bill made to Beldon Hall on the Sunday. That settled, and the larder and meets of the respective hounds being consulted, then came the question who they should ask,—whether Mr. Romford and his sister, or Mr. Romford alone; Mrs. and Miss Hazey thinking they would do as well without Mrs. Somerville; Mr. Hazey, on his part, contending that they would have no chance of getting Mr. Romford without Mrs.

Somerville. Mr. Hazey was sure Mr. Romford wouldn't come alone. Didn't look at all like a man to dress up after hunting, to turn out again in the cold, to trail across country in the dead of winter for a dinner. He would be too careful of his carriage horses for that. Mrs. Hazey combated the objection by saying they could ask him to stay all night, and made some deprecatory remarks about the trouble of having women and their maids; adding, that Mrs. Somerville would, most likely, have some fine costly sensitive creature, who would be far more difficult to please than her mistress. But Mr. Hazey adhered to his opinion, that if they wanted Mr. Romford, they must ask Mrs. Somerville also; and dreading the "I told you so" if they failed in securing Mr. Romford, they were obliged to accede, and invite Mrs. Somerville as well.

So it was settled that both should be asked, Mrs. Somerville by the ladies, and Mr. Romford by the gentleman; and as the cards for the next week's meets of the hounds were just about to be issued, a lawn meet was made for Tarring Neville on Mr. Romford's non-hunting day. Then Anna Maria proceeded to draw up an elaborate but apparently off-hand document, in the familiar strain, on behalf of mamma, inviting her dear Mrs. Somerville to give them the pleasure of her company on Wednesday, and stay till Friday. And after several alterations of phrase, and careful guarding against Mrs. Somerville coming alone, she got the draft to her and mamma's liking; and, drawing out a sheet of super-fine cream-laid note-paper (slightly scented), proceeded, with the aid of a new pen, to copy it in her best hand-writing for sending. The new pen, like most new pens, didn't go freely at first; it was like a newly-shod horse wanting to find its feet, and the first note was condemned at the third line. The second was found no better, for she put two *n*'s into Wednesday; and in the third attempt the tiresome pen made a trip and a splutter at the word pleasure, and she couldn't think of sending that either. The fourth, however, she got to her mind, and presented to her mamma for approval. Thus it ran:—

"Tarring Neville.

'My dear Mrs. Somerville,—It will give us sincere pleasure if this should be fortunate enough to find you disengaged, and if you would accompany Mr. Romford here on Wednesday, and stay till Friday. I fear we cannot offer you any great attractions; but the hounds will meet here on Thursday, and we hope you will bring your horse, and partake of the pleasures of the chase with the Hard and Sharp Hounds. Mr. Hazey joins in kind regards, and hopes to see you, with, my dear Mrs. Somerville, ever yours very sincerely,

"MARY HAZEY."

And Hazey, albeit of the cozening order, was rather puzzled how to address our friend Mr. Romford, whether as "Dear Romford," "Dear Mr. Romford," "Dear Sir," or how. "Dear Romford" would have done well enough to a three-days-a-week master, with a subscription; but here was a four-days-a-week one, with an occasional bye, who was going to devote his subscription to a charitable purpose. Then, if Hazey was to "sir," "dear sir," or "my dear sir" him, Mr. Romford might think it rather stiff; and, altogether, Hazey thought the best plan was to take the middle course, and "Mr." him, address him as "Dear Mr. Romford." So our master, having made up his mind on that point, echoed his daughter's letter without the flummery; adding, that he had a stall for Mr. Romford's horse, and thought he could promise him a good fox. And Mr. Hazey sealed it with a fine butter-pat-like coat of arms seal of many quarterings, many stags, many rings, many falcons, the whole surmounted by his crest of a lion with a kitchen-poker-like-tail. Then the letters went to the post, and expectation presently stood on tiptoe, speculating whether they would come or not; Mrs. Hazey saying they would, Mr. Hazey taking the other side, and the boy Bill going halves with his father in a sixpenny bet on the event.

Facey was at the kennel when the letters came; but Lucy saw by the postmark that they were from the same quarter, and anticipated the contents of her brother's by her own. She was all for going, all for taking Leotard, all for making hay while the sun shone. But knowing that Facey would require a little coaxing, she didn't meet him open-mouthed with his letter, lest Chowey, or Swig, or some of the queer ones might have gone wrong at the kennel, but kept it quietly in her workbox, till, having made a hearty dinner off hot beef pudding and Edinburgh ale, he had got half through a pipe and a whole glass of gin in his smoking-chair before she began.

"Oh dear!" exclaimed she, as if she had quite forgotten it until that moment, "I've a letter for you," rising, and pretending to bustle for it in her workbox.

"Letter (*puff*) for me " (*puff*), growled Facey. "Who can it be from?" taking the pipe from his mouth. Facey didn't like letters; he thought they might be disagreeable ones.

"Well, I think it's from Mr.—Mr.—what do they call him? Hard and Sharp, you know?"

"Oh, Hazey," said Romford, comforted by the sound, and turning half round in his chair to replenish his glass.

"Yes, Hazey," replied Lucy, producing the letter, and giving it to him.

"Read it," said Romford, handing it back to her.

Lucy broke the seal and did as desired; while Facey resumed his beloved pipe.

"See him —— first," said Facey, when she was done reading.

"Oh dear, but I should like to go!" exclaimed Lucy.

"But you're not axed," replied Facey, with a knowing leer of his little pig-eye.

"Yes, I am," rejoined Lucy, producing her card.

"Humph!" mused Facey, after a pause. "Don't think that'll pay!"

"Why not?" asked Lucy.

"Oh, bother of getting there—costs I don't know how much! Can hunt here, eat here, drink here,—do everything here that they propose doing there."

"Oh, but consider the society," observed Mrs. Sidney Benson, interposing in her daughter's behalf.

"Fiddle the society," said Romford; "oi can't make anything of the sort out of it."

The fact was, Facey had thought the Anna-Maria project over, and saw the imprudence of the idea. Dalberry Lees was clearly the place for his money.

Still Lucy returned to the charge. She wanted to go and air some of her fine clothes; and if the money was the only obstacle, she thought she could get over that.

"Might ride our own horses over, and send Dirty with our things by the Oldbury coach," observed she.

"Ay, but it's about as much as oi can manish to mount

myself with my own hounds," observed Facey, "without goin' to see other folks. Besides, Swig lamed Oliver Twist the last day we were out, and Bounding Ben and the grey are both coughing."

"Well, but you might ask H. to mount you," continued Lucy; adding, "I dare say he'd be most happy to do so."

"Not quite so sure of that," said Facey, looking down at his big legs; "rather above the mounting size, you see."

"Oh, but then you're a careful rider," rejoined Lucy, who was not easily turned from her point.

"That's as may be," said Romford; "but, havin' a pack of hounds of my own—perhaps the best in England—with both wittles and drink in abundance, I don't see what earthly use it is goin' over there to get the very same things that one has here. That's not what they call the economy of labour."

The fact was, Facey was just a man for his food, and no more. He didn't want his appetite whetted and petted and coaxed; and, having suffered the persecution of two parties, was not at all inclined to venture on a third. Besides, he had spent eighteen shillings in getting to Dalberry Lees, and that would serve him the rest of the season. Of course he hadn't given Independent Jimmy or the servants at the Lees anything; but, still, the vehicle and the gates there and back had come to that amount. "It was payin' for being made miserable," he said. What good did it do him dinin' off plate? He could eat off pewter quite as well, if not better. As to a fine bed, it was all lost upon him: he was none the better for snoozin' in one—could sleep in a barn, for that matter—under a haystack, if it didn't rain.

"Oh, but society—the pleasures of society! A little change, you know, is always agreeable. It doesn't do for people to live too much alone—get awkward and stupid," urged Lucy.

"Well, *you* can go," said Romford. "Dirty and you can go by the coach, just as well as Dirty alone."

"I'm afraid they've blocked me for that," replied Lucy; "they've only asked me if you go; besides, it wouldn't look well for me to go by the coach, you know—coaches are only for common people."

Puff, whiff, puff, went Mr. Romford, meditating the matter. "Coach eighteenpence, Dirty, say a shilling—

two-and-six; two-and-six there, two-and-six back—five shillings: not worth the money," resolved he, turning in his chair. He then tried the expense of the other course—Dirty by the coach, Lucy and himself to ride. "Coach for Dirty, say two shillin's or p'r'aps one-and-nine, if they made a stiff bargain; then, two horses found for the night, say save eighteenpence apiece at home by that; two selves found, dinner and breakfast each—put it, then, at two shillin's a head altogether, that would be four shillin's, and three shillin's would be seven shillin's; seven shillin's saved, except the one-and-ninepence or two shillin's for Dirtiest of the Dirty's fare—say five shillin's saved; but then there would be no end of trouble and persecution, and eating and drinking things he didn't want."

Lucy, however, combated all objections. She would arrange matters; she would see and pack up his things, so that he should have nothing to do but get on to his horse and accompany her, and when he arrived at Tarring Neville he would find his things all laid out on the sofa before the fire, ready for putting on.

And Facey, despite all his prudence, having a lively recollection of the blue-eyed lady, and not altogether disinclined to see her again, at length gave a sort of silent assent, which Lucy immediately clenched by writing to her dear Mrs. Hazey, accepting Mr. Hazey's and her very kind invitation for her brother Romford and herself; adding, that they would ride their own horses over, and she would send her maid by the coach, if her dear friend would have the kindness to send somebody to meet it.

So Mr. Hazey and his boy Bill lost sixpence between them on the event.

And, on the appointed day, Dirtiest of the Dirty was seen getting into the dribbling Oldbury coach at Beldon Hall lodges, on to the roof of which was then piled a quantity of luggage, looking as if the owners of it were going on a visit for a week. Dirty wore her Dalberry Lees pearl and ruby ring quite ostentatiously. The passengers being strangers to her, she of course thought she was equally unknown to them. So she bounced very considerably: telling them her lady was a nobleman's daughter; that she (Dirty) had lived with her two years; that when they left Beldon Hall, they

were going to stay with the Queen at Pimlico Palace,
and afterwards with Mr. Harker Tentrees at Bromley-
by-Bow. Indeed, she talked so imposingly, that, what
with her tongue and her fine attire, if she had not
admitted her servitude, and also got in at the Beldon
Hall lodges, her fellow-passengers would have doubted
whether she was a Dirty or some young lady on a visit
to our master.

Then, at a somewhat later hour of the day, Mr.
Romford and Mrs. Somerville emerged on horseback from
the Beldon Hall stable-yard—Mrs. Somerville on the
redoubtable Leotard, Mr. Romford on the èqually
valuable Everlasting : our master having previously
put the stable establishment under the surveillance of
Mr. Proudlock the keeper ; who, in his turn, was secretly
watched by Billy Balsam ; and Billy by Lucy's lynx-eyed
mamma, Mrs. Benson.

Old Mother Benson, though not good enough to take
abroad, was very useful at home : for, being of a
wandering disposition, she was always trotting about,
and turning up where nobody expected her.

Lucy, we need scarcely say, was got up with the
greatest care, looking more as if she was going to ride
in Rotten Row, or along the esplanade at Brighton, instead
of fighting her way across country, unseen, perhaps, by
any one.

Mr. Romford, on the other hand, was the sportsman
in mufti, deer-stalker hat, rough brownish tweeds, and
rusty Napoleons. Thus attired, they set out on their
travels, timing themselves so as to reach Tarring Noville
towards dusk, in order to have as little of that terrible
winter night's entertainment before dinner as possible.
And having a good eye for counting, Mr. Romford made
a detour that not only enabled him to fix his landmarks
upon it, but also carried him clear of those troublesome
obstacles to some people's progress yclept turnpike-gates.
So he reached Tarring Neville just at the time he
proposed, and, landing his sister at the front door under
the proper reception of the butler and footman, he led
Leotard off with his own horse to the stable, in order
to see them properly put up for the night before he
thought of himself. " Men can ask for what they want,
horses can't," was Facey's aphorism ; and he always made
a point of seeing to his horses himself, a precaution that

was more practised by the last generation of sportsmen than by the present one.

No one, to see Mrs. Hazey's reception of Mrs. Somerville, would have imagined for a moment that there had been any objection made to asking her, so fervent and enthusiastic it seemed to be; the only thing that at all damped the ardour of the greeting being the non-appearance of our hero Mr. Romford at her heels. This passing cloud Mrs. Somerville speedily dispelled by saying that her brother had just gone round to the stable, whereupon the glow of enthusiasm was renewed, and the seductive blandishments of the teapot recommended. Mrs. Somerville declined tea, also the alternative of a glass of sherry and a biscuit, observing that she had lunched just before they came away; whereupon the conversation was turned into the weather-groove, from which it naturally ran upon the roads and the state of the country.

Mrs. Hazey was afraid Mrs. Somerville would find the roads very dirty?

Oh no, she hadn't; they came by the fields. "That splash," said she, looking at one on the side of her habit, "was got coming over Cuckfield Common," and thereupon she held it to the fire to dry.

Mr. Hazey and Mr. Romford then presently entered the drawing-room, after whom came the boy Bill, who had been loitering in the stable to see whether Facey's horses were quiet to dress or not; and next Miss Anna Maria came sailing in in all the radiance of a recent toilette. Then, after a cast back upon the weather, the roads, and the state of the country, the gentlemen diverged upon the never-failing topic of hunting—each master magnifying his more recent runs, and the ladies discussing the taste and discrimination of milliners, and the probable shape of the approaching spring bonnets and mantles. At length the conversation began to flag, and Mrs. Somerville, whose thoughts had been running for some time on an unpacked box, containing a charming evening dress she had brought for the occasion, gladly adopted Mrs. Hazey's suggestion, that perhaps she would like to see her room, and gathering up her habit becomingly, she followed her hostess up the staircase and along a passage to where a partially opened door disclosed the gleam of a newly stirred fire. There, on the sofa,

lay the charming evening dress, which ten minutes
before had been decorating the elegant person of Dirtiest
of the Dirty, who thought she looked uncommonly well
in it. Mr. Romford too, having got his candle, was
conducted by his obsequious host to the other state
apartment, which he presently perfumed with a strong
smell of tobacco. He then proceeded to decorate himself
for dinner—scarlet coat, white vest, black trousers, such
as he wore at Dalberry Lees. And he really looked
very civilised. "Devilish handsome," as he said, when
he came to examine himself in the looking-glass.

CHAPTER XXXIX

MR. HAZEY'S HOSPITALITY

MR. HAZEY reversed Dr. Channing's or somebody's
recorded opinion that, "not what a man *has*, but
what he *is*, should guide us in estimating his true value,"
for Hazey only looked to what his acquaintance had—
we mean in the way of wealth. Hence, any man with
plenty of money was sure to be a hero in Hazey's eyes.
Nothing so contemptible in his opinion as poverty. Nor
birth, nor rank, nor taste, nor talent could compensate
for this fatal deficiency. "Poor man—very poor man,"
he would say, with an air of compassionate pity. Hazey
dearly loved to talk about his own money; tell how
much he had in railway shares, how much in Turkish
scrip, and how much in Danish bonds and new hotels.
In travelling, he generally studied his banker's pass-book
as a work of light reading for the rail, confidentially
revealing to his next neighbour the amount of cash
standing to his credit. "Humph!—not a bad balance,"
he would say, pointing to the figures—£1490, 2s. 8d. or
£2013, 17s. 1d.—"not a bad balance for a mere country
gentleman to keep;"—Hazey omitting to mention that
two-thirds of it were on a deposit receipt bearing three
per cent. interest, or as near three per cent. as he could
screw out of those who had it. With feelings such as
these we need scarcely say he issued his invitations on

the £ s. d. principle, baiting his trap as well with the inducement of having the great Mr. Romford as the temptation of meeting the rich widow, Mrs. Somerville. And Hazey having been good enough to report her reputed jointure of two thousand a year, paid quarterly, all the unmarried men in the country had been trimming their whiskers and bucking up their garments in consequence. Brisk widows are always in demand. Still Hazey's house was never in great repute, for his cookery was only indifferent, and his cellar composed of cheap and second-rate wine. So he had to fire off a good many supplementary notes after the first issue; for people, like porpoises, generally come in shoals, or decline coming altogether. Mr. and Mrs. Joseph Large couldn't come. They had a party at home. So they had, but it consisted only of themselves. The fact was, Large wasn't pleased as to Mrs. Large not being taken out first on a former occasion, and had resolved not to go to Tarring Neville any more.

The Rollingers were extremely sorry they couldn't come; Mr. and Mrs. Chipperfield were the same; and young Mr. Anthony Hallpike, who was one of the catches of the country, declined rather unceremoniously, as young gentlemen will do sometimes.

Then the tide of refusal took a turn, and they got some acceptances. Mr. and Mrs. Cropper would have great pleasure in, etc.; Mr. and Mrs. Gowleykins would be most happy; Mr. Hibberbine had the honour; and Mrs. Stirry and Miss Winkler had the same; the Rev. Mr. Matthew Makepiece, the worthy Rector of Slavington-cum-Starvington, was also at their command. Then Mr. and Miss Makepiece, who at first were only invited to tea, were promoted to the dinner-table. Next there came a little contretemps; for the Pannets of Sycamore Hill, who at first were afraid they would not be able to come, Uncle Joe (from whom they had great expectations) having volunteered a visit, now wrote to say that Joe would put it off; and this, too, after the Hazeys had invited the Dumbletons to supply their places.

However, it all came right at last; for the Dumbletons had bad colds, touches of influenza indeed; and the Pannets were not only better looking, but dressed better; in addition to which, Pannet was a water-drinker, which Dumbleton was not, indeed far from it, being one of the old sticking headachy order, who never could be got away from the dinner-table. And Gritty, the cook, was then weighted with a party of sixteen, which might be increased to eighteen or twenty, according or not as the Beddingfields of Woldingham Manor, and Mr. Bonus, who had as yet not answered, came or declined. But Gritty, like all the common cooks, was not easily overpowered. Only give her plenty of rum for the sauces, and she would undertake to get through anything.

Well, Mrs. Hazey having duly arranged all the sauce and other matters in the morning, and Hazey having told Basket how to deal with the wine, they were free to enact the parts of disengaged host and hostess; receive their dear Mrs. Somerville and Mr. Romford when they came, then dress themselves diligently, and prepare to greet their equally beloved out-of-door friends when they arrived. Miss, of course, knew nothing of any of these domestic proceedings, and the boy Bill was equally ignorant.

And, as the reader perhaps cares not to follow the elders to their respective apartments, see Mrs. Hazey reject her pink satin for her amber *moiré*, or Hazey substitute a pair of candle-light kerseymeres for the brand-new "Nicols" that Basket had laid out for his adornment, we will suppose that the worthy pair have at length descended into the drawing-room, where, with a well-swept hearth and a semi-illumination, they patiently await the coming of the company, wondering whether the clocks are right, and, if so, how they will be by other people's. Hope nobody will think it necessary to come late—half-past six quite late enough for dinner in winter. Hark! there's the sound of wheels! followed by a lull and a ring and a rush in the passage.

Mr. and Mrs. Gowleykins, of Cock-a-Roost Hall, were the first guests to arrive; fat Gowleykins with a Gibus hat and diminutive tie, Mrs. Gowleykins with a hoop that made her look like "the Great Globe itself." It was with difficulty she could get herself compressed into a seat, and then there was a great balance bagging over the arm. Gowleykins was a big, bald-headed, butter-like man, who straddled and tried to look easy, though feeling extremely uncomfortable, and most heartily wishing himself back at Cock-a-Roost Hall. He was a rich man, having, as Hazey afterwards informed Mr. Romford confidentially, full five thousand a year, which, coupled with a delightful simplicity in horsy matters, made him a most valuable ally to Hazey. He didn't get less than fifty pounds a year out of the laird of Cock-a-Roost Hall —fifty pounds at least, all but the couple of sovereigns or so he gave the groom every Christmas to keep his master's heart soft and emollient.

Mr. and Mrs. Cropper, of Cowleyshaw Hill, Mrs. Stirry, and Miss Winkler followed the Gowleykins, the two former having taken up the latter at their residence at Oaklands Grove, greatly to the prejudice of all three dresses. Cropper had growled the whole way at the unreasonable absurdity of crinolines, devoutly wishing that they and some of their inmates were at Jericho. He, too, was a moneyed man, variously estimated at from two to three thousand a year; and though he didn't hunt—indeed his beer-barrel-like figure almost precluded the idea—yet Hazey managed to squeeze a pony out of him for the Hard and Sharps under the plea of patriotism —aiding the noble sport of hunting, which Hazey always maintained it was the bounden duty of every man to do. Scarcely had Cropper's thick legs carried him round the now assembled circle, and brought him up safely on the hearthrug, .than the door opened on the voluntary principle (that is to say, without the intervention of servants), and in rolled Mr. Romford in the full array of the Larkspur Hunt—scarlet tick, clean white vest, black kerseymeres, patent leather boots with elastic sides, for which latter elegancies we do not exactly know to whom he was indebted, but to a firm in St. James's Street.

Then Mr. Hazey, acting the part of bear-leader, made up to Mr. Romford, and, getting him by the arm, forthwith began wheeling and circling him about, introducing him to this person and to that, supplementing his proclamation of names with an aside commentary upon their wealth, such as, "Deuced warm fellow that—has his five thousand a year, if he has a halfpenny" (meaning old Cock-a-Roost); or, "That's a capital fellow, full of money, subscribes to the hounds, and does everything a man should do." But the great object of Mr. Hazey's admiration was Mr. Bonus, now of Shaverley Place, but formerly of the Stock Exchange, a gentleman who still retained a lively leaning to his old pursuits, being always ready for a deal, in which he generally managed to be successful too. "Wonderful fellow," whispered Hazey to Romford, as, having effected the introduction, he led him off towards the lamp as if to show him the picture of a favourite hunter above—"wonderful fellow, turns everything he touches into gold. Do believe he gets ten and a half per cent. for every halfpenny he has. Is chairman of the Half-Guinea Hat Company, one of the best specs going. Bought a cow of me that our people could make nothing of. Only gave me six-pun-ten for her, and—would you believe it?—she reared him two calves and made him twenty puns' worth of butter besides."

This interesting genius was a slightly built, middle-sized, yellow-haired man, who might be almost any age from thirty to fifty. The most remarkable feature about him was a skew-bald fan beard, formed of alternate tufts of yellow and white hair, just like the fringe of a kettle-holder. He was a single man, and a good deal courted in the country.

And now the door opened again, and in pops Mr. Daniel Dennis, the stop-gap of the neighbourhood, a "rus in urbe" sort of youth, little remarkable for anything save living opposite a weathercock. "I live opposite a weathercock," he was always telling people out hunting. "I live opposite a weathercock, and I saw at a glance this morning that the wind was at north-east;" or, "The weathercock opposite my lodging has been steady at south-west these three days, and I predict we shall soon have rain."

Lucy, who understood stage effect as well as any woman, did not essay to descend until several successive wheel-rolls up to the door and rings of the bell led her to think the company would be about assembled, though she was informed as to who was arriving through the medium of Dirtiest of the Dirty, who had it from Hyacintha, Mrs. Hazey's maid. So she amused herself, during the progress of an elaborate toilette, with listening to the details of the internal economy of Tarring Neville,—who was mean—who was awful mean—who there was no a-bearin',—and in speculating on the probable appearance of Mr. and Mrs. Cropper; what Mr. Bonus would be like; what Mrs. Gowleykins would have on; and whether Mr. Dennis was good-looking or otherwise. At length a passage clock struck the quarter, and after a final glance in the cheval glass, Lucy took up her white kid gloves and

fan, and sailed majestically out of the room, leaving Dirty
to rearrange her things and extinguish the six wax-lights
with which the apartment was illuminated. " No use in
stinting oneself," thought Lucy, as she quitted the blaze
of light. She then made the grand descent of the softly
carpeted staircase, and was presently where Basket the
butler, glass door-handle in hand, stood guard, as well
over it as over a covey of flat candlesticks on the adjoining
table.

The door opened, and our magnificent prima donna
sailed graciously into the room, radiant with smiles,
radiant with inward satisfaction, and dazzling with
costly jewels. Her new toilette completely threw in
the shade the shabby silks, satins, and velvets of the
other ladies. They began to wish they had been a little
smarter ; Mrs. Cropper, that she had put on her violet ;
Mrs. Beddingfield, that she had not come in blue. And
then they blamed the gentlemen for advising them not.
Meanwhile, Mrs. Somerville having made a hasty survey
of the scene, and satisfied herself that there was no one
there to compete with herself, either in the way of looks
or attire, dropped her black Spanish lace mantilla off
her beautifully rounded shoulder, and proceeded to smirk
and smile and show her pearly teeth to the company :
" Mrs. Gowleykins, Mrs. Somerville ; Mrs. Somerville,
Mrs. Beddingfield ; Mrs. Cropper, Mrs. Somerville," and
so forth.

Masters of hounds are generally pretty punctual, as
well at their meets as their meals, and Mrs. Somerville
had scarcely concluded her floating teeth-showing gyra-
tions ere Basket sailed noiselessly into the room and
announced in a whisper to Hazey, as if imparting a
profound secret, that "dinner was ready." Then Hazey,
who had got sidled up to Mrs. Somerville, as if he were
going to make an attempt on her pocket, offered her his
red arm, whereupon the other gentlemen began pairing
off with the respective ladies they had had indicated to
them as dinner companions : Mrs. Cock-a-Roost with Old
Cropper, and Mrs. Cropper with Three Thousand Five
Hundred a Year ; Ten-and-a-half-per-Cent. with Miss
Winkler ; Facey ultimately brought up the rear with Mrs.
Hazey. By, however, one of those scientific manœuvres
known only to great strategical commanders, Anna Maria's
capacious dress, like Cassandra Cleopatra's at Dalberry

Lees, was found extending itself half over Mr. Romford's chair, and this though her order of going would have indicated her place to be at the other end of the table; but ladies are always very obliging where there is any business to be done.

Grace was then said by the worthy Rector of Slavington-cum-Starvington, and forthwith soup began to circulate from each end of the table. Sherry of course followed soup, and then came the fish—a dish of smelts, and turbot with lobster sauce. Hock and Moselle then succeeded, and the gentlemen began to feel a little more comfortable. The ladies, of course, had dined at luncheon-time, and, like Willy Watkins with his hunting, now only ate for conformity. Indeed, we often wonder for whom the great overpowering dinners are provided. If we follow a man to his club, and see what he orders, we shall find that soup, fish, and meat constitute the dinners of nine-tenths of the whole. Tarts, sweets, savouries, are in little demand. But when a party of men sit at one table, instead of at several tables as they do at a club, there seems to be an idea that the accumulation of appetites requires greater appeasing, and makes it necessary to have an infinity of food.

If people find certain dishes at one end of a table, they may be pretty sure what there will be at the other. For instance, a sirloin of beef is pretty sure to be faced by a turkey, whilst a roast leg of mutton generally involves some boiled chickens at the other. Then the ham, tongue, sausages, and so on, follow as a matter of course. Roast beef and turkey was the order of the day at Tarring Neville, for which there was a pretty equal demand; but Facey, not being much of a carver, willingly relinquished the honour of assisting Mrs. Hazey to Mr. Pannet, who sat on the opposite side of the table; thus enabling him to devote his attentions to Miss Hazey. But Facey was prudent and calculating. Anna Maria was certainly very pretty. Fine head and neck, beautiful brown hair, elegant figure; but then there was that confounded "Boy Bill" and another cub or two elsewhere. Besides, Hazey would live for ever, and Mrs. H. looked like a tough 'un too. Altogether he determined to take the curb of his admiration up a link or two.

Some people seem to think if they get a certain muster of guests together, and place a profusion of food before them, that that constitutes society, and that they may sit staring, just as the master of a union workhouse sits staring at the paupers.

Hazey was one of the silent sort, unless he was talking of buying, or selling, or exchanging; and as he could not hope to interest Mrs. Somerville with a disquisition on horse dealing, or favour her with a sight of his banker's pass-book, he began telling her the quality and price of the various things on the table, explaining that the candles were genuine wax, and the oil the finest sperm. He also drew her attention to his crystal, and next told her how he got his linen direct from the manufacturer in Belfast, without subjecting it to the troublesome attentions of the middleman. He was a regular bargain hunter, and was so proud of his exploits that he ¦could not keep his own counsel—even letting out that his champagne was of the cheap order—a most injudicious proceeding, seeing it was sure to deteriorate the flavour. If people do give cheap wine, they should keep the price to themselves.

We will not persecute the reader with a description of all the dishes and delicacies that Gritty's moderate abilities furnished, still less with the hard-featured dessert that followed, the component parts whereof were chiefly apples and pears, nor yet with the burthensome conversation that accompanied the whole. It was just one of those sort of dinners that those who have never seen any better would think good, and those who knew what dinners ought to be would think bad. Friend Facey, however, got through it with much more ease than he did the Dalberry Lees'one, and Lucy thought it a great deal better than spending the night with her old mother at Beldon Hall. And she was half sorry when an ominous lull enabled Mrs. Hazey to catch her eye, and with the usual gesticulation moved the adjournment of the ladies; but then she sailed out with the air of an empress.

CHAPTER XL

HOW TO SPELL CAT

OF course, on the retirement of the ladies from the
dining-room, there was a readjustment of seats at
Mr. Hazey's festive board; and our distinguished
master, Mr. Romford, between whom and his brother-
M.F.H. there had been a long interregnum of highly
garnished table, now got together, Mr. Romford occupying the seat of honour just vacated by Mrs. Somerville,
having the yellow and white fan-bearded Ten-and-a-half-
per-Cent. on his right. Next Ten-and-a-half came old
boozy Tom Pennant, then the Rector of Slavington-cum-
Starvington, flanked by Daniel Dennis, and opposite sat
Joe Beggingfield, Gowlcykins, Cropper, and others, all
anxious to hear the stories of our master, who looked,
indeed, as though he were surcharged with them.

Basket the butler, with his attendant aide-de-camp,
having assisted in the new arrangement by the distribution of chairs, glasses, and the marshalling of decanters,
now reduced the illumination by extinguishing the
extraneous lamps on the sideboard and elsewhere, and
presently withdrew, leaving our friends to fraternise
through the instrumentality of music, politics, literature,
fox-hunting, the fine arts, or what not. Of course the
wine had to circulate once or twice before anything of a
conversation could be expected, during which time those
who had anything to say for themselves began looking
out for a subject, while those who had not prepared to
act the part of sand-bags, by examining and disposing of
the wine.

Mr. Bonus—that is to say, Ten-and-a-half-per-Cent.—
having carefully manipulated his funny fan beard, and
found that every hair was right in this very peculiar
half-inch fringe, now gave a slight ingratiating turn of
his chair towards Mr. Romford; and, after a glance at his
hirsute profile, as Romford sat rocking himself in one of
Hazey's rickety chairs, apparently thinking of nothing,

though in reality scanning every thing and person in the room, Mr. Bonus ventured to ask, in a very deferential tone, if Mr. Romford ever looked into the Derby betting.

"Whiles," replied Facey, pulling out a sample of his beard and holding it up to the light. "Whiles," repeated he, re-establishing his chair on all-fours, and scrutinising Ten-and-a-half-per-Cent. attentively.   Derby betting! thought Facey (who could spell Reindeer with any of them).   That looked like business; and passing the favourites quickly through his mind, together with the bets he had pending, he was considering what temptation he could afford to offer Mr. Bonus, when his host interfered with his wine. Hazey wanted to talk about his wine; and the price of wine and the prices which horses are at in the betting ring not harmonising, Ten-and-a-half-per-Cent. was obliged to retire his subject. They, however, mutually booked each other for a venture on a future occasion; Bonus thinking himself better informed than Facey, and Facey having an equally confident opinion of himself.   Now let us harken to our host.

Hazey, who, like Bonus, was a sort of general broker—dabbled in anything—and was always running about at sales in the summer, picking up curious old port, curious old furniture, curious old anything that was cheap, now took his innings with Romford.

Formerly hosts used to persecute about their port, their rich fruity port, their tawny port, their bees'-wingy port, their five in wood and twenty years in bottle port; but since the Chancellor of the Exchequer has opened the flood-gates of the Continent, each connoisseur has his own particular wine that nobody else can acquire. Hazey had several anonymous sorts, each so superior that our party soon resolved itself into a tasting one.   The fact was, Mr. Hazey wanted to sell his brother-master a batch of Burgundy for about double the price he had given for it; and though Mr. Romford cared very little about wine, having, indeed, an abundant supply of Lord Lovetin's, yet, as Hazey was pressing and anxious, he said he didn't care if he took ten or twelve dozen, provided Hazey would deliver it for him at Beldon Hall.   And as Hazey could load back with coals from Splutterton Colliery, he agreed to the terms; and before Ten-and-a-half-per-Cent. could get his own Derby subject renewed, Hazey was at Mr. Romford again with a description of a perfect picture of a horse he had just picked up—far more than up to Hazey's weight—equal to Romford's, in fact—that he wouldn't mind selling, if Romford knew of any one who didn't care for putting his hand pretty deep into his pocket for price. And our master said he knew plenty of people of that sort; he himself didn't mind what he gave, so long as the animal was really good; and, altogether, he talked in a very liberal, encouraging sort of way. Emboldened by this, at a later period of the evening, after he had beaten about the bush a little as to their respective countries and covers, Mr. Hazey asked his guest if he would mind giving up Lowfield Banks to him; whereupon Facey, gathering himself up, replied fiercely, "No! would as soon give you an inch off my nose!" an assertion that rather startled Mr. Hazey, but still gave him a very favourable impression of Mr. Romford's sporting determination. It was clear he wanted sport. Hazey would have negotiated, at all events, if he had been Mr. Romford; tried to have got a horse, or a hound, or something to boot. But every man to his mind, thought Hazey.

And now poor Ten-and-a-half, who had been doomed to hear Mr. Hazey monopolising the rich victim, taking advantage of the lull caused by the slight ebullition of temper, turned again to our hero, and in the same bland voice as before, asked him if he ever did anything in the speculative way, Ten-and-a-half having some shares in a certain hotel company that he wouldn't care to be out of, and also a venture in the oil wells of Austria, that were not likely to yield the necessary interest; but Hazey, quickly recovering from his back-hander, turned again upon our distinguished master with an Italian wine—better, in fact, than the Burgundy; but which, Hazey said, would require a purchaser to dip his hand deeper into his pocket to procure a few dozen of. Facey, however, to whom price was no object, having got a clean glass, after a stare at its colour and an approving smack of his great thick lips, said he wouldn't mind taking ten dozen of it. "Say twelve," replied Hazey, who had booked him the larger quantity of the former. "Twelve be it," yawned Facey, with the utmost indifference.

It was now friend Facey's turn to have his innings;

and, after raking either side of the table with his inquisitive little pig eyes, he folded his hands behind the back of his head, and balancing himself on the hind legs of his chair as before, asked, with a *dégagé* sort of air, "If anybody knew anything of one Mr. Jobbins— Mr. Jonathan Jobbins?"

"Oh yes, I do," replied Hazey. "Jobbins, of Harefield. Bought the worst horse of him I had ever had in my life—Flash-in-the-Pan; you remember him, Gowleykins?"

"Indeed I do," replied Gowleykins, who had some unpleasant green-pea soup reminiscences of him; said horse having run away with Gowley, and soused him in a horse-pond all over green weed.

"Well, but what about Jobbins?" asked Hazey, anxious to run a fresh scent.

"Oh, nothin' 'ticlar," replied Facey, "only had a letter from him, complaining of moy hounds having killed his cat; and how do you think the ignorant beggar spelt the word 'cat'?" asked Facey, now settling himself down on all-fours of his chair. There was a dead silence, each man thinking how it would be.

"I'll bet a guinea none o' you can guess!" exclaimed Facey.

"I'll take your two to one," at length drawled Ten-and-a-half-per-Cent.

"No—even bettin'," said Facey—"even bettin'."

"Come, I'll bet you," said Hazey, who thought he had it.

"Done," replied Romford. "How was it, now?"

"Why, K-a-t," replied Hazey, spelling it.

"Nor, it wasn't!" said Romford, smiling.

"I'll bet you now," said Ten-and-a-half-per-Cent., who thought the chances were reduced.

"Done!" replied Romford, coolly adding, "a guinea, mind!—a guinea."

"A guinea," nodded Bonus.

"Well, then, how was it?"

"Why, K-a-double t," replied Bonus.

"Nor, it wasn't," chuckled Facey.

"Double or quits!" now exclaimed Mr. Hazey, thinking he had it at last.

"Done," replied Romford, with the greatest indifference.

"C-a-double t," spelt Hazey.

"Nor, it wasn't," chuckled Romford again.

Mr. Bonus then took a long-drawn inspiration, and thinking there were but two other ways, viz., K-a-tt-e and C-a-tt-e, made the same double or quits offer.

"Done," said Romford, thinking he might as well exhaust the subject.

"Then K-a-double t-e," spelt Bonus.

"Nor, it wasn't that either," laughed Romford.

"Come, I'll have another turn," cried Hazey, thinking to save something out of the fire.

"An even guinea," said Romford.

"Done," said Hazey. "C-a-double t-e," then spelt Hazey.

"Nor, it wasn't," chuckled Romford again.

"Then how was it?" exclaimed several.

"Why, C-a-t, to be sure," replied Facey, laughing—in which all but the losers joined. They were glum.

"Well, but you said he was an ignorant beggar," observed Bonus.

"Well, he may be an ignorant beggar, and yet know how to spell cat," replied Romford.

"Ah! but you put it as if not knowing how to spell cat constituted his ignorance," rejoined Bonus.

"To be sure!" replied Facey, "that's the way to do it."

A general chuckle then ensued. Very slowly the purses came out, and very reluctantly the sovereigns were counted, the chairman of the Half-Guinea Hat Company absolutely offering to pay in pounds, an indignity that Mr. Romford could not brook.

"Out with the shillin's!" said he, and the shillings he got. Having tried all the coin on his plate, he deliberately put them into his waistcoat pocket, saying, "it would do very well to pay 'pikes with," and again established himself on the hind-legs of his chair as before. He thought he had done a very good night's work.

Then as the circulation of the bottle became weaker and more languid, and men began to twist, and turn, and writhe about in their chairs, all indicative of present satiety, Basket, the butler, at length put an end to the negotiations and commercial transactions of the evening by appearing with a loftily borne coffee-tray, whose jingling cups clattering around acted the part of the bell that rings the merchants out of the Royal Exchange in the City of London. Up rose the majority of the guests, some to the coffee, some to the water, some to the sherry, some to the fingering and adjustment of their collars, their variously shaped beards, and shirt-fronts. And all being apparently ready for a move, Mr. Hazey duly dissolved the meeting by making for the door, and saying, "Then, shall we join the ladies?"

"With all my heart," replied Romford, chucking his napkin ostentatiously on to the middle of the table, as, if to let people see he was not going to pocket it, when, without any bowings, after you-ings, or any nonsense of that sort, he just stalked boldly out of the room. The rest then followed as they liked.

The drawing-room had now received a great accession of light, and if Mrs. Hazey's opinion of the importance of her guests might be inferred from the number of candles she was burning in their honour, it must have been very great. Independently of the heavy ordnance—the cut-glass chandelier—there was scarcely a bracket or holder of any sort without its burner. If Hazey hadn't sold the twenty-four dozen of wine, he would have grudged the expense amazingly. As it was, after counting the guests, he began calculating how much the light would cost per head; and this, too, while he was pretending to keep up a running commentary with Mr. Beddingfield about his damaged barley. But here we are in the radiant apartment, and must devote ourselves to the ladies.

About the centre of the lady-circle, under a perfect blaze of light, reclining gracefully on a luxurious yellow and gold ottoman, with her beautiful foot resting on an elaborately worked floss-silk cushion, sat our Jermyn Street friend, looking as though she had been nursed in the lap of luxury, and had never known anything of debts, or duns, or difficulties, now giving herself up to the enjoyment of the hour without the slightest care for the future. She was about tired of the ladies; indeed, she often said that the only thing that reconciled her to being a woman was, that she could not by any possibility have to marry one; so she slightly raised her person, and contracted her dress, as if to indicate that any gentleman might come and talk to her who liked. And Mr. Hazey, as in duty bound, was presently by her side, now asking after her horse, now after the hounds; and now, as Mrs. Hazey, in her company exertions, got out of hearing, expatiating on the elegance

of the jewellery that encircled her swan-like neck and
beautiful arms.

The chairman of the Half-Guinea Hat Company,
though somewhat chagrined at his loss in the dining-
room, hovered round, greatly taken with her appearance
—thinking to captivate her with his yellow and white
beard, through which he had quietly run the pocket-
comb in the passage.

Next Mr. Facey Romford's great scarlet shoulders were
seen converging upon the piano, and then Miss Anna
Maria's beautiful white ones were seen descending towards
the music stool, while Mr. Romford stood over as if
to let the fair one try to excel the dulcet notes of the
lisping syren at Dalberry Lees. And if Mr. Facey could
be won by a girl with such a "beastly brother Sam"
as the boy Bill, it is but due to Miss Hazey's charms
to say that she would have accomplished the victory,
for he thought of her well that night, and awoke still
thinking of her the next morning. She quite sung
herself into his good graces, thus indeed showing that
"music hath charms to soothe the savage breast." How
he wished he had brought his flute—would have given
a guinea to have brought his flute—would never go from
home again without his flute—would like to have
"'stonished these beggars with his proficiency."

And the ladies, with that fine delicate perception of
business that they all possess, now began to withdraw
themselves and their cohorts quietly, so that when Miss
Hazey arose and turned round for laudations after her
third song, she found the room greatly thinned. Then
Mrs. Makepiece, who owed Mrs. Hazey one for her
assistance in capturing young Mr. Busswell for her Sophia
Jane, came gallantly forward, and, seizing Miss Hazey
by both hands, thanked her most fervently for her
beautiful music, and begged she would favour them with
one more song—just *one* more—before she (Mrs. Makepiece) went. Whereupon, after a little pressing, and a
"come, you may as well do it," from Mr. Romford, Miss
turned again to the instrument, and our master mounted
guard as before. Mrs. Makepiece watching and inwardly
calculating that Miss would very soon be Mrs. Romford,
and Miss preferring to humour Mr. Romford's encore to
limiting herself to the one song that Mrs. Makepiece
had prayed, that lady, and her plain but very amiable

daughter, presently withdrew noiselessly, leaving the chaunts in full swing; and when Miss Hazey again arose for commendation, she found the men clustered round the sherry and soda-water tray, Mrs. Pannet watching to see that Mr. Pannet didn't take equal parts of whisky and water for his nightcap. Then Anna Maria, as she drew on her new white kid gloves, gave Mr. Romford such a loving look, when, in reply to his request for another song, she said, "Not to-night, please," adding, *sotto voce,* "*another time,*" as quite captivated the Facey heart, and made Mrs. Somerville (who, too, was on the watch) almost wish she hadn't come. Cassandra Cleopatra was extinguished for that night at least, thus showing that ladies are not always wrong in hoping against hope —in never giving up a man short of the church door.

And the last Rose of Summer—to wit, poor Ten-and-a-half-per-Cent.—having at length taken his departure, there was a general winding-up of watches, fearing it was late, and talking of breakfasts the next morning, Hazey being now anxious to get all parties away to bed, seeing that the extensive illumination they were then indulging in could not be kept up at less than twelve or fourteen shillings an hour. So Mr. Hazey, after two or three ineffectual movements, at length observed, that perhaps Mrs. Somerville would like to go to bed, to which our fair friend assenting, as indeed she could not well do otherwise, there was a brisk lighting of candles, and good-nighting, and our fair tragedy queen sailed off under convoy of Mrs. Hazey, arriving in her bedroom just as Miss Dirty finished her tour of the bedrooms, helping herself to a light blue smelling-bottle from Anna Maria's toilette-table, an emerald ring from Mamma's, and a pair of shirt sleeve links from the boy Bill's.

She then helped her mistress to undress and get into bed, retailing to her all the gossip and history of the lower regions of the house as she proceeded. And as one state bedroom is very much like another state bedroom, and one night passed in a country-house is very much like another, in the interests of the chase we will leave the Tarring Neville one to the imagination of the reader, and proceed to describe Mr. Romford's day with the Hard and Sharp hounds.

CHAPTER XLI

THE HARD AND SHARP HOUNDS

MR. HAZEY being, as we said before, duly impressed with Mr. Romford's importance, not only as a sportsman but a man of great social position, had marshalled his forces with an eye to general effect. Jawkins the huntsman, and Peter the whip, commonly called Peter Simple, were charged to put on clean ties and polish their boots to the utmost extremity, while Silkey the groom was cajoled into doing his best with the horses by the promise of an excursion to Kittlefield fair on the Monday. The hounds, too, were most carefully drawn—drawn as well with an eye to pace and endurance as to the more obvious qualities of colour and size. There is no master of hounds, however insignificant, who does not think he can astonish his friends with his powers, or with something about his establishment.

Jawkins was well named, for he was a bustling, noisy, shallow, show-off little fellow, continually holloaing and blowing his horn. As he never went to see any other pack of hounds but his own, he was perfectly satisfied with the Hard and Sharps, and had no doubt Facey would be equally pleased with them. If he, Facey, wasn't, he'd be no great judge, Jawkins thought. He was a good hand at puffing and selling hounds, and was in fact the Silkey of the kennel. Peter's nickname of Simple describes him. He was a silly fellow, a man that might be made to do almost anything.

What with Jawkins in a fuss and Peter in a flurry, a fox had an uncommonly good chance of escape. Peter had passed from place to place with great rapidity, sometimes getting through half a season, sometimes through a whole one, but never through two, till he came to friend Hazey. Still Peter was a smartish young fellow, and, like the gentleman who sat a horse with firmness, ease, and grace until the horse began to move, Peter's deficiencies were not apparent until the hounds began to hunt. Hazey, however, had him at his own price, and Peter was not only willing to make himself generally useful during the week, but also to go, too, for the letters and papers on a Sunday.

But here they come—hounds, horses, and all ; Jawkins on Catch-'em-alive-O ; Peter on Robin Adair, with Silkey riding Valentine for his much respected master. They trot gaily over the greensward, pass down the dip in the park to the well, and, making a bold sweep round the now leafless birches, come smartly up to the front with the air of the Inns of Court Volunteers. Here they halt for admiration ; and now the inmates of the house, having duly satisfied nature, rise from the débris of breakfast and make for the windows, while the butler and footman come into the room to rearrange matters for any chance comers. Mrs. Hazey and Anna Maria alone maintain their positions at the table—Mrs. still presiding at the handsome melon-patterned tea service, while Miss takes charge of the coffee.

And now the door bell begins to twitch and tingle and ring, according to the status and nerves of the party pulling the brass knob—Ten-and-a-half-per-Cent. making the house resound with his summons, while little Mr. Sheepshanks scarcely makes himself heard. In the guests come, straddling and clanking their spurs, and frizzing up their side hair, all thinking themselves uncommonly killing. Then, after bobs and bows and shakes of the hand are exchanged with Mrs. Hazey and Miss, the new comers apply themselves vigorously to the viands, and the process of deglutition is again in full force. And the cry is still, "They come, they come !" till Gritty the cook almost begins to fear for a famine. But as the kitchen-maid butters her last batch of hot rolls there is a sudden lull, neither entrance nor breakfast-room bell resound. The run is over, and Gritty retires to the cupboard to recruit with a glass of "Matchless Old Tom Gin."

And now, after certain mysterious looks and nudges, something is said about the "weed," and forthwith the return match of hand-shaking and grinning is played, and after a scramble for hats, caps, and whips in the passage, a certain sound then indicates and a scratching noise announces fire, and, the front door being hurriedly opened, a group of aspiring youths rush out and range

themselves under the Italian-columned portico of the
house for an inaugural smoke. Here they are presently
joined by others, who have also beat a retreat, until the
steps are as crowded as those of the Rag on a Derby
night. And they whiff and puff and smoke and blow a
great variety of curiously shaped clouds. At length the
pent-up torrent of humanity is burst by Mr. Hazey
appearing with his distinguished guest, Mrs. Somerville,
on his arm, followed by Romford with rather a formidable
looking whip under his. The crowd then start and dis-
tribute themselves, some going up to the garden, some
along the holly walk, others going down to stare the
hounds out of countenance. And Facey, thinking to see
their performance in the field, follows smoking suit, with
his old brier-root pipe, and wanders away to the stables.
Hazey then lionises Lucy; shows her his ducks, points
out Spiceington spire on the hill, and Lord Dundreary's
seat in the distance. Meanwhile the equestrian plot
thickens. The heavy subscribers, men entitled to be
late, come cantering up, whom Hazey greets with a
fervour apportioned to the price and punctuality of
their payments. And now an exclamation is heard of—

"There! there's my boy Bill!" from Hazey, pointing
out his son turning on to the lawn on a good-looking
grey—"there! there's my boy Bill! Show me the man
that turns his son out better than I turn out my boy
Bill!" Then, taking young Mr. Heslop aside, he whispered in his ear, "That's a horse that would suit you now
—safest, most temperate animal I ever was on; and *cheap*,
too," added he in a still lower key, with a squeeze of
Heslop's arm.

"Well, but what do you call cheap?" asked Heslop,
who knew that it was a term of various interpretation.

"Well," said Hazey, scrutinising his victim attentively
—"well, I'll tell you in two words—I'll tell you in two
words—but first let me say that it's no use offering me
less than I ask. I want eighty guineas for him, and I
won't even take punds."

Hazey had given eight-and-twenty for him about three
weeks before, and had spent an hour in vainly endeavour-
ing to get the seller to give him a sovereign back.

"Hem," mused Mr. Heslop, who wanted a horse for
about the price Hazey had given. "Hem, I'll see how
he goes."

"Do," rejoined Hazey, and he took an early opportunity of telling his boy Bill to keep near Mr. Heslop, and show off his horse to the best advantage, keeping clear of water, of which the beast was rather shy.

But here comes Lucy on Leotard, accompanied by brother Romford on that magnificent good-for-nothing weight-carrier Everlasting, closely followed by the curious yellow and white fan-bearded gentleman, Mr. Bonus, *alias* Ten-and-a-half-per-Cent., on a very inferior looking shrimp of an animal. Ten-and-a-half is much struck with Lucy, and does not think the less of her for having two thousand a year. Would make it into four, if he had her, in no time. He doesn't know whether Mrs. Somerville looks best in a morning or evening costume. The habit is very becoming to her, but then how elegant looking she was in full dress overnight. There were plenty of other gentlemen equally enamoured, but Facey kept a watchful eye on the whole, looking as if he was ready either to kick or strike.

Hazey, on his part, is much struck with Everlasting's magnificent appearance; above all with his fine arch neck, telling how lightly he would play with the bit and bend to the bridle. Hazey had noticed the gag in the Baker's mouth on the hag fox day, and guessed what his peculiarity was. Here, however, there seemed to be no mistake; light free action, undeniable shape, fine shoulders, beautiful head, full of intelligence,—altogether as fine an animal as ever he set eyes on. And Hazey felt flattered at Mr. Romford bringing such a horse into his hunt—evidently one of his best—and showing that he thought the Hard and Sharp hounds required some catching.

And now, time being up, and a quarter of an hour's law being given to boot—for Hazey was always in a greater hurry to leave off than he was to begin—all parties having at length got together, the cavalcade moved off in a cluster, hounds first, Hazey next, supported on either side by Lucy and Facey. Great were the hopes of the Hard and Sharpites that they would astonish our master. If they only had a chance, they thought, they could not fail to do so. Mr. Romford's might be good hounds, but theirs, they were quite sure, were better. In fact, nothing could be better than theirs. Then they criticised and made their commentaries on Lucy. Deuced handsome woman she was—best turned-out woman they had ever seen. Most perfect model of a lady's horse she was on. Then there were inquiries as to whether she rode, so that they might not be cut down by her. But this question could not be answered. Bonus, however, believed so.

Hazey, in a general way, was never in a great hurry about finding, preferring one run a day to two, as indeed did most of his field; but on this occasion he stretched a point, and stopped a greater extent of country than usual, right up to Hawkworth Hills indeed. So, after making two or three insignificant places safe, as he called it, he gave the word for Rockwoodside; and forthwith the bump of earnestness began to develop itself in the increased bobbing of the caps and the extra working of the elbows and legs of Jawkins and Co. in advance with the hounds. Then the field got their horses short by the head; the steady old hunters bobbing on at their case, the fractious ones pulling and fretting in a very disagreeable way to their riders.

So the gay cavalcade passed along Narrow Lane, round Grindstone Quarry Hill, and through the Scotch fir clump at Cornbrook, to avoid the great staring toll-bar at Latchford Law. Hazey never disturbed a 'pikeman if he could help it.

Fortune generally favours a master of hounds anxious to show sport. She is more considerate to them than she is to the "racing gents," who are frequently drenched with rain and other unpleasantnesses. Not that rain can do foxhunters any harm; but fortune is generally propitious to them in other things,—good fox, good scent, good country, good find, good finish; all the "goods" the gods can provide, in fact. The sport is generally either very good or very bad.

And now the subsiding caps in front denote the approach to the cover, and the words, "Here we are!" presently passes along the line. Jawkins next pulls up, and Peter Simple presents a broadside to the field, to keep them off the valuable hounds. "War horse, Rachel!" cries he, taking a left-handed cut at the delinquent. "Have a care there, Prosperous!" hitting him, as he had missed the other.

The cover was a beautifully retired one,—just the sort of place in which a peace-loving fox might be expected to dwell, being an angular five-acre wood, lying in a dell at the junction of three grassy hills. Whichever way a fox broke, he was sure to be viewed by the whole of the field, —a great encouragement to those who, perchance, might not see him at any other time.

And now being all ready for the fray, Lucy, Facey, field, and all, Mr. Hazey gives a nod to Jawkins, who gives another to his hounds, and away they dash into cover, as if each one knew the whereabouts of the fox and meant to have him by the neck in no time. Hazey's hounds were always very keen at the beginning, but their ardour very soon cooled.

"*Yoicks, wind him!*" cheers Jawkins, as much to show he is huntsman as anything else, while Peter Simple cuts away to a corner up which Reynard sometimes slips unperceived. And scarcely has Peter got there ere a very cool, collected, ruddy-coated gentleman, head in air, with brush extended, comes trotting up the ride below, looking as if he didn't exactly know whether the noise he heard proceeded from the hounds or from some hawbuck exercising his lungs. But the sight of Simple's sapient countenance satisfying Reynard on that point, he gave his well-tagged brush a sort of defiant whisk in the air, as much as to say, "Now, old stupid, what are you staring at? Why ain't you lookin' arter the cows?"

"*Tally-ho!*" now screams the excited Simple, in a way that would infallibly have headed a pusillanimous fox, but this gentleman being one of the flying sort, and having, moreover, no great opinion of Jawkins' abilities, merely increases his speed, and, passing up the gorge between the hills, makes his way into the open. "Gone away! gone away!" screamed the half-frantic Peter, and then what screams, and whoops, and yells, and shrieks resound from the far end of the cover, how the pullers begin to get the bits in their mouths, and the funkers to look out for their leaders. "Which way! which way!" is the cry. "Where's Smith? where's Snooks? where's Noakes? where's Tomkins?"

Meanwhile the hounds, having got a capital start, shot well ahead, making the possibility of being overridden or even pressed upon quite extinct, for the scent is first-rate, and the country most favourable. So they race, and fling, and press, and snatch the scent as if one had as good a right to it as another. It was just the sort of day to make a third-rate pack look like a first-rate one—Hazey saw that, and so did Facey, though cunning Hazey pretended to deprecate the scent, halloaing to the hounds to get "for'ard," as if they were not doing their best as it was.

Mr. Facey Romford, who thought to do the grand and consequential—the General M'Murdo of the review—found it necessary to put along rather faster than he expected, so getting his horse firmly by the head, he established himself in his seat, and hustled along as if he was out with his own pack. Lucy, too, scuttled along, closely followed by Hazey, the latter now looking alternately at her and her horse. He thought he never saw a neater couple. And though he had no intention of unduly risking his neck—seeing he kept Jawkins to do the dangerous—still he followed in her wake, not liking, in the first place, to be beaten by a lady, and thinking, in the second place, to see how she and her horse performed. He was all for appraising an animal, whether it was for sale or not. It kept his hand in. Besides, there is no saying what may happen. But the pace was too good for much observation, indeed, when our prudent master came to the third fence—a rough boundary hedge, with the usual briery entanglements, over which Mrs. Somerville hopped without disturbing a twig, he began to wish he had not committed himself to the speculation of following her. What matter did it make to him how she rode. Confound the ugly place, he should like to turn away. "Come up!" exclaimed he to his horse, in the sort of half-resolute way that indicated a shirk, and Valentine, taking him at his intention, swerved to the left, while Ten-and-a-half-per-Cent. took it in his stride. Hazey then seeing old Mr. Gallinger going as if for a gate, followed suit, and was presently enjoying the perspective of more gates in the distance, with the majority of the field cramming away on his right. Up and down, up and down they went,—now a coat, now a cap, now Mrs. Somerville's hat and habit. The hounds were a long way ahead, pressing up the gently rising ground of Cowslip Grange, then through the fir plantations of Fawley, without dwelling a moment, and onwards, still pointing due north up the sloping side of Bullersgreen, and over the brook at Ravensdowne stone-pits. Here a most acceptable check ensued, for Everlasting had been gently intimating to Romford that the rising ground did

not agree with him, and Facey did not wish the information to go any further. So he turned his horse's head to
the air, and sat motionless, thankful that Jawkins had
to make the cast and not him. Everlasting had taken his
fences very well, and being a horse of enormous stride
had kept Romford in a becoming place. Leotard, too, had
gone well, and had left old Ten-and-a-half-per-Cent.
immeasurably in the lurch. The roadsters, and shirkers,
and craners now seeing a pause, pushed on in hopes of
getting another chance of being again left behind.

Jawkins, nothing daunted by having the eyes of
England upon him, now lays hold of his hounds, and,
assisted by Peter Simple, proceeds to make a cast that
he thinks will greatly edify Mr. Romford—give him
something to talk about when he gets back into Doubleimupshire. And as fortune sometimes favours even the
foolish, and there is no very impeding fence in the way to
make Jawkins think the fox has taken an easier line, he
presently hits him off at a cattle gap, and away the
hounds go with a screech!

"Beautiful! beautiful!" ejaculates Hazey, adding, "I
hope Mr. Romford saw that."

Then they all fell into place, Hazey leading (so long as
there is no leaping), Facey and Lucy a little to his right,
with the boy Bill on the eighty-guinea grey behind them.
Bill has handled the horse so neatly and well that
Heslop is half inclined to bid sixty for him. And now
they are all at it as before, jumping and spurting and
shirking; red coats and green coats and black coats; white
boots, hot boots, brown boots, and black boots. The line
is more favourable to the grand horse Everlasting, being
slightly on the slope, and Facey puts him along without
fear of a failure. It was only up the steep that he
showed his infirmity, and degenerated into a shut-up.
But Facey did not keep horses to look at; and if they
could not go with the hounds, they could go back to the
place from whence they came. So he just stuck his
spurs into Neverlasting, as he called the horse, and sent
him along in the independent sort of way of a huntsman
who is not hunting the hounds—acting the gentleman, as
poor Sir Richard Sutton used to say on those occasions.
Meanwhile Jawkins, who is greatly pleased with his own
performances, cheers and hurries on his hounds, hoping
the lady will tip him a sovereign if he gets her the brush.

"Dash it! what a grand thing it would be if she gave him a sovereign," thought he, holloaing the hounds on. He would buy Mrs. J. a twelve-and-ninepenny bonnet that should quite cut out Mrs. Silkey's. "*For-rard on? for-rard on! hounds*," cries he to the racing pack. "What business had Mrs. Silkey to give herself the hairs she did? A huntsman's wife was far afore a grum's in point o' greatness. Hark to Columbine! hark! *that's the way on 'im!*" shouted he, as Mercury now pushed to the front. "A grum was a mere under-strapper to a huntsman,—had to bring him his 'oss, and take away his 'oss, and clean him his 'oss, and clip him his 'oss, if he required to have him clipped. Silkey be singed! Mrs. S. too—Hupstart 'ussy!"

And now, what with pressing and cheering, and thinking of the bonnet, aided by stain of a flock of sheep on a piece of very water-logged land, Jawkins managed to get his hounds right beyond the scent, and the flush of the former successful cast onwards being still full upon him, he holds them on till they are quite clear of the line. The fox has turned short to the left to avoid a conference with the driver of a coming coal-cart. "*On, on, on!*" however, cheered Jawkins, waving them forward with his arm, still thinking of the bonnet, the hairs, and the consequence. "Who the deuce was a grum's wife?" muttered he.

"Hold hard!" now cries Mr. Hazey, holding up his hand, seeing the fast-expiring energies of the pack. "Hold hard!" repeats he, fearing for the finish.

"'Old hard!" shouts Bill, who has been nursing the grey along very judicially. And hold hard it is generally.

Meanwhile Mr. Romford, who is very long-sighted, has viewed the fox stealing quietly along among the straggling gorse bushes on the rising ground some distance to the left; but it being no part of his duty to assist the operations of a rival pack, nor yet to test the enduring qualities of the grand horse Everlasting, he keeps his own counsel, and lets Jawkins persist in his mistaken cast forward, which ends, as Facey foresaw, in hopeless and unbroken silence. Jawkins then gives them a wide swing to the right, and ultimately by a back cast crosses the line of the fox at the base of the hill along which Mr. Facey had viewed him. Then great was the applause of the admiring field at the skill of the huntsman, and the staunchness of the pack. "Best hounds in England," they said. And

they all got their horses by the head in anticipation of a
stinger. But the goddess Diana said "no." Moreover,
she whispered to Hazey, "You call the four miles you
have come, seven, and let Mr. Romford and his sister
depart in peace. They'll run you down, whatever you do,
so you may just as well close as you are." And in pursu-
ance of that decree, the scent became weaker and more
languid. Indeed, only two or three of the old stagers
could hold it at all, the rest of the pack being obliged to
take it on trust. And though Jawkins cheered them, as
if his noise would assist their endeavours, yet it was
obvious to every one that unless the fox despised them
sufficiently to await their coming up, they would never
overtake him. Mr. Romford and sister Somerville, therefore, dropped their reins on their horses' necks preparatory to a stop. Our Master had taken his bearings from
"Ten-and-a-half," and he found he was going from home
instead of towards it. Had the fox been travelling "t'other
way," there is no saying but Facey might have holloaed
them on to him, even though they were driving him into
his country, where he might find him another day. Here,
however, there was no inducement to stay, Facey having,
as he said, appraised the establishment to ninepence, and
wouldn't know them better if he stayed there a month.

So Lucy and he quietly withdrew to the rear of the
field, and as Hazey now pressed on to contribute his quota
of science to the huntsman, telling him which way he
thought the fox was gone, they availed themselves of
an intervening plantation to retire altogether, mutually
agreeing they had had enough of old Hazey and the Hard
and Sharp hounds.

They then struck across country in search of their way
home.

CHAPTER XLII

THE FAT BOY OF PICKERING NOOK

THE news of Mr Romford's expedition to Tarring
Neville soon reached Dalberry Lees, and caused a
profound sensation in that quarter. Both Mrs. Watkins

and Miss looked upon it with grave suspicion, for though they did not admit Miss Hazey's beauty—indeed, thought at times she was rather plain—yet they both confessed her dangerous powers of coquetry, and dreaded lest she might have ensnared the innocent Mr. Romford in her wiles. If Mrs. Watkins had only known he had been, going, she would have given him a hint as to Miss Anna Maria's propensities—she was a regular flirt, and nothing else.

Now the only thing they could do was to endeavour to eradicate the mischief. Doubtless Mr. Hazey's hounds had been a source of great attraction; but, then, they could not hope to get Mr. Watkins to set up a pack to counteract the impression they might have made. It was a pity that fox-hunters hung so together. And then the recollection of the non-arrival of the bag fox occurred and Mrs. Watkins wished that might not have some thing to do with it,—if so, Mr. Castangs had a great deal to answer for. However, the Watkinses had the advantage of propinquity; and, rich as Mr. Romford was, he might not be insensible to the advantages of an heiress—one, too, without any brothers, who were always great bores. And Mrs. Watkins considered long and anxiously how to reinstate themselves in the sporting graces of the great master of Beldon Hall. At length she hit upon an idea, which, if not quite orthodox, was, at all events, well calculated to mislead a lady. And, for the purpose of fully explaining matters, we must here indulge in a little geography.

If the reader will take a map of England—a Bradshaw, for instance—and cast his eye up to where Doubleimupshire shoulders Snoremboremshire in friendly familiarity, he will perceive a confluence of railways converging upon a dot denoting the once elegant and retired little town of Pickering Nook.

Before the introduction of steam, Pickering Nook was one of the quietest little places in the kingdom : one doctor, no lawyer, two milliners, and an occasional pedlar with the latest London fashions. The inhabitants were chiefly elderly ladies and people who loved retirement and the musical note of the nightingale. Now it is hiss, screech, whistle—hiss, screech, whistle—morning, noon, and night. Five railways run right into the very heart of the little town, severing it like a starfish. It has become a perfect ant-hill of industrious locomotion. People seem to go to Pickering Nook in order to pass to every other place.

Nook! Nook! Nook! Who doesn't know the familiar cry? Pickering Nook is only its name upon paper. It is never called anything but Nook by the porters.

When the first bisecting line cut right through the town, severing old Mr. Mellowfield's garden, it was said that the place was ruined for ever: no one could live there after.

Mr. Mellowfield, who had retired from the troubles of fish-curing to enjoy his filberts and Madeira in the evening of life, was so shocked at the invasion of his privacy, that he nearly choked himself with anger as he waddled about with a plan of the premises, detailing his grievance to everybody that would listen to him : and nothing but a strong application of golden ointment could have got over the difficulty. Ten thousand pounds for two thousand pounds' worth of property mollified him.

The next line of railway had fewer opponents ; the third one, less ; and so on in a diminishing ratio. But the extraordinary part of the thing was, that what at first was looked upon as an intolerable nuisance by the natives, was presently regarded as an absolute advantage by a stranger, an affluent young gentleman, much troubled with obesity, which none of the ordinary remedies could reduce. In vain he tried walking, and riding, and rowing, and swimming, and cricketing, and Turkish bathing,— he never could get himself below eighteen stone and a half. Fox-hunting he didn't like, because of the wait and uncertainty ; hare-hunting had the same objection— he got chilled between the heats, and, moreover, disliked the monotony of road riding. Starving was very much at variance with his inclination, and even by living upon fish, or biscuits and grapes, he seldom got more than half a stone off his weight—nothing to a man who had turned twenty. He didn't like it : he was afraid he should get too fat. Not that he was too fat, then ; but he was afraid of becoming so. It is a comfortable circumstance that people never do fancy themselves too fat : they are sometimes afraid of becoming too fat, but they are never too fat at the time—just the right size, in fact ; only hope they will be able to keep as they are.

This stranger was young Mr. Stotfold, of—we don't exactly know where—a gentleman who was commonly called Squeakey Stotfold, from his having a most disproportionate voice to his body. It was more like the shrill note of our friend Punch, when plying for patronage, than the natural voice of a human being; and the sound of it always made people start and turn round, short round, to see what was coming. Well, young Stotfold being very fond of his food, was afraid that he might ultimately get too fat; and at length his medical adviser, Mr. Slopperton, hit upon a plan that should procure him the exercise of hunting without its drawbacks and disadvantages. He proposed that his patient should set up a pack of staghounds, and hunt from railway stations: nothing to do but load and enlarge his stag wherever he liked. No asking leave, no paying damage, no propitiating farmers, no preparation—no nothing, but just do what he liked. If one place got too hot to hold him, he had nothing to do but pack up his traps and away to another. And, glancing at the map—as we requested the reader to do—the convergence of lines upon Pickering Nook pointed it out as one of the most eligible spots for that sort of pursuit in the kingdom. From it Mr. Stotfold could shoot out north, south, east, and west—up into Snoremboremshire, down into Doubleimupshire, out on either side, with plenty of stations, and a great variety of country. Nothing to do but look at his Bradshaw. Hunt at any hour of the day: express train, mixed train, slow train, goods train—they were going at all times of the day. And old Mr. Mellowfield's house, close to the station, being vacant, Mr. Stotfold installed himself in it, with a most miscellaneous kennel of hounds, and some of the strongest, roughest-going horses in the kingdom. There was nothing too rough-actioned for Stotfold to ride: the more he bumped, the more exercise he got, the more he could eat—and eating was the object, not hunting; he hunted to eat, in fact.

Many travellers, we dare say, have seen our friend lounging about the station at Pickering Nook, or smoking his cigar on the triumphal arch that connects the up lines with the down, looking as though he were lord of all he surveyed, and as if everybody who saw him must admire him. He dressed in the brightest, gaudiest colours: pea-green coat, with canary-coloured vest, sensation ties, Garibaldi shirts, leathers and tops. He was always attracting attention by ventriloquising the guards and railway-porters, as it were, with his extra-ordinary voice. All his non-hunting days were spent at the station, in chaffing the attendants, and flirting with the pretty girls in the refreshment-rooms.

At the time of our story he was just turned five-and-twenty, though he did not look so much, having a fine light, cauliflower-like head of hair, shading a plump, blue-eyed, pink-and-white round face, that would have looked more at home under a bonnet than a hat. Whiskers he had none, and very apocryphal moustache, with which, however, he took considerable pains,—frequently feeling if it was all there, and trying to coax it into a ram's-horn-like curl at the corners.

He had been at the "Nook" since the beginning of the season, hunting and trespassing wherever he liked—procuring himself a certain amount of ill-will from the farmers and people, more on account of the unmannerly conduct of some of his stags, than the mere hunting proceeding. One stag in particular, called the Benicia Boy, had been very unruly, having upset a clothes-basketful of children out airing in Reislip Green Road, knocked an old milkman over with his cans, and starred the lofty mirror in Mrs. Sarcenet's millinery shop in Shelvington with his great unprincipled head. Still, a stag-hunt being a novelty, many people asked the fat boy to their places; while the fact of his being a bachelor did not lessen his attractions.

With a lady like Mrs. Watkins, who knew no better than proclaim that her husband only hunted for conformity, and who thought to ingratiate herself with such a sportsman as our hero by sending for a bag fox from town, it may readily be supposed that the fat boy's establishment would be very deceptive; and it now occurred to her anxious mind, that if she could get Mr. Stotfold to come to Dalberry Lees with his stag-hounds, they would not only retrieve the former disappointment, but also ingratiate themselves very considerably with Mr. Romford. She thought a stag-hunt would be the very thing to tempt him with; make such a nice change from the foxhounds; and the more she thought of it, the better she liked it. And, without consulting friend Willy, she determined to carry out the idea.

Migratory masters not being very ceremonious, though

none of them had even seen the fat boy, yet Cassandra
Cleopatra "Dear Sir'd" him on behalf of her father,
inviting him to dine and stay all night at Dalberry Lees,
and turn his stag out on the lawn the next day.

The invitation came opportunely, for somehow Squeakey,
who was not often asked twice to the same place, was
beginning to feel the .want of society other than the
Nook afforded, and he gladly instructed Tomkins, the
stationmaster — to whom (not being a good speller
himself) he gave £5 for conducting his correspondence—
to accept the invitation on behalf of himself, his stag,
and his hounds.

And, having thus laid the foundation of another
"uproar," Miss Cassandra was presently at her desk again,
on behalf of mamma, inviting her "Dear Mr. Romford"
to come to meet a brother-master of hounds; saying
it wasn't Mr. Hazey, but not telling him who it was.
And Romford, albeit very wary, and not at all anxious
to meet any of the masters of hounds whose kennels he
had laid under contribution for hounds, considered, on
reflection, that none of them would be likely to visit
such a muff as old Willy; and Anna Maria's charms
having now somewhat paled before the effulgent light
of Cassandra Cleopatra's ducats, he, too, accepted the
invitation, and so made the Dalberry Lees ladies
supremely happy.

CHAPTER XLIII

MR. STOTFOLD'S ESTABLISHMENT

TAKING it in a galloping point of view, there is no
doubt that the stag-hunter has a decided advantage
over his brethren of the chase, whether fox-hunters or
thistle-whippers, in always being sure of his game. He
is like a man with his dinner in his pocket, sure of a feed
wherever he is. Whether the stag-hunter's game will run
or not, is another question; but the same may be said of
the fox and the hare. Still, the stag-hunter never has
a blank day; he is sure of seeing the animal descend,

at all events, and if he won't condescend to run, the true
sportsman has the same privilege that the costermonger
had with his donkey "vot vouldn't go"—namely, the
right of "larruping him." To the fair sex the stag is
truly invaluable; and we should think the ladies would
poll twenty to one in favour of the stag over the fox.
They see the actual animal that has to be hunted, instead
of having to draw upon their imaginations for the idea.
Then, look at the independence of the thing. While the
fox-hunter's anxieties continue all the year round, aggravated by perfidious keepers, faithless friends, and are
never more acute than on the particular morning of the
meet, the stag-hunter turns about in his bed with the easy
indifference of the sluggard, conscious that he, at all events,
will be all right, and can lay his hand on his game on the
instant. No trappers, no shooters, no unpunctual earth-
stoppers, disturb the calm serenity of his repose. He is
not afraid of the foot people molesting the cover, or of
lazy sportsmen stopping short by its side. The hare-
hunter may go flop, flop, flopping about the country, peering into all the bushes and tufts he comes near, without
finding what he wants; but the stag-hunter has his proud
beast under lock and key, and has only to shoot the bolt,
give him a kick, and set him a-going.

Then there is something fine, wild, and romantic in the
idea of stag-hunting, heightened by the pictures one sees
of the performance,—the forest glade, the boundless moor,
the impassable-looking ravines, the glassy lake, the horns,
the hounds, the hubbub. It is the happy confusion of
fiction with fact, the blending of the glories of the past
with the tameness of the present, that tends to keep the
flag of stag-hunting flying in the ascendant. Still, as with
Stotfold, so with other masters, many people did not care
to see the staghounds a second time. They like to say
they have seen a stag-hunt, and having seen one are satisfied, and don't let out that things were not quite what
they expected. And now for our friend Mr. Stotfold.

We wish we could accommodate the sporting reader
with a list of Mr. Stotfold's staghounds; but, unfortunately, the same difficulty presents itself that we
encountered at the outset of this story with regard to Mr.
Romford's pedigree—namely, that we did not know anything; the fact being, that Mr. Stotfold did not keep any
list. That, however, is in reality of little importance;

for his huntsman, Jack Rogers, being a liberal of the first class, did not burthen himself with much nomenclature either, and just called the majority of his hounds by any name that came first into his head, so that the Cheerful of one day might be the Careless of another, and perhaps the Countess or Caroline of a third.

Mr. Stotfold generally had about five-and-twenty couple of hounds in kennel, hunting from eighteen to twenty couple, according as the exigencies of the rope and the casualties of the chase operated on their number. He did not begin with a whole pack, but bought a lot of drafts at the hammer, which were vacillating between the Indian market and the tan-yard. These came in pretty cheap—some three or four and forty shillings a couple; and a hound being a hound in Mr. Stotfold's estimation, he limited himself to three guineas a couple in future— three guineas being his outside price. Of course he got some for a great deal less—for nothing, in fact, sometimes; it being common among huntsmen, when they had a head-strong, skirting, babbling, incorrigible animal that they could make nothing of, to exclaim to their whips, "send him to Stotfold! send him to Stotfold!" Hence, as may be supposed, he had a very miscellaneous assortment of crooked-legged, blear-eyed, broken-coated, loose-loined, flat-sided malefactors in his possession.

Two very remarkable hounds, however, he had—namely, Wideawake and Wiseacre; not brothers, as the alliteration would lead one to suppose, for they were as dissimilar as it was possible for animals to be, but so christened respectively on account of their extraordinary powers and performances. So long as Jack Rogers, the huntsman, had either Wideawake or Wiseacre before him, he was pretty sure that the stag was before the hounds, and made himself perfectly easy about the rest of the pack. The reader can therefore do the same, and dismiss the rest as a lot of makeweight incorrigibles, possessed of almost every mental and bodily defect hounds are capable of. We will now describe the flower of the pack, in case any of our readers would like to breed from them.

Wideawake was a yellow or light tan-coloured hound, with bright hazel eyes and a very Spanish-pointer-like head and expression of countenance. Indeed Jack Rogers, who was a bit of a utilitarian, used to say he wouldn't despair of making him point still. He—the hound, that is to say—

stood twenty-five inches high, with a drooping kangaroo-like back, terminating in a very abruptly docked tail, looking, indeed, more like an Italian iron, as used in laundries, than a hound's stern. Nor were his personal defects his sole demerits. He ran mute, and being a queer, unaccountable-looking animal, was as often taken for the stag as for a hound. "Yeas, ar seed him," the countrymen would reply to Jack's inquiry if they had seen the stag, "yeas, ar seed him ; short tail and arl, a-goin' as hard as ivir he could lick."

Wiseacre was quite a different description of animal, being of the bull-dog-like order, black and white in colour ; very much the sort of animal one sees chained under a carrier's cart. He was short and thick, with a big bald face, loaded shoulders, crooked legs, and flat feet. Unlike Wideawake, he was of the vociferous order ; and though he did not throw his tongue prodigally, he yet did it in such a solemn sententious sort of way as always to carry conviction to the pack. He could hunt both the stag and Wideawake, and run under Wideawake's belly when he came up with him. Between the two, Jack reckoned he could catch almost anything ; Wideawake making the running, and Wiseacre keeping the clamorous party on the line.

And it was a fine, cheering, invigorating sight to stand on a rising ground—Rounhay or Greenley Hill, for instance—and view the whole panorama of the chase. The noble but unantlered monarch lobbing and blobbing across country, making for all the railway stations, cabbage garths, and horse-ponds he could see, with the deficient-tailed Wideawake leading the boisterous pack by some hundred yards or so, while sedulous Wiseacre plied his nose diligently (doing a little skirting occasion-ally), to recall his comrades in case they overshot the joint scent of Wideawake and the stag, Jack Rogers and his plump master crashing and cramming after them. And now for a word about Rogers.

Jack Rogers, as we will now take the liberty of calling him, began life as a circus man, being attached to the then flourishing *troupe* belonging to the late Mr. Nutkins, so favourably known throughout the southern counties ; and Jack was great both in the saddle and the sawdust, enacting the drunken huzzar with the greatest fidelity, and throwing somersaults without stint or hesitation.

Unfortunately, however, he had a difference with the clown, Mr. Smearface, who, instead of visiting Jack with imaginary cuts with his whip, used to drop it into him with such a hearty goodwill as caused Jack, who was amazingly strong and an excellent boxer, to thrash him, not figuratively, but literally, within an inch of his life. To escape the consequences that seemed likely to ensue, Jack bolted to Boulogne, where he presently became boots at the " Roast Beef of Old England Hotel," a house, we need hardly say, greatly frequented by the English. Here Jack took to learning the language, and adapting himself to the manners and customs of the country, whereby he greatly bettered his condition ; for the English like to get a lesson in French for nothing, and Jack, being a sharp, clever fellow, adapted himself to their humours, calling himself Jean Rougier, getting his ears bored, wearing moustache and a good deal of bristly hair about his round, good-humoured face. At length Jack tired of " mossooing," and returned to England at the active age of forty, just as old Father Time had shot the first tinge of grey through the aforesaid bristly jet-black hair. He then became a valet to a young gentleman of the name of Pringle—Billy Pringle—whose mother was what the servants call a " quality lady "; that is to say, a lady of rank,—to wit, the Countess of Ladythorne, wife of the Right Honourable the Earl of Ladythorne, of Tantivy Castle, in Featherbedfordshire. Here Jack—or rather Jean, for he still retained the *persiflage* of the Frenchman —did very well, having plenty of society and little to do, beyond cheating the young gentleman, who was a very easy dupe. Unfortunately for Jean, however, his master's mother, before being a countess, had filled the honourable office of a lady's maid, and was well versed in the mysteries of servitude generally, and resented Jack's premature abstraction of clothes and constant purchase of infallible recipes at his master's expense,—recipes for making boots black, recipes for making boots brown, recipes for making boots white, recipes for making boots pink, recipes for making gloves white, recipes for making gloves drab, recipes for making gloves cream-colour, and so on through the whole catalogue of cleanable, renovateable articles of attire.

And, having hired Jack for her son when she was not a countess, but a Mrs., her ladyship was very plain-spoken with Jack, who, being full of beans and independence, as these sort of gentry generally are, threw up his place at once, saying it was far too "mean and confining for him," and cast himself upon the world at large generally, little doubting that he would very soon be sought after. Somehow or other, though, Jack was out in his reckoning, and though he plied both the French and English characters assiduously, and was often apparently within an ace of being hired, yet somehow the engagement always fell through at the last moment, and the seedier Jack got, the quicker came the refusals. One gentleman to whom he offered himself as a French valet wanted an English one ; another to whom he offered himself as an English one wanted a Frenchman ; a third wanted a taller man, a fourth a thinner man, a fifth a younger man—all requirements that Jack could not comply with. The fact was, that though he was a dark-complexioned man, there was a certain indication about his nose that it would have been well if he could have purchased a recipe for removing. Though he always placed himself with his back to the light when under examination, yet somehow the parties generally got him coaxed round to the window before they were done with the scrutiny. And then came the thanks and the sorries, and the tantalising promises to write if they thought more of him, as if any of them ever meditated doing anything of the sort after they had once got rid of him.

There is nothing so deplorable as a seedy valet. A man had fifty times better be without any than have one of those painfully brushed glazey-clothed gentlemen, who look as if the whole concern had been bought second-hand. Jack, having in the days of his prosperity indulged in bright colours, went more rapidly downhill than the wearer of soberer garbs would have done, and at length he got so shockingly shabby that the gentlemen's gentlemen began to hesitate about passing him on to their masters when he went to look after a place. He was a very different Jack to what he used to be at the second tables when, in the full adornment of jewellery and latitude of presumption, he bullied the pages, and found scarcely anything was good enough for him. Now he was only too glad to sit down in the hall amid the general ruck of servants, and get what he could on the sly.

At this juncture it occurred to Jack that there are

other ways of obtaining a livelihood than by valeting, and, though valeting certainly was the easiest and pleasanter line of all, he had no objection to his early professional career, and bethought him of trying his luck in the sawdust circle once more. Accordingly he sought out Mr. Crackenthorpe, the manager of Crackenthorpe's Royal European Hippodrome, and offered his services as a general performer ; but twenty years had made a striking change in Jack's elasticity of limb. Instead of coming cleverly through the paper balloon, after throwing a somersault, he hit his head against the hoop, and sent it flying into the pit. Then, having accidentally slipped from his saddle when rehearsing the part of Billy Button the tailor, he could not regain his seat for some seconds, and was so blown with running alongside the brute and trying to pacify him, that Mr. Crackenthorpe lost all patience, and left his *locum tenens* to bow him out at his leisure. Jack then withdrew from that line entirely, and after driving a country doctor about in his pill-box for three months, who worked him both day and night, he was next found as the odd man at Skidmore's Livery and Bait Stables in Pont Street, Pimlico, with twelve shillings a week and a hay-loft to sleep in If Sir Bernard Burke, having exhausted the vicissitudes of families, were to turn his hand to the vicissitudes of servants, he would not find a more chequered or eventful career than that of our distinguished friend Mr. Rogers.

But it is a long lane that never has a turn, and Jack's turn came at last. One fine summer's afternoon in the height of a London season, when every jobmaster could send out double the number of vehicles he could supply, and when every caitiff with a coat to his back was elevated to the rank of a coachman, one summer's afternoon, we say, as Jack was clattering about Skidmore's yard in the wooden clogs of servitude, with straw bands wrapped around his ankles, our squeaky friend Mr. Stotfold came rolling in in a high state of excitement, demanding first the master, then the mistress, then the ostler, then the helper, then anybody he could see. He had just bought ten couple of hounds at Tattersall's, and didn't know how the deuce to get them away, or what to do with them when he had got them away. And, as luck would have it, there was nobody in the yard but Rogers—Rogers attired as aforesaid—"but needs must," says the proverb, "when a certain old gentleman drives," and our master had no alternative but to address himself to Jack. He told him candidly how they had knocked the hounds down to him, and how he wanted them housed.

Now, Jack had a turn for the chase, and when with Mr. Pringle at Tantivy Castle, on a visit to his late master's noble mother, the Countess, had cultivated the acquaintance of Mr. Dickey Boggledike, Lord Ladythorne's huntsman, and knew all about boiling and feeding and kennelling, at least thought he did, and gladly volunteered his services to Mr. Stotfold.

"If Jack could only get a man to mind the yard while he was away, he would go for them himself," he said, and a job brougham coming in at the moment, he transferred his responsibility to the driver, and, divesting himself of his *sabots*, put on an old puce-coloured livery vest, now worn almost black, and proceeded on his way to the Corner, inwardly hoping his employer might prove as simple as he looked.

The hounds were in two lots of five couples each, now, however, clubbed together like a bunch of onions, pulling and striving, and straining all ways to be off they didn't know where to, and Jack, seeing the position, summoned the intelligent bare-footed man in the old green-collared Surrey hunt coat and cap, who haunts the passage, and directing him to divide them (Jack thinking it would be better for Surrey man to be bit than him), each then seized the tow rope of five couple, and separating them proceeded up the entry, and down Grosvenor Place with his charge, amid cries from the attendant street urchins of "Talli o! talli o! A hunt! a hunt! Vere do you meet? Vere's the stag? Have you seen my 'oss? Crikey O! vot a hugly man!" meaning, of course, Mr. Rogers. The "hugly" man, however, had his hands too full to be able to resent the indignity, and, moreover, saw the fat boy's large figure looming in the rear.

"Handsome is that handsome does," says the proverb, and the way our friend managed his hounds, and above all the skilful compliments he paid Mr. Stotfold on his judgment in buying such a nice-looking lot for so little money, completely ingratiated him with our master, and made Mr. Stotfold glad when Jack hinted that he wouldn't mind giving up the capital place he then had under Mr Skidmore and coming to him. And Jack, not overrating himself—indeed, putting his services rather low, Squeakey and he quickly came to terms, and Jack left his *sabots* in Pont Street for the man who came after him. He then became a huntsman—huntsman to Mr. Stotfold, master of staghounds, in which capacity the reader will now have the goodness to view him.

He had a capital time of it, too, for his master being ignorant enough to hire him, was ignorant enough to keep him also, and a peripatetic stag-hunter like Mr. Stotfold was not troubled with those too critical fields that raise or lower the fame of a huntsman, according to the sport he shows. Jack was not only huntsman but master of the horse, buying the meat for the kennel and the forage for the stables, making up in overcharge on the articles what he considered himself underpaid in the matter of wages.

Hunting on what the swells call the scientific principle was quite beside Jack's mark. Nevertheless, he could ride —ride over almost anything, and also blow the key-bugle, and seldom or ever had he occasion to play—

" Oh where and oh where is my Highland laddie gone ! "

in consequence of losing his stag. If he whiles, as he said, let the hounds have a bite of its haunch, it was to make the lobbing gentleman more agile in future, Jack being of opinion that if a hound once put his fangs well into him, the stag would take care not to let him do it again if he could help it. At least, Jack knew he wouldn't if he were the stag.

Such, then, was the gentleman now invited by Mrs. Watkins to meet our distinguished sportsman Mr. Romford, and obliterate the recollection of the Castangs disappointment.

CHAPTER XLIV

MR. STOTFOLD ARRIVES AT DALBERRY LEES

RAILWAYS are capital things for long distances, but they don't do much for short ones. It is a grand thing to fly from one end of the kingdom to another in a day, but, for anything within ten miles, there is nothing like having one's own horse or conveyance. With them there is no hurry or confusion, ten minutes is neither here nor there, but one minute makes all the difference with a railway. It is very provoking to see a train gliding smoothly out at one end of a station as we come hurrying in at the other ; yet such things do happen with parties wearing even the best regulated chronometers. But if railways do little for travellers, they do less for visitors, who are generally set down either far too early or much too late—extremes greatly to be deprecated. It is tiresome in the short winter days, when there is no alleviating turn to take round the farm or the garden, to have to consume the intervening time before dinner in the house, still worse to meet the first course leaving the dining-room, all hope of one's coming being extinct.

Neither of these casualties, we are happy to say, awaited our friend Mr. Stotfold, for, having consulted his amanuensis, Mr. Tomkins, the stationmaster at Pickering Nook, that official chose him a train that would not only set him down in good time, but secure him a conveyance to Dalberry Lees, "It being no fun," as Tomkins truly said, "to have to walk several miles in the dark." This was a through train, and many of the passengers having come long distances and made themselves comfortable, were not inclined to be disturbed, certainly not to admit a stranger of our friend's dimensions, so the usual artifices were resorted to, dummies exhibited, and babies plied at the windows, it being a well-ascertained fact that there is nothing so efficacious as a *babby* for keeping men out of a carriage. But Loggan, the guard, always had a place in reserve for a "gent" like our friend, and now obsequiously met and led him along the line to a newly painted carriage, in the centre compartment of which were only an elderly lady and her handsome, but slightly *passé*, daughter, who he knew would have no objection to the introduction of such a stranger as Squire Stotfold ; indeed Loggan rather thought that the two travelled for the purpose of picking up an eligible young man if they could. And the fat boy having squeezed himself in sideways, squeaking his apologies as he got himself seated, proceeded to unfold his rug and set his tongue a-going on a sort of general issue expedition—weather, crops, concerts, balls, picnics, the usual staple of unmarried conversation—making himself what the ladies call very agreeable, or very forward, according as they or another is the object of attention.

But it was a short-lived triumph, for they had hardly got the full swing of conversation established ere the slackening speed of the train announced a coming stop, and it presently pulled up before the now familiar Firfield Station. Loggan's rosy face then appeared at the carriage window, announcing to our master of staghounds that his railway journey was at an end. Mr. Stotfold had, therefore, to tear himself away from his newly found friends before he had even run them to their homes. With a radiant smile to each, out then he rolled, wrapper and all, and presently began squeaking for a porter—"Porter ! Porter ! Porter !"—attracting all eyes to the windows to see such a jolly cockatoo, all green and yellow and red, fo the fat boy did not seem to think he could make himself sufficiently conspicuous. The train presently sped on, and having given up his ticket, he began squeaking for the bus.

Independent Jimmy stared with astonishment as the fat boy's great stomach came looming along, tightly buttoned into a bright green double-breasted cut-away coat, with a buff vest, yellow leathers, and rose-tinted tops ; his short neck being adorned with a bright scarlet sensation tie, secured by a massive blue and gold ring.

"Bus, bus ! where's the bus ?" squeaked he.

"Bus !" growled Jimmy, eyeing him, adding, "sink ye should have a barge."

But the fat boy still continued his vociferations.

"Are ye gannin' to tak' the whole on't yoursel' now ?" demanded Jimmy.

"No, only me and my man," replied the boy, pointing to a grinning little ear-ringed Frenchman, all teeth and hair, like a rat-catcher's dog.

"Ar dinna think we can hould any but yersel'," replied Jimmy, "ye're se fat," added he, looking him over.

"Hut," snorted the boy indignantly, half inclined to kick him ; "an impudent busman talking to a master of staghounds in that way."

"Why, then, ar tell ye what, ye mun just wait for the melon frame," replied Jimmy, "for there are two women, 'maist as big as yoursel' with their hoops, who want to be gannin' wi' me."

"Melon frame!" squeaked our friend; "melon frame! what the deuce have I to do with a melon frame?"

"It's the private carridge," explained Jimmy, "and ye'll ride far comfortabler, and besides be set doon at the Dalberry Lees door, 'stead o' bein' left by the side of the road with the bus," and Jimmy's master appearing at the moment, bearing a basket of live geese, Jimmy jerked his head at our fat friend and said "here's a gent wants to be gannin' wi' ye."

The melon-frame door was then opened, the wraps were put in, and the fat boy squeezed himself in sideways, leaving his valet to see to the luggage. All being presently adjusted, "*Jip!*" cried the driver, and away they drove from the station. Twenty minutes brought them to Dalberry Lees. Here, though Mr. Stotfold, master of staghounds, expected to be the hero of the party, yet he was not so in reality, being in fact only auxiliary to Mr. Romford. Indeed, if it hadn't been for our foxhound master, Stotfold wouldn't have been there at all. So, when he rolled into the drawing-room after his name, and found Mr. Romford, who had somewhat recovered from his Tarring Neville fever, playing the flute to Miss Cassandra Cleopatra, he took him rather smally, just as a master of foxhounds might be supposed to take a master of harriers. In this he was somewhat confirmed by finding Mr. Romford in mufti—tweed ditto suit—instead of being arrayed, as he himself was, in the costume of the chase, Stotfold thought a master of hounds should always look like his work.

Stotfold, indeed, had not ascertained his exact status as a master of staghounds, and having found his name when he advertised his meets at the top of the list of hounds, along with the Queen's, a baron's, a baronet's, and so on, thought himself entitled to look down upon the followers of all other branches of venery, and looked down upon them accordingly. He talked of the Queen and I, Davis and I, Bessborough and I, etc. Nor was Stotfold's ignorance peculiar to himself, for Mrs. Watkins, fully believing she was going to give Mr. Romford a great treat, would not anticipate his delight by telling him the name, so Mr. Romford was kept in a state of pleasurable excitement.

The reader will therefore readily imagine that it was with no very satisfactory feelings that our Master was interrupted in the middle of his accompaniment on the flute of Miss Cassandra Cleopatra on the harp in the popular air of "Dixey's Land," by the announcement and entry of this extraordinary contribution to the chase. Facey started, for his puffing and blowing had prevented his hearing the ring and arrival, and, as he sat with his back to the door, it was only by Miss Cassandra Cleopatra breaking off abruptly to do the honours in the absence of mamma, that Facey was sensible of the presence of a stranger. Up he got too, and, instead of finding Lord Who-knows-what, confronted the before-mentioned fat boy.

"Mither Romford, Mither Stotfold," lisped the fair lady, and as soon as Mr. Stotfold relinquished her soft hand, which he claimed just as he would that of one of the nymphs of the Pickering Nook Station, he tendered his own to Mr. Romford.

Romford looked unutterable things, for, besides the disappointment of a good introduction to a master of foxhounds, he had had a bill sent in for two new gates which he was sure the fat boy had smashed the last time he enlarged his quadruped at Pine Hill Clump, besides which he owed him one for the trespass in his country. So Romford just gave him two forefingers of his left hand, holding his flute in his right one as if he was going to break it over his head. The ceremony of introduction thus over, Facey then resumed his seat, and the fat boy having looked round the room to find a chair large enough to hold him, at length wheeled one up to the scene of the music, and composed himself in it. Miss then rang the bell to let mamma know Mr. Stotfold was come, thinking it better to have four people in the room than three. Mamma presently came sailing in, and received the great stag-hunter in state. Still she saw by Mr. Romford's face that all was not right. It wore much the same sort of aspect that it did on the unfortunate bag-fox morning.

Not so, however, Mr. Stotfold's. From living so much alone, he had a pent-up torrent of words to discharge, and, having now got a listener in Mrs. Watkins, he opened the floodgates of his vehemence and squeaked and chatted away with the utmost volubility, in the midst of which Facey and Cassandra resumed the interrupted melody of "Dixey's Land." Before they concluded, friend Willy made his appearance, nursing and feeling his side hair as usual, and then Mr. Stotfold had another victim to his noise.

We need scarcely say that this being what Facey would call a "bye-day," Lubbins had not the satisfaction of displaying her cookery, and the thing was very flat and unprofitable compared to the former occasion. The fact was, Mr. Facey had been over with his flute once or twice since then, and Mrs. Watkins hoped things were gradually drawing into the family circle line; they, therefore, only sat down eight to dinner, Mr. Tuckwell, Mr. Horsington, and Mrs. Dust, near and short-notice neighbours making up the number. Mrs. Dust, of course, was engaged to help to keep the course clear for Cassandra. But if the party was small, the noise was great; the fat boy going in at everything that was said, and giving his opinions in the most authoritative way. When, however, the ladies retired, the real amusement commenced, for not content with lauding the stag-hounds, he must needs sneer at the foxhounds, which of course got Mr. Romford's back up, who held fox-hunting to be the finest sport in the world. So the evening did not pass very harmoniously, and Mr. Facey was glad when he found himself back in the drawing-room.

Let us now pass on to the next morning.

CHAPTER XLV

THE BENICIA BOY

"OH, mamma, there's Lorrimer, the latheman's cart!" exclaimed our lisping friend, looking out of the window, as they all sat at breakfast the next morning. "I'll get him to examine my black lathe scarf."

"Laceman!" squeaked Stotfold, looking out, adding, "no; it's my deer-cart."

"Deer-cart!" replied Miss Watkins, jumping up and running to the window, adding "deer-cart, is it? Why, who'd have thought of a deer keeping a cart?"

Squeakey was right, however. It was indeed the deer-cart—the deer-cart followed by a most heterogeneous assemblage of foot-people, collected from the various villages through which it had passed on its way from the station. High up on a solitary seat sat the driver, dressed in Lincoln green, lording it over the old white horse as though he were driving four-in-hand. The lofty vehicle, which was painted dark green, was ventilated from the roof, and displayed on its side, in white letters on a black ground, the walking advertisement of "AUGUSTUS STOTFOLD, ESQUIRE'S DEER-CART, PICKERING NOOK." The vehicle, as Hood says in his "Epping Hunt," was—

> 'In shape like half a hearse—tho' not
> For corpses in the least;
> For this contained the deer alive,
> And not the *dear deceased* !"

Then a deputation from the stables having met the procession, and fixed upon the exact spot—a slightly rising ground just before the mansion-house, where the noble animal might be enlarged in full view of all the spectators—Lincoln green wheeled the cart round, and dropping his reins on the old white horse's back, prepared his own mouth to receive the contents of the then coming cup—

> "And letting go the *reins*, of course,
> Prepared for *heavy wet*."

The drain over, he returned the mug, and then rising in his little seat, began flagellating his own chest with his arms, causing the Benicia Boy, for it was none other than the mischievous fellow inside, to stamp and thump with his feet, to the terror of the little boys who expected to have him amongst them directly. The more the man thrashed, the more the deer stamped, doubtless expecting every moment to be ejected from his comfortable carriage. And, now, where are all your visions of rousing the antlered monarch from his lair, ye enthusiastic souls? Or where the wild expanse of country, ye romantic ones? One view of the deer-cart on the smooth lawn has dispelled them all! Yet nobody likes to exclaim, "Wot a go!" But see! here comes Jack Rogers and the hounds! Jack about half-seas-over from the ovations he has received on the road. His cap is cocked jauntily above the left ear, his pink is thrown carelessly open, even to the exposure of a much-stained buff vest, while his badly cleaned boots seem on the worst possible terms with his dirty Bedford cords, hardly indeed inclined to approach them at all.

He is riding a great raking, white-heeled, cock-throppled chestnut, who throws his snaffle-bridled head up and down in a way that would look very like spoiling Jack's beauty if he had any. A little behind the pack comes a diminutive man, in a red coat and drab gaiters, riding a most powerful dray-horse-looking brown for the fat master. This is a horse called "Hatter-his-heart-out," from his notorious rough action, a quality that, while it has caused his ejection from other stables, has procured him admission into Mr. Stotfold's, whose idea of a hunt corresponds with the familiar label on a doctor's bottle, "When taken to be well shaken."

Jack Rogers wishing to have his kennel "sweetened a little," as he calls it, an operation of not very frequent occurrence with him, has brought out all its contents, young and old, big and little, wild and steady, coupling up the most incorrigible, and ruling over the whole with a formidable loose-thronged whip, held ready for immediate action. Jack is evidently of honest Sancho Panza's opinion, "that it is good to have command, if only over a flock of sheep"; so he rides in the middle of his curs, looking as solemnly wise as half-drunken men generally do. The hounds raised a wild cry as they caught sight of the deer-cart, and would infallibly have broken away had not Jack distributed sundry telling cuts amongst the thick of them, thus converting their cries into howls. This second scene of the grand sporting drama again roused the inmates of the house, and as the ladies now withdrew to put on their bonnets, Mr. Romford crowned himself with his drab wideawake, and, providing himself with a good cutting whip from the armoury in the passage, opened the front door, and vaulting the rails, proceeded to where the noisy group stood baying—towling, howling, and scratching themselves. We don't know whether it was] instinct or chance, or the effect of previous instruction, but Jack gave our Master of Foxhounds such a salute with his cap as seldom falls to the lot of any man in mufti.

It wasn't a touch of the peak, or a rise, or a lift, but a bold bodily take-off from the head, with a fine aerial sweep that nearly brought his cap in conjunction with his cock-throppled horse's ears. The hounds, too, increased their vehemence, so that altogether there was a very pretty reception.

Mr. Romford, who was used to caps, good, bad, and indifferent, just jerked his hand in return, and proceeded to cast his scrutinising little eyes into the body of the pack—a very slight inspection satisfied him that he had never seen such a collection before.

"Nice-looking lot of hounds," at length said he, addressing Jack, who sat cockeyly on his horse, waiting the customary compliment.

"Yes, they are," replied Jack, "very nice-looking lot of hounds—good as they look, too."

"Set of rubbish," muttered Romford, turning half round on his heel.

"Want a little dressing here, don't you?" asked Romford, rubbing his whip down the back of a desperately dull broken-coated hound.

"Ah why he scratched whiles," replied Jack; "but it's nothin' to signify."

"Isn't it?" thought Romford. He then took another good stare at the pack.

"Are they any particular blood?" at length asked Romford, not being able to recognise the slightest family likeness amongst them.

"Well, no," replied Jack; "we just pick them up here and there. That one," pointing to our before-mentioned yellow friend Wideawake, "is from the Kensal Green Kennel—one of the best hounds p'r'aps in England. There's another," said Jack, pointing to Wiseacre.

"Good as he's ugly, I s'pose?" muttered Facey.

Squeakey and Willy Watkins now joined the gay throng, the latter in a desperate funk; for if fox-hunting was formidable, stag-hunting, he understood, was tremendous—always went straight. Still he essayed to keep up his courage; and advancing, whip under arm, as he drew on his white buckskin gloves, he proceeded to return Jack Rogers' vehement salute, Jack being now further fortified by a couple of glasses of Dalberry Lees rum.

"Monstrous nice pack!" exclaimed Watkins at random,

"Monstrous nice pack!" hardly knowing what he was saying, but wishing most devoutly that he was coming in from hunting instead of going out. "Oh, dear! Why was there ever such torment invented?" thought he.

"Well, and how's the Benicia Boy this morning?" squeaked Stotfold, as soon as his huntsman's attentions were directed to him.

"Oh, why, he seems pretty hamiable, I think," replied Jack; "but I've brought Old Scratch in case he shouldn't run."

"Ah, which have you here?" squeaked the Master.

"The Boy," replied Jack. "Scratch is shut up in the lamp-room at the Galliburn Station."

"Hope they won't let him out?" squeaked Mr. Stotfold.

"No fear of that, unless he comes out at the skylight; for I've got the key of the door," said Jack, producing a large ringed key from his coat-pocket as he spoke.

"All right," squeaked the Master, adding, "p'r'aps you may as well be going?" Then turning to Mr. Watkins, he asked "if there was any place where they could put up the hounds while they turned out the stag?"

"Oh yes," replied Mr. Watkins, rather taken aback at the question, his idea being that they all started fair together. "Oh yes; put them up somewhere," adding, "ask my man;"—our friend not exactly knowing whether they should be upstairs, or downstairs, or in my lady's chamber.

Away then Jack trotted up to the stables, and the interest of the scene was again concentrated on the deer-cart. There it stood as solemn as before, looking like a double-tailed tadpole, with its two tapering lines of spectators bearing away from its body. If the horsemen mustered meagrely, the deficiency was amply supplied by the foot-people.

It seemed to have attracted all the idle population of the country, and the cry was still, They come! they come! Joiners in their paper caps, shoemakers in their leather aprons, grooms in their fustians, gardeners in their shirtsleeves, all agog to see the wonderful wild beast. The fair sex, too, were duly represented; and besides a Barcelona "crack-'em-and-try-'em" nut-merchant, there were two orange-girls, and an unlicensed dealer in spirituous liquors. Expectation stood on tiptoe as to

what the solemn-looking deer-cart contained, one thinking
the stag would be like a unicorn, another that he would
resemble a goat, a third that he would be like Billy
Batson's ram. Still, whatever it was, they all seemed
disposed to give him a wide berth, by keeping a most
respectful avenue open for him instead of giving him
a chance of sticking or eating any of them up when he
came out.

And now, as our fat friend waddled round the corner
from the stables, the commotion increased; the deer's
coachman moved his van a few paces to arouse the noble
animal, whose formidable feet might now be heard stamping upon the boards of his equipage.

The fever of excitement was then at its height. The
gaping rustics stared wider than ever, the big boys stepped
back a pace or two, and the little ones trembled, many
of them wishing themselves at home again. But when
the fat boy squeaked the order to "*Let 'im out!*" there
was a feeling of disappointment throughout the throng;
for there were neither horses, nor hounds, and those
who expected to see the stag start off directly,
thought he would be over Rainford Hill before they
could ever get them out. On this point, however, they
were presently undeceived, for though the door was
opened by the old gentleman in charge, creeping cautiously
along the top of the van and shooting the bolt, yet no
deer appeared, and those who durst take a peep in from
either side, saw a rather donkeyfied-looking animal backing its hind-quarters against the far end of the vehicle,
as though it wanted to be out that way. But the old
gentleman in green, who had a long whip, much at the
service of the animal, proceeded to administer the butt-
end through the ventilator; and after sundry downward
thumps, producing a series of indignant snorts and stamps,
it at length operated beneficially, causing him to jump
out, and, head in air, to trot leisurely down the avenue
of spectators, amid the derisive shouts and yells of the
mob. In truth the Benicia Boy was not a very wild or
imposing-looking animal, his coat being dull and worn in
parts, while one of its sides was powdered with whitening
caused by a restive rubbing against the wall of its town-house
in Pickering Nook. Still the Boy could go when inclined,
and had given our fat friend some severe leads out, indeed
on one or two occasions had been lost altogether, or Jack

Rogers having got rid of his master had pretended to lose him, in order that he might indulge in a drink, and resume the sport on the following day. But the Boy was not to be depended upon—sometimes he would go, and sometimes he wouldn't, in which latter case, of course, there was nothing for it but the donkeyman's alternative that we mentioned before, of larruping him, an unbecoming proceeding with a beast of venery.

All anxiety about his now immediate escape was speedily dispelled by the leisurely trot he now took about the lawn—looking this way and that, as though he hardly knew whether he would go on or come back to his box. He seemed quite easy about the matter, very unlike an animal put on trial for its life. At one time, indeed, he looked as if he would make for the garden, but there he was frustrated by the intervention of the kitchen-maid going down from the house for the vegetables. He then looked in at the dairy, and finally trotted off down the carriage drive, past the gaudy-gated lodges, and so on to the turnpike.

The ejectment of the stag over, the excitement of the scene seems to collapse. Those who want to see more of him follow in his wake; but the majority stay behind to talk him over, and criticise his performance. At all events, there is none of the wild enthusiasm caused by the sudden start up of the hare off the fallow, or the hustling, bustling, get-away-close-at-his-brush of the fox from the cover. On the contrary, there is a vacuum between the turning out and the laying on, that may perhaps be advantageously filled up with a cigar. So, as the semi-theatrical gentlemen say, with a smile and a bow, when they want to break the performance in two, "there will now be an interval of ten minutes, if the reader pleases."

CHAPTER XLVI

THE STAG-HUNT

BEING now refreshed, we return with ardour to the chase. The Benicia Boy, as the reader will remember, is away—trotting gaily along the road, startling the horsemen and astonishing the foot-people, sniffing the fresh air as if it were more agreeable than that of his box. Our sportsmen are up at the stables, Mr. Romford adjusting the stirrups of the saddle on one of Willy Watkins's horses for himself; Mr. Watkins, already on his horse, most earnestly wishing himself off; and grinning Jack Rogers, all eager for the fray, thinking how he will astonish the natives.

The first thing that now struck our Master of fox-hounds was our squeaky friend Mr. Stotfold vociferating for the rope—"Where's my rope? I haven't got my rope! Get me my rope!" as if he was bent on immediate self-destruction.

"Rope!" exclaimed Romford; "what the deuce do you want with the rope? Have your hunt out first, at all events."

"For the take, to be sure," squeaked fatty, laughing now, receiving a coil of rope from a servant, which he slipped into a large inside coat-pocket, just as a clown in a pantomime disposes of a goose or a few yards of sausages. The boy then gave his fat self a hearty shake as if to ascertain that all was right, and thinking it was—money, keys, watch, buns, cigars, rope, and all, he next began squeaking for his horse.

"Now, then, I want my horse! Get me my horse! Where's my horse?" And forthwith the dray-horse-like brown emerged from the side-stable for our Master to mount. But this wasn't so easily managed as thought, for Willy Watkins had abolished the steps at the end of the stable as antediluvian, without providing a substitute, and Stotfold's legs being short, and his horse high, he hopped about with one foot in the stirrup, without daring to attempt the grand final hoist.

"Get me a pail! Get me a pail!" at length squeaked he, relinquishing the effort, and forthwith two helpers rushed out with a pail each, while a third punched and pushed the punchy horse up to where they stood. Stotfold then made a bold effort, and landed in the happy haven of his enormous saddle, and began shuffling and working himself about like a jockey trying to establish a seat. At length he got one to his liking, and Romford having mounted his horse, things at length seemed all ready for a start. But the fat boy, instead of ordering Jack Rogers to liberate the pent-up pack in the straw-house, pulled his cigar-case out of his breast-pocket and deliberately selecting a weed, began squeaking for fire wherewith to light it—"Has anybody got any fire! Has anybody got any fire!" demanded he, and Facey, who had just lit his pipe, handed him it, and the fat boy proceeded to imbibe and blow up a leisurely cloud, instead of pursuing his deer as hard as he could.

While all this was enacting, Brisket the butcher, and two or three other horsemen—or, more properly speaking, ponymen—who had met the Benicia Boy, were having a most enjoyable hunt. At first he seemed inclined to sulk, but Ballinger the carter's whip being freely administered, awoke him to a sense of his danger—if not of his duty—causing him to put his best leg first, and eventually to place two or three stiffish fences between him and his pursuers. The farther the Boy went, the farther the field were now left behind, and as the Benicia Boy passed through the orchard at the back of Mr. Tithemtight's rectory, the last of them left him, and he was only incommoded by farmer Badstock's cur. This he presently disposed of by a rush and a stamp of his foot, and then went trotting leisurely over the clean linen on Mrs. Martindale's drying-ground, from whence he passed into Mr. Ketherington's nursery-garden, and had a dance among the winter-cabbages and Brussels sprouts.

The sound of voices and of horses' hoofs on the stones now roused the inmates of the straw-house, drawing forth a joyous yell, and when Jack Rogers shot the bolt, every hound bounded out full cry, and spread in all directions. Bouncer made straight for the dairy, Rantipole rushed into the scullery, while Prodigal and Poulterer dived up to their ears in the pig-pail.

"Get on, and blow your horn!" now cried Romford,

anused to such riotous proceedings, and dropping his whip-thong, he proceeded to lay it into the offenders with hearty goodwill. Jack Rogers aided his endeavours, and by the time the fat boy appeared in front of Dalberry Lees, he had as many hounds about him as if he was making a cast. Unfortunately, however, Miss Watkins's Shetland pony was careering about the park, and certain anonymous hounds, thinking, perhaps, he would do as well as the stag, proceeded to charge him with vigorous determination, while a few others broke away at a cow. Then the horn and whips were at work again; the fat boy inflated his cheeks till they looked like bladder-balloons, and Rogers and Romford raced round the respective detachments of deserters to whipcord them back, at which Willy Watkins's horse denoted his delight by sundry squeaks and bounds in the air that nearly sent our friend over its head—"Oh, for Mr Stotfold's weight to keep him down!" thought Willy.

The rule of Mr. Stotfold's hunt was for the Master to hunt the hounds as long as he could, after which Mr. Rogers was at liberty to take them, and, both carrying horns, the arrangement answered very well, as Jack was always ready to face any place his master declined. And Jack, who was a bit of a courtier, always magnified his master's performance.

"That was a most terrific jump you took into the Adderley Road, just below the windmill," he would say; or, "I never saw a man ride over a brook better than you did over Long Kitlington Burn—wouldn't have had it myself at no price;" the said burn at its best being about three yards wide, with sound banks on each side.

But let us pursue the Benicia Boy.

There not being much chance of a scent where the pre-liminary hunt had taken place, the fat boy had nothing for it but to cast on till he came to virgin soil, and it was not until he neared Farmer Badstock's fold-yard that the redoubtable Wideawake dropped his stump of a stern, and Wiseacre endorsing the movement with his tongue, the rest of the pack were good enough to take their opinions from him, and, gradually closing in, at length assumed somewhat the appearance of a pack. "Hoop!" screeched Jack Rogers, cheering them on, as if it was the most brilliant move that ever was made. He inwardly hoped Mr. Romford saw it.

The Benicia Boy, as was his wont, had taken a turn round the country before deciding which line to adopt, astonishing sundry country folk by his appearance among them. Old Tommy Cobnut cutting fern in Brambleton brake for bedding for his pig, young Johnny Gooseman taking his colt to the shop, sundry girls playing at pitch-halfpenny at the low corner of Farmer Hoggin's field, instead of pulling turnips at the high one—all of whom stood staring with their heads up, wondering whatever the Boy could be. One said he was a donkey, another that he was the devil, a third that he was a Kyloe. At length the notes of the horn, and the cheer of the hunters came wafted on the breeze, and first one pedestrian and then another telegraphed the line of the chase to our friends with their hats or their hoes or their arms.

Jack Rogers now began to grin, for he saw the stag was going to run, and he thought Mr. Romford couldn't fail but to be highly delighted with the entertainment. Indeed, like Jawkins with Mrs. Somerville, he almost fancied Mr. Facey might tip him.

"*T-o-o-ld* you so!" exclaimed Jack, rising in his stirrups; "*t-o-o-ld* you so!" repeated he, pointing with his whip to where Wideawake was now leading, as usual. And Jack cheered the allied forces to the echo. Then,

Invincible Jack and invincible Jowler,
Invincible Tom and invincible Towler,

all laid their heads together to assist in the grand consummation of the catch.

The scent was now strong and good. They all seemed to enjoy it ; even the generally mute ones threw their tongues occasionally, and the skirters closed in for their share of the fun. So they raced along Galloway Lane, down Dinlington Hill (astonishing a gipsy camp at the turn), and, striking away across Castle Kennedy Common, made for the dewy vale of Horbury Heath beyond. This was one of the misnamed, or rather nature-changed, countries—like many commons, chases, and meres, which now present nothing of their original state ; and Horbury Heath, instead of being a wild, desolate track, frequented only by plovers and poachers, was a rich alluvial soil, with stout quickset fences and very wide, uncomfortable-looking ditches. Now, the Benicia Boy was fond of leaping, and made for the thick of these impediments, bucking and bounding as if they were so many skipping-ropes, to the great discomfiture of many of his followers. Here Mr. Willy Watkins, having sorely scratched his face, declined any further distinction. At Brailsford Bank, however, the field was presently recruited by the appearance of our coatless friend, Independent Jimmy, who, having now got a young iron-grey in lieu of Mr. Hazey's old horse, thought to try if he could do anything in the hunting way. So, on meeting the stag bobbing along, he unharnessed the young horse from the melon frame, and tying his aged companion up to a gate, was ready mounted, bare-backed, blinkers and all, when the tailing hounds came toiling up.

"He's on," said Jimmy, jerking his head the way he had gone, and on they went along the grassy siding of the road, which the boy had run on, in preference to the hard. Mr. Rogers was now in command, the fat boy having fallen in arrear at some of the more formidable places, and his rough-actioned horse, Hatter-his-heart-out, having worked him up into a considerable stew.

So far the Benicia Boy had kept clear of the towns, and would most likely have continued that course if they had not come in his way; but the pretty little village of Cherryford standing on rising ground, temptingly diversified by green slopes and gardens, was too inviting for an enterprising stag to withstand. So, taking the village diagonally, he passed through Mr. Collupton's flower-garden, over Mr. Hopkin's bleaching-field, into Pansey's nursery-ground, and from thence into a high beech-hedged slip of ground, interspersed with swings, hoops, and gymnasiums. This was neither more nor less than the playground at the back of Miss Birch's finishing and polishing seminary; and, in all probability, the Benicia Boy would have passed quietly along the passage, through the centre of the house—the *vis-à-vis* doors of which stood invitingly open—and so out on to the lawn in front, but for the wretched jingling notes of the old school piano, that parents buy so often over in the course of their children's education, causing him to stop and listen attentively, to hear whether it was his old friends the hounds or not. Retreating a few steps, with a slight digression to the right, brought him in front of a plate-glass window, at which, after contemplating himself attentively, he made a most deliberate dash, landing handsomely in the drawing-room, clearing the globes and a model of Vienna. What a crash and commotion was there !

" *Murder ! thieves ! murder !* " screeched Miss Birch, hurrying down from her bedroom.

" *Thieves ! murder ! thieves !* " roared the cook.

" *Pollis ! pollis !* " squeaked the page, rushing frantically out the front way.

But, before any extraneous assistance could arrive, the redoubtable Wideawake came bounding through the window too ; and the Benicia Boy, seeing his old enemy, rushed at the now open door, passing over the prostrate body of Miss Birch, and making along the passage for the front of the house, without waiting to read the beautiful rainbow-shaped blue and gold *affiche*, Miss Birch's Finishing and Polishing Academy, exhibited conspicuously in the garden, he cleared the iron rails at a bound, knocking off the hat of the pedestrian postman as he passed with the letters. The cook then having closed the drawing-room door on Wideawake (who did not like again facing the window), the immediate progress of the chase was arrested.

The cock-throppled chestnut having got into difficulties, Jack Rogers was glad to catch at a holloa, which lead him clear of the small enclosures around Cherryford village ; and now, getting his horn, he clapped forrard with his hounds, to lay them on at the windmill, where the view was just given to the south. Here they hit upon a scent untarnished by Wideawake, who, Jack candidly admitted (in reply to Facey's uncomplimentary observation, that he ought to be hung), was " rather o'er swift o' foot for them that day ; " and Wiseacre led the long-drawn line with his accustomed vigorous energy. But Wideawake was the dog the Benicia Boy most dreaded, for he was in the habit of haunching him unawares ; whereas Wiseacre, like the filial Irishman who never kicked his father when he was down, always gave him timely notice of his coming. Still, Wideawake had his use, in keeping the stag going when he might otherwise be inclined to soil or to sulk. Being now pent up at Miss Birch's, the Boy soon found he hadn't him in his wake, and began taking things in the easy, leisurely sort of way that a crow takes a gamekeeper on a Sunday, or a fox trots away before a party of shooters on a week day. There the noble animal might be seen going like a galvanised donkey, now trotting, now bucking, now trotting again; passing from pasture to fallow, and from fallow to wheat, in the open, undisguised way of a quadruped that is not afraid to be seen. He hasn't robbed a hen-roost, or run away with an old fat goose. He got his living like a gentleman, not like one of those skulking marauders called foxes, who were continually attacking people's poultry, and committing petty larcenies of that sort. He was above such work; could carry his head high—and high he did carry it. So on he went at a stilty trot as before.

At length the Benicia Boy, having traversed some eight or nine miles of country, which at the old posting price of eighteenpence a mile, and threepence to the driver. would come to some fifteen shillings and ninepence, possibly bethought him he had done enough for his dinner, and, being no longer tormented by the impetuous Wide-awake, began casting about in search of repose. He did not want to break any more windows, for he thought he had scratched himself in the side at Miss Birch's, and would rather prefer a barn or an outhouse with some clean straw in it. So he skirted the side of Hackberry Hill —half field and half moor—staring complacently round the country in search of what he wanted. There was a church steeple in front, denoting a village, another to the left, with a third in the rear. The latter, however, wouldn't do, for he heard Jack's horn, with the occasional accompaniment of the hounds—*yoou, yoou, yap, yap, yoou, yoou,* they went.

Just at this moment the picturesque outline of Pipe-ington Tilery presented itself, stretching its long length half across a five-acre field, offering every accommodation, including a mud-bath, that an aristocratic stag could desire; and thither our unantlered monarch decided on entrenching himself. So, sinking the hill, he struck boldly across country, not trying to take the tilery in the flank, but going right at the centre, spoiling as many green bricks as he could in passing over the drying ground. He then blobbed down into the spacious mud-bath between it and the tilery, and began swimming and cooling himself in its yellow waters. Great was the commotion the descent caused in the tilery. Tom Sparrow, the boy in charge of the pug-mill, who saw him coming, and thought it was Geordy Crosier's trespassing donkey, now stared as a hen stares when her ducklings take water. The moulders ceased their labours, the wheelers dropped their barrows, the clay-diggers their spades, and the firemen left their furnaces. It was confusion all and consternation. What the devil was it? The cry of the hounds and the cheer of the hunters presently enlightened them; and, looking to the left, they saw the gallant pack streaming down Hackberry Hill, closely followed by Rogers and Romford, and the man on the grey.

"Sink it'll be a stag!" exclaimed one.

"So it will!" roared another.

"That fat man's from the Nook," rejoined a third.

"Keep him in! keep him in!" was now the cry, as the Benicia Boy struck out boldly for the tilery. Then they hooted and shooed him, and pelted him with clay.

If the hounds tailed, so did the field; and Rogers, Jimmy, and Romford alone rode with the pack.

"He's taken soil!" exclaimed Jack, now pointing with his whip to the tilery commotion, as Romford and he galloped down Hackberry Hill together.

"Soil, is it?" said Romford, "it looks to me very like water."

"Oh, that's what we stag-hunters call soil," replied Jack, inducting Romford into the science.

"Do you?" rejoined Romford, thinking they might as well call it by its right name.

"For-rard! for-rard!" cheered Jack, thinking that Romford cannot fail to be highly delighted with the performance. Jack then looks back for his master.

And sure enough, on the now almost white-lathered Hatter-his-heart-out, comes the fat boy, puffing and blowing and looking very like a peony. He has indeed had a tremendous gallop, Hatter-his-heart-out having acted well up to his name, and nearly shaken him to pieces. Since our master, Mr. Stotfold, declined the dangerous in favour of Jack Rogers, he has had a good deal of rough fencing to contend with alone; none of the leaders of the chase doing much for their followers in the way of breaking the fences, and the heterogeneous group who united their fortunes with his, expecting "red coat" to do all for them. So he had nothing for it but to throw his magnanimous heart over each fence, and follow it as quickly as ever he could. And though Hatter-his-heart-out was a desperately rough galloper, he was a very smooth leaper; measuring, however, his ground so closely, as always to make the fat boy think he was going to let him down, thus keeping him in a state of constant labour and excitement.

Indeed but for the honour and credit of the thing, he should have preferred stopping before; for though it was undoubtedly a good thing to get a good gallop, yet the operation might be overdone, and the appetite injured instead of promoted. What he wanted was, to bring it home with a bloom upon it that would entitle him to oysters and porter and a substantial repast after. That he thought he had got before he came to the windmill, consequently all that had taken place since was what might be called work of supererogation. And now that he saw the prospect of a close, his flagging spirits rose within him, and getting Hatter-his-heart-out short by the head, he stood in his stirrups giving a squeaking cheer to his followers as he pointed out the strange confusion in the vale below. He then made for the tilery as hard as ever he could. What a hubbub was there! Clowns from all parts had turned up to the scene—clowns from the ploughs, clowns from the harrows, clowns from the hedges, just as the rough turn up in London at the prospect of a row—Willy and Harry and Jackey and all.

They thought the stag was going to be killed, and that they might come in for a slice. So they hemmed the Benicia Boy in on all sides, determined he shouldn't get away, despite Squeakey's urgent entreaties that they would let him land. Then the before-mentioned rope was produced from Mr. Stotfold's inner pocket, and Hatter-his-heart-out being resigned to a lad, our master commenced lassoing the stag with clumsy dexterity. Now he was near him, now he was wide; now he was near him again. At length he lassoed and landed him, amid the cheers of the populace. Instead, however, of sticking and skinning him as the countrymen expected, giving the head to Willy, the neck to Jackey, and the haunch to Harry, Mr. Stotfold began staring about, squeaking for the carriage. He wanted the old gentleman in green again.

"Have you seen my fellow?—have you seen my fellow?" demanded he, running from party to party.

Have you seen my fellow?" asks he, rushing up to

Independent Jimmy, now standing by the side of the panting iron grey.

" Nor, arm d—d if iver ar did," replied Jimmy, bursting into laughter.

At length the carriage was seen stopping the way at the top of Cinderby Lane, and a man of the place was induced by the promise of a shilling to go and conduct it through the field to the tilery. The while it was jolting its way down the rutty road, nearly tilting old Solomon out of his seat, our fat friend cast about on foot fishing for compliments on the length and severity of the run.

"Capital (puff) gallop," said he, cooling his cauliflower head by taking off his cap. "Excellent (gasp) run," continued he, mopping his brow with a yellow bandana. "Never saw the old (puff, gasp) Benicia Boy in such (puff) before. Can't have come less than twenty miles— twenty (puff) miles in (puff) and twenty minutes."

Then he approached Mr. Romford, who he thought ought to have come to him.

"Well, and what do you (puff) of it?" asked he, still continuing the mop of his greatly perspiring brow.

"Well oi, ha-hem-haw, think it's just about the ha-hem-haw sport oi know," replied Mr. Romford; adding, "oive half a mind to set up a pack myself to hunt the same day as the foxhounds, in order to draw off the superfluous of the field."

And the fat boy, feeling the compliment, but fearing the consequences, blurted out in reply—

"Don't, my (gasp) feller, I'll (puff) mine down whenever you (gasp)."

And thereupon he tendered his fat hand to Romford, who concluded the bargain with a shake.

The deer-carriage then came jolting down to the tilery, and a feed of oats in front and a kick behind soon sent the Benicia Boy back into the place from whence he came, amid the jeers and cheers of the populace.

Just then the sound of lamentation arose high above the shouts and clamour of the crowd. It was Jack Rogers bewailing the loss of his favourite hound, running about wringing his hands, asking if any one had seen him. "Seen a yellow pied hound with a short tail—a yellow pied hound with a short tail?" But we need scarcely say that nobody at the tilery has, for Miss Birch having kept the redoubtable dog safe under lock and key until her strong job gardener came, he administered such a bastinadoing as sent the old dog scampering home, with his short tail between his legs, as hard as ever he could. In vain, therefore, Jack whooped and halloaed, and twanged his horn. No Wideawake came.

"Oh, he'll cast up," at length squeaked Mr. Stotfold, getting tired of the wait. "He'll cast up," repeated he, making for where Hatter-his-heart-out was still being led about by the boy. Then, getting the horse into a clay hole, he made a vigorous assault on the saddle, and having settled himself in his seat, he chucked the lad a shilling, and drawing his thin reins, with a touch of the spur put his thick horse in motion.

The hunt was then up; the disappointed chaws returned to their clays and their clods; anxious Jack Rogers moved off with his hounds, still casting about for the lost one; and Mr. Romford was surprised to learn from Independent Jimmy that they were only five or six miles from Dalberry Lees.

"Ar'll show you the way," said Jimmy, jumping on to the bare-backed grey; and taking a line of his own, irrespective of either gates or gaps, he proceeded to make his way across country.

"Ar think nout o' this stag-huntin'," observed Jimmy, running the grey at a great on-and-off bank, with a wide ditch on each side.

"Nor I," rejoined Mr. Romford, following him.

"When you've catched the stag, ye're ne better off than ye were afore," observed Jimmy.

"Just so," said Romford.

Jimmy then angled a wide pasture at a trot, and was presently contemplating a rough, bush-entwined, rail-mended-fence with a too obvious brook on the far side. Jimmy ran the grey at a rail, but, hitting it with its fore feet, it landed on its head, shooting Jimmy well over it.

"Greate numb beast!" exclaimed Jimmy, jumping up and catching the horse as it rose. He then pulled the rail out for Romford.

A few more fields brought them to where Jimmy had placed his second horse; which now having reached, he prepared to resuscitate the melon-frame, leaving Mr. Romford to pursue his journey without him.

"Ye can't miss yer way," said Jimmy, jerking his head in the direction of Dalberry Lees. "Ye can't miss yer way. Just keep axin for the biggest feuil in the country, and they'll be sure to send yer to Lees." So saying, he gave our master a nod, and turned away to the right.

Mr. Romford then rode on, and having a good eye for country, soon took his bearings, and without troubling any of the country people with the inquiry Jimmy propounded, speedily found his way back to the glittering gates. Then having arrived at the house, he alighted at the front door and desired a footman to take the horse round to the stable; which saved him an interview with Gullpicker, Mr. Watkins's Melton groom, whom nobody would have at Melton. Then Miss met him, all radiant with smiles, so glad to see him safe back; mamma was delighted to hear Mr. Romford say he was much amused with the hunt, and altogether she thought they had made a great hit in having the fat boy down. And out came the flute and the harp for "Bob Ridley."

CHAPTER XLVII

MR. STANLEY STERLING

MR. FACEY ROMFORD had now got pretty well settled in his saddle in Doubleimupshire. He had seen most of the great guns of the country: the Watkinses and the teapot-handle man, and had now extended his acquaintance to the fat boy and the interesting family of the neighbouring master of hounds, Mr. Hazey. He had also established a nodding and "how-are-ye" acquaintance with the non-hunting Fuller, and Fowler, and Binks, and Brown, and Postle, and Hucklebridge, whom he prudently sir'd or mister'd in blank, instead of risking a shot at their names, and perhaps making a bad hit. There is nothing people dislike so much as being misnamed.

The country, if not first-rate, was fairly sporting: good enough for those who lived in and knew it, and yet not good enough to tempt peripatetic sportsmen out of their ways, unless, indeed, they happened to have a billet with

some one in it. This immunity from strangers was a
great comfort to Mr. Romford, for some men are troubled
with such a mania for pack-seeing, that there is no saying
but an inquisitive stranger might have strayed from the
other Mr. Romford's, and instituted an invidious comparison between our master and him. Not that any one
could take exception to our friend's hounds, or his horses,
or his system of hunting; but they might have raised the
question, Which was the right Romford?—asserted, perhaps, that Facey was not the man who lived at Abbeyfield
Park, which would have been very discouraging and
difficult to gainsay. A master of hounds ought not to
have his attention distracted by extraneous matter—
especially a master hunting his own hounds, as our
friend did.

Like most countries, Doubleimupshire varied a good
deal : some parts of it being good, some of it indifferent,
and much of it bad. The lowlands were deep and boggy
with great false-bottomed drains, large enough to hold
both horse and rider; but, then, these very drains
contributed to the sound riding of the uplands, they
being, in fact, the receivers and conveyers of the superfluous water that fell. Then there were the Bentley
Hills, over which hounds raced; and the Heckington
and Stanborough vales, where they dwelt, requiring all
the Romford science and energy to get them along
Taking the country, however, as a whole, the soil was
favourable to scent, as the staple of it was generally
good. And Romford's hounds could solve the difficult
problem, "Which way has he gone?" in most parts
of it.

The best part of the country, undoubtedly, lies between
Shervington Bridge and the town of Farmington Hill ;
but, then, it was infested by game preservers, who were
generally suspected of Dalberry Lees practices, with
regard to the illicit production of foxes. Formerly
three fields out of every four in this part were ploughed ;
but, since the repeal of the corn laws, the system has
been reversed, and three fields are now in old grass or
clover ley, for one that is under the plough. The enclosures, too, are large and roomy—twenty and thirty
acres each, with not over and above strong fences ; but
the land is deep and holding—or what Mr. Otto Musk,
the Leicestershire swell who got straggled there, once

described as "flat, dirty, and unpleasant." Still, there were no fences mended with old wire-rope in it, and the brooks are generally fairly jumpable—at least, when not flooded.

But we will indulge in a day in this the most favoured locality, and select a meet at Independent Jimmy's friend, Mr. Stanley Sterling's, he being about the only real sportsman on that side of the country.

Mr. Sterling was a comfortable man, and was waited upon by a woman. After that, we need scarcely say he was a bachelor : for where is the lady who will submit to be tended by one of her own sex, if she can possibly help it ? Well, Mr. Stanley Sterling, was a comfortable man, and was waited upon by a woman. He lived at a pretty, old-fashioned, gable-ended, grey-roofed place, called Rosemount Grange : where there was always a spare stall for a horse, and a hearty welcome for a friend. Moreover, there was generally a good wild fox to be found in his cover, Light-thorn-rough, at the back of the house, the next morning.

Let us also suppose that Mr. Facey Romford—lured, perhaps, by the fame of Mr. Stanley Sterling's nutty sherry, ruby port, and comfortable *ménage* generally—has come over to Rosemount to be handy for the meet on the morrow ; and that Mr. Freeman, of Shenstone Burn, commonly called Old Saddlebags, and the clergyman of the parish, form the *parti quarré* for the evening.

Freeman, who is hard upon eighty years of age, has hunted all his life, and looks more like sixty than what he really is. He is a stout, square-built man, with silvery-white hair shading an extremely rubicund face, with strongly marked lines, and whipcord-like muscles : a little, twinkling grey eye lights up an intelligent countenance.

In marching order—that is to say, the day before hunting—Mr. Freeman travels in his red coat and other hunting things, having his horse-rug rolled up before him, and the aforesaid saddlebags, containing his dress things, underneath him. Thus accoutred, he makes for the house of the nearest acquaintance he has to the meet, where Bags and his horse are always heartily welcome. Compared with the pyramids of luggage with which a modern exquisite travels, Saddlebags' wardrobe would seem strangely deficient ; but Bags had lived in times

when locomotion was difficult, and people had to think
what they could do without, and not what they could do
with—which, after all, is a great ingredient in travelling.

And yet to see the old gentleman come down in his
nice black dress coat, frilled shirt, and clean vest—the
latter vying the whiteness of his hair—with black shorts,
silk stockings, and pumps, no one would suppose but he
had come in his carriage, with a valet to boot. There he
stands before Mr. Stanley Sterling's bright parlour fire
with a beech-log on the top, as radiant and sparkling
as the fuel itself. There, too, is Mr. Romford, looking
him over, thinking what a man he is for his years ; and
now in comes the Reverend Mr. Teacher, the vicar, and
the party is complete.

Mr. Stanley Sterling did not attempt side-dishes, but
let his cook concentrate her talents upon a few general
favourites. Hence the ox-tail soup was always beautifully
clear and hot, the crimped-cod and oyster sauce excellent,
while the boiled fowls and ruddy ham ran a close race
with the four-year-old leg of roast mutton, leaving the
relish they give for the "sweet or dry" to support their
claims for preference. Beet and mealy potatoes accompanied the solids, and macaroni and mince-pies followed
in due course. A bottle of Beaujolais circulated with the
cheese. They had then all dined to their hearts' content.
As Romford chucked his napkin in a sort of happy-go-
lucky way over his left shoulder, he thought how much
better it was than any of the grand spreads he had seen.
Grace being said, the plate-warmer was then taken from
the fire, the horseshoe-table substituted, and each man
prepared to make himself comfortable according to his
own peculiar fashion.

And as each succeeding glass of bright port wine
circulated down Mr. Saddlebags' vest, the old man
warmed with sporting recollections until he became a
perfect chronicle of the chase. He seemed to remember
everything—when Mr. Princeps had the Hard and
Sharps—when Mr. Tedbury had the Larkspur—when
Sir Thomas Twyford had a third pack that hunted all
the country east of Horndean Hut, and so across by
Broad Halfpenny woodlands to the town of Cross Hands
in Marshdale. Then he got upon the subject of runs.
That tremendous run from Trouble House to Wooton
Wood, eighteen miles as the crow flies, when nobody

could get near the hounds for the last two miles save little Jim, the second whip, on a Pretender mare—the best animal that ever was foaled—no fence too large or day too long for her. Or that *magnificent* day from Scotgrove Hill to Wellingore, when some of the crack men of the Hot and Heavy Hunt were out, and they ran from scent to view in the middle of Heatherwick Moor, thirteen miles, without allowing for bends,—the finest men with the finest finish that ever was seen! To all which Mr. Romford sat listening as he would to a lecture. Facey dearly loved to pick up such stories at the end of a stinger. He kept weeding his chin till he almost made it sore.

Dinner having been at six, at nine o'clock precisely—for foxhunters are generally pretty punctual—Bridget the maid re-entered the room with the tea-tray, just as the second bottle of port was finished, thus putting a stop to the veteran's recitals and causing him to fall back on the sherry. A game of whist followed tea, and Mr. Teacher having taken his departure, Mr. Facey retired to his comfortable couch with five shillings more in his pocket than he brought. "Not a bad night's work," muttered our master, as he added a couple of shillings to it that he had of his own. He never gave house-servants anything, alleging that he could take care of himself,—nor stable ones either, if he thought his horses would fare as well without his doing so.

CHAPTER XLVIII

MR. STANLEY STERLING'S FOX

BREAKFAST at Rosemount Grange was conducted pretty much on the London Club principle, each guest having his separate *ménage*—viz., two teapots, one containing the beverage, the other the hot water, a small glass basin of sugar, a ditto butter-boat and cream-ewer, together with a muffin or bun, and a rack of dry toast. A common coffee-pot occupied the centre of the round-table, flanked on the one side with a well-filled egg-stand,

and on the other with a dish of beautiful moor-edge honey. On the side-table were hot meats and cold, with the well-made household bread. Hence each man, on coming down, rang for his own supply without reference to any one else—a great convenience to foxhunters, who like riding leisurely on instead of going full tilt to cover.

On this auspicious day, however, it was "all serene," as old Saddlebags said, the master being in the house, and the hounds having to meet before the door; so they dawdled and talked as people do who are not in a hurry and are sure of being in time. Mr. Romford was the only one who felt any concern, but this was not the uneasiness caused by the fear of unpunctuality, but alarm lest the redoubtable servants should arrive in a state of inebriety. Lucy, however, had undertaken to see them safely away from Beldon Hall, and the strong persevering man, who bought Mr. Romford's horse, was charged to look after them on the road. And very creditably they both fulfilled their mission, for as our master was deeply absorbed in the dissection of a woodcock's leg, the click of a gate attracted his attention, and looking up, he saw the gay cavalcade pass along the little bridge over the brook into the front field, in very creditable form—Swig sitting bolt upright on his horse, and Chowey preparing his succulent mouth for fawning operations on the field.

The sight acted electrically on the party: Mr. Sterling finished his tea, Mr. Romford took the woodcock leg in his fingers, and old Bags quaffed off his half cup of coffee at a draught. They were then presently up and at the window. Bridget went out with the bread, cheese, and ale on a tray, while Mr. Sterling unlocked the cellaret, and produced cherry brandy and liquors for those who chose to partake of them. In came Bonus, and Dennis, and Bankford, and two or three other never-miss-a-chancers. Meanwhile our host and his guests are off to the stable, where the horses are turned round in the stalls all ready for a start. They mount and away, Romford on the Baker, late Placid Joe, Bags on his eighteen-year-old bay horse, still called the "colt," and Mr. Sterling on a five-year-old iron grey of his own breeding. Thus they come round to the front, to receive the "sky scrapes" of the men, and the "mornins'" and "how are ye's" of the field. Then more horsemen came cantering up, and more went into the house. At length the time being up —say a quarter to eleven—and Mr. Facey making it a rule never to wait for unpunctual people, be their subscriptions ever so large, now gives a significant jerk of his head to Swig, which, communicating itself to Chowey, the two instantly have their horses by the head with the lively hounds bounding and frolicking forward the way the horses are going. The foot-people run and open the white gates, the parti-coloured cavalcade follow in long-drawn file, and the whole are presently in front of Light-thorn-rough — a cover so near the house and yet so secluded as almost to look like part of the premises. A deep triangular dell of some three acres in extent, abounding in blackthorn, gorse, broom, and fern, presenting in every part dry and most unexceptionable lying. The bridle-gate leading to it was always kept locked, and there was no foot-road within three-quarters of a mile of it. Here indeed a fox might repose. Some persons are always certain that covers will hold a fox—even though they may have been shooting in them the day before—and keep repeating and reiterating the assertion up to the very moment of testing its accuracy. "Sure to be there!— sure to be there! Certain as if I saw him!" perhaps with a view of hiding their delinquency. Mr. Stanley Sterling was not one of the positive order. He knew the nature of this wild animal too well to be bail for his appearance. So in answer to numerous inquiries if they are likely to find, he merely says he "hopes so," and then takes up a quiet position for a view, a point from whence he can see without being seen himself.

"*Cover hoick!—cover hoick!*" now cries Mr. Facey Romford, and in an instant he has not a hound at his horse's heels. The "Hurl's" man, and the man with the mouth too, have deserted him, the former to take up a position by the beeches above, the latter to hide his ugly face in the dip of the dell.

"*Eleu in there!—eleu in!*" cheers our master, as Gamester and Woodbine take a flourish towards a slope of close-looking gorse.

"Very likely place to hold a fox," observed he to himself, pulling a sample out of his beard and inspecting it. "Please, gentlemen, keep together! and don't hollao!" now cries he, looking round at the chatterers,—

Mr. Bonus asking after Mrs. Hemming's horse, Mr. Daniel
Dennis wondering if it was going to rain. He has got his
best coat on, and forgotten to look at his weathercock to
see whether it is a safe venture or not.

Like the Ashby Pasture gorse in Nimrod's celebrated
Leicestershire run, the cover soon begins to shake in
various parts, the obvious effect of some twenty couple
of hounds rummaging about it. The vibration increases
with more activity towards the juniper bushes in the
centre of the cover.

" *Have at 'im there !* " cheers Mr. Romford, with a crack
of his whip, as if to awake a sleeping fox from his trance.
" *Have at 'im there !* " repeats he, in a still louder key, now
standing erect in his stirrups, contemplating the rich sea
of bright undulating gorse. The vibration of the bushes
increases, varied with the slight crackle from the snapping
of rotten branches in the more open parts. "Fox, for a
'underd," muttered Mr. Romford, now buttoning the
second top button of his "tick,"—"Fox, for a 'underd !"
repeats he, and scarcely are the words well out of his
mouth ere the short sharp *yap, yap* of Pincher the terrier
is followed by the deep sonorous voice of old Thunderer
proclaiming the fact. "Hoick to Thunderer ! hoick !"
cheers Mr. Romford, now standing on tiptoe in his
stirrups, gazing intently on the scene, his eyes raking
every corner of the cover, like Daniel Forester's on
dividend-day.

And now the melody increases—twofold, threefold,
fourfold, fivefold, tenfold—now it's all melody together—

"More nobly full and swell'd with every mouth,"

as Somerville—not our fair friend, but the poet—sings.

"Now," as Romford asks, "where are all your sorrows
and your cares, ye gloomy souls ! or where your pains
and aches, ye complaining ones ! One halloa will
presently dispel them all."

"Hark ! there it is ! Tally-ho ! a-w-a-ay ! Tally-ho
a-w-a-a-y—a-w-a-ay !" The "away" stretched to the
length of the rope-walk. It's Daniel, the Right Honourable the Hurl of Scamperdale's Daniel, halloaing at the
very top of his husky voice, each succeeding note becoming
louder and better.

And now little Tom Chavey unfurls at once his pro-

boscis and his flail-like whip, and with repeated "Get
away, hounds'—get away!" seconds the sporting-like
twang of Mr. Romford's horn. Then what a scatter there
is of the late combined forces. The late clustered
phalanx is dissolved; its component parts are flying here,
there, and everywhere, each man looking after his own
particular leader, to whom he trusts for that knowledge
of the country that his flurry effaces. Where's Jack?
Where's Joe? Where's Tom? Then Mr. Saddlebags rises
greatly in public estimation, and whispers are heard among
the uninitiated of "Stick to old Bags!"—"Follow Bags!"
—"Bags knows every inch of the country." And the
octogenarian gets the colt by the head and slips out at a
corner into the grass fields on the left of the cover.
There he commands the pack as they break—Thunderer,
first, Resolute next, Prodigal third, all the rest in a
lump. Thunderer strikes the scent by the side of the
wall, Prodigal endorses his dictum, and the rest of the
pack adopt the same. Away they go like beans. And
just at the critical moment the Honorary Secretary, who
is riding a bay runaway with a dead side to its mouth,
which has passed through half the hands in the country,
gets the Pelham bit between his teeth, and charges into
the thick of them, knocking over Rosamond and Rallywood
and scattering the rest right and left.

"Rot ye!" roars Romford, flourishing his whip, as he
bounds over the stone wall that separates them—"rot
ye! what are ye after now? C-o-r-n-found ye, you
riband-dealer," adds he, as he gets up to him, "what
brings yer out here?" exclaiming with a scowl, as he
passes on, "you should be condemned to shop with two
old maids for a month!"

Then, as the astonished hounds get themselves
scrambled up, and the pack gathered together, our master
caps them on to where a countryman is halloaing the line
of the fox from a gate.

"That's him!—that's him!" shouts the man, as
Traveller and Trumpeter strike the scent just as the body
of the pack come up, when, heads and tails being again
united, and the scent first-rate, every hound settles to his
fox, and away they go with the stream of the chase at a
very high pressure. "Away!—away!" is the cry. The
hounds seem to fly over the country like pigeons, now at
Oakforth Green, now at Broadpool Banks, and anon at

the wooden bridge over the Brent. Romford is with them; Swig and Chowey not far off; and Stanley Sterling is a little on the left, each going on his own particular line. The Baker has had the benefit of two holding clayey fallows, and may now resume the taking name of Placid Joe, while Mr. Sterling's five-year-old grey, after a few tail-first presentations, begins to face his fences, and seems to enter into the spirit of the thing. He gathers courage as he goes. That is more, however, than some of the field do, for Bonus and Brankford, and two or three others who started with the hounds thinking it was a case of plain sailing, begin to tail off as fences supersede field-gates, and occupation-roads run out into the privacy of fold-yards. Then there is a grand divergence either to the Corsenside Lane, down which Mr. Saddlebags' broad back may be seen hustling along in *extremis*, or in the direction of Heathery Top, towards which Mr. Hubbock, the fat farmer, is gallantly leading. Either way will bring them to Berrington Hill, for which, if the fox is not pointing, he "did ought to be." But the leaders are right! Ah, yonder yokel, leaning on his plough-stilts, has seen him pass through the sheep on the netted-off turnips, sending the stupid muttons scampering together in a crowd. Now they wheel about as if they are going to charge. Chaw halloas at the top of his voice, regardless of the fact that the hounds are in as full cry as the racing nature of the pace will admit.

"Hold your row!" shouts Mr. Romford, brandishing his whip, but he might as well speak to the winds. The hounds, however, heed him not, and bustle forward on the scent with lively intrepidity—now Liberty leading, now Lucifer, now Old Sportsman coming to the front with his unerring nose. A sheet could cover them. Facey eyes them with pleasurable emotion, for he knows he has at least one man in the field who will appreciate their performance.

"For-rard!—For-rard! that's the way of him!" shrieks he, as they again stretch into telescopic point towards the head. "There they go for the Darby!" shouts he.

Now he takes a startling stone-wall, at which the Baker bounds so as to hit his rider's head against the branch of an impending ash and knocks his old hat right down over his nose.

"Rot the beggar!" exclaims Romford, spurring him across a rough fallow, extricating his head as he goes. He is now with the sheep and the chaw. The hounds rather falter on the turnips from the stain of the former, and the latter would infallibly have exercised his lungs again, only Mr. Romford, keeping outside the nets, holds up his hand and enjoins him to silence, threatening to cram his whip down his throat. Old Sportsman applies himself diligently to the dilemma, and presently pilots them on to pure ground beyond.

"That's the way on 'im!" cries Chaw, unable to contain his delight.

"Oi know it," retorts Romford, digging his spurs freely into the Baker.

The hounds snatch themselves into progression, and away they strive as before,—Liberty leading, with Lucifer and Lavender contending for places. They are all of this year's entry—or rather stealing—and he couldn't have had better if he'd bought them.

"What's the use o' botherin' and breedin' and buyin'," thinks Facey, eyeing them, "if ye can have such as these for axin' for? For-rard!" cheers he, "for-rard!" as Benedict and Brilliant now press to the front. "For-rard, all on ye! Wouldn't take a hatful o' money for ye!" adds he, now sousing himself luxuriously into his capacious saddle. The Baker and he have fairly settled the moot question which is master, and go quite amicably together.

Meanwhile the M'Adamites and riders to points poured on in their respective pilgrimages, each hoping to jump with the hounds at some convenient point or other of the now prosperous chase, and be able to say they were well up at Howell Burn, or close to the hounds down Dovecot Lane.

This independent customer of a fox, however, we are sorry to say, did not conform to the long established custom of the country, and instead of crossing Fairyclough Fields, through Winforth Rig, and out at the back of Mr. Heavycrop's farm at Milkhope, which would have joined Saddlebags' tail at Monkridge side-bar and Hubbock's a little farther on, with head in air and distended brush, he took over the fine grassy moorland country, straight for Roughfield Hill, some three miles to the north; and the farther Bags and Hubbock went, the farther they got apart from the pack. At length, pulling up on Marygate Green, Mr. Saddlebags, shading the sun from his eyes, sees the last of the field disappearing over the brow of Ravensdoune Hill, each individual horseman looking about the size of a marble.

"Bad job," muttered the old man, pulling the colt short round, amid the "Which way-ings?" the "Oh dear-ings!" and "What a bore-ings!" of his followers. A pilot, like a prophet, never gets thanked. If he rides his tail right, they take the credit of it themselves; if wrong, then they blow him up sky high. "Bad job," muttered old Bags, putting the colt at a stiffish, newly switched fence. "Come up!" exclaimed he, spurring him freely, as the old horse winced and intimated his objection to the thorns. Then, perhaps thinking the fence the lesser evil of the two, he just bucked himself over into the next field. Bags then saw his line, and set off as hard as ever his horse could lay legs to the ground. Some follow, some say he is an old fool, and pull up, having had enough of the fray. Hubbock then takes another line, sorely pressed by his partisans.

Meanwhile, without the slightest regard to the ease or convenience of his followers, this truly game fox proceeds at the most punishing pace through the open-bottomed fir woods of Brakenside Law, without dwelling a moment, and onwards, still pointing north, up a portion of Kidland Hill, from whence a commanding view of the surrounding country is obtained. Here, having apparently surveyed the

"Strange confusion in the vale below,"

heard the distant cry of the hounds, the cheer of the hunters, and taken his bearings, he had apparently come to the conclusion that he would be safer in a country that he knew than in taking a turn over the other side of the hill on which he now stood. True, he had been there once or twice on predatory excursions; but when a fox is encumbered with an old fat hen or a goose on his back, he hasn't time to pick his way to the best advantage. So our friend thought he wouldn't venture any further that way. And being a fox of a good deal of decision and much firmness of purpose, he immediately turned his head to the west, and, running along a convenient sheep track, had a fine panoramic view of the trouble they were taking to catch him,— the clamorous hounds still pressing on in a cluster, Mr. Romford yoicking and cheering them, Mr. Stanley Sterling, in close attendance on Romford, Daniel Swig and Chowey riding side by side, and two or three horse-men—one in scarlet, two in dark clothes—labouring and sorrowing after them, inwardly wishing the hounds would throw up. Enough is as good as a feast, thought they. Then along a sandy streak, denoting the township road between Wandon and Ratchford, might have been seen, if he had not been in too great a hurry to look, the broad black back of Mr. Hubbock, leading the variegated *posse comitatus*; while the fortunate Bags creeps up with his cohort along the more favourable line of Woodridge and Stobfield House.

But a southerly wind wafts the melody of the hounds stronger and fresher than our friend likes to hear it, and not wishing to give his pursuers the unnecessary trouble of eating him, he casts the country quickly through his mind, and resolves to be indebted to his old friend, the badger at Brockholes, for shelter and hospitality. So, stealing quietly down the hill, and crossing the Bowershield Road unseen, he runs the "flat, dirty, and unpleasant" plain, with its holding drains and deep ravines. Then, having exhausted its conveniences, he creeps over the marshes to Ewesley, and at the back of the Punch Bowl at Newfold. So he makes a wide circle of Birdshope, skirting the tempting glades of Rosserton Wood, which, however, he is too hot to enter; and, skirting its eastern corner, he comes in sight of his projected point, the badger's burrow at Brockholes.

If the badger is at home, he may have a fight for the berth; but still that is infinitely preferable to being dis-brushed, dismembered, and *who-hoop'd* by Mr. Facey Romford and his curs. So, putting his best leg first— and he had four uncommonly good ones—he tottled away in right energetic earnest, stopping occasionally as he reached rising ground to listen what was going on behind. At first he thinks "all is serene," then that he hears the noisy wretches far behind, next that they are coming his way, and finally, that he had better be going. So away he trots as before. And at a good, steady, holding pace, never fatiguing himself, but husbanding his strength, lest he should either have to fight at the door or pass on in search of repose. He presently reaches the sandy, oak-root-entwined entrance at the high point of Thristleton Wood, where, with right foot erect, he pauses for an instant and listens, to be quite sure that the hounds are coming. He thinks not. All is still. They have apparently had enough of it. Not the first time he has beaten a pack of hounds. Yet hark! *Yap, yap, yough, yough!—For-rard! for-rard!* there they are again. Confound their pertinacity! how they stick to a fellow's tail. What a shame! Forty great hounds setting upon one fox. But it was no time for moralising; so, being at the mouth of the badger's earth, he just popped in, taking his chance of a fight at the door.

Fortunately for our fox, the badger was a great, fat, plethoric animal, fond of ease and good living, and having several chambers to his burrow, he had laid up in an inner one, so that our friend had nothing to do but pop into an unoccupied room near the entrance. He was an unsociable badger, and seldom saw company. And scarcely had our fox got himself suited, than the loud baying of a hound filled the whole cavern with noise, causing the badger to growl and plant his great head at his bedroom door for self-defence. And further withdrawn, but still most uncomfortably near, arose the general clamour of the pack, the whole now crowned with stentorian yells of "Who—hoop!" and "who-hoop!" It was the voice of old Romford, backed by those of Chowey and Swig, and the badger, being now fully alive to his situation, makes a vigorous dash at the intruder in his entrance hall, and sends Ringwood yelping and yammering out to his comrades.

Then there was a council of war what to do, some wanting the fox dug, others "let alone," in the course of which Mr. Romford's opinion was loudly appealed to.

"He's a rare good 'un," exclaimed Mr. Stanley Sterling, anxious for his preservation.

"Is that!" gasped the chairman of the Half-Guinea Hat Company.

"Dig him! dig him! by all means," shouted several.

"Take an hour to do it," observed Mr. Hubbock; "this

is the badger's burrow, and it branches out in all directions—reaches from here to Con-stan-tinople."

"Oh, blood your hounds, by all means!" exclaimed Bonus; adding, "they richly deserve their fox."

"Blood 'em another day," muttered Mr. Romford—"blood 'em another day with a bad 'un. Doesn't do to be prodigal of good 'uns." So saying, with a "Cop, come away! —cop, come away!" to his baying hounds, he proceeded to reclaim the now panting tail-quivering Baker.

Then the appraisers began to estimate the run—time, distance, ditches, difficulties generally. One said it was one thing, another another, but they all agreed that it was extremely quick, and the fences terrible. A man who could ride over that country could ride over any.

"An hour and seven minutes, 'zactly," observed Chowey, the timekeeper of the hunt, putting on ten minutes for good measure.

"Without a single real check, only two hesitations of about a minute each," observed Mr. Romford.

"Far the best to save him," observed Mr. Sterling quietly; "far the best to save him—give us a good run another day."

"So it is," replied Mr. Romford; "so it is. Good foxes are becomin' very scarce—far too many Leadenhallers astir. Now, where shall we go for another draw?" asked he, thinking to try their mettle, not that he really meant to draw.

"Oh, done enough! done enough!" exclaimed several. "Leave well alone—leave well alone—capital day's sport —horses done enough—hounds done enough—all done enough."

"Well, then, which is my shortest way home?" demanded Mr. Romford, mounting his horse and casting about for a landmark.

"Can't do better than return with me," said Mr. Stanley Sterling, "and take a snack as you pass."

"Thank'e, I've got a captin i' my pocket," replied our master, producing a great ship-biscuit as he spoke; adding, "But are we still in Doubleimupshire?"

"Quite the extremity of it," replied Mr. Sterling, "quite the extremity of it. Close to what they call No Man's Land."

"No man's stop either, oi s'pose," muttered our master, thinking of the fox having got to ground in his country.

"Now, then," continued he to Chowey, who was trying to insinuate himself into Mr. Saddlebags' pocket, under pretence of a former acquaintanceship—"now, then, let's be going." So saying, there was a general sweep of the hounds, and horses' heads were turned to the south.

"I'll show you the short way through the fields, if you'll allow me now," said Mr. Sterling, putting himself a little in advance of the pack.

"Please," said Mr. Romford, who liked soft riding.

Mr. Sterling then proceeded to pilot him along Buttercup Pasture, through Farmer Rickstone's fold-yard, up Bushblades Banks to the Good Intent Inn, on the Woodberry Down Road. From thence an extensive view of the neighbouring country is obtained; Dozey Cathedral one way, Downley Castle another, Ritlington Clump a third.

"Now," said Mr. Sterling, pulling up short and addressing Mr. Romford—"now, your way is along this Holly Hill Road to Harpertown—there, you see the steeple straight before you; then ask your way to the Fox and Hounds at Mowlesley, and Mr. Gallon, the landlord, will direct you to Fleckney, from whence you will have no difficulty in finding your way to Beldon Hall. So now I'll bid you good-day," continued Mr. Sterling, taking off his doeskin glove and tendering his hand to our master; adding, "I'll be glad to see you at my place overnight the next time you come to draw my cover;" adding, "we'll have that badger burrow fired, or made safe somehow."

"Thank ye," said Mr. Romford, joining hands—"thank ye;" adding, "I'll beat up your quarters, and we'll see if we can't prevent his gettin' to Constantinople another time." So saying, the horses' heads diverged, under sky-scraping salutes from Chowey and Swig, Chowey telling Swig, as he unfurled his mouth with a grin, that, if he wasn't mistaken, he had seen that ere gent in Snorem-boremshire.

They then proceeded with a greatly reduced cavalcade, which kept further diminishing by withdrawals at various wayside houses. At length Mr. Romford and his men had the road to themselves, and our master conned over the run as he went, thinking with delight of the performance of the pack. If they were not the best in England, they were not far off, he thought.

And the badger presently looking out of his door, and seeing the coast clear, retired with a grunt to his bedroom, thinking what a punishment he had given the intruder; while the fox, taking a quiet survey from the door, also trotted leisurely off without saying "good morning," or thanking his host for his hospitality. And the fox slept that night at Rockwood Law, the next at Bowershield, and returned in due time to his old quarters in Light-thorn-rough. He didn't see any he liked better, and found that all places were more or less liable to be disturbed; Light-thorn-rough, perhaps, as little as any. So he again adopted it for better or for worse, as the saying is.

CHAPTER XLIX

MISS BETSEY SHANNON—MR. ROMFORD AT HOME

THE mention of mince-pies in a previous chapter will have prepared the reader for the near approach of Christmas: that festive season, when children come smiling home, with long bills in their boxes to lengthen their parents' faces; when unexpected and most wonderfully lengthened accounts come pouring in apace, and enterprising Ticks and never-dunning milliners— discarding the persiflage of patronage — demand their money "on or before Saturday next," with an urgency that looks very like a near approach to bankruptcy or the workhouse. Christmas was coming!

The interchange of cupboard love was about to take place. Oyster-barrels rose pyramidically on the counters, for transmission to the country; and cock pheasants and hares went wandering about on their first and final visit to the capital, seeking for the parties to whom they were directed. Day and night became pretty much as one, and the denizens of darkness long for the light of the shires.

This laudable yearning was largely partaken in by our before-mentioned friend, Miss Betsey Shannon, who not only sighed for the sight of

"Fresh fields and pastures new,"

but longed to see how her old friend, Lucy Glitters—afterwards Mrs. Sponge—now acted the part of Mrs. Somerville in the provinces. And as she had been useful to Mrs. Somerville, as well in rigging out her footmen as in a variety of other ways, and, moreover, knew that Lucy was not the woman to ask her down if she did not want to have her, Miss Shannon now wrote to say that, if it would be convenient to Mr. Romford and herself, she would be glad to pay them a visit at Beldon Hall. Then, as good luck would have it, the larder being pretty full, and the sport with the hounds first-rate, and Facey—perhaps wanting some one to keep Lucy quiet when he went on his fluting excursions to Dalberry Lees, readily assented ; and Lucy wrote back that they would be delighted to see Betsey down whenever she liked to come. But she said that, as they were now doing high life altogether, it would be well to abandon the name of Shannon, and adopt that of Miss Hamilton Howard for the occasion ; adding, that if she wanted any clothes to support the character, she would be glad to let her have some, as, thanks to the credit of her friend, she was very well found—better, indeed, than ever she had been before.

And as Miss Shannon is now going to play a more prominent part in our story than the mere livery-hunter and commission agent of London, we will here introduce her more fully to the reader.

Miss Shannon was now just turned five-and-twenty, her birthday being on the 1st of December, though she looked almost younger,—an extremely healthy constitution and active habits enabling her to withstand the united effects of bad air and rouge. She had long been attached to the minor theatres and City places of public entertainment, where her broad, dashing style of pleasantry procured her many admirers among the counter-skippers and " elegant extracts" of those regions.

Altogether she was a most attractive little woman, almost a sort of red-and-white edition of our friend Mrs. Somerville. What with her acting, her singing, her dancing, and modelling, she managed to eke out a comfortable livelihood, and pay ten shillings a week for her second-floor lodgings in Hornsey Road, Islington.

Well, Betsey was delighted when she got Lucy's letter, which she did after cutting her way home through a dense yellow fog from Highbury Barn ; and she jumped and danced about the room with such emphasis, that she awoke a most respectable clerk in a no less establishment than the Bank of England itself, who thought the house was on fire, and rushed to the first floor or drawing-room window, calling frantically for an "escape."

Having arranged matters, as well with the manager at Highbury Barn as with the proprietor of the Sir John Barleycorn Music and Dancing Saloon in Whitechapel, she presently left London, with three sovereigns in her pocket, and as light a heart in her bosom as ever accompanied fair lady into the country. And as the snorting engine swept the train out of town—passing from streets to crescents, from crescents to semi-detached villas, and from semi-detached villas to the magnificence of real ones, disclosing as it went real fields, real cows, real sheep, real barns, real everything,—her spirits rose to exuberance, and she thought she would never come back ; she would rather be a dairymaid in the country than have to dance for her dinner in town. And as she passed from station to station, her feelings became fortified in that line. The country was the place for her.

At length, after repeated stops, hisses, and starts, our fair friend found herself before a station that, somehow or other, she thought she had heard of before ; and diving into her lavender-coloured kid glove, she produced a little yellow-and-white striped ticket, bearing the duplicate of the name, Firfield—"London to Firfield"—upon it.

"Oh, guard ! porter ! here ! let me out !" cried she, protruding half her person through the window ; "let me out." And forthwith a sturdy porter was at the door complying with her request.

"Noo then ! where are ye for ?" demanded a coatless, pillar-post-shaped man, with a pig-jobber-like whip in his right hand. "Noo then ! where are ye for ?"

It was Independent Jimmy asking Miss Howard where she was going.

"Beldon Hall," replied our friend in a clear, musical voice.

It was lucky that our friends at Beldon Hall had the prudence to get Miss Shannon to change her name to something more aristocratic, for if she had gone into Doubleimupshire under her proper patronymic, she would never have been noticed, and might very likely have damaged the whole Beldon Hall concern. "Betsey

Shannon! What a name!" people would have said.
"What sort of people can those Romfords be, to associate
with such a person." Then her manners, though not
offensive, were rather forward, particularly with gentlemen; and altogether she required a little toning down.
This, then, she had in the much-coveted name of Howard;
for what would have been downright vulgarity in a
Shannon, became the easy manners of high life with a
Howard.

And as people are not easily stopped if they want a
thing—the standing orders of society being quite as
capable of suspension as those of the Houses of Parliament
—so the fact of Mrs. Somerville not having returned any
one's call did not at all prevent the same parties coming
again to pay their respects to Miss Howard.

Facey, we may observe, kept the gravelled ring before
the front door well raked, and could tell at a glance when
there had been callers—carriage callers or equestrian
callers; but as he could not control Miss Howard's movements, he laid it down as an invariable rule that callers
should have nothing but sherry and ship-biscuits when
they came. Sherry and ship-biscuits, he said, were
delicacies enough for anybody. He had no intention of
having his dinner ate up at luncheon-time by a party of
ravenous callers. And sherry and ship-biscuits being
more than our master allowed at first, the ladies presently
improved upon his liberality by getting Mrs. Mustard to
make a currant cake as well. Then, at the gentle tinkle
of the bell, old Balsam used to appear in his gaudy livery,
bearing a fine silver salver studded with beautiful crystal
and china accompaniments, making altogether a most
respectable appearance. And as the ship-biscuits did not
perceptibly diminish, and Mr. Romford cared little about
the sherry—Lord Lovetin finding that—he gradually
became reconciled to the ringing of his bell and the dirty-
ing of his doorsteps, so long as he himself was not personally intruded upon. Moreover, he was out hunting when
the great runs upon the house took place; and the ladies
having found out the trick about the gravel, generally
had it raked before he came home.

And Mrs. Somerville being a good judge as to who were
in earnest and who were philanderers, very soon saw that
young Joe Large was very favourably disposed towards
our auburn-haired friend, and therefore judiciously left

them alone while she herself went about her domestic affairs, or peeped through the keyhole at them, as the case might be.

Still the boy was slow, being constantly cautioned by his mother to beware of the ladies, who, she said, had very little conscience in love affairs, and though he came pretty often, still Betsey could not report much progress. Dinners Mr. Romford would not hear of, indeed they felt conscious they could not give them; but they both thought if they could have a little evening party, at which they could appear in ball dresses, it would be very delightful, and might either secure Large or spread the net wider to catch others. Ladies generally think if they can only show themselves in costly costume, that they will be sure to captivate the men, though they are quite mistaken in the matter. However, let that pass.

Well, the ladies both thought it would be uncommonly nice to have a little party. Oh dear, it would be so nice to have a little evening party. So easily done, too—such a charming house, such beautiful rooms, such nice losing-places. If only Mr. Romford could be managed—oh dear, if they could only manage Mr. Romford.

And, as good luck would have it, the chance soon came. Mr. Romford's hounds had had an uncommon run from Hoyland Hill, killing in the open in Mr. Hazey's country, with only Mr. Stanley Sterling, himself, and Daniel Swig, up, the nutmeg grey having taken a violent fancy to scrubbing Chowey's leg against a carrier's cart, instead of pursuing the pleasures of the chase, making the man with the mouth vociferate vehemently. Then Facey, having made a sumptuous dinner off toad-in-the-hole and toasted cheese, proceeded to review the run, with a glass of gin and a pipe of tobacco, from the luxurious depths of an easy-chair, breaking out every now and then in ecstacies at the performance of some of the pack as satisfied Lucy that he was very well pleased with all he had done. Then she looked at Betsey, and Betsey looked at Facey, and, seeing his humour, Betsey arose, and going to the piano began to play his favourite air, "Jump, Jim Crow." Facey was delighted: "Jim Crow" and "Old Bob Ridley" he looked upon as the two finest efforts of the imagination, and after Miss Shannon had played "Crow" over to him three times, he went for his flute and proceeded to accompany her.

Then came the "leperous distilment" as per previous arrangement between Lucy and Betsey.

"How nice it would be to have a little music here some evening," observed Miss Shannon, sipping her sherry negus.

"Wouldn't it!" exclaimed Lucy, as though the idea had just struck her.

"Such a nice house, and so well adapted for a thing of the sort," continued Betsey.

"Well, but we've had a little music," observed Facey, scrutinising them attentively; adding, "what more would you have?"

"Oh yes, we have had music, very nice music," replied Miss Shannon gaily, "but rather in a selfish sort of way, you know; what I meant was, to let other people hear us —'Mrs. Somerville at home,' or something of that sort, you know."

"'Mrs. Somerville at home,'" repeated Facey—"what does that mean? Why, you're always at home, ain't you, when you're not out, ain't ye?"

"Oh yes, but it doesn't mean that," rejoined Lucy. "It means at home to receive visitors. It means dressing up; but then there's no occasion for you to do so. You needn't dress up unless you like."

"Humph!" mused Facey, resuming his pipe, to consider how that would act. "Well, but is it a cock-and-hen club? I mean, are gentleman asked as well as ladies, or is it only a lady party?"

"Oh, certainly, a few men,—couldn't have a party without them, you know."

"And do ye give them anything?" asked he.

"Oh, just a little tea and coffee," replied Lucy.

"Tea and coffee," repeated Facey, thinking that would not do much for him.

"P'r'aps a sandwich and a glass of sherry before they go away," added she.

"Sandwich and a glass of sherry," muttered Facey—sandwiches and a glass of sherry," repeated he, thinking the latter would not cost anything. "Might have a rabbit-poie and a cheese," suggested he, thinking they would be cheaper than ham-sandwiches.

"Oh, but people don't eat cheese of an evening," replied Lucy — "only light things — confectionery, and such like."

"Humph! good things at any time, I think," replied Romford, who was a great man for cheese—good, stiff, leathery sort of stuff he used to indulge in, too.

"And what do you do then?" asked he.

"Oh, just look at each other and talk—ask Mrs. Brown if she's seen Mrs. Green, or Mr. Black if he's heard from Mr. White lately."

"What next?" asked Mr. Romford.

"Oh, well then, when you've got a good boiling you begin to let them simmer off to cards or something. Perhaps the best way will be to begin with a little music —Mr. Romford and you can open with 'Old Bob Ridley,' or any other tune; then you, Betsey, can accompany yourself on the guitar, after which we could begin to pair people off to play and sing together, or let them wander about the house and do as they like."

"Don't let them go into my bedroom!" exclaimed Facey, who had no fancy for having his valuable wardrobe or expensive toilette-table exposed.

"Oh no, lock the door," replied Lucy—"lock the door —lock all places up that we don't mean them to go into."

"And you're sure they won't make me make a speech, or anything of that sort?" inquired Facey anxiously.

"Oh no," replied Lucy, "nothing of that sort—quite a free-and-easy—a ladies' entertainment, in short. The master of the house may wander about just as if he were one of the guests."

"Well, then, oi'll wander off to bed," said Facey, rising and lighting himself a candle, observing to Lucy, as he shook hands with her, "oi think you'd better consider about the rabbit-poie and the cheese—come cheaper than ham, oi'm sure." So saying, he rolled out of the room. And as the door closed, and his slipshod feet were heard retreating along the passage, the ladies rose from their chairs, clapping their hands and jumping for joy at the idea of having an "AT HOME." They were perfectly astonished at their own success. Never thought our master would come in so easily. They little thought how much he was influenced by the idea of the fair lisper at Dalberry Lees forming one of the little musical party. The ladies then thought they had better clench the consent by sending out a few invitations; and opening a pack of "at home" cards that they had providentially had

engraved and sent down by book-post from London, they
commenced filling in the names—

" *Mr. Bonus,*

"'MRS. SOMERVILLE,

"'AT HOME,

" *Tuesday the 11th, Nine o'Clock,*

" *Beldon Hall.*

"R.S.V.P."

—to the extent of some ten or a dozen, which they enclosed
in superfine envelopes, sealed with the "Turbot-on-its-
tail" seal, and told Dirtiest of the Dirty to take them to
the lodge to meet the pedestrian postman in the morning.
This done, they retired to rest, Betsey dreaming that she
brought young Large to book before they had got half
through the evening, when other gentlemen came pouring
in apace, until she was perfectly overwhelmed with offers.
Mrs. Somerville, too, having then recently received a copy
of Crow's "Illustrated Manual of Mourning Fashion,"
dreamt that she was so captivating in a Clotilde tulle
evening dress, with its diamond-shaped bouillons, crossed
with straps of satin, that she wrote off and ordered one the
next morning without further to-do, and also a rich Zin-
garee Lyons velvet cloak for Miss Hamilton Howard, both,
of course, to be sent to the care of the Right Honourable
Lord Viscount Lovetin, Beldon Hall, Doubleimupshire.

CHAPTER L

MR. FIZZER, CONFECTIONER TO THE QUEEN

IT was a good arrangement of Mrs. Somerville's pitching
her party to the keynote of an "At home," they are
at once such elastic and compressible entertainments.
If nobody came, she was still "At home"; if half the

county came, she was there also. An "At home" may
mean anything—anything except a dinner. It may be
merely a conjurer, it may be a magic lantern, it may be
tea and turn out, it may be tea and Terpsichore, it may
be a carpet dance, it may be a quiet evening and a little
music, or it may be a ball and supper. It pledges itself to
nothing. Still, it has this inconvenience, that unless an
answer is specifically requested through the medium of
those talismanic letters "R.S.V.P.," half the recipients of
cards don't answer them, thinking it just a sort of open
thing to be gone to or not as they feel inclined on the
evening of the day. The absence of the letters is rather
indicative of its not making much matter whether the
guest comes or not. Mrs. Somerville, therefore, obviated
this by having the "R.S.V.P." on her invitations, which,
coupled with the novelty of anything being given at
Beldon Hall, caused a great sensation throughout the
country. There was no fear of any refusals, or of the
invitations not being responded to. There was no hunting
in Burke or Hart's Army List to see who Mrs. Somerville
was—everything was taken for granted. As soon as the
first surprise had subsided, the note-paper was produced,
and the answers becomingly arranged. Mr. and Mrs.
Joseph Large, and Mr. J. Bolingbroke Large, had the
honour of accepting Mrs. Somerville's polite invitation,
etc. ; Mr. and Mrs. Hazey, Miss Hazey, and Mr. William
Hazey, had much pleasure, etc., Miss Hazey thinking the
party was made for her. Mr. and Mrs. Watkins, and Miss
Watkins, had great pleasure, etc., Miss nothing doubting
that the party was made for her.

Others followed quickly, the Blantons, the Pyefinches,
the Cramberledges, the Ellerbys, the Baker-Bensons, the
Brogdales, the Bigmores, all coming, and some asking to
be allowed to bring friends, Mrs. Dust pleading for a
nephew, Mrs. Lolly asking for the addition of a lady.
Then out went more cards, and more cards still, in such
numbers that if Mrs. Somerville had not done old Ten-
and-a-half-per-Cent. out of a hundred pounds' worth of
shares in the Half-Guinea Hat Company, the outlay for
postage stamps would have been rather inconvenient.
Then came the consideration of feeding the multitude.

Old Dirty could roast and boil, but as to anything like
ornamental dishes, still less confectionery, it was wholly
and totally out of the question. She candidly said she

couldn't do it. She, however, half solved the difficulty by suggesting that her friend Mrs. Carraway, the confectioner of Hardingford, could be had over for a few days, who would be able to set out a supper fit for a prince to partake of.

"That old thing," said Betsey to Mrs. Somerville, "may be all very well in her way, but I should doubt very much her being able to set out anything superior, and in all probability she will charge you quite as much for a tenth-rate thing as a good confectioner would for a first ; so why not have a first-rate one, and enjoy the credit of it ?"

"Well," replied Mrs. Somerville, "there's something in that ; only," added she, after a pause, "where is one to get the superior article ?"

"London, to be sure," rejoined Betsey ; "London's the place to get everything. Get lions, tigers, unicorns, elephants, temples, pagodas, palaces,—all the skill and beauty of the most practised hands in each department of the sugary art."

"Ah, but how about Mr. Romford ?" sighed Mrs. Somerville.

"Ah, Mr. Romford, indeed !" ejaculated Betsey, recollecting his rabbit-pie-and-cheese proposal. "Well, that is a difficulty," added she. "Couldn't make him believe that old Dirty had made them, could we ?" asked she, after a pause.

"Oh no ; he's far too sharp for that," replied Mrs. Somerville. "Knows every ounce of everything that comes into the house, and everything that goes out of it too. One would think he had nothing a year, paid quarterly, instead of thirty thousand from land, and I don't know what from other sources."

"You don't say so !" exclaimed Betsey, who hadn't heard of such money. "Well, but if it didn't cost him anything he wouldn't mind, perhaps, would he ?" suggested Miss Shannon.

"Well, I don't know that he would," replied Mrs. Somerville ; "but the thing is how to do it."

"I think I have it," replied Miss Shannon.

"How ?" asked Mrs. Somerville.

"Well, then, you see, as we are only lodgers, as the Irishman said when they told him the house was on fire, I think we may as well make hay while the sun shines ; and with my fine new name and aristocratic connections, there can be no difficulty in my ordering whatever we like, and telling Mr. Romford that I stand Sam for the occasion."

"No more there will!" exclaimed Mrs. Somerville, delighted at the proposal.

"Have the things directed to me, you know—'Miss Hamilton Howard, or Mrs. Hamilton Howard, Beldon Hall, Doubleimupshire.'"

"Capital!" exclaimed Mrs. Somerville, clapping her pretty taper-fingered hands; "excellent, indeed. But we had better have in the Lovetin title, or they may take us for some of the smaller fry, and hesitate to execute the order."

"Well, I'd have it in mildly, then," replied Miss Shannon. "Say, 'at the Lord Lovetin's, Beldon Hall, Doubleimupshire'; not 'at the Right Honourable Lord Viscount Lovetin's, Beldon Hall, Doubleimupshire,' or they may think we are vulgar people unaccustomed to the nobility. They'll soon refer to the Peerage, if they have any doubts, and give him all his honours themselves."

"Then who should we give our valuable custom to?" asked Mrs. Somerville.

"Oh, Fizzer, by all means. Fizzer has unlimited means, and can execute the largest order off-hand with the greatest ease. I know one of his genteel young people, who says they do business in the most liberal, confiding way—never suspecting anybody with a handle to his name, or seeming to think it possible to be imposed upon."

"That's the man for us!" exclaimed Mrs. Somerville.

They then discussed the form of the Fizzer order.

"'Miss Hamilton Howard presents her compliments to Mr. Fizzer,'" suggested Lucy.

"No, I wouldn't compliment him," replied Miss Shannon. "Too polite; might make him suspicious. Just write as you would to your milliner, in a scrawly-sprawly sort of way, saying what you want, and nothing more; leaving him a little margin for the imagination to play upon, and to enable him to suggest something himself. He may propose to supply wine too; in which case you would take him at his word, and save Mr. Romford's, who, you know, only agreed to give sherry."

And Lucy, who was a much better writer than Betsey,

whose forte lay more in her toes than her fingers, then proceeded to order a champagne supper for eighty or ninety ladies and gentlemen, to be sent to Miss Hamilton Howard, at Beldon Hall, in Doubleimupshire, on the 11th, by the train that arrived at the Firfield Station at 1.30 p.m.

The next post brought down a gilt-edged extra super-fine note, with the words, "Fizzer, Confectioner to the Queen," on the pink stamp of the envelope, informing Miss Hamilton Howard that her esteemed favour had come to hand and should be duly attended to, adding, that if there was any extra plate, or waiters, or anything else required, perhaps Miss Hamilton Howard would have the goodness to communicate her wishes to Mr. Fizzer; thus showing how grateful London tradespeople are for being handsomely imposed upon. And the note concluded by requesting a continuance of Miss Hamilton Howard's favours, which should at all times command Fizzer's best attention.

So far so good. They had now got supper, plate, and extra servants if they wanted them. The minor adjuncts only remained. Lucy was now in her glory.

CHAPTER LI

MRS. SOMERVILLE "AT HOME"

FORTUNE favours the brave; and the ladies at Beldon Hall seemed to be particularly lucky, for a bright sunny day went down with a blood-red sky, giving goodly promise for the coming frosty night. And indeed, before Mr. Romford reached his kennel, after a fairish run in the lower part of Doubleimupshire, the ice began to crumble beneath his horse's hoofs, and the air assumed a crisp consistency that as good as said, "Mr. Francis Romford, my good friend, your invincible hounds will not be out again in a hurry." Nor in truth did our master care much if he stopped for a while and took stock, for several of his subscribers paid the usual convenient tribute of respect to his great riches by withholding their subscriptions, and Facey would like to have them collected. How could he ever build his hospital if they didn't pay? In addition to this, he had two or three lame horses, besides some that were getting rather light in the girth; and as Mr. Goodhearted Green had expressed his intention of being in Mr. Romford's "shire," as he called it, towards Christmas, Facey would like to have them plumped out a little before Goodheart came. So he resigned his horse to the strong persevering man, and fed his hounds without note or comment on the future. Two things Facey eschewed—hunting in wind and a frost; and he saw plainly enough that he was in for the latter. He therefore resolved to succumb without contending with the elements—a step that it would be well if other masters were to adopt. With feelings such as these, he now waddled down to the house at a sort of half-running, half-walking kind of gait.

The first thing that struck our master as he approached the Hall was the disordered state of the gravelled ring before the door. When he left home in the morning it was nicely raked, but now there were the marks of two if not three carriages upon it. "Rot it!" exclaimed he, "they'll never be done with their callers continually battledoring and shuttlecocking the cards," thinking what a consumption of sherry and captains there would have been. "Straw, too!" added he, as he advanced farther and found a few blades, also some paper shavings. "What the deuce are they doing with straw?" Facey little thinking what two cargoes of goods Independent Jimmy had brought from the Firfield Station, from Mr. Fizzer's. But when he opened the door, and found a fire blazing on either side of the great entrance-hall, his consternation knew no bounds, and he thought the quiet evening and a little music had indeed assumed vast proportions. There are, however, people who will attempt to carry off anything with a matter-of-course air, and by going boldly in they oftentimes parry, or at all events break, the force of a blow. When, therefore, Mr. Romford came striding into the breakfast-room, nursing his wrath as he walked, Miss Betsey Shannon essayed to take the wind out of his sails by exclaiming, "Oh, Mr. Romford! Oh, Mr. Romford! haven't we made an improvement in the hatmosphere of the 'ouse?"

"Made two great blazing fires, I see," replied Facey gruffly ; adding, "but I don't know that that will be any improvement in my pocket."

"Oh, but it's worth all the money," rejoined Miss Shannon, "especially on a cold frosty night like this ; and when, too, you have a few friends coming to take tea and spend the evening with you."

"Well, well," rejoined Mr. Romford ; "but there's reason in all things—reason in all things. No use making two fires when one would do. Folks can warm themselves just as well at one fire as at two. And who's been at the biscuits?" demanded he, reverting to his original gravel grievance.

"Nobody," replied Lucy boldly.

"*Nobody!*" retorted Facey. "Coom, that won't do ; bin two, if not three carriages here, oi'll swear."

"Oh, that's Independent Jimmy with—with——" faltered Mrs. Somerville.

"With what?" demanded Facey.

"Oh, just some things for Miss Shannon," replied the lady, recollecting herself.

"Things for Miss Shannon!" retorted Facey. "Why, he must have brought half creation."

"You see, now," interposed Betsey, playfully taking him by the button of his red coat as she spoke—"you see I've a cousin in the confectionery line, and he has lent us some little sugar ornaments and things to set the supper-table out with.

Facey.—"Supper-table! Why, I thought we settled there was to be a rabbit-pie and some cheese—I mean sherry and sandwiches?"

Miss Shannon.—"Oh yes—sherry and sandwiches too ; but you know these are just ornamental things, not meant to eat, you know ; and as my cousin offered them, why, we thought we might as well have them, specially as they cost nothing."

"Cost Independent Jimmy's journeys, at all events," replied Mr. Romford, thinking what a lot of rabbit-pies the money would have bought. However, as he couldn't say Miss Shannon might not do as she liked with her own, he turned the conversation by exclaiming to Lucy, "And what's there for dinner, lass?"

"Resurrection pie and roast apples," replied Lucy.

"Resurrection pie and roast apples," repeated Facey,

adding, " well, let's be at it as soon as you like, for oi'm very hungry, and ready to be doing."

" They'll be ready as soon as you are," replied Lucy, glad to see he was inclined to expedite matters ; adding, " p'r'aps you won't mind taking your pipe in the bed-room ?"

" What for ?" demanded Facey.

" Oh, only because we should like to have this room or a cloak-room."

" Cloak-room ! " replied Facey ; " why the deuce can't they put off their cloaks in the hall ? What are the two great rousing fires for, I wonder ?" asked he, reverting to the old grievance.

" Oh, but then the ladies must have combs and pins and looking-glasses, to arrange their hair and simpers," observed Miss Shannon, coming to the rescue.

" Dash them ! they surely don't mean to dress their hair here ?" replied Facey.

" No ; but then to see it's all right after the jolt of the road, you know."

" Gentlemen don't understand these things, you see,' added Miss Shannon.

" Don't oi ?" growled Facey, as if he understood a good deal more than she thought. He then rolled out of the room, wondering what the deuce the women were after—why they couldn't have a few friends to tea without all that kick-up.

It was only an uncomfortable meal as far as Lucy and Betsey were concerned, for they were anxious to expedite matters, and durst not open their mouths on the subject of the coming entertainment; while Facey seemed to dawdle over his dinner, a most unusual circumstance with him, who generally gobbled it up like a hound. If he only knew how anxious they were to get rid of him, he surely would be good enough to go. Oh dear, what a deal they had to do ! And there ! he was taking another slice of cheese. At length he gave his great mouth such a sounding smack as indicated he was done, and, turning short round to the fire, he stuck out his legs as if preparing for his pipe. Lucy then rang the bell for Dirtiest of the Dirty and as she cleared the things away, Lucy took advantage of a lull in the noise to ask if Mr. Romford's fire was burning.

" Yes, mum," replied Dirty.

"Hang these 'at homes,'" growled Facey; "they seem to make a man not at home. Light me a candle," added he, seeing there was no help for it. He then rose and slouched off in his slippers, muttering something as he went about "women and the price of coals."

"Thank goodness he's gone!" exclaimed Betsey, almost as soon as he closed the door.

"Hush!" rejoined Lucy; "you don't know what quick ears he has. Now he *is* away," added she, as she heard him turn up the passage leading to his bedroom. The ladies then laid their heads together to expedite matters— so much to do, and so little time to do it in. The fact was, Facey should not have had any dinner at home that day. And to aggravate matters, there came notes from parties begging, as the greatest possible favour, to be allowed to bring others, or exchange samples, with the weary bearers waiting for answers, and of course retarding matters down below.

Eight o'clock now struck—quicker, if possible, and more impulsively than usual—and it wanted but an hour, one short hour, until the grand company would be entitled to come; and there is always some stupid gawk who arrives at the exact moment, doing as much mischief as a score of people would do. But, thanks to Mr. Percival Pattycake, Mr. Fizzer's head man, things were well forward, which they would have had little chance of being if the Dirties had been in command, for they were all so bent on admiring themselves in their well-distended white muslin dresses, with cherry-colour sashes and little jaunty caps, as to be perfectly forgetful of the fact that they were meant to do anything but giggle and amuse themselves.

Very pretty they all were, though Dirtiest of the Dirty was decidedly the belle of the party, with her sylph-like figure, large languishing eyes, pearly teeth, and beautiful hands. She, however, felt rather hurt that, as a lady's-maid, she was not allowed to wear a low-necked dress. "There should be a distinction made," she said, "in favour of upper servants."

Billy Balsam and Bob Short, too, got into their shorts in good time; and Billy was so disguised by his powdered head and gaudy livery, that none of the Lonnergan family —not even old "Rent-should-never-rise" himself— recognised him.

But the great metamorphosis of the evening was that of our gigantic friend Proudlock, the keeper, whom Lucy had induced to put on a splendid green-and-gold French chasseur's uniform that Betsey had got down from the same unhappy hook-nose who supplied the liveries. There, with defiant false moustaches and a lofty feather-plumed cocked hat, Proudlock stood at the front door, receiving the carriages as they came up, striking awe and astonishment into the minds of the beholders.

One thing, to be sure, had been omitted in the arrangements, namely, to provide stable-room for the horses and refreshments for the servants. And as carriage after carriage set down, with the usual inquiry of the giant where they were to put up, the coachmen were told that he didn't know anything about putting up. Indeed, it never seemed to have occurred to the ladies that they would want anything of the sort. "As strong as a horse," is a familiar phrase; and what did it mean but the power of resisting hunger and cold. Besides, how did the cab-horses and things do in London? Who, in the midst of preparations like these, could think of such things? "Drive on!" was therefore the order of the day. And now let us look at matters inside the house.

The two ladies dressed together, taking an hour and a half for the operation, at the end of which time they severally appeared in very chaste and elegant costume

Let us now suppose them downstairs, all ready for the ring-up of the curtain of company.

Hark! it's evidently a frosty night, for the notes of the stable clock reverberate through the house as though it were inside the mansion. One, two, three, four, five, six, seven, eight, *nine* o'clock! Mrs. Somerville "at home" at nine o'clock, and now she's due! Then, having snatched a parting glance at herself in the mirror, and feeling comfortable on the score of looks, she takes her delicate white kid gloves and richly embroidered feathered fan off the mantelpiece, and approaches the door of the reception-room, accompanied by Miss Hamilton Howard, each inwardly hoping that Mr. Romford will be pacific under the violent surprise that awaits him—the blaze of light, the great gathering, the gorgeous supper, the—we don't know what else besides.

Hark, again! Carriage wheels sound on the now

frozen gravel, and yet it's only five minutes past nine. The noise ceases, but the momentary calm is only the prelude to a most boisterous ring.

A country footboy has got the brass bell-knob in his hand, and pulls as if he were going to pocket it for his trouble. A tremendous peal is the result. It shakes the nerves of everybody in the house,—Dirties, Lucy, Facey, and all.

"There! there's somebody!" ejaculated Lucy and Betsey, as they both got into position, Lucy before the door, Betsey a *leetle* behind, ready to advance as soon as Mrs. Somerville's smiling demands were satisfied in full.

"Dash my buttons, here they come!" exclaimed Facey aloud to himself, now in the last throes of his neckcloth. "Dash my buttons, here they come! and I not half dressed yet. Shouldn't wonder if it's Cass herself," said he, thinking how she would pout if he was not ready to "Bob Ridley" her.

But he is all out in his reckoning. Cassandra Cleopatra, at this identical moment, is getting laced into a most elegant toilette of straw-coloured Chambéry gauze with six flounces of tulle; and Spanker's man is just putting the harness on to the carriage-horses, to convey them to Beldon Hall.

No; it is the noble family of Lonnergan — Lord Lonnergan of Flush House, accompanied by his amiable wife and accomplished daughters, who, however, have not been able to persuade papa that there is no occasion to come to the exact moment they are asked for. His lordship insists upon the contrary; adding, that he once missed the mail train in consequence of being half a minute behind time, and he has always made a point of being punctual ever since. So he confronts the gigantic Proudlock, who passes the party on to the figure-footmen, who in turn conduct the ladies to the breakfast-room door, where the sylph-like form of Dirtiest of the Dirty, now arrayed in white muslin with bright cherry-coloured ribbons, receives them; and his blue-coated, short-breeched lordship is ushered into the library, where the other Miss Dirties, similarly attired, preside behind a well-garnished tea and coffee table. These beautiful girls his innocent lordship surveys with all the respect that old Don Quixote regarded the muleteer's wenches; thinking, if not princesses, that at all events they were Mrs. Somerville's servants. But he declines both tea and coffee, having had both before.

And now the Honourable Lovetin Lonnergan, who had come on the box of the carriage, having got out of his wraps and joined the ladies, summoning the old lord from his survey, advances up the passage to the radiant music-room, preceded by both Balsam and Short.

"Mr. and Mrs. Lonnergan and the Misses Lonnergan—Mr. Lovetin Lonnergan," announces Billy Balsam in the orthodox way he had been taught; and forthwith there was a great bending and bobbing and showing of teeth, with introductions to "my friend, Miss Hamilton Howard." And both his lordship and the honourable were much struck with the ladies' beauty.

Ring, ring, ring, went the door-bell, and the giant was again astonishing the arrivals: Mr. and Mrs. Brogdale and Miss Brogdale this time, closely followed by Romford's suspicious friend Miss Mouser, who did not let any doubts she had upon our master's genuineness prevent her begging Mrs. Watkins to get her an invitation to his house. Then came the Blantons and Mr. Finch, the gentleman our master called Mr. Felt.

And now, Mr. Romford having descended from his bedroom, arrayed in all the magnificence of purple and fine linen, with a smart cambric kerchief in his hand in lieu of his old snuff-coloured bandana, found a cluster of ladies and gentlemen around our fair friends, quite as many as, with a slight addition perhaps, Facey thought would constitute a party—quite as many, at least, as he expected to be asked when he gave his consent to have one. Who the deuce was going to find sherry and sandwiches for the whole county? But still Billy Balsam kept piloting in more, mangling their names, and some-times exchanging them altogether when he had two sets in hand, calling Mr. Tuckwell Mr. Brotherton, and Mr. Brotherton Mr. Brown, in the most arbitrary and un-charitable way. The carriages now came so quickly that the bell ceased ringing, and Billy had hardly time to receive one consignment from Bob Short and pass them to the Dirties, ere another party wanted to be passed from the Dirties to the music-room. Not so our fat friend from Pickering Nook, who seemed to think he had got among the fair damsels at the refreshment-room there, and kept laughing and talking, or rather squeaking, first with one Dirty and then with another, as though he were going to stay there.

But here comes the weaselly-looking chairman of the Half-Guinea Hat Company, with his yellow-and-white beard carefully combed out, and his failing crop of sandy hair made the most of towards the top. He grins as though he has quite recovered from his "cat"-spelling loss at Tarring Neville, and was easy about the hundred pounds' worth of hat-shares Lucy had got. The fact is, he has just made a great hit in buying a piece of land with a favourite clump of trees upon it, which he threatened to cut down unless certain parties paid for their standing, and amongst them he has got three times as much as he gave.

"MISTER, MISTRESS, AND MISS WATKINS!" now announced the Dalberry Lees' figure-footman in a loud authoritative tone at the front door, as though he were telling the giant something he didn't know. Mister, Mistress, and Miss Watkins had indeed come at last; and now, getting out of their opossum and black bearskin wrappers, they descend slowly and deliberately from the well-appointed carriage, as though they did not care who they kept waiting behind. Having seen them into the middle of the entrance-hall, the coachman then further procrastinates matters by demanding to know where he is to put up his 'osses. On being told by the giant that he knows nothin' about 'osses, he indulges in some coarse invectives against the 'ouse generally, and with a vindictive cut of his whip at length moves on from the door. Mr. Lolly's one-'oss shay then crawls up. Then came the Kickons, the Bigmores, and a gentleman in a gig. Meanwhile the ladies, having dropped Willy at the tea-room door, proceed under the guidance of the two figure-footmen to the cloak-room, where they remove the last wrap that conceals the artistic triumph of Madame La Modiste. Miss, indeed, looks well.

The Watkinses declining tea, which indeed they had taken before they left Dalberry Lees, proceeded, duly heralded by Balsam and Short, to the reception-room, about the centre of which, and as nearly under the richly cut glass chandelier as would escape any wax-drops falling on her dress or beautifully rounded shoulders, stood Mrs. Somerville in the full blaze of light and admiration, receiving the compliments of the men, and undergoing the scrutiny of the ladies.

There too, a little on her left, was Betsey Shannon, now, of course, Miss Hamilton Howard, the centre of attraction to three young gentlemen at once—viz., Bolingbroke Large, Sick-mouth, and the Honourable Lovetin Lonnergan. But Betsey had *esprit*, or what she called chaff, for them all, and played her cards so well that each fancied himself the favourite, and wondered why the others didn't go away. She had held six men in tow at Highbury Barn before now, to say nothing of a fiddler and the cornet-à-piston in the orchestra. So she smiled and laughed and twisted and turned to show herself off to the greatest advantage.

And now the concentrated gaze of the room is diverted from the new comers towards our great master, Mr. Romford, to see how he greets the reputed new mistress of Beldon Hall. Miss Mouser up with her glass, for hers was the eye that never missed the shadow of an ogle or the echo of a sigh. Mrs. Brogdale put on her spectacles, and Mrs. Bigmore her nose-glasses. On Romford comes like a great wave of the sea, until he reaches the reef of the family party. Then Mrs., then Miss, then Mr. have him alternately by the hand. Miss is very smiling, for she now feels assured that the whole affair is in honour of her. He wants to show her the house to advantage, before he asks her to share it with him. Miss Mouser says, with a dig of her sharp elbow into Mr. Blanton's ribs, "There's something in it, I'm sure." She then shifts her place and proceeds to take a sidelong survey—"Clearly something in it," she says to herself, as she watches the sparkle of the lisper's eye. But her triumph was of short duration.

"MR., MRS., AND MISS HAZEY, AND MR. WILLIAM HAZEY!" now announces Mr. William Balsam, piloting the party well up to the mistress. Then there was a fresh ebullition of feeling, more smiles, more bows, more curtsies, more shakes of the hand. Miss looks lovely, quite eclipsing Miss Watkins both in beauty and dress.

Miss Mouser is at her with her formidable glass, for she doesn't like her mother; Mrs. Bigmore is at her with her double ones, for she doesn't like her father; and Miss Watkins is at her with her supercilious eyes, for she doesn't like herself. A good many others, too, gave her saucy stares, for she was far too pretty to be popular, and Mr. Hazey himself was not much liked either. Mr. Romford, however, consoles her for all the curling lips by the fervour of his greeting, quite satisfying Miss Hazey that the party was for her, and her only. If Cassandra Cleopatra could have felt the pressure of his great hand, she would have thought little of her own chance of preferment. But our lisping friend is not going to surrender without a struggle, and watching her opportunity, she sidles up to our host, and asks, with a glance at the piano, if they are not going to have a little music.

"Oh, to be sure!" exclaimed Facey, now recollecting what the party was for—"oh, to be sure! Oi'll get moy flute, and we will 'stonish the natives together."

"Your flute is in the music-stand," now exclaimed Mrs. Somerville, who had been listening to the rivals, and feared lest Facey might go out of the room and upset all the other arrangements.

"Is it?" said Romford, "then let us be doing," offering as he spoke his red arm to Cassandra, who joyfully accepted it, flaunting her dress at Miss Hazey just as a peacock flaunts his tail when he's not upon over good terms with the hen.

Then there was fresh nudging and looking and hushing, and whispering of "What's up now? Going to have a little music, are we? What, a concert, is it?" with mutterings of "Oh, *she* can't play a bit, nor he either," as the two approached the piano.

Miss Cassandra now draws off her closely fitting white kid gloves, and depositing them with her fine lace and ciphered kerchief at the corner of the instrument, takes her voluminous seat on the stool, while Mr. Romford screws his old flute together, and amid hishing and hushing the audience form a semicircle behind, preparing for the punishment; and Mrs. Somerville stands on guard near the door to receive the fresh comers, closely attended by Ten-and-a-half-per-Cent., chairman of the Half-Guinea Hat Company, with Betsey and her beaux for a vanguard behind.

And now Mr. Romford, having got his greasy old instrument licked and sucked and put together, proceeds to blow a few discordant puffs and squeaks, while the fair lady runs her light hand up and down the notes of the piano, as if to test the quality of her consignment.

All being at length ready, with renewed cries of "hish, hush," the sound of voices gradually subsides, and as the now attracted company are expecting some fine Italian air, away the musicians go with Facey's favourite tune of "Old Bob Ridley."

"Why, what tune's that?" whispers one.

"Don't know," mutters another.

"Surely it's not 'Old Bob Ridley,'" says a third.

"Believe it is," adds a fourth.

"Hush!" cries a fifth.

If Facey's Oncle Gilroy really damaged his wind by making him play the flute to him when a boy, he had a great deal to answer for, as we make no doubt the assembled company thought, for a more impotent exhibition was perhaps never heard, even though Cassandra Cleopatra did halt and help him along over the weak places, instead of hurrying on and showing off on her own account.

Still the lameness of the performance did not prevent the assiduous toadies expressing their gratification and thanks to them both when they were done, even though they inwardly hoped they might not have to undergo any more of such music.

But Facey, who had a firm conviction that he had mistaken his calling and ought to have been a flutist, received it all as well-merited laudation, and as soon as he had sufficiently recovered his wind, whispered to Cassandra, "Now let's 'stonish them with 'Dixey's Land.'"

And Miss gladly obeyed, much to the comfort of some and the disquietude of others; and away they went more briskly than before.

During all this time the guests still kept arriving, Mr. Telford, Mr. Stoddart, Mr. and Mrs. Pinker bringing Miss Reevey, and Mr. Baxton his two daughters and a gawky nephew, and when Facey turned round he was astonished to find such an assemblage. There could not be less than sixty or seventy people in the room, and Sweet William still kept piloting in more. Bowman and Barker and Lightfoot and Lorington, and we don't know who else besides.

"Well, the ways of the women are wonderful," muttered Romford, surveying the gathering, thinking he would not be caught giving his consent for another quiet evening with a little music. Then the question where the

sandwiches were to come from struck like a dagger to his
heart. "Where, indeed," thought he. "A 'underd and
fifty people at least," mused he, glancing round the room.
"Terrible field, indeed."

But Cassandra did not give him much time for reflections, for, knowing the power of her rival, she arose, and
placing her delicate white arm within his red one,
she lisped in his ear, "Now take me to the tea-room,"
determined that he should not be charmed by her music,
at all events.

"Tea-room !" muttered Facey ; adding, "I don't think
there is one."

"Oh yes, there is," rejoined Miss Cassandra, piloting
him into the thick of the crowd—"oh yes, there is ;"
adding, "your people offered us some when we came."

And as she worked him on, they came upon the break-
water formed before the door, now shored up behind by
the substantial figures of "Rent-should-never-rise," Mrs.
and the Miss Rents, Fatty Stotfold, and other stout ones.

Then, having at length penetrated this apparently
impervious phalanx, they came upon where the enterprising ladies were receiving at once their guests and
the homage due to their own distinguished beauty ;
and Mrs. Somerville, looking round, confronted the
tall figure of her brother shouldering his way, with
Cassandra Cleopatra clinging affectionately to his side.

"Oh, where are you going, my dear ?" exclaimed she
anxiously, laying her hand on his arm.

"*Tea !* Where's the tea ?" muttered Facey.

"*Tea !* — there'll be—— " Here Mrs. Somerville
faltered ; she would have said sandwiches, but she felt
it was of no use further disguising the matter, so she
substituted the word "refreshment"; adding, "and I
want you to take in a lady."

"Humph !" growled Romford, wondering what was up ;
muttering down his arm to his fair friend, "you'll get
some gruel presently."

So Miss Cassandra was impounded—impounded, too,
in the most unpleasant way ; for Anna Maria, availing
herself of the familiar artifice peculiar to orators and
gentlemen troubled with a determination of words to the
mouth, got up a call on herself for some music, which,
after a certain amount of coyness, she acceded to, and
was presently playing and warbling in the place of her

predecessor. It is but justice, however, to Cassandra to
state that she talked as loud and made as much noise as
ever she could; and as it is easier to find fault than to
do better, she criticised Anna Maria's performance very
severely.

At length the music ceased, thanks were tendered,
curtsy made, and all parties began to think it was time
for something else.

Mrs. Somerville then braced herself up to the utmost,
and approaching our master, asked him to take Mrs.
Hazey into the dining-room.

"Dinin'-room!" muttered Facey, who thought the
thing would be done on a tray where they were. He
then did as he was bid, muttering as he went, "What's
up now, as the frog said when its tail dropped off."

CHAPTER LII

MRS. SOMERVILLE'S SANDWICHES

WE left our friend Mr. Romford piloting one of his
expectant mothers-in-law along from the music to
the refreshment room, under a mixed effusion of compliments from her, and speculations of his own as to
what was going to happen next.

Mrs. Hazey was now satisfied—indeed, revenged. She
saw how it was: Mr. Romford was civil to Mrs. Watkins,
but marked in his attention to her. It was clear the
party was made for them (the Hazeys), though the
Watkinses thought to appropriate it. That silly, conceited girl (Cassandra Cleopatra) was always trying to
make other women believe that the men were in love
with her.

They now got to the door of the lofty "forty by thirty"
dining-room, resplendent with light, glitter, and glare.
Along three-quarters of its entire length, flanked in at
the ends, was arranged a most sumptuous supper-table,
interspersed with beautiful fruit and flower vases, alternating with the most exquisite confectionery.

Before the elegant young gentleman in black, with the

costly jewellery on his vest, and his curly dark hair parted elegantly down the middle, stood a noble design of the royal arms—a perfect trophy—the whiteness of the sugar lions being relieved by the rich colour and gilding of the numerous flags and arms.

Half-way down, on Pattycake's right, arose a grand memorial of our Indian Empire, in the shape of a noble elephant, fully accoutred with its howdah, or castle, filled with sporting men, going out against the tiger; while a similar position on Pattycake's left was occupied by a barley-sugar pagoda, surrounded with bon-bons.

At the far end, on the right, was Britannia, ruling waves of sugar, and her car drawn by dolphins, red, white, and blue.

On a crimson velvet-covered shelving stand at the back of the room arose a perfect pyramid of plate, commencing with the massive shields and salvers of olden times, and gradually tapering away into the cups and vases of the present. It had been so long locked up, that it almost seemed to stare, as if quite unused to society. Its noble owner, however, would have stared far more if he could have seen it.

The entertainment was, indeed, what Mrs. Watkins's cook (Lubbins) would call a "grand uproar."

O'er all this sumptuous elegance Mr. Fizzer's head man, Mr. Percival Pattycake, presided, having a Dirty on each side of him, and the figure-footmen towards the ends of the table.

Old Dirty was kept below to wash up, whilst Dirtiest of the Dirty wandered about the rooms, pocketing sugar and picking up what she could.

Mr. Romford started convulsively when he got to the dining-room door, just as if he had seen another "woman in black"; for, however bold the Beldon Hall ladies were, he did not think they dared have ventured on such a step as this.

Mrs. Hazey, too, stared with astonishment, and inwardly thought it would be

> "A very fine thing to be mother-in-law
> To a very magnificent fox-hunting Bashaw."

The pressure, however, from the crowd behind was too great for much soliloquising, and the huge pent-up wave

of society pushed on, and presently broke against the
entire length of the supper-table, all equally anxious to
be at the eatables. To see the onslaught that was made
on the hams, and the tongues, and the turkeys, one could
not help wondering what they would have done if there
had not been any supper. Nor were the jellies, the
creams, or the custards a bit more neglected. " Munch,
munch, munch," was the order of the day. At length the
light artillery of bon-bons began to sound through the
room, which, however, was quickly silenced by the more
congenial fire of champagne. Fiz, pop, bang ! went the
corks from the right, left, and centre. Fiz, pop, bang !
repeated others, and forthwith black arms, and red arms,
and fair arms, presented glasses across the tables to check
the now overflowing exuberance of the bottles. Nor once,
nor twice sufficed to repulse them—back came the glasses
as though they had never been filled. The first glass, of
course, was said to be good ; the second middling ; and
the third "gusberry."

Mr. Romford having now what he called got Mrs.
Hazey hanked on to her husband, while he, wandering
about alone, muttering to himself, "Where the devil do
the chickens come from ? where the deuce do the hams
come from ? where the dickens do the turkeys come
from ? " He knew that Betsey Shannon's friend had only
undertaken to supply the ornaments. And Facey felt
just as if he was going to get the stomach-ache. At this
interesting juncture the fair Cassandra Cleopatra came
tripping up, all smiles and radiance, though somewhat
troubled in spirit, and presented arms at him in the
shape of a bon-bon.

The champagne fire now became weaker and more
languid, but the hubbub of voices and the cracking of
bon-bons supplied the deficiency. Fizzer had sent down an
unlimited supply of them, which ladies presented to gentlemen and gentlemen to ladies with the most undaunted
courage. Crack, crack ! shriek, crack ! sounded through
the spacious apartment, to which the occasional boom of
the champagne corks acted like artillery. Ten-and-a-half-
per-Cent. and Mrs. Somerville pulled one together, in
which was the following prudent hint :—

" Be not too forward in touching toes under the table ; some day
you will make a grand mistake."

while "If-father-would-but-die" was unremitting in his attention to Miss Hamilton Howard, looking as happy as if father was dead. The red or auburn-haired lady, as the case may be, was in her glory! Mrs. Somerville, too, was surrounded with beaux, all anxious for a smile from the beautiful widow with ten thousand a year, as they now called it. She thought how happy she would be if she could have such a party every night in the year. People seemed to amalgamate better than they usually do on these sort of occasions. They all appeared to have specific engagements, and to be more bent on forwarding their own little affairs than watching how other people got on. Miss Mouser, to be sure, kept on the alert with her eyeglass, but they seemed to regard her much as people regard a policeman in plain clothes, or a wasp deprived of its sting.

Meanwhile the Dirties and footmen, under the direction of Mr. Percival Pattycake, replenished the tables and arranged the garniture for further assaults — mangled remains were removed and replaced with uncut viands: Fizzer did the thing well.

Facey, who had now imbibed several glasses of champagne, was sufficiently elevated to be able to treat the matter in a philosophical over-shoes, over-boots sort of way, though when he looked at the temples and towers, and other triumphs of confectionery, he couldn't but think of his proposed rabbit-pie and cheese. "Wonderful work," muttered he, with a chuck of the chin to himself, as a fresh crop of champagne took its place on the table. "The ways of the women are wonderful, added he, as a boar's head and plovers' eggs came sailing in, as though the resources of the house were inexhaustible. "Wonder how many Philistines there are here," continued he, glancing round the crowded room. "Rather keep them in prayer-books than champagne," added he, looking at the long line of empty bottles ranged against the wall below the plate trophy.

And now, having inducted the reader thus far into the evening's entertainment, we will take leave to branch off briefly to another subject, promising that if he would like a glass of champagne in the meantime he can call for it, and he won't get it.

CHAPTER LIII

THE INVASION

WHILE all this frolicsome feasting and gaiety was going on inside the house, things wore a very different aspect at the door. The night, as we said before, was cold and frosty, with a keen cutting crescent moon ; there was no accommodation either for man or horse, and the gravelled ring was so blocked with carriages that the coachmen could not get their horses moved about to keep them warm. It was a deadlock from end to end. Under these circumstances the whole cavalcade resolved itself into a committee to discuss the meaning and probable duration of an "At home." One servant said it was a sort of a tea-drinkin', another that it was a kind of a fiddlin' concern, a third that it was just a ladies' clothes show, a fourth that they met to exchange characters of servants ; but Mrs. Watkins's London Johnny assured them it was only a sort of a morning call thing performed at night, to which people could come and go just as they liked. At the same time he said, " undoubtedly genlmen's servants and 'osses ought to be provided for ; porters and such-like might take their chance."

Whereupon a stentorian voice, that could belong to no one but our popular friend Independent Jimmy, struck up from the moon-shaded side of the ring, declaring "it didn't see what for gentlefolk's husses and things"— meaning by the latter term "servants"—"what for gentle-folk's husses and things were to be treated differently to other people's, seein' that other people's husses might bring quite as great company as gentlefolk's ; " and there being two postboys in the ring, they declared in favour of Jimmy's "unadorned eloquence." Whereupon a brisk and rather acrimonious discussion ensued as to the relative social position of public and private servants, Jimmy contending that the man who wore his own "claes," and knew when his day's work was done, was far more respect-able than a powder-monkey Peter, who had to fetch and carry "arl day, and arl night tee" if required. Where-upon several of the Jeames *de la Pluche* tribe retorted that

Jimmy, and such as him, were little better nor galley
slaves, putting three days' work into one, and living like
criminals ; to which Jimmy retorted that if the work
was hard and the fare poor, he was always in health,
which was more, he'd be bound to say, than many of them
were, "with arl their dish-lickin', pot-wollopin' laziness."
And so the debate proceeded from divers parts of the ring
—now a butler speaking, now a footman, now a tea-kettle
groom, Independent Jimmy generally replying to their
observations without reference to the fact of his having
spoken before.

When the argument was about at its height, the
sound of music came softened through the Hall to the
carriages.

"Hist !" exclaimed Jimmy ; "hist ! arm dashed if
they're not dancin' ! Sink !" added he, "but they'll
keep theirsels warm, whativer they de by us," Jimmy
stamping severely in the bottom of the melon-frame box
as he spoke.

Then there was a louder waft of music, and a louder
still.

"Ay, that they are !" exclaimed Mrs. Watkins's
footman, listening ; "and we may be kept waiting here
till 'daylight does appear.'"

"Wonder wot time they'll be thinking of us," observed
Mr. Large's butler, who would have sent the footman
if he had thought they would have been treated so.

"Wonder !" ejaculated Mr. Tuckwell's man ; adding,
"should have been out before, I think."

"Certainly," growled Mr. Bonus's servant, who, being
on board wages, was inclined to indulge.

"Just you slip in, Tom," said Mr. Brogdale's coachman
to his footman, "and see if there's anything to get ; "
adding, "if they don't mind about people's 'osses,
they surlie might think o' the servants freezin' and
starvin' in this way," the many-cape-coated speaker
flagellating his broad chest as he spoke.

And Tom, nothing loth, descended from his rumble,
and forthwith commenced worming his way among the
carriages, making his way for the back door, with which
he was well acquainted, having, when a policeman, been
a suitor of Dirty No. 2's. So he opened the door and
entered, just like one of the family. Nay, he did more,
for knowing the ways of the house, he groped along the

passages till he came to what would have been the invisible door in the dining-room but for the Miss Dirties' finger-marks, who had established a short-cut that way for carrying coals to the breakfast-room. This, then, he opened, and entered the gay, lightsome apartment.

Now it so happened that when Tom came in, Mr. Percival Pattycake, who was much smitten with Dirtiest of the Dirty, had resigned his post of commander-in-chief to Dirty No. 1, while he and Dirtiest of the Dirty carried on a flirtation in the deserted room; and Tom appealing pathetically to Miss Dirty's softer and better feelings, she just told him to help himself off the supper-table, whereupon Tom clutched a couple of capons, together with a tongue and a bottle of champagne, with which he returned triumphantly to the carriages. The sound of his coming, with the demand for a knife, caused quite a sensation in the ring, indeed all the way up the line towards the stables; and forthwith delegates were appointed from several of the vehicles to go on a sort of *qui tam* excursion into the house, and see what they could get as well for themselves as the coachmen.

Away they flew, like a flock of pigeons, as though they hadn't tasted meat for a month, and Lord Lonnergan's young man knowing the ways of the house too, he soon brought them, by certain circuitous ways, to the aforesaid invisible but dirt-defined door. Dirty No. 1 had now paired off with the fat boy, leaving the whole paraphernalia, ornaments and all, exposed to the mercy of the enemy. The intruders immediately set upon it. Mr. Blanton's young man turned a lobster salad into his livery hat, and restoring it, with a kerchief over it, to his head, next helped himself to a pigeon pie, and a bottle of seltzer water, mistaking it for curaçoa. The Dalberry Lees footman pounced on a shape of orange jelly, a nest of plovers' eggs, and a pine-apple; Miss Mouser's young man ran off with a spongecake porcupine, all bristling with almonds; Mr. Lolly's servant with a dish of Norfolk biffins; while Mr. Beddingfield's great clown of a coachman took an uncut ham in his hand, and the beautiful Elephant and Castle ornament away under his arm. Up to this time the triumphs of confectionery had been respected, partly perhaps because they did not look like man's meat, and partly because there were more tempting-looking things to be had on the table. Now, however, Mr. Beddingfield's servant's bad example was followed by Mr. Kickton's man pocketing a pair of turtle doves, to eat with some cheesecakes and a bottle of sherry.

The return of the marauders to the carriage ring was hailed with enthusiastic applause, and other adventurers were encouraged to proceed.

"You go in, Sam! You go in, Joe! You go in, Jimmy!"

"Nor, oi'll not gan in," said Independent Jimmy. "If they don't send oot, oi'll not gan in ; oi've got a crust o' bread i' mar pocket," added he, diving into his dirty old Witney coat as he spoke.

Fiz, pop, bang! now went the champagne corks from the carriages, and great was the demand for a suck at the bottles, and entreaties for a fair distribution of the food. In the midst of the clamour a spluttering cry of woe arose, causing a cessation of eating for the purpose of listening.

"Hush! what's that?" was the cry.

It was the voice of the great Mr. Spanker, the Dalberry Lees coachman, who has taken a huge bite out of the pine-apple without peeling it, filling his mouth full of needles and pins, as he afterwards described it. At first it was thought the worthy gentleman had taken a fit, then from the heaving of his shoulders that he was choking, and three or four smart whacks were administered on his back before the real cause was discovered.

And now, while they are prescribing for his much-blistered mouth, one giving him champagne out of a bottle as they give water to a racehorse, another recommending seltzer water, which was in no great demand, a third telling him to stuff his mouth full of cotton wool, let us return to our invited friends within the walls of Beldon Hall.

CHAPTER LIV

THE BELDON BALL

THE scene now changed, and Mr. Facey Romford, who thought he had exhausted all the wonders and surprises of the night, was doomed to undergo another apparition more startling and dazzling than any of the rest. This was neither more nor less than the beautiful gold-and-white drawing-room, brilliantly lighted up for a ball. The chair-covers, the brown holland bags, yea, the cut pile carpet itself had disappeared, and a searching radiance reigned supreme. It was no light for dirty gloves or dashed dresses. The cut-glass chandeliers fulgurated their sparkling lustre; while every sconce, every bracket, every available standing-place for a lustre supported its bunch of finest spermaceti, as well to show off the beauties and elegances of the apartment itself, as the beauties and elegances that were expected to enter it. And so quietly and secretly had the arrangements been made, that not one of the party, scarcely any one in the house, knew what was going to happen. Old Dirty and a daughter (Dirty No. 2) had removed the rolled-up carpet to the house-keeper's room, and washed the floor a few days before; but beyond this, Lucy and Betsey had kept the key and their own counsel, and did the rest of the decoration themselves, even to tipping the candles with spirits of wine, in order to make them light more readily. It was only on the afternoon of the very day that Chasseur Proudlock was inducted into the secret, and told to light up as soon as ever the guests went in to the supper-room; and then, having done so, to throw the door open for them to enter as they returned. And it was on their homeward voyage—Mr. Romford now convoying Mrs. Watkins, with Cassandra Cleopatra, steering her voluminous petticoats, by his side—that the first dawn of what was going to happen burst upon him.

Facey started as the flood of light shot across his path; a shock that was further increased by six well-dressed musicians slipping in before him, and hurrying up to their places in the bay. These were part of the produce of the chairman of the Half-guinea-Hat Company's hundred pounds' worth of shares in that excellent specula-tion, and out of which Mrs. Somerville had wheedled Mr. Bonus. But of that little transaction Mr. Facey knew nothing.

There, however, were the musicians, there the ball-room, and here Mr. Romford with his assiduous ladies.

"Oh dear, what a beautiful apartment!" lisped the Dalbery Lees charmer.

"Splendid!" ejaculated Mrs. Watkins, now lost in

astonishment at its size—fifteen feet longer than hers, and much higher.

Just then the pressure from behind carried them onward, and a surprised and now hilarious crowd entered the room, spreading over its ample dimensions, all anxious to try the merits of the beautiful floor. All was surprise and excitement.

"Oh dear, how charming!" "Was there ever anything so nice!" "Did you ever?" "No, I never!" "How kind of Mrs. Somerville to give us a ball."

And our hostess, who had tarried behind in the supper-room, ostensibly for the purpose of attending to her guests, but in reality to let Mr. Romford break the ice of this, the great finishing stroke of the evening, without her, now came up leaning on Willy Watkins's arm, attended by Ten-and-a-half-per-Cent., while Betsey Shannon, a little in the rear, distributed her smartness among the Honorary Secretary, young Large, and the Honourable Lovetin Lonnergan. Then, as the latter reached the radiant room, there were fresh exclamations of surprise. "Oh dear! how nice! how beautiful!" and they all wanted to dance with Betsey at once. She then surveys the scene of her exertions complacently, and inwardly congratulates herself on the fact that the Facey face exhibits nothing but the surprise that might be carried off by the use of his favourite aphorism of "verily the ways of the women are wonderful?" And wonderful they certainly were upon this occasion, converting a quiet evening and a little music into a splendid ball and supper.

Meanwhile the musicians have been tuning their instruments, young gentlemen drawing on their gloves (some wishing they were cleaner), others taking furtive glances at themselves in the mirrors, and all things conduce to an opening. The fiddlers are now in form, the assorted couples single themselves out from the crowd, the bystanders retire, the music strikes up gaily, and away they all go with a gallop.

Mrs. Somerville leads the way merrily with Willy Watkins, closely followed by Betsey Shannon with Bolingbroke Large, while the undying one starts off with Miss Hazey.

The long-secluded room is soon in a perfect petticoat whirl. The ball is well established; every Jack has got his Jill, and is ingratiating himself to the utmost of his

ability. Red coats and black coats mingle with blue
dresses and green, while yellow ones and white ones complete the scene. Here we might paraphrase Mr. Romford's
favourite apostrophe of Beckford on the fox breaking
cover, and say, "Now, where are all your sorrows and
your cares, ye gloomy souls? or where your pains and
aches, ye complaining ones? One pint of sparkling has
dispelled them all!"

Even the fiddlers seem infected with the common
enthusiasm, and stamp and shake their elbows with con-
vulsive energy. It is to be hoped that they have some
extra fiddle-strings in their pockets, for it would be a pity
to put a stop to such a party for want of a little fore-
thought.

The ice is now fairly broken, and even Mr. Facey
Romford resigns himself to the *abandon* of unrestrained
gaiety. He doesn't care a copper for anything.

"Go it, ye cripples! Newgate's on fire!" he inwardly
exclaims, as he sees the blooming ladies and light-footed
beaux rushing and floating and frolicking about the room.
Though no great performer himself, he encircles the
lisper's smart waist with his great red arm, and goes
boldly in for a dance, bumping against this party, thumping against that, stamping on t'other fellow's toes. But
the pace is too good to apologise.

And now the thick-winded ones begin to stop. Willy
Watkins first falls out, and his example is speedily
followed by Bolingbroke Large, who has been going in
distress for some time. The latter is quite blown; Betsey
feels him heaving: puff—wheeze—gasp—just like old
Jugglebury Crowdey running after a poacher.

"Come and have some refreshment," says she, now
acting deputy mistress of the house. And the youth,
being too much out of breath to reply, she leads him
away; and fortunately they re-enter the supper-room just
in the height of the before-mentioned foray of servants,
and as Mr. Beddingfield's servant is disappearing with the
Elephant and Castle. Betsey, seeing what has happened,
rang the bell violently, disturbing Mr. Percival Pattycake's *tête-à-tête* with Dirtiest of the Dirty, and causing a
general rush of attendants to the room. Mr. Pattycake is
greatly distressed at the loss of his magnificent elephant,
and forthwith offers a reward of ten shillings for its
recovery; whereupon Billy Balsam goes out among the

carriages, and offers the choice of half a crown or a constable to the man in possession, who prefers taking the half-crown; but the castle having been lost off the elephant's back in the transit, Mr. Pattycake refuses the full compensation, saying the castle was the most valuable part of the concern, and he would only give half-price.

Betsey now walked away with young Large. "Now let you and I have a spin," said she, putting herself in form for the Antelope Gallop, as they approached the ball-room door, starting off with a score directly they got within the portals. But Large was only a little better for his refreshment, and made a very poor response to the twinkling movements of Miss Shannon's pretty feet, so she very soon, what she called, "stopped the tap," and without much ceremony claimed the hand of the Honourable Lovetin Lonnergan, who, however, did not come up to her now champagne-inspired mark as a dancer. But as she was bent on business as well as pleasure, she thought to see what a little perambulation would do; so when the dance was done she walked him away, making a tour of the rooms, the passages, entrance-hall, and all, and finally brought him up at the familiar supper-table, now again in full array with the regulation complement of attendants —Dirties, footmen, Pattycake, and all. Here, after a glass of champagne apiece, they began to pull bon-bons, and the Honourable Lovetin presented Betsey with a sparkling sugar-plum, with the following motto:—

> "Before you take this pleasing sweet,
>   Let our fond lips together meet."

"Couldn't do it here, you know," whispered Betsey, smiling; but though she took him another excursion, and even asked him, when in the now deserted cloak-room, if he knew how to spell the word "opportunity," he did not rise to the invitation. Having heard of Mr. Romford's "cat"-spelling exploit, he thought there was some catch in it, and began, o-p-op-p-o-r-por-oppor-t-u—

"Ah! that'll do, Solomon," said Betsey, turning him round for the door.

And now Mrs. Somerville re-enters the supper-room just as Mr. Percival Pattycake popped off the last bottle of champagne, to whom he delicately intimates the position

of affairs. Then Lucy passing round the table to the
before-mentioned invisible door, summons him to follow
her, and after rebuking him for his master's non-fulfil-
ment of the order (as people do who are not going to pay
for a thing), she gives him out a couple of dozen of Lord
Lovetin's best sparkling, telling him she would deduct
the price of it from Mr. Fizzer's bill, he having contracted
to supply supper with unlimited wine, at so much per
head ; a safe venture for Lucy to make, seeing that Fizzer
was not there to contradict her.

If people who give bad wine, hoping their friends
won't discover it, were to see how really good wine is
appreciated, they would find their mistake, and perhaps
amend their ways. Upon this occasion Lord Lovetin's
wine had not been up very long before it became bruited
in the ball-room that there was a very superior supply of
champagne going, and troops of panting dancers came
pouring in, all anxiously asking for the popular beverage.
Non-dancers, too, were attracted by its merits. Mr.
Tuckwell, and Mr. Lolly, and Mr. Finch, and Mr.
Roxton, and even Lord Lonnergan himself might be seen
exalting his great excommunicated double-chin as he
quaffed off a bumper of the Beldon Hall supply—little
thinking whose wine he was drinking. Then this
improved excitement, coming at an opportune time,
infused fresh spirits into the party ; all

> " Went merry as a marriage bell,"

the right men getting the right partners, and swinging
up and down and round about with redoubled energy.
Even old Facey warms with the exercise, his knock-knees
smite each other vehemently, and he gets over the
ground better than before. He has divided his favours
very fairly between the lady competitors ; if he has
galloped with one, he has waltzed with the other.

So far so good—still there was a little deficiency in the
arrangements. The people outside were still wholly
unthought of. Facey couldn't think of them, because he
didn't know how they were coming. Lucy didn't think
of them, because few ladies ever do think of those things.
Betsey didn't think of them, because it never occurred to
her that the guests wouldn't come in street-cabs, which
would stand all about just as they do at Highbury Barn,

and altogether there was a singular dereliction on the part of the promoters of the party for the comfort and accommodation of the outsiders.

All people, however, are of consequence to themselves, and coachmen and footmen are no exception to the rule. It aggravated them to hear the sound of mirth and music inside, while they sat blowing their fingers, or flagellating their chests with their arms to keep the circulation alive. Nor was their dissatisfaction at all diminished by the report made by the invaders of all the fine things they found in the house. To guard against a second foray all the outer doors had now been locked and bolted, and the gallant green-and-gold Chasseur had retired within, to peep over the Dirties' heads at the door leading into the ball-room—his stalwart figure and handsome uniform making a showy background to the nicely dressed Dirties in front. And while he was thus pleasantly engaged, whispering his soft nonsense in their ears, a noisy peal came off the front-door bell that sounded as if the Lord-Lieutenant himself had arrived. A second peal, equally vociferous, followed close on the heels of the first—nay, before the first had time to get its heels well out of the way. The grand Chasseur, whose astonishment at the evening's proceedings had only been equalled by that of friend Romford himself, little doubting but it was some very great personage indeed, shook out the gay plume of his cocked hat, and restoring it with a military air to his head, summoned the two figure-footmen to precede him and open the door, while he drew himself up to his utmost altitude in front to receive whomsoever happened to come.

The lofty doors flew open, and in the noble portal stood coatless Independent Jimmy himself, whose temper having got the better of him, he had come to demand what time he was wanted.

Proudlock stepped back scornfully, shocked at the *rencontre*, for of course he knew Jimmy, though Jimmy didn't know him.

"Noo then! What time's ar wanted?" demanded Jimmy, thumping the butt-end of his great pig-jobber-like whip furiously against the marble flags.

"Wanted! What do I know about your wants!" replied Chasseur Proudlock, indignant at the idea of having answered such a ring.

"Sink! D'ye think ar's gannin' to let mar husses stand starvin' there arl neet?" roared Jimmy at the top of his stentorian voice.

"Hush! you'll disturb the dancers!" exclaimed Proudlock, waving his right arm imperiously for him to depart.

"Sink! but oi'll gan in and see," said Jimmy, pushing his way past Balsam and Bob Short, and making direct for the giant himself.

Proudlock, perhaps thinking that his military costume might intimidate, put himself in an attitude of defence; whereupon Jimmy, dropping the pig-jobber whip, at him in an instant, and planting two well-directed blows, laid him sprawling on the flags, with his right eye closed, and what the pugilists call the claret cork taken out of his nose. The giant fell heavily, and roared lustily. Oh, how he did roar! He stopped the music, and brought the dancers trooping into the hall to see what had happened. Then Old Dirty was found raising him up, with Dirty No. 2 applying a white kerchief to his nose.

"Who's dead, and what's to pay?" demanded Betsey Shannon, pressing forward through the crowd, leaning on the arm of the boy Bill.

"That imperent Jimmy has beat him most brutal!" exclaimed Old Dirty, casting an indignant eye at our imperturbable friend.

"What a go!" exclaimed Betsey, turning short round on her heel, having little doubt that Proudlock deserved it. He then got raised up and slunk off.

"Why, he's a regular Tom Sayers!" said she, looking at Independent Jimmy's stout frame, adding to Bill, "now take me back to the ball-room;" and away the two tripped in a waltz.

Great was independent Jimmy's astonishment at finding who he had been fighting with. "Sink! ar arlways said ar could polish him off in three rounds," said he, picking up his whip, and preparing to depart. Then suddenly recollecting what he had come for, he exclaimed, "Ar say, what time's ar wanted?"

"Oh, not this hour and fifty minutes yet," replied young Mr. Bigmore.

"We won't go home till morning," exclaimed the Honorary Secretary.

"Sink! it's amaist that noo!" roared Jimmy.

But he might as well speak to the winds.

Then the dancers galloped and waltzed back to the ball-room, the stately ones following slowly and demurely, wondering what would be the result of the evening's enjoyment. There were evidently many flirtations on foot; but would any of them ripen into an offer? They would see. Mrs. Watkins and Mrs. Hazey were equally confident of the success of their daughters. If Mr. Romford had danced one more dance with Anna Maria than he had with Cassandra Cleopatra, still Mrs. Watkins had the satisfaction of knowing that he had sat out a quadrille with her daughter, and also taken her (herself) in to the supper-room.

And now the musicians, having imbibed a gallon and a half of strong ale, and had some of the cheese that Mr. Romford proposed giving his guests, set to work as if they were going to fiddle the house down. And the dancers seem as if they were ready to assist them—the fat boy himself entering with avidity. So the ball is resumed with great ardour.

The supplementary champagne sustains the credit of the house, and people generally admit that they never saw a thing better done. Mrs. Somerville promised to be a great acquisition in Doubleimupshire, and Betsey Shannon was equally popular. It would be a shame to let them go out of the country. Long might Romford continue to hunt it. He was just the sort of man they wanted. And so the whole thing was a great success.

And best of friends, however, must part; and as our guests, unlike Goldsmith's

"—— dancing pair, that simply sought renown,
    By holding out to tire each other down,"

had higher aspirations than the mere movement of the moment; so first Mrs. Watkins, and then Mrs. Hazey, were shocked at the unwonted lateness of the hour, and Willy and the boy Bill were respectively told that they must look after the carriages directly, while the rivals were whispered that they must stop dancing at the end of the quadrille, as it was time to go home. And neither of them thinking to be able to complete the victory that

evening, they were content to retire simultaneously, each
feeling satisfied that none of the remanets could touch
her. So with a smiling "I pity you" sort of air, Miss
Cassandra Cleopatra presently sailed past her opponent,
closely followed by Willy and mamma, the latter giving
Anna Maria a half-saucy salute, that as good as said,
"You won't be mistress here, my dear." And Facey, who
had smote his knock-knees with dancing till they were
sore, gladly furthered the departure by tendering his red
arm to mamma, who whispered her gratitude to him for
the beautiful ball he had given her daughter as they went
along, first to the cloak-room, and next to the carriage.
Then, having got them tucked in, the lady to whom
allegorically he

> " —— had given his hand and heart,
>   And hoped they ne'er again might part,"

squeezed the former most affectionately ere she drew up
the window-sash. Spanker then touched the ready greys,
and away they bowled from the door, just as the stable
clock struck four.

"Wonderful work," muttered Facey, as he rolled back
into the house.

The Hazeys were then just emerging from the cloak-
room, and Facey having paid them the same tribute
of respect that he had paid the Watkinses, he returned
to the ball-room to see if he couldn't, in publicans'
parlance, get his house cleared. He gave a great un-
muzzled yawn as he entered the apartment, that as good
as said, "Oh dear, but I'm tired of it." Nor was his
anxiety to be done diminished by seeing that ugly old
Bonus twirling Mrs. Somerville about in a waltz, while
Betsey Shannon in vain tried to get the reader's old
friend, Robert Foozle, to follow.

"You are not much used to waltzing, Mr. Foozle,
I think?" said she, stopping short.

"No, I'm not much used to waltzing," gasped Robert.

"Better have some lessons in waltzing, I think, Mr.
Foozle," said Betsey.

"Yes, I'd better have some lessons in waltzing, I think,"
rejoined Robert.

"Ah, come to me some morning, and I'll spin you
about," said Betsey, now slipping away from him.

Whish, crush, bump! fatty Stotfold and Miss Lonnergan now knock Robert clean out of the ring. Facey then gives another great yawn.

It is melancholy work watching the decadence of a ball, the exhaustion of the dancers, the struggles to be gay against the ability to be so, the decline of the dresses until none but the shabbiest remain, the flickering of the candles, the droppings of wax, perhaps the premature demise of a lamp. All these symptoms now followed in rapid succession at Beldon Hall. The fat Misses Lonnergan got partners, the thin Misses Pinker exhibited their steps, and even Miss Mouser was induced to stand up in a quadrille. Still the thing was wearing itself out apace, and if it hadn't been for the aftermath or chaff as to the lateness of the thing, they would all just as soon have been in bed. So, sooner than give in, they danced and grinned till their cheek-bones ached.

At length the last of the crinolines disappeared under the guidance of our athletic Master, and nothing remained but those few male lingerers who so seldom get to parties that they never know when to go away—who stick to the supper-table so long as any vestige of anything remains.

Lucy and Betsey, now dreading the reckoning, stole away to bed as soon as they saw Romford's broad red back disappearing with his last convoy, and our friend, on returning, seized a sherry glass, and, holding it up in mid-air, exclaimed in an Independent Jimmy sort of tone, "Come, gentlemen! Oi'll give ye a bumper toast. Fill your glasses, if you please!" an invitation that was most readily complied with, in hopes of its being the precursor to a final carouse, when Facey speedily dashed the cup of hope from their lips by adding, "Oi'll give ye our *next* merry meeting!" an appeal that was too urgent for the most inveterate sitter to resist. So they quaffed off their glasses in silence, and, like the sick man's doctor,

"took their leaves with signs of sorrow,
Despairing of a drink to-morrow."

Silence then presently reigned through Beldon Hall, broken only by the airy tread of the pretty Dirties puffing out the candles, and the heavy tramp of the massive footmen bearing off the plate and the weightier articles of ornament. Facey then retired to rest, hardly able to realise the events of the evening. Nor did a broken harassing sleep contribute to the elucidation of the mystery. He dreamt all sorts of dreams—first that a Jew bailiff, dressed in white cords and top-boots, stepped out of his gig and arrested him for the supper bill just as he was finding his fox in Stubbington Gorse— that nobody would bail him, and he was obliged to leave his hounds at that critical moment. Then that all the musicans were sitting on his stomach, vowing that they would play "Old Bob Ridley" till he paid them for their overnight exertions. Next that he had backed Proud- lock an even fifty to lick Independent Jimmy, and that Jimmy was leathering the giant just as he liked. Lastly, that Mrs. Somerville was off with old Bonus, and that Facey's horse Everlasting stood stockstill and refused to go a yard in pursuit of them.

Other parties had their dreams. Lovetin Lonnergan dreamed that "father was dead," that he was in possession of Flush House with all the accumulations, and was just going to the coachmaker's to order a splendid blue-and-white carriage to take Miss Hamilton Howard to church; while young Joseph Large, between parox- ysms of the cramp and broken sleep, dreamt that Miss Howard was his, and was coming to adorn the halls of Pippin Priory. Robert Foozle, too, dreamt that he had got a wife without his mother's leave, and was greatly rejoiced when he awoke and found it was not so.

CHAPTER LV

MR. GOODHEARTED GREEN AGAIN

THE day after a ball is always a feverish, uncomfortable affair. It is far worse than the day before; for you have all the confusion without the excitement caused by the coming event. Nobody knows when to do any- thing,—when to get up, when to breakfast, when to lunch, when or where to dine. On this occasion the sun itself forgot to rise—at least, to shine; and those who slept with their curtains drawn and shutters closed, might have skipped the day altogether.

Jack Frost was as good as his word; and when Facey awoke, he found the landscape folded in Jack's icy embraces. "No hunting for me," said he, as, casting aside the bed-curtains, he saw the head of Roundforth Hill powdered with a sprinkling of snow., "No hunting for me," repeated he, turning over on his side; "but oi'll have a look at moy list, and see if oi can't bring some of my non-paying subscribers to book. No notion of carryin' on a country for the mere pleasure of the thing, and treat them into the bargain. Oi'm summit like the barber," continued Facey, soliloquising, "who put up for a sign—

> 'What! Do you think
> I shaves for a penny
> And axes to drink?'

but when the customer, having been shaved, wanted to drink, too, the barber read the sign—

> What! Do you *think*
> I shaves for a penny
> And axes to drink?'

Oi'm not goin' to hunt a country for nothin', and give them balls too.

> 'Shave for a penny, and ax 'em to drink.'"

So saying, our Master turned over in his couch, and presently subsided into a broken, fitful sort of sleep. Thus he remained until half-past one in the afternoon, a thing he had never done before; no, not even after the most ardent harvest dance, at which festivities he used to be a great performer. He then got up, and dispensing with a shave, jumped into his lounging-suit of grey tweed, and proceeded downstairs, as well to test the severity of the frost as to get a mouthful of fresh air before breakfast. Passing over the still bloodstained flags, he arrived at and opened the front door. What a gravel ring was there! So different to the nicely raked thing he usually kept. It looked as if all the horses in the country had been trampling and pawing upon it. There was the pine-apple, with the great bite taken out, just as Mr. Spanker, the Dalberry Lees coachman, threw it away. There were champagne bottles strewed all around, also the bottle of seltzer-water standing upright on the window-sill, and the elephant's castle lying crushed to atoms, just as it was when Mr. Kickton's carriage-wheel passed over it. The invaders hadn't even been at the trouble of taking the borrowed ale-horn back into the house, but had chucked it down to take its chance in the general *mêlée*. A keen east wind wafted straws and paper shavings about in all directions.

"Bless us, what a sight!" exclaimed Mr. Facey Romford, looking at the débris spread over the battle-field. "Declare it will take a man a month to put this ring right. All the way up to the stable the same mess," added he, following up the line with his eye. "Well, if this doesn't cost something, I don't know what will! Sooner Betsey's cousin than me!" So saying, our friend picked up the pine-apple and the horn, and, wheeling about on his heel, re-entered the house, and rang the bell for his breakfast.

It was all very well ringing, but there was nobody to answer the bell; nobody but Old Dirty, at least, and she didn't care to come. The fact was, the breakfast-room, as indeed all the others, were just as the company had left them; no fires lighted, candles as they were blown out, lamps as they were extinguished, chairs as they stood, some wide apart, others close together; everything, in fact, but the supper-table was *in statu quo*. This was clean swept, Mr. Percival Pattycake, aided by Dirtiest of the Dirty, having packed up everything worth carrying off, and being then far on his way back to town, with the score of a hundred and ten people who had partaken of the Beldon Hall hospitality.

Facey rang again and again before Old Dirty came, and then she had nothing to show,—said the girls were all in bed, and declared they wouldn't get up that day. So Facey had to go down into the kitchen and get his breakfast there, fearing to await the dribbling assiduities of Old Dirty. And as he was busy making what the Frenchman called a "grand circumference" of toast for himself, first Betsey, and then Lucy, dropped in "quite promiscuous," and a disjointed conversation arose, interrupted by the occasional entry and exit of Old Dirty, respecting the grand entertainment ; Facey fearing that he would be let in for the cost, Betsey assuring him he had nothing to fear, as she and her friend had made it all right with old Fizzer. And though Facey did not see how a young lady who sang and danced for her maintenance could afford such a proceeding, yet knowing that the "ways of the women were wonderful," he hoped for the best, and proceeded with his breakfast. This over, he looked at his watch, and finding it was nearly three o'clock, he gave up the idea of a stroll with his gun after the woodcocks, or anything else that turned up, and slouched away to the stable.

Among other miscarriages—or rather, misplacements—of the occasion, was that of the Beldon Hall letters. The correspondence of the house was not very large, being chiefly confined to invoices, with a slight sprinkling of refreshers in the way of bills delivered, though nothing at all approaching a regular "dun"; but it so happened that there was a letter from Goodhearted Green himself, dated from Wallingford, saying that he had just purchased a most desirable weight-carrier, only a difficult one to mount, which he would be glad to bring to Beldon Hall himself, and pass a few days in Mr. Romford's agreeable company. And this letter, instead of being placed on the hall-table, was laid on the library chimney-piece, and the first intimation Facey had of the coming guest was seeing a man of the Goodheart cut, riding a very superior-looking roan horse up towards the stables. At first Facey thought it was Billy Barker, the brewer ; then, that it was Harry Blanton, the tanner ; next, that it was very like Goodhearted Green.

"And Goodhearted Green it is," said he, running up and seizing him by the hand just as he was preparing to dismount. Then, as Goodheart saw there was unusual surprise, he proceeded to inquire about the letter, when mutual explanations and welcomes followed. Facey was very glad to see Mr. Green, and Mr. Green was very glad to see his good customer, Mr. Romford. Then the two looked at the strawberry roan. He was, indeed, a fine horse, up to any weight : corky and cheerful looking, but with rather a sinister cast of the eye when any one approached him.

"Has but one fault," said Goodheart complacently ;

"has but one fault—kick people over his 'ead as they
mount; but easily hobviated," added he; "easily hobviated—strap up a leg as you mount," producing a strap
from his pocket as he spoke.

"Well, but you can't ride him across country on three
legs," observed Romford.

"True" assented Goodheart. "True; but then it's only
a momentary ebullition of spleen. Soon finds out when
he has got his master on his back, and then a child might
ride him—ride him with a thread."

"Well, we'll try him," said Romford, now calling to
Short, who came rubbing his eyes, still half-stupefied with
his overnight exertions. "Here, take this horse," said
Romford, "and put him into the five-stall stable, and
send some one down to the Hall to say that Mr. Green is
come, and bid them get a bed ready, and some more
sheep chops for dinner."

The strong, persevering man then departed with his
new charge; and Facey, turning to his friend, said, "Now
let you and oi take a turn of the stables."

The two then entered the more genial atmosphere, and
were presently deeply absorbed in the discussion of the
condition and performance of Ben and the Baker, the
peculiarities of Perfection, the deficiencies of Everlasting,
the action of Oliver Twist, and the looks and eccentrici-
ties of the rest of the stud.

Lucy and Betsey were sorry that Mr. Green had not
come in time for the ball, which they felt certain
he would have greatly enjoyed; while Mr. Romford's
anxieties were directed solely to the continuance of the
frost, fearing Goodheart might not get a turn with his
brilliant hounds.

The ladies received Mr. Goodheart very cordially
feeling that he would be useful in warding off any
further attacks about the ball, and as Facey would not
hear of any extra expense being incurred for entertaining
him, they did their best to make a great man of him by
putting him into the best bedroom, one that Lord Lovetin
himself would not have accorded to any one under the
rank of a duke, or a prince of the blood-royal, at least
There, under a magnificent temple-like canopy, nestled the
old horse-dealer, a man more accustomed to the deficiencies
of a garret than the delicacies of a dressing-room.

Still Goodheart was a versatile, agreeable man; and

being only a lowish sort of fellow—the son of a cabman—
of course he had a great knowledge of high life and Court
proceedings, and could tell more of what was passing
at the Palace than any lord in waiting : so, what with
small talk for the ladies, and horsy talk for Facey, they
got on very well together; and Goodheart was found to
be a very agreeable addition to the party.

CHAPTER LVI

THE INFIRMARY BALL

THE Beldon Ball made a profound sensation in
Doubleimupshire. It was talked of far and near.
Those who were there lauded it to the skies; those who
were not, set about contriving how they could establish
an acquaintance with our fair friend, Mrs. Somerville,
so as to get to another if she gave one. There was no
longer any doubt or hesitation in the matter. No more
" Pray, who *is* this Mrs. Somerville ? Do you know
anything about Mrs. Somerville ? Have you called on
Mrs. Somerville ? Are you going to call on Mrs. Somerville ? Do you know if Lady Camilla Snuff has called on
Mrs. Somerville ?" It was all, "Oh dear, do you know
Mrs. Somerville ? I should *so* like to know Mrs. Somerville ? Charles, my dear, I must have the carriage to go
over and call on Mrs. Somerville ! " Then, on the Friday
following, the old "Doubleimupshire Herald," a muddly
county paper that seemed to edit itself, varied its quack-
medicine advertisements with a list of the lady patronesses for the forthcoming Infirmary Ball, in which Mrs.
Somerville's name headed the commoners, coming before
Mrs. Watkins, Mrs. Large, Mrs. Brogdale, and many
others who thought themselves very great ladies indeed.

And this interpolation had been made, notwithstanding the ball had been fixed and the names published
for some weeks before. Then came a letter from the
secretary, requesting to know how many tickets he might
have the honour of sending Mrs. Somerville, which
brought the matter fairly on the *tapis*—that is to say,

under the cognizance of Mr. Romford, whose little pig-eyes had detected the advertisement, though he had not thought proper to mention it. Bold Betsey, as usual, led the charge, taking advantage of a lull that occurred between the consumption of a couple of bottles of Lord Lovetin's best port, and the adoption of gin and pipes by the gentlemen. At first cunning Facey pretended not to hear, being busy with his baccy ; so she addressed herself to our friend the horse-dealer, who commenced business with a cigar.

But Green was not quite happy in good society. He was conscious that he rather knocked his H's about. Indeed he and his friend Billy Slater, the hatter of Bermondsey, had gone to the sign of the Mermaid at Margate only the summer before the period of our story, and Goodheart being spokesman had addressed the land-lord (a cousin of Skittle's), who was smoking a Manilla with ineffable ease at the front door, demanding to know if they "could have a couple of good hairy bedrooms." Whereupon the landlord, taking his cigar from his mouth, replied with a supercilious smile, "Well, I don't know ; I can rub a couple with bear's grease for you, if you like." And it was this not knowing whether to put the H in, or to leave it out, that made Goodheart uncomfortable. He knew that it was either one way or the other, and his anxiety to be right very often made him wrong. He, therefore, did not care to show off at the Infirmary Ball, and the long list of fashionable patronesses had no attractions for him. But the ladies, who saw the advantage, were all for going, and of course could not do without the gentlemen. Oh, what was to stop them from going ? There was no hunting, and it would be some-thing for them to do. The melon frame would hold four, or two inside and two out if the gentlemen objected to the crinolines, and the cost of the conveyance would be all the same for four as for two. Then in answer to Goodheart's objections that he wouldn't know any one, Lucy reminded him she was a lady patroness, and her brother, Mr. Romford, hunting the country. Lastly, Goodheart played his real card, namely, "that they would smoke him and blow him," which would be prejudicial to the Beldon Hall ladies, as well as to himself. This argument rather told. Lucy was on her preferment, and must not do anything to bring her down the ladder of society. The associate of countesses, and viscountesses, and honourables must be discreet. Then Betsey Shannon, whose counterfeit abilities were first-rate, and who knew the advantages of a high-sounding name herself, suggested that Mr. Green might go under an assumed one, or a title if he liked. And this idea being unanimously applauded, things began to get into the grooves that Lucy and Betsey wanted them. Facey thought it would be good fun to humbug the Larkspurites; and they began to consider what they should call Mr. Green—Lord Topboots, Lord Silverpow, Lord Gammon, Lord Horseley, Lord Thorough-pin, Lord Spavin, Lord Stringhalt, Lord Glanders, and a variety of similar names.

"No, no," interposed Betsey, seeing they were making fun of it, "that will not do ; he shall not be a lord at all. That will only set them looking into their Peerage, and pulling him to pieces."

"Let him be a Sir,—Sir Somebody Something; and then if they say 'he's not a Bart.,' you can say, 'no, he's a Knight'; and if they say 'he's not a Knight,' you can say, 'no, but he's just going to be made one,' or put it off in that way." And this idea being applauded too, they began to try on other titles, just as Mrs. Sponge tried on names when she changed hers from Sponge to Somerville. Sir Reginald Rover, Sir Arthur Archduke, Sir Timothy Trotter, Sir Peter——

"No, no," said Betsey, "let's have something that is neither too fine, nor too low—something that will sound so natural as not to create suspicion or inquiry, that will come trippingly off people's tongues."

"Suppose we call him Sir Roger de Coverley," suggested Mrs. Somerville, still thinking of the ball.

"No, that would be too theatrical," said Betsey ; "but we might call him Sir Roger something else—Sir Roger Russell, Sir Roger Brown."

"Sir Roger Ferguson, s'pose," said Facey.

"Very good name," rejoined Betsey, "very good name. Your servant, Sir Roger Ferguson," said she, rising and making Goodheart a low curtsy, just as she curtsied for an encore at Highbury Barn.

And the man of the H's finding there was no haltera-tive, was at length obliged to submit, and ultimately came into the humour also of having a star to decorate his coat on the occasion. This Betsey Shannon undertook to procure from the same quarter as she did the liveries and the uniform for Mr. Proudlock the keeper.

Behold, then, the auspicious evening—a bright starlight night—with her now noble horse-dealer arrayed in a gentlemanly suit of black, relieved by his glittering star and snow-white head. Mr. Romford, on the other hand, was gay and gaudy, scarlet Tick, white vest, with his El Dorado shirt puffing out in front beneath a white tie, altogether a very passable swell, and on very good terms with himself.

The ladies, we need scarcely say, were quite differently dressed to what they were at the Beldon Ball, for who can be expected to appear twice in the same costume— certainly not Mrs. Somerville, or her fair friend Miss Hamilton Howard (*vice* Shannon), who had all the resources of London dressmakers at their command. Nothing to do but send off the order, and have the things down in no time. The coroneted Beldon Hall note-paper was as good as gold in the London market, and Madame Elisa & Co. could never see too much of it. It was always lying about their show-rooms.

Considering that there was so much money in Double-imupshire, so many teapot-handle-makers, so many Ten-and-a-half-per-Centers, it was strange that they should have no better ball-room than what the old town-hall at Butterwick, built on the principle of Goldsmith's

> "Chests contrived a double debt to pay,
> A bed by night, a chest of drawers by day,"

supplied. Nay, indeed, it had harder work than the chest of drawers, for it served as well for a corn and butcher market as a town-hall, while by closing up the interstices between the great stone pillars on which the brick edifice was raised, and opening a temporary stair-case on the left, the lower part of the hall served for a theatre as well. So that, on an occasion like the present, the ball-comers might hear Hamlet junior objurgating his too too solid flesh, or get their toes trod on by the ghost of Hamlet senior stalking off the stage at cock-crow. Nay, indeed, at certain times—for instance, when an army was in motion, the setters-down had to wait for the nick of time before they could effect a passing at all, just as children at the seaside have to wait till the reced-

ing wave gives them a chance of getting after their
outward-bound boats. On this occasion a leathern-lunged
Richard was roaring for his horse just as our Beldon party
entered—"A horse! a horse! my kingdom for a horse!"

"I'll suit you!" exclaimed Goodheart in the same tone,
ignorant of the situation, and forgetful of his greatness.
The side scenes passed, and the sort of scaling-ladder staircase ascending, the adjuncts to the ball-room were little
better than the arrangements down below. There was no
cloak-room for the gentlemen, who had to hang their hats
and wraps up in the passage, while that for the ladies was
of the smallest, most circumscribed order, being, in fact,
the apartment occupied by the market keeper and his wife.

The ball-room, however, was large and lofty, seventy
feet by fifty, open up to the dark oak rafters of the roof.
The walls were decorated with town and country notabili-
ties—some in peers' robes, some in aldermanic honours,
some in plain clothes—all the work of first-rate country
artists, quite ready to set Mr. Ruskin and all the Royal
Academy at defiance.

Of course a great man like our Master was hailed long
before he got into the ball-room, and as Goodheart (now
Sir Roger) and he stood waiting for the ladies—wondering what the deuce they were doing— Facey had an opportunity of introducing the Baronet to some of his acquaintances—Sir Roger Ferguson, Mrs. Telford ; Mr. Bowman,
Sir Roger Ferguson ; Sir Roger Ferguson, Mr. Lightfoot.
But it was when the line of march was formed, and the
gay coloured party appeared improvingly at the doorway,
the decorated Sir Roger bonuing Mrs. Somerville, our red-
coated Romford escorting Miss Shannon, that the fever of
excitement arose.

The opening dance was just over, the couples were
sweeping the floor with their trains, while the *chaperones*
sat by criticising their partners, some feeling satisfied,
others thinking they could have made a better selection.
In a semicircular bay at the high end of the room, wherein they adjusted as well the weights and scales as the
consequence of the county, was an imposing array of
diamonded dowagers, looking terribly severe in their
dignity of state. These were the titled patronesses, whose
magnetic influence attracted sovereigns from the pockets
of parties little accustomed to voluntary contributions.
Even Ten-and-a-half-per-Cent. himself has been drawn.

As the Beldon party entered the room, and gradually approached the crescent of consequence, eyeglasses were raised, and inquiries were—"Who are these?" "Who have we here?" eliciting whispers of—"Oh! this will be Mrs. Somerville." "This will be Mr. Romford's sister." The first questions being quickly followed by—"Who is this with her?" "Who is the man with the star?" A question that was not quite so easily answered.

On, on, our gallant party went, just as Lord Cardigan went against the cannon, only instead of charging right into them, they now wheeled round, our fair friends feeling satisfied that the dowagers could not take any more exception to the backs of their dresses than they could to the fronts. So they sailed slowly down the room again, looking out for admiration as they went.

Before, however, the party had got half-way down the room there was a run upon our fair friends, Ten-and-a-half-per-Cent. claiming Mrs. Somerville, while young Joseph Large and Lovetin Lonnergan hastily disposed of their then partners in order to be first for Miss Howard. Large, however, got the lady, Lovetin not being able to find his partner's *chaperone* so soon as the other, but Miss Howard made it all right by a sweet smile, and saying, "I'll dance next dance with you, Mr. Lonnergan." So Lovetin stood by, admiring her elegant figure and performance, thinking if father *would* but die he would marry her and set her up in Flush House to-morrow. Then came Lovetin's turn — a quadrille — and Miss Howard was equally assiduous with him, for, with a father to die on each side, there really was not any great choice between the two thick-headed suitors. Large then had the pleasure of looking on and seeing that "lout Lovetin" getting all the sweet dimple-making smiles and smirks which, with a certain quantity of eye and tongue work, constitute what ladies call flirtation. Then, as they couldn't both dance with her at once, they began to engage Mrs. Somerville for what Facey called the "bye days," and she adroitly insinuated to each that he was the special favourite, and that Miss Howard did not care a halfpenny for the other. She also intimated Miss Howard would have a large fortune from her grandmother, who was very old and much addicted to drink. Thus quickened, each resolved, if possible, to steal a march upon the other.

Facey and Sir Roger were thus left alone, and Facey renewed his introductions of his friend—Mr. Cracken-thorpe, Sir Roger Ferguson; Sir Roger Ferguson, Mr. Elsome; Mr. Thomas Tongue, Sir Roger Ferguson. And Mr. Tongue, who was a general acquaintanceship man, believed he had had the honour of meeting Sir Roger before at their mutual friend Lord Lumbago's, if he mistook not; a fact that Sir Roger then perfectly re-collected, and was much obliged to his friend, Mr. Tongue, for reminding him. And Sir Roger tendered his hand very cordially in return. Then the two old friends walked about the room, and when people afterwards asked Tongue who that was with the star, he replied, "Oh, that's my old friend, Sir Roger Ferguson; haven't seen him these twenty years, never since we met at our poor friend Lord Lumbago's."

And Sir Roger Ferguson, being now pretty well laid in for acquaintance, told Romford not to mind him any more, but to get himself suited with a nice useful little short-legged woman, and go in for a dance. And the lisper making the grand entry just at the moment, our hero claimed her fair hand at once for a waltz, which he executed so clumsily as to draw forth a mental observation from Sir Roger that Mr. R. must be a better hand at riding than he was at dancing. And the dowagers, having now reconnoitred Sir Roger from afar, and thinking he was a nice wholesome-looking man with his clean linen, snow-white head and roseate hue, began to negotiate for an introduction, and think of admitting of his star into their august circle, for which purpose Lady de Tabby, who was a regular pedigree-monger, instructed Mr. Thomas Tongue to tell his friend that a cousin of Lady Ferguson's would be glad to make his (Sir Roger's) acquaintance. And, though there was no regular Lady Ferguson for Lady de Tabby to claim relationship with, yet he went boldly in for the intro-duction, and was presently seated between Lady de Tabby and the Honourable Mrs. Freezer, to whom he was presently introduced by her ladyship. And Lady de Tabby, not driving the relationship scent beyond the first brush, Sir Roger let it drop also, and was presently engaged in criticising what he called the "field"; this girl's looks, that one's figure and performances. Some he thought clever, but others, he said, wanted condition sadly. Thus Romford gained credit by Goodheart, and Goodheart lost nothing, except, perhaps, a few H's, which the noise of the room concealed as they fell.

Meanwhile the ball proceeded with great vigour; the floor was good, barring certain sockets about the centre of the room, used for setting up the apparatus of conjurers and chairmen of quarter sessions, which those who had hit their toes against once, took care not to come in contact with a second time if they could help it, and though the three-and-fourpenny tea was a poor substitute for Lord Lovetin's Cliquot champagne, so freely dispensed at Beldon Hall, yet it was better than nothing, and served to make a break in the evening's amusements. And in due time Sir Roger Ferguson sailed grandly up the middle of the room with Lady de Tabby on one arm, and the Honourable Mrs. Freezer on the other, looking as consequential as a Lord Mayor in full fig. And Lady Camilla Snuff, who was in pretty much the same line of business as Lady de Tabby, and of course didn't' like her, wondered who the pushing, tuft-hunting woman had got hold of now. Both the ladies in possession thought Sir Roger very agreeable, though he did not reciprocate by singing

"How happy could I be with either," etc.

The fact was, Sir Roger would rather have been in bed.

And Mrs. Somerville played her cards so well between the rival suitors that Lovetin Lonnergan, who was the more ardent and impulsive of the two, screwed up his courage during the dancing of the "Lancers" to sound Betsey Shannon if she would accept him conditionally —that is to say, accept him and keep the thing snug until father would be good enough to die, which he insinuated could not be very long, as he was seventy-six years of age, and getting very shaky on his pins. And Betsey, having the *grande ronde* of the dance to consider the matter in, recollecting that Large had a father too, a tougher-looking one than Lord Lonnergan, and that an offer was an offer—a good thing under any circumstances, she made as pretty a downcast simpering acceptance as she could raise, and at the conclusion of the dance was led, not to the hymeneal altar, but to a smoking hot Gladstone claret cup now placed on the tea-table at the lower end of the room, wherein they pledged each other their troth.

"Mrs. Lovetin Lonnergan, your very good health."

"Mr. Lonnergan, your good health," whispered Betsey, turning her beautiful blue eyes full upon him. So they clenched the bargain.

Then meeting Mrs. Somerville, who was now fanning the flame of young Large's ardour, telling him about the rich grandmamma addicted to drink, Betsey gave her a knowing look which, with a slight sideways jerk of her pretty head at her partner, as good as said, "I've captured this cock."

And the Honourable Lovetin Lonnergan, flushed with success and the influence of the claret cup, looked at his opponent in a triumphant sort of way, as much as to say, "I pity you, old boy!" But Large, nothing daunted by the haughty appearance of the tenant in possession—on the contrary, rather encouraged by the agreeable intelligence just conveyed by Mrs. Somerville —returned his supercilious stare with another, and a tolerably loud exclamation of "What a lout that young Lonnergan is!"

And now Mrs. Somerville, having primed them both, and Sir Roger Ferguson having got rid of his tabbies, Mrs. Somerville and he did the consequential up and down the ball-room together, eliciting bets from the acute and censorious as to how long it would be before she was Lady Ferguson.

"Too old for her by half," said one.

"Ah, but a 'star' will compensate for all that," observed another.

"Fresh old fellow, too," muttered a third.

"What will old Bonus say?" asked a fourth.

"Never marry such an old rat as that," said a fifth.

Then the music sprang up again, and Sir Roger and Mrs. Somerville stood criticising the performers, remarking on this one's head, that one's shoulders, t'other one's feet. People do not work themselves so severely at a pay ball as they do at a gratis one. They seem as if they could get enough for their money, and having had it, go away. Whether it is the absence of the Cliquot, or gooseberry, as the case may be, or that they think it does not look well to stay too late, we know not;

but certain it is, that there is always a great deal of fore-thought and arrangement about getting away.

On this occasion the stately patronesses began to move first; and Sir Roger Ferguson's services were again enlisted in calling up and putting them into their carriages, which he did with the ease and agility of a London linkman. Then all the *chaperones* began looking at their variously going watches, trying amongst them to cast the nativity of the time, followed by rushes at their panting yet avoiding charges, urging them not to engage themselves for any more dances, assuring them, perhaps, that the carriage had been called up a dozen times, or that it was an hour and a-half later than it really was. So at length the effervescence of the evening gradually died out; and, in lieu of sparkling eyes and twirling gauze, hooded nun-like ladies were seen hurrying along the passage, enveloped in the wraps and disguises of the night. Then came the descent of the scaling-ladder, the groping past the wings of the now deserted stage, and the ascent into the great family coach, or the squeeze into the curiously contrived turbot-wells of modern times. Away they drive, amid the varied thoughts and reflections of the hour. Those who have done well hug themselves with the recollection of it; those who have done little make the most of that little, and, casting forward to the future, hope for better luck another time. Foremost in the happy party was our friend Betsey Shannon, who could hardly wait until the melon frame got clear of the jolty cobble-stones of Butterwick ere she announced to her fair companion (Sir Roger and Facey being outside), that she had brought him to book.

"Well, which?" exclaimed Lucy, who had forwarded both their suits so evenly as to be unable to say which was likely to be the winner.

"*Lovetin!*" replied Betsey, with emphasis.

"Bravo, Lovetin!" exclaimed Lucy, clapping her pretty hands. "Bravo, Lovetin!" repeated she. "Ah, now! if father would but die," she added, with a laugh.

"Well, it's not to be till then," rejoined Betsey.

"Ah, but I wouldn't stand that," said Lucy. "Make him marry you now, dear, and keep it snug till father does die, if Lovetin likes. 'Safe bind, safe find,' is a capital maxim."

"Well, but suppose he won't?" said Betsey, who did not like to lose the chance of being Mrs. Lonnergan.

"Then take t'other chap; he's quite as good a catch as Lovetin, only his pa is a little younger; but then, on the other hand, they say Pippin Priory is a much better place than Flush House."

"True," ruminated Betsey, "true;" adding, "either would do very well."

"He's sure to offer," observed Lucy, "sure to offer. I'm only surprised he hasn't done it to-night. I primed him up that you were a member of one of the oldest families in Wales, and had a boskey old grandmother at Leighton-Buzzard, who would leave you a hatful of money."

"Indeed," laughed Betsey joyfully. "Anything better than dancing at Highbury Barn. If Large has the pull in the face way, t'other has it in the figure."

"Oh, all cats are grey in the dark," rejoined Lucy. "You catch one of them, and get a home of your own; for there's nothing so bad as dependence."

"True," assented Miss Shannon.

The two ladies then leant back in the carriage, each following a line of scent of her own; Betsey thinking what a dash she would cut at Flush House (for the Honourable had inducted her into the anticipated carriage splendour), Lucy thinking how to play Large off against Lonnergan, so as to secure one or other for her friend. At length Lucy spoke, breaking in upon an imaginary carriage airing that Betsey was taking with her lovely Lonnergan.

"Oh, I would make him marry you off-hand now," said she, reverting to her former position. "If he won't, Joe Large will. Indeed, as I said before, I only wonder he didn't offer to-night."

"Well, I think he will," replied Betsey; "only, as he seemed to be leading up to the point, that stupid matter-of-fact hatter came up, and would have me to dance with him, and stuck to us till I did."

"Stupid marplot!" muttered Lucy; "these sort of boobies think that people come to balls to do nothing but dance; whereas every one knows that the real business of a ball is either to look out for a wife, to look after a wife, or to·look after somebody else's wife. However, never mind," continued she, drawing the buffalo skin coverlid up to her chin, "never mind. Large will come to call before long, and then we will see what we can do, for 'sharp' must be the word—first come first served, the rule. Such chances as these don't occur every day ; and though people are good enough to take us at our own price at present, yet there is no saying how soon a change may come, and then they would be equally furious the other way ; so we must just strike while the iron's hot, and capture one or other of the idiots."

So saying, she gradually sunk off in a doze, and the next thing that occurred was the tapping of Independent Jimmy's great knuckles at the melon-frame window, announcing that they were back at Beldon Hall.

"Noo, then, get oot !" said he, clattering down the harsh iron steps, and leaving them to effect the descent as they could.

The ladies and gentlemen hurried into the house, and discarding their wraps, they awoke Dirtiest of the Dirty, who was dosing over the breakfast-room fire, dreaming of Percival Pattycake. They discussed the events of the evening over some of Lord Lovetin's best Cognac brandy ; and at twenty minutes to four, Mr. Romford moved the adjournment of the debate.

CHAPTER LVII

THE COUNTESS OF CAPERINGTON

MRS. SOMERVILLE was right in the advice she gave Miss Shannon, when coming home from the Infirmary Ball, to get married as quick as she could, for things at Beldon Hall had gone so extremely well that Lucy feared a reverse.

She thought it was too good to last. We often see things in this world go so smoothly at first that there seems no chance of a failure, when all of a sudden they take a turn, and down they come with a run. Certainly, amongst them our friends at Beldon Hall combined as much duplicity as could well be contained in a party of four. First there was Mr. Romford, acting the turbot-on-its-tail, deceiving poor Lord Lovetin, Lord Lonnergan, and all ; then there was Mrs. Sponge, calling herself Mrs. Somerville ; and Betsey Shannon, arrogating the distinguished name of Hamilton Howard ; and now the old Clerkenwell "'oss dealer," Mr. Goodhearted Green, passing himself off for a baronet.

All or any were liable to be detected at any moment—Mr. Romford by Lord Lovetin's making his long-meditated journey to England, Mrs. Somerville by the frequenters of theatres and cigar shops, Miss Shannon by half the counter-skippers in London, and Sir Roger Ferguson by any stray tourist or stableman with whom he had ever done business.

The only way our friends bore up against the accumulation of deceit was, by never thinking of the consequences. Enough for the day was the evil thereof, they all felt. There was no disputing one thing, namely, that they had been most wonderfully favoured, and that people seemed quite as much inclined to deceive themselves as they were to deceive them. But a day of reckoning always comes at last, though in this case neither man nor woman was the immediate cause of its advent.

Leotard, the wondrous Leotard, the cream-coloured lady's horse, who has already played such a conspicuous part in our story, was now destined to fulfil still greater achievements. The last we heard of him was, when the boy Bill satisfied himself of his paces by private trial at Tarring Neville, while Mr. Romford and Mrs. Somerville were regaling after the hunt with the considerate Mrs. Watkins's bag fox. Since then Mrs. Somerville had ridden Leotard with varying success and satisfaction, the horse sometimes going remarkably well, sometimes only middling — oftener, perhaps, middling than well—at other times ill, or rather not at all. Lucy, however, never risked an open rupture with him. If she found he was going to be queer, she went home with him, pretending that his way was hers also. So the horse maintained his reputation for beauty and docility. Mrs. Somerville and her horse were always greatly admired : people were proud to open the gates for her.

Foremost among the horse's admirers was Independent Jimmy's friend, Mr. Hazey, or Second-hand Harry, as he was commonly called. Hazey was always on the look out for horses, not so much to supply his own wants as to know where to lay hands on them, in case he could place them to advantage,—that is to say, get a little more for them than he gave. He was always touting, and sneaking, and "do-you-know-anything-to-suit-me-ing?" every man he met. Cheating in horses has become quite a science. Formerly the dealers had the monopoly, but what they now facetiously call the "gentlemen" have trod heavily on their heels of late. They are more skilful, more unscrupulous, and, we really think, lie better. The fact is, the real professionals haven't time to concoct the ingenious and elaborate schemes now hit off by the disengaged idler. Moreover, the amateurs have access to society that the dealers have not; know the haunts and habits of victims better, and how to cajole them.

What is the waste of a week to a man who has nothing whatever to do but sit in the Park and pick his teeth with a quill? But time is money with a horse-dealer. He may have to be in Edinburgh, or Exeter, or Horncastle, while the other gentleman is arranging his plant.

Hazey had a great connection in what Mr. Thackeray would have called the "Roundabout" line—many touts, many spies, many stable sneaks, many idle gentlemen, looking out for him. He knew how to keep the lower order of veterinary surgeons in good humour, so as to get them to pass almost anything. One of his cardinal rules was, never to tell where a horse came from. If he bought him in Cheshire, he would declare he came from Shropshire; if he came from the east, he would say he came from the west. In this there was good policy, for there is nothing so easy as to find out all about a horse, provided you can but find out where he comes from. Every ostler and helper can tell you something, and they generally speak truly, too. Tommy will "mind" his being foaled; Jacky will remember his being backed; Tomkins can tell when he was shod; and plenty will remember when he first came out with the hounds, with Willy Winship on his back, who, of course, showed them all the way.

Now, as ill-luck would have it, among Mr. Hazey's many miscellaneous friends was the well-known Captain Coper, late of that distinguished corps, the Horse Marines, who, at this juncture, knew a man who knew a "female woman" who knew a gentleman who knew the Right Honourable the Countess of Caperington, and her ladyship wanted a horse—a perfect lady's horse— for which her noble husband would give any reasonable price. And a lady in that position not being likely to remain long unsuited—at all events, unsolicited—she was presently besieged with horses of all sorts and sizes ; bay horses, brown horses, black horses, a great variety of horses ; but unless a party is properly introduced, that is to say, has made a satisfactory arrangement with the middle-man, he has very little chance of effecting a deal, and the Countess had rejected horse after horse that might have suited her uncommonly well if they had not been crabbed by the go-between, who, of course, had not been properly propitiated.

At length Captain Coper (who had then lately been rusticating "over the water") heard of her Ladyship's want, and bestirred himself to supply it. Resolving in his capacious mind the various parties he had done business with, he came to the conclusion that Mr. Hazey, being a master of hounds, would be the most likely (supposing they could agree upon terms) to supply the deficiency and obtain a long price. So he wrote "Dear Hazey" a letter, asking what he had in the lady's horse line, and the percentage he would stand for an introduction to a real live Countess in want of a perfect picture of a horse. And Hazey, albeit he had a horse or two that had something in the habit line, to wit, Bill's gallant grey, and a bay that dug its toes into the ground at each tenth step, and shied at everything it met on the road, yet he still thought they were hardly up to the exalted honour of carrying a countess—no doubt a pretty one, as countesses always are. If she had been a commoner, he would have tried it on with these, declaring there were not two such paragons in the world, and were both so good that he didn't care which he sold.

But a countess might be made available in a variety of ways : she might call on Mr. Hazey in London—she might present Anna Maria at Court, perhaps, which would be extremely agreeable. And the thought of Anna Maria presently brought Mr. Romford to his recollection, and in due course came Mrs. Somerville and her beautiful cream-coloured horse. "Ah, there now !—there was an animal !" mused Hazey, with a chuck of his chin ; " the very thing, if Mrs. Somerville would but sell him. And there was no saying but she might sell him—didn't see why she shouldn't sell him. He was sure he would sell him if he had him, and could get a good price." Then the recollection of Facey and the hospital for decayed sportsmen rather checked him. They might be extra-independent, to be sure, but still he didn't see why he mightn't sound them; so be set Bill to set Silkey, to set Storey the horse-breaker, to set big Rumbold the veterinary surgeon of Burchester, to ferret out what chance there was of Mrs. Somerville selling Leotard.

And now, whilst they are busy prosecuting their inquiries, we will say a few words respecting the Countess of Caperington herself.

The Right Honourable the Countess of Caperington, we need scarcely say, was not always the Countess of Caperington : no, nor anything approaching one. In fact, she began life as an actress, as Miss Spangles of the Theatre Royal, Bungington. Here her beauty and ardent coquetry captivated a fast young baronet, the late Sir Harry Scattercash, of Nonsuch House in G —— shire. Miss Spangles became Lady Scattercash, and did the honours of the house with great liberality so long as there was any house to do the honours in. All the sock-and-buskin tribe had a hearty welcome at Nonsuch House, and long and serious were the symposia that ensued. Mrs. Somerville, then Lucy Glitters, had the run of the house, and it is not unlikely that what she there saw taught her how to manage matters at Beldon Hall. And of all the sock-and-buskin tribe none was more truly welcome than that celebrated actor Mr. Orlando Bugles, late of the Surrey Theatre. Bugles had a bed whenever he liked to run down : nor was he shy in availing himself of his privilege.

Drinking, however, is only a question of time, and sooner or later has always the same ending. Worn out with debauchery and premature decay, Sir Harry Scattercash presently departed this life at the early age of thirty-two, and where could the lovely widow seek for solace than on the manly bosom of Mr. Bugles. Lady Scattercash married him. But beloved Orlando, we are sorry to say, took to evil ways also—brandy-and-water was his bane too; and twice in three years Lady Scattercash found herself a widow. Having seen Bugles buried, "b-e-a-u-tifully put away," as she described it, she again came to town, and presently terminated an engagement at the Lord Lowther music saloon by running away. The next thing heard of her was, that she had become the Countess of Caperington ! How this came about nobody knows but the Earl and Countess themselves, and being a lady before the marriage, this match excited far less attention than it would have done had it been contracted with Miss Spangles. Sir Charles Bridoon, the next taker of the title, or the Ladies Caresson, the Earl's sisters, might complain and say, "Who *is* this Lady Scattercash ?" but the world at large were content to take her Ladyship as a true and correct countess. And, indeed, so far as looks were concerned, she was an ornament to the Peerage, for she was just in the full development of womanly beauty —fat, fair, and thirty, with as much ease and vivacity as Betsey Shannon herself. The Earl was as proud of her as if he had married her first-hand, and was never tired of contemplating her beautiful face under a variety of bonnets. Not only bonnets, but hats, caps, hoops, everything that appeared in the chronicles of fashion. When her Ladyship's carriage drew up with a dash at Mrs. Slyboots' the milliner's, in the commercial town of Worryworth, there used to be such a commotion raised in the shop, to the neglect of all the rest of the customers, Mrs. Boots breaking off in her recommendation of thirteen-and-ninepenny bonnets for two guineas, with "Mary !" "Jane !" "Susan !" to her elegant young people who were serving, "look out !— look out ! Here's the Countess of Caperington coming !—here's the Countess of Caperington coming !" as if all people's wants were to succumb to those of her Ladyship. Then there was such curtseying, "your Ladyshipping," and worshipping, as if nobody's custom was worth anything compared to her Ladyship's.

Our business at present, however, is to get the Countess a horse ; so, leaving her to turn over the contents of Mrs. Slyboots' shop at her leisure, we will proceed to inquire after Mr. Hazey's success in the equestrian line.

CHAPTER LVIII

THE DEAL

MR. RUMBOLD, the veterinary surgeon, did not take
much by his journey to Beldon Hall. The fact
was, Mr. Facey had his servants better drilled than to
give information to people merely because they wanted to
have it; and our friend being a bit of a vet himself,
Rumbold was just about the last man he wanted to see
hanging about his stables. Nor was Hazey more successful with either Jowers the blacksmith, or Mr. Golightly
the exciseman: for Chowey spun one of them out of his
stable, and Swig the other. And Captain Coper being
exigeant,—having, as he wrote, many applications from
other parties anxious to suit the fair Countess with a
horse, Hazey was obliged to "Dear Romford" our hero,
and to have recourse to the lie applicable to the occasion.
Thus he wrote :—

"TARRING NEVILLE.
"*Thursday Night.*

"DEAR ROMFORD,—I chanced to hear out hunting to-
day that Mrs. Somerville has some thought of parting
with her cream-coloured horse (Blondin, I think she
calls him); and I write to say that if it should happen
to be the case, I think I know of a lady who would be
likely to be a purchaser. Of course, at this time of year,
ladies' horses are not in great demand; but I think, with
a little management, we might get what is fair and right,
which I am sure is all that either of us would think of
requiring. I hope this sale, if true, is not a sign of Mrs.
Somerville's departure, for we can ill afford to lose so
ornamental an appendage to our hunting-fields and to
society in general. Mrs. Hazey and my daughter beg
their kind regards to her and Miss Howard, with, my dear
Romford,—Yours very truly,   H. HAZEY.
"FRANCIS ROMFORD, Esq.,
    "BELDON HALL, DOUBLEIMUPSHIRE."

The letter came very opportunely, for Sir Roger
Ferguson was still at Beldon Hall, which enabled our
master to arrange with him the price of the horse, as well
as to use Sir Roger as an incentive to the intending
purchaser. There is generally a fat goose in every hunt,
who is the reputed purchaser of all the horses that other
people want to sell, and your regular "sticker" for price
can never give a direct answer, without first indulging in
a great, long exordium as to what said goose will give.
So Sir Roger was now selected to fill the honourable post
of puffer to Leotard. Lucy therefore wrote, on her own
account, to say that her horse was for sale, and, by a
single coincidence, their friend, Sir Roger Ferguson, was
anxious to purchase him for a Park hack for himself;
but, hearing that a lady wanted him, with his usual
gallantry, the worthy Baronet consented to waive his
preference, and let Mr. Hazey's friend have the refusal of
him. Then, without saying anything about the horse's
merits, defects, or peculiarities, she branched off upon the
weather, hoping the frost would soon give, and enable the
poor pent-up foxhunter to take the field! and reciprocated
Miss Hamilton Howard's and her own good wishes to
Mrs. Hazey and family, and volunteered to send Mr.
Romford's and Sir Roger's also.

Then, in a postscript, she adroitly added, that Sir
Roger had offered £150 for Leotard, at which price Mr.
Hazey could have him.

The answer rather staggered friend Hazey, for £150 was
a London price—quite an immense one in the country,
where they expect to get two or three horses for that
money; added to which, Hazey's own profit and Captain
Coper's regulars would bring the price up to a couple of
hundred. Then, on the other hand, there was a Countess
and a Baronet to operate upon; and, all things considered,
Hazey thought he should not be doing himself injustice
if he wrote Coper word he had a perfect animal at
command for £175; adding, that the Countess must be
quick in her decision, for there was a Baronet after the
horse, who didn't stick at price. Hazey then gave a very
minute description of Leotard, so glowing and flattering
that few could resist him.

Coper was a dashing dealer, always rounding his figures
and going for guineas, and immediately made Hazey's
£175 into two hundred guineas, at which price he wrote

the man who knew the "female woman" who knew the
gentleman who was acquainted with the Countess of
Caperington, that a perfect lady's horse could be had.
He also copied the descriptive part of Mr. Hazey's letter,
and dwelt on the fact of the Baronet's competition. And
the offer, in due course, came to the Countess. Now, two
hundred guineas is a longish price for a hack; but then it
is a price that carries such respectability with it as almost
to supersede the necessity of circumspection. Who would
think of asking two hundred guineas for a horse that was
not something out of the common way? A twenty-pounder
is always a suspicious animal; but three-figure horses sell
themselves. Moreover, the Countess fancied the cream-
colour; thought she would look well upon it, with its
flowing mane and tail; and so there was nothing for it
but to have it. A cheque was therefore transmitted by
the circuitous route that the message had come. Coper
then docked off his "regulars"; Hazey took his; and,
finally, Mrs. Somerville received a hundred and fifty
pounds for a horse that Goodhearted Green had bought
for the various sums of thirteen pounds, twelve, and
eleven.

Not that Lucy got the money; but Mr. Hazey's cheque
was drawn in her favour; and she had to endorse it ere
Mr. Romford and Goodheart could manipulate the money,
according to the peculiar arrangement that existed
between them.

CHAPTER LIX

THE DISASTER—THE LORD HILL HOTEL AND
POSTING-HOUSE

THE Earl and Countess of Caperington were staying at
their seat, Caperington Castle, enjoying the old-
womanly sport of battuing, when the wondrous Leotard
arrived. Here they were, entertaining a semi-dis-
tinguished party—not quite good enough to advertise,
perhaps, but still very sounding in titles. Two or three
dowagers, who lived half the year at their own expense

and half at other people's; some distinguished foreigners, some equally distinguished Englishmen. The guests being chiefly of the adhesive order were about tired of each other; consequently anything that created conversation was extremely acceptable. Leotard now furnished some.

He was greatly praised and admired by all — all excepting Mr. Bustler, who called himself his Lordship's stud-groom, though the stud only consisted of a few ponies. Bustler had not been properly propitiated in the £-s.-d. transaction, and thought Leotard had been punctured for a spavin, though nothing of the sort had ever been done. Indeed, if Leotard's mental qualifications had been as good as his bodily ones, he would have been a very nice horse, and well worth a hundred pounds. But, like many bipeds, he could better bear adversity than prosperity, and as soon as ever he got his condition up a little, back came all his bad qualities. He then would not do anything he didn't like, and if coerced, resented it. He then either kicked the party over his head, or, in the language of the low dealer, "saluted the general"—that is to say, reared up on end.

Now Leotard, with a perversity that had always distinguished him, went perfectly well on the first days of trial; the Countess's way being apparently his, and the Countess's pace also. When, however, he became better acquainted with the roads and the country, he began to exercise a judgment of his own; and one day, when the Countess wanted to canter across the grass sidings of the Rosendale road, to meet the overladen market coaches, Leotard insisted upon taking her to Tewkesbury. Not that he had any acquaintance at Tewkesbury—indeed, we dare say if she had pulled him up for Tooksbury, as she called it, he would have insisted upon going to Rosendale. It was just a spirit of contradiction—a sort of equine awkwardness that nobody could account for. The Countess, however, had a spirit too; and, moreover, had no idea of a horse, for which her noble husband had given such a liberal price, presuming to exercise a will of his own. So she just administered the whip—one, two, three; but before she got four the horse was up straight on end, and the Countess was down over his tail. It was just Mrs. Rowley Rounding over again. Then off went the horse, full tilt at first, but not finding himself pursued, he relaxed into a snorting, tail-distended, head-diverging trot, as though he were surveying the landscape —much after the manner of the Benicia Boy. General chasers made a "click" at him, as they called it; but Leotard evaded them all, and entered Caperington Park just as the noble Earl and his party opened fire on the rabbits on Fourburrow Hill. Then there was such a commotion, and sending off, and running heel, to track the offender back to the site of the dissolution of partnership. The Countess, however, had tucked up her habit, and one of the before-mentioned overladen market coaches coming up, she hailed it, and made three on the box, sitting between the coachman and a puffy butcher from Bassetlaw. Thus she met the affrighted party, easing their minds but not her own, for she was very angry with the horse, and wanted to give him a good whipping. When, however, she saw him stand and deliver Mr. Bustler like a shot, she thought she had better do it by deputy; still more so when she saw a helper share her own fate. The horse was then unanimously pronounced to be vicious.

At this juncture there appeared upon the scene our rosy-gilled, silvery-haired friend, now no longer Sir Roger Ferguson, but the old original Goodhearted Green, of Brown Street, Bagnigge Wells Road. Goodheart was so overcome with grief at the Countess's misfortunes, that he could scarcely find utterance for his sorrow. "Oh dear, he was distressed! he was 'urt! he didn't know the time when he had been so put about! Hadn't slept a wink for two nights for thinkin' on't. The Countess ought never to get on to such a quadruped again. He knew the 'oss— wicked, mistetched animal, that had been turned out of half the stables in London. People that sold such 'osses ought to be indicted for conspiracies." And after a good deal of similar palaverment, he concluded by saying he thought he knew a man who would give fourteen or fifteen pounds for him; which Goodheart affirmed was more than he was worth. And though it certainly was a miserably dejected figure to take for a two-hundred-guinea horse, yet, when he won't do anything for his keep, what is the use of him? So they just let him go, hoping to get something back from Coper and Hazey. Coper, of course, could not be found; and though Hazey liked countesses, he loved money more, and could not bear to part with his beloved gains. It was hard to lose the profit of his labour, especially when he believed the objection to the horse was founded partly on caprice, and partly on incompetence. The boy Bill assured him that nothing could go better than the horse did the morning he tried him at Tarring Neville; and certainly Mrs. Somerville rode him with the greatest ease and composure. If the Countess had given more for him than she liked, that was no reason for dissolving the bargain. Many people expected more than they got, and those who knew the least about horses always expected the most. Hazey had had many such, but none of them had ever got a halfpenny out of him. He didn't sell hands, only horses.

The horse, we need scarcely say, was soon back into Beldon Hall, undergoing the treatment and discipline necessary for keeping him in something like subjection; and when Mr. Hazey heard that Mrs. Somerville was riding him as usual, he gained confidence in his cause, and asserted boldly that the horse was as quiet as a lamb, and had doubtless been ridden injudiciously, or spoiled by mismanagement.

The Countess felt piqued at this announcement, conceiving that it conveyed an imputation on her horsemanship; for though she was not in reality a good rider, yet she thought she was, and perhaps was more sensitive on the point than if she had really been one. The Earl, too, backed her opinion, seeing that she sat well on her horse and looked the equestrian; and the party generally favoured the view that the horse was vicious. Hazey, however, held out the other way; and for once believing his own story, stated that the fact was capable of proof, for the horse might be seen with the Larkspur Hounds almost every day in the week; Mr. Hazey, perhaps, not thinking that any one would be at the trouble of making the long journey for the purpose of seeing. Here, however, he was mistaken, for railways have annihilated distance; and having got a locality to work upon, the Countess talked and fretted, and fretted and talked, till she worked herself up into a resolution to go and see. If anybody would go with her, she would really go and see. She would like uncommonly to go and see. She thought it would be very good fun to go and see. And a lady in that mood not being likely to remain unescorted, especially when she paid the expenses first, Major Elite, and then Mrs. Mountravers—both staying guests—volunteered their

services to accompany her into Doubleimupshire. And as
none of them had ever been there before, or had the
slightest idea how to get to it, the expedition furnished
abundant food for conversation; first to find out what
part of Doubleimupshire Mr. Romford hunted; secondly,
how it was to be got at; and, thirdly, where the meets of
the hounds were.

To this end maps, and books, and "Bell's Lifes," and
"Bradshaws" were consulted, and calculations made for
train meeting, and crossing, and catching. Then came
the sorting and packing and arranging for the journey,
the Countess taking as much luggage as in former times
would have served a traveller to India, all, of course,
directed—so that they who run might read—"To the
Right Honourable the Countess of Caperington." Then
there was such a to-do about her Ladyship's man, and her
Ladyship's maid, and her Ladyship's this, and her Ladyship's that.

At length they got started as well from the castle as
from the neighbouring station of Lilleyfield, and, after
numerous halts, and stops, and changes, with the usual
variations of speed peculiar to different trains and systems
of railway, they found themselves, towards sunset, contemplating the tall spire of Dirlingford Church from a
dumpy little station about a mile from the town. Railways which make some places ruin others, and Dirlingford
had suffered the latter fate. The railway seemed to have
sucked all the life out of it—taken it all up to Pickering
Nook. So few passengers stopped there that the solitary
omnibus did not meet every train, and now that the
driver had got a haul in the graceful person of the Countess
and her attendants, he seemed appalled at the quantity of
luggage. Didn't know how he should ever get it up.
Independent Jimmy would have had it on during the
time this one was looking at it. At last, with the aid of
the porter, he got it accomplished, and the party being
now seated—"Where to?" was the question. "Head
inn!" was the answer.

"That'll be the Lord 'ill, then," said he, and, hurrying
round to his horses, he mounted his box and drove down
to the town.

The Lord Hill Hotel and posting-house, at Dirlingford, was a good sample of the old-fashioned wayside inn,
now fast disappearing before the march of modern civilisa-

tion. It was a great gaunt four-storeyed, small-windowed, red-brick house, standing right in the middle of the High Street, its front door reached by an iron-railed flight of steep stone steps. On the right of the door was a caged bell that had announced the coming of many a carriage ; on the left the name of the landlord, John Scorer, with the words "neat wines, neat post-chaises" below. Above the door was the sign of the house, the "Lord Hill," a faded warrior in full uniform, powdered and pig-tailed according to the prevailing fashion of the day.

At one time it kept twelve pair of post-horses, besides a few that worked on the farm, and seven long coaches changed horses at it twice a day. Great were the gains from the unfortunate victims whom necessity compelled to take the road in those days. They were treated much like cattle at a market, pushed and squeezed and fed any-how. It was for the great magnates of the road that the landlord's attention and civility were reserved. Then, when the bow-legged "next boy out" descried the coming carriage, he gave the caged door-bell such a ringing as caused a similar commotion in the house to that which attended the coming of the Countess of Caperington to Mrs. Slyboots' the milliner's, at Worryworth. The Lord Hill was convulsed.

And the mention of her Ladyship reminds us that we have got her and her party in the Dirlingford omnibus, from which we had better extract them as soon as we can. One disadvantage of the now universal use of public con-veyances undoubtedly is, that consequence does not get properly attended to. When that the maid dresses so much finer than the mistress, it is difficult at first sight to distinguish between them—to say which is which. The Countess, however, was not one of that sort, and always dressed as became her exalted station, and the bus had scarcely stopped at the Lord Hill Hotel and posting-house door ere it was bruited throughout that a great lady had come. Then down went Scorer's pipe on the inner bar table. Mrs. Scorer adjusted her antiquated frilled cap in the looking-glass, the old bed-gowned chambermaid, Rebecca, slid downstairs, holding on by the banisters, and Timothy, the bald-headed, short-breeched antediluvian waiter, with something between a napkin and a duster in his hand, waddled out of the commercial room to join the commotion in the passage. Great was the bobbing and bowing and curtseying and your Ladyshipping, great the gesticulation to induce them to get forward out of the way of the now coming boxes, and ascend the narrow staircase to the gloomy regions above. Of course there wasn't a fire in any of the rooms, "but they would light one directly," Scorer said. And to this end Rebecca began to strike a light with a flint and steel in the "Trafalgar," declaring she could get one sooner that way than with a lucifer-match.

The Lord Hill·was a close, frowzy old house, from which every breath of air seemed to be excluded by heavily dressed curtains before the never-opened windows. The sitting-rooms were large and low, their lowness being further aggravated by most oppressively heavy mouldings on the ceilings. It was enough to give one the nightmare to think of such ceilings. As to those grand old temples of suffocation, the large four-post beds in the small rooms, the large boot-jack, the diminutive towel, and insoluble soap, they are yet to be found in most countries, and need not be described. We also pass by as well the order for, as the incidents of, the mutton-chop dinner—the offer of everything, with the reduction to nothing; the battered copper-betraying side-dishes, the green hock, and dull needle-case-shaped champagne-glasses, with the strong, loathsome cheese that followed the dry, unpalatable tart. Let us suppose the evening spent; the long wax-lights replaced by short ones, and our tired travellers off to bed, to sleep, to dream, or perchance be bit by bugs.

Those who have watched the progress of public convey-ances, seen how the fastidiousness of former times has gradually disappeared before the lights of common-sense and utility, can have little doubt that another great change is coming over the nation in the matter of domestic economy. The universality of travel; the extreme diffi-culty of getting servants at home—the hopelessness of managing them when got; all tend to show that clubs, which answered so well for gentlemen, are about to be extended to families, in the shape of the magnificent hotels now rising up all around, where, if people do pay for accommodation, they at all events get an equivalent for their money.

CHAPTER LX

SPITE OF ALL AND STAND AGAINST ALL

MR. FACEY ROMFORD, like most good sportsmen, eschewed show meets: he also avoided making them at inns or public-houses. He had no fancy for being waylaid by skirmishers on the look out in the highways and byways, to bring in all they could catch to be stuffed with a second breakfast before he had half digested the first. Still less to have his hounds pressed upon or ridden over by pot-valiant horsemen fresh from the joys of the tap or the table. Hence some of his meets were rather ambiguous, especially to strangers, of which, however, there were few came into the country. A bridge, a milestone, or guide-post were all favourite places of his; but among the anonymous ones was a place called Spite of All, whose locality was difficult to fix. The name was not very promising, suggestive more of the tenacity of the squatter than the politeness of the country. And Spite of All was one of those troublesome encroachments against which the Lord Lonnergans of former times used to be content to issue their edicts without seeing them enforced. Spite of All had therefore become a freehold, and had to be respected, notwithstanding it stood on the domains of a duke. But it so happened that Spite of All was not the only place of this description in Doublcimupshire. On the north-east side was its duplicate, called Stand against All, and people in the hurry of the moment were very apt to mistake one for the other. There was an obstinate resistance recorded against each, with a triumphal reten-tion by both the parties in possession.

Well, the meets of Mr. Romford's hounds for the week were: Monday, Raw Marsh; Wednesday, Thorncross Hill; Friday, Spite of All; Saturday, the tenth milestone on the Larkspur Road. Friday is generally considered an unlucky day; at all events a day that people do not generally choose for their pleasure expeditions; and it was unlucky on this occasion; for if the meet had been transposed, Friday the tenth milestone, and Saturday Spite of All, Mrs. Somerville would have been at Spite of All, and not at the road meet, while, in consequence of the confusion of manner and ideas, the Countess would have been at the road meet, and not at Spite of All, so they would never have met, for Mr. Hazey picked up another customer for the Leotard horse before the Monday.

But we anticipate.

One might as well ask a hairdresser or a haberdasher about the meets of the hounds as the waiter at an inn, but attached to the Lord Hill Hotel was an antediluvian postboy—one Benjamin Bucktrout, the last of the twelve who had driven from that door—whose geographical knowledge was said to be great. Bucktrout was an illustration of the truth of the old saying, that nobody ever saw a dead postboy, for if he had been anything else he would have been dead long since. As it was, there was little left of him but his chin and his hands, save what people might conjecture was in his jacket and boots. And the Countess of Caperington, who was accustomed to have everything arranged for her, told her maid Priscilla, when she herself retired to her great tabernacle of a bed, to find out how long it would take to go to Spite of All, and to call her accordingly. Then Bucktrout being appealed to, declared he knew the place quite well, and that it would take him an hour and twenty minutes to go there, part of the road being, he said, in a very indictable state of repair. And so he was ordered to time himself to be there at 10.30 to a minute, the Countess never allowing any one to be unpunctual but herself.

Accordingly next morning, Bucktrout, having made himself as great a swell as he could,—scrumpy red jacket, with blue glass buttons and tarnished silver lace at the black cotton-velvet collar and cuffs; questionable breeches, with seedy boots, turned round a very passable queen's-coloured barouche with a gorgeous crown on the panel, drawn by a pair of high-boned, hard-featured white horses, the usual accompaniments of wedding festivities. Then the footman and Priscilla the maid, and the landlord and the landlady, having made as much fuss and preparation as they could, what with cloaks and cushions and furs and foot-warmers, stood waiting the descent with a graduated sliding scale of spectators tapering away from the doorsteps down to the kennel. And, after a sufficient pause old Timothy announced that the " Countess was coming ! " the " Countess was coming ! " Then all was eyes right and attention : Bucktrout, subsiding in his saddle, contemplated his horses' ears, while John Thomas stood bolt upright, holding the carriage door in his right hand. Priscilla occupied the other side of `the steps to assist the crinolines in their ascent into the carriage, while the rest of the party ranged themselves in a semicircular *tableau*, after the manner of actors when the curtain is going to fall. The great people get in, the voluminous clothes are arranged, and the door closed quickly to prevent an egression.

" Right ! " cries the gold-lace-hatted footman, as he jumps into the rumble, and away they bowled up the grass-grown High Street of Dirlingford, drawing many fair faces to the windows, and eliciting many ejaculations of " Who can those be ? " " Who can those be ? " " Bless us, what swells ! "

Bucktrout did his best to keep the old nags up to their collars as they pottered over the uneven cobble-stones of the street, not knowing how a judicious display might tend to take the wind out of the sails of the opposition spicey greys at the Golden Fleece inn ; but as they got upon the level surface of the Silverdale Road, the old gentleman gradually relaxed in his exertions, until a very gentle rise in his saddle alone denoted that the horses were not walking—indeed, at one time, they looked as if they were all going to sleep together.

Bucktrout was a ruminating old boy, and between cogitations as to whether he should drag down High Higson Hill, or risk it, where he was likely to get his dinner, and what the Countess would be likely to give him over his mileage for driving, he directed his attention to the question of getting to his destination. "Stand agin All," muttered he—"Stand agin All ; that'll be by Fitzwarren, and round the old tower to Happyfield Green and Ringland."

"Stand agin All—Stand agin All. Sure it was Stand agin All that they said," continued he, rubbing his nose on the back of his old parchment-like glove as a sudden thought came across his mind, whether it was Stand agin All, or Spite of All that they said. "Sure it was

Stand agin All, they said," repeated he, giving the led horse a refresher with his knotty whip, as if to get him to coincide in that view. Still Buckey had his doubts about it, and as he jipped and jogged he began, like a prudent general, to think how he should manage matters in case he was wrong. "Spite of All and Stand agin All were very much alike," he said; "one as bad as the other a'most; couldn't make much difference which they went to. Most likely it was one of those things they call picnics, where folks make themselves as uncomfortable as they can, and call it pleasure. Sure, for his part, he would like to sit at a table with a clean cloth before him, and a knife and fork to eat with, instead of his fingers." Then he gave his own horse a dig with his spur, by way of preserving the balance of pace.

Meanwhile the Countess and party, having timed themselves as well as they could by their watches, began looking about for the usual indications of the chase—foot-people in a hurry, grooms with their masters' horses, sedate gentlemen jogging on with their own. The Countess expected to see the naughty Leotard pop up at every point. But no; neither pedestrian, nor equestrian, not even the man with the colt in the breaking-reins appears. Major Elite suggested that perhaps Mr. Romford's half-past ten meant eleven. Many masters of hounds, he said, were very unpunctual.

The road, which for some time had been twisty and turny, to say nothing of what the Countess called "cogglecy" presently became worse, being formed of nothing but soft field stones ground down to excellent housemaid's sand, and after a slow tug through its laborious depths, the old screws came to a standstill just opposite where another road branched off at right angles, and the veteran Bucktrout, turning half round in his saddle and pointing to a wretched mud cottage with a thatched roof built into a bank, announced with a grin and a touch of his greasy old hat, "Please 'um, this be Stand agin All."

"Stand against All !" exclaimed the Countess. "That's not the name of the place we want to be at ! *Spite* of All, not Stand against All !"

"Well, mum, it's all the same, mum," replied Bucktrout, now satisfied of his error, but determined to brazen it out. "Some folks call it Spite of All, you see, my leddy, and others call it Stand agin All, you see, my leddy. It's the place you mean, the place they had the great 'size trial on aboot, before Lord Chief-Justice Best and a special jury, which doubtless you've heard tell on." Bucktrout thinking it immaterial whether the Countess saw the cause of one assize trial or another. Both places had been in Court.

But here we may observe that Spite of All would have felt rather humiliated by the comparison, for while Stand against All let its smoke out of the four-square-paned window or the rickety door, Spite of All had a fine fire-brick chimney rising boldly out of a substantial grey roof; two fairish windows, and a door that a moderate-sized man could get under without stooping. Moreover, Spite of All was in a good country with fine wild foxes, and Facey Romford knew where to find them.

Be that as it may, however, here were our friends at Stand against All, and though Bucktrout's assertion had an air of plausibility about it, yet there were no hounds to back the decision.

"Well, it's very odd," said the Countess, looking about with concern.

"Must have mistaken the day," observed Major Elite.

"No," rejoined her ladyship firmly; "I'm certain I'm right. Friday, Spite of All; Saturday, the tenth milestone on the Larkspur Road."

"Or the hour," suggested Mrs. Mountravers, looking at her watch, which, however, afforded little assistance, for it was standing at half past two.

Bucktrout now stood up in his stirrups, contemplating the country like a whipper-in waiting to view a fox away. Nothing to be seen. Stand against All seemed to have it all to itself.

"Knock and ask," now said the Countess, addressing herself to the footman as though she were at the door of a Belgravian mansion.

"Please, my lady, who shall I inquire for?" demanded he, touching his fine cockaded hat, as, having descended from his perch, he now stood at the carriage door.

"Ask if the hounds are coming here to-day," replied her ladyship.

"Yes, my lady," said the footman, trotting off, taking care of his shoes as he made for the rickety, weather-beaten door of the miserable hut.

Rat, tat, tat, tat, tat, he went at the frail wooden fabric, as though he were going to demolish it.

"Who's there?" roared a stentorian voice, that a westerly wind wafted in full force to the carriage.

"Please, do the hounds meet here to-day?" asked the footman in his mild company accents.

"No, you ass!" roared the poacher, for it was none other than Giles Snarem, the notorious leader of the night gang, whose second sleep he had thus disturbed.

"Come away!" cried the Countess—"come away!" satisfied there was a mistake somewhere.

The order was satisfactory to old Bucktrout, who feared if the inquiry was prosecuted any further it would tran- spire that the hounds were at Spite of All, whereas he had driven the party to Stand against All, though he was certain about the action being tried before Lord Chief- Justice Best, because one of the high sheriff's javelin men lodged at his house, and told him all about it—indeed, he believed the javelin man had been of great assistance to the judge in trying the case. At the word "home," from the footman, he therefore caught his old screws short by the head, and turning the carriage round, what with flagellating one horse and spurring the other, he managed to make them plough through the heavy sand at a much better pace than they came. A respectful distance being thus established between Stand against All and our travellers, he presently relaxed into his old jog-trot pace, and having stopped to refresh himself and horses at the Barleymow wayside inn, he trotted into town with as much dash and vigour as he could raise. Those terrible greys at the Fleece were always haunting his vision, urging him and his horses beyond the decaying powers of either.

Arrived at the Lord Hill hotel and posting-house, the first thing he did after setting down was to run and look at "Bell's Life" in the bar, and finding Mr. Romford's hounds advertised for Spite of All, he told the landlord he had better book the journey to Spite of All, and then there would be no mistake in the matter.

"All right," said he; "all right," scrambling out crab fashion. "Spite of All, and Stand agin All 'ill be all the same thing—same thing—place they had the 'size trial on about afore Lord Chief-Justice Best and a special jury."

So that day's journey went for nothing.

CHAPTER LXI

THE TENTH MILESTONE ON THE LARKSPUR ROAD

FOILED in her first effort to get a sight of the redoubtable Leotard, the Countess of Caperington returned
with vigour to the charge, sending, immediately on her
return from Stand against All, into the commercial room
of the Lord Hill hotel and posting-house for the old
well-thumbed map of the county, and searching with
avidity for the next meet of the hounds. Fortunately
for Bucktrout, neither Spite of All nor Stand against
All had obtained their present notoriety when the map
was published, consequently they were not on it to
contradict his assertion that they were one and the same
place; and her ladyship having placed her pretty forefinger on the extensive stain denoting her then locality
at Dirlingford, she proceeded to make a very scientific
cast to the east in search of the diminutive town of
Larkspur, formerly the residence of the Doubleimupshire
hounds.

"Here it is!" at length cried she, looking up, "here it
is! right to the north-east of this place," and getting a
cedar-wood match out of the lighter stand, she proceeded
to measure the scale in the corner of the map, and then
the distance from the before-mentioned greasy mark on
the side.

"Oh, quite within distance," said she, "quite within
distance; not above twelve miles from here at most, by
Burbury and Cracknel."

So saying, her ladyship dismissed the map, and ordered
the dinner for that day, and the carriage for the next,
with one and the same breath. And now leaving the
reader to imagine a repetition of the former evening's
performance, we will pass on to the following morning,
and suppose the Countess and party again taking the
field in the Lord Hill carriage in all the glories of
consequence and dress.

Bucktrout had increased his magnificence by adding a

pair of tarnished red and white rosettes to his antediluvian horses' heads, and sat cockily in his brass cantreled saddle, thinking how he was taking the shine out of Peter of the Golden Fleece, and his greys. Then after the fuss and preparation, gaping and staring and starring of the former occasion, the Countess and her friends came downstairs, and with due importance got themselves seated and adjusted in the carriage.

"Right!" again was the cry, and the low part of the High Street was this time enlivened with the sound of carriage wheels. If people in London ran to the window to look at every vehicle that passed, what a time they would have of it.

Bucktrout rode with much more confidence than he did in going to Spite of All, for he knew his way, and moreover was certain that he was going right. So he rose cockily in his saddle, now admiring his left-leg boot, now looking into the flowing rosettes at his horses' heads, now whipping and spurring the old nags into activity. If he wasn't cutting a dash he didn't know who was. Jip, jip, jip, he went as if they were a pair of five-year-olds instead of being nearer five-and-twenty. The road was good—turnpike all the way: none of the sandstone quagmires, with great boulder stones turning up like flitches of bacon every few yards, that impeded their progress the day before.

They had not gone many miles ere the first indication of the chase appeared. This was a tight-buttoned, blue-coated groom riding a well-conditioned brown horse, between whose sleek coat and the rider's tops there seemed to be a species of honourable rivalry as to which should be the darkest. The horse had it, perhaps, but only by a shade or two. Formerly grooms couldn't get their boots white enough ; now they can't get them dark enough. Such is the mutation of fashion.

"All right to-day," said the Countess, eyeing the unmistakable symptom. Bucktrout then passed him at a half-cantering trot.

The plot presently thickened. At the Burbury side bar two grooms were paying their own and their hack-riding masters' tolls, and a little farther on a knot of miscellaneous horsemen were regaling themselves at the door of the Good Intent inn with early purl and other delicacies. Some people can drink at any time.

Bucktrout spurts past them as if he despised such performances. The country was evidently getting alive.

Ah! there's a red coat! Only a seedy one, to be sure, as the first red coat on the road generally is, but still a red coat, thus openly proclaiming the nature of the coming entertainment. It is little Tommy Squirt, the Union Doctor, who is deceiving himself, as Independent Jimmy would say, that he is passing for a great man, though in reality he is only offering himself for a figure of fun. A badly turned-out man in red is always a deplorable object; doubly so when the horse and the coat are equally bad, and all the appointments show that the colour is expected to do everything. On he jogs his badly clipped mouse-colour very gingerly, having both corns and a curb to take care of. And now the brute trips in a grip just as the carriage is passing, causing an outburst of laughter from the party.

Then the turn of the road reveals another red coat— a red coat on a grey—a rat-tailed grey this time. It is our old friend the Chairman of the Half-Guinea Hat Company, who has become very assiduous in his attendance on the Larkspur hounds of late. He has got himself up with extra care, with his all-round-the-chin beard combed carefully over his blue tie, like samples of yellow and white worsted on a stall.

"What an ugly man!" exclaimed the Countess in passing, quite loud enough for Bonus to hear.

"Isn't he!" assented Mrs. Mountravers in the same tone.

"Wonder he doesn't dye his beard all the same colour," observed Major Elite, whose turn it now was to stare.

But we are now ascending the slightly rising ground of Cracknel Green—a rise so gentle that it was not until the establishment of railways that it was found out not to be level. Bucktrout's horses, however, who have wonderfully fine shoulders for detecting the collar, feel it at once, and gradually relax into a walk. Half-way up stands the ninth milestone, calm and serene as milestones always are, but causing the ladies to start and adjust their bonnets, and Major Elite to button his gloves and feel his collar. They are presently overtaken by a large party of horsemen, some in black, some in red, some in green, who stare and wonder who old Bucktrout has aboard to-day. Though they all admire the Countess, they think the Major might be very happy with either.

And now the indubitable level being obtained, Bucktrout has no excuse for further nursing, and at the word "Trot!" from the Countess he gathers the old horses together, and with the aid of the spur, the whip, and the voice, is presently at the

> "Delightful scene!
> Where all around is gay, men, horses, dogs;
> And each smiling countenance appears
> Fresh blooming health and universal joy."

Our foxy-faced Master has just turned into a large pasture on the right of the road, the hounds looking blooming and well. Daniel—the Right Honourable the Hurl of Scamperdale's Daniel—sober and solemn; and little Chowey, the man with the philanthropic mouth, contracting and dilating his proboscis as though he were considering whom he should kiss. Romford rides the redoubtable Placid Joe, Swig the water-objecting Brick, and Chowey the wriggling Oliver Twist. They now take up a position well into the field, and give the hounds ample space to roll and be criticised.

Then there is the field, large, parti-coloured and gay, as fields generally are when the meets of the hounds are by a turnpike side, and carriages and horsemen can commingle. There are two or three gigs, and two or three phaetons, some containing gentlemen, who on peeling will prove horsemen, while others will follow in their vehicles as far as they can, and then go away.

"Turn in here!" cried the Countess; "turn in here!" as the hesitating Bucktrout pulled up at the field-gate, and looked round with a grin.

"Yes, my lady," said he, now gathering all his energies to steer through the gate without a collision against either post. He just managed to do it.

"Who have we here?" said Romford to Mr. Joseph Large, who still patronised the pack at great personal inconvenience.

"Don't know," replied Large; adding, "it's the Lord Hill chaise."

"So I see," said Romford, who had long booked the old horses for the boiler.

Then, as the carriage approached and drew up before the pack, Facey, seeing the ladies were pretty, raised his hat, an example that was immediately followed by

Chowey and Swig with their caps. Chowey half thought the Countess was an old acquaintance, but for once he couldn't hit it off.

Then as the hats and caps subsided, there was fresh inquiry as to who the strangers were, and a sending of Todd on the sly to ask Tomkins, and a similar expedition by Large to Ten-and-a-half-per-Cent., who now came up on the rat-tailed grey. None of them, of course, could tell. But here comes some one who can, viz. our fair friend, Mrs. Somerville, who, entering the field by a gap at the opposite corner, confronts the carriage as she advances, mounted on the wondrous Leotard.

Lucy wondered who the strangers were—then she thought she had seen that face before—very like Lady Scattercash's—couldn't be Lady Scattercash—yes, it was Lady Scattercash.

"How do you do, Lady Scattercash?" said she, riding up to the carriage door and tendering her hand as she spoke. But the Countess, who had had the advantage of a quiet carriage seat for the survey, had realised Lucy before Lucy did her, and her displeasure at seeing the horse going so quietly was not at all diminished by the familiarity of *that person* calling her Lady Scattercash, when she was in fact the Countess of Caperington. So she neglected the proffered hand and preserved a stolid scornful stare.

"I think you don't know me," said Lucy timidly, withdrawing her hand as she spoke.

"Yes, I do," replied the Countess haughtily. "You are Mrs. Sponge—Lucy Glitters that was—most pernicious woman!" added she, with an upward curl of her lip.

If the Countess had stabbed her to the heart she could not have inflicted a more deadly wound, for there were horsemen all around, every one of whom, Lucy felt sure, would hear what was said. The words perfectly rang in her ears—"You are Mrs. Sponge—Lucy Glitters that was—most pernicious woman!" She was indeed Mrs. Sponge—Lucy Glitters that was; but she felt that it was not for an old comrade like Lady Scattercash to upbraid her. She would not have done so by the Countess. And, turning her horse short round, poor Lucy burst into a flood of tears.

Notwithstanding the unwonted sight of a lady in tears in the hunting field, we believe if it had not been for that

long-eared Chairman of the Half-Guinea-Hat Company,
Lucy's misfortune might have escaped observation. He,
however, being down-wind, with his ears well cocked as
usual for a catch, heard the ominous, "*You are Mrs.
Sponge!*" coupled with the denunciation "*most pernicious
woman!*" and immediately put that and that together for
a story. Not that he went bellowing about the country
exclaiming, "I say, this is not Mrs. Somerville, but Mrs.
Sponge, the wife of our friend Soapey Sponge," but he
innuendoed it, which was just the same thing. The story
flew like lightning, and in a very few days was all over
Doubleimupshire. But a great deal may be done in a few
days, and ere the bubble finally burst a great deal was
done in this case. But the *dénouement* of all this spirited
conduct deserves a separate chapter.

CHAPTER LXII

THE FINISH

IT was an eventful morning to other parties besides our
friend Mrs. Somerville. When she got back to
Beldon Hall she found the fair auburn-haired lady had
played young Joseph Large off so successfully against
Mr. Lovetin Lonnergan as to make the latter consent to a
clandestine marriage, of course to be kept profoundly
secret until it pleased father to die. And Mrs. Somerville, feeling the pressure of circumstances and the precarious nature of her own position, at once set about
furthering the arrangement, not by ordering those
voluminous mountains of clothes and dresses that
generally mark the coming change, but by quietly procuring a marriage licence and an obliging clergyman to
use it.

Then, to make surety doubly sure, and completely
baffle old Lonnergan should any reports get into circulation, Mrs. Somerville suggested that Miss Howard should
be married in a feigned name, and hit upon that of
Shannon. "Elizabeth Shannon, say," as if quite accident-

ally; and Lovetin thought the idea rather a pull in his favour if anything, being greatly goaded by the persecuting importunities of that disgusting Joseph Large, who, he felt sure, would marry her at any price.

The Registrar, holding the document firmly in one hand while he presented the palm of the other, said in an unbroken breath, "Two pound twelve and sixpence, and I hope it will make you both very happy," his happiness evidently consisting in getting the two pound twelve and sixpence. And Lovetin paid the money (which "Old-Rent-should-never-rise" wouldn't have done) without asking for discount. Lord Lonnergan would certainly have had the sixpence, if not the two and sixpence off.

It would not interest the reader to follow the worthies through the consequences of their mutual disappointments; suffice it to say, that there was presently an uproar, though not of Mrs. Lubbins's order, both at Dalberry Lees and Beldon Hall.

Our sprightly friend Betsey Shannon had the best of it, for here was real wealth and an easily managed husband.

Of course the match was not kept secret—as what match ever is?—but its announcement was not attended by any unpleasant consequences. The fact was, that though father was not obliging enough to die, yet his faculties failed just at the very time, the first indication of which was the conviction that Betsey Shannon, now Mrs. Lovetin Lonnergan, was a great City heiress; and Mrs. Lonnergan, always trusting her great man implicitly, received her daughter-in-law at Flush House with the greatest cordiality. There Mrs. Lovetin was most comfortably located, everything going on most harmoniously, thus contradicting the assertion that there never yet was a house built large enough to hold two families.

The old Lord used to sit in his easy-chair contemplating Betsey's beautiful figure and complexion, muttering aloud, "Ah, lucky dog, Lovetin, lucky dog; always told you to stick up for the money. Beauty and breeding are nothing compared to blunt." Then he would burst out with the old favourite aphorism, "When has a man got enough money, Lovetin? When he has got a little more than what he has. Ah, lucky dog, lucky dog! Be as rich as Rothschild—rich as Rothschild, my boy."

But we are occupying ourselves with a minor hero to the neglect of our great master, Mr. Romford.

When matters burst up at Beldon Hall, Cassandra was indignant exceedingly, and we need not say that there was terrible disappointment at Dalberry Lees, crimination and recrimination.

"If he didn't say himself he was the owner of Abbey-field Park, everybody did for him, and he never contradicted it. Turbot-sitting-upon-its-tail on a cap of dignity, forsooth! What business had he to seal his letters with a turbot-sitting-upon-its-tail on a cap of dignity? Downright imposition. Gaining credit under false pretences. Ought to be transported. So said Mrs. Hazey.

But Facey, as the reader has seen, was a man of energy and determination. He was yet young, vigorous, and ungrizzled—not at all trammelled with nice feelings or delicacy—and having got in the bulk of his season's subscriptions for the hounds, he sold the balance to our friend Ten-and-a-half-per-Cent. for fifteen shillings in the pound, and without indulging in any further blandishment about founding the hospital for decayed sportsmen, pocketed the money, and got his hounds and horses away a few hours before poor Lord Lovetin's bailiff threatened to seize for the quarter's rent. Indeed, his Lordship had his misgivings almost as soon as he let his place, particularly with regard to not restricting Mr. Romford from the use of the cut pile carpet that Mrs. Emmerson and he differed about.

"Fox-hunters," his Lordship said, "might scrape their feet and wipe the thick of the mud off their boots at the door, but there was a deal that stuck to the upper parts of the legs that he knew dropped off here and there as it liked at its leisure." All this would tread into the carpet and furniture generally, and he questioned that Mrs. Mustard would look very deep for hidden dirt.

Now were his anxieties diminished by the non-receipt of the quarter's rent when due for Beldon Hall, which, having been let by himself, he expected the pleasure of manipulating without the mulcting process as it passed through Mr. Lonnergan's hands. Indeed he had promised himself the pleasure of buying a new black Lyons silk waistcoat with the percentage so saved, an article of raiment that he was greatly in want of. In fact, he had marked two or three down in the Palais Royal that he thought he could compass; but then, like a prudent viscount, he did not like spending the money before he got it. Now he wished he might not be thrown naked and houseless on the world when he had long been looking forward to comparative ease and comfort in his old age.

But his anxieties were not thoroughly aroused until meeting little Jack Lounger in the Rue de la Paix, reading a letter from England, with an account of the splendours of the Beldon Hall ball, which not being insured, it instantly occurred to his Lordship that Romford would infallibly be burning the place down. "Burn it down to a certainty!" exclaimed he, thinking he saw it all in a blaze, and flames bursting out simultaneously from every window, just as they did at Camden House—"burn it down to a certainty! Statuary, marble, Sèvres china, clocks, cabinets, Apollo, Daphne, and all. That sort of work wouldn't do; he would be reduced to beggary in no time. Great as would be the expense, and ill as he could afford it, he really thought he must go over to England and see how matters stood." He mistrusted Lonnergan, who he thought would be sure to side with the tenant. And accordingly, after due consideration, his Lordship went with a return-ticket, available for one month, by rail to Boulogne, and then by one of the General Steam Navigation Company's ships to London Bridge Wharf, thence on by rail again to Firfield Station, altogether to the damage of two pound five. Serious work for the silk waistcoat!

It was evening when his Lordship arrived, and Independent Jimmy was at the back of the station, as usual, catching the passengers as they came out, just as a butcher catches sheep coming out of a fold.

"Noo then! where are ye for?" demanded Jimmy, getting hold of his Lordship.

"Beldon Hall," replied the viscount.

"Then *get in!*" exclaimed Jimmy, jerking his capped head towards the open omnibus door. "Noo then! where are ye for?" inquired he of another. And so he went on till the stream of humanity ceased to flow.

He then climbed up on to his box and cut off: shortly after which the process of setting down, "Noo then, this is so-and-so, get oot!" commenced. "Noo then, this be Beldon!—get oot!" at length said he to his Lordship. And his Lordship got out accordingly, slipping his bag into the lodge to be sent for as he passed. He then slipped up to the house by the back way.

Being a lord, and feeling the advantage thereof ; moreover remembering Frank Romford's peaceable demeanour at school, and recollecting also that he himself was on a visit of inspection ; his Lordship thought he had better assume a little more intimacy than really existed, and affect to come upon his tenant in the way of a friendly, agreeable surprise. So, without ringing, he opened the door and let himself into the house. The spacious hall was dark and gloomy—not even a solitary tallow candle illuminating its monotony ; but if a man can find his way anywhere without a light, it is in his own house ; and feeling rather comforted than otherwise at the absence of an illumination, his Lordship passed through the echoing hall, and entered the vestibule beyond. Here a light under the bottom of a door indicated residence ; and after a momentary pause, he gave a gentle tap.

"*Come in!*" roared Romford, thinking it was the strong, persevering man who cleaned horses. "*Come in!*" repeated he still louder, the first summons not being obeyed.

His Lordship then did as desired, and disclosed a tableau of considerable strength and variety. Before a bright, partly coal and partly wood, fire, on a small round table of the finest buhl and red tortoise-shell, stood Facey's old friend the gin-bottle, flanked with a half-emptied tumbler and a well-stocked bag of tobacco ; our master was stretched at full length on a richly carved and gilt sofa, covered in old Gobelin tapestry, the elbows and back in green Genoa velvet, smoking his pipe at his ease. On the left of the table, shaded from the fire by a clothes-horse containing sundry articles of male attire, sat Mrs. Somerville, in a reclining chair covered with rich purple and amber satin damask, darning a pair of Mr. Romford's old stockings. Having a good front view, each started with astonishment at the sight of the other.

However much boys may change as they grow up into men, there will generally be some distinguishing feature by which they can be recognised ; but under no possible process could the little dark-beady, black-eyed Romford of his Lordship's early days have grown up into the great shaggy Herculean monster that now arose from his lair before him.

His Lordship started, for he thought to give his old schoolfellow an agreeable surprise; and Romford started, for he was not accustomed to intruders, and didn't want to be troubled. They then stood staring at one another like Spanish pointers, each wondering who the other was.

Lord Lovetin at length broke silence. "Beg pardon," said he, "but I thought it was Mr. Romford."

"Romford it is," said Facey, yawning, and stretching out his great arms as if to show the intruder what he had to contend with. (He half thought it was somebody come after old Fog's £50.)

"But not the Romford I was at school with," observed his Lordship, eyeing him intently.

"Don't know who you are, to begin with," replied Facey; "but moy name's Romford," observed he; "*that oi'll swear to.*"

"I'm Lord Lovetin," replied his Lordship mildly.

If his Lordship had put a pistol to our master's head he could not have given him a greater shock; and forthwith all his acts of omission and commission rushed to his mind with terrible velocity: the trifle of rent, the conversion of the coach-horses, the spurious sister, the turbot-on-its-tail seal.

We need not follow our friends through the *dénouement* that ensued on the discovery by his Lordship of the mistake he had made in jumping to the conclusion that there was only one Mr. Romford in the world, nor relate how Mr. Facey Romford not only insisted upon sitting rent free during the time he had been at Beldon Hall, but also upon receiving a handsome bonus for going out, which his Lordship, albeit almost heart-broken at the sacrifice, thought it better to do than submit to any further devastation and deterioration of property. Oh, what a shock it was to him! Knocked ten years out of his life, he said. The more his Lordship saw, the less he liked what had been going on.

The place was indeed in shocking confusion: everything converted into what it was not intended for. Betsey's old brass-eyed Balmorals stuffed into the richly carved Indian cabinet; a pound of sugar and a nip of tea placed under the shade of the figured and flowered Dresden timepiece, now left without any protection; a statuary marble figure of Psyche crowned with Facey's tenpenny wide-awake; and Mrs. Somerville's dirty goloshes tucked under the arm of a companion figure of Cupid. A majolica cup, with crest and coronet, was filled with shot; and in a Sèvres tray, with turquoise and gold border, reposed a battered old powder-flask.

And here let us say that we take shame unto ourselves for not as yet having introduced the noble viscount personally to the reader. Take then a short but faithful sketch, executed in the field in the detective style. Say five-and-forty years of age, five feet ten inches high, sallow complexion, long visage, dark hair, thin on the top (like the passionate gentleman's in "Punch"), dark hazel eyes, arched eyebrows, narrow feet and a very narrow mind, short whiskers and long spiral moustache, stoutish build with a military air; dressed in a complete "ditto" suit of brown, with a French wallet slung over his shoulder, and a peaky French travelling-cap held in his hand; added to this, a peculiarity when speaking of shrugging up his shoulders continually.

The news soon spread that his Lordship had cast-up—dropped in "quite promiscuous," as the saying is, and was very ill-pleased with all he had found.

The Dirties had come in for their share of the censure, and promulgated what passed pretty freely. And when a story once gets admission into a house, it soon finds its way into the drawing-room.

Still Facey had his friends in the hunting-field, men who said he was the right Romford—the right man in the right place, as far as they were concerned. He could kill a fox with any one, and had as good a pack of hounds as ever came into a country. If he wasn't a man of much blandishment, as Independent Jimmy said, still he could go across country like a comet; and nothing pleases people so much as a dashing, fearless rider.

Facey, moreover, who, as our readers will perhaps have seen, had assurance enough for anything, went on in his usual routine way, hunting his country with great fairness and impartiality, contending—with some degree of plausi-bility—that nobody had anything to do with anything but his hounds. They might hunt with him or not, just as they liked, he said; but he would be master of his own house (as he continued to call Beldon Hall), so he just advertised his meets as before.

And indeed, but for a certain interesting circumstance

2222222222

we don't know but he would have continued to hunt the country up to the present time, and that circumstance we shall now proceed to relate. Amid all the snubbing and cold-shouldering that ensued, one house remained firm and faithful to our Facey, and that was the house of our distinguished friend Willy Watkins. Nobody there would hear anything against Mr. Romford. They didn't "want to hear anything against Mr. Romford." "They wouldn't hear anything against Mr. Romford. They begged that nobody would trouble themselves to tell them anything against Mr. Romford. The world was made up of spite and ill-nature, and people generally spoke from an interested motive." (This latter observation was levelled at Mrs. Hazey.) "Lord Lovetin was a notorious screw, and doubtless wanted to cheat Mr. Romford. Mr. Romford was quite right in resisting him." And poor Willy was sent out hunting twice a week, in order to keep up appearances; this, too, when the now diminished 'fields made the risk extra hazardous in the way of fencing, few caring to break them for him.

And considering how the men were divided in opinion as to whether Mr. Facey was the right Romford or not, there is nothing extraordinary in a lady who knew so little about hunting as to suppose that a bag fox, or a day with Mr. Stotfold's stag-hounds, would be acceptable to our master, mistaking the controversy about the keenness for the real question as to the ownership of Abbeyfield Park, and as there was a doubt about the matter, giving the benefit of the doubt to the party she was interested in—viz., to our Mr. Romford. As the men couldn't marry Mr. Facey, they didn't care whether he was the owner of Abbeyfield Park or not; but it made all the difference to Mrs. Watkins. There was, when she made her mistake, a very natural one. He was the right Romford to the gentlemen, but not the ladies.

So Facey continued to visit at Dalberry Lees with his flute, taking an occasional spin for a perch in the Trent as he passed; and nothing could be more cordial or encouraging than the family.

The reader will be surprised at the promotion of the match under such circumstances, but the cause is easily explained. The fact was, that the accounts from Australia had latterly been very discouraging. The worthy papa had been much outwitted of late, and had made some very improvident speculations, as well with Willy's money as his own.

Nor were the Honourable, and the lady *who was very nearly an honourable*, the only ones who sought the secret services of the Church at this memorable epoch. Strange as it may seem, our most sagacious friend Facey led to the hymeneal altar our lofty-minded friend Cassandra Cleopatra, with the full consent of her august parents. Nay, it was difficult to say whether the Watkinses or Facey were most anxious to hurry on the match, the Watkinses considering that Cassandra would be perfectly safe with her ample dower out of Abbeyfield Park, while friend Facey thought it would be a very good thing to have Dalberry Lees to fall back upon when matters should burst up at Beldon Hall.

Our fair readers will perhaps think that there is not sufficient inducement here shown for our lisping friend foregoing that greatest triumph of female life, the excitement and preparation of a grand wedding. Men always wish them over as quietly as possible : ladies can never make fuss and display enough. Well, but there was a reason for it, notwithstanding, as we have before intimated. The fact was, that the worthy old convict whom we left in the colony to manage his own and his son-in-law's affairs, while the latter and his wife, or lady, as her husband called her, came over to England to see if there was anybody good enough for the daughter, had had the misfortune to make some very bad speculations, and had lost the greater part of that wealth which Willy had lost the greater part of his hair in obtaining.

It was not, therefore, desirable to undergo the manipulation of the lawyers on Cassandra's account, and they could therefore hardly ask Mr. Romford to submit to it on theirs. They had no doubt at all that Mr. Romford was very rich, and that it would do uncommonly well. And Mr. Romford, not being inclined to write for the title-deeds of Abbeyfield Park, or indeed to have any unnecessary hiatus in his hunting, agreed that it was far the best to manage matters quietly, and then go to London and have a flare-up in the spring. People get far more for their money there, he said, and he knew everybody in London—Smith, and Brown, and Bates, and all.

The Romford stud sold uncommonly well, as it naturally would where its good qualities only were known. Placid

Joe passed into the hands of Mr. Hazey for £90, and having borne him triumphantly through the thick of his own hounds, quickly passed out again at a loss of £60. Hard day for poor Hazey. He thought to stick him into Sir Theophilus Thickset at a considerable premium.

Mr. Joseph Large bought the fine weight-carrying bay called "Everlasting," but which declined against the hills, and was very well suited, the horse being always as ready to stop as Large was himself. So they agreed capitally together. Large gave £80 for him, teapot-handles being rather on the rise at the time of the sale.

Ten-and-a-half-per-Cent. bought "Perfection," the nutmeg grey, with a partiality for scrubbing its rider's legs up against carriage-wheels; and the brute having subsequently made rubbing posts of the postman's gig, Linseed the doctor's fly, and Marrow the butcher's cart, his owner was at length constrained to come to the conclusion that he had better send "Perfection" to Aldridge's, where he was knocked down for a £10 note— his character being perfectly well known to the frequenters of the Repository.

When Facey and the Watkinses came to the knowledge of the *doo* they had practised on each other some sharp passages were exchanged, and a family war was on the point of commencing, when the name of Willy Watkins made its appearance in the *Gazette*. Facey was not the man, he said, to kick a foe when he was down; so it was agreed that all matters of difference between them should be buried in oblivion, and that Romford and wife should start forthwith to the Antipodes, and look after the old convict and the wreck of Willy's property. This resolution was forthwith acted upon: and, strange to say, almost the first person our hero met in the streets of Melbourne, just opposite Bright, Brothers, & Co.'s store, at the corner of Flinder's Lane and Bond Street, was our estimable friend Mr. Sponge, the runaway husband of the all-accomplished Mrs. Somerville, who has played so conspicuous a part in our story. Soapey—looking as brisk and spruce as a man who has lit on his legs and can hold up his head before anybody—very different to the Mr. Sponge who bolted by the backway from the cigar-shop in Jermyn Street; and though that "sivin-pun-ten" was still standing against him, it did not prevent Mr. Sponge hailing his creditor with unfeigned cordiality.

And indeed he had good cause for looking brisk, for he too had been to the diggings, and, not far from where friend Willy Watkins feathered his nest, had pitched upon some uncommonly good nuggets, which he had now come to Melbourne to sell. People who will pass each other on the grand street of life—the Parks or Pall Mall, for instance—will fraternise uncommonly on a Swiss mountain, or at the Antipodes. So it was with our distinguished heroes.

Of course Facey knew nothing about Lucy, and, upon the principle that where ignorance is bliss 'twere folly to be wise, Soapey was not extra-inquisitive about her. To the credit of Betsey Shannon, who had gained such an ascendancy over her sapient husband as a spirited young woman like her ought to acquire, Mrs. Somerville had a capital billet at Flush House, where she was treated with the greatest respect by the old buff-vested Lord and his Lady. They thought Lucy was second only to Betsey in beauty and breeding. But dependence is irksome, and Lucy presently longed for a crust of bread and a crib of her own.

The attainment of these *desiderata* shortly afterwards presented itself in the following letter from Betsey Lonnergan, who had gone up to town for a few days, leaving Lucy in possession of Flush Hall :—

"MAWLEY'S HOTEL,
" *Wednesday*.

"DEAR LUCY,—I write to say we shant come home till after the turn of the week, as Lovetin and me am going for a couple of days to Fokestone to see a cousen of his.

"You mustnt be dull, but keep your spirits up like a little brick as you are.

"Now for some news, which will make your back hair stand out like a Chinese man's pigtail. I were setting in our carrige at Carling's the sighgur shop's door in Regent Street, whiles Lovey had gone in to get some weeds, when who should I clap my eyes on but Bellville as 'used to was' with us you know afore he went to Orstralia—(is that right ?—well, if isnt, you know what it means).

"Bellville went to lead in tragedy, you know, up at the diggins', and a pretty tidy pike he has made on it. He was dressed quite like a swell—blue frock coat, with brade

and frogs and a poodle collar, and his trowseys were tite,
à la Charley Mathews, only they had brade down 'em too.
Mustash, of course, and all that. Well, he stares at me
and me at him, till he sees me smile, and then he offs with
his tile and makes up to the carrige-door. After a short
scene of surprise, he asks, '*Commy foe?*'—Quite correct,
eh?

"'Of course,' says I, with a frown; and then we both
laughed, as you may fancy.

"Well, B. told me what 'tremendous success' he had
had—thought him Macready in disguise—gave him half
share of the house, and a clear 'Ben'[1] every month—and
he has made mopusses enuff to come back quite india-
pendent.

"'What's that to me?' says you, 'or to Betsey Shannon'
now she's the bride of another?'"

"This is what it is. In course of conversashun he asked
after you, and why you and Soapey had parted. I told
him the truth—how Soapey had bolted and left you to
shift for yourself. 'Then,' says B., 'I can give her the
cue to find him again, if she wishes it. He's doing furst
rate at Melburn; and if she's short of rowdy to pay her
passige out, I'm ready, for "Awl Lang Sign," to lend it
her.'

"There, my dear, that's something for you to think
about till me and Lovey come home again—and here he
is, ready to take me to the Canterbury, where I have
teased him to go this evening.

"Bless you, dear, and please see that fires are kep in
our bedroom and my *bodore*. Good-by.

"Your affectionate friend,
"BETSEY LONNERGAN."

Lucy did not long deliberate over the contents of her
friend's letter before she decided to share the success of
her Sponge. She resolved to discard the assumed name
of Somerville, and set out for the Antipodes in search of
him; so, following in the wake of the Romfords, she
presently found him, and both Facey and Soapey gave her
a most cordial greeting.

The voyage out had agreed with her, and she was looking, if possible, handsomer than ever. Soapey took to her
without hesitation, on the sensible principle of letting

[1] *i.e.* half the receipts, and a benefit free of charge.

"bygones be bygones." And Facey, who was a capital manager, so long as he hadn't the old lady to contend with, had, with the aid of twins, got the lisper into such subjection and good order that Beldon Hall was all ignored—never mentioned.

Indeed, Mr. Romford didn't see why, saving the elegance of the name, Lucy shouldn't have called herself Mrs. Sponge instead of Mrs. Somerville.

And we are happy to say that old Granby Fitzgerald's defalcations were not so utterly ruinous as were at first expected. There is something saved out of the fire for Willy, while Facey, with his natural aptitude for taking care of himself, has secured a trifle also; which, with what he took out with him, makes him up quite a purse. The last account heard of Soapey and him was that they were going to set up a bank in Collins Street East, under the firm of

"ROMFORD AND SPONGE."

Good luck attend their exertions, say we ! We expect to hear of their setting up a pack of hounds together next.

THE END

THE WORLD'S CLASSICS

A Select List

Peregrine Pickle
Edited by James L. Clifford
Revised by Paul-Gabriel Boucé

Roderick Random
Edited by Paul-Gabriel Boucé

Travels through France and Italy
Edited by Frank Felsenstein

R. S. SURTEES: Mr. Facey Romford's Hounds
Edited and with an introduction by Jeremy Lewis

Mr. Sponge's Sporting Tour
With an introduction by Joyce Cary

WILLIAM MAKEPEACE THACKERAY: Barry Lyndon
Edited and with an introduction by Andrew Sanders

Vanity Fair
Edited by John Sutherland

IZAAK WALTON and CHARLES COTTON:
The Compleat Angler
Edited by John Buxton
With an introduction by John Buchan

OSCAR WILDE: Complete Shorter Fiction
Edited by Isobel Murray

The Picture of Dorian Gray
Edited by Isobel Murray

A complete list of Oxford Paperbacks, including books in
The World's Classics, Past Masters, and OPUS Series,
can be obtained from the General Publicity Department,
Oxford University Press, Walton Street, Oxford OX2 6DP.